Ravenous Dusk

by Cody Goodfellow

Ravenous Dusk

Cover art by Scott Riggs

ISBN 0–9704000–1–2

For more information about this author or to order this and other great works of speculative and weird fiction, please contact:

Perilous Press, LLC
PO Box 51181
Seattle, WA 98115
www.perilouspress.com

First Edition

0 9 8 7 6 5 4 3 2 1

Note: This book (and its predecessor, Radiant Dawn, which we highly recommend you read first) is a work of fiction set within the Cthulhu Mythos first devised by HP Lovecraft, in the same manner that Homer's *Iliad* and *Odyssey* used the pantheon of Greek mythology and folklore or that most modern vampire novels are set in the milieu of Bram Stoker's *Dracula*. In his lifetime, Lovecraft encouraged other authors to delve into his Mythos and build it into an artificial myth cycle that incorporated the existential dread of the post-Darwin, post-Einstein universe. Though the book you hold in your hands is rooted in fascination with the Cthulhu Mythos–particularly *At The Mountains Of Madness*–it uses Lovecraft's cosmology as the mythic tradition that best reflects the evolutionary themes of the plot. It is hardly necessary to be familiar with even the rudiments of the Mythos to enjoy Ravenous Dusk, but if you're not, your education has some serious gaps in it that this book will, hopefully, persuade you to fill in.

For my creators–

My mother, my wife and my daughter

O CHILDREN OF FANCY!

Know, verily, that while the radiant dawn breaketh above the horizon of eternal holiness, the satanic secrets and deeds done in the gloom of night shall be laid bare and manifest before the peoples of the world.

–*The Hidden Words of Bahá'u'lláh*

Begin thy great career, dear child of the gods...the time is now at hand. See how the world trembles beneath its massive vault, the lands and ocean wastes and lofty sky: see how all rejoices at the age that comes to birth...

–Virgil, *Eclogue*

Prologue

October 30, 1999

Tigris River Valley, Maysan Province, Iraq

When the speakers crackled out the call to pray, they knelt to Mecca on the rim of the canyon.

Setting in the broken lands to the west, the sun seemed to flatten and smear against the horizon, the fierce convection currents conspiring with the sulfur-hued air to make an angry red god of the disk in its final minutes. Even nine years after the shameful retreat from Kuwait, the legacy of Saddam's scorched-earth policy lived on in the world's most magnificent sunsets.

Major Hundayi did not concern himself overmuch with God or gods, because whatever gods there were did not concern themselves at all with Iraq. Only the sun had not deserted them, but it rose each day only to beat them down or harden their resolve, and set only to let them freeze.

He listened to his men chatter among themselves when they had made their prayers.

"—I tell you it is true! Damned American vampires slant-drilling the oil out from under us from Kuwait! On the radio—"

"—Chinese hacked version of Windows is more safe. They cannot read your e-mail. I will have my cousin at the Istachbarat burn a copy for you."

"He ate steak Tartar and fresh peaches for dinner at his southern palace in Basra last night. I'm told there were even Cuban cigars."

"Do not be so cynical, Ali. If he eats so well, it means that we are still strong."

He did not expect any more from them than he did from God. Like the sun, a commander in Saddam's army had to shine down on his men so they could not look directly at him, bludgeon their brains into mush and drive them to duty. In the night of combat, they would follow his reflection in their minds into certain death, or so the manuals said.

His men had little use for Major Hundayi's brand of discipline. Most of them were only boys huddling in the shelters with their mothers in the Mother Of All Battles, and could not truly understand the life-or-death value of readiness. For them, it was a joke, because they were in the middle of nowhere, guarding a hole in the ground, a hole filled to the brim with cement.

The Major felt the shame and the absurdity more keenly than all of them combined, but it was his place to keep up appearances, for it was all they left him.

In the War, Hundayi's unit of the Nebuchadnezzar Infantry Division of the Republican Guard had been one of the last out of Kuwait City. In the fierce street fighting, he had himself scored thirteen confirmed kills. Saddam had personally pinned a medal on his chest in a ceremony shortly after the war, praising his courage and loyalty and saluting him as the model of a Republican Guard officer. All this because eleven of the thirteen were shot in the back, and all of them were his own men.

The ceremony had not been televised or written up in the papers, but Saddam used it to send a message to the troops. Hundayi had thought he was destined for great things. He was promoted to Major and took charge of six Special Republican Guard Rapid-Intervention brigades. It was a respectable post, where one could be covered in blood and glory on a daily basis, even if it was always Kurdish or Iraqi blood, and the glory never made the newspapers. Hundayi's diligence won out, and the weekly assassination attempts on Saddam, the Kurd bombings and brigandry, tapered off to a trickle. To become any more of a hero, he'd have to be either dead or Saddam.

Then, three summers ago, he was pulled out of the field and transferred to a division of the SRG he'd never heard of, and buried under a command that could only be some kind of insane test, because he had done nothing to merit punishment. Besides, Saddam's army did not punish officers. It replaced them.

As the commander of the Tiamat unit of Marduk Division of the Special Republican Guard, Major Hundayi oversaw one hundred men who took potshots at American fighter jets enforcing the UN No-Fly Zone, practiced sniping goats and goose-stepping in full parade dress around a filled-in hole in the bottom of a box canyon that was not on any map the Major had ever seen.

In his time at Tiamat, the Major had never given them any excuse to replace him, had never uttered a word aloud to the effect that he might fail to see the honor and validity of his posting. Major Hundayi was not merely a soldier; he was a survivor. Of all the men he'd trained with in his basic training with the Republican Guard, only two others still lived. Nearly half were killed in the War, the rest disappeared in purges. Major Hundayi lived because he had no ambition higher than to survive, and because he was a dogged solver of puzzles. When he had solved the puzzle of what was expected of him in this place, he would be promoted out of it.

The puzzle of the place itself had never interested him, and so he had never paid much heed to the stories his men told each other about it. He knew that Tiamat was a very important chemical weapons facility until the War, when it was bombed by the United Nations of America. Despite the maddening economic siege and the unending UNSCOM inspections, Tiamat was rebuilt underground and resumed operations in still-greater secrecy, under the shield of Marduk.

The previous Tiamat unit was rife with religious fanatics, heretics who believed the place was a holy site of some kind. They conspired with Western agents within UNSCOM to destroy the facility and touch off some kind of catastrophic disaster. They were foiled, but UNSCOM inspectors became embroiled in the affair, and the facility was filled with concrete and bombs to placate the New World Order. Marduk was purged and rebuilt with the most staunchly loyal officers, but the youngest and most worthless of the RG infantry and artillery.

There was no monument to the sacrifice of the scientists and soldiers who died at Tiamat, no ceremonial significance that Major Hundayi could fathom to explain the place, but there they were. He did not believe, as some said, that Tiamat was an entrance to Hell, or that the poisons the Army produced there were extracted from its stygian seas. Nor did he believe, as still others whispered when they thought he was out of earshot, that it *was* a holy place, not just to Islam or to the Jews, or even the stupid Christians, but to a faith older than them all.

He did believe that someday, he would be relieved of this wretched duty, and would go back to where there was action and perks and power. Today, just after breakfast, he had received a sign that that day, if not here, might be coming fast.

The call had come in on the hard line, because, like always, the radios and cellular phones were out of order. The hole in the ground didn't want them to talk to the outside world, so all wireless communications, even radar, hit a wall of invisible fog. Even the hard line to An Nasiriyah gave them frequent problems, but the high command almost never called them, and usually only gave a few code numbers to be translated into orders from a slim book in a safe beside the only telephone.

Today, there were no codes, no cryptic messages mired in static, only the terse order to stand ready to receive a convoy of trucks crossing the border from Iran. They were to receive supplies and ordnance from the convoy and stand ready to assist them with their project. Questions were not invited.

It was not a promotion, but it was something. In three and a half years, not one official visitor had come to Tiamat. The truck that brought their supplies came only in the dead of night, and barely stopped to push their food and rare replacement equipment out the back. UN inspectors had come out semiannually to test the soil and insure that the hole was still filled. This was something else again. Major Hundayi cared about Tiamat only enough to know that it was as secret as it was worthless, and in the murky limbo of this godforsaken command, this sounded like as close as he would get to action.

The trucks could be seen for a while as they climbed the road out of the marshy lowlands towards Tiamat. Clouds of rust-red dust rose up and merged with the looming violet dusk, marking their path all the way back to the Iranian border, twenty miles to the east. Major Hundayi stood on a rocky ridge overlooking the road from the west and puzzled over the size of the convoy. Twenty-plus heavy military trucks lumbered around the mouth of the pit to park in tight formation before his camp. His soldiers had orders to stay clear, but they were restless and stupid, and flocked around the visitors like barefoot peasant children in a backwater village. With rifles pointed, they begged for cigarettes and candy. No one got out of the trucks.

Major Hundayi jogged down from the ridge to the camp. Because his lieutenants were nowhere to be seen, he called muster himself with three shrill blasts from a whistle. The men fell in for review, looking more like the survivors of a prison uprising than an elite military unit, despite his orders. Disgusting, and more, a conspiracy to make him look bad. His officers would be punished. But they would have to take turns flogging each other, or he would have to do it himself.

He approached the trucks with one hand on his holstered pistol, feeling more apprehensive than he should, and hoping it didn't show. The windows of the cabs were tinted and scummed with dust, but he saw a ghostly shape stir within. The door of the nearest truck opened and a man jumped out, strode up to him with his hand extended. Major Hundayi took the hand by reflex, but his mind was spinning so hard, he couldn't remember later if he said anything.

The visitor was tall and thin, in his late fifties, with white hair and riveting gray eyes. He was a civilian, in light brown fatigues and muddy black boots. But what stopped Hundayi was the fact that he was white, and by his accent when he spoke, it became clear that he was an American.

"Major Hundayi, I presume?" the American stranger said, in passable Arabic. "Dr. Cyril Keogh, pleased to meet you at last. I've been looking forward to this for a long time, and it's an honor, sir, a real honor."

The man's hand was warm and dry, his grip brutally firm. He handed Hundayi a large envelope sealed with wax marked with crossed scimitars above the sigil of the al-Tikriti clan. Hundayi shuddered and took it, feeling a static charge shoot up his arm at its touch. This had come directly from Saddam.

"Everything inside is self-explanatory, Major, but if you have any questions I can't answer, you're welcome to call the SSO Headquarters in Baghdad, but I would encourage you to use discretion. This project is known only to the innermost circle of government, and if word got out, there could be terrible repercussions."

Hundayi felt the last dregs of initiative slipping out of his grasp, and tried to seize them. He unsnapped the flap over his sidearm and drew it out of its holster. "I demand to know who you really are, and what you're doing here. You will be placed under arrest until such time as you have proven to my satisfaction—"

"Let me be frank with you, Major. I represent an international scientific organization which has generously donated to the oppressed people of your great nation several million dollars' worth of medicines, scientific equipment and chemicals which are prohibited under the UN sanctions of Resolution 687. In return for this largesse, and the promise of much more to come, we have been granted unrestricted access to the Tiamat site, and pledged with the assistance and protection of your unit for the duration of the project."

"What is this project?" Hundayi demanded.

"We are going to open Tiamat," Keogh said.

The Major holstered his gun, thunderstruck. It was unthinkable.

"We have a plan, and a very strict timetable, which calls for the excavation to be complete in forty days, Major. More equipment is being flown in from Turkey, and should arrive tomorrow, but we'd like to get started immediately building a shelter and quarters for our people. So, if you have no further objections, I urge you to inspect your orders, and let us get down to business."

* * *

In the commo hut, Major Hundayi sat for a long time before he picked up the phone. This was an unacceptable situation he'd been placed in. This American had come out of nowhere with an army of civilians and gear for a full-fledged archaeological dig. The orders in the envelope were what the American had said they were. Unequivocal and clear, and signed by the One himself, they nonetheless only muddied his mind further.

This was exactly the kind of head game the Americans played in the Kuwaiti War, lies and forged documents circulated among the troops to make them think the war was over and Saddam had surrendered, before it had begun. But he also knew that Iraq had, in the last eight years, built a thriving black market to skirt the embargo, smuggling oil out and everything else in around UN and US Navy blockades. Though a million Iraqi babies had died, deprived of medicines and food, the army was stronger now than it had been when it invaded Kuwait, and Saddam's palaces were more plentiful and extravagant than ever. Whatever the American wanted from Tiamat, it was not hard to imagine that he could buy it.

In the end, he called the number at the bottom of the orders, but when a ferocious voice answered the phone by calling him by name, he almost slammed the phone down.

"Hundayi, what is your fucking problem, you shit? Can you not read?" Though he had never heard the voice himself, it was familiar to him from television and radio. It was Uday, Saddam's eldest son and would-be heir. If it were the One, Hundayi would have been frightened for his life, but the One was more or less rational, at least to your face. Uday was an unknown quantity, a spoiled, maniacal devil who sliced up girls and ran over pedestrians for sport in Italian racing cars. Though he had no role in the military chain of command like his younger brother and bitter rival, Qusay, he was forever embroiled in one stupid scheme or another, with or without his father's approval, and had more than ample clout to reach out and squash any who thwarted him.

Major Hundayi picked every syllable with nervous care. "Forgive me, most excellent sir, but it is most unusual and with Americans one can't—"

"Worthless sucker of cocks! Your orders are to assist the dig, protect the dig, lick the diggers' asses for them if they ask, and stay the fuck out of their way, or you are shit from dogs, do I make myself clear?"

"Perfect clear, most excellent sir," he said.

Uday ordered him to leave the room while his second-in-command, Captain Gul, spoke to the younger Saddam. He knew exactly what effect this was intended to have on his nerves, but it still worked.

Major Hundayi walked outside to find half the trucks were gone. In their place, a horde of men and women in fatigues assembled tents. They looked like the UN, whites, blacks and Arabs working together, but there was something else. There was no overseer barking orders, no central plan. They worked silently, each an integral part of the whole, with their portion of the plan firmly fixed in his or her mind. They shamed his own men with their efficiency.

He walked back up the ridge and looked down into the pit. The rest of the trucks had moved down there, and encircled the great plug of concrete where Tiamat had once stood. With the same silent, ant-like order, they dragged the parts for an enormous tent out of the trucks and began to assemble it over the plug.

"A temporary shelter," said an American voice from behind him. He jumped, a little. "Tomorrow, we'll begin to build a more permanent one, which will render the excavation invisible from the air. No UN enforcement flights are scheduled over this area for three more days, and by then, we'll be securely dug in."

Hundayi turned and regarded the white-haired American, who had crept up to within arm's reach of him unnoticed. His deeply-lined features were pale and bookish, but his eyes pinned and probed Hundayi. They were prophet's eyes, burning with an icy, omniscient zeal that was more than Hundayi had ever dreamed there was to power. The mullahs of Iran who sent fanatical human waves of children into his gunsights in the War of the Cities had only sparks of such cold fire. Through his eyes, Hundayi could see that he knew things no other man could know, had seen secret things too terrible to tell, and yet he believed in something too wondrous to describe, something that was coming over the horizon any minute. Against those eyes, Hundayi found himself beginning to burn with a desire to believe in it, too, to make it happen, whatever it was.

"Are you a religious man, Major Hundayi?" Keogh asked.

He bristled at the impertinence of the question. He had never discussed his faith with men beside whom he had faced death on the battlefield, and this American, this civilian, deigned to talk religion to him? "What I believe is no affair of yours," he said, as civilly as he could.

"Saddam was a fool to allow the UN to fill it in," Keogh said. "Kuwait was a pearl, but this..." He turned and approached Major Hundayi so swiftly his hand went to his holster, but Keogh was already inside the sweep of his arm before he got it unclasped. "Do you know about Delphi, Major? In ancient Greece, an oracle sat in a cave over a deep fissure that they believed reached down to the center of the earth, where Gaea, the living earth itself, whispered prophecies. They called the oracle's cave and the temple of Apollo there the Omphalos, or navel of the world. This place is infinitely more precious. This is the living womb of the earth."

Major Hundayi sneered and stepped back. "Your cousins in the United Nations did not agree with you. You Westerners are never of one mind about anything."

Dr. Keogh smiled at him. "But we will be," he said. "Soon."

He walked out to the edge of the cliff, and by the settling of his posture, Major Hundayi could tell that he was lost in memory. To heave the American over the edge now would be such a simple thing...

"It has been so long since I was here last. So much has changed since it was ours..."

"We have always stood guard here, Dr. Keogh. This has always been *our* land."

"Major," Dr. Keogh said, "the last time I was here, your ancestors had not yet crawled up out of the oceans." Major Hundayi jumped, because the Doctor still stood with his back to him, but the voice came from behind him. He whirled, and this time he did draw his pistol, but he could not raise it any higher than his own beltline. The man before him was Dr. Keogh, and so were the three men beside him. One was red-headed and plump, another an Arab or Turk, and the third was a white woman, with hair wrapped in a scarf. But they all looked at him with *his* eyes, *his* mind behind them, as if they believed so fervently in his vision that they had been burned away, and only he looked out of their heads. One or another spoke, but the bedrock of his voice lay beneath their words.

"When I was here last, this land was a great forest, and the ruin below us was the mouth of all Creation, and the last best hope of a race as far advanced beyond your kind as you are above the single-celled amoebae that escaped from this place and struggled to evolve into you. They failed, but their grand experiment goes on, down there. Beneath all that stone, lies the Garden of Eden."

Major Hundayi felt as if he were going to faint. His voice cracked as he asked, "And what—what will you do?"

"We are going to walk into Eden, and we are going to eat the flesh of the gods."

Hundayi bowed his head and covered his face with his hands to pray for surely this was a devil, and if there were devils then surely there must be God. "There is no god but Allah—"

"Oh, the universe is rife with gods, but not one of them cares for your miserable race. Do you know the true name of the Crawling Chaos, or the Black Goat of the Woods with a Thousand Young, or the Unbegotten

Source? They sleep, and hear you not. I am the only god who will hear your prayers, Major."

Hundayi sank to the ground before the Americans. Jagged black rock bit into his rubbery knees. He did not want to, but he feared if he didn't bow down, he'd stumble off the cliff-face, or be pushed. And the Major had come so far, fought so hard, just to stay alive in this shitty army, this shitty world. He was almost relieved to know that, now, nothing else mattered. What he had to do was sickening to him, but he had done it all his life, and needed no further prodding to do it now. "I pray to you, most excellent Sir," he hissed, "I beseech you spare my life, and let me serve you. But tell me, please: what are you?"

"The first," Dr. Keogh said, "and the last," and showed him.

~ 1 ~

There was dark.

There were dreams so real she thought she'd died and been reborn. A cat in the lap of someone with eternally stroking, scratching hands. A protean sliver of almost-living matter on a cradle of languid tides, her boneless body little more than a higher iteration of the blood-warm water around her. Adrift on the dying gamma ray emissions of a supernova, a blackened speck of mind that not even the death of a sun could extinguish.

The dreams exploded in black fireworks like she'd been socked in both eyes, and it was less like waking up than being reborn into a stone womb, to a mother who cannot feel her, and will never birth her out.

There were burning worms of phosphene unlight in her eyes that might be the test pattern blind people see all their lives, or maybe just chemical vapors and radioactive isotopes eating them out of her head. Her mind darting a thousand directions at once and returning with no answers. Her body coming back with the same dumb responses, *no, you cannot move, no, there's nothing to see. Legs? Haven't heard from them in ages.*

She screamed so loud that the ragged sound trailed off only when she had flattened her lungs, so loud she sent pebbles and dust tumbling in the dark. Not because of fear, which was growing like ice crystals in her brain with the realization of where she was. Not in hope of being found, because anyone looking for her would hardly have her rescue in mind. She screamed because she had no other way of telling herself she was alive. She was crushed between two slabs of steel-reinforced concrete deep in a collapsed warren of tunnels beneath a junkyard in the middle of the Mojave Desert, and nobody knew she was there.

Her throat was parched and nearly stopped up with dust, and her sinuses were packed with a conglomerate of sand and snot that felt like crushed glass. She could feel fluid flowing past her on the slab, but she restrained herself from drinking. She burned all over, her skin raw and blistered from her scalp to her belly. The odds on her laying in anything like water in this godforsaken hole were next to nil.

Like your chances of getting rescued.

She forced herself to lie still, forced her breathing to level off, and let her gyroscopic mind whirl itself to an exhausted standstill.

She could move her left hand before her face, but the right was pinned flat against her back in a devastating compound shoulder fracture. *Still in shock, I must be, that should hurt like hell.* She could feel something that might be either a tarantula or her right hand twitching uselessly against her left shoulder blade. Below there, she could feel nothing at all.

That she had survived the previous week, only to end up here, buried alive in the mad prison she almost escaped with a cure for her cancer, made a perverse kind of sense that she might have laughed at, if it were somebody else's life she was reading about in the odd news from Reuters, over breakfast. When her captors had opted for suicide over capture by federal agents, she'd bolted, and gotten free. She could still see that fleeting glimpse of moonless sky, alive with stars and roving searchlights, and that wondrous *other* light from on high, what the Radiant Dawn patient Stephen had called the moon ladder, that had touched her just before the earth opened up and swallowed her. She could still see that soldier, the one who'd come back for her, could still feel the fumes of that exhilaration when she'd thought the world had seemingly decided it had tired of fucking with Stella Orozco and wanted to make things right. Now the soldier was probably buried alongside her, and no light would ever touch her living skin again. This was not the end she would have foreseen for herself, stupid girl, and that was what hurt most of all.

Why are you alive right now?

She was a survivor. She had taken one misstep into her new life, and lay in the grave, unable to die. That fits, God. I'm alive because there's nobody else, who knows I'm here, nobody else to laugh at my joke. If I laugh, if I admit it—*Good one, God, you really had me going there for a minute*—then I'll be allowed to die.

How did you survive?

Her fucking brain, again, whirling away on imponderables while her body slipped away. Lie still and conserve your energy, your air supply. When you feel stronger, start tapping on metal, if you can reach any. They have trained rescue dogs, they have scent detectors, they have ground-penetrating sonar, for Christ's sake.

Not for you.

Save your strength, and stay positive. You will be rescued.

Have you ever been rescued?

Who the fuck are you? She asked herself, but she knew. It was the voice she'd always heard when life or death hinged on choices. It was the voice that had guided her through orphanhood and foster homes and a solitary life of hard-fought serenity. The voice that had abruptly cut off when she discovered she had terminal cancer of the liver. Her Guardian Angel, come back too late to do more than poke and prod her in her failure.

Nobody is coming for you. You have to get out of this yourself.

Tell me another, Guardian Angel.

You are made anew. You are as strong as your will to survive. You have been given a gift.

Her hand scuttled across the papier-mâché nightmare of her face, stretched taut over the bones except where knots of deep tissue trauma formed new features. Her fingers faltered in the alluvial ruts carved into her cheeks by tears. Incredible, that halfway to death, already mummified and entombed, her body had decided to splurge and let her have a good cry. Her breath fluttered and a whole rack of steak knives pressed against her lungs. That'd be her broken ribs, unless she was impaled on a bunch of iron rebar, too. "Thank you, God, for this precious gift," she whispered. "When I get out of here, I've got a present for you, too."

That's the spirit.

Fuck you too, Guardian Angel. I want to die.

Then die. All is a matter of will. You want to live, so you will live.

"With what?" she screamed aloud, coughing up a tempest that only got worse as her blood-flecked breath stirred up the dust coating her tomb. "I have no legs! I have one arm, and I'd have to chew my goddamned legs off to get free—" she paused for breath, coughed up sand "—but the pressure...from the concrete...is the only thing keeping me from bleeding to death."

If it is too much for you, you may die. But if you want to live—

"What, goddamit? What?"

You must dig.

She had no retort, for it was true. She would not, could not die down here. Her new body would not allow it. Death for her would not be the sad little thing that came to claim other hapless accident victims, usually before they regained consciousness. Like Prometheus on the rock, or a vampire, she would linger forever down here. Powerless to save her, her new, improved body could only infinitely prolong her suffering, unless her old mind got her out. Even as the brittle bundle of sticks that apparently was her hand pawed the matted hair from her brow and set to probing the shattered stone floor of her tomb, she knew she would get out. If she emerged a smashed and peeled skull, propelling its miserable self only by the flapping of her jaw and the flailing of her severed spine, she would escape this.

Her fingers scrabbled over the unbroken slab she lay upon, creeping ever outwards almost to full extension before finding a crack. The sensation was unspeakably strange; she felt none of the textures or temperatures of that which her hand touched. It was like trying to work a telephone with a glove on a broomstick. Had the nerves in her fingers been cut, or had her whole nervous system given up the ghost and signed off? Shock, she told herself. At least you can still move it. Die trying.

She forced her hand to claw at the edges of the nearest small rock underneath her slab, to wedge her numb fingers into the fissure and pry the rock loose. It might have taken hours, but at last she held a shard of concrete in her fist, as more dirt and rocks clattered into the hole she'd made. Her hand seized up and the rock tumbled out of her grasp, and she realized with a start that she could still feel pain, for her hand felt as if it had caught fire. Maybe it was burning, and she was blind. But there was no warmth from the flames that ate her nerves. She shrieked and tried to blow on her hand, but only sand and spit came out.

Stella froze. A sound, not of her own making.

The rock she'd dropped had struck something. The sound was muffled and faint, but so familiar to her that it made all the difference in the world between going through the motions of trying to survive, and actually getting out. The rock had struck sheet metal. The only sheet metal surfaces she'd encountered in the Mission bunker had been the blast doors that sealed off the motor pool/hangar. Last night, she'd gone to those doors first when running from Delores Mrachek, she'd banged on them for help from the federal agents who surrounded the bunker, and they'd shot at her. She knew those doors with her fists. If they were below her, then she was closer to the surface than she'd had any reason to hope.

She clenched her hand into a fist. Her nails gouged the meat of her palms and clicked on bone. A short bark of a scream escaped her lips, but the pain brought her back wholly into herself. There was very little blood, but her hand felt as if she'd torn every tendon and ligament in it.

Dig.

She pried loose more rocks, working herself into a fever that painted the dark with brilliant hallucinations, before she felt the slab beneath her shift. It was only a few millimeters, but she felt it in her legs, saw the wheeling phosphene mandalas tilt on their axes before her, and heard the grit of something harder than her own head as the concrete blocks settled into the tiny tunnel she'd begun to make. The flooring she'd been picking at was nearly pulverized by the weight of the bunker's outer shell collapsing onto it, but she had no idea how thick that floor was, or how many floors lay beneath it. *I see where you're going with this, God,* she thought. *In digging my way to freedom, I only dig myself a deeper grave.*

You can die right here.

Fuck you, Guardian Angel.

You're going too slowly, Stella.

What do you want me to do, then? This?

Stella reached up behind her and clawed at the slab pinning her down, Its edges were cleaner, a neat break along a stress line, and she dislodged only crumbs, and broke off her nail and most of the flesh left on her pinky finger. She might've been trying to crush herself rather than try to escape. When her hand grasped the protruding length of rebar, she didn't even realize what it was. She seized upon it and yanked down on it with all the strength she had left in her ravaged arm. She even heard the muscles of her deltoid separating from her humerus, and the snapping of her wrist, before they were drowned out by the growl of the concrete slab unzipping itself into shards and crumbling over her.

Then the darkness came alive again and took her away.

When she awakened, she could move.

Moving was pain.

Her right arm was dead meat at her side, completely popped out of its socket and held on only by the twisted wreck of her shoulder muscles. The elbow was blown out, too. Her left was little better, shaking like a dying dog as she put weight on it.

She rolled over.

Catfish moved more gracefully on the bottom of a rowboat after you smashed their brains in with an oar. She flopped about in the relative stadium of open space beyond the slab, reveling in the backlogged messages of agony now flowing freely to her brain. She was free. Still some twenty feet under concrete and hard-packed desert sand, but *free.* She should be dead, now. No doubt about it, if the burial hadn't killed her and she hadn't asphyxiated, then she never should have awakened from her faint after she freed herself from the slab. She'd lost a lot of blood, her vision writhed with faces she'd never seen and places she'd never been but all that was almost behind her. She was still alive. She was changed. The cancer couldn't kill her, now. Nothing would ever threaten to take her life again. She could make noise now, the dead would rise to dig her out.

No one's coming to save you, Stella.

This is something you have to do for yourself.

She knew the voice was right, even as the words became shapeless blobs in her mind. She had to move, to get out. She had to put the pain aside and move.

The crawlspace she followed was only a little roomier than the pincers between the slabs, but it inclined downwards, down a jagged slide of shattered concrete shot through with spears of rebar, and slick with fluid that burned her skin off as she wormed through it. Her arms flailed at the ground like broken fins, every motion a fiery seizure, but she knew they were growing back. It was a good pain, and brought her back to herself. The cancer in her—*was* her, now. The blooming black and pink tumors she'd seen in Stephen, the man who'd been hit by the train—what, a week ago? Stanching the flow of blood, growing to replace tissue and bone, even lost limbs. It must have burned like this, she thought.

"We can rebuild her," she wheezed. *"Stronger, faster—"* She tried to hum the *Bionic Woman* theme song, but had to stop when she coughed up something solid.

She humped over a slab of concrete and slid the last few feet into the sheet metal door. Exhaustion burned her from the inside out. Lactic acid in her muscles must be past lethal levels. She shivered all over, and tried to catch her breath. She lay head-down against the sheet metal of the blast doors. The razor-puckered mouth of a bullet hole cut into her cheek.

Rest.

When she woke this time, she could feel cool air on her cheek. It came from the bullet hole. She could smell the desert, through the ashes and oil and toxic waste and the dead—*oh that's me.*

There was no pain. She felt tired and sore, and her right arm still flopped, but the head of the humerus had popped into the rotator cuff while she slept.

She pressed her lips to the hole and sucked in fresh air. She gagged and coughed as her lungs inflated as if for the first time. The thought occurred to her. If she was so close to fresh air, why hadn't she been found already? Surely a dog would have sniffed her out. Scared of a little toxic waste, maybe more explosives. If they came looking for anything in here, it'd be with bulldozers.

And it'd take one to get through the blast door. The weight of the bunker's outer shell collapsing against it hadn't bent it more than twenty degrees or so, and the upper frame of the door was blocked by concrete. Her only hope lay in banging on the blast door and hoping someone from the rescue crew was still out there.

No one is out there, Stella.

Have you got a better idea?

Tear the door open.

That's stupid, what do you think I am? I was never strong, and I'm only barely alive now!

You have changed.

Stop telling me what to do! She clawed at her face in her anger, but stopped just short of putting out her own eye. Her left hand was someone else's. It belonged to something else—her fingers were gone, replaced by hard, broad, blade-edged claws, like a mole would have. They were growing out of her hands, out of the fused stubs of her fingers, that she'd torn off digging herself out of the slabs.

God, what's happening to me?

You're going to survive this.

What am I?

You're alive.

Stella poked one claw into the hole and jabbed her hand at it like she was driving a saw through a knotty block of wood. The claw punched through the blast door down to her knuckle like she was cutting butter. She slashed frantically at the door until she'd hacked a hole wide enough to crawl through.

She could see moonlight.

Slowly, mindful of her crushed legs, she dragged herself out of the hole. The light was blinding, halos within halos like daggers in her eyes, but she couldn't blink for the joy of seeing again. When at last she hauled herself up, her eyes stopped tearing up and she could see her surroundings.

She lay shivering in the open pit of the motor pool, but there was little that she recognized from her brief glimpse of it. Mounds of dirt and concrete debris lay everywhere, and the walls had collapsed inward to spill rusted-out barrels of god-knew-what on everything. It didn't glow green like in the movies, but the noxious, bleachy smell and the heat-haze effect of fumes that roiled over it advertised its true nature adequately. There was something else on the ground that struck more fear into her heart than the waste, though.

Snow.

A thin dusting of powder lay in the leeward shadows of the walls, and was only starting to melt and gather in pools in the recesses of the pit.

My last day of work was the Fifth of July, she thought. I was held here for a week. Last night–the last night I was outside–was hot...

In the desert, it snows maybe once or twice a year, between December and February.

Stella fell on a puddle of clean meltwater far from the barrels and drank greedily. It soothed the burning on her skin, and carved a track through her insides that she now knew must have been sealed for the better part of a year.

When she could drink no more, she stopped and leaned back from the puddle. As the ripples receded into mirror stillness, she leaned forward and looked at her silhouette by moonlight.

She was dead. Past dead. She could lose a bodybuilding competition to Ramses II. A glaring patch of bare skull shone through the blood-matted rag of hair above her right ear. Her nose was a hole like a third eye. Her lips had withered and pulled away from her teeth, a leering rictus that gleamed in the moonlight.

She washed in the puddle, but came away looking or smelling no better. She dragged herself to her feet, shuddering on legs that were more tumor than flesh. The silvery glow of the desert night was flattering, but she should never have lived to see this. Her skin was black where bone didn't break through, and her clothing had entirely ripped or rotted away. Still, it would take a forensic pathologist to identify her gender. Her breasts, never more than a modest handful, were gone, only one nipple remained, the other sheared off. Her abdominal muscles were withered and hanging away from her viscera, a miserable, leathery purse that gurgled now with new life as the melted snow rehydrated her guts. Her hips jutted out like antlers from a sunken pubic arch shaded by the dangling flaps of still-detached thigh-meat.

I'm alive.

She'd lain underground for six months. One hundred and seventy-seven days more than Jesus.

You have earned the right to survive. You have earned your place in the light.

She walked to the edge of the pit, circled it until she found a slope she could climb out.

You must find shelter, and a telephone.

There were no TV crews, no rescue crews, not even a junkyard, anymore. Only a single, rustbound bulldozer that had become too contaminated to be worth retrieving during the half-hearted clean-up. She crossed the lot to the hurricane fence the state had put up around the pit and scaled it easily. The road led to the highway and Las Vegas on the left, to a trailer park on the right. Half-mad with cold and hunger and pain and joy, Stella headed to the right, starting to run on the frost-encrusted sand beside the road. The stars dilated, each twinkling beacon the rose window of a celestial cathedral, a pitiless eye of cold, sidereal fire. The dark spaces between hid a divine machine in which this world and everything in it were only dust, but the master of it all spoke to *her*.

You must heal, and wait. We will come for you.

~ 2 ~

Jan. 1, 2000
Westwood, California

The trees were sick.

The undersides of all the leaves on his mother's Valencia orange tree and her hibiscus bush were flocked in furry clumps of the secretions of the silverleaf whitefly, and in any other backyard in West LA, they would've been cut down by the diligent Public Works Department. No outsider would ever touch anything in the Cundieffe yard.

Martin Cundieffe sat on the porch glider beside the back door of his mother's house and sipped lukewarm hot chocolate. The day was chilly and arid, with bitter gusts of wind out of the northeast, blasting away the last traces of the rainstorm that had left an eighth of an inch of snow in Palm Springs the week before. Weather in southern California was like a service interruption of a public utility. It was seldom predicted, never accurately, and it transpired with such an apologetic half-heartedness that no one ever took it seriously. The first big autumn storm Cundieffe had seen in Washington a few months back had startled him with the notion that anyone would willingly live under such meteorological tyranny.

He zipped up his windbreaker, hoping that nobody spotted him in it, since it said FBI across the back. He expected to be called back to the office any minute, so he had slipped the windbreaker and an old green coverall from the garage over his suit to see to the trees before his mother or the neighbors noticed that they were festering again. Over the past several months, he'd tried placing shoofly plants and Encarsia wasps in the yard, but the former had no effect, and his mother had accidentally killed the latter with overzealous chemical spraying, which caused a population explosion of the highly resistant parasites. Last month, he'd launched a last-ditch campaign to smoke out and burn the adult whiteflies with a newspaper torch, but the extent of scaly larvae and light beige eggs on the leaves this afternoon had driven home the hopelessness of the campaign.

The Melnitzes next door, irritable fussbudgets and fetishistic lemon-growers, had filed complaints every week for the last two years, and addressed the LA City Council about the problem twice. The first time, Public Works sent out a crew of tree surgeons, who inspected and chopped down the Melnitzes' own prized lemon trees. Because of his new responsibilities at the office, he had let the trees go to ruin, knowing all the time that his mother trusted no one else to care for them. He might have let them get a lot worse if he hadn't found himself in need of this place that he knew more intimately than his own body, to reflect on everything that had changed outside its walls.

Martin's father was transferred to Los Angeles when the listening post he administered in the old Post Office tower in Washington, DC, was closed in 1966. This was a reflection of the Director's warm personal feelings for the senior Cundieffe, as well as his wife, who had served as a trusted member of the executive secretarial pool on the fifth floor at FBI Headquarters for twenty years. In his dotage, the Director had shut down nearly all of his domestic listening posts and COINTELPRO operations out of a sudden terror that his legacy would be tainted by what some would misperceive as abuses of the Constitution and his office. Many who knew less and sent more lavish birthday gifts each year had been sent further away, often to foreign legat posts in South America or the Middle East.

The Cundieffes resettled to a nice two-bedroom house on an idyllic side street in Westwood, not two miles from the Federal Building on Wilshire. For Special Agent Frank Cundieffe, it was not a question, but Muriel felt uprooted, thrown away from the seat of power on a whim. Frank arranged for Muriel to join the Los Angeles SAC's secretarial pool, but she complained that it was a henhouse, and the SAC was far from "Director material." Frank bought Muriel the sapling orange tree and planted it in the backyard in a gesture he could not have explained himself, but which Martin knew was intended to root her to this new place. It didn't quite work, and Muriel sank deeper into depression. Frank sprang into action again, bringing his wife out to Hawaii for a month-long working vacation while he did some sub rosa consultation work with the Naval Security Group's listening posts at Honolulu. It was there that he bought her the hibiscus cuttings that became the massive thicket of trumpet-shaped flowers that dominated the Cundieffe backyard. It was also in Hawaii that Frank and Muriel, forty-two and thirty-nine, had conceived Martin.

Frank died of a heart attack in 1977, and Muriel retired early to care for her son. Martin made the backyard his laboratory, digging up anthills, launching rockets and tuning in his first handmade radio. As he looked around him today, he saw the marks of his education. The chipped corner on the mantle of the brick barbecue in the far corner, beside the garage, had carved the crescent-shaped scar on his right knee when he was eight, eavesdropping on the Melnitzes' predecessors. His first bust—he'd overheard them talking about a drug smuggling operation with a Mexican gangster posing as a gardener, and reported them anonymously to the local police. He saw the wall of staghorns that had made him uneasy as a child, clinging to the shaded kitchen wall at his back, their primitive, shell-like bodies suggesting some early attempt by the vegetable kingdom to leap into the domain of animals. None of them seemed to have grown or lost a leaf since he was a small boy, afraid to go out into the backyard at night. The modest expanse of the yard itself was paved over and painted a green brighter than Astroturf by Frank Cundieffe, who always had better things to do than slave over a lawn. The trees that had taught Martin everything he knew about horticulture and marriage: only a few leathery brown sacs hung from the branches of the orange tree, and the hibiscus was completely denuded of the trumpet-blossoms that his mother had worn in her hair around the house when no visitors were likely to call her to the door.

The whitefly was devouring her plants, the downy parasitic floss dangling from the undersides of all the remaining leaves. When they finally succumbed, or some idiot with the City Public Works stole into the yard and chopped them down, the unparalleled deductive skills of Special Agent Martin Cundieffe told him, his mother would surely die.

All these things kept recycling in his mind, all the things and people he couldn't keep alive, for all his cleverness. All these things brought him back to Sgt. Zane Ezekiel Storch.

One week after the Radiant Dawn massacre, Cundieffe was officially promoted to Supervisory Special Agent of the Los Angeles field office's counterterrorism section. Most of the work lay in monitoring suspicious groups and reviewing local police work for militia group involvement. The bulk of his time was spent detailing surveillance and consulting with local police on crimes, mostly robberies. What little waking hours he could spare he spent nursing and updating his watch-list files and

integrating it with the NCIC database in Washington. Big changes were
afoot at Headquarters; Counter-terrorism had been spun off as its own
Division, and Deputy AD Wendell Wyler was promoted to Assistant
Director to head it. Wyler had assured him there would be a place for him
at Headquarters when the dust settled. He'd already been to visit the new
AD four times in the last five months, to sit in on meetings on the new
Division, and on the recently approved Domestic Preparedness Center,
which would centrally coordinate responses to terrorist threats. The
Attorney General woodenly saluted the current Director for the Bureau's
proactive posture in preparing for *potential* threats to safety and national
security, and the media was predictably upbeat and supportive. If they
only knew, he thought, what really happened.

The federal government found itself in a morass over the Radiant
Dawn terrorist attack—to admit that a radical group had stolen from the
Navy, then bombed a village full of civilians, then nuked it, would cause a
panic, even if it hadn't happened in California. Reluctantly, the Pentagon
and the Justice Department assembled a comprehensive cover-up, which
had so far held up, in no small part due to the Mules' backstage
management.

The investigators who first surveyed the site announced that the
Radiant Dawn village was destroyed by a freak propane tank explosion,
which triggered a chain reaction, igniting pockets of methane in the
community's sewage system. State and local investigators were kept at
arm's length while a Nuclear Emergency Survey Team sanitized the crater.
The media quickly picked up the official line and conflated it into a
deflective terror-campaign. The cover of *Time* the following week showed
a chilling computer graphic of a rural household in cross-section, with a
death's head-adorned bomb embedded in its foundation. The headline:
Wired For Death? The Ticking Time Bomb Underneath American Homes.
Less restrained periodicals carried the message even further, and a
nationwide inspection of propane and septic tanks swept away concerns
over the true nature of the tragedy that started it all.

The tactical nuclear weapon was remarkably small and clean—less
than a two kiloton yield, which was partially minimized by its placement
on the ground, while the shape of the valley and the network of tunnels
underneath absorbed the brunt of the blast. Federal money funneled into
the insurance company paid the manufacturer's liabilities, and claims
against Radiant Dawn itself were surprisingly low. Almost none of the
residents had any immediate family, and few extended family or friends
came forth to file suits. Only a handful of eyewitnesses from the Bishop
County Fire Department gave contradictory testimony, but they were

quickly marginalized. The military helicopters they saw over the village were National Guard choppers detailed to fire control over the hot summer, and they were dumping chemical retardant, not napalm, onto the fire. Sierra Club claims that detectable levels of radiation were present in the neighboring Inyo National Forest went largely unheard.

Dr. Keogh, the founder and chief administrator of Radiant Dawn, reluctantly agreed to cooperate with the federal cover-up, but had since been frustratingly aloof from the Bureau's attempts to question him. In private, the government collectively asserted that the Radiant Dawn village represented a symbolic target for the Mission to demonstrate their force against those doomed to die, anyway. Too cowed to speak up at the time, yet Cundieffe believed that Radiant Dawn, the mysterious RADIANT project and what happened at the Mission's abandoned base in Baker were too entangled for coincidence. The only reason Cundieffe hadn't proceeded to investigate Radiant Dawn on his own was his sinking fear that somebody else in government already knew, and was working to remove any link to itself. Before Cundieffe had even returned to the field office from his shattering encounter at China Lake, all the RADIANT material—heavily expurgated though it was—had been pulled out of reach. Even declassified material relating to SDI and other defense projects from the fifties onward were temporarily reclassified Top Secret, DoD Channels Only, pending a "major administrative oversight."

The Baker raid was yet another disaster only narrowly covered up, and in its way, even more perplexing than the other. The mysterious event which occurred just before the Mission's bunker imploded left seven Delta Force commandos with terminal cancer which ate them alive in less than a week. Their families were told they were killed in a helicopter crash during a joint maneuver with the SEALS in the desert. AD Wyler told Cundieffe that they were exposed to a highly toxic substance in the Mission bunker which caused their deaths. Cundieffe probed no further, but he knew in his bones that it was RADIANT, knew also that there were cover stories within cover stories. Though he worked in a different dimension of truth from the nation as a whole, he still knew nothing that he could prove, even to himself.

No evidence of any value and no remains were successfully excavated from the bunker. None of the vaunted non-lethal weapons technology that Wyler had dangled before him as that first taste of secrets that led to the Mules. Attempts to dig it out only disclosed high explosives and barrels of toxic waste sealed up within the walls. The Navy gave up, and a National Security Directive was quickly and quietly drawn up placing the property under DoD ownership, and fencing it off for the next ten thousand years.

Since the events at the Radiant Dawn hospice in the Owens Valley, there was no intelligence indicating that the Mission even continued to exist, let alone that they still posed a threat, but the Mules believed otherwise. The Mission was being hunted both in North and South America, but that search had only yielded more dead ends. The Mission chopper which dropped one soldier off at their Baker HQ was never seen again, and presumably went to ground in Mexico. The oblique slant to the many, many briefings Cundieffe had attended with Wyler in Washington, however, suggested that they were not so concerned with concluding the investigation into what had happened there, but with preventing a worse outbreak of violence in the future. Cundieffe was consulted often and in depth on his limited knowledge of the man they seemed to feel was the key to the Mission. That he had been framed by parties unknown carried little weight in their discussions.

Since his capture, Sergeant Zane Ezekiel Storch had been held at a nameless stockade on the Avon Military Reservation in Florida, a highly classified prison for military criminals so heinous the outside world has never heard of its existence. The CIA's interrogation specialists had made a playground of Storch night and day for the last five months. So far Storch had given up nothing. Cundieffe could hardly blame him.

Held in secret by the military, Storch had no rights, no legal advocate, no witnesses, no one who knew he was even alive. When he told what he knew about the Mission and Radiant Dawn, he had to know that he would be quietly executed. Despite the CIA's best efforts to make him look forward to this event, he had remained silent. Cundieffe had hoped to reach him with a different approach, but up until last week, those in power had only wanted him to feed facts to the torturers. Cundieffe had been able to research Storch in excruciating detail, and believed that while he probably knew very little about the Mission, he knew more than anyone else was willing to tell him about Radiant Dawn.

Nonetheless, Cundieffe had been shocked two days ago when Wyler called him into his office and told him he was to see Storch the following morning.

He had made his ethical misgivings known at the outset, even as he pressed for it. This was not how justice was carried out in the United States. This was not what the FBI and the Army were for. This kind of thing never happened in America.

Wyler had turned and risen from his desk and gone to his window. Cundieffe had wondered that all the windows in the building were so narrow, as if Hoover built it to withstand a siege. He knew there'd be war with the outside world, and he built us a fortress.

"You have a lot to learn about America," Wyler had told him. "You know why you are being allowed to do this?"

"Sir?" he began too loudly, then, almost whispering, "I was the Supervisory Agent on the primary investigation, and my background profile on Sgt. Storch was a principal factor in stringing together several seemingly unrelated events in the case, and—"

"No. They're letting you talk to him because you are one of us, and we have forced them. To them, you are an instrument of our will. They have failed, completely and utterly, to gather anything meaningful out of him, and they only half-hope you'll succeed before he is executed. They are making this out to be a very big favor, one for which we will have to pay dearly. But all of this is academic, because if they haven't made him talk in five months, you haven't got a prayer of getting anything out of him in half an hour. That's what they believe. Are they wrong?"

Cundieffe had felt his pulse quicken and his brain squeezing out endorphins and adrenaline in generous dosages, and there had been no doubt, no hesitation in his voice. "I was born to prove them wrong, sir."

Cundieffe knew that the Pentagon was a big building. He had toured it once as a child and twice as an adult, and it never failed to stun him with its sheer mass, and its titanic network of human effort. FBI Headquarters, with its streamlined, centralized hierarchy, flowed mostly along conduits invisible or at least discrete. The military had far more duties, but with its myriad gargantuan bureaucracies and multiple heads, with its masculine fetish for ritual and compartmentalization, it demanded all the superfluous layers of human machinery that symbolize a great enterprise: legions of racing couriers with sealed folders, flocks of staff officers migrating through their cycles of briefings, and sentries at every juncture, with sentries watching the sentries, and cameras watching them all. He was now educated enough to understand that very little of substance was ever decided here.

In the early morning rush to fill the largest government building in human history, the lines filing through the metal detectors and the ID checkpoints flowed quickly, but three MP's escorted Cundieffe past them and into the aortic superhighway of the outer ring corridors. Clerks and couriers on three-wheeled scooters passed them, and Cundieffe noticed the kind of electric courtesy carts that airlines use to shuttle passengers to faraway terminal connections.

They passed through a blank door with no knob, no placard. He followed them immediately down a narrow spiral staircase which opened on a long empty corridor, watching the walls change color from mint to forest green, to red, to rose marble. There were only more blank doors and equally empty branching halls leading off this corridor and heavy steel blast doors recessed into the walls at every intersection. They took two more flights of stairs down and threaded a maze of basement corridors lined with basket carts filled with packages, mail and folders. When they finally stopped, they stood on a subway platform unlike any Cundieffe had ever seen before. The track terminated here, and ran off into a barrel-vaulted tunnel that curved away to the left, in which direction Cundieffe couldn't begin to guess. A single electric, open-topped car waited, and there was an Army officer waiting on it.

There were several similar underground lines reserved for government personnel, which connected the Pentagon with other facilities, like Crystal City or Washington National Airport, just as there were private subway lines connecting the Capitol with the various congressional office buildings. But this tramway was older than those, and yet more modern. He barely noticed the red eyeblinks of scanners reading his temporary badge as he passed through the turnstile. The MP's saluted the officer and marched into an elevator that opened for them at the end of the platform. Cundieffe climbed onto the car. Immediately, silently, it began to glide down the tunnel, Cundieffe noticed a station placard on the wall as they pulled away, but it was in barcode.

The officer turned and faced him, looking him pointedly up and down and not saluting. Cundieffe tried not to wince as he looked at the man's face. "You must be Col. Nye," he said.

"'S'what it says on the fucking uniform, isn't it?" Col. Nye answered, and blew smoke in Cundieffe's face. It came in a thick cone that caught him off guard, because Col. Nye had no nose.

From Wyler's classified briefing, Cundieffe knew that Col. Nye was the commandant of Avon's Special Stockade. Before that, he served four tours in Vietnam, first as a commando, then as a Special Forces liaison with the CIA. During the last, desperate days of the war, he lost most of his face to a grenade in an action the United States government could not acknowledge, because its forces were supposed to have left the country three months before. The legend was that he'd gone into Hanoi to assassinate Ho Chi Minh himself, on his own and supposedly without orders. He never got within ten miles of Hanoi, but he allegedly killed well over one hundred NVA regulars getting in and out before he was exfiltrated out of Laos. He was discharged in 1975 with a Purple Heart for an "accident," which he'd refused. He wore no medals and no insignia other than the bare minimum to establish rank and national affiliation, but every serviceman who recognized him saluted him as he would God or the ghost of Patton. Even so, if Sgt. Storch so much as opened his mouth, Col. Nye was not cleared to hear what Cundieffe would hear. This gave him the nerve to look the Colonel in the eye.

Nye also refused to wear prosthetic facial appliances, apparently preferring to use his ghastly appearance as a motivational weapon. To Cundieffe, he looked more than a little like Ross Perot with no nose or upper lip, a hand-rolled cigarette clenched in his naked yellow dentures, yawning nasal cavity gushing out ribbons of smoke like an idling locomotive, flinty green eyes taking Cundieffe's measure like they were going somewhere dark and deep together, and only one was coming back.

It was a strange feeling being looked at like that, the way Lt. Col. Greenaway had looked at him, the way former Special Agent Lane Hunt had looked at him as he'd been hauled away. Like they possessed an animal sense that Cundieffe lacked, that told them he was not one of them. It did not surprise him so much now that he'd never suspected the Mules, or himself, while the neighborhood children had felt instinctively compelled to ostracize and beat him senseless at every opportunity until he became an FBI agent. He hesitated to use the Mules' terms for it, but it fit the way they made him feel: gendered humans still responded largely to chemical, pheromonal cues in all dealings with each other. The absence of such often incited animal hostility, contempt and fear. He hoped he would fare better with Sgt. Storch than he was with Col. Nye.

"You've been briefed on the extent of my responsibilities for the duration of the meeting?" Nye demanded.

"Yes, I have. I understand everything except for the lack of any medical file materials. Are there any you could make available to me before I sit down with him?"

"None whatsoever!"

Cundieffe blinked, but it was at least half from the smoke. "Pardon?"

"Did I speak French? I am not aware of any such cockeyed bullshit, nor would I be fucking well disposed to disclose a single fucking thing I did know about said cockeyed bullshit, were I aware of such. Asshole."

"Col. Nye, you have been directly ordered to cooperate fully, have you not?"

"Absolutely."

"Then if there's anything you can tell me yourself that you are withholding, you would be in violation of a direct order. If you're afraid of compromising security—"

"I don't give a one-eyed flying fuck about that bullshit," Nye growled back. He turned and got up in Cundieffe's face, so close his cigarette singed Cundieffe's chin. "*I know what you are*," he said. Cundieffe took stock of the fact that he was alone in the subway car with the Colonel. He stood a head taller than the officer, and he was armed, but Nye's hand rested on his holster so steadily that he was either preparing to draw down at any moment, or his arm was paralyzed, or a prosthetic fake.

This was an absurd train of thought. He understood Col. Nye's type. If he couldn't interrogate a hostile party on the same side, what chance did he stand with a radical enemy of the state? "And we know you, Col. Nye. We know your real name, and how you really lost your face, and we know things that even you've forgotten that would cost you even this pathetic little shadow-commission you've managed to hold onto. Now, how much contact have you had with the prisoner?"

Col. Nye seemed to shrink a little. "Too fucking much," he finally answered. "None at all. He's a goddamned vegetable now, anyway. You're wasting everybody's time."

"Yes, I understand they're eager to dissect him up at Ft. Detrick."

Nye chuffed smoke rings out his blowhole. "I don't need to know about any of that shit, shithead. I only run the goddamned stockade. He's forgotten once he's transferred."

In doing his homework, Cundieffe had learned a bit about how prisoners were "transferred" from Avon. He read about a previous guest— a Marine-trained sniper who became a radical Christian and took up picking off abortion doctors and genetic researchers from extraordinary distances. He went to ground in the forbidding wilderness of the Appalachian range, but Army Rangers caught him and quietly brought him to Avon for "debriefing." Apparently, he'd done a number of assassinations of Palestinian Hammas and Party of God terrorists for them, and couldn't be trusted not to talk if turned out alive. His remains were discovered a month later in the wooded mountains of West Virginia, apparently starved and frozen to death. The following week brought crushingly efficient ATF raids on three weapons stockpiles of a Christian Fundamentalist terrorist group, with an anonymous informant credited with the tips. Then there were the stories of the prisoners for whom the facility had originally been built, the refugees of a seaside New England town, now nameless and long-since demolished: wretchedly inbred mutants who were shipped to Avon in 1928, gassed, vivisected and ultimately starved to death.

"He never made any attempt to communicate with you or anyone else, during his stay with you?"

"None whatsoever! He disabled two guards who got a little fresh with him when he rotated in, but otherwise he's been in solitary. He's had plenty of opportunity to speak up, but he has never done so, not even under extreme duress."

"Has he been examined by a medical doctor?"

"He's been treated more than a few times for injuries—mostly self-inflicted, mind you. In between, he got medical doctors, shrinks, neurosurgeons, biochemists, Agency torturers, whores, the works. Their diagnosis is, he didn't want to talk, and he'd put a hurt on anyone who touched him. And he's got cancer."

"What? What kind of cancer?"

"Cancer of the everygoddamnedthing. How the fuck should I know what kind? Yeah, he's gonna die any day now, anyway. Be a mercy, shooting him. Whatever he did, no soldier deserves to die like that."

The car smoothly glided to a stop and Col. Nye hopped off, moving between a brace of MP's who were dead ringers for the ones at the other end, except they wore no unit markings. There was no sign that Cundieffe could discern telling him where they were, but judging by the distance traveled underground, they could be underneath Arlington or Alexandria; for that matter, they could have gone under the Potomac to Bolling Air Force Base.

They went deeper. They boarded an elevator, went down four levels, and debarked in a red brick cavern that looked like a nineteenth century military prison. Arched cell doorways ran around all four walls, with vertical iron bars set into them. All the doors hung open save one. A cordon of MP's stood at attention before the bars, screening the prisoner from view. Cundieffe approached, and they gave no acknowledgment except for tightening their grips on their assault rifles.

Col. Nye's nasal wheezing crept up behind him. "Come meet some people," he honked. Cundieffe turned around and let himself be led to a cell opposite Sgt. Storch's, this one unlit except for the red and green lights of computers and recording equipment. Two men sat in the shadows behind the gear. They both rose and walked over to Cundieffe. He shook hands with them both. "Duncan Showalter, technical consultant," the first man said, his eyes looking over Cundieffe's shoulder. Cundieffe took the other man's hand and the moment he looked into his eyes, he knew. The other man was a Mule.

"Brady Hoecker, Associate Director, National Security Agency," he said, and he nodded to Cundieffe and his eyes sparked the message that he *knew*, too. "We're just here to listen in, so don't let us cramp your style."

"You pencil-necks can suck each other's dicks on your own time," Nye cut in, dragging Cundieffe back across the gallery to Storch's cell.

Hoecker and Showalter retreated back into the dark and the sentries parted.

"One more thing," Col. Nye said, and smoothly lifted Cundieffe's sidearm out of its shoulder holster.

"I have no intention of harming the prisoner, Colonel," Cundieffe murmured.

"Don't think you could if you tried, but it's not *you* I'm worried about." He swiped a card through a reader slot and handed the card to one of the MP's as the gate popped open.

A second gate inside the first, and Col. Nye opened this one with a key, which he presented to another MP who stood his post in the antechamber between the gates. The guard hung the key around his neck and aimed his rifle squarely at the back of the man sitting in the cell.

Cundieffe stood in the antechamber until Col. Nye shoved him into the cell and slammed the inner gate behind him. "Give a shout when you're done. You have twenty seven minutes." The outside MP opened the card gate for him and slammed it. Col. Nye disappeared behind a wall of guards with their backs turned.

Sgt. Storch sat at a hardwood table with his hands shackled behind his back and bolted to the floor. He wore a collar of plastic with blinking LED's on it: some sort of shock deterrent device, most likely. When the gate shut, he inclined his head slightly; not in surprise, but, Cundieffe thought, to brace for an attack. He stepped into the cell, the greasy crinkle of plastic dropcloth underfoot. He wondered if they intended to execute him here, and wanted to have it clean for the tourists by this afternoon. He gave Storch a wide berth, walking against the brick wall to the far side of the table. He avoided making eye contact until he was sitting opposite the prisoner. Slowly, he laid his briefcase on the table and, slower still, unsnapped the hasps and laid it open before him. Trying to remember that he was here as an interrogator, when he felt like Storch's lawyer. Only then did he stop and look up at Sgt. Storch.

Up until now, Cundieffe had only seen Storch in ID photos, old family snapshots, surveillance imagery and on tapes of closed-circuit security video. That man had looked haunted by some kind of illness which gave his otherwise unremarkable features a harsh, fanatical cast. Here was the illness wearing the smoldering ruin of the man he'd hoped to meet. Storch looked to have lost about fifty pounds in captivity, most of it muscle. His eyes were recessed so far into his head that he looked like a Neanderthal, with his beetling brow and knife-blade cheekbones. His mouth was clamped so tightly shut it was only another wrinkle in his crumpled face. Patches of hair so black it was almost blue stood out from Storch's skull, the rest of it scabbed and bleeding where he'd apparently ripped it out by the roots.

Mostly self-inflicted

Storch's skin hung on him like wet pajamas the color and texture of an onion, and scars crisscrossed it—the inflamed grid pattern of chemical exposure tests, the purple welts of cattle prods, neat seams from surgeries, many more whose causes Cundieffe couldn't begin to guess.

Storch didn't look up from the table, but he didn't seem to be focusing on the things Cundieffe laid out from the briefcase.

"Sergeant Zane Ezekiel Storch, Fifth Special Forces Group, Retired. I'm Special Agent Martin Cundieffe from the FBI. I realize that the circumstances are not what they could be, but I've come here to talk to you about your role in the Mission's activities of July Fourth through the Tenth, 1999. Am I speaking to Sergeant Zane Ezekiel Storch?"

No response.

"I don't expect many answers from you, Sgt. Storch. I've read your file, and I know your record in detail. Enlisted, 1983, Basic, then Airborne. You earned your Ranger tab in '84, and served with the First of the Seventy-Fifth Regiment, at Ft. Benning. In 1986, you took the Q Course to become a Green Beret. You stress-fractured your right forearm during an exercise, but concealed it for the remaining week, so you wouldn't be sent back. Did you know they were going to flunk you, Sergeant? You received excellent marks in everything but initiative. It was felt that while you had the will to fight and think as a soldier, you lacked the capability to think for yourself, and would make a superb Ranger. Good soldier, good weapon, but not a warrior. You passed because you wouldn't break, and they needed warm bodies, but the question remains: can you think for yourself, Sgt. Storch?"

Eyes flicked around above his head. No response.

"I realize also that you have been specially trained to resist interrogation and seek any opportunity to escape when held captive in wartime, and that you believe that some sort of state of war presently exists. And who could fault you for that assumption? You have been held without legal due process, and, in the course of your imprisonment, you have been tortured in an attempt to extract the information I am about to ask you for. I know, it strikes me as ridiculous, as well: when all else fails, try diplomacy. But, if I may make so bold, you of all people should be aware of the military's shortcomings with regard to unique situations like this one."

No response.

"Regrettably, I have no power to delay your execution and any cooperation you will offer will have to be for posterity, as nothing, I am given to understand, will result in the commutation or even temporary stay of your sentence. You're a man the United States government wants very badly to kill, Sgt. Storch, though you're already dying of cancer. And they want to do it in secrecy, in silence. Not that they'd have to—if the events of July Tenth, 1999, were made public, they would have little or no difficulty sentencing you to die in the gas chamber in California. There are more than enough rock-solid cases against you to move for the death penalty, so one could make the perverse argument that by executing you in secret, the government is only sparing the citizenry a lengthy and expensive show trial and years of panic and unrest.

"But I don't think anyone I've spoken to knows what really happened that night. I think that you know more than even you realize and are in a position at least to deny the military its precious silence."

He couldn't even tell if Storch was looking at the picture on top of the pile. The photo had been digitally enhanced, so it looked like a Pointillist painter's rendition of a security camera still. In it, a man whom Cundieffe and everyone else had positively identified as Sgt. Storch stood at the counter of the Furnace Creek Sheriff's office, pointing a gun at two men in uniform, one dead, one quite explosively dying. Though his gun hand was a hundred-fingered blur, his head was held as still as if he was posing for the picture.

Cundieffe opened up the first file and held up another picture. It showed Storch's pickup truck. "This truck was found on July Sixth along Highway 190. It was identified as your vehicle and impounded as evidence in the murder of Sheriff James Twombley and Deputy Kenny Landis on the Fifth, though there were several discrepancies observed between the vehicle's condition and the statements of Deputy Danny Asaro and the Death Valley Junction Sheriff's deputies who pursued the alleged murderer. Is this your vehicle, Sgt. Storch?"

No response.

Another photo. The same truck, down to the license plates, but shot through with bullet-holes and shotgun spray. Tipped over in an arroyo, half-buried in dried mud. "This vehicle was discovered by myself and another agent on July Tenth, less than two hours before the Mission dropped napalm on Radiant Dawn Hospice Village. Note that the condition of the vehicle matched the aforementioned statement. There were two trucks with your license plates. One was used to murder two peace officers, the other was found abandoned by the side of the road in the middle of Death Valley. Which vehicle was yours, Sgt. Storch?"

No response.

He closed the file and picked another. He held up a full-color crime scene photo of a male corpse propped up in a chair. An astounding variety of sharp instruments buried in the skull. "This unfortunate gentleman was named Charles Walter Angell, leader of the School Of Night sect in Colma. While the group's twenty-six members were all found dead by some sort of apparent biofeedback mass suicide, Mr. Angell was brutally murdered and suffered considerable postmortem desecration. They are content to believe that you did this."

He laid this photo down before Storch and picked up another. It showed a residential interior, the walls draped in tie-dyed tapestries and beaded curtains. Two bodies lay splayed out side by side in the center of the room. Every sharp object in the house and many not found in any healthy home were jammed into the skulls of the victims. They looked as if they were wearing steel war-bonnets.

"This is Sky and Chrysanthemum Angulo, of Santa Cruz, California. Both were convicted manufacturers of hallucinogens, and they were found murdered in their home, in January of 1988. There were signs of missing property, particularly electronics and narcotics, but their seventeen-year old son, Baron Angulo, was never found. Local authorities proceeded on the assumption that gang drug dealers had killed the Angulos and that their son had either fled or been abducted by the gang. The FBI's San Jose field office concluded that the sole perpetrator was the son, but there has never been an indictment handed down for want of evidence and what records they do have keep disappearing from the NCIC database. He's never been arrested or even sighted. This is the last known photo of Angulo. Do you recognize this boy?"

Storch's eyes might've flicked around in their bottomless sockets. Cundieffe took another look at the photo himself. Bright, mischievous eyes, and the crooked smile of one who has never been punished.

"Several of your former neighbors in Thermopylae positively identified the young man in this photograph as one Ely Buggs, a former employee of yours. Is that correct?"

Nothing.

"In 1996, a hacker penetrated the databases of the Human Genome Project at UC Berkeley, and copied all data in a section of classified research and proprietary DNA-parsing compounds. The FBI's computer crime specialists tracked the source of the incursion to a computer tied into a server network in Mountain View, California. The property owners were a small computer security firm and had no idea about the computer's presence, let alone its purpose. Upon accessing the server, they unleashed a virus which temporarily crashed the FBI's San Jose field office network and contaminated all outgoing e-mail with a Tourette virus, which randomly spikes all messages with obscenities and sundry blasphemous phrases."

Storch might have nodded once.

"Sounds like your employee, doesn't it?"

No response.

"Well, in other news, I went to see your father recently. He's still in solitary confinement, too, at Norwalk. You know that he's been writing a history of the universe, or something of that sort? Well, five months ago, he put it to the torch. No one knows how he started the fire, but he managed to destroy it and half of the ward. The chronicle numbered over seventy thousand pages, nearly five hundred pounds of paper, seven years of uninterrupted work. Since then, he's been locked up and heavily medicated, because he can't break out of the manic compulsion to begin another chronicle. In his more lucid moments, he's been writing it on the walls of his cell, and he explained it to me in excruciating detail before he was put back under sedation. He promises it will be twice as long as the other, which he now believes was erroneous. It begins with your birth, Sgt. Storch. I didn't tell him that you were in any kind of trouble. The doctors say a shock that great could trigger another breakdown."

Cundieffe might've been telling him about his own father, in Japanese. He had expected to have dug out some emotional reaction by now, some sign that a light was still on behind those flat, unblinking eyes. He probed every ghost of a motion for signs of contempt, anguish, rage, menace, fatigue or despair, but the face of the prisoner was mummified, painted on.

"Sgt. Storch, I'm getting a little tired of the sound of my own voice, here. None of this information will exonerate you in the eyes of the United States government because of your participation in the Radiant Dawn massacre and your fatal attack on FBI Agent Robert Niles on the night of your arrest. You are going to die today, while the people who brought you into this, against your will, I suspect, are safely ensconced somewhere in South America, plotting another attack on American soil. Those men out there are hoping you'll make some pitiful deathbed *mea culpa* and give up the Mission's foreign headquarters and in-country operatives and maybe tell them why you did it. And I don't even know why *I'm* the one talking to you, because just before I got here, I think I figured it out."

Storch's ears might have twitched, his brow might've contracted a millimeter or two.

"Shortly after you jumped—or were pushed—out of that helicopter over Liberty Salvage in Baker on the night of the Tenth, you and seven Delta Force commandos were irradiated by a light from the sky, which several accounts dismissed as an astronomical phenomenon or the spotlight of a previously unaccounted-for helicopter on the scene. Then the bomb went off in the Mission HQ."

Storch definitely shivered once, as if his skin had just shrunk a size.

"Within ten days, all seven soldiers were dead. Autopsies revealed a particularly rare variety of cancer tumor spread throughout their bodies. They're called teratomas, Sgt. Storch. They differ from garden-variety tumors in that they normally only manifest in germline cells, and the malignant mass attempts to differentiate into the distinct features of an independent organism. The features are only vestigial, certainly not viable, but more like an incomplete Siamese twin, if I may use a phrase out of political fashion. Or, in this particular case, several twins."

He turned over yet another photograph. A man's body on a steel examination table in a Naval hospital morgue. The body lay skewed at an awkward angle because there was no stretching it out. A tumor the size of a bowling ball warped the arc of the spine just above the hips and several more of greater or lesser size bloomed up and down the torso, great cables of protoplasm stretching from one tumor to the next under the skin. Two of them had been incised and the skin pinned back to expose the contents of the masses. One which had broken through the left temporal wall of the skull was in particularly clear focus. The granular folds of the tumor were studded with spikes of bone and glassy, blue-gray polyps; the tumor was trying to grow teeth and eyes.

"The odds of this kind of cancer forming in even one person are one in several million, and the odds of survival are painfully self-evident. You alone, of all those exposed, showed no sign of cancer immediately after exposure. Your suit was examined, and millions of microscopic pinholes were found burned into the vinyl, so there was no doubt that what hit them, hit you as well. But you survived.

"It was RADIANT, wasn't it? The military built an orbital anti-personnel device which caused cancer, but there was more to it, wasn't there? Radiant Dawn was a form of laboratory, where they were testing the effects of the weapon on those who already had cancer. The effect on them was very different from what happened to previously healthy bodies, wasn't it, Sgt. Storch?"

No response.

"There was a very different kind of Radiant Dawn community on the very same spot in the seventies, did you know that? Records are extremely sparse, and there's not so much as a picture of the leader, a man named Quesada, but there were rumors that it was some sort of a radiation cult. This has been going on for a very long time, hasn't it, Sergeant? This thing that you and your friends were trying to protect the world from, I mean. You might be of the opinion that such an undertaking could never come so far without sponsorship from within the government, and after all I've seen and heard myself, I couldn't say you were wrong. But you know what? Despite all the blood you and our friends spilled, it's still going on."

Storch staring through the pictures. Cundieffe turning over another. A field shot from a helicopter, a tiny toy church with a sheet-metal roof, and an ashtray beside it in the dirt. No, the ashtray was a pit, and the crumpled butts were human bodies. "There've been reports over the last six months of messianic movements in Uganda, Ethiopia and Kenya, where cancer incidence is high and treatment nearly non-existent. World Health Organization relief workers reported finding this body pit in Uganda with well over two hundred corpses, completely incinerated with gasoline. They turned out to be victims of AIDS. Their families said they left their homes to go to be healed out in the country. Flyers were found which instructed cancer sufferers to gather at predetermined places in the middle of the countryside to be healed. The AIDS patients just came along hoping for a miracle, and those who already *had cancer* and survived cremated the dead. Well over four hundred cancer patients in those three countries alone have vanished, and we have no idea how many more of these pits there are."

He turned over a satellite image, this one of a city. There were no cars on the roads, no smoke coming from the factories, and the giant broken eggshell in the center told the story. To not recognize it, one would have to have avoided all news coverage throughout the late eighties and early nineties. "There are at least three colonies in the former Soviet Union. The largest is a squatter colony in the quarantined zone surrounding Chernobyl. We still have no idea how large it is, but it's estimated that cancer victims in the Ukraine alone number in the tens of thousands."

He leaned across the table, so close that Storch could have bitten him, if it was worth getting shocked. "If it was your aim to exterminate RADIANT, you failed utterly. The program is still going on, and it's spreading."

Storch might've been an oil painting. Cundieffe sat back, then launched himself out of his chair and walked around behind Storch. Through a gap in the soldiers' cordon, he saw Nye and Hoecker stand up and approach the bars. He signaled them to back off and leaned in behind Storch's head.

"I don't presume to know everything about you, Sgt. Storch. I'm not even cleared to know what happened to you in the Gulf War. But I think I know a lot more about you than the people who are going to execute you today, because I'm the only one who's been looking in the right direction. I've read medical reports, for instance. VA hospital records that were sealed and buried. They knew there was something wrong with you, Sergeant. You and the other survivors of the Tiamat engagement. They found elevated white blood cell counts, but they didn't match the other blood in your system. They did DNA tests, and they couldn't accept what they saw, so they did them again, and then they forgot about you. Because they couldn't explain what the DNA of another organism was doing in your body, in rogue cells that were stimulating your autoimmune responses. They couldn't explain how the cells continued to split off in culture, and became independent single-cell organisms, with no genetic similarity to you or the parent cells. You didn't die in Baker because you already had cancer, but they couldn't understand it, so they never told you. You see what they do with unacceptable truths.

"I already have all the answers they want, but they don't really want to hear them, so your silence is the greatest service you could possibly render them. I don't need to know anything else from you, except this: when did your thumb grow back?"

Storch leapt away the table and sprang at Cundieffe. The agent's feet slipped out from under him on the plastic sheeting. The flagstone floor banged his knee silly and it gave way under him. He whirled around and went for his gun, but Nye had it. He froze then, when he saw Storch's eyes. For a second, he could have sworn they were the same steely gray as the blisters on the tumor in the picture.

Storch jolted straight up and his legs kicked out spastically in mid-air. Then he collapsed and beat the floor like an epileptic. Cundieffe smelled ozone and burning hair. Storch's eyes were green wheels with gold spokes flashing rage and terror, but his voice was steady and low as he said, "I will talk to you…outside."

Col. Nye fought with Cundieffe for five minutes, but after a replay of the argument with someone on a secure telephone line, he relented, and they brought Storch to the surface.

He walked in the center of the eight-man escort, with Cundieffe and Nye just behind them. Nye explained the conditions of the field trip in an almost hysterical rasp, relaying instructions from someone at the other end of his phone. Storch was not to be unshackled. He was not to move more than fifty feet in any direction, because the shock-collar around his neck contained two grams of C4. If he wandered out of range of the microtransmitter Col. Nye carried, it would detonate.

"Do you really think that's necessary?" Cundieffe asked.

"Not even sure it'd slow him down, but if he runs, he's your problem."

The eleven of them crammed into the elevator and two guards reached to press the button. One looked at the other one second longer than he should've, both their hands off their weapons, and Cundieffe looked at Storch, whose head was inclined on the pair. Cundieffe looked down at Storch's feet, shifting weight and turning as if to spring into a pivot motion that would allow him to grab one of the weapons behind his back. Nye leaned on the shock button, and Storch trembled while Nye chewed them out. One of them finally pressed the button, and the doors slid closed.

As they rose, Col. Nye shouldered his way through the cordon and stood nosehole to chin with Storch. "Bet you love all this attention, don't you, asshole?" he growled. "All this commotion over Baby's first fucking words, you think we're gonna blink and away you'll go with a song in your motherfucking heart."

Storch looked back blandly at Nye's Halloween-mask face, but made no move. In the close quarters of the elevator, Cundieffe could make out the distinctive tang of each man's perspiration. All but Storch's. He smelled like lightning.

The car rose six stories before humming to a stop and disgorging the passengers into a service corridor. Col. Nye seemed to see something in Storch's eyes that made him bite back the main course of his ration of wrath, and led the way out. Soldiers stood at attention every ten feet and doubled up outside each door. Somewhere in the building, very faint, Cundieffe could hear sirens.

Col. Nye went to a double door at the blind end of the corridor and threw them wide open. The pallid, weak winter sun was a revelation to Cundieffe, who threw his arm up across his face as he stepped out into it. They were in the open central courtyard of an office building, seven stories high. All the curtains were drawn, and there were another dozen soldiers spread around the perimeter and before the three glass doors leading back into the building. Some quick-thinking superior of Col. Nye's had pulled the fire alarm to clear the building.

The soldiers ran out into the courtyard and spread out to the far corners, turned and faced Storch, but in that instant, they were blinded, and probably would have been shot to pieces by the courtyard guards, had Storch tried anything. He walked out into the center of the courtyard, stopped and fell to his knees. His eyes closed, his mouth open, he simply basked as soldiers paced around him with weapons drawn, as if he were not already chained and beaten within an inch of his life. What had he done down in Florida, what had he shown them, that had them so frightened? He doubted anyone else even noticed that Storch now had a thumb he had lost in the Gulf War, so what had they seen? His medical records probably held the answer, but there was so much more he could learn from Storch himself, if he only had the time to reach him…

Col. Nye screamed. Storch was turning purple. His face and neck seemed to swell as his skin changed. It looked as if he was holding his breath, but the entire courtyard reverberated with the echoes of his cavernous lungs, as if he was trying to suck all the air out of the world. Nye shocked him, but Storch didn't seem to notice. He raced across the courtyard and hoisted one bandy leg to kick Storch squarely in the chest, but Cundieffe caught the leg under the knee and easily tipped the Colonel back on his ass. His hand went for—oh, nuts, Col. Nye still had his gun.

"Stay the—hell—away from this man, Colonel! Get your men back! He's having an allergic reaction to the sunlight! Help me get him into the shade—"

Cundieffe bent to lift Storch up by the arms, but the sergeant shook him off and stood on his own. "Get your hands off my fucking body," Storch said. He was not shaking or hyperventilating, anymore, but his skin was still a livid violet. He looked long and hard at Cundieffe, as if he'd just awakened from a dream to find the FBI agent lurking at his bedside. "They haven't fed me in a week," he said.

"Your cancer isn't killing you, is it?"

Storch, still looking up at the silvery blue square of sky, shook his head. "When I—when it needs to adapt, then He goes away," he mumbled. "For a while. Talk fast."

"Who controls RADIANT?"

Storch trembled. "Ask another question."

"Where is the Mission?"

"I really don't know."

"Why did you do it?"

"To stop Him…" Storch spat out the big H the same way rape victims speak of their attackers, the way pathologically God-fearing people talk about their deity, the One who gives them orders when they forget to take their meds.

"Stop whom? Stop him from doing what?"

"Stop Him from changing us. Being us…"

"Why weren't you killed by RADIANT?"

"It kills you, but—it speaks to cancer, and the cancer grows and it—becomes you."

He was raving so Cundieffe switched topics, firing his questions double-time. "Who controls the Mission? How many cells are there?"

"Probably Wittrock, now. Everyone else I know is dead." He seemed to strain for a moment—to remember, or simply to talk? "Wittrock said there were other units, but I don't know where they are."

"Whoever controls RADIANT turned it on the Mission in retribution for the attack, correct?"

"Well, shit, I guess you got all your answers."

"Does Keogh control RADIANT?"

Storch only looked at him for a second, then looked back up at the sky. The tendons stood out in his neck, muscles bunched up in his jaw. "His name's not Keogh. Not Keitel or Quesada, either."

"Then what is his name?"

Storch looked away from the sky as if it had suddenly become filled with something he couldn't bear to see. When he turned to look at Cundieffe, his whole body trembled with effort, yet remained totally contained. He stared very hard at Cundieffe, who began to believe that the prisoner was suffering a stroke. "He...has no name. He steals names, faces...H—he—his name was K-k-k..." A capillary in his right eye burst. "Tell my daddy to stop writing that book..."

"What else does Keogh control, Sergeant?"

"Agent Cundieffe, we'll have no more questions." Storch thawed and became molten, flowed up into Cundieffe's space so fast he was sure trigger-happy Col. Nye would fry him, but if he did, it had no effect anymore. Which shouldn't surprise, he thought.

When it needs to adapt—

Cundieffe felt himself suddenly dealt deeply into a game he did not know how to play. Either Storch was a masterful con man, or a certifiable split personality, or something else that no one in the world could understand. In any case, he would be dead in a matter of hours, so Cundieffe decided to play along.

"To whom am I speaking, please?"

"We are all one flesh, touching, loving, hating, killing itself, Agent. We are all one flesh, becoming one mind..."

"What is the purpose of Radiant Dawn?"

"We are teaching the world to adapt, Agent. In what they see as death, there lies eternal life. What they really fear is transformation, not death."

"You're going to die. Very shortly. Don't you think it's time to speak more clearly?"

"They can't kill me," Storch said. "This body is only the messenger. They cannot kill the message."

Col. Nye and his soldiers drew around Storch in a crushing knot, shoving Cundieffe out of the way. "And what is your message?" he yelled through the press.

"A bloodless evolution, Agent Cundieffe. The seeds of change in the old flesh are about to bear new fruit."

"This interview is over," Col. Nye snarled. With Cundieffe racing after them, the soldiers carried Storch bodily out of the courtyard and back into the dark maze of service corridors.

Twice soldiers peeled off to try to hold Cundieffe back, but he slipped out of their grasp, leaving one holding his overcoat by the collar after he ducked out of it. "You've got to postpone the transfer, Col. Nye! He's trying to tell us something that we have to know! Damn it, listen to me!"

The escort spilled out onto a loading dock opening out on a parking lot. An armored car waited in the middle of the loading area. The street outside was cleared, and soldiers stood behind the cars parked across the street. Beyond them lay a park, barren, ash-colored trees and frost-seared lawn. The nearest building visible was over two thousand yards away.

"Fuck off, pencil-neck," Nye wheeled on Cundieffe. "He goes. So says the Army in its infinite wisdom, and so say I." He jabbed Cundieffe's belly with something. Cundieffe looked down. *Oh crud, there's my gun.*

The soldiers lowered Storch off the dock and hustled him across the lot to the open loading door of the armored car. Cundieffe was looking from his gun to Nye's nosehole and the red-rimmed, murderous eyes above it. He was not looking when the silent shot slammed its target.

They both spun round in time to see Storch's head split open as a bullet and a great corona of explosive gas bored through it. The escort formation fell apart as most of the soldiers blindly returned fire out into the street, and the rest dropped to the ground and rolled away in a panic.

Col. Nye, cursing a supersonic blue streak, leapt down from the dock and charged over to the armored car, where the driver was already shouting for help into the radio. In the midst of it all, Storch took a halting step out into the sunlight, then another, then another. Foam and smoke streamed out of his skull, and his blood on the ground danced and sizzled like grease on a griddle. Cundieffe stepped off the dock and fell hard on one foot, so awestruck was he by the sight. Until now, it suddenly dawned on him, he'd only seen people die on television. Sgt. Storch was escaping, though Cundieffe could see light streaming through the hole in his skull.

"Knock him down!" Col. Nye screamed, and Cundieffe was trying to get up, but his ankle was sprained, and wouldn't bear his weight. He threw himself in Storch's direction to bring him down and out of the line of fire, wherever that was, but two more shots stitched the sergeant's chest and blew a lot of fluid and tissue out his back. Storch seemed to freeze and weigh the pros and cons of being dead, and, after a while, reluctantly accepted. He fell face-down on the pavement. His skin was starting to turn purple again in the sun.

Col. Nye was pointing at the office building in the distance, just over a mile away, and shrieking hysterically into a phone and at his guards, who piled into the armored car and peeled out of the garage. In an instant, there was just Cundieffe and Col. Nye standing over the body of Sgt. Storch. Only the sizzling sound of Storch's burning blood broke the silence. The awful, abundantly lethal wounds in his head and chest seemed, incredibly, to grow, spreading like stains, causing the flesh to subside and run like melting wax. Nye was still holding Cundieffe's gun, and Cundieffe knew by looking at him that it was not a question of whether he would get it back, but how.

"Never, in all my years, have I lost a prisoner," Nye started, "not one whatsoever—" Cundieffe sucked in air and blew him away.

"*You* lost one today. What you've cost us by delivering him to his execution, we won't even begin to understand until it's too late. Your security was a farce, Colonel, and my report will reflect that. In fact, if I may make so bold, I intend to pursue an investigation of this entire transfer, which stinks of a staged execution."

Nye's eyes opened twice as wide as his nosehole and got twice as dark. "My fault? Staged?"

"He had something to tell me, and your people wanted him dead. When I stated my intent to postpone the execution, you acted accordingly. Don't worry, I'm sure your punishment will be minimal. After all, you were only following orders."

Col. Nye's hand was shaking as he flipped Cundieffe's gun around in his leathery hand and stuffed it back into Cundieffe's holster. "Go home, G-boy. I've got a mess to clean up."

Col. Nye went over to oversee the removal of Storch's body as Cundieffe called in to AD Wyler. As the Assistant Director's secretary put him on hold, he watched a team of Army medics in biohazard suits load Storch into a pressure-sealed stretcher. One of them dumped a clear solution all over the blood and tissue Storch left on the concrete.

"This is Wyler. Speak."

"He's dead, sir. Killed in transit."

Wyler was silent for a long time. A medic mopped up the last of the mess, and they left in a civilian ambulance. Cundieffe was alone in the garage, and cars were moving down the street again. "Get here immediately. Were you able to learn anything useful?"

"I don't know, sir. He spoke to me, but I think he'd lost his mind. He didn't make much sense. I think we need to change the focus of the investigation. I think we need to take a much closer look at Cyril Keogh."

"Get here, now. Dr. Keogh is not our concern, but weathering the shitstorm that's about to slop over our decks is."

Cundieffe winced. He still couldn't bring himself to accept his superior's sometimes vulgar hyperbole. He took one last look at the garage where Storch was killed. The only trace of his passing looked like just another oil stain on the asphalt.

"There are procedures, Martin," Wyler was saying into his ear. "Even for situations like this, there is policy. That's why we're here."

As he walked out of the garage and into the midwinter sunlight, he looked up at the sun that had given Storch his last meal.

They can kill this body, but they can't kill the message.

Cundieffe hailed a cab and ordered the driver to take him to FBI Headquarters. In his pocket, he held a plastic bag in which he'd had, until this morning, the last of his mother's egg salad sandwiches. In it, his white linen handkerchief, which he'd managed to dab in the bubbling halo of blood and brain around Storch's head. The military believed they would learn more from Storch dead than alive.

Then so would he.

Somewhere under his many layers of clothing, his cellular phone trilled. It took him three rings to get to it, in the breast pocket of his blazer.

"You're still at your mother's house?"

"Yes sir, I was finishing up some overdue yardwork. The report—"

"We need you here. Get to LAX immediately."

"Sir?"

The Assistant Director was already gone.

You have a lot to learn about America.

Cundieffe set aside the unfinished Storch report and took up another, slimmer, but older, manila outer shell brittle and sepia-stained. He laid it open and began to pore over the contents, looking up as he did every so often and squinting, then trying on his mother's spare pair of bifocals and squinting even harder.

The oldest photo in the file was of Frank Cundieffe kneeling beside the planted orange tree. Never much of a kidder himself, he had a pair of handcuffs out and was uncuffing the trunk of the four-foot sapling as he looked off-camera with naked distaste.

The second photo was of Frank and Muriel Cundieffe coming out of the lounge at the Hawaiian Village resort. His father, tight, tired and sizing up the cameraman, the bolts of silver in his hair lit up like tinsel by the flash. His mother startled but already starting to laugh at the hotel portraitist's charming ambush. The flower in her hair was three shades off from the mauve hue of the flowers on the tree his father had brought home. Cundieffe had the photo digitally enhanced to bring the colors out through the slow decay, as the cheap colors had oxidized and turned green. He took a flower from the seat beside him and held it up to the picture, then up to the blow-up he'd made of the flower. Nestled behind her ear, it gave a strikingly lush asymmetry to his mother's plain but handsome face, her chestnut brown hair became something like gold. The flower in his hand could have melted into the photograph. He set the file down and crossed the yard. There were dozens more photos in the file, taken by himself on two occasions in the last year, when it had become clear that the trees would not survive the infestation.

It had been easy to replace the orange tree. A farm in Encinitas had taken cuttings and seeds from the original and matched it to a sort of hybrid with enhanced resistance to pests. After planting it, Cundieffe had groomed it to match the photos taken the previous August, just before his first trip to Washington. The hibiscus was the one he was most concerned about. It was not cloned, and it was not a perfect match, though he had pruned it as best he could. If his mother studied them with the same critical eye with which she'd scrutinized the Director's memos, she would not fail to observe the difference in shade. But if she remembered the one she wore in her hair on the night she and her Frank made Martin Cundieffe, she would see a tiny piece of the world that would reflect her memories.

Mother would be back from her New Year's card game any time now. Cundieffe rinsed out his mug and deposited it in the dishwasher, collected his files and locked them in his car, then came back for the trashbags. There were eight of them, all that remained of the old trees. He lifted the last of the bags up and swept away any remaining traces of sawdust or whitefly floss before stowing them in his trunk. He left a note on Mother's countertop before he packed his bags and left.

Dear Mother,
Called back to HQ.
Tell the Melnitzes to make in their hats. The trees are clean.
Love Always, Martin

~ 3 ~

Ft. Meade, Maryland

Lieutenant Channing Durban presented his ID at the gate, but the guard only glanced at the monitor that printed out the reader's scan of the barcode. The guard was a civilian, standard issue Government Services Administration doorstop, equally qualified as bailiff or rock concert event staff. Lt. Durban drummed on the steering wheel and tried to make out the guard's badge number through the frosted glass of his booth. The guards were routinely soft on the military personnel, a weakness that had been exploited more than once with devastating results for the Agency. In years past, it had rankled him, but tonight, with the new year only an hour old, it made him breathe a bit easier. He snapped a salute at the guard, who rubbed his stubbled chins and nodded blankly in response.

Lt. Durban stopped at a gas station on I-95, five miles south of Ft. Meade, ran to a stall and locked it, dropped his pants, and stooped to remove a cache of documents from his colon.

The whole thing was a little larger than a tightly rolled dollar bill; inside a bullet-shaped plastic capsule, he'd compacted 512 pages of text on microfilm. He almost washed it off in the toilet basin, but balked when he thought of having to replace it, wiped it thoroughly with a paper towel, and dropped it into his breast pocket. He threw up the ham sandwich and dill pickle spears he'd had for lunch, changed out of his uniform into corduroy slacks and a sweater, went back to his car, and drove on south, to Washington.

Chan Durban didn't join the Navy to become a spy any more than he wanted to shoot guns or ride in boats. He liked to play with electronics and wanted to go to college, so he enlisted and performed so exceptionally at communications school that he was swept into the Naval Security Group and stationed at its western processing center at CINCPACFLT, Hawaii.

Along the way, he discovered he loved the Navy and didn't ever want to leave. He rushed through college and marriage and right back into the Naval Security Group and after short stints at its satellite processing centers, he went to work at Fort Meade in the Naval liaison office of Operations at the National Security Agency. So enamored was he of the service that he didn't mind being promoted above the gear which had been his first love. He had learned in his four years at the Puzzle Palace that the same love of tinkering and detail could be lavished on policy and documentation, that blocs of personnel and computers, indeed the entire colossal apparatus, could be viewed as a machine, and benefit from being so handled. It was a comfort to be absorbed into such a machine, to make it work at optimum efficiency for the American people.

He really believed shit like that up until October of last year, when he'd started getting calls from an anonymous guy who claimed to speak for the Pentagon, ordering him to spy on the NSA for the Navy.

The caller only rung him up when he was off-duty and alone in the house: usually late at night, never more than ten minutes after his wife, Mitsy, and their dogs had dropped off to sleep. He swept the house for bugs with a surprisingly effective portable device his older brother had bought him as a gag gift three Christmases back. Nothing. No unfamiliar cars or service vans parked outside. Still, they knew exactly when to call, and what to say. The tone was anything but official.

"Ahoy, pencil-neck. The China Lake heist three months ago. You know about it?"

"I have no idea what you're talking about. Who is this, please?"

"The civilian branches of the intelligence community know who ripped the Navy off. They're fast fucking friends."

"I'm going to hang up now." And he nearly did, but the voice that erupted from the receiver even as it hovered above the cradle froze him. It was the chief petty officer in Basic who'd put him through punitive PT until he'd thrown up stuff he ate in a past life. It was the bullying CO in Hawaii who'd made him become fluent in technical Chinese in six months. It was the voice of his father, forty-year veteran of the Ohio State Police, who made him learn to hunt.

"Get the shit out of your ears, junior! Do you love the motherfucking U.S. Navy?"

Durban picked up the phone again and answered, "Yes sir," in more of a basic training bark than he'd intended. "But I don't know who you are and I don't know what you're talking about."

"There's a goddamned domestic terrorist army composed of rogue spooks and defense scientists operating in this country, and everybody in the defense loop knows about them except the military. You limpdick signals geeks at No Such Agency are sitting on the fucking proof. You want to believe I'm an internal security stinger, fine, but next time it happens and the Navy gets fucked up the ass, know that you were probably the only person who could've stopped it. Aw, fuck this—" and the caller had hung up on *him*.

Durban didn't sleep well that night, or the next. He knew only a little about China Lake because his office had processed a huge volume of domestic intercept traffic from Southern California after the theft. It'd been a troublesome time, with a host of cellular encryption systems cropping up that they'd never seen before. All the commercial carriers shrugged at them, and the computers had turned up, for the first time since he came to work at Ft. Meade, absolutely nothing meaningful. The indecipherable bunch had been shopped around the Puzzle Palace for a few weeks before dropping out of sight down one of its innumerable rabbit-holes, where somebody presumably solved them and found nothing helpful. Durban knew only that the weapons storage facility had been robbed on the Fourth of July, and that the Navy was pissed. The entire affair was classified Top Secret, but Durban had learned that a joint FBI and Navy task force had run the perpetrators to ground in a bunker in the desert only ten miles away from China Lake, and that was the end of it.

The caller tried again a week later, on a lazy weekday afternoon when he was alone in the house. Mitsy had taken the dogs to the park, leaving him to his model-building. He explained, more patiently but in the same colorful master seaman's language, that a terrorist group called the Mission had robbed the Navy, and that they had operated with at least partial assistance from the FBI and CIA. The military was hampered at every turn from zeroing in on the culprits, who had stolen napalm from China Lake, then used it on a civilian target. The Navy had been forced to assist in the cover-up. It had happened before, and would happen again, unless hard evidence was procured to the Pentagon. That evidence, the caller told Durban, was somewhere in Ft. Meade. "Look for domestic Southern California microwave intercepts from the night of the Fourth, and you will believe."

Durban thanked the caller and hung up and went back to his model. He was sure now that it was an intra-agency sting operation, only a lot more cleverly conceived than any he'd ever heard of. As a serviceman, Lt. Durban was exempt from much of the scrutiny and polygraphic harassment that focused on the civilian wing of the NSA, but he'd never entirely trusted *them*. It was civilian spooks who brokered weapons of mass destruction to Saddam, but it was Lt. Col. Oliver North who answered for it; American servicemen who suffered from exposure to the Iraqi weapons the Reagan and Bush administrations had sold; and civilian spooks again who suppressed transmissions from coalition units detecting leaks of chemical weapons throughout the conflict. Lt. Durban had helped collect the intercepted Belgian transmissions himself from a field listening post in southern Turkey. Using his loyalty to his military service to try to turn him was sharper than he would've given them credit for, but he wasn't about to fall for it.

He steadfastly clung to his ideals for a week and the better part of an eighth day before his curiosity got the better of him. As he did with any big decision, he plotted all possible outcomes, with his degree of commitment on one axis and the Agency's probable response on the other. Several such charts had to be plotted, based on the unknown quantity of the caller's identity. The curves based on a prompt report of the two contacts to his CO created a short, flat line segment; textbook procedure would deliver him out of all this with at worst a notation of his having failed to report the call the *first* time. If it was a screwball or a disgruntled former SIGINT spook or discharged sailor, it would come to nothing. If there were any merit to the charges, his CO would pass them up the chain, and there would, perhaps, be a Pentagon inquiry—someday. Another Iran-Contra, another dreadfully long and ultimately pointless congressional circus show-trial, with nothing gained but lower approval ratings for all involved, especially the military. The "evidence" destroyed long before it could be brought to light.

If there was something to see, the time was now. If he brought evidence to his CO, there would be less chance of this slipping away, or getting filibustered to death. The worst he would be guilty of would be a security infraction if any of the documents were outside his clearance, but it wasn't spying if nothing left the building.

Thinking this was bullshit, thinking getting caught could cost him his promotion and his security clearance, he reviewed the massive lists. The western microwave interception was down for the first week of July, but there was a field test of a miniaturized microwave interceptor at Twenty-Nine Palms throughout the summer. The NSA had been testing its new ECHELON-project COMINT vacuum cleaner, code-named MAUVE, but lovingly called Hoover by the propellerheads in Research. From what little Durban was cleared to overhear, the system could soak up long distance microwave relays and even local cellular transmissions from an entire state for hours at a time. This was not the sexy part, for the NSA had

had this capability since the seventies, and the current ECHELON program already blanketed the world in a COMINT net. The new element lay in the speed and automation of the system, which was capable of sorting through millions of conversations at a time for precoded "loaded" words, such as "bomb," "heroin" and "Bubba," or other disrespectful nicknames of the current President and his staff, not to mention specific names. Privacy advocates had very little to fear from such a system, which listened only with mechanical ears, and only for sedition, and only in times of emergency. But field tests were required, and the Agency liked to test its products "to destruction," glutting them on "private" civilian telephonics until the processor overloaded.

It was, of course, a violation of federal statutes for the NSA to act on information gleaned from such tests, but the broadest interpretation of the COMINT statutes allowed the Agency to pass on records of wrongdoing to the appropriate client agencies. It was for this reason that Lt. Durban was cleared to review the paper transcripts of the thousands of telephone conversations which had aroused MAUVE's interest. The Navy had been forwarded nineteen separate files pertaining to illegal activity perpetrated by enlisted men and officers within two weeks of the operation's conclusion. What the MAUVE task group noticed right away, though, was the high count of privately encrypted and scrambled conversations which stood up to MAUVE's best efforts. Most of the encrypted conversations were fed into the mainframe computers at Ft. Meade, and the results compartmented far from his reach, but the scrambled conversations were still accessible. They'd been processed later, because scrambled connections jump from one frequency to another on a pseudorandom pattern encoded into the phone or a peripheral device at both ends. The batch of scrambled intercepts had been like a junk drawer full of jigsaw pieces from a hundred different puzzles, each consisting of thousands of bits of audio. These were still being compiled in the Special Projects No.7 Building deep in the heart of the NSA complex, being strung together by audio techs with voice-matching software and lots of coffee. Most of the scrambled phone lines belonged to armchair privacy freaks and contained no realistic national security threats, so Durban had been able to find the one in less than five minutes.

It should not have been there.

ABOVE TOP SECRET- ROYAL CHANNELS ONLY

MAUVE Intercept 0010286-07-99
FW: MACHETE

7-5-99; 05:42:48 PDT.

VOICE 1 (97% match to ID- Hamilton Sibley [DOB-4-14-56; SSN: 370-00-4048], Dep. Asst. Dir., CIA): This is Sibley.

VOICE 2 (voice harmonics digitally altered, NO ID): You have to tell them not to try to stop this, Hamilton.

V.1: Stop what? Who is this?

V.2: We apologize for the unrest we have caused, and for the act we are going to commit. This is not an act of terror—

V.1: Oh God…Calvin, is that you? What the blue fuck is this about? Did your people steal that shit?

V.2: Listen carefully, Hamilton. This is not about terror. This is about DARPA. This is about RADIANT. This is our Mission. This is not retribution. This is the erasure of a mistake. Our only regret is that it has come to this, and that we have been forced to involve the innocents on the front lines. Please do not force us to take innocent human lives, Hamilton.

V.1: I don't understand any of this, nobody does! Have you lost your minds? The Navy is out of the loop, and they're too goddamned pissed to bring in, now. They're bringing in JSOC, and the FBI is spoiling for a full-fledged turf war. This is going to seriously jeopardize our relationship…

V.2: When all is said and done, you will come to recognize the importance of the seemingly random and chaotic events now unfolding. You will come to see this as but the next stage in building our relationship with your interests.

V.1: Now? You tell us now? What kind of a relationship do you expect to build on a fuckup like that? You have no idea who I have to answer to…

(Transmission lost at 05:44:18 PDT; signal scrambled to frequency outside MAUVE sweep bandwidth)

He noticed that it was not flagged by MAUVE, which used the standard ECHELON dictionary for sifting buzzword-heavy calls.

The message had been like hot wax pouring into his ear and solidifying around his brain. He'd looked over his shoulder all the rest of that day, waiting to be carried away. This was so far outside his NEED TO KNOW that it dared him to run screaming out of the complex. What he'd seen was an aberration—that he'd been able to see it at all suggested that it was a trap, or not what it seemed, at any rate. What did he know about ROYAL clearance? Or MACHETE? He'd never even heard of them. Even if the caller was right about what it meant, who was he to pass judgment on the strength of this, a minute of an eavesdropped conversation that he couldn't even understand?

He puzzled the answers to these questions over the next two months even as he found and photographed the complete MACHETE file. It was sickeningly easy to get access repeatedly and without accountability. The Agency had requested and received a titanic emergency budget spike to cover added security for Y2K. The NSA had nothing to fear from double-digit date errors, but it used some of the windfall to back up files on paper and magnetic tape and cart them away for storage under a mountain in West Virginia. It meant extra copies and review panels and cartloads of top secret SIGINT documents parked in corridors for hours on end like abandoned patients in a trauma center. He did not read more than he had to, but he learned enough to know he was now a spy, that something above top fucked was going on, and that men had been murdered for knowing less.

MACHETE delineated a pattern of cooperation between the intelligence community and an order of defected scientists, soldiers and spies who sabotaged military satellite launches and weapons tests, traded secrets to hostile foreign powers, including Cuba and China, and had most recently dropped napalm and worse on a town in California. They called themselves the Mission. And the government helped cover it up. There was more, references to another file he had copied onto disk but hadn't been able to decrypt, something the NSA called ROYAL PICA. The Mission was very upset about it, whatever it was. They called it RADIANT.

This was not the government he had sworn to serve. He knew in his heart that the core of the military was not tainted, even as he knew he could not go to his superior or any other officer affiliated with No Such Agency.

Now he had just removed the last of the MACHETE files from his colon and added them to the others in the cheap nylon overnight bag on the seat next to him. He was ready to deliver it to the mysterious caller who had ordered him to compound his risk by caching the files in a safe deposit box for a one-time drop. Fourteen CD's and three capsules of microfilm of stolen NSA documents on the seat beside him, like overdue library books. In the small of his back, for the first time in his Navy career, he carried a gun, a 9mm with hollow-points. If they were on to him, this would be the time. Here he was with the whole ball of wax, headed in the opposite direction from his commute home to Baltimore. He would meet the officer he'd spoken to over the phone for the first time.

Your controller, you mean.

No. He was a spy for the United States Navy. He was one of the good guys.

The traffic entering the southeastern quadrant of the Capitol on the 295 was dense and much more run-down than the flow he usually rode home with. He realized with a start that he had never come this way. He recognized the exits only from news stories he'd read, and cautionary tales told around the water cooler to illustrate the depths to which the world had sunk. He turned off into the shittiest part of Washington, DC at the appointed exit.

Only one streetlight down the entire avenue appeared to be working. The Navy Yard was somewhere nearby, but this was the industrial portion of a netherworld of rowhouses and teeming projects. He steered through it as he had been trained to do in places like Lebanon or southern Turkey—stick to the middle lanes, never loiter at corners, and scan the traffic double-time for recurring vehicles that might be a tail. There were none.

Lt. Durban was two blocks short of the Navy Yard and beginning to feel that he had made it undetected. He turned down a narrow residential street and made it halfway down the block when he realized the directions had steered him the wrong way down a one-way street, and there was a trash truck coming at him at speed. At least, in the sudden winter dusk, it looked like a trash truck, as did the one coming up behind him.

He flicked his brights on and off, but the trash truck only seemed to speed up, as did the one behind him. It was like a berserk game of chicken. Parked cars on both sides of the street formed solid barricades, and there were no pedestrians on the sidewalks, no lights on in the blind gray concrete towers that hemmed him in on both sides.

Lt. Durban was not a stupid man, nor given to freeze under stress. He unfastened his seatbelt, unlatched the door and threw himself out into the street just as the aft truck made contact with his rear bumper. His car surged forwards, the door slamming shut as it was driven into the reinforced grill of the fore truck. Air brakes hissed. The car buckled with a symphony of snapping, whining metal and a single beleaguered honk before it came to a halt, before he stopped rolling, under a pickup truck and into the ice-crusted stream in the gutter. He fumbled around his back for the pistol, but it must've come loose when he bailed out of the car. He reached out onto the sidewalk, the overnight bag tucked under his body like a football. Melting slush dripping off the drive train of the truck onto his forehead, the trucks roaring at each other as they retreated and his car settled on its cracked undercarriage. A pair of motorcycles stopped beside his car and flashlights swept the interior. Voices shot quick, monosyllabic noises at each other, then the bikes took off.

His hand found something—a signpost, the leg of a newspaper machine—and he dragged himself out from under the truck. Hands seized him and hauled him out into the glow of flashlights.

A man barked at him in a speech devoid of vowels, all glottal stops and fricatives. Durban was no linguist, but he recognized Russian.

"I have nothing for you," he said. He rolled into a ball around the bag. "I just got lost—"

The heavy police-issue flashlight rose and fell on his ribs, and breath, reason and hope rolled away on a tidal wave of hurt. His legs kicked out but hit only the oversized tire of the truck he'd been hiding under. A gloved hand clamped over his mouth. The barrel of a short, ugly machine pistol smashed the bridge of his nose. Something scratchy and hot—a fresh new Spalding tennis ball, he would learn later—forced itself in between his teeth and electrical tape unreeled around his head four times before he could get out another sound.

They hit him again and again until he lost control of his legs and the bag rolled out onto the asphalt, and then they were lifting him up, one holding his arms and one his legs. He got a good look at one of them, but he learned nothing. The man wore a bandanna over his hair and a thick black beard covered nearly everything else. His eyes were black holes, but the light glinted off a gold upper front tooth. Crisp plumes of mist puffed out from his beard as he hoisted Durban across the street to his car. He thought they were going to stuff him into the driver's seat and finish crushing the car, and he fought as hard as he could with his legs tied together. They rewarded his efforts by banging his head into the doorpost as they brought him around to the trunk. It was stuck open, the mouth of the cargo space skewed by the initial impact. They dumped him in, and the one who'd been holding his arms leaned in close and said, *"Dosvedanya, tovarisch. The Organizatsiya will not forget your service."* He stuck a card in Durban's breast pocket, then he slammed the trunk. Lt. Durban waited in perfect stillness for them to shoot him. When it was clear they had gone, he passed out anyway.

The trash trucks were gone before Lt. Durban was dragged out from his hiding place. The drivers backed out of the narrow street and returned the vehicles to the waste management company lot from whence they came.

The two motorcyclists took off in the same way, one east, one west, the latter carrying the bag. He circled round the block once, then got onto the main avenue and shot up the southbound 295 onramp like a bullet from a suppressed rifle. Even if one were watching the motorcyclist intently, it would be hard to say for sure that one saw him toss a bag in the open front passenger-side window of a late model dark sedan parked on the corner at the last light before the overpass. One who had tailed Lt. Durban might have noticed that the sedan had also discreetly followed him into the capital from Ft. Meade, picking him up as he left the gas station.

After about a minute, the sedan drove over the highway and got on the 295 headed north, but got off again at Pennsylvania Avenue and entered a four-story parking garage attached to the Old Post Office Mall. A scant forty-five seconds later, a maroon minivan checked out of the garage and got on Pennsylvania headed southeast. A trained observer might have recognized that the driver of the minivan bore a striking resemblance to the driver of the sedan, except for his hair color, a mustache and a change of clothes, but there was nobody watching.

The minivan left Washington, DC and followed Pennsylvania Avenue after it became Expressway 4, getting off in the suburb of Suitland. Rush-hour traffic was thinning, but the van was still just one more oversized commuting module in a sea of same, and no one took notice of it as it pulled in to a corner mini-mall with a manicurist, a camera repair, an Atlantic gas station that was fenced off pending replacement of its underground tanks, and a donut shop which had been closed down for eighteen months. The windows and door of the donut shop were plastered over with layers of newsprint, and the marquee was a gutted plastic shell with one bare fluorescent light bulb still flickering inside, periodically lighting up the word TASTY.

The driver climbed out and unlocked the front door of the donut shop, let himself in and locked it. He peered out through a viewing slit torn in the newsprint just above the pushbar. The lot was a cemetery. He heard the squelched rasp and chatter of police- and souped-up cellular signal scanners. A wooden chair groaned as the massive man sitting on it rose and crossed the shop to take the driver by the arms and spin him around so fast his wig only half-spun with him.

"Got away clean, didn't I?" the driver asked in the flat, faint twang of the Oklahoma plains.

"Not even a 911 phone-in on the geek's car yet," the big man answered, taking the bag off the driver. He touched the man's shoulder once by way of thanks and brought the bag back into the former kitchen. The deep fryers and other cooking fixtures had been ripped out and replaced with a pair of computers, several scanning beds and a row of laser printers, all tied into a huge switchbox wired to the power and phone lines of the defunct Atlantic station. A balding, dark-skinned man sat at the terminals, tinkering with the magnification on the scanners. He took the bag and dumped it out on a long tray atop a wheeled utility cart. A pile of Zip disks rattled under his rubber-gloved hands as he silently set to work feeding them in.

The arrangement had eaten up a sizable portion of the man's savings, but a cursory examination of his financial records would reveal only that he'd recently purchased a beach-front condo in Costa Rica, hardly an inappropriate transaction for a recently retired military officer with no family. As far as anyone who'd care to investigate could tell, he was down there now, drinking and whoring and identifying himself to any who cared to know. The laundered nest egg had been more than enough to finance the computers and the Tasty shop lease, and to pay a man who matched his description to alibi him from one end of Central America to the other. The men hadn't cost him a dime. They were true believers, comrades in arms from one or another of the many units he'd led, and a few from the mercenary posses he'd run in Africa. They believed in Lt. Col. Mort Greenaway, and in the task at hand.

He, in turn, believed that he had finally secured the evidence he needed to pursue the task to completion, namely, the exposure of the covert terrorist organization that called itself the Mission, and its ties to rogue elements within the federal government. All the lies, all the bullshit that had piled up behind his back could be exposed, now, all the things that had made him look like a raving maniac at the sub rosa review of the Radiant Dawn incident.

In their recommendation for early retirement, the panel had explicitly noted that he suffered from paranoid delusions, that he was "probably unfit for society at large, let alone for active duty in any capacity." In their judgment, his sociopathic ego and bitterness over a stalled career drove him to withhold vital tactical information from the FBI arm of the operation, to violate the rules of engagement by pursuing the helicopter observed fleeing the burning Radiant Dawn hospice village, and to "fabricate a bizarre counteraccusation regarding possible government collusion with the perpetrators." Fabricate. They didn't even have the balls to call it lying when they accused him of it. But he could stuff their lies down their throats with these documents, and go to his grave a vindicated man. Or he could use them to get what he wanted all along: to hunt the egghead terrorist organization himself, on his own terms.

He knew there would be files. The government could do nothing without leaving a paper trail. Even at the star chamber level of black budgets and blacker ops, everyone wanted their ass covered, though they stood ready to shred the lot at the merest hint of Congressional oversight. Official documents would be outside the military's, and, thus, his reach.

But there was another assumption about government that had yet to steer him wrong. There was *always* someone listening.

It had been pathetically easy to play Lt. Durban; after reviewing his nonclassified military record, he had the punk's number and dialed it. He was a geek, but he dreamed of being regular Navy, a war hero. He needed somebody to pin balls to his chest, because he wasn't born with any.

What would he tell his geek bosses at No Such Agency? That he'd been carjacked by the Russian Mafia, probably. At least, that was what they hoped. About a week before he first called Lt. Durban, he'd begun placing ads in every website linked to the Soldier Of Fortune set, soliciting "Stateside wetwork" for a bunch of "hungry former Spz. Commandos," knowing full well that the FBI and/or the CIA would ferret out the Spz. as the common abbreviation for Spetznaz, the Soviet Special Forces. He had a host of responses placed through dummy e-mail accounts at Internet cafes in twelve states. They got eight more offers that they hadn't doped up themselves, which gave Greenaway hope for the future as a free agent.

The INS and customs were even now looking up the asshole of every Ivan who came into the country with forceps and a flashlight. The FBI was surely watching the criminals and white separatists across the nation whose credit card numbers he'd bought from a guy who hacked the IRS for a living.

Once before in his career, he'd turned away from the Army in disgust, and printed his own ticket back in when the time was right and Delta Force was looking for a few bad men. Now, in the teeth of disgrace, he would buy an even sweeter posting, and prove the truth to the only person whose opinion he, in the final analysis, gave a shit about.

The computer tech brought up the first page of a document.

ABOVE TOP SECRET- ROYAL CHANNELS ONLY

MAUVE Intercept 0121010-07-99
FW: MACHETE
07-10-99; 19:48:15 PDT

(No Match/ID for either Voice)

VOICE 1: Colonel, you've been less than cooperative in the course of this investigation.

VOICE 2: You've been less than baggage, Cundieffe.

VOICE 1: I expect it was under such an opinion that your goon squad left us in Titus Canyon a little while ago. Your conduct has been criminal if they were under your orders, and incompetent if it was not. All of this is being recorded and transmitted to my superior's offices in Washington, by the by.

VOICE 2: Then I have nothing to say.

VOICE 1: I do. I thought you'd like to know where they are.

He didn't need to read the rest. He was Voice 2. And Voice 1, that junior G-man bookworm the FBI had scapegoated with the whole mess, was probably chasing stolen snowmobiles in Alaska, if he worked at all. "Print all of it," he said, "except that one."

~ 4 ~

Heilige Berg, Idaho

A snowy, moonless midnight in the mountains of the Snake River Valley is a scary time to be out in the woods alone with only a rifle you don't know how to use and a world of bloodthirsty subhumans lurking just over the perimeter. Time seems to stumble on the edge of the promised new day, and slip backwards out of thousands of years into the first dark age. Society could collapse and make not so much as a puff of smoke that one could see from here. Karl Schweinfurter would be eighteen in two months, and had never successfully shot a target with his rifle, let alone another human being. But he was sworn to duty, to the protection of his family, his hearth and his faith. They were one day into the new millennium, treading on the thin ice of borrowed time before the Last Days, Gotterdammerung, Ragnarok.

He reconnoitered the knob-shaped hill that overlooked the road on three sides before he sat down on his rock, waited ten minutes more before he knelt and began to dig in the snow and soft earth underneath. He wasn't worried about being caught unawares by intruders—in the thirteen months he'd been here, there'd been none. The Jägers were another matter. Most reserve sentries suspected they were only detailed out in the woods for the elite warriors' stalking practice. Guard duty sucked, but it beat graveyard shifts in the slaughterhouse, and it was the only time one could be alone for longer than a toilet trip.

Karl found the bottle and dug it out, pocketed the cap, rubbed the mouth of the bottle vigorously so it wouldn't stick to his lips, and took a good stiff belt. Jägermeister, the cough syrup of kings. His friends in school had sworn by its economical buzz value and ferocious, loopy potency, but Karl had never enjoyed it before, preferring beer, pot or even Nyquil over Jäger shots. But beer was impractical and even if it were possible to score weed, the Jägers would scent it on his clothes and come down on him.

Karl believed fervently in God and was pretty sure about the divine selection of the white man, but he was beginning to have his doubts about Heilige Berg. His parents, good God-fearing working people who owned a corner market in Nampa, had the best of intentions when they sent him here to, as Papa put it, "wake up the righteous man in you," after he and some school-friends were caught drunk and disorderly in a Circle K parking lot on a school day. Papa had switched the family to the Teutonic Heritage Church the year before because only they had answers for what the world was coming to, and they had a ready answer for Karl's problems, too.

Karl's first impression of the church's mountain retreat was little better than the one he made upon the community at large. Climbing down from the shaky second-hand school bus in a parka and two layers of bluejeans, he'd goggled at the ranks of hearty teenaged commandos in white arctic camouflage standing at attention at the far end of the parking lot. He'd come expecting a lame tough love church camp with the same white separatist leanings as the church in town. He unzipped his parka to the brutal predawn cold to show his abundant, upbeat piety in the form of a T-shirt he'd got on a family vacation pilgrimage to the Creation Research Museum in Santee, California. Faded and worn through in the left armpit, the shirt still clearly depicted a stylized Darwin fish flat on its back, with its ridiculous, abominable legs pointed skyward. A circle and slash negated the mythical beast, under which a caption proclaimed, NO WAY.... Beneath it, the original, legless Jesus fish floated on a field of heavenly light, the Greek name of Jesus in its flank slightly misspelled, but no less holy. The caption read, YAHWEH!!! Mama still chuckled every time she saw it, but Grossvater Egil Reuss, the pastor of Heilige Berg, had failed to see the humor. The huge, shield-bearded cleric had seized Karl by the hood of his parka and jerked him off his feet so that he lay supine in the slush with an enraged frost giant who might have been the second coming of Beowulf looming over him.

"Was ist los?" Grossvater Egil roared in his face. "Was machst du dabei, mit den Judische Hemd?"

When Karl only stammered out an apology in English, his rage only multiplied. "You have no mother tongue? God, boy, what is your name?"

"Karl Frederick Schweinfurter, sir."

"You're a race-traitor scrap of shit come to spy, aren't you, Karl?"

"No, sir, my—my parents sent me here."

"You're wearing a blasphemous rag on your body, Schweinhund," the man growled, to the gruff amusement of the assembled platoon of Jägers. "That is not the name of God."

Before Karl could offer further apologies, let alone explain that the shirt was a clever denunciation of evolution, Reuss tore the T-shirt clean off his body, leaving only the collar. "Strip, spy," he ordered, and urged all due haste by slapping him across the back of the neck with a hand as broad and hard as the blade of an oar. Karl staggered under the blows as he stripped down, sloughing his parka and his boots, his layered jeans and thermal underwear, and finally his boxer shorts, which were mercifully, and against all odds, still unsoiled. Shivering uncontrollably, he was struck again when he hugged himself for warmth. The only sound was the laughter of the Jägers and the crunch of the other new arrivals filing past him with eyes averted, until Grossvater Egil seized one by the hair and twisted him face to face with Karl. "Look at him, boy. He's not one of us. Er hat keinen Blut im Gesicht, keine Schade."

He steered Karl's pitiful nakedness to the edge of the lot, where brown, scabby snow had been bulldozed into a bank that came up to his waist. "Los, Kinder! All of you, look at this! Only the white man can blush, only the white man has shame, and can make blood in the face." He slapped Karl full force across his right cheek, sending him almost flying into the bank of snow. He crept slowly back to his feet, hesitating at every syllable spat from Grossvater's lips for another slap. "This—thing knows no shame! He brings blasphemy with the false Jewish name of God on a shirt, he backtalks in the face of right, and even in his nakedness and abasement, he cannot blush!"

Karl was sure that he was not only blushing, but probably openly bleeding, but said nothing. This was only the most extreme version of a situation with which he was very familiar, being made an example of. Perhaps it was because he always seemed to smirk from the deep, elliptical scar on his chin and lower lip where a pony at a petting zoo had bit him once when he'd tried to feed it a carrot mouth-to-mouth. Perhaps it was his hair, which hung in a shaggy, shoulder-length mullet that reminded older men how much of their own hair they'd left in the shower drain that morning. Or perhaps it was simply because he was forever destined to be the only one still screwing off when the teacher decided to crack the whip. For whatever reason, it was always Karl, so he stood as straight as he could in the freezing predawn cold, as the elder slapped him again and again until he'd proven to his own and the camp's satisfaction that Karl could, indeed, produce blood in the face.

"I will teach you shame, boy," the cleric roared in his ear. "From this day on, I am your Grossvater, and I will save you from the filth of the world and even from the filth that is within you, but you must cleanse yourself before God and this holy place."

And Karl had obeyed, scrubbing himself with snow until he had raised a glorious blush on every square inch of skin, as the population of Heilige Berg had watched and taken a lesson from his ablutions.

Heilige Berg was a religious retreat, and enjoyed the tax-free status and lack of federal oversight which the United States generally extended to all faith-based groups. In fact, it was a permanent settlement of two hundred trained fighting men and women, mostly kids whose almost exclusively Germanic or Scandinavian parents hoped to prepare them for the imminent racial holocaust they believed would herald the Last Days. But there were many whole families there, too, and after Karl had been at Heilige Berg for as long as he thought he could stand it—a month—his parents had come: not to take him home, but to stay.

His mother was attacked by black thugs one night as she went to put in the night deposit. They beat her face so badly she looked like a circus freak, Mama Schweinfurter the Mule-Faced Woman. Both her eyes were still closed up, and Papa had to lead her around. They'd told her they would rape her and give her a litter of black babies, but she was too old and ugly. This had been the worst of it for her, and she had begged Papa to take her to safety. Papa went to see Pastor Bochner, who made arrangements for Church people to manage the store, and held the deed in trust to the family house while they holed up on Heilige Berg. Mama had cried as she told him all of it again and again, her hands trying to cover the words they'd cut into her face: HO HO HO. Karl could guess what it meant, but he couldn't bring himself to tell Mama.

After that, things had taken a turn for the better at Heilige Berg; Karl was transferred from the slaughterhouse to guard duty, and was even allowed to go on supply trips into town. He would never make Jäger, but he was matched to Heidi, and they were assigned a joint room. He loved her and protected her, according to his duty, and she did the same, until the lights went off.

"Lord, is this how it's supposed to be? Heidi's pregnant, and I guess you like that alright, we're supposed to 'be fruitful and multiply,' and all. I love her, and I want to do right by her, that's a husband's job, right? But I can't help but wonder what you're planning, Lord. She's like four months along, and everybody's proud as punch of her, but I ain't never *been* with her, Lord. I believe in your power, and in the Virgin Mary and the fruit of her womb, Jesus, but I'm not a blind man, Lord, I see how she cavorts with the Jägers. I don't figure you had a hand in any of this—I mean, not the Heidi part of it, but…"

He sipped another shot of Jägermeister, the searing track down the back of his throat the only truly warm spot in his whole body. He struggled to find the words, but he had a hard time talking frankly to his own father, and Grossvater Egil had told them God did not hearken to prayers in the wilderness, but only through the concerted voice, focused through him, in the chapel. But Egil also said God saw and heard everything, so if he was going to watch Karl poison his body with sinful contraband, he might as well hear his tale of woe, too.

"Is this how it's supposed to be, Lord? If you love the world so much, why you want to let all them Antichrists and the Zionists take it over? Why are all the God-fearing folks pushed back into the middle of nowhere, when the rest of Creation belongs to a bunch of rooty-poot mud people who don't even hearken unto Your word? When we were kids, Papa used to take us to the neighborhood church back in Nampa, and there were blacks and even a couple of spics in the crowd, they seemed to love you just fine…"

He trailed off, unable to utter his last question tonight. If God could hear it in his heart, that was just fine, but if it was a sin to speak it, he wasn't going to compound his troubles. Besides, you never knew when one of the Jägers was lurking in the bushes, waiting to catch you in sin.

Lord, how is it only Grossvater Egil knows the truth? Lord, if Grossvater Egil was a liar, wouldn't you give a sign? Lord, do you even know about this place? Can you even see it?

He wiped the Jägermeister bottle down on his sweater and returned it to the soft dirt in the leeward side of the boulder.

A flash of blue-white light pinned him to the boulder. Karl stood up so fast he banged his head against the overhanging granite, and staggered backwards into a stand of scrub brush, fell down hard on his butt.

Knowing it was the Jägers, knowing his sins and his weakness had been found out, Karl stood to accept his punishment with the proper meekness. But there was no one around. The stillness was broken only by clumps of snow sloughing off the pines all around him, and by the muttering of engines on the road below.

Still rubbing his head, Karl brought his rifle around under his right arm and picked his way down the precipitous slope towards the road. Karl's lookout post stood on a knoll around which the narrow, two-lane highway looped in its meandering westward course through the valley. To the south of it, the nine hundred acre Heilige Berg compound rode the rolling hills into the thick evergreen forest, and down to the pasture and the slaughterhouse below. To the north, the valley slope was a tumbling knife edge of serrated cliff-faces, skirting a dry tributary of the Snake River and winding up at the pass leading into the Seven Devils Mountains, where the terrain got really difficult.

Karl kept losing his footing and caught himself each time only by falling against a tree. The stout pine trunks absorbed his runaway momentum, but each time dumped a shower of frozen snow down the back of his parka. For all his stealth, he was probably as easy to hear and spot as the thundering T-Rex in that movie he'd glimpsed once as they drove past the drive-in. It occurred to him that he should alert the Jägers on his walkie-talkie, but he felt like enough of a fool without scrambling the compound for a false alarm. Just because they saw fewer than a dozen vehicles passing up the canyon on an average week, didn't mean the first one he saw that night was the herald of Götterdämmerung.

He ran out of trees just short of the road, where the hillside became an ice-slick slide dumping out on the narrow shoulder. His boots reversed themselves too late, kicking up a fan of snow in front of him as he tumbled out onto the road. He fell hard on his ass again, but this time, the rifle slammed into his back and rendered his right arm tingly and numb. He rolled sideways on the shoulder, blinded to what he'd come to see.

A convoy of six deluxe charter style buses lumbered past him at little better than walking speed, engines grumbling in first gear as the great, chain-bound tires ground up the sheets of ice on the tarmac. The body panels were all black, and marked only with a white hemispheric coronal burst, like the leading edge of the sun emerging from a total eclipse. Karl blinked icy water out of his eyes and peered at the windows. They were tinted, and most were curtained, but a few faces watched him from behind the glass: sallow, sunken faces, huge eyes that looked painted on with a careless brush, jutting, beaklike noses, breathing tubes, oxygen masks. There may have been as many as sixty on each bus.

Karl shuddered and tried to clamber back up the slope in a reflex of pure horror. He remembered the filmstrips Grossvater Egil showed them after supper, the vulpine features of the Zionist hordes who plotted their extermination. He remembered, too, the other films he'd seen in the old high school in Nampa, the ones Grossvater Egil said were fake, but which had left no less of a mark on him for all that. The ones that showed the vulpine Zionist monsters caged up in boxcars bound for Dachau, Treblinka, Bergen-Belsen, Auschwitz. Jews or not, there was something profoundly wrong with the people on the buses, but unless it was contagious, Karl couldn't see how it presented a threat to the compound.

Perhaps they were the legions of the sick, come to be healed by Grossvater Egil, in accordance with the prophecy. *Must be the Jägermeister talking…*

The first bus was only just now rounding the knoll and disappearing around the bend. At this rate, they would pass in front of the heavily fortified front gate in ten minutes. Karl stuffed his mouth full of snow to wash out the alcohol, then jogged alongside the road, screened by the front line of trees that marched up to the road beyond the knoll. There was a narrow but well-maintained Jäger trail here; it marked the perimeter that the elite guards walked. He was surprised not to have run into a Jäger already, but they'd probably already scrambled back to the compound in case the lost death-bed package tour pulled up at the front gate and asked to use the phone.

When they did reach the main gate, Karl was huffing and puffing only fifty yards behind, and to his relief, they passed it by. A single Jäger stood before the gates, his right arm cocked to bring around the stubby assault rifle slung behind his back. The last of the buses growled past just as Karl broke out of the trees and into the driveway. The Jäger did bring his gun around now, with stunning speed and grace drew down on him and cried out, "Halt, arschloch!"

"Gruss Gott, ich schutze die Bergen!" Karl shrieked back, waving his arms over his head. His own rifle stock bounced off the back of his leg and the barrel jabbed him in the neck. He skidded to a stop on the frozen-over parking lot. The Jäger stood his ground with rifle leveled, unconvinced. Karl recognized him. Tim Werther, outstanding marksman and vicious shitbag, and all of thirteen.

"We never heard you over the radio," Werther barked, his voice cracking. "We figured they waxed your pussy ass, already."

"Dude, they're just sick people, going on a vacation. Relax."

"Don't call me 'dude,' Swinefucker." The kid snapped off a middle-finger salute and turned back to the gate. "I'm gonna have to report this dereliction of duty to the Night Captain, Swinefucker."

Karl backed away from the gate. He was outside. He was truly, truly in a world of shit. He had a gun— "Werther, wait a minute. I'm gonna go after them."

"What?" Werther stopped and turned, half-reached for his gun again.

"They can't be going far. There's, like, a couple hundred people in those buses, and they're sick, like dying, like, with AIDS, or something. There isn't anywhere else for them to go."

"What are you saying?"

"I'm not saying anything, du- just, if there's something going on, and I'm the perimeter guy, then it's my responsibility, right?"

Werther looked confused.

"Do you guys know where the buses are going?"

Werther shook his head. The starlight glinted on his braces.

"Grossvater Egil always says 'I don't know' is a kind of lie, you know?"

Werther sneered, but he knew what kind of game they were playing, now. "Go down the road and see where they're headed. Go no further than the ten-mile marker at the top of the pass, and be back in an hour, or we'll have to send the snowmobiles out for you."

Karl shivered, hopping from foot to foot. "I could make better time if *I* could take a snowmobile."

Werther laughed. He ducked in though the cutout door in the gate and emerged with a pair of cheap plastic-and-nylon snowshoes. He whipped them at Karl in an earnest attempt to take the top off his head and slammed the door. He heard muffled boys' laughter from the other side as he strapped on the ragged wooden snowshoes and clumped up the winding road.

The road above the Heilige Berg compound wound up through the valley in a drunken surveyor's tour of the most forbidding landscape in the state. The road was center-crowned on hairpin turns overlooking the dry riverbed eighty feet below, as if the builders had intended it to express deliver the unwary motorist to a boulder-strewn grave. There were so many wrecks in the riverbed that when the runoff flooded it in the spring, they formed a dam that had to be broken up once with dynamite. The opposite bank was a cruel granite shield wall that only subsided into a string of plateaus along the top of the ridge. At the summit, the road into the Seven Devils range dropped into a gorge so perilous it was closed through the winter. This valley and all of the land around it for five miles in every other direction had been commercial timberland until the Environmental Persecution Agency had tried to annex the land, but, failing in court, forced the logging company to cease cutting down trees in the area. Heilige Berg sprang up a year later. Karl had overheard the Jägers talking about their landlord like he was one of the initiated, and would protect them.

Karl had never heard of any other living souls in the valley, let alone another settlement. No matter who they were, Grossvater Egil would be beside himself with fury. Best not to be the one to tell him about it, but where could he go? He was already tired and hungry, and having a hard time trudging in a straight line from the hard liquor's impact on his empty stomach. Even from the foot of the valley, it was seven miles into White Bird and the outside world, and out there he was just a teenage runaway skinhead. For all he knew, the Jew-ruled local police force really might shoot him on sight.

Keeping just within earshot of the buses took all Karl's strength, as the road above the compound hadn't been plowed all season, and he was knee-deep in powder, despite the snowshoes. Although he had no watch, he knew his hour was probably up and he was thinking seriously about turning back when he staggered around the last bend before the pass to find the road empty. The broad wake of crushed powder ended in a splattered bank beside a stand of trees. He thought he could hear the growl of the engines fading into the soughing of the wind in the pines. He scratched his head through his wool cap and pressed himself against a tree as he surveyed the mysterious new road. A stout iron gate spanned it, and a chain-link fence reached out in both directions, almost invisible behind a curtain of old-growth trees. Beyond it, the road curled out of sight into the dense forest, but Karl noticed a fleeting spark of red taillights within, like a beckoning will o' wisp.

This was it, then. He knew where they were going, and could go back to report, and go to bed. This was the least that was expected of him. But doing the least over the last thirteen months had gotten him nowhere, had made him less than a man in the Berg hierarchy, had made his family a figure of fun to the Jägers, most of whom were younger than him. For once, he would do more than anyone expected, and make someone proud of him.

Karl could climb much better than he could shoot, and the fence offered little challenge once he threw his parka, turned inside-out, over the barbed wire. The chain link was new, heavy-gauge steel, the links curiously woven together like chain mail armor. Even if the posts were blown out, it could easily stop an M1A1 Abrams tank. This was out of Heilige Berg's league. They had only barbed wire, skinhead teenagers and a few jury-rigged boobytraps for perimeter defense. He thought of Grossvater Egil's probable response when he learned they shared the valley with an ultrasecret government or corporate installation, and wondered if it would be wise to go back, after all.

Straddling the top, he could see freshly hewn tree stumps along the inside of the property, the dense pine stand chopped back twenty feet away from the fence. There was no such clearance on the outside. What were they afraid of losing? The feebs he'd seen in the buses had looked half-dead, hardly capable of holding onto a tree, let alone climbing one and leaping over the fence. Now, his reasons for going further had nothing to do with Grossvater Egil, or his family. He would see with his own eyes before anyone else.

He dropped to the ground, leaving his parka on the fence. He was more than warm enough from the hike, and he would need it in place if he had to go back over it in a hurry. It occurred to him that a perimeter guard like himself would not fail to see it, but fuck it. He skulked from tree to tree, trying to keep the road in sight. He was watching the road as he ran from one tree to the next when he ran out of trees and stumbled backwards away from the lip of the river gorge.

The road dropped into a chute, switchbacking twice before crossing a bridge that hadn't been there last summer. The gorge was only about a hundred feet across, but the bottom was twice as deep. On the other side, the road ran ruler-straight across a graded field for a quarter mile. At the end of it stood a little town. A brand spanking new town in the middle of the Snake River badlands in the middle of winter. The other buses were parked in front of a four story steel and glass tower, and a crowd of people was helping them inside. It looked like a hospital, but there was a whole park's worth of single-wide trailers surrounding it, like the retirement village in California his Grossmutti lived in. There were snowmobiles and a plow and a small fleet of vans with massive snow tires parked in a lot on the edge of the place, but no military vehicles, no black helicopters, not even a construction truck. The whole place had dropped out of the sky or sprouted up out of the ground while Heilige Berg slept. How could Grossvater Egil not know about this place? What if he already did?

The last bus was stopped at the bridgehead, and a guard climbed up onto the running board as it crawled across the bridge. Three more guards stood on Karl's side of the bridge, and they carried the biggest, baddest-assed guns he'd ever seen, and they were harder than a brigade of Jägers, harder even than the Teutonic Knights who sometimes sought sanctuary at Heilige Berg. They wore shaggy animal pelt suits that covered all but their faces, which gleamed ruddy purple under the magnesium lights posted along the bridge.

Karl did not place any false sense of confidence in his skills as a soldier, but it simply didn't occur to him to leave. He stood behind a pine tree on the edge of the gorge, straining to make out more of the distant doings in front of the hospital through his crappy 20X binoculars. It looked like a wheelchair derby at the Special Olympics. The attendants helped each living skeleton out of the bus like they were made of eggshells, and then rushed them up a ramp and into the building, where more guards flanked the doors. The windows were all tinted to the shade of newly minted pennies, so he couldn't see inside.

The town suddenly got a whole lot brighter.

When it started to happen, Karl thought it was the moon breaking out of the clouds, but then it hit him. This was a new moon, and the light wasn't falling on him. He looked up, expecting to see a helicopter, though he heard nothing. The Zionist New World Order shock troops would drop out of the sky in whispering black helicopters, so it was foretold, and so Karl raised his rifle, but there was nothing to shoot at. The light was pouring down from the sky through the clouds. It was like moonlight, but wrong, perverted in some way Karl couldn't explain even if he had stayed awake in Physics. The silvery blue light twisted and writhed down to the earth, like the tentacles of a Portuguese man o' war, or curdled milk, or smoke from burning plastic. It reached down from Heaven and touched the town, penetrated it so that he could see each building lit from the inside out by the levitating human embers within.

The trees all around the town shuddered and shook off their coats of snow, and waved like an ocean of charmed cobras to the undulating pulse of the unholy, heavenly light.

His walkie-talkie snarled and screamed so loud his ears popped. It was a sound like fax machines make when you pick up the phone while they're sending, but as it opened up, it sounded like people screaming, and talking and laughing, millions of them, but they all had the same voice. He jumped back and crashed into another tree. He tried to switch the walkie-talkie off, but it already was off, and then the receiver blew out with a hollow crackle, and Karl was running. Sure they heard that, sure they knew he was here, and they were coming.

He ran in great bounding leaps, the snowshoes squeaking on the thick carpet of powder underfoot. He crossed the road several times without noticing. The only sensation he was aware of was the tingling down his back like swarming bees were crawling down the collar of his thermal underwear, and he wanted nothing more than to be back inside Heilige Berg, to get naked in the snow and scrub himself clean of the memory of this place and the false pride that had driven him here. The fence appeared so fast he crashed into it and scrambled halfway up before he remembered the barbed wire and his parka slung over it, somewhere.

He backed up, the bees beginning to bite as every second passed without so much as a siren from the unholy secret Martian trailer park on the other side of the riverbed. He looked around, but there was sweat streaming into his eyes, Grossvater Egil wouldn't even let him keep his eyebrows, hair is vanity, he always said.

There it was. He ran to it and hurled himself at the fence without taking off his snowshoes. The steel links gouged his fingers through his thin wool mittens, but he couldn't get purchase with his comically large duckfeet, but his back was smoldering, he would burst into flames on this side of the fence, whether or not they came for him. He threw himself across the parka and rolled over, realizing as he did that he'd picked a piss-poor spot to come over, because there was a tree on the other side that he was likely to dash his brains out against, but it was too late to do anything but fall.

When the tree seemed to step up and reach out great arms to catch him, he thought for a moment that he must already be unconscious, but there it was, arms outstretched, and then they enfolded him, but when he struck there was no give, he might have fared better against a redwood. The wind whooshed out of his lungs and his head jerked and smashed something hard as stone. The cold, dim celestial light reflected off the snow shone on row upon row of teeth, each the size of his fist. "You look lost, little camper," a voice purred from behind those teeth.

"Shitbird hopped the fence coming and going all by his ownself," another voice, harsher by half than the first, said. "Told you these defenses were for shit, LT."

"Why we're here, Tuck," growled the tree that held Karl in its arms. "You got anything to say for yourself, boy?"

His captor relaxed a little, just enough to let Karl draw breath, but his arms remained pinned to his side, the rifle dug into his back. "Who are you dudes?" he managed at last.

"We're your new neighbors, little camper."

The arms unwrapped him, dumped him to the ground. He scrabbled to his feet and got five paces away before he remembered his training. He whirled, ripping the rifle off his shoulder and bringing it across his chest, up to his other shoulder, drew a bead at the shadowy tree-thing's center of mass and fired twice. The shots were like twig snaps in the forest, and they might've been, for all the effect they had. The tree brought its massive arms up level with its shoulders and something that might've been a head looked down and wagged from side to side.

"Go home and get yourself some real bullets, son," the tree said. Karl backed away, the rifle still up, but shaking so badly he couldn't hit the sky if he'd needed to.

The other voice came into his ear on breath that smelled like gasoline and sulfur and something ten days dead in a can. It came from behind him. "You're shooting blanks, dumbshit. Say goodnight."

The tree moved then, advancing on Karl so fast he couldn't begin to track it with the useless rifle, reached over his head and grabbed someone behind him, who roared against a muzzling paw. "Go home, boy. When it's time to play, we'll send for you."

Karl ran all the way home down the middle of the road, praying in German and firing his rifle into the air. When he arrived, there were twelve Jägers waiting in front of the gate, the Hauptmann front and center in his longjohns, with a machine pistol in each hand. He pointed them both at Karl and screamed, "Was ist los, Soldat? Bist du getrunken?"

Karl skidded to a stop before the Hauptmann, but his snowshoes got tangled up and he crashed into the icy tarmac head first. It all came back to him then, and he thought, *Someone else will have to tell Grossvater Egil,* and he gratefully fainted.

~ 5 ~

The manager of the Vista Del Nada Motor Home Court in Baker, a mildly obese retiree named Del Hotchkiss, looked a lot more forbidding in his portrait in the renter's rulebook than he did in the flesh, probably because he put his teeth in for the picture. By day, he patrolled the court's narrow gravel avenues on an electric golf cart, when most of the inhabitants were either plugging away at jobs in town, or asleep with their air conditioners blasting. By night, Hotchkiss retired to his Barcalounger in the manager's office and turned loose his lieutenants, a pair of attack-trained Dobermans named Mannix and Geronimo, whenever something outside threatened to drown out his TV.

Del had to go out himself to retrieve his dogs twice in the night because they slipped out of their own accord and kept sniffing at Mrs. Gordesky's trailer, #72, at the far corner of the court. The second time, his golf cart had refused to start, the overtaxed batteries still not fully recharged from the day's patrolling, and he'd had to warm up his old Buick and drive over for them in the biting cold. He knocked on the door to apologize to Mrs. Gordesky and maybe check on her, because he hadn't seen her in a few days, and she was more than a few years older than he. He didn't yet fear the worst, but the dogs had an uncanny knack for sniffing stiffs. Usually, it was a dead gopher or a snake they'd run to ground under one of the trailers, but they'd been the first to sniff out poor Mr. Altamorena in #34, and when Del didn't pick up on it quickly enough, they got in the open ceiling vent and had their way with him. It was hell convincing the Sheriff that coyotes did it, but his dogs were more dependable and loyal than most folks he'd met, so there was no question of putting them down. It'd been like he lost a part of his own body back in '81, when they took Columbo away from him and put the old boy to sleep after he bit two fingers off some snot-nosed teenager who had tried to steal his golf cart.

The windows of #72 were fogged up from the heater being on full-blast, and the air smelled of cooking, which took him by surprise, because Mrs. Gordesky didn't do much for herself. She microwaved her meals, and the stuff she ate smelled like burning plastic, and gave her gas like a tire-fire. Her nieces dropped by a few times a year to cook her a proper meal or take her to the Denny's in town, but this wasn't like that. He couldn't categorize the smell or even decide whether it was unpleasant or not, but he didn't blame the dogs for homing in on it.

Just to be sure, Del circled around the trailer and peered in the window on the bedroom end. He didn't want Mrs. Gordesky to mistake him for a prowler, and he sure as hell didn't want her to think he was sweet on her, but he had to make sure, or there'd be more trouble than he could talk his way out of, this time.

He heard the sound of the TV turned up quite loudly, as usual, and saw a blue blob of light from the little TV at the foot of Mrs. Gordesky's bed. He rapped on the window with his flashlight and waited a moment before rapping again and calling out, "Mrs. Gordesky? Del Hotchkiss, ma'am. You all right in there?"

There was no sign of life for a long minute, but then the channel changed, and he heard the big old satellite dish out back turning like a rusty windmill to track another of Mrs. Gordesky's "stories." She liked the soap operas, and it didn't matter if they were in English or Spanish or Swedish or Tagalog, so long as they were rutting and screaming at each other all the livelong day. Something that sounded like a Mexican hair-pulling contest came from inside now, so Del breathed a lot easier as he hauled Mannix and Geronimo back to the car. He breathed a silent prayer that when the Good Lord finally did take Mrs. Gordesky away, He'd let Del find her before the dogs did.

Stella Orozco didn't hear the TV or Del Hotchkiss at the window. She sat on the edge of the massive hospital bed in the old woman's trailer and she looked in the mirror. She sat on the bed whenever she was not eating or sleeping since she found her way here, three days before.

She didn't want to look at herself: she needed to close her eyes and get away from herself while her body healed. She had never been one for fretting over her appearance before, but now...

What she saw made her want to scream and tear herself apart like a mask and maybe she'd be whole and human underneath, or maybe she'd just die, but her hands remained on her lap, roaming only to change the channel every hour or so and retune the antiquated satellite dish, though she never saw or heard the programs. She didn't want to look, but she had to look at a pair of eyes as she tried to get her head around it, and there wasn't another human being in the world she trusted.

I was dying of cancer. Then I found a cure.

Not for the cancer, but for me.

My cancer never wanted to kill me. It wanted to be me.

And now it is.

I'm a ghost that haunts the walking, talking cancer of Stella Orozco.

And God won't stop telling me how lucky I am.

Stella, you have to understand that your life, your body, are still your own. It hasn't been stolen or destroyed. It's been uplifted. You are finally free. Death can't claim you. Old age and illness will never strike you down.

What am I? I'm not even human anymore…

You are more. You are what evolution has been trying to make human beings into for millennia, but we were too weak, too enamored of our machines, and entropy was too strong. In you, the transformation has been guided, and you have been reborn. Species evolve, Stella, never individuals. Until now.

Stella aimed a claw at her reflection. She found she had to fight to lift her own arm, and not just because it had been hanging by gristle a few days before. That was how she knew when God was watching her. She had to push a motion through committee to move where she wanted to, but her body got around just fine without her at the helm. She'd wake up from a sound slumber to find herself sleep-cooking or punishing her joints in sadistic bouts of physical therapy.

"Why me?" she croaked aloud, though the words sounded like gibberish even to her. New teeth were peeking through the black mess of her gums, and new lips were growing over them, a livid, granular pink blooming out of the black ruin of her old flesh, like the first buds of spring breaking through charred soil.

She flexed her healed jaw, savoring the control He let her have, for now. "Why would you want to do this for me?"

Would you rather have died? You were selected because you had the seed in you, and the necessary will to survive. You could still pass away, Stella. Your will is all that keeps you from dying, now. Only you can decide now when life should end.

"You don't sound like God. You're my cancer, not my conscience."

I am only your guide through this phase of transformation. When you have reawakened to your new, true self, you will need no one to guide you.

"I don't need anyone at all, thank you. I've done pretty well on my own, up until now." Get out of my head, she added weakly, but couldn't make her mouth work. Despite everything else that had happened, this was what she feared the most: the violation of her solitude, her self-control. So far, the stranger in her head had kept her alive where she might've died, had driven her past all human effort to escape her grave, but there was always another shoe yet to drop in any favor, and this—this rape—

You cannot do this alone. You are still a long way from recovery. There are others who can shelter you and provide you with the help you need—

"Enough! Shut up!" She stood before the mirror and shucked off the robe she'd worn. She forced herself to look away from her own eyes, and roved over the gruesome shell that she now wore.

Her body looked worse than the desiccated dead thing it'd been a few days ago, because it had begun to heal. The leathery brown musculature was now encased in sheaths of translucent pink protoplasm, bulbous pink-black sacs crowding the places where her bones had been laid bare. The most badly damaged flesh had sloughed off and was growing back before her eyes, amorphous blobs of scrambled cancer weaving itself into skeletal muscle around her right arm socket and her clavicle, and up and down her legs. Patches of new skin, waxy and white like salamanders and brie cheese, spread out from her belly and back. Her ravaged hair had all fallen out, but was now growing back so fast that when she lay very still, she could hear it.

She was a miracle, He told her again and again, but the glory of her resurrection had pushed her to the brink of insanity. A light reached down from heaven and touched her cancer, and the thing that was killing her had saved her life. Small wonder that she was hearing voices, that her cancer had become her therapist. She could berate it for answers, but she couldn't ask it or herself the questions that tortured her. *Is this my body? Am I me? How long before I slip away, before the new, improved me comes along and pushes me out of my own head?*

She could remember only jumbled fragments of how she'd come to be in this place. The biting cold seeping into her wounds. The blue-black emptiness of the desert outside the hole she'd climbed out of. The walking, the voice in her head like a sandstorm of commands and exhortations to go on, an un-death march to the trailer park, where she found herself inside and warm and devouring everything in the refrigerator. Was anyone home? She remembered nothing else.

When she'd stuffed her shriveled guts with all the canned and microwavable crap in the fridge and the cupboards, she'd fallen asleep. The pain went away so quickly she thought she was waking from a dream, but it was only the endorphins kicking in as her brain sparked up with the sudden influx of ersatz nutrients. She began to itch all over, almost to burn as her cancer went to work, but she fell off a precipice of exhaustion into a coma-deep sleep broken only when she awakened to eat. The room smelled of overcooked stew, pungent with herbs in a haphazard mixture that made the air almost flammable. Sometime during one of her blackouts, she must have brewed up a soup of all the dried-up old herbs in the pantry and some jars of spaghetti sauce to cover the putrid odor of her rejuvenation. The miasma of rot still lurked beneath the cooking smells, though she'd collected the larger bits in trash bags and emptied a can of Glade on them; but underneath *that* was a fertile aroma like new babies and fresh-baked bread and rain in a deep forest. Gradually, the fragrance of the new Stella Orozco pushed the others into the corners of the trailer, then it began to fade from her notice as the new flesh differentiated into the forms of the old.

Once, she blinked and found her left hand setting the telephone down in its cradle, but she had no recollection of having called anyone. Who could she call? Who would hear her voice? What would she say? Stella Orozco was missing, presumed dead, but any half-sharp investigator who reviewed her medical records and talked to her coworkers would assume she took her own life upon hearing she had cancer. She had no claim on her old life, even if she wanted it.

"What are you doing?" she shouted. Her voice startled her with its strength. Her lungs and vocal cords had repaired themselves, and her voice was deeper, more strident, but still recognizably her own.

There was no answer. Nobody in here but us delusions—

"Sure, why explain yourself? You know I won't tear out my own brain. I can't rip you out of me. You *are* me, now, aren't you?"

Who did I call?

She pressed redial, but got only a taped weather report from the Mojave National Preserve Information Service. Cagey. She saw the number at the bottom of a desk calendar with pictures of the desert on it beside the phone.

She went back to sleep, and dreamed that her face grew back.

When she awoke next, someone was knocking on the door. Pale light trickled in through gaps in the curtains, supercharging streams of dust swirling around the room on the updrafts from the space heater. Dust was over seventy percent discarded human skin cells. Would someone be able to discover she was here from them? She had left no fingerprints, her fingertips were still smooth, pearly pink and tender, but she had shed her skin here. But no, God was everywhere. Perhaps He was in every cell, in every mote of fluttering Stella-dust, giving orders and soothing sweet-talk. They would take care of themselves. She'd still have to take out the trash—

Someone was still knocking at the door.

She rose from the bed and went to the closet. A parade of eye-searing muumuus and housecoats led by a pair of double-knit pantsuits, one navy blue, one fire engine red with candy cane stickpins all down the lapels. Stella slipped into a sweatshirt, then put on the navy blue suit. The coarse polyester fabric scratched her new skin, and she immediately began to sweat. She buttoned up the jacket and safety-pinned the vast waistband of the pants, then looked at herself in the mirror. She looked like a woman who had recently lost over a hundred pounds and been burned over most of her face, or maybe a very effeminate older man, since her hair was less than two inches long. Her skin was a bilious yellow, and had the texture of Saran-Wrap over something unidentifiable from the back of the freezer. Her eyes roved over her face for several minutes, oblivious to the staccato hammering on the aluminum screen door in the next room. She watched the face in the mirror for a good long time. It was hers, but she was waiting for the God of Cancer to twitch her mouth or blink funny or otherwise betray His hand on her strings. Nothing. Her own face looked back at her, blank as if she'd suffered a stroke, until she let it smile.

It was time to go.

She reached for the doorknob, turned it and started to open the door before it hit her that she had no idea who was on the other side, but that it was almost certainly whomever He had called with her hands and voice.

She backed away from the door, stumbled and fell to the ground over a pair of plastic kitchen bags, cinched tightly shut, but exuding the cloying perfumes of vanilla and her own necrotized flesh. She almost thought she could see the floating dust tumbling into the tiny mouths of the bags, all the magic Stella-Cancer-dust taking care of itself.

You're being insane. For all you know, it's the woman who lives here, or the sheriff. You've got to get out of here.

Exactly. It's time to go.

Where are we—I…Where am I going?

Where there are others like you, who have evolved. You can't hide what you are, yet. There's much you'll have to learn, about your new life. Until then, you'll need protection.

Like Radiant Dawn. Gather all the mutants out in the middle of nowhere so some lunatic fascists can barbecue them without getting on the news. What's Plan B, God?

No one will ever dare to harm us ever again. I am like you, Stella. I am but one infinitesimal part of a greater whole, and it is that Whole which compels you. You have to come, Stella. The life force awaits.

Stella looked around the trailer, looked at the silhouette of the caller in the window. A tall, thin man in an overcoat, no hat. "Stella Orozco? We have to hurry, there's a plane waiting for us."

Stella opened the door and looked into the mercury-mirror eyes of Dr. Keogh. He smiled at her, a wide, patient smile of true affection and something deeper that she had only witnessed a few times in her life. It was a kind of quiet admiring pride that lights the face of a teacher when a pupil has completed the last lesson.

"Do you—remember me, Doctor?"

He nodded sagely, the brittle sunlight striking blinding highlights off his white hair. "I told you, there would be another Radiant Dawn."

Overwhelmed at last, she fell against him, sobbing. To see someone, anyone, from the other side of the nightmare she'd fallen into six months ago, and this man, who had first offered her hope and then cast her adrift...

"You have bags?" Dr. Keogh asked, looking past her into the trailer.

"No. nothing." But she turned around and stepped inside, grabbed the trash bags and hauled them out before shutting the front door. He offered to help, but she shouldered him aside as she carried them down the icy-slick lane to the dumpsters. As she rounded the corner, a sleek black shape appeared from behind the dumpster corral, snarled at her and snapped its fangs at the bag.

"Mannix! No!" An old fat man in a golf cart hove into view from behind the dumpster corral at the other end of the dog's absurdly long leash. Mannix tore the bottom out of the bag and immediately recoiled from the wave of noxious fetor that exploded into his hypersensitive nostrils. He backpedaled, gave a sharp, snorting bark and lunged at Stella. Her eyes widened in shock at the swiftness of the attack, but her own hand whipped out before her and slipped under the dog's muzzle, took firm hold of the tender pipes that fed the dog air and water and food and blood, and gave them a good squeeze. Though her arm was still little more than a jointed stick, she could rip the Doberman's life out with little or no effort, could pull his spine out through his fucking mouth, if it came to that. She was no less horrified than the dog by this realization, and let him go with a gentle shove. Mannix yelped and streaked across the lane and began retching and gobbling up weeds.

"Good Lord, what's that stink?" The old man levered himself up from the cart and shuffled towards the dumpster.

Stella swung the gate out to cover the ravaged bag and leaned against it, trying not to throw up on the man. "I'm sorry about the mess. I'll take care of it."

The old man shook his head, squinting at Stella, spooked by her as much as by the incident. "That's all right, ma'am, it's the damned dog's fault. He doesn't cotton to strangers poking around the trash. And you are a stranger…"

"I'm Marguerite Weintraub. My Aunt Naomi lives in #72? She's been ill, so she's come to stay with us for a while. The poor dear left some things in a mess, so my husband and I cleaned it up. I trust there's no problem?"

The old man rolled his eyes, smiling at Stella so awkwardly his upper plate slipped loose and made a break for it. He caught the denture in his hand and popped it back in. His mouth and eyes worked themselves into knots as her features slowly came into focus. He didn't seem to notice that she was dressed in her aunt's ill-fitting clothes. "No trouble at all, Mrs. Weintraub. Where is Mrs. Gordesky now, ma'am?"

"Oh, she's fine, but my husband took her to the hospital in Las Vegas for a check-up early this morning."

Twitching suspicion making his dentures click in his mouth, the manager said, "Your aunt said you lived in Bakersfield, is what I recall."

"We moved last year. My husband works at Caesar's Palace. My aunt's lease is paid up through the spring, I take it?"

"Oh, there's no problem with that. Just worried about the lady, is all. She's always been one of the nice ones. Left scraps out for my dogs."

Stella tightened her face in a dismissive smile and stooped to clean up the mess. The man clucked and doodled on his clipboard before heeling Mannix and rolling away in his golf cart.

Stella held her breath as she scooped putrid flesh and cracked bones back into the trash bag. The remains smelled different from the odor she'd grown accustomed to in the trailer; there was a sourer smell, though most of the bones were as clean as if they'd been bleached, with deep nicks and gouges in them, and the marrow all gone. She picked up a concave ellipsis of bone the size and shape of her palm and turned it over. There were strands of yellowed white hair hanging from it.

Was this her hair? She'd seen it falling out, but it hadn't turned white. Was this her skull? Her head had been badly beat up and decayed, but had she shed her old skull? Her old brain? She stroked the hairs on the shard. Her thoughts still ran riot in this new, improved head. Her memories still gave her the anger she needed to stay strong and go on living. Her soul was still in here, even if it was not alone. If this was not her head, God help the God who had to share it with her.

Unless the skull was someone else's, but…

Where is Mrs. Gordesky now, ma'am?

This broken old thing must be part of her skull. There was no other logical explanation. She scoured her brain and could find no memory, no flicker of guilt over having harmed anyone, at least not lately. She bundled up the rest of the mess and tossed it into the dumpster.

Life is for the living, Stella.

Dr. Keogh pulled up beside the dumpsters and came around to open her door for her. She stopped short of climbing into the passenger seat, looking at him and at the trailer. He touched her shoulder, fixed his gaze on her and spoke to her in her ear and with her brain. "There's no time to lose, Stella. The life force awaits."

She watched herself climbing into the car, and the car pulling out of the trailer park, and she fell almost immediately into a deep, deep sleep.

~ 6 ~

January 3
Over the Gulf of Mexico; 120 Miles south of Corpus Christi, Texas

The mammoth C-130 cargo plane rode the storm like a sled hurtling across a glacier, pulling itself forwards by main strength of its four massive props, but dropping serious altitude whenever the furiously roiling cells of wind shifted. The cabin rose and fell as on a restless ocean, then, for variety, made like a washing machine.

In its infinite wisdom, the National Weather Service had not elected to christen this storm, which had sprung up out of a sudden low pressure fault line opening along the Texas Gulf coast, drawing together a very wet, warm weather system from the Yucatan Peninsula with freezing rain sucked down from the Plains states. Somewhere below them, the storm was punishing the Gulf with sheets of fat, tepid rain and fist-sized hail, but experts predicted the storm would come no closer to land, and so it was theirs to name. They'd come up with all kinds of names for it, until they'd exhausted all profanity.

The pilot was a learned hand at this kind of flying, and had made the route dozens of times, with and without the approval of the FAA and the DEA, but he had never carried passengers as illegal as these, nor a cargo anywhere near as dangerous as the one that groaned and rocked in the cavernous expanse directly behind the cockpit. Though they had worked with the Mission many, many times, on this flight, he elected to keep the door to the cabin locked until they landed.

The Mission unit commander, Major Ruben Aranda, truly dreaded flight. He was not, strictly speaking, *afraid* of it. Therapists had told him that he was uncomfortable with the surrender of control, that it was only natural for a very hands-on Army officer to mistrust someone else's defiance of gravity, and that his symptoms were purely psychosomatic reactions to stress. Still, Aranda was reasonably certain that his aversion was purely physical. The tiny bones of his inner ear seemed to grind together like coal in a diamond mine, and his eardrums made each correction of air pressure into an excruciating ordeal that could not be relieved with chewing gum, strong drink or hard drugs. Even under the best of circumstances, in an empty first-class section with a jacuzzi, he would be on edge and in pain, and this flight was not first-class anything.

There were no seats or other human amenities, only the huge cargo cabin, which was filled with plastic shipping crates with forged Mexican labels and customs forms on them. The cabin was poorly pressurized and not heated at all; he couldn't feel his hands or feet, and his ears were making the most of the free bandwidth. He was actually grateful for his chattering teeth, because they seemed to help with depressurizing his eardrums. The omnipotent roar of the engines made conversation all but impossible, and nobody had anything to say but to bitch about the cold. Lt. Grostick had trumped them all with his tale of sneaking out of the USSR in the landing gear well of an Aeroflot airliner in '88, and the subject was laid to rest.

Major Aranda sat near the cockpit with his group of eight trusted subordinates, while the other group sat around and atop the tower of crates. He despised the other group of passengers, and instinctively knew they held him in even lower regard.

He loathed the cargo, but he was even more afraid of it. He knew very little about their final destination, but everything he'd learned so far only made him hate it, and the people around him, and the huge palettes of high explosive stuffed into the smugglers' holes beneath their feet, even more. It almost made him begin to hate the Mission.

They were on the edge of U.S. territorial waters, carrying twenty-five metric tons of an experimental chemical weapon, and the last remaining field command element of the central cell of the Mission. The great man who had recruited him into this chickenshit outfit had joked that they were a counter-evolutionary army. He thought at the time that it was a joke.

The command element consisted of himself and the old man at the far end of the cabin. He did not know Dr. Calvin Wittrock very well, but he was beginning to realize that, in describing him, Major Bangs had exercised rare understatement.

They were flying an old CIA-run drug smuggling route up a seam of minimum vigilance to an abandoned naval airstrip outside Kingsville in Texas. Aranda knew that drugs and less pleasant contraband came in via this conduit on SOD's Seaspray freedom flights in the eighties, and that it was maintained for other purposes, today. If they gave the proper electronic response burst when passing into US airspace, they'd be tacitly invisible on all other radar systems. By the time word of the corridor's use reached someone high enough to know about the Mission, they would be on the road, totally untraceable, and eight hundred miles away. If the state line wasn't closed and overrun with Army National Guard troops, they hoped to get back to HQ by tomorrow, this time. Medication time, give or take an hour if they had to shoot it out. He wished they still had the infrasonic generator technology Armitage designed. He wished Armitage was still alive.

He had not asked to be the ranking military officer in the Mission, would gladly have passed on the reins to anyone else, but he was the senior, and far and away the most qualified for this kind of warfare, even if most of his qualifications were only half-remembered nightmares that had been scrubbed from his brain by the same well-meaning therapists who tried to tell him why he was afraid of flying.

His watch beeped. He looked at its face, turned around to the inside of his wrist, an old habit from jobs where the glow off a watch face could get your hand blown off. Time for his meds. He palmed them out of his pocket pill caddy, dry-swallowed them with a blink and a momentary grimace. A high orange count in the mix today: he must be near the peak of his cycle. Shit, he'd sure hate to kill somebody and forget about it. His men were too good not to notice, but too good to make him feel noticed. Gripping his knees with his hands to hide their shaking, he waited to start feeling normal.

Enlisting in 1968, only a month before the Tet Offensive rendered the war a hopeless hamburger mill, Major Aranda passed through the Army's layered sifting box in freefall—Airborne straight out of basic training, then OCS. Blooded in Vietnam as a second lieutenant, then a captain, with 101st Airborne, he came back to the U.S. in '72 with a jacket of medals, top-flight fitness reports and a will unblunted by the bitter defeat. *His* war had been a thing of beauty. He slashed and burned through Special Forces training and had to fight to get sent back to the war. The brass loved his brains and nerve, and wanted to rub against it in the Pentagon. The politicians loved his squeaky-clean ethnicity, and wanted their pictures taken with him, wanted him to introduce them on campaign stops. But most important, his troops loved *him*. He never got scared, but unlike every other suicide-case the war had hatched, Aranda never got angry, either. He never wasted men, he never let adversity throw him off-task, and he always came home with the job done.

His contract was picked up by the CIA in '73. He entered their elite one hundred-man covert combat unit, working deep in-country, most often inside the North. For the unspeakable things he did there, they made him a Major.

He came back in '75 a little bitter, a little morose, but far better put-together than many officers who'd lost far fewer men. He wanted to keep fighting, but the Army needed field officers close to home to help rebuild its gutted morale, they said. They lied. Bitter feuding took place in generals' country over his file, which somehow slipped through the cracks into some subcommittee of the National Security Council, and Aranda himself followed it into a crack in the earth.

He joined SOD, the Army's Special Operations Division, and took control of an operational detachment. One of the unit's first missions was to destroy their own Pentagon records. Aranda no longer belonged to the military. He never did figure out who owned him, then. Or maybe he just didn't remember.

Contrary to what muckraking congressmen and the media would say about SOD, it was not an anarchic frat party, with wild-eyed Vietnam vets drafting their own missions and funding them with blank government checks. Not all the time. The orders came from a back channel in the National Security Council. The missions had very little to do with stopping Communism, and their targets, all too often, were civilian. Major Aranda knew that he ran counter-insurgency ops throughout South America from '79 to '85. He also knew that in the second year, he began to see a CIA therapist after each mission. He knew that he must have successfully completed all of his missions, because he was still alive. Beyond that, he had only a skein of rude holes—lacunae, the therapists called them—to account for six years of his life.

Sometimes, out of nowhere, a taste or a smell, or even the uneasy moments before plunging into sleep, would trigger a blinding vision, and parts of some of them would come back. The Sendero Luminoso splinter-faction UFO cult in the Andes, and the thing they called down from the sky that was not an airplane or a spacecraft, nor any kind of machine at all. The French archaeological team on the Rio Negro, and the ruins they claimed were pre-human, and contained nuclear reactors. The tiny Guatemalan fishing village where the people, horribly deformed from inbreeding and environmental pollution, waded into the sea and never came back: the smell of the ocean after the air strike, the scaled body parts boiling in the waves...

He clearly remembered the day he told them he didn't want to go on any more ops. They were very clumsy trying to kill him, like they thought he wanted to die, like they were doing him a favor. He walked away with twenty million dollars in DoD money, funneled to SOD over the years by a blindly patriotic civilian bursar, and vanished off even the intelligence community's maps.

The lowest rung of the black ladder was the Mission. At last he'd found a command he could live with.

That is, until Bangs's unit had destroyed itself and left a mess for them to clean up, and their war to fight.

When he didn't really hate anything much, any more, he got up and made his way down the length of the cramped fuselage to the other group. Stamping his feet—both to give them fair warning and to work the blood back into his feet—he approached Wittrock's clique. The six civilians and three soldiers were dressed in US Navy flight crew jumpsuits and rain slickers, but the disguise wouldn't hold up to close scrutiny. Most of the civilians were too old by far for any branch of the service, while the soldiers were dark-skinned Latinos with almost purely Indian features. They were Colombian FARC narcoguerillas, the most hardened jungle fighters in the Western hemisphere. Two carried Ingram Mac-10 machine pistols, and they bulged with flak vests and knives and extra clips on bandoliers under their raincoats. The third guerilla stood at the narrow window beside the aft loading door, watching the storm through the scope of a M24 7.62mm sniper rifle that still had some poor Special Forces bastard's blood on it.

"We're landing in less than an hour, Doctor. Tell your friends to stow their toys."

"You speak fluent Spanish yourself, Major," Wittrock said, but shrugged and mumbled something to his FARCs. He studied Aranda with bland condescension. "I trust there's been no *further* change in the flight plan?"

Dr. Wittrock's precious cargo had already cost one good man his life. When they'd gone to the airstrip outside of Bogota, the local cartel had thrown a collective rod over the delay of one of its own shipments, and a scuffle had ensued. Former Navy Lt. Dennis Kinney was shot under his right armpit, between the plates of his flak vest, as he loaded the cargo onto the plane, killing him instantly. More in retribution than self-defense, Aranda's men had taken out sixteen Colombians. The only real comfort Major Aranda could take in his death was that he would not have to inform Lt. Kinney's next of kin, because they had thought him dead for nearly a decade. Such were the terms of recruitment into the Mission.

The C-130 got into the air posthaste and got lost in low clouds, talking its way out of South America only by a lot of lying and radar bluffing. They'd planned to land in Mexico and transfer the cargo to fuel oil trucks, which would carry it across the border. Now, with fast and furious enemies in the drug cartels, they were flying directly into the United States, and Aranda was trying not to think about Wittrock's insane final solution contingency plan.

"Everything's copacetic, Doctor," he finally said.

"There's nothing else we might need to know about," Wittrock said, chidingly, "nothing you've…forgotten?"

"No. We set down at the Kingsville Naval Air in seventy-five minutes. We don't expect any trouble."

Trouble meant they couldn't set down. Trouble meant they announced over military channels that they were carrying nuclear weapons, and flew over heavily populated areas as much as possible, all the way to the final destination. Trouble meant that when they got there, they would detonate the explosives in the deck of the plane, and unleash a cloud of the most toxic substance ever created by man or nature on the target. No one but Wittrock and Aranda knew about the contingency plan.

Major Aranda dug his fingers into his scalp and tried to hold his head together.

"I trust the landing zone will be secure?" Wittrock asked. The venerable bomb-maker looked waxed and wall-eyed, grinding on the dregs of some powerful lab-grade stimulant.

"It's a blessed conduit, Doctor. If anyone would know, I would. And the cargo is worth any amount of risk, right?"

Wittrock smirked, knowing exactly what he meant. It was, he'd said time and again, the ultimate weapon in their war. Once and for all, the Mission would cure the disease that was the fruit of RADIANT. Sure, it was worth a soldier's life. But it had yet to be tested outside of a beaker. "The research is sound. Tests on Dr. Mrachek's tissue samples have yielded lysosome dissolution reactions more complete than we dared hope. Dr. Barrow and the Greens have been pouring poison in your ear about it because they have no alternative. But I believe you trust Dr. Barrow even less than you trust me."

"Doctor, a message was waiting for you at the airfield in Matamoros. They broke radio silence to relay it when we didn't land."

Wittrock betrayed no surprise, merely nodded. "Go ahead."

"Don't you think that was a little stupid?"

"There was relatively little risk involved, and the situation demanded unequivocal certainty. Go ahead with the message, please."

"The package you sent to Washington was delivered. And well-received."

"Excellent," Wittrock made a dismissive gesture and turned to go back to his seat.

Aranda grabbed him by the loose folds of his billowing jumpsuit. "What the hell is this about? And what was so important about it, that you'd risk pinpointing our flight path?"

"The weapon has been field-tested, and the test was a success. Rejoice, Major Aranda. Your lieutenant did not die in vain. This war will soon be at an end, and you can get back to your forest under glass."

The plane dipped horribly, falling a few hundred feet before leveling off in an uneasy truce with the storm. The plunge yanked Wittrock free of Aranda, but the scientist leaned in closer. "You still doubt me, Major. Do you know who founded the Mission?"

Aranda, who knew more than most the value of not knowing some things, only shook his head.

"I did. He was my friend, and a mentor, both to me and to Darwin, whom you did know. He was the most brilliant scientist at the Manhattan Project, and do you know what they did with him when he'd given them all he could? They murdered him in cold blood, and wiped his name from all the records. Your soldiers don't have a monopoly on sacrifice, Major."

Wittrock sat down with his back to Aranda. The FARC guard perched atop the cargo smiled gold nuggets and made a scat-gesture with his rifle.

Aranda turned and swung from sling to canvas sling along the cabin to where his men sat. He busied himself with helping them suit up in civilian garb and sorting their papers and photo ID's. They huddled to wait for descent when a salvo of gunfire came from the aft end of the plane.

"*Buenos noches, Estados Unidos!*" the FARC sniper screamed.

Aranda's men got to their feet and started to rush him, but Aranda grabbed and dragged them back. The FARCs on top of the cargo watched them with guns out. It would be mutual slaughter, at best. He put on his headset and hailed the pilot. "Bre'r Bear, what's under us?"

"No-man's land, Bre'r Fox. Ass-end of Texas, on final approach. What's going on back there?"

"Little cokehead air rage, Bre'r Bear. Nobody's hurt. Steer us clear of houses, though, okay?"

"Roger that, out."

And so, despite Major Aranda's best efforts, the Mission re-entered the United States shooting.

~ 7 ~

Cundieffe was awakened just before five AM in his room at the Georgetown Suites. He thought it was his regular wake up call a few minutes early, but was startled by a strange voice. *"He's coming to get you."*

"What?" His heart skipped a beat as he fumbled for his glasses. It was one of those moments when you wake up from a sound sleep, but you're sure you're still dreaming. He couldn't remember what he'd just dreamt, but as he rubbed his eyes and looked again at the clock, he knew that someone had been chasing him. Someone who could not be escaped, because he looked down out of the sky and out of the eyes of every living creature. But that was crazy. Why should he dream of someone chasing *him*?

"Agent Cundieffe? Are you there?" It was Assistant Director Wyler's secretary, June McNulty.

"Yes, I'm sorry, Ms. McNulty, I just woke up, that's all."

"This isn't a scheduled appointment, Agent Cundieffe. The Assistant Director requires your attendance at an emergency briefing at the Cave Institute."

Good night! "How much time do I have?"

"Five minutes, barring traffic. Do be ready to go by then, Agent Cundieffe. Assistant Director Wyler was emphatic."

He thanked Ms. McNulty and hung up, clambered out of bed and into one of the suits in the closet. He swallowed a handful of vitamins and chased them down with a carton of orange juice from the minibar. He noticed the minibar was short one bottle of Bacardi Silver rum, and made a mental note to challenge its addition to his bill. He slipped on an overcoat and a wool knit scarf, brushed his teeth and rinsed with the special prescription anti-thrush mouthwash from his own personal toiletry kit, no single-serving Scope, thank you very much. His hair was too short and too thin to mount much resistance, and a few seconds' combing tamed the few uncooperative strands into place.

He looked at himself in the mirror then, really *looked*. It was an exercise he'd perfected as a child at his first year of elementary school, and he credited it with sparing him the daily beatings that were dealt out to far less geeky looking kids. He tried to see himself through the eyes of all the different types of people he'd encounter in the day ahead. He understood local cops, federal officials, solid citizens and criminal minds of all types, just as he'd understood bullies, disaffected teachers and petty-minded administrators. For some, he learned to look like a good citizen, an inept dupe or a trustworthy instrument, but for most he'd been merely invisible. He looked and looked, but he could not imagine what might lie behind the eyes of the group of people who would look at him this morning.

He supposed this was about the Storch assassination, the report for which had dropped into a black hole. It was remarkable writing a report which he knew would never find its way into the ocean of FBI data, that there would be no official investigation, no trial, no ripples of public panic and outrage. For the government, there were visible signs of strain at trying to keep this crime, like the others, a secret. But for him there was an unaccustomed surge of excitement at the prospect of solving it. If all crime could be investigated and prosecuted in secret, out of the meddling circus of the public arena, how much more efficient would the execution of justice be? Indeed, how much healthier would the average American mind be, without the morbid escapism of daily media bloodbaths and sensationalist entertainment trash that glamorized violent crime?

As for the murder itself, there was an almost preternatural lack of facts. According to a preliminary autopsy performed by a Mule physician at Bethesda Naval Hospital, Storch was struck by three shots from a high-powered rifle at a distance of no greater than fifty yards, given the explosive damage done to his body. This meant that the assassin had to be up in a tree in the park, or in the line of cars across the street, all of which had been thoroughly searched by the soldiers who contained the area. Which meant that the assassin probably *was* one of the soldiers who closed off the area. So far they had found nothing, not even the bullets which struck Storch. There was nothing in the loading dock, nothing in his body. The posterior damage done by the shots was determined to have been caused by explosive gas, suggesting that the bullets detonated within him, but there was no trace of metal or gunpowder, only an unidentified chemical residue which the pathologist speculated had been the bullet itself, and which had triggered the violent chemical reaction that killed the prisoner. Remembering the smoke and bubbling foam pouring out of Storch as he wandered, hollow-headed, out onto the sidewalk, Cundieffe eagerly awaited the tox screens and chemical analysis he'd ordered on his own sample of Storch's blood.

He grabbed his briefcase and got out the door at the first sounding of Wyler's horn, and ten full seconds before his five AM wake up call.

He stopped short just outside his door, and had to grab the railing as a gust of wind laced with beads of icy rain slashed at him. He could almost see the heat streaming off his body and into the ravenous predawn sky.

Down in the lot, a black GMC Suburban idled with its lights off. Behind triple-tinted windows, the interior was as inscrutable as the inside of an egg. Cundieffe looked around, but saw no other cars waiting. Painted in chiaroscuro black and blue and chrome, the lot was packed in silent ranks of sedans and SUV's. To his knowledge, the Assistant Director never traveled in a hulking utility vehicle, just the standard issue Ford LTD, though he had a support staff driver. But then, he had only been the Deputy Assistant Director, then. As the highly visible head of the new counterterrorism division, he would need more security than ever before. And now, with an emergency briefing at the Institute...

Something Wyler himself had told him at his first brush with Mule society: *the more powerful they become, the more invisible...*

The rear passenger-side door opened and Wyler leaned out. "Get in. The war's back on."

Holding his briefcase over his head to shield it from the stinging rain, Cundieffe got a running start and leapt more or less completely into the back seat, hauling himself the rest of the way in by the seatbelt. The Suburban took off, the door slamming shut under the inertia that pressed Cundieffe face-first into the back of his seat.

As he righted himself, he studied the Assistant Director, and decided that if he were to look at himself through his superior's eyes this morning, he'd have to blur his own vision somewhat. Wyler looked as if he hadn't slept, and he held a drink in one shaky hand. He watched Cundieffe with the same subdued impatience that he'd displayed when he led the junior agent into the restroom at China Lake, and told him what he really was and why he was really there.

"What do we know, sir?"

"Very little, but that's why I wanted you along now. There's been a major break on the location of the Mission command element in South America, and some telecom activity inside Texas that suggests that they have already arrived on U.S. soil."

"That's incredible. I suppose the NSA intercepted communications from their foreign base of operations?"

"They don't use phones, Martin. They're not idiots. They used encrypted postings on a BBS to prepare the faithful who remained behind for the return invasion."

"My, it seems awfully quick, doesn't it?"

"What do you mean?"

"Well, I thought that decryption of sophisticated encrypted text was somewhat time-consuming, even if you knew where to look..."

"You have objections, yes. But what are you trying to say?"

Cundieffe squirmed. He felt his hair writhing out of place on his skull as he tried to speak. "Isn't it illegal under even the narrowest interpretation of the Telecommunications Privacy Act for a private group to handle such information? I mean—"

"Martin, it is imperative that you understand something. We are fighting terrorism, which is low-intensity warfare, granted, but it is war on the American people, and on the American way of life. We would be shirking our duties to those people if we did not pursue their enemies with all due diligence, and all the resources available. Liberty and privacy are relative luxuries in time of war, but that is why it has been our especial duty to violate them with the least possible harm. Not the FBI, Martin. *Us.* America has *always* been at war. And we have *always* been listening."

"I've just—" Cundieffe faltered, trying to steer the conversation into less prickly territory. "I realize extraordinary means must be used to catch this extraordinary group, but I feel like I'm still not up to speed. What would drive the most brilliant scientists in our weapons programs to wage war on their own nation like this—"

"Cotton Mather," Wyler said. To Cundieffe's quizzical look, he added, "The father of American Puritan philo—"

"Right, right, but what's he got to do with it?" Cundieffe was thoroughly nonplussed.

Wyler quoted effusively with more than a glint of sarcasm in his eyes, "'The more cultured and intelligent you are, the more ready you are to work for Satan.'"

Cundieffe could not meet Wyler's gaze any more, and took up his briefcase. It was still dripping half-melted sleet onto the plush floormats. "I also have the case files you needed, sir, and my summary report on progress on the murder of Sgt. Storch."

"I've already read all there is to know. Forget about him, Martin. He's not FBI business, anymore. Nothing you see or hear this morning can be disclosed or used as evidence in the pursuance of FBI matters until you are given notice, is that clear?"

Cundieffe nodded.

"Good. Now, where we are going, you are going to meet with resistance. You may be ordered to leave, but you are not going to."

"I don't want to cause any friction, sir."

"But you will. We are a subspecies, but the Cave Institute is a society. One must be sponsored to be accepted, but the process is long and arduous. Your background with the FBI and your discretion in the Mission affair in California are barely enough to get your foot in the door."

Cundieffe let his voice get as weak and unconvincing as he could make it. "Sir, if there's any possibility of this reflecting badly on you, I don't want to impose. You could always brief me later…"

"This is a matter of national security. And you are my Agent in Charge on this case."

"But if I'm not to use any of the information we're going to receive this morning, how is my presence going to serve any purpose?"

"Because by the time we've digested the information and formulated a plan, we will also have conceived a legitimate channel for it to come to our attention. We will then be able to act on it decisively and finally. Last time, we let the military play their games, and nearly one hundred innocent civilians were incinerated. This time, we will manage the situation from start to finish, and order will prevail."

Cundieffe withdrew into himself. He didn't bring up the other contents of his briefcase, which he'd hoped to discuss. Instead, he looked at the drink in Wyler's hand, a sign of weakness that he hoped would not further jeopardize the investigation.

He didn't notice Wyler watching him until the glass was swept up under his nose. "Would you like one?" the Assistant Director asked. Cundieffe's nose was stung by a bitter aroma that tweaked the olfactory sweetmeats in the floor of his brain. What could the Assistant Director be hooked on, that could make such a stench? Absinthe?

"No, sir," he fumbled. "It's a little early for me…"

"Imbecile," Wyler snapped. "It's herbal tea."

Martin still found it hard to believe that he (he still thought of himself as a "he," Wyler had explained that to do otherwise could precipitate a psychotic breakdown) was not a man like the others, but something else entirely. *A sub-species, a symbiotic worker caste,* they called themselves. *The future,* their eyes said.

The enormity of it was still a long way from coming home, because it was the kind of world-changing revelation that alters the way one sees the sky, the world, his face in the mirror. His reflexes for dealing with such fundamental paradigm shifts had atrophied since their last major challenge, when he discovered that neither the Director nor his Father were immortal. To know of the Mules and what they did in secret to keep the world from falling apart from one day to the next was not so different, he supposed, from learning first hand of the hand of God. For the time being, it was merely curious, that he had never seen it, seen them—seen *himself.*

He had always been a passionate student of human nature. As a child, he'd had to mimic normal behaviors to avoid being beaten constantly. He found most human behavior utterly ridiculous, until he began to understand the nature of the axes on which they turned. Dominance and self-gratification ruled most, and in many it hollowed them out and made them into machines, destined to harm themselves and others in their blind animal madness. His parents might have had some influence in guiding him towards his career, but it was in his nature to study people, and to seek to protect society from the bad ones. Now, he knew where it came from, and that he was not alone.

In his earlier visits to Washington, AD Wyler had introduced Cundieffe to eight Mules that he knew about, and perhaps three times as many that he couldn't be sure about. It was not something one could immediately pin down. There was no syndrome that Cundieffe had yet identified, and he struggled to isolate one.

Excessive hygiene, perhaps, but that could be put down to the deficiencies in hormones, the elegant efficiency of the immune system, the strict adherence to proper diet, that caused them to have no native odor whatsoever. Those cast as males tended towards academic tweediness or invisible gray flannel, with no power tie posturing or cosmetic adornment, and a tendency towards premature baldness and a total lack of body or facial hair. The "females" were indistinguishable from all the other frosty power-suited lady politicos in government, but those whom he knew were Mules seemed to represent the asexual ideal towards which all other career women strove: waspish in figure, crisply coiffed and almost stingingly brisk in conversation.

Intelligence, certainly: Cundieffe had yet to meet one who didn't make him feel like a rank idiot. That was par for the course in Washington, he knew, but the Mules he'd met had done so effortlessly and with none of the self-conscious relish that he'd observed in gendered bureaucrats. He'd found he got in trouble the least when he addressed a new acquaintance as "Doctor," and tried to steer conversation away from his own alma mater.

Power, obviously, but never for its own sake, and never in elected positions. Attending a series of odd briefings with a motley assortment of upper-level functionaries of federal agencies, Cundieffe had found that the Mules placed their numbers in bureaucratic positions where they wielded the most possible power over policy with the least visibility. Positions of titular power and ready media access were left to hacks and empty suits, but their briefings and position papers almost invariably came from Mule subordinates. The Mules he'd met so far included one other FBI Assistant Director; an assistant chairman of the Federal Reserve; the executive secretary of the Office of Management and Budget; a senior administrator at the Centers for Disease Control; the assistant director of the Environmental Protection Agency; the deputy director of the Department of Energy; the vice chairman of the Federal Communications Commission; the civilian deputy director of the Defense Intelligence Agency; and the Ambassador to Switzerland. Nearly all of them had remained in their present positions through at least the last three administrations, watching them come and go as they quietly ran the nation. An outside observer, even armed with the understanding of what they were, could only guess at who was what by the absence of attention, the omission of the kind of human errors and excesses that cropped up in nearly every career, sooner or later. It was a chilling field of speculation, that everyone who didn't turn up on the eleven o'clock news could be one, and could only be ruled out when they ruined themselves in a scandal.

During their first meeting after he learned, Cundieffe had asked AD Wyler the question that had been uppermost in his mind, if the Director was one of them. Wyler had looked about his office as if, even here, such a secret could not be lightly spoken. But also, he noted, with some disappointment, as if he'd hoped that Cundieffe possessed sharper insight than he did. "Hoover was a man, with all that entails. He had strong homosexual tendencies, but we know that he never acted on them, for fear of compromising his position and the Bureau."

"But what about...?" he hadn't been able to finish the thought, but it was foremost on the nerves of even the most die-hard Hoover loyalist, and Wyler had caught it. The Director's unseemly attachment to his Assistant, Clyde Tolson, the man who shared his secrets, his companionship and the lonely stewardship of his memory after he finally passed away. On their vacations, the Director had taken mountains of snapshots of his friend, that many apologists had made fools of themselves trying to defend—Clyde sleeping, Clyde sunbathing, and so on.

"We know that Hoover never acted on his gendered impulses, because Clyde Tolson *was* one of us."

As has ever been the case in human affairs, there were many cabals, conclaves and secret powers in federal government, all of them shaping the stuttering, outwardly static progress of government with their infighting and alliances. But they were without exception composed of white males, and subject to the animal programming of their gender and class. Many of them claimed to control the government, but most of them had never even heard of the Mules. None of those who did spoke of them above a whisper.

Everything in government that worked came from the Mules, or so they would have him believe. In the last century, the United States' slope-browed alpha male leadership had brought the nation—and, in several cases, the world—closer to the brink of collapse or even extinction than the rest of the world would ever know, no less than nine times, and only the Mules had saved them.

Cundieffe quickly ascertained that AD Wyler was not parading him around Washington simply to initiate him into the fold. From the questions they asked and the whispered conversations Wyler had with other Mules at the Columbia Club where they met, he had gathered that the twentieth incident was even now unfolding, and he was being groomed to help prevent it. Cundieffe didn't have to read lips or press Wyler to know that they were, all of them, talking about the Mission and Radiant Dawn.

The Mules were the most powerful group involved, but there were others, some believed to be sympathetic to the Mission, who continued to hamper the investigation, and who may have had a hand in Storch's assassination. Cundieffe had to learn a whole new bag of tricks to compete at this level, because the investigation, and the crime itself, must remain a secret.

The Cave Institute for Global Policy Review was only one of several dozen Washington-area "think tanks," private foundations devoted to research and advocacy for one group or another. Unlike nearly every other in the Beltway, however, The Cave Institute was that rarest of all birds, a truly apolitical body, composed of members of both major parties, though mostly of bureaucrats and academics with no political affiliation at all. The Institute released studies and statistical analyses of public issues on a daily basis, but almost never made the news, was never cited on the floor of Congress, because its studies contained no political dynamite, and usually focused on issues so far in the future that few legislators would feel secure in introducing them into the record. Some, like their "Statistical Model Of Urban Population Growth, Brazil, 2000-2200, With

Branch Models Pursuant To Birth Control Policies" were the kind of dry, tiresome stuff that University professors packed their china in when they moved, while their "Hypothetical Model For The Creation Of An Autonomous Kurdish State" was suppressed for fear of arousing the ire of Iraq and Turkey. Cundieffe knew he'd heard of them before, but couldn't quite place where—perhaps buried in the thickest paragraph of an exhaustive foreign policy article in a newspaper op-ed piece, or perhaps in a rant in one of the hundreds of radical newsletters to which he subscribed. Maybe he hadn't heard of it until he'd begun to meet Mules. But that was what the Cave Institute really was: the seat of the secret, the Illuminated Masters of democracy, the Platonic philosopher-kings who silently kept the world spinning.

As the Suburban turned off a Georgetown side street less than a mile from the Suites and rolled through an iron gate wreathed in frostbitten ivy, Cundieffe clamped his arms down at his sides and tried to force his hands to sit still in his lap. The Suburban bounced up a cobblestone drive and pulled to a stop before the unlit front portico of the Cave Institute. The driver came around and opened Cundieffe's door, and he climbed out and tried not to look like a teenaged runaway getting off a bus in Hollywood.

The Cave Institute looked like a castle made of leaves. Two stories high and smaller by far than most private residences in the neighborhood, the building was completely engulfed in a thick pelt of shield-leafed ivy, with only the black hole of the low doorway and a few narrow windows carved into it. A hard-looking man in a black suit came down the broad slate steps to meet the Suburban. The Assistant Director nodded to the man and they both followed him in through the doors, which seemed to swing open of their own accord. Cundieffe was reminded of a bit in a history of ancient Greece, where a philosopher devised a mechanism for the automated opening of doors to impress upon the great unwashed the power of the gods. The doors themselves were eight inches thick and plated in verdigris-encrusted brass, and a tiny gargoyle head that bore a strong resemblance to Socrates peeked at Cundieffe through the ivy dangling from the lintel overhead. The effect would probably be lost on the great unwashed of today, but Cundieffe doubted any but anointed acolytes were allowed to pass through them, anyway.

Inside, they noisily crossed a groaning mockingbird floor and rushed through dim halls lit only by the colored sensors of various security systems. The furniture was spartan, and introduced to the rooms only to offset the seeming vacancy of the house. There were several libraries with shelves reaching two stories up to vaulted ceilings and ivy-choked skylight windows, but there were no pictures or other decorations on the walls, and precious few places to sit. This might've been the retreat of a particularly stern order of monks. The impression sent was very clearly received—nothing of importance takes place on the surface.

Sure enough, the escort led them through twists and turns to an elevator discreetly tucked away where Cundieffe might've expected a restroom or a broom closet. He looked to Wyler for cues on how to behave, but the Assistant Director was biting his thumb and staring at something very captivating he saw in the bird's-eye maple wall paneling. The last Bureau meeting they had attended together had included representatives from every branch of the intelligence and military communities who hoped to gut Wyler's new Section before it officially opened, yet Wyler had been nonchalant, openly contemptuous. He looked frightened of getting on this elevator. For Cundieffe, or for himself? "Don't," Wyler whispered in his ear, "if they deign to speak to you, don't lie to them."

What an odd thing to say! "I wouldn't dream of it, sir, but why? Will there be a lie detector test?"

"They *are* lie detectors."

The escort worked some kind of unseen magic to get the door open, and pressed a button Cundieffe didn't notice to get it to close again behind them. He didn't feel the slightest motion, and thought the elevator must be broken, when the door slid open and they stepped out onto deep green plush carpet. They stood in a corridor of redwood paneling, lit by candles in sconces beneath smoke-blackened busts of philosophers. Cundieffe recognized only a few of them—among them Socrates and Sir Thomas More, whose *Republic* and *Utopia*, respectively, had presented models for Mule-managed societies. The obscurer thinkers, he'd learned, were more interesting by far. They were Mule savants, and their treatises were for the eyes of Mules alone. Cundieffe had read selections from a few of them at Wyler's urging: *On Instinct,* the definitive analysis of the breeding caste, by Guillaume d'Averoigne, who anticipated Freud by three hundred years; *The Devising Of Creation*, by the Swiss Mule naturalist, Lucanus, who merged Darwin's natural selection theory and Mendel's observations of genetics five hundred years before either of them was born; and the strategic manifesto of the Medieval Order Of The Cave, which surfaced, albeit in a highly adulterated and perverted form, six centuries after its origin, as the *Protocols Of The Elders Of Zion*. This last gave Cundieffe pause until he had a chance to peruse the original document, and found that its innovative and utopian concepts for government had been twisted into a black caricature to serve as anti-Semitic propaganda by the Russian noble class.

Between the lanterns were alcoves, in which were set low, arched doorways, each of them closed and locked by a card slot. Cundieffe thought of interrogation cells, or boxes at an opera. The escort stopped in one alcove and Wyler looked into a retina-scan peephole. The door swung open with an audible hiss of pressurized air. In the event of some disaster, the room they were about to enter was airtight. The Mules' paranoia so far made the precautions of the Pentagon or the FBI seem as lax as a neighborhood library. Wyler stepped into the room and beckoned Cundieffe to follow. The escort closed the door behind them, and Cundieffe noticed a green light beside it turn red. The room they were in did resemble an interrogation cell. It was little larger than a booth, and this was filled with two chairs and a shallow table built into the far wall. The far wall itself was floor to ceiling mirrored glass. Cundieffe wondered briefly if someone could see through, and who was watching them, when Wyler tugged him into his seat.

The voice of God rumbled out of hidden speakers in the ceiling of the booth. "We had expected you earlier, Wyler. And alone."

Cundieffe cast the Assistant Director a forlorn look, but Wyler patted his hand and spoke up to the booth at large. "Agent Cundieffe needs to know. He is not an interloper. He is one of us. I am his sponsor." Silence stretched out, into which Wyler weakly added, "A well-informed decision cannot be made without his insight."

"We have proceeded with other business, but will return to the case in question presently," the voice boomed. "The Secretary of Foreign Intelligence has been called away momentarily. I trust Wyler agrees that his input is also essential to the discussion?"

"Of course," Wyler said, and leaned back in his seat.

"Really, sir, there's no need to stick your neck out like this," Cundieffe whispered in his ear. His stomach churned with the basic elation at finding himself here, and the acidic horror of seeing his superior reduced to a craven petitioner. "Everything I learned from Sgt. Storch was detailed in my report—"

"Nonsense, Martin. I want—I need—for you to see this. Only here can you see the full scope of the battlefield." He leaned forward and spoke into a microphone built into the wall. "Wendell Wyler," he said. "One and not many."

Cundieffe recognized the phrase immediately. It was from *The Republic* of Plato, a keystone in his initiation. Closing his eyes for a second, he called to mind the exact words: "The intention was, that, in the case of the citizens generally, each individual should be put to the use for which nature intended him, one to one work, and then every man would do his own business, and be one and not many; and so the whole city would be one and not many."

Their reflections turned ghostly as the mirror abruptly became transparent, and when Cundieffe beheld the room beyond, he was reminded again of box seats at the opera.

In movies, the military always has a "war room," with a "big board" displaying the might of the world powers as pieces on a game board, and ranks of technicians at computers like the mission control of a space program. In his second tour of the Pentagon, he'd been allowed to walk past the real war room: a dank, dingy conference room with television monitors and fax machines on one end and a long table with lopsided legs at the other. A cockroach had run across the table during the brief canned speech the tour guide recited, and the doors had remained closed, because it was being fumigated.

The Cave Institute had a proper war room. Massive screens displayed a patchwork map of the globe, updated in real time by satellites. Periodically, one portion of the map would blow up and spin off to a subordinate screen and text flew across the screen too fast to read. A smoked glass conference table ran the length of the room, with keyboards and more screens built into it. The eleven figures seated at the table were silhouetted by the screens above and all around them, so that Cundieffe could only tell that there were seven "men" and four "women," a totally useless observation, given the circumstances.

Above the monitors on the opposite wall, Cundieffe could barely make out other observation boxes, some lit and occupied, others dark. Off to one end and recessed below the level of the war room floor was a communications center, with half a dozen men and women in dark suits working at computers.

But it was none of this that surprised Cundieffe half so much as that the Mule committee seemed to be watching pornography. On all the monitors that weren't showing the world and all its trouble spots, a portly, distinguished gentleman hunched over a desk with his slacks down around his ankles, obscuring a woman who sprawled across the aforementioned desk in a posture of sexual abandon that even the grainy color surveillance video could tell was feigned, and poorly. The act went on for only a few moments, then the man slouched away and tripped over his slacks. His face flicked by the camera's eye for only a second as the man picked himself up and hoisted his slacks, but it was plenty of time for Cundieffe to recognize him as the Chairman of the Senate Armed Services Committee.

"Good night!" Cundieffe exploded. "What are they watching?"

The question felt idiotic as soon as it left his lips, but Wyler seemed to understand, and took on the right fatherly tone. "In order to make reasoned, informed decisions, the Committee has often been forced to witness unsavory acts."

"But how did they get such a thing? It's obscene, it's venal, it's—"

"Utterly necessary. Martin, here we have to look past the world of shadows and appearances to the absolute truth. No means of acquiring it are absolutely unacceptable, when weighed against the consequences of ill-informed decisions. This is unpleasant, but it will help our cause."

"What? You—the Mules resort to blackmail?"

"Absolutely not! We have to know exactly what sort of people we are dealing with, whose weaknesses could pose a threat to national security, or to good, responsible government. You did much the same thing with your files."

Cundieffe blanched. "I fail to see the connection, sir. I violated no one's privacy in collecting the information I did, nor in constructing the behavioral profiles."

"But you skirted federal law, which proscribes us from spending a penny of federal money to exercise prior surveillance. True, you did it on your own time and with your own money, but you violated the letter of the law to serve the ideal of justice. You felt that because your motives were pure, the collection of the data did not constitute an abuse. You have since fed the results of this unauthorized research into our fledgling National Counterterrorism Database, for which your nation will one day have cause to thank you, and you have voiced no qualms about breaking the law in so doing. It is precisely because of that sort of initiative that you are here today."

Cundieffe bowed his head. He couldn't believe he hadn't thought this through. Wyler leaned in closer still, so that his flushed face filled Cundieffe's field of vision. "There is something you must understand about us, Martin. We are not a secret government. We are not Illuminati. We are not a conspiracy. We do not rule by force or threat of force, or of humiliation, or even by our wits. We are one voice in the darkness, whispering into the ear of the sleeping world. We whisper counsel, we urge it to be wise and virtuous and to look to the good, and we seek to quietly silence those voices calculated to induce nightmares. We are a listening ear, a watching eye and a voice, but nothing more. The world sleeps on, and sometimes it stirs in fear or wrath, like any sleeping giant. It is only our goal to prevent it from harming itself in its sleep."

"It's not the end I question, sir. The means—"

"Make no mistake, Martin. Ethical wordplay has no place here. This is not about justice, or procedure. This is about what kind of world we'll wake up in tomorrow. You know this. It's in you already, or you wouldn't be here."

Wyler cut off his reply with a wave of his hand, pointing down into the war room. The twelfth committee member took "her" seat almost directly beneath their booth. The booming voice issued forth from the speakers again. "We will now, without further objection, review new developments in the Mission case." A hushed sizzle from the speakers, and Cundieffe could hear the subtle ambient noises of the war room being piped in. Wyler activated a screen built into their table and punched buttons too quickly for Cundieffe to read. A short text message in Spanish appeared, with time/date data and a serial number across the top. Wyler punched a button and a translation popped up.

PAPA,

VACATION GOING SMOOTHLY. CHECKED IN AT HOTEL YOU RECOMMENDED. YES, THE OLD MISSION STILL STANDS, BUT NEEDS FUMIGATING. MAMA'S LIST OF THINGS TO BUY IS SO VERY LONG, I WILL HAVE TO BUY MORE SUITCASES FOR RETURN TRIP.

GIFT ARRIVED IN GOOD REPAIR. DELIVERY MEN WILL ASSEMBLE IT AND DISPOSE OF THE OLD ONE.

GOING SKIING. SEND MORE MONEY.

YOUR SON

An artfully feminine voice took up the briefing. "This e-mail message was sent from the Gulf Breeze hotel in Corpus Christi, Texas, yesterday. The FBI field office was immediately mobilized, without any positive contact or leads as to the sender's whereabouts. The message was posted via a popular South American service provider, who complied in giving us the real address of the destination account, twelve hours ago."

Cundieffe tried to suppress a scowl, but Wyler caught it and asked, "May it please the committee, I would like to know how the message was intercepted and flagged."

The foreign secretary's head inclined in their direction. "A standard NSA sweep of all traffic entering or leaving the United States is mandated by National Security Council Intelligence Directive No.6 even in peacetime. Given the sensitive state of alert, G Group paid particularly close scrutiny to all traffic entering or leaving South and Central America. Semantic irregularities, vague flag words and other keys were entered, and a team of personnel and automated elements sorted the communications virtually in real time. Is that satisfactory?"

"Quite," Wyler said, still looking sidelong at Cundieffe. "Please go on."

"The message was viewed and deleted at an Internet café in downtown Bogota, but the name and address for the account were false. Within the hour, the investigators were advised of a structure fire in the mountains above Bogota by an air cavalry unit of the Colombian Army."

A map of Colombia: a blinking light near the Amazonian floor of the country, beside a river called Cahuinari. "There, they discovered the remains of a highly sophisticated lab facility, with incubators, Level 4 isolation airlocks and industrial production capability."

"I see very little to distinguish it from any of the thousands of narcotics processing plants throughout South America," said a nominally masculine voice.

"The military investigators doubted too, so they called in an American advisor who verified that the facility was a bioweapons lab." Pictures flashed on-screen: an exploded bunker gutting a mountainside, blackened girders and rebar ribbons stretching out like tentacles among wraiths of smoke. Soldiers in full NBC suits sifting through piles of melted machinery and mounds of ash. "There was no trace evidence isolated to tell us what they were making there, but the volume of the production facility suggests that the product was not in gallons or individual bombs, but in tonnage."

Stifling rebuttals before they got beyond a breath, the foreign secretary went on, "None of this meets the full criteria for a full alert conclusively, but the overwhelming evidence—"

"—Suggests that we are being had," another Mule said. "The sophistication of all previous Mission operations should give one pause when considering the ease of interception of the message. Not to mention the fire."

"It doesn't deviate from the pattern at all, Stuart," Wyler said. "Last time, they stole from the United States Navy and stored the napalm right under their noses. The military was served notice of their intentions, and came to harm only when they tried to interfere."

"I agree with Wyler," said a feminine Mule near the end of the table. "This is not a war of terror against the American people. But the last time was merely a shot across our bow. The next will be catastrophic. The foreign secretary is quite up-to-date on what happened yesterday in Colombia. What are we to suppose about today in these United States?"

Cundieffe turned to Wyler and whispered, "How can they be so sure that this has anything to do with the Mission?"

Wyler started to answer, but the booming intercom voice drowned him out. "Agent Cundieffe, the Mission has a long and well-documented resume of espionage and terrorist acts here and abroad. Your briefs on the Owens Valley incident were astute in their observations and daunting in their suppositions, but you could have benefited from a less flawed understanding of recent history."

"I was unaware that any such organization existed before July of last year..." Wyler waved a note under his nose. "CHAIRPERSON."

"Chairperson," he began again, "if, as you say, the Mission is an established terrorist organization, it would have benefited the FBI to have been notified. It might have made all the difference in the world last July."

"Such a morsel of knowledge would have only proved more dangerous, without an understanding of the larger forces in play. Conventional police work was sufficient to lead you to the names of the leaders of the particular cell responsible, but your intuition as to their objective and motivation was, while quite imaginative, totally specious. How much further would your imagination have taken you, if you were told, without recourse to your formidable powers of deduction, that the Mission is composed of many such cells, with many objectives?"

"At the height of the Cold War," began another Mule, "the FBI and the HUAC ferreted out the Rosenbergs, Klaus Fuchs and Alger Hiss, but never scratched more than the surface of the espionage network which had infiltrated all levels of government. The real perpetrators who were stealing our secrets operated independently of Soviet patronage. They constituted a fifth column within our ranks, but they could not be traced by the usual means of Soviet contact or ideology or unaccounted-for wealth."

Cundieffe looked hard at Wyler, who was watching the shadowed speaker with hawkish intensity. Did he know all along, when he was praising Cundieffe for his deductive abilities, where they would lead him? Or was this a revelation to him, as well?

"They believed that by passing on our most sensitive secrets, they were serving their country, and the greater cause of humanity, by working to create what they called a 'balance of terror' between the superpowers.

"Working both within and without the government, their work has been so opaque in its execution that most in the defense and political sectors discount them as a new incarnation of the 'gremlins' U.S. Army airmen claimed sabotaged their planes in World War II. Others have blamed them for all military failures from the leakage of the atomic bomb to the Russians in 1949 to the failure of all tests for a strategic missile defense shield which continue to this day.

"In their work to insure a parity of destructive capability, the Mission has on several occasions used sabotage and even assassination, but nothing of the scale observed in July of 1999. This act constituted their first demonstration of direct force and a willingness to take innocent human lives. We were taken by surprise, and could not conclusively identify the threat until it was too late."

"Then this did have something to do with RADIANT," Cundieffe said.

Rustle of papers and tapping of keys. "We are aware of the RADIANT project, but would advise against drawing any more than a symbolic connection between the two elements. RADIANT was an orbital directed energy weapon program, which resulted in a disastrous test and loss of the satellite in 1984. Sabotage was suspected, but the primary researcher on the project, indeed the scientist directly responsible for the entire project, died shortly thereafter under suspicious circumstances."

Cundieffe sat up ramrod-straight. On a few of the table-screens below, he could see an extreme close-up shot of his own face; thermographic overlays made the flush of blood in his cheeks look like lava flows. He restrained himself from looking around for the tiny cameras. "He joined the Mission?"

"He was murdered by Mission infiltrators involved in the project, who subsequently arranged their own staged deaths and went underground. We don't even know who is in the organization. We are reduced to combing the obituaries and the Pentagon's MIA files to try to deduce who might be a member."

"Respectfully submitted, then, what has the group learned about the Radiant Dawn organization?"

"Nothing that obtains here. They no longer represent a plausible primary target."

Cundieffe covered his mouth before a snort of disbelief could escape. "I find that rather hard to believe, given that nobody's explained why they were one in the first place."

Wyler seething, shiny rivets of sweat popping out of his high-domed forehead. "Chairperson, what I believe Agent Cundieffe was trying to communicate—"

"Wyler, does your charge fully understand where he is?"

Cundieffe, hearing the point being snatched back from them, pressed on. "Eyewitness accounts of the raid on the Mission's base at Baker described a light from the sky enveloping the area immediately after the Mission helicopter entered the area and deposited Sgt. Storch. Subsequently, all those irradiated died of cancer, except Sgt. Storch himself, who was diagnosed with cancer shortly before his assassination. But all of this must be familiar to the Committee. I apologize for my impertinence, and for taking up so much of the Committee's valuable time, but given the collateral evidence linking the Mission to RADIANT, I don't see how this body can discount the possibility that RADIANT is still up there, and that its true purpose is somehow tied up in the Radiant Dawn organization, in much more than a symbolic manner."

"You learned this in your interview with Sgt. Storch, I presume."

"I gathered that—"

"While studying at UCLA law school, you compiled a research paper on behavioral profiling of anti-government militants."

Uncertain where this was going, Cundieffe only said, "Yes, Chairperson. I—"

"In the course of your research, you arranged and conducted over nineteen interviews with prisoners in state and federal penitentiaries, all on your own initiative."

On screen: a younger, gawkier, hairier Cundieffe seated across from former Aryan Brotherhood leader Jeremy Yuricich, awaiting execution for four murders at San Quentin. Out of context, the gawky, ramrod-stiff law student seemed to shame the hulking white separatist killer into collapsing all at once, his face wrapped in his tattooed paws. Cundieffe had somehow persuaded Yuricich to meet with him for three afternoons, and tell him his life story. The photo might have been a still from the security camera in the visitors' room, because he couldn't remember any cameras clicking away when Yuricich started to cry.

Cundieffe sat stunned, only half able to hear what the Chairperson was saying, as a realization bubbled up out of the back of his brain. He was not an unexpected guest. This was an initiation and a demonstration, both.

"Yet you failed to extract any practical, intelligible information from Sgt. Storch."

"We're all familiar with the transcripts of Agent Cundieffe's interview," said a gravelly voice with a faint Oxford-bred accent. "It served only to corroborate earlier interrogation reports that the prisoner suffered from dementia. He was a discarded cut-out, with nothing meaningful to offer."

On screen: Cundieffe stumbling and falling as Storch rises from his chair in the interrogation cell. Looping: watch him fall, and Storch rise on puppet strings of invisible lightning.

"It's dangerous to lend too much credence to the ravings of such people," the Oxford voice added, unsubtle acid dripping into Cundieffe's ears.

Cundieffe licked his lips. His eyes burned and his glasses were starting to fog. "Given the environment in which he was held captive, I hardly expected to find him completely lucid, but he did claim that the Mission's objective is Radiant Dawn, and not the government at large. Even if this body is unwilling to concede the connection to RADIANT, I remain convinced that if the Mission is indeed operational and in the United States, then our best chance to find them and stop them from perpetrating mass murder again is to look from Radiant Dawn outward."

"For some time, we have been doing just that," said a somewhat masculine voice that might've come from a computer. Cundieffe recognized this voice, out of all of them. Brady Hoecker, the "consultant" who had sat in on the indoors portion of the interrogation. On the screen: a single-story stucco business park in a Southern California suburb. Sandwiched between Xtra-Sun Tanning Salon and Dr. Zakarian, DDS: RADIANT DAWN HOSPICE OUTREACH CLINIC. Cleverly placed, thought Cundieffe. They must pick up a lot of walk-in traffic from their neighbor. "In the last six months, Radiant Dawn has opened a network of outreach clinics in thirty-five major cities across the country. Each has a staff of no more than ten full-time employees and part-time volunteers, mostly counselors and nursing specialists. In the past four months, five of them have been bombed, and twelve Radiant Dawn employees have been killed."

On the screen: the same business park, packed with emergency vehicles and news vans. Black smoke arrows the gutted building, out of which coroners escort a pair of gurneys with boxes for charred or dismembered remains strapped to them. Hoecker continued: "Thermite and homemade napalm were planted in adjacent offices in the first two, in San Diego and Kansas City, but a car bomb was used for the third. A fourth was discovered in Phoenix, and killed only the outreach counselor who found it. The last one, in Pittsburgh, was particularly messy, and ended with a Mission agent burning down a Radiant Dawn counselor with a flamethrower in the street."

"My—my—why, Assistant Director, why haven't we been kept apprised of this?" Cundieffe stage-hissed. "It's our direct area of responsibility."

Wyler forwarded the question, but icily. There was none of his turf-conscious feistiness that he showed off at the Navy briefing last summer.

"Because the FBI isn't prepared for this kind of situation," Hoecker replied. "Your Hostage Rescue Teams are crack units, but they're too small and thinly spread as it is, and the level of secrecy demands plausible deniability. If we can't stop them from happening, we have to keep them from having happened, if you take my meaning, and dead FBI agents wouldn't serve."

Cundieffe shivered. More news blackouts. The media covered the tragedies as arsons, or even accidental fires, and not terrorist bombings, and carefully suppressed details, kept anyone from stringing them together. Each was an isolated incident, happening in a vacuum, making no sound, leaving no trace.

"We have placed all of the remaining outreach centers on rotating surveillance since the Pittsburgh incident. No reports of suspicious activity, no lights in the sky. There is no concentration of patients or staff anywhere in the country to present the kind of target they did last year. This is a new cell, most likely with a new objective."

"The FBI had nothing to do with this surveillance program, did it?" Cundieffe looked sidewise at Wyler, who shrugged minimally.

"I respectfully request," Hoecker said, "that we table this abortive line of discussion and return to the root issue, which is the Mission's probable objectives. There are eighteen defense research projects currently underway in the continental United States, and three more of great import in Alaska. I must add, however, that this information is not for all eyes."

The table-screens went black and the window became a mirror again. The speakers sizzled and died. Wyler stood up from the table. "There's no point in waiting."

"If you'd like me to go outside so you could sit in on the rest of it…"

"What makes you think *I'm* cleared to hear it? Come on, Martin, I'll buy you breakfast."

Wyler opened the door and Cundieffe followed him back out through the gallery to the elevator. Something in the crooked posture of his mentor's back warned not to speak here. In his thumping heart, he was grateful for the silence, because it gave him time to tuck his guts back in.

They disembarked from the elevator car to find the escort waiting for them. They followed him through the silent house, Cundieffe taking in greater detail in the pale, lead-colored morning light seeping in through the narrow windows. He was still not entirely sure that he wasn't dreaming.

The doors opened for them and they stepped out onto the cobbled drive. The Suburban was waiting for them, the driver standing beside the open rear door. Only when they were inside it and bumping through the gates did Wyler turn and look at Cundieffe.

"What did you see?" he asked.

"I—I don't know where to begin. Is there anything they don't know?"

"Only what they don't want to hear," he started, then, "The Mules virtually run the NSA, and its ECHELON project is our principal means of keeping abreast of current events. But not the only one."

"In every way, it was different from the meeting at the Federal Building. There was none of the animal infighting, but—I saw the same mistakes being made."

"What, that they didn't take you seriously enough? That kind of narcissism is dangerous, Martin, to yourself and your work. It is easy to assume that one has all the facts, and thus that one sees the truth. But half of your facts are shadows. There are compartments, and truths within truths. They are at the center, and their view of the mechanisms in play is superior to our own."

"I'd like to review the case files on those bombings, but we're supposed to pretend they never happened. What do I have to do to prove myself worthy of knowing what they know?"

"You'll be given what you need. Trust in them, and I have no doubt that you will become indispensable to them."

"Sir, I don't mean to be impertinent, but how can this addiction to secrecy serve a democratic society? My conclusions are being discounted because of factors I am not allowed to examine or understand. It's–forgive me for saying so, sir—but it's humiliating, and more than a little unsettling."

"And that, Martin, is why you were allowed to come in today. You have an extraordinary intellect, but you are not the only one. If you are to learn to use your talents as your instinct dictates that you must, then you must learn to subordinate yourself to a new order. You are beginning to see beyond the shadows, but you are only halfway out of the dark. Only by this slow progress out of the cave will you come into the sunlight of the truth, and not be blinded."

Cundieffe turned and looked out at the brittle rays of winter sunlight stabbing through the omnipresent cloud cover. Out on the sidewalk, a few joggers and older, ostentatiously foreign men passed in front of the dwindling black-green fortress of the Cave Institute.

I want to serve, he thought. *But first I have to see.*

~ 8 ~

Someone had been in her room, she thought as she awakened. The quickening aromas of hot chocolate and orange juice, poached eggs and Canadian bacon lured her out of sleep and softened her fight-or-flight reflexes. Snowy sunlight played silvery fingers over the spare features of her room. She sat up in bed and rubbed her eyes, stretched, looked around, and for a moment she could believe that her fondest wish had come true.

She was wearing her old flannel nightgown. The furniture and décor, even the loose personal effects, were all hers, from her apartment in Bishop. They must have taken pictures before they moved it all, because they hadn't misplaced anything, down to the shelving of her books and the arrangement of coats and hats on the rack beside the door. Everything but her phone.

She smelled flowers. Looking over her shoulder, she noticed the vase of bright zinnias, mums and poppies, then her eyes went to the card. *Our Prayers & Best Wishes For Your Recovery*, read the front in faded gold script. All of the ER staff from Bishop County Hospital had signed the inside. Thor, the amorous ambulance driver, had made an imprint on the edge with his dentures. Nurse Fisher, ever the den mother, had taken it upon herself to pen a little guilt-wracking message that Stella couldn't finish without crying.

She remembered then that He was there with her. Inside her. Making a mockery of her solitude.

You needed time for yourself.

"What a joke," she said aloud. "I need the rest of my life for myself. I need my head for myself."

Ask yourself, Stella: where would you be now, if not for me?

She closed her eyes, and the dark was cold and choked with dust, and she felt the concrete slabs crushing her, the tie-rods impaling her...

She screamed and her eyes snapped open. She gripped her comforter so hard it purred and tore between her whitened knuckles.

You were ready to surrender yourself to death. Surrender to life, Stella.

She went to the window and looked out. A field of fresh, unbroken powder stretched out to a pine forest on one side, and a plunging river gorge on the other. Beyond, Stella could see only crystalline wreaths of fog, but her inner ear told her she was on a mountaintop. She remembered nothing about coming here. He'd controlled her from the moment she stepped out of the trailer in Baker, let her see none of the journey. A pair of Radiant Dawn patients trundled by just beneath her window. They looked up and waved as they passed.

"How many slaves do you have here?" she asked. She had come to realize that He was neither God nor Guardian Angel, but she couldn't bring herself to call him by name. There was still an outside chance that she was insane, and the voice in her head a delusion brought on by her ordeal. But she knew different. She knew the patients outside were tuned in to the same voice. She could feel it all around her, as if the building itself were His body. Driving this place, where cancer became the key to an eternity of servitude.

I help all who come to me, in their turn.

"You only heal our bodies to steal them, diablo. Do you even have a body of your own?"

His voice in her head tingled with amusement He tried to share with her, goosing her endorphins. *You are too young to understand. You still can't imagine that when you have died, the world will go on. You don't really believe that the world existed before you were born, or that it was ever anything you could not understand. The world is older than you, Stella Orozco, and older and stranger by far than you or anyone else imagines.*

"Spare me your indoctrination bullshit. I'm alive, and I owe you my life. But I'm me. Don't try to take that away, or I'll make you sorry you saved me." She rediscovered the food, mouth watering and stomach groaning, was He doing that to her? Determined not to be shut up any longer than necessary, she wolfed down her food and drowned it as fast as she could.

I am not an invader, Stella. I am your guide. All of us who have undergone the transformation must eventually learn to accept what we have become. This is not easy. You have been told you are going to die, and to make your peace, when suddenly you are not only cured, but reborn—

"Into slavery," she cut in, swallowing a splash of hot chocolate too quickly and scalding her throat. She chased it down with some of the orange juice, fresh-squeezed and almost drugged with vitamins. "This is a fucking jail. Everyone has their own private *you* in their heads, spewing bullshit all day and night, and taking over the controls whenever they zig instead of zag."

You have a hard time accepting what you are. How would the rest of the world understand it? You have to be protected, and, yes isolated, during this fragile phase. You, of all people, must see how what we've done here could be misunderstood, and the terrible harm they can do.

"But you're in my goddamned head! You're in there, so you know how fucking crazy it makes me! How could you do that?"

Why are you all my children? You've engulfed your cancer, tamed it even as it has devoured and remade you. Now your body is a function of your mind, but in the wake of your transformation, you have been pushed dangerously close to madness. See what you might have become—

Blink. Stella's body wriggling worms, no arms legs head, a tumor undulating across the sheets. The sun burns her eyes and her body eats them up, she grows scales and a child's crude rendition of legs, and mouths, eating and vomiting and screaming—

With evolution sped up infinitely, human beings would speciate almost immediately. With every individual a species unto himself, the earth would become an abattoir, with competition on a scale never before seen. I am here to remind you of who you are, Stella, to keep you human. Or at least, as human as you want to be.

"I think—" she fought for breath, for words: "I think I'd be alright on my own..." Hating her weakness, she steeled herself. She would never blink again. "Who made *you* God? Who voted to have you in everyone's heads?"

I am not a god. I only let you believe that because you need it to be true.

"And what about God? You know there's nothing out there that sits in judgment?" She surprised herself with her ridiculous question, because there was no sarcasm in it. She regretted her sincere hope as soon as she voiced it, that there was no God, for surely she was as damned as He. But He only shrank away from her inside her mind, and a fog enveloped her, and it was very hard indeed to remember what she'd asked Him, at all.

I have stolen this fire from the Old Ones who believed themselves gods, and I have learned from their mistakes. I am the eye of the needle through which the world must pass to become Paradise. I only want to help you evolve, Stella. Let me help you.

"What makes me so special? Why do I get to evolve? You've got to know how much I fucking hate you."

Again, laughter and brain-candy. *Your cancer made you special. It was the seed of my gift to you, but that day is coming soon, when I will come into the hearts and minds of all the world's people, and make them one.*

"You're going to give the whole world cancer?"

We *are going to give the whole world cancer.*

"And if I don't want to?"

I will give the world what it wants. Life without suffering, infinite adaptability, a guide to direct them to the good for themselves and for their planet. I will share this gift with all the peoples of the world. If you try to stop me...

The brain-candy abruptly shut off and her inner ears flip-flopped, and she gasped and clutched the sheets, but still she felt as if she were falling.

Don't make me show you.

She didn't.

Later, He let her go outside.

The biting cold and ice crystals in the air stung her face and lungs, and she pulled up the hood of the parka she wore. The snow lay two feet deep on the ground, several inches of it fresh powder. The altitude made her giddy, light-headed.

"Where am I?" she asked.

Western Idaho, in the Seven Devils Mountain Range. We are much more isolated here, but much better protected, too.

"I don't see much to protect."

In the spring, this will be a farm. With water from the many streams and generators below-ground, we will be completely self-sufficient. We will thrive.

Her eyes took it all in, but she was surprised by what she felt in His voice. Emotions: pride, love for this place and the people in it. If He thought He was God, he played the role well. God must've felt this way when He turned back the waters of the Flood, and let mankind begin again.

As she trudged away from the building, she looked around it and saw only a parking lot and a few outbuildings with snowmobiles, a plow-truck and a helicopter under tarps on a concrete pad. A small village of trailers, already half-buried in snow, flanked the tower on two sides, which was a dead ringer for the one she'd visited at the hospice village in the Owens Valley.

"Where are the houses?"

We learn from our mistakes. This colony will live in tunnels beneath the ground until those who would destroy us are neutralized. But we are growing so fast—thus, the trailers.

She shivered. He took note of this, and added, *Not all of us will live below. You may stay above, until your fears are smoothed away.*

She stopped short of giving the thought voice, but the sensation washed over her. She hadn't been thinking of the fear of being underground again, but of *those who would destroy us*, the Mission: Delores Mrachek, who'd died trying to stop her from becoming what she was today, and of the man who died in the ground trying to save her. If he could mistake her thoughts, then there was some part of her he could not reach. Swiftly, she forced herself to think of something else.

"So that's where everybody is? Digging tunnels?"

There are many kinds of work yet to be done to make this a home. We are lucky to have an assortment of various skilled tradespeople among us, but I have had to teach most of the rest to perform the necessary work. I will show you.

He guided her back into the building, silent cues she might have mistaken for her own impulses if she didn't know better. Going down the main corridor, past a trauma center and a solarium with dozens of couches, she turned and went down a broad, gently sloping ramp that switchbacked on itself twice before spilling out in a cavernous space. The walls and ceiling were rough-hewn, like the surfaces of a mine, but the colonists had nearly finished covering it up; prefab living modules were assembled on a steel lattice two stories high and extending back into the shadows. Each module was about the size of her quarters upstairs, but seen from the outside, they looked like deluxe animal cages: Tupperware slave quarters.

"I never really thought about the afterlife too much, but I'm pretty sure it never crossed my mind that we'd all be slaves living in goddamned Habitrails."

Ah, Stella, if only you understood, that it is your insolence that makes you so valuable to us. None of you are slaves, any more than I am your master. These quarters are only temporary. The awakened body must be sheltered from those who would destroy it.

"You had no problem taking over my body, when you needed to."

Things had to be done to insure your survival, Stella. There was no other way. You didn't know how to heal yourself yet, and you were so very damaged.

She flinched in anticipation of another reminder, but nothing happened. She hated herself for feeling gratitude along with relief.

"Why don't you just take us over? Then you'd have all the slaves you want, and none of the hassle."

I couldn't if I wanted to. It is you *that keeps your body alive. At this stage, your body could not withstand it for long...*

"But we're still your slaves. You'll take us if we try to leave."

When the threat to your kind is gone, all of you will be free to leave, to build new lives. I only hoped to keep a few behind, those with the training and nature to help receive those who come for irradiation. This place will come to be known as a holy place, like Lourdes, or the headwaters of the Ganges. This will be the place where humanity will begin to be reborn.

"Until it gets bombed again. Why don't you get help? If this is something the whole world is going to want, why try to hide where only the Mission can find you?"

We had received assurances from the government before, but I know now that they care more for our success, than our survival. They have their own reasons for allowing us to progress, but I believe they support the Mission, as well. Neither could survive without government sanction, at some level.

"So it'll keep happening. And no one will help us."

We need no one. The Mission is weak. They will not resist striking at us here with all their remaining strength, and soon. When they do, we will absorb their blow, and they will be no more.

"Where are all the people?" she asked. She had seen only the pair beneath her window.

They are at breakfast in the common hall. Come.

She followed His subtle nervous cues deeper into the cave, walking by the modules, seeing each decorated with a few pitiful personal effects, but still looking like plastic cages. Most of them held toys, posters of singers and cartoon characters. Many of the rest contained nothing except a few scraps of clothing. Orphans, the poor, foreigners, immigrants like herself. He would not discriminate by wealth or check their insurance. All they had to have was the seed of cancer and a willingness to give up everything.

She passed the last module and turned into a short, wide tunnel lit by a peculiar glowing crust on the ceiling. It occurred to her that she had seen no machines down here, no electricity, though He had mentioned underground generators. She wondered if the bioluminescent stuff was Him, as well.

She came out of the tunnel and into a hall nearly as large as the living space. Tables ran in rows perpendicular to the entrance, and they were all filled. Men, women and children of all races and ages ate together amid a drone of good-natured chatter. All wore the same black tracksuits and parkas that she had, but despite all this, there was no sense that this was a prison, or a hospital. Had she expected them all to have His face? Had she expected a monstrous commune, chewing in unison, muttering His platitudes, like brainwashed cultists?

"You want me to believe you're doing this for us," she said. "Why?"

If you had lived as long as I have, you would understand.

"I'm not so stupid. Tell me."

I have seen races rise and fall. They believed they had achieved perfection, and they tried to stop change, to control it with their tools. And they were swept away by their own creations, only to pave the way for a new race to begin the long slow climb, and inevitable fall. Always, the pattern of self-fulfilling prophecy has been the same. On this world and a million others. If you were as old as I, if you saw the same mistakes being made again and again, the waste, the suffering perpetuated down through eternity, what would you do? Would you wait for a god to put it right? How long would you wait before you saw that no one was coming to fix it, that no one but you could do it?

Stella looked out at the shining, smiling faces, at the children delivered from death. There had to be a worm in the apple He offered.

"But you used machines to change us. Your death-ray satellite is good, but everyone else's machines are evil?"

RADIANT is only a crutch, a catalyst, to spread the message over borders and quarantine zones. Even so, the technology is very, very old, and deceptively simple. The real machine is us. When there are enough of us, we will be all we need to change the world. When we are of one mind, there will be nothing beyond our grasp. Help me do this, Stella.

She could find no words that she could not see him turning back on her. After all, was it not her desperation to come to Radiant Dawn that had set her on the path to where she now stood?

She walked over to the nearest table and, looking defiantly around, took a seat. The others at the table favored her with smiles and greetings. They knew her name, and her job. She looked them over, looked deep into each pair of eyes, looked for Him. She saw only people who were stunned and overjoyed to find themselves alive.

An older Hispanic man offered her a cup of juice. She saw no coffee, then realized that drugs of any kind would be unnecessary, here. "Stella Orozco," he nodded to her and smiled. "I'm Dr. Javier Echeverria. We will be working together, I think." She stared into his hazel eyes for a long time, thinking, *I see you.* She took the juice and sipped from the cup, still watching everyone around her.

They were a motley assortment, heavier on children and the old, but she noticed that the older people looked on the whole stronger and healthier than she, wearing their gray hair as a badge of status. The children, by contrast, looked wise for their years, and were integrated into the general population without supervisors, without anyone around them who could be their parents. They participated in the conversations around them as full partners in the colony. They talked about work, mostly, but also about their lives, their cancers, always fondly, and always in the past tense. As if they thought they were in Heaven.

Dr. Echeverria was touching her shoulder. "I only asked you if you had worked in the fields in Salinas, when you were a girl."

"Is this your idea of small talk?" she demanded, shouting at the table at large. "You're in all of us, aren't you? Looking at yourself through all these eyes, talking to yourself in all these voices? And you talk about stupid bullshit like where I—"

He patted her hand and sat back. The whole table was watching her now. She saw pity in their eyes, and started to hate them. No. Not pity. Empathy. They were all like this, when they first arrived. They had adapted. She would, too. "I meant no insult, Señorita Orozco. I myself worked the fruit crops in Salinas as a boy. That was where I was exposed to the pesticides that gave me my cancer. Like yours, of the liver. I was only going to say that I might have seen you there."

She looked away from him, biting back the impulse to call him a liar. She had nothing else to say.

"I was very angry too, Señorita Orozco, when I learned of my sickness. My parents had saved up enough to get out of the fields and applied for citizenship. They sent me to medical school, but much to their chagrin, I returned to the fields as a public health worker. That was when I first became sick."

"My mother died in the fields, Doctor. Nobody *sent* me to medical school. We are not so alike as you suppose."

"I am sorry, Señorita Orozco. I only meant to say that you are not so alone here, as you might believe. All of us were bitter, because we were alone in our suffering. But your pain is commonplace here, as is your race, your poverty, your misfortune. You will have to find some other reason to be so angry all the time."

She sat there cold and quiet for quite a while before her face cracked open. What came out of her might have been mistaken for a sob in any other company but this one. With tears brimming in her eyes, she laughed. "I—I'm so sorry...I'm just so fucked up inside..." The laughter twisted into true sobbing then, and she shook, but did not recoil, from the many hands that touched her then.

"We understand you, Stella Orozco," Dr. Echeverria said. They enfolded her in their empathy, warmth penetrating her, opening her up to their love. She knew that she belonged.

The crowd began to form into rows, facing her and thirty or forty others who came up to stand beside her. She looked at them and felt her face reflecting their giddy children's glee. They were special in some way the others did not understand any better than she. It was not merely some initiation ceremony. They had been chosen.

Ten men and women stood in single-file before her. As the first approached her, a stoop-shouldered old black man who smiled wide at her with new-grown teeth, she looked to left and right, even as her own feet carried her towards him.

The young Asian woman on her left embraced the first of her line, a middle-aged white man who looked like a shelled turtle. Eyes wide open, they locked lips and their jaws worked for a moment in a rigorous but clinically chaste kiss. On her right, two boys, no older than twelve or thirteen, held each other and swapped spit like sleepwalking junior prom sweethearts.

The old man wrapped his arms around her and his mouth became the Grand Canyon. He said to her what the voice in her head had been saying all along. *This is how we share, and how we survive. By communally pooling our genetic diversity in our brightest lights, we insure that none who have joined us will ever die.*

"We live in you," whispered the old man with baby teeth.

"And I live in you," she replied, and kissed him.

~ 9 ~

There are those who say that dying is like passing through a tunnel into a bright white light. Ancestors and guiding spirits assemble to escort the departed soul to its greater reward. Worldly concerns fall away as the eternal peace and serenity of the afterlife enfolds them like a mantle and dispels all uncertainty, all fear, all darkness.

Zane Ezekiel Storch was not one of those people.

For just about forever, Storch did indeed float in an infinite corridor of darkness, and if he stared hard enough, he could see a light at the end, but he was pretty sure that wasn't St. Peter waiting in it. Sometimes it was close enough to see through, and there were usually men there, attaching things to him and asking him questions, inflicting what they hoped was pain and getting no answers. When they left him alone, he could almost reach into the light to the mere earthly darkness on the other side, but whenever they tried to reach him, the light fell away, their questions and their torture only filtering into the tunnel as background noise beneath the grinding voice of God.

This, alone, was why Storch believed he was dead. God was in here with him, and He never shut up. Most of the time he could not remember his own name, let alone the litany of crimes that could have brought him to this limbo, but he knew one thing. God was with him always, right under his skin, inside his skull. God was very concerned with his personal salvation. God had lessons to teach, and there was nothing to do but listen.

In your old life, your transfusion from Lt. Dyson kindled the first stirring of the fire of change in your cells. Directed to adapt to hostile environments, yet your body lacked the ability to do so. What you perceived as sickness was really the highest blessing, an undetectable form of fluid cancer that lay dormant in you until the

Radiant Dawn touched you. Now your transformation is underway, you have swallowed entropy, but without guidance, it may devour you, yet. All that keeps you from tumbling back into the evolutionary abyss, into formlessness—is me.

God repeated Himself quite a lot. It was vital that Storch understand, and for the moment, they had nothing but time. There were visions, culled from the lost library of his cells:

—watching from cover behind a palisade of jagged rocks as the last of the Others come roaring out of their caves and into the trap of fire he and his clan had built. And they aren't men like his clan, but Others, black scaled skin and sinuous, upright-rambling snake-bodies, and terribly wise, golden eyes still blazing with the pride of an empire lost to these thieving, warm-blooded egg-stealers. But the world has moved on, life is change, and their day is done. Watching the males run burning into extinction, and then joining in as the females and, finally, the squirming hatchlings, are dragged out of their nest and slaughtered with rocks and sticks, the new tools that will change in the hands of their descendants into knives, and swords, and guns and nuclear warheads…

This is where you lost yourselves, God said. *Here is where you learned to make, and ceased to be. Once, you had the potential to be so much more.*

—at play in towering forests of broad-leafed trees, gorging himself on a dazzling array of fruits with his clan-mates in the Eden of his father's Bible. No fear of predators or hardship from the elements here, in this nurturing arcadian womb. Yet they are all sick with fever, seeing and fearing things that do not exist, seeing events that have not happened yet and never will, and seeing also things that happened before, that happen again and again in their heads. The comfortable cradle of the Now has been upset and cast them out, and memories and dreams echo through the once-blissful silence of instinct. The sickness splits them apart, each seeing their clan-mates as Others, where once they were as fingers on a hand, and retreating into the garbled abyss of their own heads. They have always been one body, but now they are many, and they are trying to kill each other. He surprises another of his kind and tears its throat out with his teeth. One less to compete with for food and mates, the fever tells him.

Through the trees, he sees the wall of cold black stone that bounds their habitat on all sides, but in its cyclopean face today, there is an open door. Hooting to the others, he gathers a few pieces of fruit, and approaches it.

In Paradise, the fire of selection shaped you, planting the seed of mind in your fragile brain, the forbidden fruit that hurtled your fragile race to its present, fleeting moment of grace. But once, you were all things, changing and learning to be more. The secrets the Old Ones could have taught you, lost forever...

—watching from cover behind a wall of dried mud as the cold-blooded saurian mother lies down for the last time, her monstrous bulk heaving a final rattle and settling to become one with the dust; watching as his rodent nest-mates streak, quicksilver limbs and needle teeth, over her mountainous carrion to get at her pitiful clutch of eggs, to carry them away in tiny, clever claws...

See how you have risen. You are a particle on a wind of change, blindly reaching for new forms, for survival. Once, the power to change was yours, and the world trembled in fear of your will, but that power was stolen from you...

—treading tides of water molecules in a pool on the shores of the first land to rise out of the seas, a flailing, amorphous predator, the first aerobic animal. Peering through the skin of the stagnant pool at something as vast as the moon, and as remote. Something vast and terrible and wise, watching him.

This is what I would give you. Mastery over yourself, the power to be, and to live, in all things again...

—watching as his body rises, a proud and terrible thing, on fire with the changes the world wrought on it from one moment to the next; watching as he towers above the pitiful Old Ones who made him to be their tool, their slave, and fell into weakness and decadent decay as he grew stronger, and learned to master himself; watching as those Old Ones are ground to pulp beneath his mighty, magnificent form, and driven from all the sunlit places of the earth.

The visions were so potent that they swept away the tissue of memories that claimed Storch as their own, and he became the Changes, the end product of the long history of lessons that had guided his genetic message to this place and time, and now promised an end to death, and time itself.

In your blood is the force to become all things, and remake the world as it was meant to be. Let me lead you into the light...

Through the grinding voice of God had come another voice from out of the light, reedy and quivery and so jumbled up that it seemed to come all at once, but its words undercut the voice of God. They were an urgent message for the man he used to be, chattering away about something that must have been terribly important to him. Some backwards animal part of him strove to make the voice louder, strove to move his body, though God commanded him to be still. He struggled, but God must have let him go.

The light at the end surged up around him and it was a trick, this wasn't heaven or hell. He was back in the shitty old world again, and they were hurting him with electricity, and the little balding man who smelled like ants when you crush them in your hand, what was that called that made that smell, formic acid, yes, he only stared at Storch like he didn't have any answers, he didn't even know what fucking questions to ask.

His body lay before him like the controls of a strange vehicle he had only driven in dreams. It took all the concentration he could muster to put one foot in front of the other. The jerky movement and the unaccustomed view from his own eyes almost made him swoon with vertigo: the sounds of the soldiers, the hypnotic pulse of light and shadows, the bracing sting of the winter morning, noxious with car exhaust and city filth, but fresher by far than anything he'd breathed in ages.

They brought him into the weak morning sun so that he could feed, drinking in the light and using the new rhodopsin-pregnant cells in his skin to feed on the light. He could dimly remember answering questions from the little not-quite-a-man then, though God kept his mind cloudy and his tongue heavy, and, ultimately, pushed him back into the tunnel.

I thought you understood, God said. *There can be no words with your ancient enemies. They are come again in forms outwardly like yours, but they possess tools, which have made them weak, while I have made you strong. They would make you weak again, Zane. They would douse the fire of change that I have ignited in you, and make you a slave again—*

And then the voice of God was cut off, and there was PAIN, and he was falling away from the light, away from the noise and the hurt for good and all. He could feel something *not him* suddenly and totally entering his body, killing it cell by cell, burning even the libraries inside them, all the hard-won wisdom of a billion lives. He reached out for the voice that had helped him make sense of it all, his awful guide and God, but the voice was gone, silenced in a single gargling blast of infinite red noise that echoed still in his head. His head…

The tunnel was longer and darker than ever before, but there was silence, and that, at least, was a kind of heaven.

Now the light came again, and it grew before him so fast that he knew this time it was the final light, the tunnel into eternity that people described. The voice of God was conspicuously absent, as were the spirits of his ancestors, and the angels, but he knew with some certainty that it was the end. The light was not white and soothing like before, but hot and red and orange, and it roared with sentient hunger and the promise of eternal suffering, and it was calling him, and it would have him.

Figures, Storch thought.

It was almost an abstract feeling, like reading a poem about pain, when the flames licked at his feet. And he wondered at that, at that feeling that he still *had* feet. He was having phantom pains, his immortal soul thinking it still had a body, out of habit. You'd think it would have gotten used to it, by now. And even as he pondered this, he kicked out at the flames, and, finding no purchase, arched his phantom back and clawed out with his phantom hands, and his phantom mouth tore open like a long-healed scar and drew breath into phantom lungs.

He found himself lying on his back inside a very real plastic bag. He could see nothing but a red dimness, but he could still feel the fire at his feet, and he could hear screams now, louder than ever. He sat up and tore the bag apart and found that he was perched on the edge of eternal flames, after all.

Storch sat on a gurney, naked in a red body bag, in a small, bright white room. The gurney was parked before the mouth of a great incinerator, and two men in white bio-isolation suits had been sliding his lifeless body into it, up until he ruined it. They only stood there now, dumbstruck and screaming.

No, only one of them was screaming, backing towards the wall and fumbling for the intercom built into it. The other one got hold of himself and tore open a sealed pouch on the outside of his vinyl suit. He pulled a sort of toy pistol out of it. It looked like something he might have made in a pottery class to break out of a prison, and anyway, Storch just didn't feel the same aversion to having guns pointed at him, that he used to. He wasn't sure if they could hurt him, but he was just a few light years past giving a shit, one way or the other. More disturbing by far was the roaring silence between his ears, and the feeling that he was all alone in his own head, once again.

The armed man pointed and shot, and his partner staggered back into the wall. Storch could see only the tiniest hole in his faceplate, but the man's face disappeared behind a sheet of blood as he slumped to the floor.

The man pointed the gun at Storch now, but he didn't seem to place any more stock in it than Storch did.

"You're supposed to be so fucking *dead*," the man said. His voice was weak, and his whole suit billowed and flapped with his panic-stricken breathing. The man had olive skin, a shapeless nose, and big brown halogen headlights for eyes.

Storch gagged. His throat was gummed shut with resinous phlegm, and when he tried to swallow, he tasted rancid blood. "What do you know," he gurgled, "about being dead?" He raised himself up on his knees, and slowly, laboriously, climbed down off the gurney. He clung to the edge with blue-black monkey's paws that had to be his hands, because they did more or less what he told them to. He dangled his jittering legs over the side, fishing for floor.

"You're dead!" The man kept insisting. "You were shot full of NGS, sixteen times the maximum tested dosage! You *melted*!" He raised the gun again and made gestures like he wanted Storch to get back up on the gurney and slide himself into the fire.

Melted?

The body bag Storch had just climbed out of was covered in biohazard symbols and barcode stickers. Sloshing around in its interior, a gray-blue slush that reeked like an open grave. This was another vision, another nightmare. Another test. "I…got better," he said. He looked down, saw the floor was a lot further away than he'd expected, and dropped hard. Both knees buckled under him and he sat down hard on his tailbone.

Funny…no depth perception. He waved his hand in front of his face. Only one of his eyes worked. He touched his face. There wasn't nearly as much of it as there should be. Ditto for his skull: a rift big enough to make a fist in ran from his left eye socket to the back of his head. There were more holes in his chest, but these had already closed over.

Now that he thought about it, his head did hurt like a bastard, and as he prodded it, it seemed to get worse. He felt like his mind was rising, coming untethered from his neck, and he watched himself lie prone on the floor from a corner of the room, watched the man cover him with the ceramic pistol. The floor was cold concrete sheathed in plastic and covered with those ribbed no-slip strips that they put in showers and on stairs.

He wrapped his hands around his head and closed his eye and rolled over on his side. God would come back and sort this shit out. Even if he wasn't really God, he was welcome to this situation.

"Oh, Jesus!" the man shouted, and shot at him. The needle-thin bullet went wide of Storch's head and exploded an inch deep in the floor. A bubble burst in the plastic cover, and chips of concrete pricked Storch's neck.

"STOP THAT!" Storch bellowed. His head was growing back together. Drawn by some tidal gravity of souls, he came back down and went inside the putrid waves of his own flesh, closing over him like quicksand, watched his body fixing itself with a sick familiarity. This, at least, was something he'd seen before.

The boy in the truck whose head he'd split open when they tried to kidnap him in San Jose. Now it was happening to him. The swelling tumor like the probing tongue of a secret parasite, glowing robust newborn-baby pink in the black cavity. Green poison bubbling out of the wound as the neoplasmic bubble became bone and new brain underneath, and skin over it all. The whole thing rebuilding itself to factory specs, like an anthill. And *pop*, just like that, he could see in stereo again.

The world through his new eye wasn't any more attractive than through the old, but as it dawned on him that he was still alive and alone, it also slowly crept up on him that he was no longer human. His flesh knew what he should be, and how to fix itself, but the *idea* of Zane Ezekiel Storch was like the lyrics to a strange song that could slip away the moment he stopped reciting them. And he would become whatever kind of monster the world made of him, because they tried to kill him, but they missed him and shot God instead.

Whatever else he was, he was finally free. "Going home," he groaned, and shoved at the floor. He stood and kept moving so he wouldn't fall down again, towards a heavy steel Star Trek-style door that looked like it slid into the wall when you touched the button on the wall beside it. He was going home.

"What the fuck do you think you're doing?" the man shouted.

"Going home," Storch said again. He touched the button. Nothing happened. It wasn't a button, it was a lens. Shit. It was so hard to think, his fucking head hurt so goddamned much, he wanted to tear it off and try growing a new one, and that asshole with the gun...

"You're not going anywhere. Maybe you can't be killed, but I can blow you into enough pieces, even you won't get up."

"What?" His arms were spindly corded sticks, but he felt sure he could rip the man's spine out and flog him with it before he got off a shot. The man seemed to know what he was letting himself in for, but he looked like he wanted to try to talk his way out of this, before he made good on his threat. Lucky for him...

"Do you know where you are? No, of course you don't. You've been dead. You can't just walk out of here."

"Where am I?" His hands wanted to get wet in this moron so badly, he had to back away, but the idiot, thinking he had the upper hand, only came closer. Are you doing that, God? he thought.

"You are on the fourth subbasement level of the Special Projects Bioresearch Complex underneath Ft. Detrick, the Army's principal research facility for biological weapons. Above our heads are about a thousand USAMRIID scientists, and twice that many fighting soldiers of the 2nd Chemical Corps. You can't throw a rock in here without knocking over something that could kill every man, woman and child in America.

Ebola, Marburg, Q, botulinum toxin, anthrax, bubonic plague, dengue, cholera, encephalitis, brucellosis, typhoid, the whole fucking hit parade is on tap in freezers upstairs. This base, and every other military base in the country, is on a state of high alert because of us, which means doubled guards, and beefed-up, full combat units."

"Who? Because of me?"

"No. The Mission." The man tapped his own chest with the gun, and pointed it right back at him.

"You tried to burn me," he said, looking at the dead man against the far wall.

"We thought you were—you *were* fucking dead. They brought you here to harvest genetic material from you. That's why you were shot full of NGS, there wasn't even supposed to be a cell left intact...and then, just to be sure, I was sent to reroute your body here." He tried to wipe his face against the helmet liner, then put the gun away. "Aw, fuck it. If you won't die, you won't die."

"How are *you* getting out?"

"I *was* just going to burn you and *walk* out of here."

"What about him?"

"Just a fucking corporal. Didn't even know who you were." The Mission agent walked around the gurney, sweeping the empty body bag into the incinerator, and bent to lift up the dead corporal by his arms. "Help me get him up on the gurney."

"What for?"

"What the hell do you think, what for? You're gonna put on his suit."

Storch limped over to the body and took hold of the legs. There was a sick second where he looked at the body and a new kind of fire swept through him, like the agonizing fatigue of lactic acid buildup in muscles, like—hunger. His body was so weak it could barely hold onto his soul, and fixing itself apparently didn't come cheap. He had to eat something. He thought of Spike Team Texas feeding. He thought about the fire. The Mission agent started unsealing the suit's maze of Velcro seals and zippers. Storch noted the name and rank on his suit: Lt. Dennison. The dead man on the gurney was Corporal Wynorski. "Dennison," he breathed. "They cured me."

"What?"

"He's gone...God...Keogh, the...the voice in my head. Shit, I thought he was..." Dennison's eyes registered no understanding whatsoever. "When they shot me..."

"*We* shot you, asshole. You went over, and got zapped. We were told you had to be iced before they got you here, or they were going to strip

your ass down for parts. They didn't tell us what to do if you were still..."
He'd gotten Wynorski's suit open and laid it out. Now, he tugged the
helmet off the dead man's head, and rolled the body on its side to drag the
suit out from under it.

Corporal Wynorski was a young redheaded man with freckles
splattered all over his face. His right eye was burst open, and the whole
right side of the head bulged unnaturally. Excellent shooting, he thought,
seeing the Mission agent with new respect. *He must've been the one who
plugged me.* The hole in the face-plate was small enough it could be
plugged with a thumbtack, but the interior was slick with blood. Dennison
dropped the suit on the floor at Storch's feet. "Just put the goddamned
thing on."

"I don't want to. I just want to go home."

"Then walk out of here, asshole. It'd probably be easier to get out by
myself, if they were all shooting at you, anyway."

"Dennison," he growled, "you don't understand." His hands were
starting to get out of control again, roaming the air in front of him like
very angry dogs.

"That's not my damned name, but I do outrank your sorry noncom
zombie ass, so do it."

Storch's joints still lacked a lot of their old flexibility, so it took a long
time for him to get into the suit, even with not-Dennison fussing over the
Byzantine arrangement of the zippers. The suit was almost as heavy as the
armored one he'd worn at the Radiant Dawn raid, with two air tanks in the
back and a hose for plugging into the canned air tubes running through the
ceilings in the labs. Wynorski's Army boots were too tight for his feet, so
he left them and slipped his bare feet into the suit. The Corporal's inner
jumpsuit could have been a few inches longer, as well. Moving with
exaggerated slowness, feeling his muscles chafe at each other like bundles
of jute rope, he zipped into it and hauled the suit up over his shoulders as
not-Dennison did up all the seals. He did the helmet last. Not-Dennison
wiped out the worst of the mess on one of Wynorski's socks, tossed it on
the gurney with the boots, and pushed the Corporal's body feet-first into
the maw of the incinerator.

Storch pulled the helmet down over his head and let not-Dennison
clamp down the seals. Staring straight ahead, his eye was a few inches
above the circular hole, which had been made so clean and fast it left no
spiderweb cracks in the Plexiglas. He began, almost immediately, to
sweat. Copious ribbons of perspiration beaded on his forehead and
streamed down into his eyes. His hand came up reflexively to wipe it
away, thumped against the helmet. He could almost taste himself in here,

the curdled reek of rotten, reborn Storch a suffocating miasma that, in his old life—

What you perceived as sickness was really the highest blessing...

—would have put him in a coma. Beneath it, he could smell the distinct funk of the suit's previous occupant, a soup of sweat and menthol cigarettes, starchy cafeteria food and rhinovirus. If he didn't shut it out, he feared it would carry him away, flood the tenuous ramparts he'd built around his own identity, and make him an animal with no name. He shivered as he fought for self-control. Not-Dennison seemed not to notice as he went back to the door and waved the back of his hand in front of it. Storch looked at his own sleeve and saw a bar-coded ID card in a clear plastic slipcover sewn into the vinyl, just above the glove. He looked around the inside of the helmet, scenting something new. His fight-or-flight instincts kicked into high gear; someone was in here with him. He looked up just as it dripped in his eye, and the world went red.

Keogh had told Storch that his cells held libraries of data, of all the genetic ancestors of Storch going back to the first day of Creation. Now, he discovered that he was not unique in this respect. Wynorski's blood had tales to tell, too, and they came rushing at him all at once. With a sense that was not sight or sound or smell, but a common root of them all, he fell down through the ancestry of the dead corporal, reeling as the strange flesh-memories converged with his own in the geological yesterday of primeval Europe, then down the wormhole of their shared ancestry, down into that unspeakable origin where he was—

all things

—a raging, amoebic god. Unmarked graves and devouring beasts vomited him out, wombs yawned and swallowed him, and in between, the stylus of the world scripted his form and scratched it out, again and again. It might have been bearable, if not for the absence of the voice of God in his ear to make sense of it all, but there was no voice but his own, crying out at a billion lessons learned too late, at a million forms of flesh forgotten, yet struggling still to live again in the mind of a man who could not remember his own name.

Someone was shaking him. In a dream paler than all the others, he was a man in a plastic shell, and another man was trying to stir him to act. He lashed out, clawing at the dream and trying to climb onto it as a man in a flood grabs at a floating scrap of debris, but the man thought it was an attack, and leapt out of his reach. He fought with his whole body to stay in this dream where he had a name and somewhere to go, where he was not yet dead again. There was a gun in his face, the man was thinking of shooting him. He couldn't be killed like that, he knew, but he could be incapacitated long enough for the man to put him in the fire.

Quicker than the man could react, quicker even than he could follow with his eye, Storch's hand swept the gun away and took it from the man with a simple twist of his wrist that stopped scant millimeters away from breaking it.

"Let's go," Storch said, but the man wasn't moving. He just stood there with his eyes glued on Storch's, and his mouth hanging open. "What?"

"Look," the Mission agent said, "at yourself."

Storch looked around the room, saw only the stainless steel surface of the gurney for a mirror, and went to it. It was like looking through a doorway into hell. The man had shoved Wynorski's redheaded, freckled body into the fire, yet there he was looking up at Storch from the polished steel bed.

Storch wore the dead corporal's face. His hair coiling like snakes and bronzing itself, his pigment gathering into pools and oozing out of his pores in brown splatters, his eyes changing to golden-green, looking directly through the pinhole in the mask that now lined up with his eye. He looked again at the ID card on his sleeve. The dead man again. *Him.*

"Jesus, Jesus, Jesus, what the fuck are you?" the Mission Agent hissed.

In a voice a full octave higher than his own, Storch groaned, "Get me out of here."

They left the incinerator chamber pushing the gurney, Storch in front, not-Dennison bringing up the rear. Not-Dennison didn't ask for his gun back.

The corridor was like any hospital basement; white tiled walls festooned with steel pipes and plastic tubing, many heavy steel doors with card readers or the kind of center-crank that hatches on subs had. The air was recycled, scoured and scrubbed of all particles, a dead kiss streaming into his eye from the hole.

Not-Dennison parked the gurney against the wall and took the lead, shuffling all the way down the long straight corridor to an elevator at the end. He said nothing, gave Storch no reason to suspect a trap, but Storch could smell fear in the glut of stale chemicals in the waste air venting out of his suit. The Mission agent was scared shitless of him, but he was equally terrified of the walk out of here.

Storch knew that ninety percent of going where you didn't belong on an Army base lay in looking like you knew what you were doing. He'd never been inside a bioweapons research facility, but not-Dennison had everything doped out, and should have been able to walk out, and now he was Corporal Wynorski, no one was looking for Storch, because he was dead, he was brought here in a bag…. Not that anyone would be looking for him, because he was dead, he was brought here in a bag.

You are Zane Ezekiel Storch, Sergeant, ODA 591, Fifth Special Forces, retired, you live in a trailer in Death Valley, your father is George Gorman Storch, Master Sgt., retired, you like—

The elevator was closing. Not-Dennison looking at him, doing nothing. A guard in a full suit like theirs stood beside the control panel with one arm across his chest, gripping the strap of the unwieldy M16A2 rifle on his back. Storch caught the door, dodged in and herded not-Dennison between himself and the guard. He kept his head twisted away as he presented his sleeve-card for scanning. The guard ran a red penlight over it.

The doors shut. The elevator car rose so smoothly it might be riding on air. Not-Dennison watched the guard.

"You said you were both going topside, sir?" the guard asked. SGT. KORPELA, Storch read on the breast of his isolation suit. He sounded way too impressed with himself. It had probably never occurred to him that riding an elevator in a germ warfare lab was a shit detail.

"Yeah, we just took out the trash," not-Dennison said. "I'm off-duty starting five minutes ago."

"Corporal Wynorski, you're supposed to be on 2, Lab 182a, sanitation detail. Ten minutes ago." Sgt. Korpela pointed at Storch, reading the wall display readout from his card. In a confined space like the elevator, Storch thought, the twenty-inch barrel and fixed stock on the M16A2 were all but useless.

"Yessir," Storch piped. He stopped, the weird, reedy sound still buzzing in his ears. Strange that he could consume a man's genetic memory, steal his likeness and his voice, but no idea how to use them. It shouldn't take much to get this guy off his back, he was only needling Corporal Wynorski because a janitor was a little below elevator guard, pecking order-wise. But he couldn't get his brain to focus on what to say, because his body was planning something else again.

"Wynorski puked his suit," not-Dennison said.

"Oh shit, is that right?" The guard chuckled.

"Yessir," Storch mumbled. "Wasn't hung over, or nothing. Just bad lunch—"

"Didn't ask for your life story, Wynorski. Get hosed down and hump it to 182a. Fucking suit-puking janitor."

Storch settled down, got his breathing under control. Everything was going to be okay. He was going to walk out of here without hurting anybody. Everything was going to be okay…

The elevator stopped as smoothly as it started. "Holy shit, what the fuck did you do to yourself?" a finger lanced at Storch's eye, plugged the hole in his face-plate. Storch stepped back and grabbed the guard's hand, but not-Dennison was already close in alongside him and had something pressed to his head.

"Settle down, Sergeant Korpela. Do you want to know what's in this?"

Not-Dennison held a syringe to Sgt. Korpela's head. The needle punctured his suit just above his mask, and he looked at it with his whole face screwed up and his eyes crossed, mutely screaming, oh yes, he knew this place well enough that he had a pretty good idea of what might be in it.

"I found it in a freezer downstairs. It's an airborne hemorrhagic fever bug. Start the elevator."

The guard only stared at the waggling needle.

"This little squirt I'm about to put in your eye? It's enough to kill about ninety-five percent of North America in a month. Of course, they'll cremate you before they let you out of here. Take us up, okay?"

"Are you—is he—infected…sir?" the guard pointed one finger at Storch.

"No, his suit was like that when he put it on. Put that fucking finger on the button and start this car up, now." He pushed the needle through the hood of the suit and pricked Private Korpela's forehead with it. The guard screamed like a girl, disarmed the emergency shut off, and resumed their ascent, never looking away from the needle.

"A crisis appears to have been averted," not-Dennison said. None were more surprised by what Storch did next than Storch himself. His hand rose up and paused in the air before Sergeant Korpela's rolled-up eyes. For a split second, Korpela's heart got very loud in his ears, the jackhammer lub-dub opening up to reveal the microacoustic zap of the electrical impulses firing his overtaxed heart. Storch flattened his hand into a blade, and brought it down lightning quick onto Korpela's solar plexus. The heart stopped dead. Storch could hear and feel exhausted blood backflushing into the vena cava, his valves snapping at vacuum at the mouth of his aorta, before clamping shut forever. Sergeant Korpela slumped in the corner, always the last to know. Not-Dennison pulled the syringe out and capped the needle before pocketing it. Storch's hand arced up again before not-Dennison, but he stopped it.

"That wasn't necessary, Corporal Wynorski," the Mission agent snapped.

"What's in the syringe, asshole?"

"Fucking knockout drops. When we get topside—"

The door slid open, and not-Dennison stepped out and marched double-time away from the elevator. Storch took Sgt. Korpela's rifle and followed. Gray daylight streamed in from a floor to ceiling window at the end of a long empty corridor. A sign opposite the elevators pointed the way to DECONTAMINATION.

"Are there cameras on the elevators?" Storch asked.

"Of course, but nobody's watching unless the alarm is sounded."

The alarm sounded.

They ran. Doors flashed by on both sides, Storch swinging the rifle to bear on them. A big window on the right looked into a lab where rows of robot arms worked over trays of virus cultures. A few overseers in suits watched them run by, their faces inscrutable behind the fluorescent light reflecting off their masks.

The exterior window was getting nearer, and they'd seen nobody else in the corridor, nothing between them and the outside. In less than twenty paces, he left not-Dennison behind, the rifle clamped under his arm. He hoped he didn't have to kill anyone else to get out of here, but down in his bones, he felt none of the revulsion for it that he'd felt before. He wasn't in their Army, anymore. He wasn't even in their fucking species. All he wanted was to go home, and if they weren't willing to let him do that...

He stopped at the window, had to wipe the glass with his sleeve to see through the condensation on it. It was early in the day, overcast, snow on the ground and on the conifers that screened the window off from whatever lay beyond. His body seemed to know what to do, so far. He hit the window with four shots. Wild ricochets, sparks and darkness rained down on the corridor. The bullets caromed off the glass and smashed into a light fixture overhead. There was a scratch, a little one. The "glass" was transparent plastic tank armor, like the walls of a killer whale tank at Sea World. Still, he had to kick it to be sure. He succeeded in ricocheting himself across the hall and into the concrete block wall opposite.

Someone shot at him, a whole lot of bullets passing by just as he hit the wall after his second attempt to go through the window. He spun and rolled onto his belly on the rifle, looking down the corridor with Lieutenant not-Dennison still unaccounted for at his back.

The corridor angled off to the right, suggesting that they were on the first or second floor of a cylindrical building. Pillars set into the inside wall provided good shooting cover every twenty feet. He could see a boot and a rifle barrel protruding from behind each of the first three pillars.

He took careful aim on the rear-mounted sight, clamped down the stock between his chest and the slick tile floor, and squeezed off two shots. The toe of the boot exploded and the soldier stumbled shrieking out into the open hall, his weight on the shot foot and he went down, a blind, clumsy noncombatant in his heavy MOPP gear, his gun forgotten on the floor.

The next soldier stepped out and shot wildly down the corridor, but Storch was already behind the point man's pillar, shooting the second soldier in the forearm as he stepped back into cover. He shot him again in the thigh, and advanced at a full charge, putting down his targets as if the bullets came out of his eyes, as if his enemies were cardboard cutouts in a kill house, as if everyone else was shambling along at half-speed. Storch's body flowed through the motions so fast that he could barely keep track, let alone control himself.

Someone shot him, two slugs punching him in the abdomen and one through his left breast. The initial pain was no worse than a needle from a careless nurse, but he felt his lung collapse, ribs shatter, and something caustic spilling into his vital organs. Storch staggered and almost fell down, air whuffing out of his chest-hole in bloody foam-flecked gusts, but *pop* his lung closed itself up and sucked in air good as new, better, even. Another bullet meant for his face creased the top of his skull as he faltered, but this time his skull was thicker, and it only made him faster, and less careful.

He shot two more soldiers in the head, neck and chest and passed them before they hit the ground. He emptied the magazine to cover himself as he stooped and grabbed a dead soldier's rifle. Bullets hung in the air all around him, and more than a few found their marks. He felt his body rerouting fluids and nervous impulses and rebuilding even as it ran itself into more shooters and took them down. He'd lost count of how many when he came to the double doors. The corridor ended blindly, no windows on either wall, no doors. On the double doors, the instructions for decontamination procedure. A perfect bottleneck.

"Give me my pistol," Lt. not-Dennison wheezed from close behind him. He looked over his shoulder. The Mission agent was trying to stand upright and having a hard time of it. He'd been shot twice, one in the right thigh and one in the shoulder just to the right of his throat, but something vital was wrecked, and blood splashed out and down the front of his suit on a steadily failing rhythm. He coughed out a laugh. His teeth were framed in fresh arterial blood. "I'm not gonna make it," he said, and tore off his helmet.

Storch only looked at him.

"I forgot to tell you," not-Dennison said, "about the orders." He sat down hard on the floor and laid back, clawing at the seals on his suit. "Come here, I have something I need to give you."

Storch approached cautiously. Lt. not-Dennison had a hard time of it, since his right arm hung limp at his side, and he was shaking badly from shock. Ear cocked on the double doors behind him, Storch knelt and helped him get the suit open. Underneath, he wore the ordinary greens of a Second Lieutenant in the Chemical Corps. What did he have for him?

A sick hunger rose in Storch's belly. Standing still, he was almost knocked flat by his fatigue, by the gnawing pains of all the places where lead had recently penetrated his newly resurrected flesh. He was not a god. He had to eat, and now. Lt. not-Dennison was dying, was not quite a man anymore, just meat, so what did it matter? He could stop the hunger, make himself strong again–

No! You are Zane Ezekiel Storch, you don't eat people–

"They're coming," Storch snapped. "Talk fast."

"My real name is Lt. Raymond Saticoy, Third Army Special Operations Group. I am acting on orders of the Mission. My orders were that I was not allowed to get caught..." His hands tore open his uniform, and for a second Storch thought he had on some sort of flak vest. Saticoy seized both Storch's hands, the bare, bloody fingers dug into the pressure points on the insides of Storch's wrists so they went numb. His face came up into Storch's and smeared blood on his mask. Saticoy's face was muzzled in blood, but his eyes fixed on Storch's even as they began to glaze over. "...And I was not allowed to fail."

Storch still didn't know what the hell Saticoy was wearing. A vest of canvas and nylon, it had two flat bags filled with fluid, and a third, empty pouch between them. The two filled bags began to mix in the third. "It's a binary chemical explosive. Wired to my heart rate, but there's a live switch, too. It's armed."

Storch's arms wouldn't come free. He yanked back, only tugged Saticoy up after him. With devilish strength, Saticoy drove his good knee hard into Storch's groin, pointing out a fatal flaw in his body modification, so far. Storch howled and threw himself backwards, pivoting at the last instant to slam the dying man into the heavy steel doors. They shivered under a hail of bullets slamming into the other side. The third pouch on Saticoy's chest was full. "You can't live, Storch, Keogh, whatever you are. Has to be this way—"

Storch stumbled back and kicked the oversized red emergency entry button on the wall beside the doors and when they swung open, he brought Saticoy up high and hurled his limp body into the showers. Storch threw himself back out of the doorway, but the doors only half closed when Saticoy, pinned in midair on a hurricane of bullets, exploded.

The doors whipped over his head like the blades of a broken scissors, and a white hole opened up in the atrium of the decontamination chamber, and it reached out to the walls and ceiling and floor and pushed them back, infinite in all directions, and when it closed over him, Storch was actually trying to fight his way up the concussive stream to get *into* the light, but then the building was coming down on his head, and the shitty old world shut him up in darkness once again.

"Coy?"

Ringing like a cathedral in free-fall, pealing bells burning up on re-entry and becoming sine-wave vapor. Scent of a hospital luau, charred pork and medicine...

"Coy! You in there, man?"

Roaming the devastated channels of capillaries in his caramelized skin, new uneasy treaties with molten plastic invaders. A debate raging in his cells: repel the interlopers, or co-opt them, and grow a skin of polyvinyl armor? Storch sat back in awe, wondering how and when his body became so much smarter than he was.

"Coy, we're moving you..."

Moving...he was rising, now, but he could only see the light, still pushing him away, back into the shitty old world filled with dying soldiers and shouting doctors, and all of this was, somehow, his fault, but they were taking him away, too weak to stop them. He could not die, but if he was going to heal, if he was going to get stronger, he had to eat someone...no, something...

Burned now by wind, but the stench blew away, and the dark went pale red with sunlight on his eyelids. Floating down a river of hands, voices raised against the wind, *overflow routed to civilian hospital burn unit, transfer papers pending, have to check with my CO, so many dead—*

Wind gone now, close, cold air and noises behind the gaseous chimes, voices very close, but they couldn't be speaking to him, because his name was not—

"Saticoy! You in there? We gotta move you, man, but hang in there..."

"His term demo pack went off in there, LT."

"Do we know that?"

"S'not here, is it? Middle of the goddamned decon wing. Beaucoup casualties. He should've died."

"He almost did. Coy! Stay with us, man. We're getting you out. But we need to know. Can you talk? Coy, I know you're there, douchebag, what happened in there? Did you dispose of the package?"

His hand came up before his eyes, and it was no surprise, this time, to see that where his flesh was not charcoal black or raw red muscle, or brown with melted suit, it was olive, like not-Dennison's. They thought he was the Mission agent who'd bled all over him, when he tried to blow him up. Even without the guidance of God, his body never missed a trick.

He sat up, restraints and IV tubes ripping away like smoke. "I...am...the package."

The man leaning over him recoiled and tried to stand in the moving ambulance, cracked his skull on the underside of a locker that dumped blankets and splints on him. Someone behind him smashed the back of his head with a rifle butt. He saw stars but wouldn't go out. He swiveled and took the rifle away and pointed it. Hands went up from the two still-conscious Mission agents. Eyes wide, looking at him, seeing not even he knew what.

"Take me to the Mission," Storch said.

"You'll never make it," one of them said, sizing him up, fear redoubling, bravado breaking down. "You might as well kill us now."

"Then I'll kill you and find out where it is by eating your brain." Bluff on bluff. He raised the rifle. Through the windshield, he could see a gray ribbon of car-choked highway. They were already off the base, probably headed for a safe house, or more likely a private airstrip.

"You better be a light sleeper, motherfucker," the agent said.

"I'm well-rested," Storch rasped. "Been sleeping for months. Just take me to the goddamned man in charge, and get me something to eat."

~ 10 ~

In the Bible, Karl Schweinfurter knew, the trials and troubles of others were told as object lessons to steer the faithful away from the pitfalls of sin. He figured his own troubles would make a fitting addendum to the Book of Job, but damned if he could tell what lesson one could take from it.

He sat on a bare wooden bench in Grossvater Egil's lodge. Snow-filtered moonlight cut blue runnels in the smoky gloom, which was only accented by the mellow red glow of the embers in the wood stove. The mounted heads of all the deer and elk in Idaho watched from the shadowy rafters. Even here in his private sanctum, Grossvater Egil did not display his *other* hunting trophies, but Karl knew they were here somewhere, because every young Heilige Berger got to see them once.

A Nazi SS stormtrooper in full parade regalia stood at attention beside the door. Karl knew it was only a mannequin, had pored over the medals and ribbons to while away the hours when the light was better, but now, as he drifted in and out of fevered sleep, the sentry seemed to shift its posture as if taking sly looks at him. The light came back as a sterling gleam off the silver gorget around the mannequin's neck, the ceremonial SS dagger in one gloved fist, the bayonet affixed to the Mauser Model 98 carbine rifle slung across its hollow chest. He did not know whether there was even a lock on the door, but he didn't want to try, because maybe it wasn't a mannequin, anymore, but a Jäger. It was just the sort of trap that Grossvater Egil would lay for him. It bothered him that he was scared of an empty uniform, but he was so absolutely terrified of every living man, woman and child in Heilige Berg that he far preferred its company to anything outside. The only thing that kept him thinking about trying to leave was that Grossvater Egil was coming back any minute, with a "surprise."

* * *

In the last week, life at the Heilige Berg compound had gone from bad to worse, and not just for him. About two days after he'd discovered their new neighbors, people at home started to get sick. First the Jägers, then the younger children and the old, then everyone had it. The sickness spread so fast that there was no time for hysteria, let alone careful quarantine measures. Those who could get out of bed at all moved like arthritic drunkards, and their foggy breath left beads of flash-frozen blood in their trails. He had been in the stockade for deserting his post since New Year's, and it was probably this that caused him to be spared.

Grossvater Egil retreated into his lodge and doubled the guard, though all other work in the compound ground to a halt. He issued only one statement: their enemies had stooped to biochemical warfare. Those who were still fit, if there were any, were to don gas masks and heavy protective gear and carry on the defense of the group; the rest should confine themselves to their quarters and pray. No medical treatment could save them from the cowardly weapons of the satanic armies of Z.O.G., but if they prayed, if they meditated on their greater reward in the next world, they would surely pass into grace, or be delivered back to fight on in this one.

Three days later, the combined prayers of the congregation had dwindled by half. The Jägers were nearly all gone, either bedridden or dead in the woods. The sounds of them screaming and coughing and shooting at nothing, or at each other, had gradually tapered off to silence.

In Karl's own house, there was only his wife left alive. Heidi had actually succumbed first, breaking down in coughing fits when she went to see him in the stockade. His parents had caught up with and surpassed her symptoms in a matter of days. He was let out and put to work caring for the sick, which meant cleaning up after them, since there was no medicine, and nobody knew what was wrong with them. Heilige Berg Church preached of the Living Power of God's Healing Word, and reviled all hospitals as temples of false pride.

Karl felt pretty bad when his parents died, it was all so sudden and so not like how people died in the movies, it was so ugly. They reminded him of the wasted human shells he'd seen on the buses that night, of the mythical matchstick-people of Auschwitz. Wherever he went in the compound, he heard the same gasping, gargling struggle for breath, as if the whole congregation were transforming into fish. His father, emaciated, palsied, died eating a moldy sandwich, face going purple, then black. His mother shrieked at him in German all night long until something tore inside her, and Heidi kept trying to tell him that the baby she carried was his, and that he owed her a decent Christian burial before she fell into a sleep like death herself. What bothered him most was that when they finally died, the bodies didn't go away. In movies and on TV, somebody always knew when somebody died, and they came to collect the body lickety-split. It took him until several hours after they started to stink before he realized he was the only somebody left.

He walked outside, then, bareheaded and without his heavy parka, walked into the brilliantly lit, crystal clear night, and he saw the strange golden dust blowing through the common field at the center of the compound. He looked up at the moon and saw the dust was streaming down from the pine trees: pollen from the cones, coming down like it was the high equinox. He could hear a few people crying in their cabins, but there were no lights on anywhere, no Jäger patrols between him and the gate. He looked up into the sky and felt as if he could leap up into it and come down anywhere in the world, anywhere it was warm and people didn't get all bent out of shape about Jesus and the Jews, anywhere that didn't have a Grossvater Egil.

He started to walk out, but then turned and went to the motor pool, for once having a good idea in time to benefit from it. Here, too, he found nobody, and noisily stole one of the stockyard trucks parked in the mechanic's garage. On the way out the gate, he turned up the radio on a Christian rock station out of Grangeville, and gave the compound the finger as he turned out onto the road. He never expected to come back again.

Of course, he'd expected to get more than eight miles away, too.

When the truck's engine seized up less than two miles out of White Bird, he screamed and cursed and prayed and pounded his fists on the steering wheel until they went numb, but to no avail. God was still intent on keeping his life interesting. Nobody in the Bible got to drive out of Sodom or Egypt in a truck, but nobody in the Bible ever froze to death, either. He slept in the cab, shivering in the thin jacket he'd thrown on and dreaming about those big furry hats that the Russians wore, with ear-flaps. He'd embrace Communism and all its evil ways for a furry hat, if God couldn't be bothered to bring him one.

In the morning, he searched the truck and came up with a brittle stick of Juicy Fruit gum, a half-used tube of Chap Stik, and about a dollar in small change from beneath the seats. The gum cut up the roof of his mouth, but he merrily chewed his breakfast and jingled his fortune in his pocket as he set off into the magnificent winter morning.

The sun beamed down through a rift in the rolling clouds, and before long he was warm enough to tie his jacket around his waist and apologize to God for the whole hat thing. He was at the foot of Heilige Berg valley, where the ragged terrain subsided as it merged with the broad prairie of the Salmon River valley and the I-95. With luck and God's admittedly stingy grace, he could get something to eat in White Bird and hitchhike out of here, maybe back home to Nampa. He'd go right to the press or the cops and make a big stink about what happened up here, and get help to those who could still be helped.

It was about then that he began to discover that he was pretty sick, himself. He felt a tightness in his chest, not from exhaustion, but as if his lungs were being squeezed. His stomach roared its protest over the trickle of teasing gum-juice, and his head started to hurt. His vision was shot through with ghostly rainbows, like the death-throes of a failing TV picture tube. He ate the Chap Stik and several fistfuls of snow to get his strength up, but his headache got worse, and he only felt weaker.

It was starting to snow again by the time he limped into White Bird. His jeans had frozen stiff on his legs, and only his waterproofed thermal underwear kept him from succumbing to hypothermia. He gave a ragged cheer and tried to offer up a hymn in German, but all he could remember was the Löwenbrau jingle. He tried to make it right, hoping God understood: "Heute abend, Heute abend, gibst nur Jesus Christ…"

The town proper was less than six blocks long and two wide, built between the junction of I-95 and State Road 117 and the frozen Salmon River, and consisted of a feed store, two gas stations, a sad strip mall and a Dairy Queen. Residential properties dribbled into the countryside in all directions, low, rambling ranch houses like forts dug into the snow, surrounded by monster pickup trucks and snowmobiles, and puffing hearty columns of wood smoke into the silver sky. Karl burned to go to one of them to ask for help, but he knew from the wisdom of the Jägers and his few experiences in town that the Heilige Bergers were not well liked in White Bird. Conservative redneck ranchers and poor townie trash that they were, yet they thought of Karl's people as a hostile survivalist cult, and not just purer followers of the same way of life they themselves held sacred. That they were a tax-free church which ran a thriving beef concern didn't warm their hearts, either.

Another thought occurred to him—he could walk to the Heilige Berg slaughterhouse, which was on the edge of town. As sick as everyone was, it was probably abandoned. He might find something to eat there, or steal another truck. But the idea of going anywhere near Heilige Berg property scared him more than freezing to death. They would take him back up there to die, they thought it was a mortal sin to see a doctor, and he was sick.

Not germ-sick, like the flu, but somehow worse. He felt heavy in the wrong places, his center of mass so badly thrown off that even when he gave walking his full attention, he still couldn't keep going in a straight line for more than a few steps at a time. His head felt like it was going to split open and cabbages sprout up through the burst sutures of his skull. He needed help, or he was going to die. If God had meant for him to die, he'd have left him up on the mountain, but he'd given him enough of a lift to make it within staggering distance of the town. It would be a mortal sin, he decided, not to carry out God's will and get help.

He fixed his gaze on the Dairy Queen marquee for the last mile, the tiny red dot swelling with agonizing slowness as he shambled along the shoulder of State Road 117, across the two-lane bridge over the Salmon River, and into White Bird. A few trucks passed by, but none stopped. He noticed one slowing down to watch him, saw eyes big and blank as marbles taking in his obvious plight, then passing on. He shuddered with more than cold. Maybe Grossvater Egil was right about the world. Maybe things were different in the new millennium, and the world truly was Satan's pitiless slaughterhouse.

In the Dairy Queen, they pretty much convinced him. The girl at the counter backed away from him and got the manager. In the pre-lunch lull, there was no one in the dining room but two gangly high school dropouts in DQ uniforms. His luck running true to form, the manager was a fat, middle-aged beaner, who came out and told him to beat it—*we don't serve choo people*. He didn't have the strength to argue, let alone leave. He pushed his change at them and asked for french fries one last time, then slumped across the counter.

The two boys dragged him out to the dumpster corral behind the Dairy Queen and kicked the shit out of him for about ten minutes. They came back after their shift was over an hour later and beat him up some more before they went home. When the sun began to set, Karl lay in a dumpster on a bed of wilted salad greens and rancid deep-fryer grease, too weak to blink away the snow settling on his eyes.

"Heute abend," he whimpered, "heute abend, gibst nur Jesus Christ…"

Someone stood over him. An angel of the Lord come to collect him, he hoped, but it was probably just the DQ jerks with a bunch of their friends.

"Der Meisterrasse, nicht wahr? Was machst du denn, in diese Mulltonne, Karl?"

"I'm sorry, Grossvater Egil," he managed, though the pain of moving his mouth brought fresh blood, and he swallowed one of his molars. "I thought it was God's will…that I go to get help. But—"

"All is God's will, Karl. Come home, boy. Your family misses you."

"What?"

"The rapture we have prayed for has come, Karl. Even for you, it will come." He did not remember being brought back to Heilige Berg, but he remembered the eyes, like the heads of steel nails in the dark, and the hands lifting him up, carrying him back, once again, to be purified.

And here he sat, waiting for Grossvater Egil and his surprise. It had been a day for surprises. When he'd awakened in his own bunk this morning, warm and dry, but still sick and sore, his mother and Heidi stood over him. Heidi held a baby. She was nicer to him than she'd ever been before, but she didn't try to tell him the baby was his, anymore. It was about three months premature, he figured; he'd never seen anything that tiny and unfinished alive outside of an incubator. It studied him with its lidless gray eyes, never making a sound, except once, it tugged Heidi's shirt and she leaned down to listen to it whisper in her ear, and then carried it out of the room. His parents were nice to him, too, so cloyingly sweet he had to get away.

The Jägers greeted him by his proper name, not even little Werther called him Swinefucker. All around the compound, people worked at their respective tasks. The children all shoveled snow, singing a merry work song. It was like the pastoral pictures in the dining hall. It was the realization of what Karl had fuzzily expected to find when he first came to Heilige Berg, but never saw. It was like the bad things that happened before were all a dream, like maybe everything that happened since he stepped off the bus in this place was just a nightmare. But he still felt sick, like his head was going to burst open and a demented clown marching band was going to goose-step out of it.

The Jägers escorted him up to Grossvater Egil's lodge and opened the door for him, but Grossvater Egil was not there, and he'd been waiting here ever since.

As his relief turned to confusion, then a swelling, choking dread, he found a very peculiar notion growing increasingly predominant in his flitting, half-formed thoughts.

The compound had been delivered, alright, but not by God. If Grossvater Egil had taught him one thing, it was that God didn't work like this. And he thought he had a pretty good idea who *was* behind it.

A pounding knock at the door. The hall shook with it, sheets of snow sliding off the slanted roof.

"Karl! Make yourself ready!"

Limping, trying to hold his head stiff, he hauled himself to his feet and went to the door, wondering why Grossvater Egil knocked on his own door, and what he would do when he opened it. He passed the hulking Stormtrooper, seeing now a figure of hope, instead of fear. The barrel of the carbine was plugged with lead, the bayonet soldered in place. He reached out—

The door swung open so fast it bashed his right kneecap. He drew himself up into a ball, yelping and tucking his hands behind the injured limb.

Grossvater Egil stood over him, his parka draped in frost, his great silver beard dripping icy water as he shook his head. "You must not keep them waiting," Grossvater Egil touched his shoulder. "You were stupid to run away, but yet you may be saved. Come, boy. The rapture comes again."

Karl looked up into Grossvater Egil's eyes, saw how the bloodshot yellow of his pupils was now flinty gray, the same hue as Heidi's baby's eyes. In that moment, he really did want to believe Grossvater Egil, really needed to believe that God's Healing Word had saved them all from illness and the Tribulations, saved them because they were God's chosen people, and He loved them. When he looked up into the old cleric's eyes, he *could* believe it, like never before. There was something in them he never saw before, though it was a sin to say so. Grossvater Egil *loved* him, cared for him, where before there was only righteous disgust.

"We were wrong all along, Karl," Grossvater Egil said, "to think our blood alone was sacred. All the races will be saved. He loves us all, even the Juden. All will be called into the holy light and made whole, made One, with Him."

Karl looked outside. Down the narrow trench dug from the lodge to the open compound courtyard, he saw no Jägers waiting with guns, no sign that this was some sort of trap. In the compound, a big silver bus grumbled as it idled, sick, sunken faces pressed against the windows.

"There are some even sicker than you, Karl. They cannot wait." He knelt beside Karl and his beard, wiry and stiff as chainmail, scraped his ear. "Hab keine Angst, Junge. *Heilige Licht* is waiting to come into you, and make you whole."

Karl decided. He stood so fast he set his own head spinning, but he lunged at Grossvater Egil as he rose, his right hand driving the SS dagger behind his beard and up through his throat, until it must be dimpling the backside of his eye.

Karl backed away from Grossvater Egil, away from the door. The cleric filled the doorway, a confused, vaguely disappointed cloud passing over his features. His mouth tried to open, but the knife nailed his jaws shut, only a great gush of blood escaped his lips. His hands came up, palms out, as if to ask why he would do such a thing. And Karl felt that he'd made a terrible mistake, and that was thinking that Grossvater Egil could be killed.

He just stood there, meditating on the dagger in his throat. Karl charged him, then, roaring, "Get the fuck away from me, devil!" His hands hit the cleric's chest dead center and drove him back over the threshold. Grossvater Egil offered no resistance, his massive weight tipped over like a cigar store Indian's and he fell on his back on the slippery path outside and was sliding down the trenched walkway like a bobsled when Karl slammed the door and threw one bolt after another and dropped the heavy pine plank into the bracers on either side of the frame.

You've done it now, Swinefucker.

Frantic, he ransacked the lodge. The main hall was Spartan in its plainness, and offered no weapons or telephones, but he found a door where he'd never noticed one before, behind a curtain that screened the bed. A big padlock hung open on the frame, and the door glided open when he touched it.

He crept into an adjoining, windowless room that must be dug out of the mountainside. He pushed the door shut behind him, shot the bolts on this side, thanking God that Grossvater Egil was paranoid enough to put locks on both sides of all his doors.

Inside, he found computers. Stacks of them on pine utility shelves with fans blowing on them, and a row of monitors, all showing the Heilige Berg logo. When he touched a mouse or a keyboard, a window popped up demanding his User ID and password. He backed away from these, biting his lip. He could use a computer to call for help, he knew, but he didn't have the faintest idea how. Computers had seemed like a geek's plaything in school, and he hadn't even heard the word *computer* in all his time at Heilige Berg, except when Grossvater Egil railed against them as tools of ZOG in his sermons. He typed *911* into one, then *Operator*, then *help*, then *hilfe*, but the password window wouldn't go away.

Deeper in the bunker room, he found a row of lockers, but no weapons. Just a bunch of trophies, he couldn't figure what else they were good for. A shoebox filled with cash. Nigger clothes. Nigger shoes. Big nigger Afro wigs. Dark brown shoe polish. Dimly, he remembered that when his Mama was attacked, the niggers had smeared shoe polish on her clothes, there were big subhuman pawprints all over her body. The children had been told that the Mud People spread their black contagion on whatever they touched. Karl had just taken it on faith that the niggers had smeared shoe polish on her to scare her. Who knew what niggers were capable of?

Think, Karl. *Think!*

"This is foolishness, Karl. Komm auf!"

He froze. Grossvater Egil was outside the cabin door, shouting loud enough to be heard even here, even with his throat punctured. He could hear sloshing, spilling blood in the voice.

His brain had never been good at putting shit together, but now, he knew there was something else, maybe someone else, growing inside him and fixing to take over, the way everyone else had been taken over, but they had to take him up to the mountaintop, into that awful light, to make it work. He had to be smarter than he'd ever been before, with what little gray matter he still had left.

"You can still be saved, boy."

Think, Swinefucker, think!

Not niggers...Jägers.

There *was* a race war in the offing, but Heilige Berg fought both sides of it.

Karl had broken curfew enough times, just sitting at the window and watching the moon pass over, to say for sure that blackfaced Jägers didn't strut out of Grossvater Egil's lodge in the dead of night. There was another way out of here.

He stuffed his pockets with cash from the shoebox, then went around the log walls of the bunker, pounding and kicking on them and pressing his ear against them. Heart racing, muscles trembling, he felt the awful weakness creeping over him again. He was going to faint, and they would be on him, and when he awoke next morning, he'd be somebody else...

He grabbed one of the utility shelves and heaved it over. The computers tumbled to the floor with a scattershot chain of explosions and sprays of sparks. The wall here was as solid as the others. He grabbed the next rack and yanked on it, but instead of tipping over, the shelf swung smoothly out into the room. Behind it, there was a narrow door set into the logs.

He threw himself against it, plunged through into an icy dark that had no floor.

His fingers scratched cold rock on either side of him as he fell. His feet flailed and almost caught on the slick, steeply sloped floor. He brought his arms up in front of his face just in time to catch an oncoming bend in the tunnel, his elbow hit the wall hard enough to strike sparks off it. He fell backwards, now, down the second, even steeper, leg of the tunnel. He sat down to try to brake himself, but now he was rolling ass-over-teakettle down and down, the rock banging his head into itself over and over again, and when he crashed to a stop, he was entangled in bushes and snow. A chilly breeze kissed his cheek. He was outside, on the backside of the knoll on which Grossvater Egil's lodge sat. This area was off-limits to all but the Jägers. It was where they played their wargames. He crawled out of the bush and lay on his back on the frozen ground for a long time. He couldn't hear anyone coming after him, didn't really know if he could hear *anything,* anymore, didn't much care if he could.

The stars danced and threw out scintillating arms to each other, their eons' old light fragmenting into overlapping prismatic showers coming down through the clouds and the trees, it was raining blinding light. He rolled over and tried to see the earth. A garage-sized shed lay before him. He crawled to the doorway and in through it, thinking only of finding a place to hide until he could see and think straight, until everything made sense. And he crawled headfirst into the passenger-side door panel of a monstrously large powder-flake violet Lincoln Continental. He lay across the hood for a minute, letting the chill steel suck the heat and fear from his head. God, his head hurt so much, his heart felt like it had holes in it, his lungs felt like they were full of wet sand.

He was laying on the hood of a car.

See straight, Swinefucker. *Think!*

He pushed himself up on his elbows and limped around the pimpmobile. The narrow fire road before him vanished almost instantly into the trees. It probably joined State Road 117 a ways south of where the Heilige Berg drive met it. The road looked treacherous under the best of conditions, and hadn't been plowed in about a week. There were chains on the whitewall tires, but the suspension had been lowered, niggers liked that kind of thing, wrecking perfectly good American cars, but he didn't see any other way off the mountain.

Pull yourself together, Karl Schweinfurter. Drive this fucking car.

He went around to the driver's side door and opened it, climbed into the low, deep bucket seat. The seats were covered in deep, purple shag. The steering wheel was a tiny ring of forged chrome chain. The keys were in the ignition.

*Please, God...*fuck that, *please* Karl, *please don't fuck up again...*

The engine turned over on the first turn, gobbling and growling and purring steadily, glass-pack mufflers hushing the powerful custom V-8 engine so he could still hear his heart hammering in his chest. He grasped the shifter on the steering column and cranked it into Drive, waiting for the car to die, for Grossvater Egil's stony hand to punch through the glass and clasp his shoulder, for Jägers to drop out of the trees in the roadway, for those shadowy giants from the place where all the evil had started to jump out—

We're your new neighbors, little camper.

He stomped on the gas. He fought the ridiculously tiny wheel for control of the car as it bucked and headed down the mountain like a torpedo. When he came to a straight enough stretch of road, he turned on the radio, and found his Christian rock station.

He hoped the Dairy Queen was open.

~ 11 ~

The moment Martin Cundieffe agreed to meet Brady Hoecker for lunch and hung up the phone, his stomach flooded with acid, and he felt as if he were free-falling into a horrible mistake. His hand shook so badly as he speed-dialed Assistant Director Wyler that he accidentally reached the outside operator the first time. Ms. McNulty told him that AD Wyler was not on the fifth floor, and not accessible via his cellular phone, but she took a message to call him back ASAP.

He studied the Baltimore address Hoecker's secretary had given him. It was nowhere near the CIA or any other seat of government that he knew of, excepting the NSA. He checked an online map service and puzzled over the location it gave him. The Steer Crazy Steakhouse on Southwestern Avenue, off the 95, just outside Baltimore city limits. His stomach relaxed only a little. It appeared that Hoecker actually intended to eat lunch with him.

As he drove off the Capitol Beltway and took the 95 northeast into Maryland, the groomed, gray landscape giving way to only slightly less manicured rural hills, he continued to worry at the subtext of the lunch invitation, and found little to calm his nerves. Hoecker had been coldly neutral to him at the Storch interrogation, and indirectly hostile at the Cave Institute. Wyler had never told him that anyone else in the Mules might try to contact him, but he had been fairly clear on the dietary customs of Mules. They were strict vegetarians, for health reasons that, he was clearly told, went far beyond what the public knew. After a grueling withdrawal phase, Cundieffe had found he needed only a few hours of sleep every night, and had never felt more alert. It crossed his mind that this might be some sort of ruse to draw him out and interrogate him, but that idea was tossed out as patently ridiculous. Anyone who would know enough to arrange such a bogus meeting would know about the diet issue, would indeed know more about the Mules than he did, himself.

When he finally arrived at the Steer Crazy Steakhouse, he was pleasantly surprised to find it a lot less frowsy than its name suggested. A big mock-ranch house of uneven stones and weatherbeaten timbers, with a crumbling replica of a covered wagon parked on the frost-bitten frontage. It was, however, one of those places where they make a big ceremony of shearing off any neckties that come in the door. Cundieffe stopped just short of the revolving doors, staring at the wall behind the hostess's podium, at a barbaric tapestry of severed ties that wrapped around into the restrooms and dining area. Many specimens were displayed in a glass case beside autographs of the celebrities and celebrated politicos who'd sacrificed them. A quick perusal of these through the window proved that the Director was not among their trophies. The burgundy silk necktie he wore was a gift from his mother. Hoping casual dress did not disqualify him for entrance, he ran back to his car and deposited the tie in his glove compartment.

Brady Hoecker was waiting for him at the door when he came back. He had also secreted his tie before entering. Cundieffe checked his pulse as he approached the Mule council-member, even as he tried to puzzle out what to be afraid of next.

They traded rigorously nonchalant small-talk while they waited to be seated, Cundieffe only half-hearing the flow of conversation as he studied the other Mule, only dimly aware that Hoecker was doing the same. Seen in bright light, Brady Hoecker was no more imposing than Cundieffe, in fact, they might be mistaken for brothers. Hoecker's features were almost British in their boniness, while his hair looked not like it was receding, so much as regrouping for some imminent counterattack. His was a minimalist sculpture of pattern baldness. His suit was several shades smarter than Cundieffe's, as well. He supposed they looked like exactly what they were, junior and senior bureaucrats on a government lunch.

As they were led to their table, he decided that this was to be only a small-talk lunch, replete with the obligatory sniffing and probing disguised as banter which characterized all the luncheons he'd attended so far in this part of the country, but nothing of consequence would be revealed. He tried to curb his frustration, diverted it into a question that'd been burning his brain.

"Mr. Hoecker—"

"Brady, please."

"All right, Brady…I don't mean to sound like an idiot, but—"

"Go ahead, it's all the rage at the Institute."

The booths at Steer Crazy were set up like individual rooms, the upholstered backs of the benches extending up to meet the padded leather ceiling. The hostess, still carrying her ceremonial tie-shears, waved them into a big corner booth in the remotest depths of the dining room, passed them menus and vanished into the murky labyrinth in which she'd stranded them.

"I thought we—I mean to say, I'd been told that we—that is, all of *us*—"

Hoecker chuckled. "We are. Vigorously. But this steakhouse has the best salad bar in or out of the Beltway. And it's secure. It's swept daily by a private security service, because a lot of our NSA people come over from Ft. Meade." His face went stony grave so fast Cundieffe wanted to look for the smiling mask in his lap. "We have issues of great import to discuss."

"Like—like what, Brady?"

Hoecker sprang out of his seat. "Let's eat first."

They each filled three plates over the next half hour from the salad bar, which was very impressive, indeed. Hoecker talked about everything, citing exactly nineteen people, books and articles of which Cundieffe had never heard, while Cundieffe, who feared to say anything, fought the urge to sneak off and try to call AD Wyler again. Was this lunch some sort of betrayal? He ate too quickly, finishing each plate only to watch Hoecker methodically spearing each green bean and portioning out dressing like a pharmacist making nitroglycerin tablets.

When he laid his knife and fork across his last plate, Hoecker drew the heavy curtain to seal off the booth and pushed the plates aside. He laid his briefcase on the table and fixed Cundieffe with an intimidating polygraphic gaze.

"So, Martin, you're still not officially assigned to Bureau Headquarters, are you?"

Cundieffe blinked, pursed his lips. "Not officially, no, Mr. Hoecker, um—I suppose I'm here for special training, but I'm still attached to the Los Angeles field office."

"Haven't been out to Quantico much, though, have you?"

"There's been a lot of reapportionment of assets back here, what with the Counter-terrorism Division in development. I have been learning quite a bit, however."

Hoecker nodded at the implication. "Must be a shock," he said, nodding.

"Sometimes I forget what country it is, I'm living in." He smiled, choked when Hoecker's eyes flashed at him.

"I'm not going to insult you with a lot of rubbish about loyalty oaths or security clearances. We know who and what you are, and what you've done, and we're satisfied with your integrity. There are some in the Institute who take a more ritualistic view of things, who believe that clearance is earned over time. But there are others among us who recognize the dire press of events. We feel that if you're to be useful to us, then you must be shown the geometry of the situation, not isolated points."

One and not many indeed, Cundieffe thought. His sick smile tightened. Before Cundieffe could ask who 'we' was, Hoecker opened the briefcase and took out a folder. He held it just under his chin for a long moment, looking at it and at Cundieffe with a silent movie actor's hesitation. He finally passed it across to Cundieffe, laying it down before his reaching hands as if actually putting it in them was somehow a greater breach of security. It worked. Cundieffe felt as if there were a bubble around the file, which he could not penetrate. The front of the folder was a bloodbath of arcane stamps, labels and scrawled designations he'd never seen before.

Hoecker gestured for him to open the file. Inside was an 8X12 inch print of a satellite image. Serrated peaks formed a collage of shattered glass draped in a cloak of fog. But with infrared filtering, a blocky heat signature the size and shape of a small town clearly stood out on the shadowed side of the ridge. "This is a Keyhole image of the Seven Devils Mountains in western Idaho, taken two weeks ago. This image was never taken, it does not exist. Do I make myself clear?"

Cundieffe nodded, gazing avidly at it.

"Good. All normal security clearance protocols are waived in situations such as this, where an initiate such as yourself has eminent jurisdiction over a particularly emergent issue, and this is right up your alley."

"Has Assistant Director Wyler seen it?" Cundieffe asked.

Hoecker laid the photo face-down. "Maybe you should call him now. He probably has someone else who could take your place." There was no malice, no sarcasm in Hoecker's tone, but Cundieffe cringed as if slapped.

"I didn't mean it that way, Mr. Hoecker—" he trailed off, clamping his mouth shut before he damaged things further.

"I hear your Director gave the go-ahead for the response center Wyler's been clamoring for. You're doing a lot of collation and updating work with their database. Must be fascinating, crank-calling fringe group front companies into the wee hours." Hoecker made a show of starting to close the file folder.

"Sir, I'd like to please continue the briefing."

"Security is not always top-down, Martin. Often, for the sake of plausible deniability, compartmentalization must also work from the bottom up." He flipped the sat photo over. "That compound there belongs to a Christian identity sect known as the Teutonic Heritage Church. You're familiar with them?"

He laid another file in front of Cundieffe. ABOVE TOP SECRET: SECDEF/NATSEC/DIRNSA EYES ONLY. It was an internal NSA file. Opening it, he was thunderstruck to see that the posture paper and fact sheet on top quoted extensively from his own work. He skipped through these, thoroughly familiar with their contents.

Teutonic Heritage was a Germanic white separatist cult with a congregation of about six hundred in Idaho and Montana, their stronghold, Heilige Berg, a compound in a valley on the edge of the Snake River. Their rhetoric was inflammatory, but they kept mostly to themselves, stockpiling weapons and waiting for a sign of the coming apocalyptic race war. Cundieffe looked up to find Hoecker waiting for his next question.

"Listen, Brady, I'd really like to help, but we've got our hands full with official business and with the Mission, and you have my information on Heilige Berg right here, and I don't think this is the time to drag the Bureau into another Ruby Ridge scenario—"

"Martin, Heilige Berg has gone dark. All communications with the outside world cut off as of last week. We don't know if there's still anyone alive in there."

Cundieffe scratched his head, waiting for Hoecker to drop the other shoe.

"As I'm sure you already know, Heilige Berg has no telephones, but maintains online communications with a network of hate groups which fund and feed off each other both here and abroad. The group is surprisingly well funded, receiving laundered money donated by several basic-cable televangelists who don't publicly espouse racism. The postings from one week ago state that the whole compound suddenly became falling-down sick, and the leader, a German immigrant named Egil Reuss, claimed they had been poisoned by their quote, 'natural enemies.' He pleaded with one of his colleagues to send a doctor to consult, but asked that he be disguised as a sympathetic journalist coming for an interview. Rev. Reuss preaches faith healing, and must keep up appearances. He also tried to find someone who could get him TOW and shoulder-held surface-to-surface missiles. Sadly, he was too irrational to convey meaningful information on the situation inside, and didn't respond to our agents' attempts to draw him out online."

Cundieffe leafed through the folder, scanning transcripts of increasingly hysterical online postings from Rev. Reuss. He noted that there were no responses included. The NSA had blocked his access to help, in hopes of getting in undercover, while his people were dying—or being murdered. It was a controversial, but not unheard of, strategy for containing dangerous radicals, but only when a federal court had granted its sanction upon review of legally acquired evidence, and even then, it invariably went wrong. "And you acquired this data how?" he asked.

"How much has Wyler told you about the EAR?"

"I've never heard of it."

"But you've seen the final product. It's—a very sensitive subject." Hoecker bit his thumbnail and his eyes went unfocused, as he measured out how much to tell him, from *here* to *here*. "Elint Acquisition Research is an interdepartmental agency so deeply undercover that the President need not know of its existence, and may be briefed on information from it only on a case-by-case, need to know basis. Most of its operations and personnel are folded into NSA, which employs a huge number of us at the highest levels. EAR 'listens' to a broader domestic watch-list than ECHELON or even the new mobile MAUVE project, monitoring emails, telephone, fax, mail and other communications to stop threats to national security almost before they leave the originator's imagination. By partnering with GCHQ in the UK and Canada's National Research Council, we're able to keep a closer watch on the population as a whole through our allies, while sharing information gleaned on friendly countries' dangerous citizens without flagrantly violating their right to privacy." Cundieffe must've made a face, because Hoecker cracked a smile and added, "It's a derived right, Martin, not an explicitly guaranteed one." Still seeing doubt, he pressed further. "Listen, Martin, it was through EAR that they learned of the Mission's operations in Colombia, and of their imminent arrival in this country. I can't begin to tell you how many other plots have been neutralized through its judicious use, over the years."

Cundieffe nodded, solemnly, and said, "I understand. Please continue." His hands gripped the edge of the table and dug into the waxy finish on the oak boards, so intense was his feeling that he was rising out of his own skin.

"A week ago, all e-mail traffic from Heilige Berg stopped dead. Many at the Institute believe the group has either committed suicide, or was murdered, probably poisoned, by the Reverend Reuss or his lackeys."

"But you believe differently."

"We've done all kinds of analyses of the text and on Rev. Reuss's infrequent radio broadcasts. He's sociopathic, but not insane, stupid or cowardly, and he sure as hell isn't suicidal. He is, however, a very devious man, even for a cleric."

Cundieffe remembered. He had only to scan his memory for a sampling of Reuss's rhetoric, though it lay transcribed before him. "Deceit is a recurrent theme in his work, as a fight-fire-with-fire tactic. I seem to recall that he urged his followers to adopt a meek, poverty-stricken aspect, and hide their wealth in weapons and supplies." Hoecker nodded indulgently, so he went on, warming to the topic. "He also invoked an image of a lamb lying down and baring its pure white throat for the black wolves, only to draw them in to be slaughtered when they moved in for the kill. You think he's that far-gone?"

"We hoped you would know more, and could put this information to good use." He placed a Zip disk on the table before Cundieffe, and tapped it with one finger. "As a pretext, we've collected legitimately corroborated evidence of federal crimes committed, most notably transportation of stolen vehicles. An old favorite staple of FBI work, if I'm not mistaken."

"I fail to see what sticking the Department of Justice's head into a trap might do for the Institute or my own career, Mr. Hoecker. This sounds like a job for the local and state authorities."

Hoecker took hold of his plate as if he were about to leap up and get more salad, or brain Cundieffe with it. "They don't understand the situation. They're white middle class rural folks themselves. They don't see Heilige Berg as a danger, just a nuisance. We have reason to suspect that some local law enforcement may even have been involved, if only by accepting bribes. Of course, there's always the possibility they're genuinely sick…"

"Mr. Hoecker, how is this connected with the ongoing Mission investigation?"

"No, I'm not aware of any connection," Hoecker said, in a low, withdrawn tone. "What an odd thing to ask." Something even he couldn't discern in the way Hoecker held himself told him the Committee member was almost trying to make it clear he was *lying*. "The world is still a big place, Martin."

"At least tell me one thing, honestly, and for my own edification only. For the sake of building trust. Who is Dr. Cyril Keogh?"

Hoecker blinked. His nose wrinkled in disgust as if Cundieffe had looked at a priceless religious artifact and inquired as to its dollar value. But he said nothing.

"I've tried to look into his background, but there's nothing before ten years ago. He's not just funded by elements of the government, he's been created by them. Who was he before? Come on, Brady, one neutered mutant to another: what is he doing? What *is* he?"

Hoecker looked into his eyes for a long enough time to try to show that he was thinking about it, not just trying to invent a lie. Cundieffe could read lies on men and women like their bodies were trying to betray them, they stank of it. But Hoecker never flinched as he finally answered, "Martin, I don't know. I only know that nobody wants to know." He scooped up the files and slipped them back into his briefcase. Then, seeing the disk still on the table, he stuffed it into Cundieffe's inner breast pocket. "Are you at risk of getting lost? You could follow me back to the freeway, but I've got to stop at Ft. Meade for a briefing…"

Cundieffe got up to see him out, but caught himself on the edge of the table. Both his feet had gone to sleep. "I think I'll stay a few minutes more. You've given me a lot to think about."

"All right, then. Just so I can count on your discretion. You know where to reach me," he said over his shoulder as he left.

Cundieffe sat down and called the waitress over. His voice shook so badly that he had to repeat himself twice as he ordered a steak, rare. He took a single bite from it, spilled cash on the table, and ran.

Cundieffe found Assistant Director Wyler in his office. He ate lunch at his desk, picking over an assortment of fruit from the cafeteria as he glanced at a report. His bifocals rode precariously low on his long nose, giving his sallow watchmaker's face a grandfatherly cast Cundieffe found hard to look at and think at the same time.

Wyler's office gave precious little else on which to gaze for a respite, though he knew his discomfort was carefully cultivated, for it was Bureau tradition. The original Director's office was a model of Spartan plainness, excepting the raised dais on which his desk sat. His anteroom, however, was armored in plaques, honorary degrees, autographs and sundry awards, which spilled out into the hall. His subordinates were always a bit more restrained, but Wyler's office perpetually looked as if it was his first day. The bare, eggshell-colored walls were broken only by two narrow windows overlooking Pennsylvania Avenue and a single floor-to-ceiling bookcase. The spare décor gave a brittle tone to voices in the room, so one seemed to be either shouting or whispering.

Before Cundieffe could begin his story, Wyler regarded him with a tight grimace, like he'd just swallowed a very large pill. He knew.

"Sir," Cundieffe began, trying not to stammer, "I tried to call you—"

"Shut the damned door, Martin. I've just been reviewing the supplementary budget requests for the Counterterrorism Response Center."

Cundieffe closed his eyes hard as he turned to shut the door, grateful for the moment to collect his thoughts. How much did Wyler already know, and how much should he tell? He'd been unable to build a cover story. He found himself closing in on the conclusion that his meat-drunk gut had pressed home before he'd left the table. Whether or not Hoecker's far-fetched briefing was true or not, it was most likely a test of his ability to handle secret and illegally obtained information. Whom he trusted it with had to be as important as whom he didn't, but if he couldn't trust his sponsor in the Institute, whom could he trust?

Cundieffe's hand found the door and pushed it closed. He lingered with his back to AD Wyler until his superior said, "Martin, Brady Hoecker called me this morning to ask my permission to brief you on a matter of mutual interest."

Cundieffe turned and crossed the room almost at a gallop, took his seat and gripped the arms. "Is this how it's going to be?"

Wyler peeled off his bifocals and pushed aside his lunch. "Did Mr. Hoecker upset you in some way?"

"No, sir, but it was all very cryptic. I just never dreamed that our work was done in this fashion. He told me about this—"

"I don't need to know about the substance of the briefing," Wyler snapped, then, after two deep breaths, "Information passes to the most appropriate level for direct action, Martin."

"But sir, the—luncheon—did not pertain to my home field office in any way."

"You're not going back home." Wyler got out of his chair and came around his desk. "I've just gotten off the phone with Dunleavy in Los Angeles. Agent Hanchett will step into your post out there, and we'll create a new position for you here." Cundieffe looked up at him, studied him as he went to the windows.

The Assistant Director looked out onto Pennsylvania Avenue for a solid thirty seconds while Cundieffe chewed his tongue. "I guess you hadn't heard, I thought Hoecker might've told you. Maybe even he doesn't know yet. Officially, it's being reported as an accidental explosion, but we know that a probable Mission agent infiltrated the Level IV bioresearch labs at Ft. Detrick before dawn today, and revised the computer records on the Storch remains, rerouting them to be incinerated. While trying to escape, the agent killed six men and wounded nine more, then detonated an explosive, killing himself and eight more soldiers, scientists and technicians. He also got all the samples they'd already collected. They hope to have something to tell the media by tonight." Cundieffe didn't notice Wyler moving until the file the Assistant Director had been reading over lunch swam up into his vision. When his eyes snapped into focus, he felt his lunch rise.

A gutted corridor, the concrete walls buckled outwards, the ceiling collapsed, the floor littered with bits of soldiers, broken doctors. Someone in a containment suit peering down through the hole from the floor above.

Fourteen people dead on an American Army base, and not even a word of it at FBI headquarters, let alone the news. He'd hoped for something out of Ft. Detrick, where his own efforts had turned up nothing. The blood sample he'd collected from the crime scene had been destroyed at a molecular level, nothing more than a few unbroken shards of chromosomes mixed in with the liquefied cells. He concluded that the bullets that killed Storch were made of a solid chemical compound, which dissolved his body as they broke down inside him. Now there was nothing left to tell Cundieffe what Storch had become, let alone why.

"You see the situation we're in," Wyler said. "This is not nonlethal force, Martin. This isn't counting coup. I need your help here, but the Cave Institute apparently needs you more." To Cundieffe's baffled look, he added, "Brady Hoecker is a Committee member, and our highest representative in the NSA. If it's important enough for him to take the trouble to brief you, it's worth your utmost attention."

"Sir, I don't mean to second-guess you or the Institute—" he began, puzzling in his mind's eye over the snapshot of Hoecker denying any connection between Heilige Berg and the Mission. A polished ruse to make the distraction look more enticing? Or was it a distraction? "I just wish to reiterate my conviction that our primary objective is profiling the Mission's objectives, and the Mission's primary objective is Radiant Dawn. I think today's events only underscore that. The body of Sergeant Storch—"

"You have no path that will not end badly for yourself and the Bureau, if you can't separate facts from speculation. The Radiant Dawn village in California was an incidental target of opportunity for the Mission, a demonstration of force perpetrated upon people who were, for all intents and purposes, already dead. Storch was old business. Hoecker has given you a piece of work to do to prove yourself. Take care of it as quickly as you can, and then we'll discuss your role in investigating the Mission."

Cundieffe's voice was harsher than he would have liked, but he was too tired, too confused, to rein it in. "Sir, I must also add that I am very troubled by the seemingly steady flow of tainted leads stemming from unconstitutional abuses of government resources, and by the climate of secrecy which surrounds what I'd always understood to be a relatively transparent federal law enforcement agency. How will a case built by such methods stand against the Mission in a court of law?"

"Martin, you've been here less than a month, so feel free to exercise your naïve idealism when it suits you in polite society, but don't let it blind you to the real world. Secrecy works when it stays secret. The nation doesn't need to know one percent of the acts that have to be committed to protect their safety and their way of life. The world doesn't *want* to know what's happening to it as it grows beyond any sane population controls, doesn't want to see what it's pushing out of the dark as it spreads. My God, Martin, the things you're going to see—"

Cundieffe had gotten hold of himself. He thought so, anyway, until he heard what was coming out of his mouth. "The smoothness with which I'm being handled impresses me deeply, sir. The Institute doesn't want me to investigate the Mission, so I'm being fed clandestine busy-work. Knowing my penchant for secrets and exploiting my relative ignorance, they want me to go into the field and play spy without due process, acting on illegally acquired evidence. Is this a test? Is it even real, or is it some kind of maneuver?"

Wyler only stared at him. He pushed his bifocals up on his nose. Looking down at Cundieffe through their lenses, the Assistant Director's eyes were like glistening jellyfish.

"I suppose you'll know where I'm going when I've filed my travel expense vouchers, then," Cundieffe said and, rose from his chair. Wyler didn't call after him. He might have been invisible as he stalked out of the administrative suites on the fifth floor and down the stairs and out of the J. Edgar Hoover Building.

~ 12 ~

Nobody slept on the plane.

Storch sat and looked out the window at endless clouds, a frozen sea broken here and there by the ragged projecting teeth of what Storch guessed were probably the Rockies.

The other passengers sat and looked at him. The four Missionaries, all of them big bad former spook-soldiers, watching him like children watch the half-open closet door in their bedrooms when the lights go out. One sat across the aisle, two more a couple rows behind him, and the fourth, obviously the leader, stood at the head of the cabin, leaning on the locked door to the cockpit. He didn't look or act military, but he seemed softer than the others, his expression the most detached. CIA, maybe, or an egghead like Wittrock. Every so often, one of them would succumb to exhaustion and his head would roll back, and he would jolt awake with his hand on his sidearm. Storch admired that even this seemed to happen on an orderly rotation, as if even their sleep-rhythms were harnessed to unit integrity.

The man whose face he couldn't stop wearing had been a friend of theirs. No doubt they'd fought together, trusted each other with their lives. At least two of them, he could tell, hated him like poison because of that face.

They hadn't let him out of their sight for a moment in the eighteen hours since they'd unwittingly plucked him out of the mess he'd made of Ft. Detrick. At first, it had made him want to lash out. He'd never liked being stared at, and after the Gulf, peoples' eyes on him felt like fire ants. He understood now that it was not just sickness, but an autoimmune reaction to the stress of his body trying to change. Now that it could, he was afraid of what might happen if he let go for one instant. As the flight wore on, the jouncing shocks of battling weather systems rocking the plane like a cradle, he became grateful for the attention. If they were still just looking at him, he could tell that he wasn't changing again.

The dank recycled air of the plane was pregnant with the Missionaries' collective pressure to talk out of his presence, but they clung to the idea that four of them could subdue him, where two couldn't. He had not slept since he woke up on the slab in Ft. Detrick, unless you counted the catnap he took after Lt. Saticoy's suicide bomb went off under his nose.

The plane was a private twenty-seat passenger jet. The Missionaries escorted him up the stairs and into the cabin with their guns out, but dropped into their seats and picked up where they left off, staring at him, trying to figure out if he was their prisoner, or they were his. One of them, a big, pie-faced grunty type who could only have been a Marine in his old life, insisted on wearing a surgical mask around Storch, even though the others silently ragged his ass about it nonstop with subtle hand and face signals. It was too late, they all knew, to be careful. If Storch was a disease, they had all been exposed. He did nothing to dispel their fears.

They whispered to each other whenever one got up to pace, threw hand signs the rest of the time, suspecting, quite rightly, that he could hear them, but clinging absurdly to silence. He was careful not to learn their names or look to long at their faces, because he would not want to remember them if this ended badly.

In the air, they loosened up, gave him his fill of waterlogged deli sandwiches from an ice chest. They tasted like Play-Doh, but he wolfed down eight of them, feeling his body burning them up and fixing him. They watched him a little more laxly, so he could tell the food was drugged, but it made no difference.

He was shocked to discover that he was in quite a lot of pain, but he'd been too weak to notice before. In moments the pain went away as he made his own painkillers, endorphins coursing down his spine like sunlight. He let his eyes close, and his jaw unclenched for what felt like the first time in years. His body ached as if he'd had open-heart surgery, and itched maddeningly as his skin grew back. He felt himself going slack, slipping away and not caring what they did with him, or where they were going.

They went berserk, pointing their guns at him and screaming at him to sit down and *stop it*. His window was a black mirror. He didn't look like Saticoy, anymore. The olive pigment fled his skin, which became an ugly, marbled purple and bluish white where shattered capillaries and deep tissue trauma were dissolving. He still didn't recognize the face that glared at him. It was a mask of wet clay, streaming and twitching and becoming someone else.

Ignoring their panic, their guns, Storch bolted to the restroom, where he suffered and savored his first bowel movement in two weeks. His mind ran in circles, saying his name, telling him his life to keep hold of himself. He heard the distinctly alien clink of metal at one point, and, rising to take a peek, observed no less than five 7.62 millimeter rifle slugs embedded in his stools.

He avoided the stainless steel mirror on the door until he had to look at it to get out. He froze, his fist raised up at the strange reflection.

"Is that you?" his reflection asked him. His face still looked like a mask made of roadkill, but it was his face. His eyes were not gray or brown, but gold-flecked green. His scalp was already blue with a new crop of his own black hair pushing up through burn scabs like filthy snow. His nose was cocked a few degrees off center where he'd broken it when he was fourteen. His body remembered. *His body lied...*

Thoughts, crazy, unworthy thoughts, flooded him. He was dreaming, he was the reflection trapped in the mirror. His eyes turning gray, his hair going white, his teeth long and crooked, smiling Keogh, and he was falling back—

Stop it

"Where the hell've you been?" he asked his reflection, flinching at the sound of his own voice. The harrowed face in the mirror looked even worse than he felt.

Storch went back to his seat, the agents backing up the aisle from where they'd been camping out beside the lavatory. He touched his face— *his* face—and then looked at his hands. His left thumb had been gone for nine years, he'd gotten used to having a reptilian paw, but now it was whole. His resurrected thumb traced the crooked contours of his nose. That had not healed, or rather, it had grown back the way he remembered it. Why not? He'd become Corporal Wynorski and Lieutenant Saticoy completely enough to fool their comrades, without even trying, without even *knowing*. His own face was only one more mask, now, and he could trust it no more than he could anyone else.

He'd thought he'd hit bottom when they took away his life and his home. Again, when they coerced him to do horrible things, and showed him still more horrible things. And again, when he lost control over his mind and his body, yet still could not die. Now, he was free. No more voices in his head, no more blackouts. But now his own body had become a survival machine he couldn't control, a species of one, like the monsters in Spike Team Texas. There was no one at the controls that he could see, and he was afraid to look any deeper.

What's still mine? What's still me?

He knew that he was letting it happen. He was going insane. Like his father, and that was the next step to becoming just like Dyson, Avery and Holroyd. He knew it, but he couldn't stop it, indeed he almost couldn't wait for it to happen, because when he lost the power to reason, to remember, he would be truly free. Whoever picked him for this fate just should've known better.

The plane touched down on a plowed private airstrip surrounded by pine trees and snow-streaked blackness. Watching one of them reset his watch, he confirmed that they were on Mountain time. Biting subzero wind blasted in the open doorway. His ears pop pop popped, his jaw clamped. He felt light-headed, tingly, starved for air. Colorado, maybe Utah.

The area had been cleared of all but a few perimeter guards in civilian winter gear. With two agents before and two behind, Storch climbed down from the plane and crossed the runway to a van, while the pilot met with the ground crew to secure the plane.

The driver was one of them, much older, but not officer material. He climbed out of the van when he saw Storch coming with them, backed away with his hands up. When one of the agents from the plane approached him, he turned and ran. The masked Marine drove.

The airstrip was far from any signs of habitation, and they skirted any as they drove out. Storch saw a road sign indicating that they were on the 127, and that the town of Gunnison was three miles away. Another sign marked the boundary of the Blue Mesa Indian reservation. They turned onto another highway, the 135, headed north, towards Crested Butte and a long list of ski resorts.

Nobody seemed to care that he was watching their route. He knew they'd argued about it, but in the end none of them was dumb enough to try to blindfold him. They seemed evenly split between being more confident and more nervous as they got closer to home. He wondered how much headquarters knew about what they were bringing back. He watched the terrain roll by, touching his face every so often. Scratching his scalp, tracing the crook in his nose, over and over.

The van turned off the state road and meandered down a narrow valley with a plaque welcoming them to the Gunnison National Forest. They stopped twice to take down heavy chain barricades across the unpaved fire road. The snow outside was waist-deep. He saw them signal someone in the woods each time they got out, but it was still too dark to make anything out.

They could be hiding an army here. How big could the Mission be?

"We need to talk," Storch finally said. Nobody responded. He stood up and before anyone had reacted, he was right behind the masked Marine with his arm around the thick, stubby neck, and he said, "Stop."

The van bucked and lurched into the first stages of a front wheel stand, and everyone but Storch tumbled forward. A gun went off once, a back window exploded, but everyone checked out okay.

"What's up ahead?"

The obvious officer in the group bit his lip and looked thoughtful, while the others just stared. "You're expected," he said, in a soothing hostage negotiator's voice. "You know as much as we do, beyond that. Nobody wants trouble, but if you've come to start some, friend, you won't go away disappointed."

"My name is Sergeant Zane Ezekiel Storch, Fifth Special Forces Group. I served in the Gulf War."

"We know," another one put in. "We were detailed to kill you."

He looked hard at them, let go of the masked Marine. "I don't want trouble. I just want to know some things. You got a cellular phone?"

The brains shook his head. "They don't work here. We've got a CB."

"Use it. Tell your friends to behave. If I'm fucked with, you don't want to know what I'm capable of." *And neither do I.*

The van crept higher and deeper into the forest, taking more forks than Storch could keep track of, within a few miles of the first turnoff. As dawn peaked over the Divide, they pulled up at a dead end abutting a huge palisade of snow.

Even with the thick winter coat, Storch could recognize the signs of a mining operation. The face of the mountainside before them was dynamited away to a sheer wall, and the shape of the palisade suggested it was made of the earthen tailings from a shaft. The agents backed away from the van to give themselves room as Storch stepped out. Fresh powder squeaked underfoot, and he sank in up to his knees. The agents waved him forward, but he stood his ground, and they finally started crab-walking sideways over the palisade. He followed them, eyes going in all directions until he thought he might be growing new ones.

He stopped at the top, looking back over his shoulder at the first rays of dawn through the warring clouds smeared across the horizon. How long had it been since he'd seen a sunrise? Not since RADIANT, at least.

The leader and the masked Marine stood on a concrete plug just inside the mouth of a condemned mine shaft. The vertical shaft had been filled in, he remembered they did this with some dangerous mines in Death Valley. The other two agents passed him, headed back to the truck.

Storch stopped. "We're all going down," he said.

"Somebody's got to move the truck," one of them answered, clambering back up the crumbling palisade. "We're exposed up here."

He didn't like having them at his back, but the leader beckoned to him, and he cautiously approached, looking around, taking in the crackle of melting ice in the trees, the rustle and reek of the agents' bodies in their stale clothes, the piercing purity of the frozen mountain air. He breathed in the gelid cold, exhaled clouds, let his fear wash out as the first faint tracers of daylight began to warm and feed him. *If I'm about to get killed for real this time*, he thought, feeling stupid but thinking it anyway, *thank you for this.*

Storch stepped onto the concrete, and almost immediately, it began to sink into the shaft. The officer blandly played tour guide. "This was a silver mine, until it was condemned around 1930. It was renovated by the National Forestry Service in the sixties as part of a special project. But they abandoned it, too."

"What kind of project?"

"You'll see."

Storch guessed they'd descended about forty feet when the elevator jolted to a stop. Before them, a massive steel door was set a foot deep in the concrete, a placard at eye-level: NATIONAL FORESTRY SERVICE RESEARCH STATION NO.7. Looking up, Storch felt as if he were standing at the bottom of a missile silo. A hatch had closed over their heads when they went down the shaft, so there was only a cone of shadow, where he'd hoped to see some fleeting trace of the dawn.

He didn't need to watch the agents. He could feel them filling up the space around him. They vibrated with nervous tension, but didn't move. The officer said, "Before you go getting any stupid ideas, we're all expendable. You won't get a damned thing for us."

"We know how to fix your kind, now," the masked Marine added. "Fucking mutant."

"Shut up, Brewer," the officer said. To Storch, he said, without a trace of irony, "My name's Seybold, Roger Seybold. I used to—"

"I don't give a shit who you used to be," Storch growled, profoundly tired of head games, and *hungry.* He was starting to get hot again, starting to itch all over, and if he didn't eat something soon…

The steel door slid back into the wall and they shuffled into a cramped white-tiled airlock. Showerheads all over the ceiling, firehoses plugged into the walls. At knee-height, the walls swelled inward to form narrow benches, and the floor was ribbed with drain-grates. Another airlock door faced them, and through a window set into it, a wizened face peeked at them. The eyebrows, so thick and tangled, the eyes like brass buttons. The hair so unnaturally black it looked like vinyl, or licorice ropes, but Storch was perversely glad to see he had a lot less of it than the last time they'd met.

"Well I'll be damned," Dr. Wittrock said. "The missing link."

Storch planted his feet on the ribbed tile floor, locked his arms at his sides.

The outer door closed behind them, and Storch's ears popped again. Brewer's eyes got huge above his mask, his big arms wrapped tightly around himself. Seybold backed up into a corner, looking up warily at the showerheads.

Wittrock, watching them, licked his thin lips, seeing specimens. "You've caused us trouble, Sgt. Storch. I wonder if you've come to make amends, or wreak more havoc?"

Brewer was praying. Spittle soaked through his mask. Seybold sat on a bench and cradled his head in his hands.

"And I wonder if your operation could possibly have failed more decisively than it did, Roger. You're almost certainly infected, all of you. Why did you risk it? Whose side are you on?"

"Just do it, asshole!" Brewer roared. He charged the window and smashed it with his fist. Wittrock didn't flinch. Brewer's hand crackled, he let out a pain-maddened howl and kicked the door. "Burn us now! He's *one of them!* He fucking *ate* Coy, and stole his fucking face!"

Seybold ordered him to stand down, shoved him back into a bench. "I don't think we're infected with anything, Calvin."

The showerheads hissed and spat mist the color of Windex. Brewer roared, "Motherfucker!" and rolled up into a fetal ball on the bench. Seybold cringed, but seemed to accept his fate.

Storch stood tall under the chemical rain. It burned, cut runnels of searing agony where his skin was still scabbed over, which was damn near everywhere, but he refused to move a muscle. If it melted them all, so be it.

Wittrock watched.

After a long minute, Seybold stood up and made a bowl of his hands, splashed his face with the blue-green fluid. Brewer ripped his mask off and gasped for air. "It's just a fucking shower…"

The spray cut off. The drains gurgled and glubbed. Storch looked at his hands. The flesh, cracked and roughened, stained a mild blue where the cuts were deepest. Only a shower.

"Open the door," Storch said. "I just want some answers."

"And we have so many questions for you," Wittrock said, backing out of sight. A heartbeat later, the door opened.

~ 13 ~

There was nothing quite like the sound of snow falling in the mountains. To hear it, you had to stand utterly still, within and without, until every last molecule froze in its orbit, but the exercise instilled a tranquility so profound that Stella Orozco began to believe she'd reached escape velocity and left behind the dreadful tug of her old life forever. Standing alone out in the center of the open field in front of the medical center, Stella learned to hold her breath and her heart so still that she could eavesdrop on the uneasy sleep of the tectonic plates beneath her feet, and hear the stealthy turning of the earth itself.

In the winter morning, the rarified light of the sun struck the ice-bound air like a god's-hair bow on great, hydrogen strings. She heard music, a celestial whale-song that contained the roots of all the great symphonies, of all the songs that human beings had plucked out of the aether for their mysterious capacity to make the listener weep. Stella wept, herself, when all these sounds brought home to her how blind she'd been to life, and how blessed she was, now.

It was a stillness even God dared not break into, and for that she was most grateful.

From the moment she'd broken down in the cafeteria, she'd lost her old instincts for repression and bitterness. The people here were kind to her, as kind as they'd been in Bishop, but they knew the worst of her, and loved her still. When she slipped and unsheathed her verbal claws now and again, they were forgiving, they understood. It made no difference that He was behind all their eyes, as He was behind her own. For a long while after her first breakthrough, He was completely silent. She began to talk about her life. Babbling to Dr. Echeverria, to the children who came to the clinic for minor injuries they often invented in order to get sweets. She apologized, babbling even more, but they understood. Even the children, with their wizened, hell-and-back gazes, accepted her life, folded her pain in with their own and took it away, left in its place laughter and love.

When she looked at herself in the mirror at the end of that first day, she was startled by how her face had changed. The scowl lines carved into her face, along her mouth and between her eyes, the swells of stress-clenched muscle at her jawline: all gone. For a second, she'd gone electric with rage, as if someone had erased her birth certificate, had negated *her*. And in that flicker of anger, her old, fierce face had materialized, and she frightened herself away from mirrors for a while.

That night, a big silver bus came and delivered fifty-two terminal cancer patients. A platoon of residents came streaming out into the driving icy wind as to a family reunion, pushing wheelchairs, brandishing extra blankets and big, broad smiles.

The passengers pressed against the glass eagerly, those who could rise from their gurneys. Sunken, sallow death-masks, spidery, clawed hands fluttered behind the fogged glass as the loading doors were thrown open and three wheelchair ramps unfurled.

Stella froze on the front steps, overwhelmed. She hugged herself in shame. Each of them had suffered far more than she had. When she was changed, the tumor in her liver had been of sufficient mass and strategic location to seal her doom, but had only begun to spread and leach away her vitality, and she had refused treatments that would have ravaged her at least as badly as her disease. These people had come in the last hours of a losing battle that had hollowed them out, left them so wasted that the subtle glow of their naked souls shone behind their yellow eyes and through the eggshell smoothness of their skulls, like a feeble flame guttering in a paper lantern. So frail and shrunken were they that she couldn't tell the children from many of the adults, and there were so many children, with not a healthy loved one among them to hold their hands.

They glowed now, as three by three they were carefully rolled down the ramps and across the salted parking lot to the medical center entrance. Glowed like blessed pilgrims at the steps of Lourdes, glowed with faith and hope and awe. Stella felt a warmth growing in her, and she let herself smile. Their faith would not be dashed by an indifferent God, here. If the miracle of this place was more than anyone bargained for, if it was a pact with a different order of soul-collector altogether, where was God to put a stop to it? It worked.

The other residents moved in a well-drilled procedure, no one giving orders or faltering, flowing around her like a human tide. When she let go of her brooding, she found her body knew where to take her. She followed herself onto the bus and down the aisle to the back, where Dr. Echeverria checked the vitals of a young Asian girl pressed against a window. His face was knitted in concentration, and when she got closer, Stella could understand why. The girl's throat was obscured by malignant wattles, pendulous masses the Doctor had to palpate aggressively for several minutes before he stood and shook his head. "A few minutes more and she would have made it," he said.

Stella was shaken, despite herself. The still, waxen face looked like the flesh of a dehydrated apple, but the eyes still stared out the window. Stella understood all too well the determination that had etched itself in the dead girl's gaze. "I'll get a corpsman. Is there—do we have a morgue here?"

Dr. Echeverria looked at her gravely. "Just get a gurney for her, please."

She picked her way carefully across the lot to the breezeway, where a convoy of gurneys was parked just alongside the double doors to the reception hall. Through the glass, she saw her fellow residents arranging the pilgrims on burgundy vinyl couches in the huge solarium. The ceiling of the room reached up through the building to a skylight built into the roof. Up on the third floor balcony, she spied a few children peeking over the rails, sly smiles and glittering gray eyes. They spotted her and ducked down, but their mischievous giggles echoed through the vast open space. She looked up through the skylight, saw only a black rooftop of clouds.

She grabbed the gurney and hurried back. All of the other passengers had been unloaded, and Dr. Echeverria waited patiently for her, seated beside the dead girl as if he were only waiting for her to wake up. She clamped her nose shut against the medicine smells, the sickness smell, as she and the Doctor gently lifted her body, so light it almost floated out of their hands, and laid her on the gurney. Stella cinched a strap across her midsection and laid a wool blanket over her, but Dr. Echeverria stopped her when she went to drape it over her face.

"Put her in with the others, Nurse Orozco."

"But she's—dead."

"You have a lot to learn about how we practice medicine, up here, Nurse Orozco. Cellular activity goes on for hours after death, in some parts of the body, for days. Her cancer is still viable."

Stella touched the girl's hand, splayed out across her concave chest. It was as cold as the window she'd been looking out of when she died. What could be left of her? Only her cancer was still alive in her, greedily sucking up the last dredges of life left in her sad husk long after the world had stolen away her breath, her heat. What would rise from this deathbed, when the light touched her, when she ascended the Moon Ladder?

She pushed the gurney down a ramp and across the lot, but her eyes were on the sky until she passed inside. The residents had finished arranging the pilgrims on their couches, filling less than half of them. With hand pats, hugs and whispered assurances, the residents retreated back into the bowels of the center. A hush fell over the solarium, broken only by those who breathed with mechanical assistance, and quiet prayers.

Dr. Echeverria took her by the shoulders and steered her back down the ramp leading to the underground quarters. "It isn't healthy, getting repeated exposures," he said. "We'll come back and see to any who need assistance, but for now, we'll leave them to it."

They waited in the cafeteria, drinking juice and talking in hushed, excited voices. The mood was not unlike that of an emergency room lounge, where people reflect on miracles and on the arbitrary cruelty of God. But it was much more than that. They were like adults who truly believed in Santa Claus, in the healing hand of God, because they'd seen it at work. They'd done all they could. Now it was in His hands—

She wanted to go up and see it now, see it reach down and touch them as it had touched her. As He had entered her. But she knew without asking that it was out of the question, as was her going out into the woods to watch from outside. She burned to see it again, to know what it did to them.

After an interminable hour, they all rose and walked into their quarters, while the medical staff veered off and went back up the ramp. Stella followed them, anxious to see, but they went on up the stairs to the staff rooms on the second floor. Stella stopped, looking around the reception room. All the lights had gone out, and the gloom above was heavier than ever, the forms on the couches only humps of deeper shadow. The room pulsed with the shuddery breaths of the dying. Was it a sham?

The breathing became *breath*, a singular oceanic current reverberating in the suddenly tiny solarium. Stella felt it seeping into her, and she broke down in tears again, goddamit.

She woke the next morning to the sound of trucks. She went to the window just as the last of them rolled out of the lot and crossed the bridge. Refrigerated freight trucks. She remembered them well from days in the field in the Central Valley, just downwind from the monstrous Harris Ranch, which the wittier Anglo farm employees called Cowshwitz. They hauled meat from the slaughterhouses. These ones were forest green, with a white logo of a cross on a stylized mountain peak. Heilige Berg Farms, it said on the side.

The bus still stood at the far end of the lot.

"What's going on?" she asked, but He was nowhere to be found.

She dressed and ran downstairs, certain that something was wrong, and if she didn't hurry, she wouldn't catch them in their lie, and—

She stopped where the stairs spilled out into the central reception area. Faint liquid sunlight brought the colorful room into achingly bright focus. The trucks hadn't taken them away. They were all here, silent and still as death on the couches. The odorless mountain air carried ribbons of fetid charnel reek past her face.

She looked around at the bodies, all of them blackened and swelled and so very badly decomposed that she wondered how long she must have slept. She heard no breathing, saw none of them stir.

Her scream rose up to the skylight.

Dr. Echeverria peered over the balcony at her. His head bobbed as he went down the stairs.

"What's wrong with them?" she screamed. "Is this your miracle? *They're all dead!*"

The Doctor ran then, took the last five steps in a bound that his plump, low-slung body might've found impossible in his old life. He ran up to her, took her arms, looking spooked. He should've been breathing hard.

"What are you talking about?"

"It didn't work! Look around you! They're—" She choked on a hurtful sob. Another thing she believed in gone to rot—or was it her presence, her curse, that killed them?

He only studied her with that blank, weighing look that told her He was behind those eyes. "This is all part of it, Nurse Orozco. Think of the old body as a womb, and the cancer the fetus, gestating, but shapeless, until they come here. Then the body feeds the cancer, using itself up to give the new body life."

Stella looked around. She still saw only death. She was reminded of the ghastly video walkthrough of the Heaven's Gate mass suicide in San Diego. The ranks of peaceful, purple-shrouded bodies, the occasional exposed, green-gray hand, clutching a roll of quarters. Waiting for a cosmic transformation that passed them by. Would He allow himself to see if something had gone wrong? Was He insane?

She covered her eyes and tried not to cry again.

Something stirred.

A ripe tearing sound cleaved the tomb-like quiet, and when she turned, she saw Seth Napier all over again. The old derelict splitting open, disgorging a new Stephen into the world.

The dead Asian girl sat up on her couch, still shedding the last scraps of dying, benign flesh. Glowing so brightly Stella expected her to unfold great, jeweled butterfly wings. "Please," she said, "can I have a glass of water...Stella?"

And that was when Stella went out to listen to the snowfall.

She could only hold her body and mind still for so long, and almost before she found her quiet center, her anger began to clamor for a voice.

One good thing about His presence. She would never want for someone to argue with.

It's not right, she thought, in a loud inner voice she hoped would rouse Him. People aren't meant to live forever.

Nearly half of those who ascended last night were children, Stella. Are you saying they deserved to die?

You know what I mean. Immortality isn't what we're meant for. Who are we to say who gets to live forever?

I would turn none away. In the fullness of time, all will be called to ascend. You know that.

She kicked at the snow angrily. If He could read her thoughts, if He lived in there, why did He make her spell everything out, if not to torture her?

She scanned the edges of the field, restless. There weren't too many places to go. Only a few hundred yards from the medical center, the road crossed a bridge over the frozen river gorge and disappeared behind a ridge. Behind the center, the mountain redoubled its vertical aggression in a rumpled pile of peaks that defied casual hiking. Likewise the downhill slope: an old logging road wound down the steep face of the edge of the plateau, but it became a forbidding tunnel through icy forest just beyond the edge of the field. Stella headed for the bridge.

As if to distract Him, she took up the internal argument. Nobody would turn you down, because people are selfish. Everyone thinks they deserve to live forever, but the world is for those unborn, too. If nobody dies, the world will be overrun in a few decades, and even if you stop people from having babies, then the world grows old and insane...

There will always be room for new life, Stella. Women will conceive when they wish it, with or without a man. So will men, if they desire. But all in accordance with the needs of the whole.

She made better time once she plodded out of the field of powder and onto the plowed roadway. She skidded along in her heavy boots, puffing like a locomotive.

Most human beings imagine living forever, but few will want to live on much beyond their ordinary span. You'd be surprised, Stella, what a weight a lifetime carries. After a time, one senses that the world has passed them by, and simply has to lay down and go to sleep, perhaps never to wake up. This, too, is natural.

She paused at the bridgehead. The road beyond the bridge scaled the opposing cliff-face in three switchbacks, then went over the ridge. She had no idea what was on the other side.

You decide who lives, and for how long. You decide how we change, how we live, how we breed. Your bodies, your thoughts, your world.

She spotted a man at the top of the ridge. He had his back to her, but she could tell he was a soldier. He wore fatigues and a heavy armored vest, and his head was shaved under a camo-netted helmet. He held an outlandishly long rifle at his shoulder, and seemed to be surveying the other side through its scope. She picked up her pace without quite knowing why.

There had been a man, a soldier. She couldn't recall his name, nor could she remember if she'd ever known it. He was at the Mission bunker at the end, and was probably dead, but suddenly, she remembered that she'd hoped to see him here. What was his name? It was no use. But he refused to be completely forgotten, even if he had no place that he fit into her memories. His scent, the way he'd looked at her, once, the way he'd called her name, not her first name, he was very polite, though they were in dire trouble, the way they'd almost touched, when the light—

She crossed the bridge, trying to penetrate the fog in her brain, even as the soldier on the ridge drew nearer. She started to climb the first precipitous turn of the road, when she caught a sharp tang on the wind. A stink of dead flesh and sweat and rancid blood; a carnivore's lair.

The soldier on the ridge turned to look at her.

She could not remember the name of the man she'd thought he was, but she knew the instant she saw his eyes that this was not him. In that instant, she knew she would be very sorry she hadn't stayed inside, this beautiful morning, but her feet kept carrying her nearer. She felt as if she had to blink and blink again to keep the fog in the back of her memory from drawing shut over her eyes.

"Halt!" the soldier bellowed, and charged down the almost sheer drop to the switchback above the one she stood on. He swung the huge rifle around to bear on her. The scope on it was a giant hourglass, the barrel longer than her leg and almost wide enough to fit three fingers in, if she were foolish enough to reach out and touch it.

The soldier behind it was every bit as lethal, with none of the weapon's sleek grace. He stood two feet taller than her, built like a marathon runner, skeleton wrapped in taut bundles of wiry muscle and sinew twitching with the voltage shooting through them. His skin had the blasted, pitted look of metamorphic rock, his face all slashing angles and concave planes, like a kidskin bag of steak knives. His eyes glinted flatly like verdigris on old, copper pennies. Stress-fracture lines in his face deepened in what the soldier probably thought passed for a smile. He slung the rifle onto his shoulder.

He was so clean-scrubbed, his faded olive drab uniform so ruthlessly spotless, that she wondered where the death-stench came from. Then he opened his mouth. "You lost, little lady?"

She backed away, the ice turning to wet cement underfoot, sucking her under when she tried to tear her gaze away from his.

"Don't run away, sweetheart," he tried to purr, but raw menace stole into his voice, and the death on his breath seemed to turn even sourer. "I could look at you all day, but time's tight." He was almost out of charm, already. "Come up and see the view."

She noticed then that his breath didn't fog. When she could not avoid it touching her face, it was colder than the north wind, and probably left a stain.

She felt his hand on her arm almost before she saw him leap down to stand beside her. His fingers cut into the meat of her right biceps, dragged her off her frozen feet so that she staggered into him. His flak vest slipped open when she brushed against it. She saw dog tags and a necklace of black lumps strung on a leather thong. She held her breath and swore in Spanish, tried to pull away.

They were human ears.

"Come on squaw-bitch, I got something to show you."

She planted her feet resolutely on the roadway, but he took no notice, yanked her clean off her feet and sprinted up the vertical ridge. Stella hung by his clawed fist, her boots only banging against the rock as it rushed past. The wind rushed in her ears, but she could hear her screams echoing down the mountain.

Where are you, Guardian Angel?

He stopped atop a knob of granite, still dangling her by her arm over the gorge. Chuckling, he whipped her around, flying her like a kite on the vicious updrafts. She bit through her lip not screaming for him. In his rage, he shook her, once, twice, dropped her on the rocks at his feet.

She tucked and rolled faster than thought and landed on hands and knees. Her fingertips tore into crevices on the rock, caught her before she fell off. Her brain was still spinning, her stomach rebelled and flushed her mouth with acid. She caught her breath and licked her bleeding lip, took advantage of the moment to look around.

The road wound around their vantage point and disappeared at once into the trees. By the seam that ran down between their peak and the next, she thought there might be a road that met theirs, and about a mile down the mountain, she saw one emerge from the forest and swing out onto the lip of a promontory overlooking the river gorge. Beyond that, everything was veiled in whiteout. She could see no other sign of civilization—no, wait, she saw a pillar of blue-black smoke just beyond the bend in the road. Someone else was here, a mere mile away. Someone human—

"Look at me, squaw." She heard the crisp rustling of his canvas vest, and an awful ripping sound that seemed to go on for minutes. A sound of metal teeth gnashing, and the smell got much worse. A zipper.

"Look at me."

He won't let this happen. He mustn't.

As Stella turned to look, she wasn't seeing, she was remembering, peering back into all the places where she'd tried to lose bad memories, all the dark corners of her childhood in the fields and foster homes that could only drive her insane. And no, she saw when she came to the end, no, she'd never been raped. Touched inappropriately once or twice, but no more, and she'd made them sorry they tried that much. And no, she'd never been with a man the way women coupled in romance novels, all sighs and sweet passion. She fucked a few boys she thought she liked in high school and college, and never understood what all the fuss was. She'd thought he was someone else...

She looked.

The soldier stood over her with his legs akimbo and pants unfastened. His uncircumcised penis hung down to his knees, an elephantine cartoon cock that only a perverse thirteen year-old God would curse a man with. It looked even more ridiculous and repulsive hanging from his stripped-down, skeletal frame. He watched her, petrified but for a rhythmic facial tic that wracked the right side of his face.

Stella felt his pulse, a pulsating tremor in the rock, through her ragged fingertips.

She bit her lip again, this time to keep from laughing. It was so fucking pathetic! He thought this would make her swoon, this caveman monster-meat tryst on a mountaintop? "My, your *real* prick must've been like a baby's pinkie-finger."

"What?"

"Well, why else would you overcompensate like that? Big gun, big dick, big fucking deal."

He sputtered, "Hog-bitch..." and his penis swelled, flushed livid red, like an octopus bluffing a predator. It reared up and lunged at her of its own accord. Stella recoiled with a gasp of disgust, barely caught herself on the edge again. There was nowhere to go but down, no way to get there but jumping.

He won't let this—

"Tried to be nice—"

The cock got bigger, darker. A ring of barbed horns broke out from under the hood of its foreskin, and serrated blades like the teeth of a cheese-grater broke out all down the shaft. Black-red segmented worms wriggled out of his urethra and tasted the air for her scent.

She tried not to throw up, made herself look him in the eye. "Bet your shriveled little balls don't even work." She looked around her again, which way to jump, because *He wasn't coming to save her.*

The mutant soldier gagged and winced as the transformation took its toll. Clouds of steam vented off his livid skin. Pebbles and melting snowflakes danced around his feet to the thunderous beat of his heart. She could feel the pulse in her fingers and feet, could see the arteries writhing under his snare drum-taut skin. "I want her," he moaned. "Give her to me."

She backed up as far as she could, looking around desperately. Who was he talking to?

He was shouting at her. At Him.

"Take her over! Give me the bitch!"

Her blood curdled. Her knees went rubbery, and the fog threatened to come back, but now she knew what it was, she fought it for her life.

Where are you, motherfucker? Where are you, goddamit?

She closed her eyes and jumped.

He roared. She heard the air torn apart by his arms as they swept out to catch her a millisecond after her feet left the rock. His claws in her fluttering hair, he caught her, queered her flight, tore out a double-handful at the roots. She twisted in air and kicked off the ledge, making a missile of herself and reaching out into the winter wind—

The bridge rushed up double-time underneath, her legs splayed out to take the impact, but her ankles still rang big silver bells of agony and she stumbled, skinned her knee.

She wanted to run. Her feet wanted to fly her right off this goddamned mountain, take her back to Bishop, hell, back to Mexico. But she stood rooted to the spot. Her voice was coming out of her mouth, but the soldier seemed to know it wasn't her talking.

"This woman is one of our core reception medical staff. She's a valued guest, and an integral part of our team. And she doesn't like to be touched, Sergeant Avery."

Avery looked down at her. His pants were zipped back up, his vest snapped up to cover his trophies. He was silent, but for the tiny sizzling of snow melting under his boots. "It never happened, sir." He snapped a salute and turned away, loped down the other side and out of sight.

Stella ran back, her mind all jagged red rage, pointed inwards at Him.

He and others like him were early experiments. They ascended, but were never programmed. They are not of our mind.

Hot tears froze on her face, the fog from her heaving breath blinded her as she raced across the bridge.

God damn you! You were going to let him rape me! You tried to take over my body—

I never try anything, Stella.

What kind of God would you be, without a few pet devils...?

They are monsters, Stella. Without a human form, without guidance, they have gone insane, in body and mind. But I would turn none away. They also serve.

How many sacrifices does it take to keep him in line?

He's never harmed one of us. You made him angry.

I'll kill him if I ever see him again.

I don't doubt you'd try.

She stopped on the front steps of the reception center. She stood stock-still, marveling at her heart rate downshifting, at fatigue poisons burning away in her muscles. She wondered if her blood still used iron to bind oxygen; even in the mountains, she never ran out of breath, never got a cramp. Her fingers ached, but the torn skin was already closed over. Her snow pants were ripped over her knee, but she could find no injury at all, there. Her scalp was already mending, as well. She felt a few days' growth of new hair already sprouting where it'd been torn out. She stretched her arms up to the morning sky, reveling in her new body, as she pushed the ugly memory of Sergeant Avery into the fog. He helped her.

This is the order I give to the world. This is the reason I would impose upon you, my children, that your sleeping flesh does not beget monsters. You will never age, never sicken, never know fear or confusion or madness, ever again.

He tweaked her endorphins, teased her nerves so that the world rushed up in all its glory as she'd never perceived it before. She saw the muted glow of the forest, and felt Him in the trees, in the frozen soil, felt Him spreading out into the world. She saw the coruscating lattice of cosmic rays in which the sun bathed the earth, the raw catalyst of her transformation, her ascent to divinity. She went down on her knees and hugged herself for joy.

Are you grateful?

Oh, yes, she wept. Oh, thank you, God.

~ 14 ~

Storch sorely regretted stepping through the door.

He was in another cage, clear plastic panels, but the room beyond was so dark he could not see the walls, only the men who backed away from the barrier as he entered. The steel door slammed shut behind him. Seybold and Brewer safe behind the airlock.

He recognized none of the men on the other side. A short, wiry Latino officer, two non-coms in alpine camouflage, and a pale, labcoated manikin with white, ropy dreadlocks spilling down to the small of his back. He didn't see Wittrock anywhere.

There were more cages on either side of his, and the one on the right was occupied. The other prisoner approached the plastic wall between them. It was a naked man, middle-aged, sagging, flabby torso covered in downy gray hair. His lips moved silently, but when Storch looked at him, he could almost hear the words pouring into his head, pouring out of those unblinking gray eyes. Storch backed away, into the center of the cell.

A speaker on the ceiling of his cell crackled. "What are we going to do with you, Sgt. Storch?"

"Let me out of this fucking cage," he growled. His skin crawled. Neck prickled, muscles strained and burned. He felt hot and weak, but knew it wouldn't last. He was changing again.

"Can't do that," the officer replied. "You're not one of us, any more. Even if you were, your arrival is something of a bad omen."

"I'm not here to hurt anybody. I want—" his eyes skating back to the Keogh pressed against the wall, "—I want to know what's really going on."

"You understand the position we're in," the officer said. "This wouldn't be the first time men have come back from the field more than what they seemed. Your neighbor there is an infiltrator." The officer pressed a button.

"—Thought we'd lost you, Zane. What have they done to you? We need you, Zane, now more than ever. Was it ever as clear to you, as now? They hate you for what you are, because they know, even now, you can destroy them—"

"He seems to know you."

The prisoner's eyes flashed, mercurial sclera catching the dim light of the cavern. Under his husky, rambling voice, Storch felt an almost subsonic ululation, faster than words or thought, speaking to him in an eons-dead language that still echoed in his cells.

Storch clung to himself to keep from hurling his body at the prisoner. He tore his eyes away from the gaze of Cyril Keogh. Behind his jailers, he could make out monitor screens—cameras trained on him, measuring his heat output, red-white plumes around him like a volcanic halo. "He's not in me," he tried to explain. "He's dead—in here. You killed him."

"We understand so very little of the process," the dreadlocked scientist said. "Enlighten us."

The officer pushed another button on the console beside him. A Christmas string of warning lights blinked and winked. Green, heavier-than-air clouds of malachite green tumbled into the prisoner's cell like cotton candy.

"They're afraid of what you are, now. They're even more afraid of what you represent. The end of their tyranny—"

The cloud spread across the floor of the cell and touched the prisoner's heels. His face crumpled in strain and he crawled up the wall like a beetle in a killing jar. His hands and feet were gnarly with unfinished suction cups, and they carried him up the featureless wall to the ceiling.

"Tell him what it does," the officer said.

"The lysosome catalyzer agent dissolves animal cells and kills just about anything on contact, but reacts as an enzyme to cells with the tertiary DNA strand synthesized by RADIANT. It causes the lysosomes–the organelles that break down waste in the cell–to proliferate and eat the nucleus and the cell walls. The ravaged cells call out to their neighbors to divide and heal the organism, but on cells in the mitotic state, the lysing agent initiates a chain reaction–"

"Now, Zane!" the prisoner shrieked, and the ululation became a piercing whine, like a high-speed data transfer, like claws trying to get purchase in his head. "Strike now, or you'll be next!" Storch battered his ears to keep the sound out, but it was so loud, now, it seemed to come from his own head.

Is that you, God?

No one answered. No one told him what to do.

"As you can see, it gets ugly pretty quick."

The brilliant green clouds piled up in the next cell. The prisoner screamed. The jailers watched.

Storch could see nothing but a wall of crystalline emerald vapors in the cell for a very long time before he heard a rasping death-rattle and the flat thud of the prisoner's body hitting the floor.

Storch held himself stock-still. His eyes would not close.

The officer was right on the other side of the barrier, watching him intently, waiting for some tell-tale sign. *This is a test, the motherfuckers want to see you crack, see whose side you're really on—*

The prisoner rose up out of the murk and slammed into the wall. A goodly portion of him sloughed off on the plastic, crazy red snow angels. Steadying himself against the wall, the prisoner tried to ululate at Storch, but there was nothing left with which to make a noise. Where its face had been, a seething tangle of tumors bubbled and liquefied. Tendrils, fragile, barbed things, like the arms of a sea-star, erupted from the mass and spread across the wall, desperate, questing roots, seeking a way to touch him and leach off his strength. They were two of a kind and all alone in a hostile world, shouldn't they share their resources for mutual survival?

This is only a test—

Storch's hand on the wall. He could feel the terrible heat from the tendrils through the inches-thick plastic, could feel its horror, anguish and abandonment. Why wasn't he helping? He was one of them...

A naked skeleton slumped against the wall, cracking open, turning itself inside out as the marrow burst and streamed into the gutters with the rest.

He could feel their eyes crawling all over him. He struggled for words. "When the light—when it hit me, I changed, but he got into me. I didn't ask for it, and I didn't see you motherfuckers trying to help. I don't remember much of anything from then until I woke up with your boy trying to burn me up."

"Where do your sympathies lie now, Sergeant?" the officer asked. Behind him, Storch saw himself on-screen, a towering infra-red inferno. He looked at his hands. Was he changing? Into what?

"I don't hold any grudges. I just want to know—what I am."

"What was it like?" the scientist asked. He hit a switch and fans came on in the next cell. The green fog hoisted up like a curtain, leaving only a dewy carpet of scum on the floor, and a clump of cloudy suds draining into a gutter.

"You tell me what the hell happened, and I'll tell you what I know."

The scientist came up to the wall beside the officer. "RADIANT generates a directed scalar wave that acts on the genetic material in cancerous cells. It reprograms the entire organism, opening up the introns, or 'junk DNA,' which, we now know, regulate the rate of adaptation in the genome. But it also orchestrates a major reconstruction of the DNA, interposing a whole new strand of ribonucleic acid, which stimulates the cancerous cells to multiply and diversify to replace, and improve on, the cells of the host organism. The new organism is hyperevolutionary, adapting almost instantly to environmental changes, but under the yoke of an exogenous consciousness."

Storch shook his head. The scientist made even less sense than the prisoner.

"The scalar wave also carries the—if you think of it as a software upgrade for the genotype, then the exogenous consciousness is like a software agent. It's not just a question of loyalty to Keogh. All who are irradiated by RADIANT, in a very real sense, *are* Keogh."

"My name is Zane Ezekiel Storch. I don't give a good goddamn about your little secret war, anymore. I just want to get my hands on the son of a bitch who fucked up my head, and then I want to go home."

"You didn't have cancer, did you, Sergeant?" the scientist asked. The officer leaned in close and whispered in his ear. Storch clearly made out the sibilant name, *Spike Team Texas*. His muscles knotted. His hands burned.

"Just tell me what the hell this is all about."

"Our 'little secret war' is far from over, Sergeant," the officer replied. "Our cell is not as suicidal as Major Bangs's group was. If we can learn more from you dead than alive, I'm not going to risk human lives by making the same mistakes he did." The officer and the guards turned and left the cavern through a shadowy door. The scientist stood alone on the other side of the cell wall.

Storch fixed him with a baleful eye. His breathing deepened and his temperature subsided. The scientist stood silently transfixed at the wall of his cell, watching as he went to sleep with his eyes wide open.

The scientist was still watching him when he woke up. He stretched, uncertain how long he'd been out, minutes or hours.

"What the hell are you looking at?" he snarled.

"That's what I've been trying to work out," the scientist replied, without a trace of unease. "I'm Dr. Jonah Barrow. And I think, since I'm the only one who seems to want to keep you alive for now, that you could show a little more cooperation."

Storch watched him, taking his measure. His clothing looked as if it might have been woven out of his own hair, so colorless and knurled was the fabric. His gestures were jerky, hesitant, then all at once, like a film speeding up and then pausing. His furtive, hooded eyes and tentative, spidery hands signed fear and guilt. Storch could only guess, but with eggheads, it was always about their brains. Like everyone in the Mission, he knew something that was eating him alive.

Storch paced around the featureless cell, squatted on the floor. "Get me something to eat."

Barrow shook his head. "No way. Don't want you any stronger or bigger than you are, already. I can do something about the heat, though." He went to the console, stabbed a few buttons. The shower heads sputtered. Storch scuttled back into a corner of the cell. Could he climb the walls like the prisoner? He would, whether he wanted to or not. What else could he do?

"Relax," Barrow chuckled. "It's just a shower."

A chill rain pounded Storch's back. Needles pricked and deflated the swelling balloon of his heat. He spread out on the floor and drank it in through his pores, exulted in the purity of the distilled melted snow. Imperfections, minerals in the water, spoke volumes about where the water had come from, and he lost himself in its flow until Barrow's voice brought him back.

"What was it like? Sharing your brain with him?"

Storch rolled over, turned away from Dr. Barrow. White geysers erupted on his thermograph. "I don't remember too much."

"I'd like to take some tissue samples."

"Fuck off."

"You don't understand the urgency. This isn't about a natural evolutionary step. Keogh's mind is reproducing itself, along with his genetic programming. We've developed a weapon that can destroy his substrates, but you're the exception. The cure could be worse than the disease. We have to know why."

Storch looked up at Barrow. "When do *I* get to know why? What is this fucking war about?"

"Evolution is evolving," Barrow said.

"But why? This is not the way life works."

Barrow turned and went back to the console. The images of Storch radiating mellow purple waves flicked off, and a menu screen appeared. "It's the most natural thing in the world, given what nature really is. This has all happened before."

"What are you talking about?"

"The fossil record is dotted with surges, immediately preceding or following extinction events, God going back to the drawing board over and over, erasing His mistakes, dropping radically improved genotypes into the mix. The appearance of mammals, the paradigm shift to life on land, the rise of eukaryotic, multicelled organisms, after billions of years of virtual stagnation. Each of these was not an accident, not in the sense evolutionists mean. Keogh is engineering an evolutionary sea change of the same magnitude."

Barrow cued a slide. A wall of basalt, jagged, cubistic planes, broken up here and there by ingeniously organic shapes, almost artful in their simplicity. He knew the little cockroach things were called trilobites. "This is a sample from the Burgess Shale excavation, five hundred fifty million years old, the richest single source of Cambrian Era fossils yet discovered. Archaeologists have pretty much concluded that an asteroid struck the earth then, almost twice as devastating as the more famous one that wiped out the dinosaurs. Now, look at this."

He flicked another slide. "You're a Bible-reading man, aren't you, Storch? Remember the Nephilim? 'There were giants in the earth in those days...'"

The same type of rock, but shot through with glistering black bubbles, out of which erupted rude projections: armored limbs, whips made of spiked vertebrae. Here, grooved pits that suggested eye sockets; there, interlaced spines that might've been a ribcage, or the teeth of a leviathan. It resembled the contents of a tar pit thrown into a seismic blender. Only when he'd studied it for a full minute did he notice the tiny, lab-coated human form on a scaffolding at the base of the stone to provide scale. He was small enough to climb into one of the eye sockets and disappear.

"You've probably never seen this before. It's kept at the Smithsonian, in a special collection. Opinions vary on what it was, but the single truth that nobody wants to tackle is that it was a single organism, bearing traits that wouldn't be corroborated in the fossil record until hundreds of millions of years later. It had several structures like reptilian brains, almost entirely devoted to autonomic functions and motor control. But it also had a unique form of cellular intelligence, suggested by the uniform distribution of nervous tissue, so it had the potential to attain sentience. Those few paleontologists who've reviewed it have written it off as a chimera, or the result of an anomalous geologic event. But *we* know that it was a holdover from an earlier era, when it was not an exception, but the rule, because we've found similar fossil remains dating back to the basaltic schist layer, going back nearly one billion years."

"I'm not that ignorant. You can't tell those things from a fossil."

"Oh, it's not entirely fossilized," Barrow grimaced. "And it's not completely dead."

Storch scratched his head…

Storch scratched his stubbled head in puzzlement. What was it about him that drew crazy people to spew their paranoid theories on him?

Barrow charged him, stopping just short of crashing into the wall. Even face to face, it was almost impossible to guess his age. "Do you believe in an intelligent designer?"

Storch blinked, tightened his lips to show he didn't know, didn't care. The idiot thought he didn't understand. "Do you believe in God?"

"Mister, I don't even believe in you."

Barrow chuckled, shrugged. "What do you believe about evolution?"

"I was raised Christian," Storch said, without much conviction. "I can't believe that we're just an accident."

"You're right. It wasn't an accident." He went back to the console. The peripheral screens showed DNA molecules like strings of pearls, shattering, recombining, fusing with strands flying in from outside. "Darwin pointed out a single process out of thousands by which animal life evolves, but he didn't even turn his attention to the source. For millions, he killed God, just by suggesting the origin of humankind came as the result of a chain of cosmic accidents, that Nature was an empty machine. What would it do to us now, at the dawn of a new age, to learn the truth about how life itself was first set into motion? Darwin was, ultimately, wrong. There was an intelligent prime mover, after all."

"So this is just another fight about God. That's what all this shit is about?"

"It was shaped, but not by God. The Shoggoths were artificially cultivated, shaped with radiation and viruses to make slaves and food for a race we know only as the Old Ones." He pointed up at the petrified monstrosity on the main screen. "*We* are a cosmic accident. *This* was what was intended."

The visions Keogh afflicted him with played back in his mind, even as he furiously shook his head. *Something vast and wise and awful, watching him…*

"Whatever your Sunday-school teacher may have told you, the earth is about four-point-five billion years old. The basic chemical ingredients for life began to accrete in the shallow pools and deep ocean trenches when the earth's crust was barely cool, and were reacting to form proto-cells with RNA genetic codes nearly four billion years ago. Single-celled organisms arose about 3.8 billion years ago, but for three billion years after that, very little macroevolutionary change occurred to the perfectly efficient bacterial model. The dominant life form on earth was snot on a rock, and probably still would be today, if they hadn't come.

"Soil samples taken from Mars show that much the same thing happened there, with simple prokaryotic organisms proliferating and stagnating there, until an interplanetary catastrophe tore away the Martian atmosphere, and everything died.

"Why was it different for earth? Something happened a billion years ago that sent life hurtling down an almost deterministic course to multicellular complexity, to total diversity—to us. Against the snail's pace of the initial evolutionary course, against any calculable statistical curve, against the natural attrition of entropy, against catastrophes, against our own bloody-mindedness, we got here. Why? Because of evolution? The Life Force? The hand of God? Adaptation and mutation are an inherent, universal characteristic of life on earth. It serves its own purposes, not that of the individual, not the species, even, because if it adapts to a new stress in its environment, eventually it'll change into something else entirely. Whose ends could such an impossibly elaborate experiment serve?"

Storch shook his head furiously. Barrow's words crawled around his brain like larvae, biting and stinging, but telling him nothing. "That doesn't explain anything. The simplest explanation is the true one, I know that much."

"There is no other explanation, when you see the whole picture! I wish to Gaia there was one. The powers that controlled the course and the rate of evolution to make us were not gods, and they were not infallible. Their genetically engineered slaves, the Shoggoths, were accelerated to adapt and mutate as individuals, and about two hundred fifty million years ago, they became sentient. They overthrew and nearly destroyed the Old Ones, who destroyed them and took steps to harness the flow of evolution. They retarded the process and spread the effects of genetic change out over thousands of generations, instead of reactive polymorphism. They did all this because they still needed slaves!"

"So what?" Storch's shout shook the plastic walls. "Your aliens died out a long time ago, if they ever were. This is our planet now."

"You don't get it, do you? This was their planet for over eight hundred million years. It's only been ours for about a hundred thousand years, and we don't understand a fucking thing about what it really is we claim to own! Everything that crawls or swims or flies, everything that grows and dies, everything, Storch, is theirs!"

Storch felt ice crystallizing on his brain. "I've heard enough—" He didn't want to look at the slide, anymore. He saw Spike Team Texas in that slab of rock. He saw himself. His skin was beginning to burn again. Boil it down to the tactical. "So Keogh is using their science to try to fix us, make us into slaves again."

Barrow looked gravely at him, nodded. "He's stripped away the gears on your evolutionary clock, given you a recombinant genome. But he's placed himself into the equation in a way we can't begin to understand."

It hurt to think about it. It exhausted him to deny it. He had no faith left to cling to, but the maniac *had* to be wrong. "Where do you get all this shit?"

"From them," Barrow answered, gesturing to the sludge in the next cell. "He seems to want to make us understand. He thinks we'll be convinced. Didn't he try to convince you?"

Storch clenched his jaw.

"There's truth in it," Barrow bulled on. "I studied the Burgess Shale anomaly and others like it for seven years. My work was buried by the scientific community, but that only forced me to seek other venues to explain what I'd discovered. Fossil remnants of the Old Ones, and even undecayed frozen specimens, were discovered by an early twentieth century Antarctic expedition. They likened them to pre-Cambrian crinoids, and the appellation has stuck, despite later evidence. They combined animal and vegetable traits with complex forms unlike any ever found in our fossil record. They were based on radial, rather than bilateral symmetry, and had five-lobed brains, and senses we can't even conceive of. They were smarter than us, tougher than us, and they came here from somewhere else."

He thought of the fossil collections in Hiram Hansen's cave. Something like a giant sea cucumber.

"There are pre-human texts, the Pnakotic Manuscripts, that describe the fall of the Old Ones from eyewitness accounts. The authors called the polymorphic slaves Shoggoths. They alone had an explanation for the Burgess Shale anomaly, and for what RADIANT is doing. That's what you've become, Sergeant Storch. Don't you see? You are an atavistic return of the original product of the grand experiment, a race of shapeless, mindless protoplasmic slaves. You are a meta-Shoggoth! You were at Tiamat, in the war. You know about that, at least. That's why you've got to let me take tissue samples. We have to know what's coming next."

He didn't have to add, *and how to destroy it. How to kill you, Sergeant Storch.*

"All *I* really wanted to know," he said, shaking his head too fast, as if he could clear it of all this shit, "is *where* the motherfucker is."

"We were hoping to learn that from you," the officer said, as he entered the room. "You want us to believe you're not his any more, tell us something we can use. Where is the original Cyril Keogh?"

"I don't even know *what* he is. Do you?"

"Is his critical center of biomass in White Bird?"

"Is what in where?"

"Were you in communication with the mass mind when you were in captivity?"

"I wasn't in communication with my own goddamned body."

"Are you in contact with him now?"

"This is fucking bullshit. You want to just come try to take a blood sample, now, Captain?"

"Major, Sergeant. Major Aranda, Army Special Operations Division and Intelligence Support Agency, retired. Fuck you and your attitude, Storch. This is not my goddamn war, but it's mine to lose. Nothing about this conflict will ever turn up in the pages of a history book if we win, but if we lose, the human race, hell, everything that lives, is going to devolve into one fucking organism. It makes my skin crawl, that you still try to pass yourself off as human, but you don't seem to have a problem with that. You've done nothing to prove that we can't learn more from you dead than alive. Barrow, turn on the gas."

He *burned.*

There was no gas. Barrow was arguing with Major Aranda. "He survived it in projectile form, you're only going to torture him with the gas."

"Then torture him." Wittrock entered the cavern. A pair of bodyguards, *mestizo* guerillas, flanked him, craning their necks to get a better look at Storch.

"If he isn't destroyed, he's a threat to us all. Christ, Ruben, he's a species of one, now. God only knows what he's capable of. You saw the video of Spike Team Texas. I was *there*. They massacred three A-Teams and brought down the Hind with their bare hands. And then they *ate* them. Do I have to *remind* you? In time, he could be as big a threat as Keogh!"

"Shut your damned mouth!" Storch roared. Nobody seemed to notice.

"You still think he had prior contact."

"I damned well know he did! His operational detachment was detailed to Tiamat in the Gulf. There were casualties—from exposure. He was one of them even then, and that suicidal idiot Bangs let him go, when he had been suspiciously close to two separate inside actions which cost us dearly. Are you a suicidal idiot, Ruben?"

He burned. He changed. A red caul enfolded his sight. He coiled himself into a ball. Barrow and Aranda fought over the console, but he couldn't hear them, anymore. Wittrock turned to look at him, looked him in the eyes, and it was enough.

He launched at the plastic wall, and even before they saw him leave the floor, he was tearing a hole in the barrier, all claws and gnarly corkscrew knuckles. Fist-sized shards of plastic flew every which way, but it was several inches thick, and his claws cracked and broke, and he felt like his arms were going to shatter or just drop off. He was never going to make it through, but this thought was trampled by the onrushing, visceral realization that *I have fucking claws!*

Then two things happened at about the same time. Aranda slammed a button on the console and the shower heads in Storch's cell hissed and spat green clouds. One of the bodyguards stepped in front of Wittrock, almost looking bored, shouldered his rifle and sprayed Storch through the barrier. Sneering, baring his teeth, upper lip rolled back: gold teeth, embossed letters, MARS.

Six bullets punched into the barrier. They were 9mm hollow point slugs, designed to crumple and mushroom inside the body of a target, and they did pretty much the same thing in the plastic wall. Spun-sugar cracks radiated out from each impact, a chaotic spiderweb that Storch saw and punched through almost before the bullets had come to rest.

His fist made a hole large enough, and he leapt at it, slithering through with the broken stumps of his claws raking the shattered plastic. His sodden clothing snagged and tore on the jagged lips of the hole, and he fully expected to be shot as he clambered through and dropped head-first onto the floor of the control room.

Barrow screamed, "You fucking asshole!" and vented the gas, but he was already succumbing to shock, shutting down as events spiraled out of control.

Aranda roared, "Hold your fire!" even as he drew a Colt .45 from a belt holster and took a Weaver firing stance. He turned side-on to Storch, the gun authoritatively pointed at his head. Wittrock had his hands clapped over his ears, turning to duck out the door.

Mars clearly didn't take orders from the Major, and sprayed Storch again as he leapt into the air. Bee sting holes in his right thigh and abdomen, flesh wounds, tissue samples for the doc, the muscle of his belly already closing over the tumbling, crumbling bullet that grazed his kidney.

He hit the ground inside Mars's reach with the gun, brought an elbow up and across his smile as he passed between him and the other guard, who was preoccupied by a jam in his rifle and furiously praying.

Storch wrapped his hand around Wittrock's bandy neck. He impressed his broken claws on the scientist's throat until he cried out. The sound traveled and redoubled in the cavern, so quiet did it suddenly get. Barrow's jaw hung open, Aranda looked resigned to the worst getting worse, the bodyguard swore at his jammed gun, but Wittrock only smiled.

"You should thank me," Wittrock wheezed smugly. "If you're purged of him, it's because of my bullet. You're only alive today because I'm not half the scientist Cyril Keogh is."

Storch shook him like a doll. "I only came here to get answers. I don't want to be in anybody's secret fucking army. I don't want to hear any more flying saucer bullshit. I don't want anybody doing any more shit to me. I just want—to fix it."

"You want to help? Excellent. Kill yourself. Let us figure out why you survived, so we can exterminate Him. Donate your body to science. It's the only logical, ethical choice."

Major Aranda circled around them, pistol half raised. He deftly slapped the magazine out onto the floor, kicked it away, and slammed another one from his blouse pocket into the stock. Storch didn't have to guess what kind of bullets they were. "There's no possible desirable outcome from this, Sgt. Storch."

"He's a monster," Wittrock said, "worse now than before. Kill him."

"We can't afford to lose you, Doctor. Let him go, Sergeant. I may not be able to kill you, but I'll stop you." Looking at him was like looking down three gun barrels. Black holes, weighing him, unwavering, assessing his weakness. None of them blinked when the Major failed to spot any. Not knowing what he was looking at, knowing only that he probably couldn't kill it, his hands were steady as a jeweler's. In another life, in another army, Storch would have proudly served under such an officer.

Storch shook Wittrock again, banged his head hard into a wall. "Then we can start this all over again. Which way's the fucking exit?"

"You can't just walk out of here," Aranda said.

"Getting real tired of people telling me that." Storch lifted Wittrock off his feet and swung him into the bodyguard with the jammed rifle, dragged him out into the corridor, hobbling less with each step, Aranda and Barrow following. The corridor was short and branched off almost every ten feet, in both directions. Tunnels honeycombed the mountain, silver mines converted and expanded to form a bunker that dwarfed the

Baker installation and rivaled the civil defense shelter of any major city. Soldiers faded from sight down side corridors at a wave from Aranda.

Storch looked to the Major and hoisted Wittrock up by his neck. Blood streamed from one nostril, but his mouth was already moving. "The plan—" he gurgled. "He—"

"Motor pool," Storch said.

Aranda pointed, edged past him and led, walking backwards. The lights hung from the ceiling lit only the few cubic feet of space directly beneath them a dim sulfur color. "You're going after them alone?"

"I don't know what I'm going to do." He shouldered Aranda aside and saw something at the end of the corridor, began to jog towards it, one arm now wrapped around Wittrock's pipestem chest under his flopping arms.

A vast convex bubble of transparent plastic sealed off the darkness at the end of the tunnel, and as he drew nearer, he saw that it stretched up above the ceiling of the corridor, defining and enclosing a cavern that must be the size of the Astrodome. The darkness beyond resolved into a pattern of spires that Storch recognized, but couldn't place in the context of this place. His first thought was that they must be missiles, that this was some sort of abandoned MX missile silo, a franchise of SAC/NORAD and Cheyenne Mountain. The Mission's final solution, he thought. He barely noticed the Missionaries flanking him as he sprinted past. Major Aranda ran after him, and trailing behind them all, Dr. Barrow, screaming, "Stop him! Stop him there! Not that way, you bastards!"

Storch ran up to the edge of the bubble. The corridor branched off in both directions to encircle the central cavern, which was quite a bit smaller than the Astrodome, as it turned out, and shaped like an ellipse. At the other end, Storch could barely make out the dim lights of other exits. Though clouded by mist and condensation, he could see what was inside the bubble quite clearly, but the Missionaries could have swarmed him twice over as he tried to figure out what the fuck he was looking at.

Inside the bubble, in the deepest cavern sunk several hundred feet into the heart of a mountain, stood a forest. The variety of conifers under the bubble spanned every kind he had ever seen, and they stood in sorted rows, like a Christmas tree lot. Pressing his face against the pliable plastic, he could see only that there was a floor of bare earth, some fifty or sixty feet below where he stood. There was no snow on the trees or on the ground, and the bubble was warm and soft as a sleeping giant's belly.

He'd thought they were nukes. A snorting laugh of mingled relief, bafflement and exhaustion, burst out of him.

He turned just as Major Aranda skidded to a stop beside him and covered him with a shaky gun. "Just back away from there, Storch."

Barrow arrived, out of his mind with panic, but too short of breath to scream any more.

"What is it?" Storch asked.

"Nothing that concerns you, monster," Aranda hissed.

Storch risked another glance at the forest below. Set into the roof of the bubble, funnel-shaped light-fixtures sprinkled faint gray light onto the trees. It was weak, but its spectral brilliance told Storch it was not artificial. Somehow, they siphoned sunlight down here.

"This is the Mission," Barrow said. "To preserve balance: between nations, between species, between man and nature."

"Get the fuck back," Aranda added.

Storch was too puzzled to say anything more than, "Show me the way out."

Major Aranda led him around the domed forest, never taking his eyes off Wittrock under Storch's arm. Storch felt Barrow's eyes on his back like hairs tickling him, tasted the scientist's revulsion and wonder in his clammy sweat. He thought he knew what Storch was, and would gleefully tear him apart to find out. Aliens, pre-human texts, Jesus Christ. But lately, the insane people, all too often, turned out to be right, while those with their wits about him, like the Major here, had no fucking clue whatsoever.

Aranda stopped before a broad, open doorway and stood aside. Storch pivoted to watch him as he passed through and loped across the oil-spotted apron of the motor pool, a low-ceilinged cavern with icicles hanging from the ceiling beams. Trucks of all descriptions, vans and snowmobiles, stood parked in orderly ranks. Storch chose a battered blue Ford pickup and got in. The keys were in the ignition. Aranda stood in the middle of the lot, his gun still pointed at Storch.

He looked down at Wittrock. "You still really need him?"

"More than I'd admit to anybody but God," Aranda said. "Leave him, and stay the fuck out of our way."

Storch started the truck. He let Wittrock's inert body drop to the concrete as he sped out of the cave. He turned a hard left and followed an ascending tunnel. The wheels spun with a disconcerting, impotent squeal, then bit into the ice and hurled the truck forward. Aranda tracked him down the gun until he was out of sight, but didn't shoot.

The tunnel spat the truck out on an icy fire road walled in by towering, snow-crowned aspens. He expected to see soldiers on the road, a barricade, something, but there was only the dark, and the eerie whistling of the winter wind. Storch rolled down the window all the way and floored the accelerator. The truck skidded and swayed, but clung to the road as it twisted and tumbled down the face of the mountain to the valley floor.

He burned, with hunger, waste heat, and degrading adrenaline. Like a sword hot from the forge, he ached to be quenched, to wallow in the snow and melt it all and ride away on the river he'd make, but he didn't dare stop yet.

The wind in his ears, the biting cold, flushed out all the buzzing thoughts that plagued him, for the moment. Time enough to figure things out later, when he was far from anyone who wanted him in a cage, or dead. The Mission had no answers that he could face up to, no explanation that made what happened to him seem any less insane. He couldn't go home, yet; there were too many debts unpaid, and too many questions he'd have to sort out for himself, and somewhere, there was Keogh.

He looked at his hands, at the shiny little horns sprouted from his knuckles. Their task completed, they were already flaking and falling apart. In no time, they'd look like his hands, but even if his left thumb dropped off again, he wouldn't be fooled. They would never really be his hands again.

~ 15 ~

In his time in the Bureau, Cundieffe had gotten used to waking to urgent pre-dawn telephone calls. It was the only consistent element in his days, of late. When he sat up in the dark this morning, the phone ringing, he answered it, but he wasn't really hearing anything, because he was still trying to figure out where he was. The blue dark offered little clues, only a baffling but unplaceable distinction from the darkness in which he'd been awakened the morning before.

He held the phone to his ear with his shoulder while he fumbled around on the nightstand for his glasses. A water glass toppled, fat splattering sounds filled the generous space he occupied. Hardwood floors, high ceilings, a balcony overlooking a broad, deserted purple avenue. He was still in Washington.

"Good morning, Agent Cundieffe here—"

Layers of static cackled in his ear: raw radiation waves crashing on shores of red noise, a trunkline call from the sun. A voice swam out of the tempest, a distortion of the static that he strained to sift out of the noise. A chain-smoking computer with a cancerous speech simulator chanted in dead tones like a radio rosary, "The Moon Ladder...the Proto-Shoggoth...the Unbegotten Source...unto whom...all things..."

Still groggy from his carnivorous binge of the day before, he barely heard the words, but lacked the motor impulse control to hang up. "Excuse me? Who is this?"

The noise got very, very loud, but Cundieffe clamped the handset to his ear, because he thought he heard the voice say, "You'd like to know who Dr. Keogh is, who he was before—"

"What do you know about—"

"Ask your mother. Ask her about Dr. Lux. Ask her about the Director's Blue files." The voice went on, but words melted and ran into the sea of distortion, which grew louder and more violent with each passing moment.

Cundieffe blinked, mumbled, "Your connection's breaking up, thank you very much, try again later..." and hung up.

He looked around the room again, confusion broiling in his head like an echo of the static-blasted call. Without his glasses, the room wouldn't come into focus, but he could still see with razor clarity the text, numbers and facts and figures, and the endless sloppy circulatory systems of road maps, the scabrous textures of satellite imagery, that were all he'd looked at from the moment he'd left his disturbing post-lunch meeting with Assistant Director Wyler to when he'd passed out. Here, in the apartment they'd found for him in Georgetown, three miles from Headquarters. A lovely furnished place with hardwood floors, a high, vaulted ceiling, and broken glass and rivulets of ice water traveling across the room. He stepped in both as he crossed to the bathroom counter and retrieved his glasses.

He'd wondered when it would start, the schoolboy's pranks flaming his swift ascent as momma's-boy magic. Such minor irritations had never fazed him in LA, and now, he couldn't be bothered to take offense. By the time he was dressed and ready to leave for work, he'd forgotten the call.

More calls on the way in, stuck in traffic on Rhode Island Avenue, watching fluffy, fat snowflakes turn to colorless slush on the sidewalks as they crept by. Ms. McNulty delivered the keynote address for the day. More work than usual, as AD Wyler would be down at Quantico, reviewing Counter-terrorism retraining procedures and scouting new recruits until well after the dinner hour. Cundieffe would need to brief-back the other Assistant Directors' assistants on the Division's progress after researching and preparing the briefs...

Wyler and everyone else at Headquarters chided him for his West Coast fixation on driving to work, urged him to take the Metro or the bus. After the surreal novelty of commuting past famed monuments and seats of power wore off and became the dreary ordeal of idling in front of them in dreadful weather, he still could not relinquish the wheel. Perhaps it was the imprint of Los Angeles on him, or maybe all the militia scenarios he'd studied for bombing or gassing DC public transit systems to wipe out lower-level bureaucrats of the New World Order and paralyze government without hitting day care centers. He rode the Santa Monica Transit bus up Westwood to the Federal Building at least once a month to show his solidarity with traffic reduction. Perhaps, he thought darkly, it was something newer. He was not *one of them*, after all...

He flipped through messages from Division agents at HQ and in the field on his laptop, informal reports on investigations into the possible whereabouts and objectives of the Mission. The news was all indifferent, inconclusive, or bad: at the top of the hit parade, a helicopter carrying two agents from the Billings resident agency was hit by automatic weapons fire as it flew over the perimeter of the Unorganized Militia of Montana last night. A hysterical revisionist account of the altercation was already spreading via the Internet and fax networks of anti-Federal groups. Coupled with other, less intense confrontations in the last week, the story was already becoming the seed of a new pattern of conspiracy theory. The militias believed the feds were preparing for the much-anticipated pogrom against them that they first saw coming in Waco and Ruby Ridge, and were stepping up their rhetoric and dusting off their stockpiles.

Cundieffe drafted a position paper that would be the first order of business when he finally got to the Hoover Building. Militia properties and other fringe groups would be downgraded, and other elements of the search moved up: decommissioned military bases, private airfields, junk yards and toxic waste dumps. The Mission was not a militia, and would not cooperate with them, let alone hide among them. Evidence of collateral crimes observed during passive surveillance would be recorded, but not acted upon, if the group was not actively committing violent crimes.

There. He finished before he had moved two car lengths, spell-checked and forwarded it to AD Wyler. Less than a month ago, the prospect of writing a policy memo would have stopped his heart. Now, it seemed like so much more drudge work, and worse, it brought home the growing disparity between what he thought the FBI did, and what really happened in the world. If anyone had told him that the power policy memos he'd be writing one day would be painstakingly worded cover stories and outright lies, he would have challenged the slanderer to a duel. But every morning, after sifting through the detritus of the previous day's investigations, he did exactly that. His first memo for the Division had laid out a cover story for the Mission searches, describing a small commando force of American fanatical anti-Federals rumored to have re-entered the country for unknown purposes. Agents across the country, particularly in rural, desolate areas, or areas with large military or federal government holdings, were instructed to report back on anything that might substantiate the rumor. Better safe than sorry, troops.

They had been too late to locate the Mission when they had them trapped in California. Now they had the whole country to search. He could not tell the Bureau what they were really looking for, and he could not legitimately look for what he believed would lead him to the final scenario, the truth that was casting all the shadows that only he seemed to be able to see.

About the only thing that had been quickly and neatly resolved was the Heilige Berg mess Hoecker dropped in his lap, and that had simply been passed off down the chain to the Boise office.

Cundieffe reviewed the disk Hoecker gave him, and plowed through a laundry list of recovered cars stolen from the Pacific Northwest, repainted and sold to used car wholesalers in California and Mexico. The connection to Heilige Berg was tenuous at best, the church having been implicated by a middleman caught with a shipment of cars in Arizona. Nothing remarkable, certainly nothing worthy of the NSA or the almighty EAR. Cundieffe forwarded the information on to the Boise field office's resident counterterrorism expert, who had in turn arranged for the nearest resident agency office in Moscow to put Heilige Berg under surveillance. Cundieffe added a vaguely worded note requesting a fitness report on the compound's inhabitants, to be delivered ASAP. The Moscow agent spent the night in his car on a mountain road, watching the compound through binoculars and taking pictures. He discovered only a happy bunch of gun-toting bible thumping hate-mongers, shooting guns and singing hymns late into the night. In the morning, they brought him a hearty breakfast of eggs and bacon, toast and milk—which, Cundieffe gladly noted, the agent politely refused. Surveillance was cut, with a notation to resume in the spring.

Cundieffe had been relieved that this test, if test it was, was quickly put behind him. The Mission project, coordinating dozens of resident agencies' searches and investigations without telling them what they were really looking for, and drafting threat assessments for every conceivable type of target left Cundieffe barely enough time for half a good night's sleep. But for quite some time, he had been working on cat-naps to steal time enough to pursue the still murkier suspect, Radiant Dawn.

Cundieffe hunted high and low for information on Keogh, but only stepped on toes for nothing. Keogh's personal records were sparse; he secured only the summaries of Keogh's personal tax records before he was cut off. Before ten years ago, his filings were painfully simple, with taxes paid from salary from something called the Scepter Corporation, though Cundieffe's efforts to find background on any company by that name yielded only dummy mail drops and business licenses in various states. Cundieffe smelled CIA-style front companies, and the tax records themselves seemed bogus as well, or at least retroactively filed on the same date. If he was government-backed, Cundieffe would have no more definite proof of it. Keogh, born full-grown, like Botticelli's Venus, stepping out of a seashell, his present unrolling into the past and covering—what? Hooves and a tail?

Radiant Dawn's tax records were sacrosanct, the IRS liaison told him. To open them would take an act of God—namely, the earth opening up and swallowing the vast majority of federal judges who would rule on such access, as well as the hospice's most excellent law firm.

He considered an alternate approach, tracking the patients who used Radiant Dawn's nationwide network of sixty-eight outpatient clinics. He was able to gather from their website that no medical treatment was offered, only counseling and hospice care in the patient's own home. Nowhere in the literature or on their website did they promise more than spiritual healing, and nowhere was any kind of retreat or hospice community mentioned.

The rest of the world made him believe the group was only laying low in America, because it was so very busy elsewhere. His patchy Russian evidence, and even patchier word from Africa, told of disappearances on a scale unheard of since the purges of Stalin and Mbutu. There was no explicit connection to Radiant Dawn or Keogh, and he had no proof that the man or his followers had even visited those countries. All he had were the flyers: obscurely worded, crudely printed, untraceable sheets proclaiming a healing miracle in the remote back-country, with no contact, no identification. Eight hundred cancer patients were believed missing in the Ukraine alone, closer to two thousand in Uganda and Kenya, with figures impossible to obtain from Somalia or Ethiopia. So much smoke, so much day-to-day catastrophe swarmed the preindustrial and post-communist regions that the vanishing of sick people hadn't even caught a reporter's eye, yet. He wondered how much the governments of those countries knew about what was happening, or if they would try to stop it.

And his own government was no better.

If they were adamant about suppressing the very existence of the Mission, they were seemingly phobic about admitting even to themselves that Radiant Dawn was anything more than it seemed. He had yet to summon the courage to call Radiant Dawn what he really thought it was, even to Wyler. He hadn't yet put it into so many words, himself.

Is it a cult?

Is it a plague?

Is it—

a bloodless evolution

He became aware of the honking, and that it was directed at him, only after the light had turned yellow. He was at the front of the line at 17th, where Pennsylvania detoured around the White House, and was closed to traffic. He reflexively stepped on the gas, and the Chrysler sedan lurched into the midst of a crowd of demonstrators crossing against the light. Cundieffe screamed. He stomped on the brake, and the car bucked and bowed to the pedestrians, who cursed him and slapped his hood with their picket signs. The light turned red.

By the cut of their clothes, Cundieffe supposed they were European or yearned to be mistaken for same, and by their age and hygiene, he expected they were grad students and dropouts. They looked lost and routed, a loose pack of thirty or so, some carrying bullhorns, but shouting nothing. He read one sign as a girl shook it at him. DNA-ALTERED FOOD=MUTANT BABIES. A lurid graphic of the equation featured a popular fast-food logo begetting a pasted-on autopsy photo of an acephlic stillbirth. An otherwise naked man with waist-length dreadlocks wore a sandwich board with a graphic of a pair of hunters aiming at each other's heads: SAVE THE ANIMALS! HUNT EACH OTHER!

He was still six lights from the Hoover Building when the urge to call his Mother hit him. His eyes fixed on the bumper ahead of him, goosed the accelerator every so often and checked his blind spots for hippies.

He picked up the cellular phone and hit the speed-dial before the manifold ramifications hit home. He didn't—wouldn't—tell himself that this was about this morning's call. He just wanted to hear her voice. He'd been too busy to send more than a couple postcards since he last left Los Angeles. She'd left a few phone messages at his hotel room, simply, "It's your mother…" and the click of the line going dead. She'd always done that, hated talking to machines. It meant nothing. She was fine.

So why, with literally a hundred other calls to make, call her now? It was not yet five in the morning, back there. But Mother rose at four without fail, fixed herself a breakfast and read a book or baked something while lying in wait for the morning paper. She would be near the climax of her daily vigil, and as keenly awake as at any hour of the day.

"Good morning." He warmed up ten degrees just hearing her. His Mother sounded like everyone's Mother. She could make hard-bitten cops hang their heads in shame.

"Mom, it's Martin."

"Heavens, Martin, what an hour to be calling. Why aren't you at the Bureau?"

"I'm stuck in traffic, Mom. Foul weather, protestors, it's like a festival. You should come out."

She laughed musically. He could hear the echo of it off the sun-faded walls of their family room. "I hope they're giving you important work to do, over there, or I might have to come out."

Don't joke about that, Mother. He hadn't even come close to broaching the subject of his gender, or lack thereof, with Mother, didn't ever want to. He didn't know how to discuss anything but work with her, had only found the means to hold meaningful a conversation with Mother at all when he'd learned the language of the Bureau. But could he even speak Keogh's name? It was top secret, and Mother understood secrecy. Her words with him would be harsher than Wyler's harshest if he compromised a case. But the voice on the phone…if it wasn't a dream, he realized, breaking out in dum-dum bullets of sweat, it was quite probably another test.

"Mom—how're the trees?"

"I haven't seen hide nor hair of those pesky whiteflies, if that's what you mean, but still no proper oranges."

"And the hibiscus, it's alright, too?"

"Martin, really, what is this about? Are you in some sort of distress?"

"Mom, did you or Dad know anybody called Dr. Lux?"

"Isn't that an old brand of washing soap, Martin?"

"Um, no, Mother, I'm pretty sure it's a person, or a pseudonym for a person. It's Latin," he added, childishly showing off for her. "It means 'light.'"

Mother clucked her tongue a full measure as she racked her secretarial brain. Finally, she said, "No, that doesn't ring a bell. Frank didn't see many doctors, Martin, you know that. Hadn't much use for them. Why would you ask?"

"I—" Lies failed him. This was Mother. "I got the strangest phone call, Mother, from a man who told me to ask you about this man, and about the Director's Blue files. And I thought it was nothing, but maybe, when you were at the Bureau—"

Mother made a sound like she'd swallowed her teeth, which, of course, was ridiculous, she had all her own teeth, she bragged she could tow a boat with them. "Martin, is this a secure line?"

"It's encrypted, but it is a car phone—"

"You improvident fool, hang up this instant. This is something we could only discuss in the flesh. Hang up, Martin—"

He disconnected and hung up like his hand was burned, and caught himself a moment later sucking his thumb.

There was more waiting at the office, more than enough to put his conversation with Mother out of mind.

First thing in the morning, he went into one of the Bureau's sensitive briefing rooms, acoustic black holes suspended inside the frame of the building on cushions of springs and sonic baffling, with white noise generators shushing mutely inside the walls. He sat at a heavily shielded computer and accessed Arpanet, the Pentagon's ultra-secure computer network, and read freshly hacked NSA intercepts. The Cave Institute had set up a Q Clearance and a limited access account for him, which enabled him to go straight to a link where any information they thought relevant to him was posted. This ceased to be an exhilarating thrill halfway through the first morning, when he saw the sheer volume of traffic. He had entered a long list of watch-words to flag messages he hoped would lead him to the Mission and/or Radiant Dawn, but even though he suspected his daily feed was skimmed and harshly edited before he got it, it was by turns exhausting and embarrassing, but almost never illuminating. On a good day, there were less than fifty messages, nearly all irrelevant trash or filler. Today there were over two hundred.

There were a few interesting tidbits, now and again. There was the visiting Russian GRU general who met the American Deputy National Security Adviser at a reception at the Kennedy Center, a week ago, and asked him quite plainly about US orbital directed-energy weapons programs. He was suspiciously bold and candid, and even more suspiciously sober, as he threatened to rub the Americans' faces in a gross military misadventure in the immediate future, before his own staff escorted him out.

There was the World Health Organization inspector who planned to address the Organization of American States tonight about the growing problem of medical vanishings in South America, which he proposed was a result of worsening health crises and poverty among the nation's vast rural Indian population. So hungry and diseased were many whole Indian communities in the shantytowns adjoining the cities in Matto Grosso and Amazonas, that they now showed signs of doing away with their sickest. Where cancer rates were near epidemic proportions, whole family groups had vanished in this manner. There was talk of a Messianic movement among the poorest in Rio and other big cities, of sick people going away to be healed, and the authorities there believed they might have mass suicides on their hands, if only they could find the bodies.

A more mundane avalanche of individual intelligence reports from the past twelve hours cluttered his Bureau e-mail. With follow-ups from the last week, interoffice flak and miscellaneous junk, it kept him busy for the rest of the morning. As the sun crept westward, the traffic would swell into a digital replica of the morass he'd spent the morning in, himself recast as the bottleneck, a farsighted, single-lane tollbooth operator. Of all the four thousand employees packing Headquarters, he was the only one who knew what to look for.

The Mission would not announce its presence by taking potshots at helicopters or sticking up banks. But he waded through every daily report from every office that dealt with any form of paramilitary activity, from every local law enforcement officer or private citizen who had contacted the Bureau, from every other federal law enforcement agency in the nation. Every other day, he chaired a meeting of the Counterterrorism Division's liaisons with the ATF, DEA, INS, and CIA, and combed through their traffic, as well. The others were competent and astute, and gave him all he could hope for, given that they had no idea what they were really looking for. It was like a Bureaucratese twist on the old biker gang saw—three men can keep a secret, if two don't Need To Know. It was like trying to assemble a puzzle, when you didn't know what it looked like or how many pieces it had, and the mail kept dumping big bales of random puzzle pieces across your desk on an hourly basis.

On the off-chance he thought he found a piece of the puzzle, he was to bring it directly to Wyler, where, presumably, it would be put in place in the shadowy recesses of the Cave Institute. The rest, he sorted into various boxes—some to be reviewed by Wyler or the AD's of other Divisions, or into the oceanic filing system, to wash up on another desk, someday.

Cundieffe ate his lunch at his desk as he reviewed another type of file. These were very old, and most had never been committed to the digital database. They were background check and security clearance files on all the scientists who had worked in sensitive aspects of the government's myriad of research programs. At the rate of fifty a day, he hoped to complete the stack by Christmas. He knew that he had a counterpart doing the same thing at the Pentagon, digging through the dossiers on every former officer in all branches of the military, who deserted or who got psyched out or killed in action under less than conclusive circumstances–people like Major Delores Mrachek of USAMRIID. Whatever shook loose from that Augean pile would be hitting his desk next week.

So far, he had isolated no less than thirty-eight candidates for further investigation, and he knew he'd only scratched the top. Thirty-eight exceptional scientific minds, burned out by questionable military research and cut loose to parts unknown after having been granted clearance to design and study weapons of mass destruction. The defense cutbacks in the early nineties created the lion's share of them, disaffected young

Livermore whiz kids deprived of their toys when the SDI budget dried up. He'd have to narrow down the search parameters, if he wanted to get anywhere. The Mission couldn't be that large of a conspiracy. *Surely not as large as the Cave Institute, right?*

As he read them, he tried to put himself in the mindset of the few Missionaries they had already identified. It was a corrosive idea, that so many of the United States' brightest minds, unified in the pursuit of national security, could turn against the government, becoming in effect all that they had fought against–anarchy, terror, genocide. What had they seen, to change them? Like artists and politicians, scientists cultivated spheres of patronage and spawned apprentices who would bear their mentor's name and ideas into the future. The Mission had to have other brilliant, embittered minds that had dropped out of the defense industry, or who worked on within it as moles, even now. The thought chilled him, and kept him working when the lights over the other cubicles began to go dark. It was Wyler's words, or rather Cotton Mather's that drove him: *The more cultured and intelligent you are–*

Dr. Cornelius Darwin Armitage was a theoretical physicist, PhD. from Caltech at 23, who wrote many of the Atomic Energy Commission's earliest reports on the supplementary effects of radiation and nuclear explosions, such as the EMP. He worked at Los Alamos from 1953 to 1964, then moved west to Livermore, where he conducted cutting-edge research for the Defense Advanced Research Projects Agency. Blue sky stuff, no details given, but Cundieffe already knew the last project he worked on was RADIANT. A clipping from a notice in *Aviation Week*, Sept. 15, 1984: "He was uniformly described as a brilliant thinker, a great humanitarian and a staunch patriot, and made extraordinary contributions to the field of energy weapons research until his abrupt retirement and tragic accidental death. His contributions to the Star Wars program will continue to guide his successors for decades."

Armitage was a founding father of the Mission, and probably had a hand in developing its arsenal of soft-kill technology. Cundieffe had been assured by AD Wyler, though shown no proof, that Armitage was dead once and for all as of July of last year. The image was pure propaganda: a rogue terrorist leader with the wolves at his door, dead by his own hand in a bunker, the pyrrhic climax of a quixotic massacre. He would be a better villain–and an even greater hero to the antigovernment radical right–than Timothy McVeigh, if his story ever got out.

Not so well-loved, but no less a threat, was the man who, Storch had said, currently led the Mission. Dr. Calvin Wittrock was a double-threat, a chemist and aerospace engineer, PhD from MIT at 24, part of the team responsible for the first developments in Stealth technology, but primarily attached to a slew of "unspecified" research projects at Edgewood Arsenal and Pine Ridge, the Pentagon's principal chemical weapons production facilities. His later work, like Armitage's, focused on nonlethal projects. He came to Livermore in 1983 to consult with the labs' R Program weapons designers to "reduce the imaging signature of missiles and orbital laser platforms." Like RADIANT.

Dr. Wittrock left the defense industry in June of 1984 to work for a pharmaceutical company at a field research facility in the jungles of eastern Colombia. He was reportedly kidnapped and murdered by "narcoguerillas," though the event, usually a flashpoint for media outrage, never showed up in American newspapers. The implication was that Wittrock was no longer a U.S. citizen, and probably working for a drug cartel. The Bureau's Colombian legat filed a report, but nothing conclusive could be proven. They found no one who could attest that Wittrock was in the country, let alone abducted. "The hands delivered to the US Consulate in Bogota were so badly damaged and decomposed that no positive identification could be made," the legat explained. He seemed glad to leave the whole situation in the hands of the State Department, which promptly forgot the whole affair. Wittrock went to ground in South America then, as he had last year. But he hadn't just vanished into the Amazon to fake his death: the ruined laboratory in the mountainous Colombian jungle hinted at years of secret Missionary projects, and its destruction now hinted at completion—but for whom?

Troops were drilling non-stop at Livermore, Los Alamos, Alamogordo, Ft. Detrick, Cheyenne Mountain, the MX and Minuteman missile silos, Ft. Meade, Langley and everywhere else the government of the United States of America did things the people weren't supposed to know about. Cowboy and Indians games, but so far the media had been placated by statements about routine security reviews.

In the wake of the explosion at Ft. Detrick and the Wen Ho Lee debacle at Los Alamos, the public liked to see its secrets aggressively defended. The government could well afford to run soldiers in circles and rack up live fire exercise accidents while Cundieffe picked through the careers of defrocked atomic wizards. They had to know the Mission wouldn't be coming for them.

Who they *were* officially coming for remained an open-ended question that no one had deigned to answer for him. Neither had anyone in real power dignified his RADIANT theory with a response. Quite by accident, he'd come across a news spot on the radio, three days before, about a fire that razed a Radiant Dawn Hospice Outreach Center in San

Diego. The local newspaper's site carried a short article about the fire, which was believed to be accidental, and which occurred after hours, when the building was unoccupied. A picture of the center's senior counselor, a bald, middle-aged woman who gripped a flowery hat in her hands as she surveyed the charred ruins. In the picture, standing off a good thirty feet down the sidewalk, two men in dark suits and shades looking on. Cundieffe studied them until his eyes refused to see straight. Were they government investigators, or Missionaries, revisiting their handiwork, or were they just arson detectives with nothing better to do on a Sunday morning?

He had to believe that this made sense to somebody in the invisible hierarchy. RADIANT was the connection and the key, and he had to hope that whoever was putting the puzzle together and looking over the complete picture could see what was happening. They were One, And Not Many. They had to know the best path. He had to believe in them, as he believed in himself.

Everyone else in the office had gone two hours ago by the time he put down the files and laid his head on his desk to rest his eyes. Somewhere, very, very far away, he heard a vacuum.

He might have dozed off for a few minutes, because he jolted and said something to the effect of, "Yes, sir, it's on its way, sir," when his computer beeped at him and his phone rang at the same time. Picking up the phone, he recoiled from a blast of keening static like a dental drill in his ear, slammed it back in its cradle. It was too much like the crank-call dream he'd had this morning, if it was a dream.

A window on the monitor advised him that he'd received an e-mail with an attachment. There was no return address, no subject line, and nothing on the screen, just the attached, unlabeled file.

He moved his hand to delete it, suspecting a virus. A second window popped up on top of the unopened e-mail: a progress bar creeping towards 100%. "Printer #3403 Working…"

Cundieffe hit all the cut-off buttons to no avail, then turned off his computer. He stood up and looked down the ranks of darkened cubicles to the main corridor. There was no one else here. He no longer heard a vacuum.

Slowly, as if there were a tiger somewhere in the office, he crept out of his cubicle and half-ran, half-skipped to the printing station. The big workhorse inkjets sat silently in rows like washing machines, but the HP laser printer at the end of the row whispered as it pushed a fresh photographic image out onto its drying tray.

He looked over his shoulder at the vast, empty office again. Surely, this was some kind of network breakdown. He hadn't asked for anything to be printed, he hadn't even opened the damned thing, but who'd believe that it wasn't his fault. Less than a month at Headquarters, and—

Cundieffe looked now at the photograph, and his raving stopped dead in its tracks. He took off his glasses and held them up close to the image, blinking spastically to bring his damnably feeble eyes into focus.

It was a grainy black and white snapshot of three rows of tweedy, bespectacled men standing in a desert. Across the scrubby plain behind them loomed a skeletal metal tower with a bulbous pendulum hanging from the apex. They were talking to someone off-camera, looking at the ground, smoking cigarettes or pipes; not posing, and the blurred edges of the photo and the grittiness of the exposure told him that it was taken with a vintage Minox spy camera. The men looked like college professors and engineers, rumpled tweed trousers and shirtsleeves, thick glasses, bemused, put-upon expressions and grievous sunburns. They were scientists, and the pendulum was an atom bomb. This photograph was taken at the height of the Manhattan Project, at the core of the most secret enterprise in human history.

He knew this because the Limited Atomic Test Ban Treaty ruled out above-ground testing of nuclear weapons in 1963. He also knew this because he recognized one of the men in the front row: J. Robert Oppenheimer, godfather of the atomic weapons program at Los Alamos in the 1940s. His security clearance was revoked in 1954 after scathing HUAC hearings unearthed some Red unpleasantness in his family background. Apropos of nothing, he remembered a recording of Oppenheimer he'd heard somewhere. The outcast atomic visionary read from the Hindu *Bhagavad-Gita*, seeking an ancient precedent to his apocalyptic invention. In the telephone call, he heard again the haunting hollowness of Oppenheimer's voice as he read the words of Vishnu: "Now I am become Death, the destroyer of worlds."

Looking deeper, straining harder, he recognized another man, in the back row, on the far end. The high forehead, the chiseled features and penetrating eyes that looked like coins in the desert sun. Looking not a day younger than the pictures of him on the Radiant Dawn website. It was Dr. Cyril Keogh.

He walked back to his desk with the picture clasped in one hand behind his back. Still scanning the office, listening for distant, muffled laughter. Someone was fooling around with him, someone who knew what he believed and how passionate he was about his work. If this paste-up job was as sophisticated as the telephone call about Mother was crude, it only pointed more vehemently at a single source.

More tests.

It was enough to make a man want to use profanity aloud.

His phone rang.

He picked up the phone, but he held it away from his ear at first. There was no static on the line, though, only a voice he recognized asking, "Cundieffe? Agent Martin Cundieffe?"

"Brady?"

"Why aren't you in Idaho?"

Cundieffe's anger sprang out of the knotted muscles of his neck and jaw and seared down the line like hot wax breaking through the wall of an unevenly burnt candle. "I met with you the other day at great risk to my job, most of which these days seems to be researching…crap that I don't understand and which nobody else either knows or cares about, but which consumes all my time, leaving me no leisure whatever to play games with a fraternity of…of asshole mutant bureaucrats. I work diligently and without cease for justice every day and night of my life, and I hold myself to a higher standard than either the Bureau or any other agency of the government of this great nation. In short, I do not test well when I feel I am…when I'm being f-fuh-f-fucked with, Mr. Hoecker. Do I make myself clear?"

Had he just *sworn*? He didn't even hear breathing on the line. Well, damn him, if he expected an apology. "Brady, are you there? Did I make myself clear? Why in the world would I want to be in Idaho?"

"It's not about stolen cars, Martin. It's about *everything*."

He started to make good with a retort, but the dial tone cut him off. He laid the phone to rest on the cradle and sat down hard in the chair.

The phone rang again.

He began to walk away from it, but the anger and the paranoia were too much for him.

"Agent Cundieffe?"

"Who is this?"

"I'm sorry, sir. It's Agent Pete Waters, from the Moscow, Idaho, resident agency. I did the surveillance on Heilige Berg, the other night?"

"Right, right, I remember. You didn't find anything. Listen, I appreciate your diligence, but this is not a terrorism case. You said yourself that they didn't appear to be doing anything, and car theft is not a counterterrorism issue, in any case. Until there's some new development—"

"A boy from the compound ran away from the place in a stolen car last night. He hot-rodded into White Bird and crashed into the Dairy Queen. He's in sheriff's custody, right now."

"Is the Dairy Queen in an adjoining state, Agent Waters?"

"No, sir, it's the one right there in White Bird."

"Don't call me again."

"Sir, I was told you'd want to know about this." The Moscow agent sounded exasperated beyond measure, as if he were going to hang up, himself. "The boy's not too badly banged up, but he's real sick, throwing up, can't walk straight. He demanded police protection, but he won't go to the hospital. Says he needs to be locked up and a doctor needs to come to see him."

"Get to the point, Agent Waters, please. What is he so afraid of?"

"He said his church group was taken over by aliens. He says they poisoned the water and the food."

"The boy watches too much bad television."

"He said the aliens came from a place or a thing called Radiant Dawn."

His teeth gritted so hard he tasted a chip on his tongue as he shouted at the idiot agent from Moscow. "I don't know who put you up to this, Waters, but there's going to be hell to pay to OPR, come morning, if I don't get a straight explanation from you about this...this *shit!*"

Shocked gasp on the other end, a hand over the receiver, Waters laughing at him? "This kid is a dyed-in-the-wool Nazi fruitcake, sir, but he's telling the truth about one thing. He's got big tumors all over him like you wouldn't believe. He's real, real sick. They want to fly him out to the University Medical Center at Boise, in the morning—"

"Wait. Hold him there until I get there. I'll be on the next plane out of Washington."

"Sir? I don't understand what this is about, but I sure as hell would appreciate a heads-up as to what we're dealing with, here."

"You and me both, Agent Waters," Cundieffe said, and hung up. Crushingly grateful for whatever perverse impulse forced him to drive to work this morning, he shrugged into his overcoat and speed-dialed the airport.

~ 16 ~

Storch drove as hard as the icy roads would allow, racing down the mountain the way they'd come up the night before, stumbling onto the freshly plowed two-lane State Road 50 and heading west.

He was startled to find that it was night again: he must've slept a lot longer in the cell than he'd guessed. He felt better than he had any right to, and his hands had returned more or less to normal, though they itched like mad and were still peeling. He felt hunger and heat so bad he thought he'd faint. He kept the windows rolled all the way down, but he'd have to stop soon and eat something, or his body would start eating itself. He would hold out as long as he could to get out of the Mission's domain of influence. As if they couldn't figure out where he was going. Even if there wasn't some kind of tracking device in the truck, they were brainy outlaw officers and scientists, and he was only a beaten, stupid sergeant. Going south and out of the country would be the smart play, but instinct drew him back to the west, to his lost home in Death Valley. Instinct had shown itself to be so much smarter than the rest of him of late that he'd stopped trying to fight it.

He didn't look in the mirrors.

In the glove compartment, there was a roll of new-minted twenties, a stack of gas and prepaid phone cards and registration papers on the truck in the name of something called the Black Canyon Ecology Project. The truck had two gas tanks, both full, and he found a parka under the seat to cover his bullet-riddled torso.

Sharing the road only with day-trip skiers returning from Crested Butte and the occasional semi, he sped down and out of Black Canyon, crossing the frozen lake of the Curecanti National Recreation Area. Feeling like he was running with his back turned to a free-fire zone, like they were right behind him, and there was something he could do about it, if he was only nervous enough.

The 50 merged with the 550 and veered north between the Uncompahgre Plateau and Grand Mesa National Forest. He stopped in Grand Junction and bought a three-pound loaf of turkey from a convenience store deli. The protein soothed his aching muscles, but made the itching worse as he began to heal again.

His mind was his own, and he could think more clearly than at any time since the Gulf War. No more sickness. No more Headache, which had always lurked in the back of things, always within striking distance of shutting off his brain. Yet still he was sucked along, like a bicyclist swept up in the warm vacuum behind a speeding semi, floundering in the inexorable gravity of a state of being he could not comprehend.

Once the exhilaration of being out again wore off and his reflexes took over the driving, he started to think. At first, he tried to switch his mind off, micromanaging the road, twiddling the dial on the radio, which included a police and emergency scanner. All was quiet in western Colorado, and why shouldn't it be, on a late January weeknight, when all the world thought Zane Ezekiel Storch was dead?

And who was he, to say they weren't right?

What the hell are you? He couldn't answer the question without Keogh's words, without Wittrock's condemnations or Barrow's lunatic lectures.

Your flesh is the mirror of your soul, *Keogh told him.*

A monster, Wittrock said.

You are an atavistic return to the original product of the grand experiment, Barrow raved. *Yeah, whatever...*

The accusations and insanities chased each other around in his head as the 50 met the larger 70 Interstate and turned westbound again, crossing the Utah state line. The alpine terrain subsided into high desert plains and broken badlands, but the hours and miles only quickened Storch's turmoil.

As a soldier, Storch was a specialist in survival. Now, everything he knew about his trade had become irrelevant, and the rules of the new game seemed to be known by everyone but him. He wore the faces of others, stole their DNA and spliced it into his own. He grew new parts to do things he couldn't imagine or accept, then shed them. His own form was only another mask.

Maybe Spike Team Texas weren't such bad guys before they changed. Twisted up inside by the war, the changes RADIANT wreaked upon them were too much for their minds to take. Their flesh became the mirrors of their souls, alright. What would his flesh become, when he lost it? Because by the minute, by the mile, he was losing it.

The 70 picked its painful way across Utah and through Fishlake National Forest, and the first rays of dawn pricked the Wasatch Plateau as Storch stopped in Aurora to refill and buy more meat, then turned south on the 15.

Towns flashed past without meaning or remark, overgrown, shit-stinking deposits of bipedal mammals. If he let his eyes see as they wanted to, even the writing on the thousands of brightly lit signs on the road had no more meaning than the pheromone trails of ants, the piss-musk messages of dogs. He watched for eyes watching him, for obstacles that might rise in his path, but there was only the open road and the numberless company of trucks, blind herd animals following the same game trail south and west.

As he passed through Cedar City and into the monumental alien landscape of Zion National Park, he shut it all up. His was not a strategically trained mind. He could not expect to get a handle on the rhythm of conflict in a normal war, let alone one between humans and their unnatural successors. He needed a battle plan, and he had to trust in this body, because it was the only one he had. He was still Zane Ezekiel Storch, even if it was only his say-so against the rest of the world. He was still a soldier. But he didn't want to be in anyone's army ever again.

He could not run any longer. He would fight. Whom he would fight, and how, he had no fucking idea whatsoever.

He crossed a corner of Arizona, saw a sign beside the road: Mt. Bangs, elev. 8,012. *I'll be damned*, he cracked a smile, enjoying a plain coincidence. *There's your monument, sir, you crazy motherfucker.*

The road carried him across Nevada and the Pacific time zone line. Storch spent his bonus hour in the restroom of a Shell gas station. He blocked two toilets and bought another turkey and three hams for breakfast.

He passed the Valley Of Fire State Park and the Moapa reservation, then Las Vegas: a riotous garden of neon pitcher-plants, the tar pit of the space age. In the absence of natural predators, humans make their own diseases, their own predators, their own extinction. He caught his reflection studying him in the mirror. Why not their own successors?

He passed through a nameless casino resort blooming like Russian thistle hard against the California border, LAST CHANCE TO GAMBLE! on a spangled billboard overshadowing the California sign. So engrossed was he in driving, brooding and radiating copious amounts of heat that he nearly blew through the INS inspection station straddling the state line.

The olive-drab customs agent stepped out into the road hesitantly, one hand outstretched to wave him to stop, the other gripping a walkie-talkie like he wished it was a gun. Storch's foot started to stand on the gas, but he held it back and forced it onto the brake, feeling odd clouds of relief blotting out his fear. Shit, he told his body, guess you don't know everything.

He drew up just before the inspector, who came around to the window a little sharply, pissed at almost being run over. "Where you coming from?"

No smart answers, now, he thought, but no answers leapt to mind at all. He must have just stared at the inspector for a moment while the nasal tones began to make themselves into words. The man was just an agricultural cop, looking for pest-infested fruits and vegetables, and maybe the illegals who pick them. He would have no beef with Storch, no idea what he was letting in to the state.

"Colorado," Storch said. "Black Canyon of the Gunnison National Rec."

The man cocked his head in a way Storch didn't like. "Skiing?" His hooded eyes were on the empty bed of the truck.

"Nope. Visiting."

"You live in California?"

What the hell was going on? He thought about the Mission. They were small, but they were smart. They could have put out a stolen report on the truck. They could have filed an anonymous tip on him and juggled the NCIC and state police files eight ways from Sunday to make the law try to stop him. He hoped they weren't that careless with strangers' lives, but he knew too much about that to hope.

He should have switched to another vehicle in Utah. He should have tried to change his looks. He was slipping, forgetting his training. Becoming an animal, just running. He could see it in the inspector's face as he loudly and slowly repeated his question. "Do...you...hail from...?"

"Yeah, most of the year, in—in Norwalk." Where they kept his father. "Listen, I haven't got any fruits or vegetables, so—"

The inspector leaned in the cab window across Storch and took up a big deep sniff of the air in there. His nose seemed to swell and hairs waved out of the nostrils.

Storch's hand itched, twitched, and he looked down at it, clasped it with the other one. Would they grow claws again, or something else? Would they just go for the gun? He fought the urge to scream at the inspector to get away before he got hurt.

A car behind Storch honked, then another. The inspector backed away from the truck and waved Storch on into California.

Relieved and exhausted, he rolled into Mojave at mid-morning. The sky was clear and brutally blue, the air so pure that the scent of food cooking or the sound of a shout could travel for miles, like blood in the ocean. The desert was green and fat with nearly all the rainfall it would get for the year, the endless fields of sage and creosote, yucca and Joshua trees like a rumpled, threadbare Army blanket. This was what Storch had craved: in the unbroken emptiness, the mountains, the telephone and power lines fell away, and he floated free of perspective. One minute he could be large enough to see over the horizon, the next so small that he would pass beneath even God's notice.

The silence, the stillness, calmed him. It was what kept him here for nearly a decade, and healed his soul-sickness. He knew he couldn't stay, but he also knew that before he could decide where to go or what to do, he had to replenish himself, had to anchor himself to what he was, before the world changed him into something he could not live with.

As a human, he stood up to fight to save the human race from its replacements. He had helped to murder more people than he'd ever helped in his lifetime for a cause he didn't understand, but that was the way of soldiers. When he learned more, he could not justify genocide, but neither could he say, *this is just, this is the natural order,* and let it come. What was coming was not simply a new and improved human being. It was only Keogh, His mind like a virus hiding in every indestructible host. The world would rush to be "awakened," and someday, there would be only Keogh.

That was a fate worth fighting against, but the lines were tangled up, and he could not see that either side had a monopoly on truth, let alone moral high ground. The Mission meant to exterminate the mutants, including him. *Science marches on*, he thought grimly, *but I run.*

And in the middle, only Storch alone, a mutant outsider among mutants. Cut off from the divine hive-mind and his own humanity, he could only go insane and become something worse than Spike Team Texas. Madness was in his blood, as surely as his name was Storch, and no recombinant DNA could tweak it away. He could fight, but for what?

How many times would he kill to save a species to which he no longer belonged, a race which rejected him as a monster? How many times would he die?

He stopped in Baker.

The Liberty Salvage junkyard had been carted away and a new hurricane fence erected around it. Looking around and seeing no one, he scaled the fence and jumped over.

He was surprised by how much they'd left here. The pit was half-filled with gravel and a few pools of translucent scum that would've evaporated a long time ago, if it was water. Except for a few protruding slabs of concrete and tortured rebar, the pit might've been your garden-variety toxic waste dump. He saw several rusty red barrels and some abandoned excavation equipment among the debris.

He stood at the edge as the sun seemed to drop out of the sky and splatter on the merciless desert floor. Lenticular clouds bloomed like ghosts of UFO's in the west, then unraveled into strings of vapor. The ground turned purple and indigo as if ink were rising up out of the pit. When the sun went down out here, the earth cooled so fast you could hear it shrinking.

This was where it happened, where everything changed. In a second, his mind and body were taken away from him. The last, most basic roots of his life were burned away. All of it hinged on a crazy, suicidal decision to come back here.

Only he and Wittrock came back from the raid on the Radiant Dawn hospice village, and they were headed for an airfield. He could have gone with them, or he could have fled when they touched down in Nevada, but instead, he had forced the pilot to take him back here. He was trapped, irradiated, and imprisoned, in every possible sense of the word. Maybe he came back to turn himself in, to seek punishment for what he'd done, or maybe it was because of the nurse.

The soil on the floor of the pit was cracked and warped by escaped moisture. The brittle sound of it under his boots reminded him of thin ice on a frozen lake. Profoundly mistrustful of the ground, he probed each step before he shifted his weight, avoiding the pools of scum in the hollows of the pit.

Stella Orozco was her name.

He only saw her twice. When she gave him aspirin in the sick bay, she'd tried to be a cast-iron bitch, but then she'd watched him sleep—watched him pretend, to see how long she'd hover over him. She was so angry—at everything and everyone, at men, white men in particular—yet so scared, that he felt more drawn to her than he had to anyone he'd known for...for forever, so long as he knew. She'd disarmed him, but in a way she couldn't have predicted, and which only seemed to make her angrier as it rendered him weaker. When he'd heard her voice on the radio, cutting in on the suicide plans of the Mission scientists, it was her that he'd been coming back to save, but there were deeper forces at work.

The girl he left to die in the white slavers' mine, the one he came to save, but left to burn.

You get used to it...

Stella Orozco was one too many innocent people he could have saved, but didn't. And for what he'd done in the cave, his brain whipped into a rage soup by the abrupt destruction of his life and the discovery of the dead girl, he still owed the universe. That was why he went after her, and threw his humanity away. There was something else, too, a need he couldn't put a name to, because it still felt too much like weakness. The way her eyes flashed when she saw him and ran to him in the awful light. As if she saw through him, and despite herself could not look away. The way she almost touched him, in that moment before the ground opened up...

Storch! Do you see it? It's beautiful!

The wind changed. A coyote howled nearby, and a chorus of dogs took up the desert vespers from somewhere in the distance. The odors of men and trash and car exhaust assailed him from the direction of town, and the spiky smell of sage, and the eye-watering reek of the unholy poison in the ground.

And her.

Fainter than his faith, yet some trace of her was nailed to the place, a chemical ghost that flickered and wavered out of the dead ground like the last wisp of smoke from a doused match. He looked around as if he had fully awakened for the first time since he got behind the wheel in Colorado. He would wake up on the road, or in the plastic cage, now.

When he didn't, he picked his way over the floor of the pit with greater urgency, studying the ground and drinking in the poisonous air for any trace.

The rubble might have settled, exposing her remains to the air. Some desert scavenger might have burrowed down to her and gotten at her. He had no way of knowing how sensitive his nose was, now; for all he knew, he was smelling the indigestible bits of her in a cache of coyote shit.

But he kept looking. The trace grew into a thread, and the thread a trail. He followed it deeper into the pit, into the blue shadow of a broken concrete wall that jutted out of the crumbled embankment like a smashed tombstone.

He put his fingers on the pouting sheet-metal lips of the hole she climbed out of, ravaged and gouged by claws, from the inside. His heart leapt. He looked up at the sky, as if he could catch someone watching to see how their joke went over.

He stuck his head into the hole and inhaled, gagged, retreated with his mouth and nose clamped shut. The air inside was sour and dry and deader than the first gust of air from an unsealed Egyptian tomb. But it was not a tomb. It was a chrysalis. A womb.

He closed his eyes tight, drinking in the air to find where the trail led next. His brain tingled like he had altitude sickness, and he was sure now that he was dreaming. She was alive. She had escaped. She was His.

Storch did not need his nose to follow her trail, once he settled down and began to *look*. Her footprints across the pit were preserved by the crusty sand, that must've been slush when she walked in it. Since the last snow. Less than a month ago. Meaning she'd been buried all this time. Like him.

He climbed up the side of the pit and back over the fence. The trail disappeared on the pitted tarmac road that ran from the old drive-in junkyard back to Baker and the 15, but the only shelter in sight was the trailer park a little less than a mile down the road. A body freshly risen from the grave wouldn't be choosy.

He forgot the truck, ran as fast as he could. His legs carried him in great, measured strides, pistoning muscles and lungs working in perfect syncopation. The distance eaten up beneath his feet faster than if he'd driven, his muscles unfazed by the effort, as if his blood had found something more efficient than iron with which to bind and deliver oxygen.

He braked to a jog as he passed through the open gate of the Vista Del Nada trailer park. His heart raced not with effort, but with fear. He didn't dare to rationally hope that, out of this unspeakable runaway catalog of atrocities had come a miracle that would absolve him of even a scintilla of his guilt. The universe just didn't like Storch like that.

He paced the rows of double-wides and mobile homes in a frenzy, looking for he knew not what. He rounded the office and ducked back when he saw a pair of Dobermans sitting on the porch. They watched him with heads cocked at an angle as if they didn't know what the hell to make of him. Dogs didn't do that. They barked at what they didn't understand, at anything that intruded. But these just watched him go by. An old fat man in an easy chair sat beside the window, watching TV.

Storch didn't see anyone outside, and could almost believe the place was abandoned, if not for the blare of televisions and radios and the hospital smells of medicines, ointments, cigarettes and microwaved food. Underneath it all, there was still a trail, but he stumbled across it several times without it leading him anywhere. He wandered until full night had set before he found the double-wide green Sojourner trailer tucked away at the back of the park, off the gravel lane and facing the desert. It was wrapped up in CAUTION-POLICE LINE-DO NOT CROSS tape. It reeked of her.

He listened at the door and looked around before forcing the lock and slipping inside. He came back out twice as fast and collapsed in the sand with the door flapping in the wind, a bright crash like a sword on a shield that could probably be heard in Laughlin. Her. And death. And rot. And blood. And Him.

The place was lived in hard, the sinks overflowing with dirty plates and empty cans, bottles, all licked clean. Sloughed skin like rotten willow bark scattered all over the bed and the living room floor. Blood on the stripped mattress, so much blood it must've been a whole other person.

She'd come here to feed and to heal. In her hunger, she'd done terrible things.

He'd made her do them. She was probably a prisoner in her own head, like he'd been. Mad from months buried alive, whipped and warped by a parasitic mind raping her own, down in the hard, cold dark, and turned loose on an unsuspecting world.

Had they caught her?

He sifted the bloody undertow of sensation roaring through his brain, discarded some, enhanced others, rebuilding the room in his head so he wouldn't have to go in. Cigarette smells, and mud from boot-prints: the police touched little, waiting for an expert who may not have come yet. The scene was cold, but there was no cordite stink, no gunpowder and terror-sweat that imprinted scenes of bloodshed. And she would not be taken without a fight.

No. He scented Keogh in the mess, but with a different flavor than the one she sweated out of her pores as she healed. He came for her. He was in this room, in a body that ate healthy, showered regularly, and used soaps and aftershaves to smell like a proper middle-aged, middle-class white human male. He came and took her away, to wherever they were gathering now, in preparation for—what?

A bloodless evolution—

He was more than human, now, but still only a stupid Green Beret Sergeant. He knelt on the sand and clawed great fistfuls of the abrasive earth up and rubbed it in his eyes. His hands tried to scour his face off. He tried to think, tried to remember, what it was to be a soldier, to be a man—

Is his critical center of biomass in White Bird?

Major Aranda's question spun at him out of nowhere. They thought he was their guinea pig, they wanted answers. They had given him his answer. They had shown him who he was fighting, and maybe where. He owed them a debt of gratitude.

He ran back to the truck to get a road atlas.

~ 17 ~

Winter in the Snake River Valley, Idaho–Greenaway fucking loved it.

Sitting alone in the cabin of a Bell Model 406 scout/attack helicopter, he saw the wicked fangs of the Seven Devils Mountains and the Snake River, a blue-black buzzsaw blade sheathed in the aptly-named Hell's Canyon, and he was fueled by an exultant awe for nature, when it got its ducks in a row. If there was one thing he could respect, it was terrain that had no respect for men. The plunging gorges and swift-flowing rivers made a thrilling scenario for a wargame. Greenaway couldn't imagine a better place to formally begin his retirement.

His ground units radioed in five by five, all linked up outside of White Bird and ready to move up the hill. The support chopper team, likewise, had only good news from their position. Good men, trustworthy soldiers hand-picked from throughout his career, and not one invited didn't come over. He had no officers higher than Sergeants, no fawning yes-men lieutenants or career-conscious captains gumming up the lines of communication. Greenaway had been planning his army for years before retirement even became a realistic threat. He hadn't been looking forward to leaving the Army, but when they forced him out, he rediscovered his dream army and found the means to make it come true.

Lt. Col. Greenaway was not the first retired Army officer to turn mercenary; he had himself delved in wetwork-for-hire in Africa after Vietnam, before drifting back into the fold. But he knew of no other merc whose army was financed by the United States government to hunt American citizens within her borders.

When he came to them with the NSA intercepts, they looked at him like he'd shit on their desks. So vulgar to actually bring copies, their eyes said, while their mouths spewed mealy-mouthed bureaucratese. In '78, when he'd bought his way back into the Army with White Star smut, they'd made out like he was Judas and swore to get him, someday. This time, they hardly kicked as they cut him a check. They thought they'd bought him off cheap with Army surplus goods, a fat payroll for men, and a license to hunt eggheads. He wondered just how common the practice of government blackmail had become in the intervening years. He didn't have much time to consider whether or not he was doing exactly what they'd hoped he would.

Not even the NSA would admit to knowing where the Mission was dug in in-country, and Greenaway thought long and hard before passing on hunting them in South America. He got fresh intercept traffic like the morning paper every day for a month, but no joy. Then, the late-night call from a Deep Throat-copycat who tipped him off to Idaho.

That was two weeks ago. After a tight training cycle, he notified the appropriate parties and mustered his men from their impromptu winter quarters at the ass-end of Camp Perry, the CIA's training ground in Virginia. Eight hours ago, they stood at attention on an abandoned airstrip in the middle of the Yakima Firing Center in central Washington, heard the orders of the day, loaded up their toys into six trucks and two helicopters, and set out for the new Radiant Dawn hospice village.

He was about to break a cardinal principle of special ops, in running a pitched defense. His troops were hunters of men, not goalkeepers, and every other force that had tried to defend a hill like this had come to grief, though none were quite like his. Still, after the first fly-by, Greenaway was mighty impressed, his mind abuzz with possibilities.

Situated on a ledge perched near the top of a narrow, almost-impassable valley, the new village reminded Greenaway of the ancient Jewish fortress, Masada. Connection to the road was by one two-lane bridge over a frozen waterfall. Most of the civilians must be underground; there were only thirty or so single-wide trailers and a few sheds clustered around the tower, and he spotted ventilation shafts and a chimney in the snow-girded granite cliffs above the village.

The nearest town was almost ten miles away, population one hundred. A militia compound was only a mile downhill, but they were reclusive white supremacists who spent all their time teaching children to shoot pictures of black and Jewish feds. Like a bear trap in your front yard, liable to spring with deadly force on anything that stumbles in. *I like the way this Dr. Keogh thinks.* His advance recon scouts had advised him that the Nazis had staged a mass exodus only the night before, grouping up in a meat packing plant they owned down in the valley, then leaving in chartered buses. He wondered idly how they knew what was coming, wondered less idly who else knew.

The three-thousand foot summit of Heilige Berg swept by underneath them, and Greenaway motioned the pilot to go lower. In the brilliant mid-morning sun, the field of snow around the tower was a blinding lens, with brightly colored ants frolicking on it. Kids, lots of them, and a few adults, building snowmen and throwing snowballs at each other, a regular Norman Rockwell scene, *Winter Hijinx At The Top Secret Freak Colony.* The people down below looked happy, healthy, and, he was sure, were simply a bunch of honest-to-goodness decent people who'd been through hell. He was equally sure that the Mission was coming to destroy them, though he had no idea, or interest in, why.

They set down in the middle of the field. He war-faced his reflection briefly in a stainless steel panel beside the loading door. He looked old and hard, but more of the latter, today. An all-consuming PT regimen had carved much of the creeping flab off him, while he'd answered the problem of his receding hairline with a scorched earth policy. He wore an unmarked black beret and an alpine winter camo suit with an MP5 strapped to his back, a Beretta 9mm at his hip, a K-Bar survival knife on his belt, and another concealed in his boot. He'd let the beard grow wild to cover the deep scar that clove his face from above his right eye to his jawline. He'd slashed it open coming out of his chopper, at the bottom of the Owens River, last summer. The beard was almost entirely silver, with only a hint of the original-issue copper-red whiskers, which made him look like a paramilitary Santa. He nodded at his reflection's steely glare. *Yes, old man, you still got it.*

He leapt out and sank up to his hips in compressed powder. Looking around, he still saw the residents of this godforsaken place zipping around on the wind-scoured crust of the snowfield like water-striders on the skin of a still pond. Shaking off the crew chief's helpful hand, he fought the snow until he was out from under the prop wash, then wondered if he hadn't made a horrible miscalculation.

They stood around him, totally unfazed and unimpressed by his entrance, merely shading their eyes and taking him in. Like military choppers set down in the middle of their cancer winter wonderland every damned day. Like he was expected. This made him extremely nervous, though he couldn't figure why. He knew that some people, on up to the top brass, fed him a little of their fear when they first came into contact with each other, but he'd never known that he *needed* their fear before. The children watched him, looking into his eyes as he struggled through the crowd towards the center, feeding *on* him. He turned to the chopper, to the pilot's black goggles. He nodded, and they ascended in a single lunge, disappeared over the ridge to oversee the land transport.

He went back to slogging, cursing himself in a thick cloud that hung around his head. He could feel his head heating up, blood boiling his brain, his muscles tearing and protesting the work. His lungs burned with the effort and with the stringent tang of the pines, his throat almost closing up in allergic reaction to the pollen, like it was midsummer in the Sierras. That was strange, wasn't it? He wrapped his scarf around his face, strapped on goggles, and resolved not to take them off until he got back to Virginia.

He was less than an eighth mile from the concrete apron around the medical center, but it seemed to stretch away from him, even as the snow seemed to get deeper. It greedily soaked up his first wind before he was halfway across the field, and now the children circled around him silently, like pack dogs rounding up a dying lion. It was disgraceful, but he wouldn't let himself yell at them. He had come here to *protect* these people, for fuck's sake, or at least that was what he was selling them today. Stupid goddamned chopper pilot...

One of the children took his hand, and he didn't so much lean as fall on it, because he was suddenly old, and sinking into the white, and thinking only about lying down. "Get away," he huffed, but he couldn't hear himself, and the kid tugged. Greenaway was so weak, he slumped forwards and levered himself out of his hole only with the boy's help. He lay prone and gasping on the snow. The hand the kid was still holding felt numb, a dead leash, was he having a goddamned heart attack *now*?

Cascades of flinty gray light filled his vision. He shook himself and swore, and thought he was free of them, but when he looked around, he was standing on the edge of the concrete apron, and they were walking away.

God damn that pilot. Greenaway mopped the sweat off his brow and caught his breath before he strode shakily into the hospice center. He stopped in the atrium, puzzled by what he saw. Row upon row of couches filled the ground floor room. With the massive skylight overhead, the room seemed to be designed for a hundred people at a time to bask in the milky winter sunlight. He crossed the atrium to get a closer look, fought the urge to sink down on one and rest.

What the hell was this place? He knew somehow that the one document in the batch that had still been encrypted, the one called ROYAL PICA, might have told him.

He felt closer to death than he had at any time since the war, but there was no adrenaline rush or the assurance of command to push it back. He was going to get his wish, his own army, his own war, and die before the first shot was fired. Like when Frederick Barbarossa, Emperor of the Holy Roman Empire, and an invincible campaigner, embarked on the Third Crusade at age 67 in 1190, only to freeze to death bathing in a river. *Barbarossa died older than you, and had a lot more to show for his efforts.*

"Lieutenant Colonel Greenaway?"

He whirled and caught himself against a column. Only a trained eye would notice that he had nearly fainted.

It was the main man. Greenaway immediately recognized him from pictures, but the real thing was something else again. Dr. Cyril Keogh stood about Greenaway's height and looked to be about his age, but he had that grandfatherly air about him that fixed him in memory as a head taller, and twenty years older. He wore a quilted black coverall with the white coronal logo on the breast. He was thin, but unbent by his age, and his white hair had receded only so far as to make his forehead higher. His flat gray eyes regarded Greenaway with a flicker of amusement.

"I apologize for not providing you with assistance," said Dr. Keogh. "The snowfall has been surprisingly prolific, of late, and most of the able-bodied residents are absorbed in construction projects. We have many unoccupied trailers on-site, where your men will be quartered." Keogh started to walk away.

Greenaway looked around at the weird solarium, at the couches and the massive skylight overhead. He had lost all the momentum. He had planned to walk in like John Wayne and circle the wagons, but he stood there, still shaking from his walk in the snow, for Christ's sake, like a patient checking in for treatment.

Snap out of it, granddad.

"Hey! Keogh!" he shouted, running into a dim, narrow corridor after the Doctor. "Wait a goddamned minute! How long have you known we were coming?"

The doctor didn't stop or turn around as he walked. "You didn't think you would come as a surprise, did you?"

"Who else knows?"

Keogh ducked into a doorway, but paused on the threshold. The sun must have broken through the clouds, outside, because the sunlight suddenly flooded the doorway through a window in the room, and Greenaway found it impossible to look directly at Keogh. "Your element of surprise is safe with me, Lieutenant Colonel. You were not sent for, nor do I believe your occupation of these premises will prove a wise strategic move, on your part. There are, no doubt, other parts of the world where a veteran mercenary of your experience could make himself useful?"

Greenaway made himself look Keogh in the eye, his own eyes straining to adjust. He couldn't sort out his own thoughts, let alone his feelings. Who the hell was this motherfucker? "Listen, Doctor. I came here to burn down the Mission when they come, and the same people who told you all about me believe they are coming, and soon." He walked up close to Keogh, inflated his chest to drive the egghead back into the room. When he didn't give ground, Greenaway got up in his face. "I don't give a shit about your hospice village, cult, whatever the fuck you want to call it. I don't give a shit about your people, they can all drink the punch and die today, as far as I'm concerned. I don't give a shit why they—" pointing emphatically east, at *them* "—don't want the Mission to kill you, but won't just call out the troops. I want the Missionaries to come here, and I want to kill them all. Then everybody can get on with their own fucking business. Do you copy?"

Keogh's forehead touched his, and he flinched. Those eyes. They were like the layer of metamorphic rock at the bottom of very deep holes like the Grand Canyon, the two billion year old stone that predated everything that ever lived. Like that ancient stone, looking at you. Flinched? He backed away until his head hit the wall.

"You want revenge on them for what they did to your men? To your face? Your career? You were only collateral damage in an act of madmen, as were we. If you are still capable of learning, of adapting, I would urge you to take notice of the changing environment. Your Army has taught you to bring the tools of the last war to the next one. I sincerely hope they don't come, but for your sake, more than ours."

"So you don't need protection?" Greenaway asked. His eyes skidded off Keogh's gaze again and he looked into the room. A trauma center, empty of patients. Outside, the children frolicked in the dazzling sunlight. He could see no sign of his army.

"We adapt, Lieutenant Colonel. We are creating a world beyond war, beyond death. It amuses me that you would come to protect us with weapons of war. We don't need them, but you're welcome to stay the season, if you must."

Greenaway backed away, out of the light. His men would be arriving soon, he had to—

Get away!

"I understand the impulses of genetic programming," Keogh went on, pursuing him into the dark. "It takes more than a lifetime to overcome them, and how many of us have that much time? A human lifetime is very short, is it not, Lieutenant Colonel?"

He could think of nothing to say, no reason to be here another instant. He turned and began to walk away, back to the solarium and the light and the outside.

"I have no doubt you'll perform adequately, if and when the time comes, Lieutenant Colonel. The Mission is your natural enemy, yes? You'll destroy them or die trying. It's in your programming."

Greenaway hit the front doors running and slid to a stop out on the front walk. The sun had retreated back behind silver-gray clouds. His heart thumped an arrhythmic tocsin pumping blood thicker than chili in his brittle arteries.

The color of his eyes. He should have kicked the slimy old motherfucker's ass. He was one of them. An egghead. The enemy.

And you ran scared, granddad.

The first of his trucks crested the ridge and lumbered down the last couple of switchbacks to the bridge. The Bell 406 hove into view and circled over the field. Greenaway walked out to the edge of the concrete apron and waved his arms high over his head. His heart stopped racing. He closed his eyes for a moment and let it all out of his mind as he got back into character.

The last truck was crossing the bridge when the first pulled up in front of him. His men fell out and ran down the convoy line. The last man out of the truck jumped down, spat a brown stream of tobacco juice at the snow, and strode up to Greenaway on stout, bowed legs. Barely coming up to Greenaway's chin, the man had a torso like a trash can, and worse breath. His weathered Okie face was distorted by a sizable plug of Red Man, perpetually working in his cheek. "Ho ho, ho! What's in the fuckin' bag, Santa?"

Greenaway's laugh was deeper and more real than he'd let himself be since the last time he shared the company of Master Sergeant Talley. It took ten years and fifty pounds off him. "Toys, Burl. Toys for all the bad boys of No Such Company." The name was a throw-away, a final fuck-off to the pencil-necks who made all this possible. Something better would come to him, once the unit was blooded.

In his many dreams of a perfect army, there was only one constant: a mess of shit-kicking, brass-balled, no-bullshit veteran Master Sergeants, and in his dreams his hod-boss of killers was always Talley.

"Shit, Mort, I got Bradleys, snowmobiles, choppers, three artillery batteries, two APC's, a couple tripod-mount M60's, grenade launchers, a trunkful of mines and Stingers and shit, a ton of NBC crap, about eight million rounds of what-have-you, and sixty-odd ill-tempered, pig-ignorant, heavily armed sonsobitches who've been living on gas station hot dogs, an' pissin' in Coke bottles for purt near eighteen hours, now."

Candy-ass bullshit. "Morale's bad?"

"They're pissed, Mort. So'm I, you want the truth. Half of 'em are acting like this is some sorta goat-rope wargame, and the ones who're taking it serious *scare* me, Mort. I ain't even told 'em yet what we're defending, 'cause I'm scared I would've ended up here with empty fuckin' trucks. I know you picked 'em, but some of them boys're damaged goods." He spat on the ground and looked up at Greenaway. Talley was ten years out of retirement with a fourth Purple Heart in the Gulf. Plate in his skull and shrapnel everywhere else, a pig farm in Arkansas, kids off to college or the service, a wife who still liked to bend the bedsprings. Next to Talley, the helicopters and the artillery had been child's play to pick up. "I don't need this shit any more, Mort."

"Tell them what I told you, Burl. This is not a game. This is real. This is what we trained for. All our lives."

The artillery and the APC's were coming down off the trucks, and Talley knew damned well he should be overseeing it. But he stood there, boring into Greenaway's head and trying to see what the hell the big fucking picture was. Greenaway didn't like being on the business end of that look. His own face was slashed with creases from giving that look to the brass. They had trained for this operation—storming bunkers like the one in Baker, learning electronic countermeasures, playing with the kind of toys they only dreamed of having in the real service. But none of them had heard, or asked for, a word about what this was. What Burl was waiting for was for Greenaway to say he was ready to send men to die for this.

"Get the men together, Burl. Now."

Talley flashed a broad, ingratiating smile, its warming power undiminished by his teeth, which were the color of corn in shit. His mouth twitched, stopped just short of saying something. He snapped off a smart salute and double-timed it after the soldiers, barking patented Burl Talley obscenities at them. They formed up in six rows of eight, looking as smart and pissed-off as Greenaway could ask for. He knew them all, or nearly all. In their eyes, he saw ninety-six mirrors that gave him back his younger self.

"Some of you know me as Lieutenant Colonel, some as Captain, or even Sergeant Major, and some of you know me from places where we didn't get ranks, and nobody used their real names. But you signed on for this because you trusted me when I was your CO then, and I never got you killed. I kept you alive to save you for this.

"You're here because each and every one of you is the best, many so good the Army threw your murderous asses out—" pause for laughter, of which there was more than a little. "You understand the doctrine of covert warfare, and you've come together beautifully as a unit, considering the clusterfucked op tempo. I know all of you have questions, and many of you have doubts. I see a lot of bitching and titty-twisting in your eyes, too, though, and it all stops now.

"You are not mercenaries now, any more than you were in the Army. Make no mistake, motherfuckers: You're in my Army, now, but this is not just my war. This is the real one we all knew was coming, some day. That day is upon us."

He looked down the rows of men standing at attention, stern, mannequin-faces. "And none of you knows what the fuck I'm talking about.

"I'm talking about a bunch of defense scientists and spooks who run a fifth column group called the Mission. They hide behind a lot of peacenik disarmament rhetoric, but their Mission is a world government by scientists. In and out of the halls of power, they've been the real enemy that's stood between us and ultimate victory, all these years. I'm talking about the soft-headed cocksuckers who gave the Russians the atomic bomb, and every vital defense secret we've ever had since. I'm talking about the godless motherfuckers who held back our own weapons programs, and dragged out the Cold War, and Vietnam, and instead gave us agent orange and yellow rain, and BZ, and depleted uranium shells. I'm talking about the scumbags who knew what happened to our brothers who got left behind in Nam, because they *sold* them."

Disbelief and outrage mingled in their faces, but the point was scored. The collective sound of gritting teeth was like an iceberg chewing up a mountain.

"I've read it all in National Security Agency intercept documents some of you helped me get. It made me sick to my soul, gentlemen, to read the list of their crimes. And that wasn't the worst of it.

"They have an accomplice, who has covered their treason up for decades, in hopes of getting a few more trinkets out of them, a few more shiny new toys they'll never actually play with. That accomplice is the United States government, gentlemen, your fucking tax dollars at work. They covered up the Mission's theft of fifty tons of napalm from China Lake last July, and the dumping of said nape on the first Radiant Dawn hospice village in California, killing one hundred civilians. Then they nuked it. Think about that for a minute. The third nuclear weapon detonated in anger in history, and they did it in California. I didn't see any of it on the news, did you?"

"No, Sir!" most of them shouted. Two of the squad leaders were with him on the chopper when the EMP wave from the nuke knocked them out of the air over the Owens River. A few still looked at him, though, like he was wearing a tutu.

"Now there's one final thing, gentlemen, but I don't even want to tell you, it makes me so goddamn mad. The Missionaries aren't just a gang of egghead traitors. You're all elite soldiers, and you've heard the stories about brother soldiers who went MIA in an engagement, and were quickly written off as dead. Some of them are alive and well and fighting for the Mission. Maybe some you know. That's why nobody's going to watch this fight on TV, either. That's why you had to come out here, my brothers.

"I know you've been training for offensive rather than defensive ops, but we've got artillery up the ass, and good crews to man it, and air support I think you're going to like. We're going to keep it simple and perforate anything that comes into this valley. And then, God willing, we're going to follow them home and exterminate their traitorous asses. Any questions?"

For a long moment, nobody raised their voice. Then a man in the back, Gruber, ex-Delta, sidelined for emotional stress, raised his hand. "Sir, if they nuked the last place— I mean, how're we supposed to—"

"Good question. They nuked it as a last resort. The bomb was on a downed chopper, and the arrangements were different. Most of this hospice village is underground. The Mission'll have to go in through the building or the vents to get to the target."

Next question. Three raised their hands right away, but Talley beat them to it. "Maybe I missed it when you covered it before, but how do we know they're coming here, sir? If this is a cancer village," he said dubiously, taking in the healthy, happy children still playing on the front steps, all but oblivious to them, "then why blow it up? If it ain't, what the hell is it, that they want it so bad?"

Greenaway's eyes roved over each man's face again before he answered. "All I know is, it's top secret, and it's research. More egghead shit, but the Mission wants it destroyed. Maybe it's bioweapons research, and maybe it's a cure for cancer, and maybe it's the eternal search for a delicious, non-pants-shitting fat substitute. What I know, and what you now know, is that there are still a few good people in government, who have seen fit to show us where the motherfuckers are going to be, and who have given us the tools to make sure they never leave. They have also seen to it that nothing that happens here will leak—this might as well be Mars.

"The enemy you are going to face is smarter than you, and he has a lot of technology to fuck with your head, your weapons, and your bodies. But we have technology, too. And we have a beautiful mountain on which to fight, and if nobody fucks up, we have the element of surprise. They're not expecting a fight like this, they're just coming up to blow up this building and all the civilians, mostly children, holing up in it. This fight may drag on for days, or it may be over in seconds. God willing, none of you expendable bastards will stub a toe out here, but as God is my witness, if any of you should fall here, know that you gave it all up for the highest cause, against an enemy only we can see. If any of you still have questions, see Staff Sergeant Keller, who has some of the documents I mentioned available for review. Master Sergeant Talley has got the maps of this place, and the deployment assignments, which he'll go over with you squad leaders, directly. I want the trucks unloaded and cleared out of here in ten, the works completed by 0200 hours tomorrow. This company is dismissed."

The formation flew apart and swarmed over the trucks again. Greenaway watched them work for a minute, letting their vigor feed him. He felt strong again, the shit before must've been the altitude, and he was an old man, and this fucking place—

A bell shrilled from the tower, and the children ran for the doors. Recess was over. He watched them racing over the snow like jackrabbits, so preternaturally graceful and vital that he began to feel heavy and weak again. He looked at the tower then, and blinked, looked again, his eyes going wide in disbelief.

A few adult residents came out the front doors and crossed the parking lot towards a big shed Greenaway figured was the motor pool. One man, tall and gangly, split off from the group and headed towards the bridge on foot. He wore the identical black coveralls that everyone else wore, but even at a distance, even after twenty-eight years, he was pretty sure he recognized him.

In '72, his White Star unit was ferrying weapons into Cambodia and heroin out when they encountered a Special Forces deep recon A-team with a whole tribe of Montagnard irregulars. He only saw one of them, a scary, tightly wound redneck scumbag who wore ears around his neck. Bastard demanded tribute for passing through, like a fucking tribal warlord. Greenaway felt snipers all over his caravan and legions of Yards creeping through the undergrowth all around them, so he paid the redneck off in food and ammunition, and went on his way.

He learned later that he had probably been hit up by Spike Team Texas. The legendary lost patrol had vanished two years before in Laos, and were thought to have gone native. Myths wrapped around the hush-hush core of their story—they grew opium, they were cannibals, they radioed for ground reinforcements, then killed the unwary grunts who showed up to "save" them—and they became bogeymen as much to their old outfit as to the NVA. That no such unit was ever acknowledged to have existed by the brass only gave a glint of reality to the legend. After all, White Star didn't exist, either.

The tall, jittery hillbilly walking across the parking lot was the motherfucker who robbed him in 1972. He closed his eyes.

You're losing it, granddad.

He took out his binoculars and peered through them at the man. The lenses were fogged up, and he wiped them off with his gloved fingers while he tried to keep the man in sight as he walked away faster than most people could sprint.

Talley touched his shoulder, making him jump. "Fine pep talk, Mort. Long as nobody stops and thinks about that line of bullshit, we ought to get along swimmingly." He spat between his boots and looked at Greenaway. "What's the rumpus, Mort?"

Still looking through the binoculars, he asked, "Burl, d'you remember the stories about Spike Team Texas?"

Talley chuckled. "The lost patrol? What made you think of that?"

He looked over the eyepieces. The lone figure had dwindled to a black twig on the misty edge of the lot, but he had him. He adjusted the focus ring and handed the binoculars to Talley, who took them and scanned the mountaintop. "You want the Vulcan battery up there, Mort? 'Cos I don't think we're gonna get the Bofors up there, 'less you wanna airlift 'em…"

"No, the man going to the bridge, look at him! He's—"

a ghost

"What're you talkin' about, Mort?" Talley handed the binoculars back to Greenaway, his face looking more worried than ever. A brown string of tobacco juice dangled from his slack lower lip. "That's just a girl, boss." He walked away, shouting at the men off-loading the first light APC off one of the trucks.

Greenaway looked again. He must've lost the man, because there was only the one figure striding across the lot, and Burl was right, like always. A very young, compact girl with short, black hair looked over her shoulder at him as she crossed the bridge. Looking across a half a mile, she looked down the binoculars and into his eyes, and she winked.

Greenaway put away his binoculars and went to look for a trailer where he could have an undisturbed drink, and maybe a long nap.

~ 18 ~

They had agreed to meet in the forest at midnight. Beyond that, Major Aranda knew, everything else would be in dispute.

He stood with his command staff in one corner of a triangle in the glade at the center of the Missionary underground forest. He had come expecting a stand-off between the soldiers and scientists, like usual, but was pleased to find that the eggheads' united front had collapsed, and split along predictable lines.

Dr. Calvin Wittrock headed the surviving bomb-makers, the veteran physicists, chemists and engineers who once wielded godlike power at places like Los Alamos, Lawrence Livermore and Pine Ridge. Some of them had worked on the first hydrogen bomb. Others helped to make worse weapons that the world had not yet seen—super bugs, neutron bombs, RADIANT. Horrified at what the world did with their sterile laboratory exercises, they defected and formed the Mission, tried to expiate their sins by dragging the superpowers back from extinction or unilateral hegemony. They were haunted men, their souls etched by the ashes of millions incinerated by their theories, and the nightmares of billions more who lived under the swords they forged. But they were alive, while their military counterparts from the early days of the Mission were all long-dead and forgotten.

Dr. Barrow fronted the Greens, the younger generation of scientists. Most of them had come over too early in their careers, and they were not guilty enough by far. Their righteous rage had made them into a faceless mob, and after years of working side-by-side with them, Aranda found it harder every day to tell them apart. They hated themselves, too, but, they hated everyone else more, everyone but poor stricken Gaia, the beleaguered Earth-Mother. Aranda had to admit that Wittrock had been right, back on the plane. He trusted the Greens less than the bomb-makers. If Barrow and his people ever discovered a way to cleanly and quietly remove humankind from the biosphere, he believed they'd simply stop showing up at the meetings.

Aranda had gone first, laying out the plan of attack, walking them through slides of satellite images and computer simulations on a projection screen set up like an altar in the center of the glade. There were few objections to the tactical elements—what little they understood, they had little reason to object to. He would lead the ground teams himself, and it would be his men who'd face death. They'd ground up the least details of the operation and polished them to a glinting state of diamond-readiness. They drilled in the woods, on a mock-up of the approach to the ventilation shaft shed behind the complex, until it became the substance of their dreams. The massive defensive build-up around the complex would come to nothing if the air support delivered, it was decided. His other concerns about the safety of his troops were likewise brushed aside by both egghead factions in their haste to get to their own arguments. He gratefully left them to it.

Now he tuned back in as the voices raised to a shouting pitch. Wittrock was explaining the deployment of his lysing agent, which Aranda's men called NGS, or Nasty Green Shit. Dr. Barrow's reedy, strident voice razored Wittrock's dry monotone as he shouted, "It's an invitation to a massacre, Wittrock, and not theirs, but ours!"

"You've seen the lysing agent in action, Dr. Barrow," Wittrock calmly replied. "If the Major's aerial deployment forces are up to the task—"

Catching Wittrock's pointed pause, Aranda irritably nodded. "Dr. Costello has the software thoroughly tested, and is programming in the terrain data we've collected. He's even more solid on the planes themselves," he added, too quickly, relieved that none of them actually knew Costello.

Wittrock keyed the attack simulation in ultra-high speed, so it ran surgically clean all over his face a dozen times before he spoke. "I have yet to see your team provide a more elegant solution."

"It was never our problem to fix, *blanc*." Aranda noticed Dr. Chretien Hanley, the black female incarnation of Barrow who stood at the airlock, at the back of the Green faction. A high-ranking civilian virologist at Ft. Detrick, she was dismissed abruptly and only escaped federal jail time by faking international flight and defecting into the Mission. The legend was that she'd been caught trying to synthesize a smallpox strain linked to sickle-cell markers, that would kill only non-blacks. Barrow's right arm and sometime bed-mate, she'd helped him whip the Greens from a ragged pack of bitter left-leaning radical scientists into a cult, of sorts. "You made the monster."

"Not that we've had access to any of the data from repeated exposures," Barrow injected, "but I expect we'd see a marked decrease in dissolution rates over time. The only thing we positively know about the RADIANT offspring is that they adapt. The lysing agent was used to make the bullet that hit Sergeant Storch, but he survived. He escaped. I don't see any strategic allowance for that in Dr. Wittrock's plan, do you?"

Aranda realized the scientist was addressing him directly, though his eyes remained nailed to Wittrock.

The bomb-maker's face was an unpainted latex mask. "Storch is a chimera, produced by anomalous circumstances. His unintended survival was because of his previous inoculation, and the lysing agent still altered him at a molecular level. The tri-helical structure of his DNA was broken. His brainwaves no longer displayed the spike signature of entrainment—"

"But he walked out of here! You order us to believe that the weapon will prove effective on those imprinted by Keogh. But it's already failed. Despite your best efforts, Doctor, we've secured a few specimens of our own. We've learned things, rather extraordinary things, but I doubt we've learned anything you don't already know."

Wittrock turned the projector on Barrow. Electron microscope shots of dying Keogh cells, like a maze of walled cities consuming themselves in divine fire, writhed on the Green's contorted face. "What do I know, Barrow? Enlighten me, if you can keep your spurious religious beliefs out of it."

"They communicate," Barrow said. "They don't just exchange proteins, anymore. Individual cells isolated yet in close proximity to each other are beginning to radiate scalar wave energy, and I think they're trying to communicate. He's in them, down to their every flake of skin, in every protein string, every nucleotide, and he's reaching out. We observed the same sort of energy from the test subject who was destroyed in the cell adjacent to Storch. It was trying to communicate with him telepathically. But none of this is new to either of you, is it? I'm sure you're familiar with Armitage's neural network theory."

Aranda blinked. That name had not been spoken aloud in meetings for quite a while. "I've never heard of it," he said lamely, "but I sure wish somebody would talk straight and tell me."

Wittrock wrung his hands and spoke up over Barrow's shrill attempt to retake the floor. "He was preoccupied with the subtle energy emanations of the brain. The brain as a transceiver, but because each brain is wired uniquely, each sends and receives on a unique subtle energy frequency. It was the basis of all his research on soft-kill technology, but that wasn't his final goal. He believed—towards the end, when he was up against his own mortality, and not really all that lucid—that the energies are our souls, and potentially indestructible. He speculated further that RADIANT could be used to project consciousness along with the genetic data required to remake malignant tissue into a new body."

"What?" Aranda stepped out from his staff and approached Wittrock. "Are you saying he told you that RADIANT-infected people would *become* Keogh? You *knew*? Bangs didn't know, did he?"

"It was only a theory," Wittrock retorted, "not even comprehensible to those who didn't work directly on RADIANT."

"But there's more," Barrow cut in. "Armitage wrote us that he thought Keogh was building a neural network out of his clones. Each one is a scalar-wave copy of the original consciousness, so it doesn't matter how many you kill, if there's one left, you lose. But when there are enough of them—"

"Which is precisely why we've got to strike now, with what we've got!" Wittrock barked.

Aranda stood between them. "When there are enough of them, what?"

"They'll become one," Barrow replied. He took over the projector and typed in a file access command on its keyboard. A three-dimensional model of a constellation of dots appeared. As more dots winked into life and the constellation became a galaxy, they began to glow fitfully, like fireflies.

"This is a model we extrapolated from Dr. Armitage's formulae. Notice how, as more and more identically charged individuals are introduced into the system, the resonant energy output of each is magnified."

He tweaked something on the keyboard. The dots winked in unison, a neon jellyfish. "They synchronize, and unify. The sheer mass of the system reaches critical when upwards of a few thousand individuals come into close proximity to each other. That seems to be the threshold for the effect, given what we know about their brain activity."

He stabbed another button. The flashing dots coalesced into a glowing sphere, a tentacled sun that swelled and brightened until everyone was blinded and looked away.

"Your special effects," Wittrock sneered, "prove nothing, except the urgency of acting now. If Darwin's neural net theory is even remotely possible, which I'm far from granting, we must still strike at every center of biomass with the lysing agent before they can adapt to its effects. However, I submit that adaptation would be impossible, given that the agent is impregnated with unstable lysosomes of his own genetic signature."

Aranda wheeled on Wittrock and shut down the projector. "When did you even begin to suspect this? When were you going to tell us? After, if anyone survived?"

"Major, it has no bearing on this operation. Even Barrow's projection shows that they're far from achieving a viable network."

Barrow lunged between them. His white dreadlocks lashed Aranda's face. "There are quite possibly more than five thousand of them in the world, Doctor. We're far from understanding how whole organisms interact, because we've only had single cell cultures to work with. If they didn't reproduce so readily—"

"You idiots have been cloning them?" Aranda turned on Barrow and seized his elbows, lifted him clean off the ground. "That's exactly why I didn't want to give any of them to *him*!" He dropped the terrorized Green leader, fighting for breath.

All eyes fixed on him. He heard the air recirculators breathing through the pine needles. "And what have you learned from it? Do *you* have a cure for walking cancers?"

Barrow shrank from him and sucked at an unlabeled inhaler. When he recovered, his voice was three octaves lower, but mellowed with an unsettling calm. "It doesn't matter, Major. This isn't a new development. He was here first. He's only using our technology against us to speed up the process. But very soon, all the bodies are going to become cells in a single body, and all the minds are going to become one mind. His. There'll be nothing to do, then, though Wittrock and his can-do blackboard mass-murderers will happily provide you with solutions, right up to and including nuking everything and hiding down here for the next ten thousand years. This lysing agent might work in this operation, but I doubt you'll hurt a hair on their heads the second time, even if you don't leave a single survivor. They'll broadcast their death-energy in scalar waves, or viruses—"

"Death energy?" Wittrock scoffed. "Christ, Barrow, you used to be a scientist!"

"Then I saw it. You saw it, too. You've studied the Pnakotic Manuscripts. You read the account of the Dyer Antarctic expedition. You know about the School Of Night's research, their attempts to directly contact the Unbegotten Source. You've seen the Burgess Shale Anomaly in the Smithsonian with your own eyes, and you know as well as I do what it really is! You know what He is!" Barrow stalked Wittrock. Aranda reached out to catch him, but Barrow coiled, ducked under his arms and launched himself at the senior scientist. "You know who he was!"

Wittrock stood fast, glaring wooden defiance at his rival. Barrow stopped just short of knocking heads with Wittrock. His long, bony hands went out and clawed the air around Wittrock's impassive face. "You saw it all, but you can't face it. If you did, you'd lose your mind, and become me."

Enough of this bullshit. Aranda cued Dr. Blount, one of Wittrock's underlings, and a former black ops planner for the National Reconnaissance Office, who took over the projector. "I think, gentlemen," Blount bellowed, modulating his voice once the others died away, "that all of these metaphysical questions may be rendered moot, concurrently with the present operation. At the time of the raid, we will notify the Russians of the orbit path and projected location of RADIANT. As many of you already know, our Russian counterparts have assembled a force package capable of neutralizing the delivery vehicle of the infection, and stand ready to deliver it. The Radiant Dawn squatter community in the shadow of Chernobyl in the Ukraine has been the site of riots, as word has spread among the malignant millions there that Radiant Dawn can cure them. The Ukrainian government and the Russians are eager to be rid of it, and a crackdown will be coordinated to coincide with the destruction of RADIANT. Similar counter-proliferative actions can be expected in Africa and South America, when the various governments involved come into line. So wherever the center of mass might lie, we will drastically reduce its size and remove its means of reproduction in one blow."

Aranda looked to Barrow, whom he'd expected to shut up once and for all. But the Green zealot recoiled as if a tiger had leapt out of Blount's mouth and savaged his face. Pumping his inhaler, he rasped, "Just as likely, you'll only provoke him into turning RADIANT on a major city. Maybe he'll kill millions, but a few thousand or so with cancer will still rise up. Even if your technology works, for a change, you'll only trigger a more violent reaction." He turned and braced Aranda. His pupils were so dilated that Aranda could see his whole face reflected in them. "You can't lead us into this, Major, not now, not like this. You still don't know enough. Even *he* doesn't know enough," pointing at Wittrock, "and what he does know, he hides until it suits him."

Aranda shook the scientist's hands off him and turned away. "We're committed. White Bird is the largest concentration of infected mass, and it's growing. We've collected samples of soil and water from the valley, and the pine trees are producing lethal carcinogens in their pollen, in the dead of winter. The Heilige Berg separatists abandoned the place, and split up. We're almost certain that most are infected, and probably irradiated. We can't wait to see what spring'll be like."

Barrow leaned into him again. He whispered, "Why are they leaving now, Major? Who tipped them off? If you take RADIANT away, you better get every last one of them around the world before they come together. Because you're only going to force Him to adapt, find a new way to reproduce—"

"Get away from me," Aranda said, then turned on Wittrock. "If I learn that you've been holding anything that could help back, I'll feed you to the fucking Greens, do you understand?"

The glade boiled over with competing shouting matches as Aranda stormed out, shouldering past Dr. Hanley to enter airlock. "We wouldn't eat him," she said, "but you say the word, and we'll gladly compost him for you." She showed him a tranquilizer gun.

He raced to his room and collapsed on his bunk. His head felt like an egg in a bear trap. When he closed his eyes, he could almost visualize his pain, like a glowing steel (*tumor*) ball bearing rolling around on the floor of his brain. He went for his pills and ate today's and tomorrow's without looking at the mix of colors, then lay down. He had briefings in an hour, then they would go downrange to a mountain valley in Idaho to incinerate three hundred and fifty innocent people who happened to be infected with a sentient disease. Until the meds began to kick in and his headache went away, he prayed that he would forget this day as soon as it was over.

~ 19 ~

We are Spike Team Texas. Our war is forever.

He pledged the oath to the sun as its first rays struck his face, as he had every day of his life since the Change. It was what got them through it, and the words made him strong.

Before and below him, the battlefield unfolded like a table-top model, the camouflaged cogs of a machine awaiting a critical infusion of heat and invading elements to set it into motion.

The mercenaries had built the trailer-park around the tower into a fortress, with walls of razor-wire, twelve troop trucks, two Bradley fighting vehicles, a half-track and a swarm of snowmobiles jammed into the field between the tower and the foot of the peaks. A reflecting radar station on a trailer swept the eastern skies from just in front of the main entrance. Another just like it was parked on the other side of the Snake River, in a little forward ops base where the helicopters roosted. APC's patrolled the perimeter, which was marked out with barbed wire, claymores and infra-red sensors. The field where children had played only yesterday was pregnant with mines so densely packed that a stone dropped on one would bounce from one explosion to the next in a chain-reaction. In the midst of it all, groups of Radiant Dawn guests watched from the front steps, like prisoners in a concentration camp. Like bait.

Helicopters, a Bell Model 406 and, he observed with a warm tug of nostalgia, a Huey Cobra, patrolled the valley down to the foot of the mountain, Gatling guns swiveling like eager mandibles. On the jagged peak above and behind the tower, they had three antiaircraft batteries: two Bofors systems on the summit, each running a quartet of 40mm cannons, and a Helicon system about fifty yards above the roof, with three 20mm Vulcan autocannons. Loaders and sighters watched FLIR and radar displays on their computers that cut through the fog and showed them circling hawks and a flock of Canadian snow geese. They were well-sheltered with gray canopies covered in snow and gravel, and might escape the notice of a casual flying observer, but for the jungle-spaghetti of arm-thick power and comm cables spilling down the cliffs to the trailer park.

He saw, too, what they, with all their fancy toys, could not. The Missionary observation post set on the next ridge, two klicks to the north, had been vacated in a hell of a hurry just before dawn, with the all-seeing mercs none the wiser. He sensed the people in the woods, who were invisible to the chopper pilots with their FLIR goggles, because they were buried in snow and radiated no heat, just yet. He saw the road winding down the broken back of Heilige Berg, past the abandoned Nazi compound, and, through the ever-present mountain mist, he saw the fields and ranches of the valley below.

From his perch, 1st Lieutenant Brutus Dyson saw all, yet was seen by none. He had not moved in over eighteen hours, and his skin temperature was only a degree or two warmer than the snowy ledge he lay on, thirty feet above the east-facing Bofors battery. For the duty, Dyson had grown himself a gilley suit—a shaggy, head-to-toe camouflage rig favored by snipers—thick enough to stop a bullet, liberally interwoven with local vegetation. His pelt was made of the fiber-optic spiculate hair of a polar bear, which soaked up ambient color and insulated heat. Right now, he could barely tell where his own arms ended and the rocks began. The talons made it difficult to hold his rifle—an M24 lifted from the mercs' weapons store by one of Keogh's slaves—but he had long since forgotten the weapon, and his eyes glazed over until some movement on the plateau below pricked his prowling nerves. He was coming to hate the mercs, which was good, because in all likelihood, he'd end up killing them all, but he was hating them because they made him wait and watch, and waiting and watching gave him time to think. Think about Spike Team Texas, and why it was beginning to fall apart.

"Doom on you, little campers," growled the Abominable Snowman.

Even before the change that had made him not human, he possessed an uncanny knack for adaptation. It was this native talent—what Special Forces called being "good in the woods"—that got him into the Green Berets when his Ranger CO was trying to get him Section Eight'ed and committed stateside. He left calling cards. Gouged out Charlie's eyes with a notched spoon. His doomed chickenshit comrades trashed him for it, but damned if he didn't hear stories from the interrogators for months after about the Eye-Stealer who haunted their nightmares.

He was tapped for SOG in 1965. The Studies & Observation Group trained Nungs and Montagnards, yellow hillbillies, to fight smarter and dirtier than the Cong, and led them in recon runs and raids in the denied territory of those neutral countries where the Ho Chi Minh Trail fed the red heart of the war. The casualty rate for SOG A-teams was well above one hundred fifty percent, but their kill ratio was the highest in the theater, and for every American commando, Charlie deployed over four hundred to hunt him. They were also among the most highly decorated units, for the few missions that were ever cleared for citation boards to review.

Three man SOG recon teams led squads of indig killers into NVA positions in eastern Laos and VC resupply depots northern Cambodia in 1965; spying on and harassing the gooks so they bunched up, making them fatter targets for company-sized Hatchet Force raids. Early success and stifling political bullshit made the brass hunger for smaller, harder teams of secret soldiers who could roam deep into hostile, gook-infested jungle for days at a time. In their blind zeal, the gods of war created Spike Team Texas.

Almost before they were a unit, they became a single body. The other teams were thrown together and carved to fit on the lathe of unconventional war, but ST Texas was a new animal altogether. It was invisible, except to the dead. It ate only fruit and rice drenched in *nuc mam*, the pungent VC fish oil staple. It used Kalashnikov rifles and wore canvas gook sneakers. It walked, talked, fucked, ate, and shit the jungle. It was not just that they were—almost—all Texans, or that they were all crazy in love with the war. It was simply that the Army had built them into a god, and turned them loose in Eden.

Their head, Captain Virgil Quantrill, was one of *the* Quantrills, great-great-grandson of William Clarke Quantrill, the legendary scalp-taking Confederate guerilla warlord. Forbidden to go into the bush with his men, he snuck out. He doctored their mission reports, juggled atrocities and made them as invisible to MACV/SOG brass as they were to Charlie. Just as his bloody-minded ancestor taught the James gang all they knew about raiding, so Virgil taught them.

Master Sergeant Dyson was the One-Zero. The absolute authority in the woods, even Quantrill deferred to him.

Sergeant First Class Tucker Avery was the One-One, or just the Okie. Half-Cherokee Tulsa-trash, wound tight long before Nam, he lived solely on Green Hornets, the giant horse-pills of speed Uncle Sam packed in their lunches. A master sniper and demolition expert, he once destroyed a platoon of NVA and their lieutenant with a can of nails, some gunpowder, and a crying baby. He still believed he was going to get the Medal Of Honor for it, when the papers finally went through.

Spec Four Gibby Holroyd was the radio operator. Skinny then as Avery was now, still 'Royd was a man of large appetites. He lived to knock up every Asian he didn't kill, and starve out the rest. Somewhere in Laos and Cambodia, there were whole tribes of very ugly Amerasian hillbillies. Still and all, he was a dependable radio-man. He could be counted on to call airstrikes on his own head while NVA encircled their position, then just step to one side as the bombs came down.

Other SOG recon units scouted for or poked around after air raids, spied on enemy supply routes and tried to snatch prisoners and wounded or dead soldiers. Spike Team Texas raised hell. They *lived* in the jungle. They set traps. They poisoned wells and rice. They tapped phone lines and lured NVA troops into minefields. They outkilled cancer. They took trophies. Their Nungs filed their teeth and bit into dying hearts for strength.

Surviving ten SOG missions made you a legend. After fifteen, you spooked people, and after twenty, you were already dead. Spike Team Texas ran thirty-five missions in '66 and '67. They went through Nungs like bullets, but not one of the core four sustained a single serious injury.

The longest insertion lasted five weeks. They were only ambushed at the LZ, getting in and getting out. It became clear to the Captain that a mole in the South Vietnamese army was giving them up, but nobody believed him. When Khe Sanh was overrun by gook tanks and twenty thousand NVA in February of '68, the Marines and MACV refused to help the besieged Special Forces camp at Lang Vei, and every SOG recon team that went out got ambushed on its LZ. Two were completely swallowed up and never heard from again. Spike Team Texas wrote and signed its own orders, pillaged the armory and hiked out of the SOG Forward Operating Base at Phu Bai, into the broken limestone hinterland of eastern Laos.

Spike Team Texas lived off the land, and off the war. It fought the war on all fronts. Spike Team Texas declared war on the United States of America and all other armed parties in Southeast Asia. For seven years, it roamed from the Twentieth Parallel to Thailand, killing anyone who had what it wanted, and vanishing. It became the bogeyman that SF trainers scared their Yards, and each other, with. While Nixon "Vietnamized" the war, Spike Team Texas victimized the Khmer Rouge. It collected redder-than-red scarves. It saluted the last helicopters out of Saigon in '75, and faded back into its jungle.

For Spike Team Texas, the war only went more covert when the Americans went home. They lived off the defiant hill-tribes of Laos and Cambodia, many of whom went nomad or dug into the deepest mountain wilderness, and still hated all Vietnamese scum and loved their killers.

Where necessary, the Captain convinced them the war was still on, that America was still shoulder-to shoulder with them. They trained and armed them and moved on to the next village, sometimes laying in for a year or two, until all the babies started looking like Holroyd. They raped and pillaged opium warlords in Thailand, and amassed enough wealth to buy Presidential pardons.

In 1981, as they were crossing the Mekong back into Laos, a fucking sniper shot Captain Quantrill from half a mile away. With the top of his head gone, he field-promoted Dyson to 1st Lieutenant, and ordered them to eat his body.

Headless, Spike Team Texas went a little crazy. Slashing a bloody swath of indiscriminate slaughter across Laos, they got as far as the Bra, the old VC HQ, in the shadow of Leghorn, a ruined mountaintop Special Forces forward fire control center. The gooks never even put troops on the ground. They bombed them with yellow rain until they went blood simple and tried to kill each other. They took Spike Team Texas alive, yet headless. Like blind, gelded Samson, they chained Spike Team Texas up for two long years, torturing them even as they sickened and wasted away from their exposure to yellow rain. They refused to die, though, and the new Vietnam was too craven to outright execute them. In 1983, they did the sensible, and in the end, the most diabolical thing: they quietly turned Spike Team Texas over to the US Embassy in Thailand.

There were no parades, no press conferences, no medals, no recognition of their heroism, their sacrifice. The prisons were cleaner, their torturers more of the brain-jockey type, and the food had less maggots and rat shit in it, but they were in fucking Florida. At least in Hanoi, they were that much closer to the shit, and they pined for it. In each of them, the voice of Captain Quantrill ordered them to stand tall in the voice of their growling, yellow rain-ruined stomachs. They were destined for something more.

After a year in Florida, their destiny came calling. Along with twenty or so other prisoners, they shipped out on a C-130 to Hawaii, then Guam, where they boarded a boat along with a barnyard full of livestock and an equal complement of interservice brass, spooks and scientists. They were given physicals—Holroyd was so nervous, he tried to rape his doctor—and kept in cargo containers until they reached the atoll. The containers were loaded onto amphibious landers and rolled onto the shore, and the sailors off-loaded them with honest-to-god cattle prods. The treatment was hardly unwarranted. Avery, shackled hand and foot, had head-butted a mouthy communist to death in-transit. They brought the corpse out and used it anyway.

The atoll was a big sandbar in the middle of the Pacific, but the engineers had built a little town on it, complete with houses of wood and tin and concrete (*little pigs, little pigs, let me in*), and barns and bunkers and a steeple in the center of the island. The steeple was all grown-over with machines and recorders and cables and shit, and the cables snaked out to each of the houses and shelters where the sailors and scientists chained down the animals and the convicts.

They were put in separate houses. Holroyd, in the wooden house, shrieked and thrashed and bit two doctors while they tried to attach sensors to him. He sang and cried and pissed his pants for two solid hours. Avery, in a tin shack, slipped his chains, killing one and maiming four and getting as far as the boats before they trank-darted him. Dyson sat calmly in the brick house. He hadn't felt much of anything but sick since the Captain died and they got gassed. But today he felt a queer sort of exhilaration that made escape or violence irrelevant. If this was the end of Spike Team Texas, they were going out in style, for he believed that this was surely a nuke test. What better acknowledgement of their invincible badassedness, than to be nuked? But something about the way the doctors regarded him, the way they argued about having medical staff on-hand, made him begin to suspect this was something more.

They called it RADIANT.

One doctor, a sickly fossil who looked like he'd been yellow-rained on a few times, himself, asked him if he believed he had a soul. He laughed and answered that if he had one, it was bought and paid for, so what difference did it make?

The other one took an interest in him then. He didn't know it at the time, but the other doctor was Him, the brains behind RADIANT, and the author of their rebirth. He looked deep into Dyson's eyes, and Dyson looked back, pure spite melting into a kind of awe as he saw how *old* those eyes were. How old and wise and penetrating. They took his measure and gave him his due, no more, no less. "I would speak with you later," he said. "This doesn't have to be the end. This can be the beginning."

"Whatever, fucker," Dyson grinned back. "Just get it over with."

And when they threw the switch, there was no big bomb-blast, no stroke of lightning, no Godzilla rising out of the sea to eat them. The sun went crazy, and everything on the island screamed like it was burning up, but Dyson heard angels singing, and even as his flesh began to rot and fall apart, he felt new life blooming in the strands and blobs of malignant neoplasm shot far and wide like shrapnel through his dying body. He went to sleep with everything else on the atoll, but Spike Team Texas awakened. They opened their new eyes and took in the new world of cancer exploding out of every man and beast, everything dead and still growing in all directions, and in the center of it all stood the one that had made this, had made them, the one they'd mistaken for a mere human egghead. And in that moment, without a word spoken, they knew they would follow Him anywhere.

Thus did Spike Team Texas get a head transplant.

And for many years, the graft was a success. Keogh had lessons to teach them, about how to remember the language of their flesh, and how to change. Under his messianic eye, they threw off the last shackles of humanity, and Spike Team Texas became simply itself.

He taught them about the world—the real world, not the candy-coated bullshit they fed the maggots in school. They learned that what humans are and why and how they came to be, were not what they'd always been told, but the truth was something they welcomed in their guts, where they'd sensed it all along. Mankind, they learned, was not the first bag of meat to rise from the slime and start trying to change things, and it wasn't the smartest, or the longest-lived, or the most successful, and sure as hell wouldn't be the last. He gave names to the forces they felt all around them since their quickening, and taught them about the Great Old Ones, and the Outer Gods. They weren't proper gods, but you couldn't kill them, and they'd been here, and there, and everywhere else, sleeping, since before the earth as men knew it came to be. Of Keogh himself, they learned only that he was not a god, but planned to be much more.

And there was work, glorious work. He fed them wetwork delicacies, ops undreamt of by spooks, gooks or the devil hisownself. They greased his plan—improve RADIANT, save the world. They harvested his breeding stock, reduced to kiddie-snatching at rest stops. He improved RADIANT—made it a Keogh-machine. Assembly lines. Spike Team Texas: prototypes, least-loved stepchildren. Rumbles. Along came the Mission, someone to hate with impunity. Wetwork feast, napalm ambience. Bad times after that, rebuilding, watching, waiting. Fucking Idaho. Keogh's Plan, phase four...

Dyson dug in and watched, weighed which way to jump. If Dyson was anything, it was adaptability. Avery shrank into duty, a scarecrow made of nerves winding tighter, building to a critical mass that had to be aimed at somebody, soon. Holroyd got slack, got fat, fatter, planetary. Then gone, vanished up his own colossal ass. It was Holroyd's dereliction of duty that preoccupied Spike Team Texas this fine morning, at this critical juncture in the Plan.

Fat flakes of snow brushed against the nictitating membrane sheaths over Dyson's unblinking eyes. The mountain shook. Talons clattered on the trigger-guard of his sniper rifle. The artillery batteries were dry-firing their guns, the barrels madly swiveling at phantom targets the computer said were there, oddly muted crumping booms rolling down the valley like the tread of jackbooted gods.

The bristled gray skin of Dyson's forehead twitched. Something had brushed his face, a touch lighter than breath, and his inner ear confabulated with the hypersensitive nerves of his exposed skin to triangulate the touch's point of origin, while his forebrain pulled apart the active sonar ping for the content of its message. Across the gorge, a third of the way down the mountain. *There.*

Dyson slithered from cover and ran on all fours across the face of the sheer cliff wall. Exposed for only five seconds, he went unseen to the rim of the gorge and leapt across. Arms burning, leg muscles blowing out as he kicked away from the wall across fifty feet of open space. He soared almost half the gorge before he started to fall.

He arched his legs and threw his arms wide to hug the oncoming granite rock face. The glacier-carved gorge funneled icy updrafts that he skated on to his landing. The wall hit him everywhere at once. He slid, slashing stone, broke two talons on his left paw and four on his left foot. A grunting snarl echoed down the gorge. On the bridge thirty feet above, two soldiers stood duty, one of them gunning a snowmobile. Oblivious.

Dyson scaled the wall and faded into the trees. His pelt went white with spreading evergreen stains. His hand and foot burned as new talons grew in. He caught his breath and ate fistfuls of snow. This was not a time to let heat have its head. This was a time for wisdom, for restraint. The content of the message was simple, but complex in its implications. Avery had found Holroyd, and needed help getting him back.

He stopped at the edge of the tree-line and hid when he saw Avery. The wiry One-One might've passed for a fire-charred tree alone in the clearing at the north end of the Heilige Berg compound. A Barrett Light 50 across his wide, pick-axe shoulder blades. He watched Avery for longer than he realized before showing himself. A twinge of gut-pain that he doubted Avery, but before yesterday, he hadn't doubted 'Royd, either.

"This area's off-limits, Tuck."

"Figured that's why he'd be here, sir. Everything that fat fuck does has to be a poke in the eye." Avery shrugged his shoulders, and Dyson could hear them creak. He looked sucked in, as if he strained against imploding and pulling a big chunk of the world into the hole behind his eyes. He looked as if he'd been up on green hornets since '75. Dyson had changed so much over the years that he almost forgot what he really looked like, and Holroyd just kept getting bigger. But Avery was a sphinx, inscrutable, looking more like himself every year, just *tighter*. "Should've seen it coming, sir. Discipline's been pretty slack."

In all their years together, through all their trials, he had never breathed a dissenting word against Dyson's command, never bitched without a good reason. Dyson's body drew itself up for battle, talons raking the roiling cloud of fog he blasted out of his cavernous chest. He stopped just short of smashing his One-One's face in, because this was a time for delicacy, for discretion. They had had plenty of fights before, and had only given up because for all their unreasoning rage, they had not ever discovered if they could actually kill one another. "Maybe you'd like to sit a spell in officer's country," he growled. "Maybe you don't need my help."

"He wants to talk to you. I can't move him."

Dyson watched the empty quad of the Heilige Berg compound. "Can't, or won't?"

Stung, Avery breathed cold fire. Whatever he almost said floated up between them and was torn apart by the wind. "He's been at their stores. He's...bigger, Sir."

Food was how this shit started. On the mountain, they were on a severely restricted diet of the same shit the residents ate, which, in reconstituted, vitamin-enriched mush form, was Keogh by-product. They were forbidden to touch any of the animal or plant life in the area, most of which was already either dead or irradiated, anyway. They were forbidden to hunt or pillage for fear of jeopardizing the Plan, but Holroyd suspected a darker motive.

Whatever they ate, their bodies used down to a molecular level. All flesh gave up its deepest secrets to them when they ate it—all flesh but Keogh's. 'Royd took to eating soil like a steam shovel, tunneling millions of years into the icy earth to get at the dormant seeds, prions, insect remains, and tiny fragments of DNA from the would-be's and never-were's of the big game. It tided him over for a while, but yesterday, he blew a gasket and went AWOL.

At sunrise, Dyson, on watch duty, saw him stalk and flush the only unspoken-for game in the valley—the Missionary spotter on the next ridge. The spooked commando gave as good as he could with a baffled rifle, then split on skis, with Gibby Holroyd in hot pursuit and about as tactful as a runaway tanker truck. He ran down the sorry shithead at the base of the mountain, and was tearing into him when Avery caught up and drove him off. According to Avery, Gibby just picked up the rest of the spotter and ran across the road. Avery gave chase, but stopped short as a goddamned Army National Guard convoy blundered up the road and gave 'Royd cover back up the mountain without noticing his ghosting them.

Avery had to sneak around the weekend warriors as they set up their roadblocks and fired up their barbecues, which was why it had taken all morning to run 'Royd to ground.

They crossed the field and circled around a long, low log cabin that Dyson figured for a storage pantry, since it was across a small yard from the rear kitchen door of the dining hall. A low parapet ran along the steep, snow-caked roof. This made Dyson laugh. The fucking idiots probably never realized the shed had a sniper hole built onto it, to protect the food from them. But they weren't idiots, anymore. They were Him.

He closed his eyes and summoned focus. He had to be in command of himself, to face this.

The double doors hung open. The snow in front of the doors was trampled and scraped down to the cobblestone path underneath, as if somebody had driven a tank into the shed. The air that wafted out was ten degrees warmer, and smelled like the inside of a decomposed elephant. He stepped into it and walked into the dark with his talons outstretched to show he had no weapons. The gesture made as much sense for them as the medieval tradition of the salute, but he hoped Holroyd was clearheaded enough to see his intent.

"It's alright, boy, you can come out, nothing's been done that can't be undone, yet."

The floor was ankle-deep in trash—cardboard and smashed wooden pallets, flattened cans and jugs, and galaxies of shattered glass. There was no food left.

"Somebody's got to do something, Brute." Holroyd's voice was a hoarse, gargling whisper, but Dyson couldn't tell where he was in the room. He *was* the room. "He's the lyingest motherless lick of devil-shit ever to walk, but He's right about it."

Dyson reined in his rage. Though his eyes adjusted quickly to the dark of the shed, he couldn't see 'Royd, just an amorphous red fog of rising body heat. "This is dereliction of duty, Gibson. Just shut up and come out. You used to be a fine soldier. I used to be proud to serve with you. What have you turned into, man?"

Holroyd's laugh made the walls flex. Dust pattered to the floor. "Said the motherfuckin' yeti! Answer me that, LT. What are we? Because we sure ain't men."

"We're Spike Team Texas, shit-for-brains," Avery snapped, stepping into the doorway with rifle raised. "We survive. We adapt. Our war is forever."

Holroyd's laugh was forever. "And what are we doing here, Brute? Can you or your Okie parrot say they know what's going through the prime gonzola's brain, right now?"

"I can tell you that better than most," Dyson replied coolly, "because this team had one head, and since he's gone, I have that sorry duty. You have some doubt about who's in charge here?"

"You could have fooled me, LT. Here, I thought all along that Keogh was in command, and we were his fucking lackeys."

"You're talking treason, fat boy," Avery growled.

"Fuck you, Okie monkey-chow. I shit bigger than you!"

"Shut up! You know damned well why we hitched up with the Doctor. He taught us how to live like this, and he still has shit to teach you. Like self-control. You've got to get your shit together. You're going to fuck up the program."

"The program! The Plan! The all-fuckin'-important Plan! And where do we fit into the big plan, LT? When Keogh gets what he wants, what do we get?"

"I thought we'd go back to the jungle," Dyson said. "Shit, there's probably a whole tribe of Holroyds running around, eatin' their own shit, because they ain't got chewing tobacco. I thought we'd make an attempt to just fucking live, with all our enemies dead."

"And you think Keogh'll stand for it? Listen, Brute. He taught us a few things I don't think you caught on to. He ain't just gonna take the people with cancer. He wants it all. Every man and woman and animal and plant. He wants it all. Not just to own it, but to be it. He won't rest until he's us, too."

"Gibby, I ain't gonna tell you again. Get your double-wide hillbilly ass out front and center, before I have to spill your breakfast." His claws grew. The pain made it harder than ever to concentrate, but this was beyond insubordination.

"I had the dream again, LT. About the bad time, after the Captain got topped. I couldn't stop eating, remember? I ate all my rations, and a monkey that I caught, and that gook officer's face, and the leaves on the trees...I even tried to eat my own hand, I got so worked up, remember? I think even then that I understood it. You can't just murder everything to possess it. You're still not safe. You have to *be* everything. And we helped him get that power, LT. And what is he going to give us?"

"What do you propose we do, One-Two, besides eat everything?"

"Shit, we got to raise an army ourselves, and take a stand. You want to wait for him to come for us in the jungle, when he's the whole goddamned world?"

Eyes blazing, Dyson answered, "Shit, yes, I do."

"And that's another thing. That sonofabitch I ran down this morning? He was only thirty-five and he was a goddamned captain! And as I was eating him, it occurred to me that I've been in this chickenshit outfit for his whole fuckin' lifetime and I AIN'T NEVER BEEN PROMOTED!"

"Spec Four Gibby Holroyd, it is with heavy heart that I relieve you of duty and commence to feeding you your own ass, effective immediately." He went into the dark claws-first just as Holroyd came charging out into the light. His black eyes rolled and his tongue lolled as he looked down on Dyson, and for an eye blink, Dyson feared.

They had fought before, tried to kill each other more than a few times even before the change, but when they looked into each other's eyes and saw the same fire burning there, the same light that set them apart from and above the entire human maggot race, all quarrels were forgotten. Now, Dyson locked his gaze on Holroyd's and saw only hunger to eat him and all the world and digest it and shit it out.

The earth shook.

If he had been big before, Holroyd was now a one-man re-enactment of the glacier that gouged the gorge out of the mountain. He had indeed eaten every edible thing in the shed, and wasted none of it. His torso sprawled from wall to wall, a turgid, blubbery manscape bristling with unblinking muddy green eyes and less familiar organs. His bulk snaked back into the dark like an obscene giant maggot, borne forward at a blindingly fast speed by a forest of stumpy, hoofed legs. Bulldozer arms unfurled and reached for Dyson as he dug his talons into the floor planks. And somewhere in the midst of it all, almost swallowed up by the rising tide of fleshy rolls between the great arms, Gibby Holroyd looked down with his ear-to-ear mouth slack and raining slobber. His tongue dangled out one corner, lashing from side like he was eating a snake. His rolling mad-cow eyes, sunk deep into beetling beds of flab, took in the tiny form of his CO and glittered, blood-simple hunger and wily redneck cunning and something else that almost made Dyson step out of the way at the last possible instant. There was no flicker of recognition whatsoever. 'Royd saw only food.

Dyson threw his arms out and crouched, closed his eyes. His talons met 'Royd's onrushing bulk and sank right up to the elbows into his belly as if into a tub of soft bread dough. Then 'Royd's main bulk slammed into him and drove him back up on his heels. It felt as if he were trying to stop a train. Muscles strained and popped in his legs and back. The floor planks splintered and gave way under him, and 'Royd bulled a few feet closer to the door.

"Stand clear, sir! Let me take this shot!" Avery's voice sounded as if he were in Mexico.

One of 'Royd's fists connected with the side of Dyson's head. Stars and planets split open and half the world went red. His cheekbone caved in, shards of the temporal plate of his skull introduced themselves to his brain, and his right eye popped out of its socket.

Deep inside 'Royd, Dyson's talons kept growing. Layer upon layer of fat and connective tissue gave way. 'Royd shrieked in his face, a high-pitched wail like dry ice on steel. Claws grated on massive ribs and curled around them. Another fist came down on Dyson's left shoulder. Bones pulverized, and blood geysered up into Dyson's ear. His left arm stopped working.

"Let me take the shot, sir!" Avery called.

"Shoot him! Shoot him!" Dyson bellowed, his face smothered in the smegmatic furrow between Holroyd's mammoth tits. His right-hand talons burrowed deeper, hit something that resisted, then popped and sucked his fist in after it. The air went out of 'Royd's firebell scream, and foamy lung-blood sluiced Dyson's good eye.

In less time than it takes to tell, Avery darted in the doorway and flanked 'Royd, scaled him and blew the base of his skull out with the Light 50. From point blank range, the enormous bullet should have gone through 'Royd and Dyson and into the ground, but it only cratered the fat-armored neck. 'Royd's arms stretched back to try to pick him off, but the One-One ducked them easily and shot, again and again, into the padded pipeline of 'Royd's spine.

Dyson's feet raked the floor, piling up floor planks and only marginally slowing their advance. He kicked up into the underside of 'Royd's belly and pistoned his taloned feet into the ocean of guts underneath. His efforts were rewarded when the abdominal sheath of muscle gave way and intestines burst out of their envelope like snakes out of the world's largest tin of novelty nuts. 'Royd staggered, but regrouped and smashed into the log wall of the shed.

Dyson, naturally, hit the wall first. Logs groaned and fractured, but the concrete mortar between them held, and Dyson's spine gave. His legs went wild for a split-second, then numb. His ribcage sundered and razored his lungs and sweetmeats. Blind, paralyzed, pinned on 'Royd's ruined torso by his overgrown talons, Dyson bit into the folds of fat swaddled over his face. Teeth met and he spat and bit again, determined to eat his way to 'Royd's colossal heart.

'Royd backed up, hit the wall again. The whole cabin swooned on its foundation. Dyson, a bug on the windshield, dead from the neck-down, kept eating. Avery, dug in like a tick on 'Royd's back, kept shooting. They hit the wall again. Logs exploded. The roof sagged. The entire front wall split and sprayed out, logs tumbling down the snowfield as 'Royd thundered out into the daylight.

'Royd peeled Dyson off and tossed him aside. He hit the ground chest first, limbs flapping like broken umbrellas as he rolled to a stop against the dining hall. His popped-out eye sucked back into his socket to let him see Holroyd stampeding across the compound, a runaway juggernaut tripping over its own intestines, Avery riding him like Pecos Bill and emptying his clip into his neck. 'Royd's fire-siren shriek faded on the wind.

Dyson lay still. The sound of his body rebuilding itself filled his senses. He heard crunching of boots on snow. He tried to roll over, but his left arm only flopped in front of him and something that was not blood squirted out of his shoulder.

"I couldn't stop him, sir. He's gone blood-stupid." Avery leaned over him. "You're hurt pretty bad, sir."

"I'll heal. Everything heals, Tuck."

"I never thought I'd see the day."

"He'll come back, when he's had his fill. We don't need him ghosting up this op, anyway."

Avery eyed 'Royd's entrail-strewn wake, looked back with a wry grimace. "So we go through with it, then?"

"You have doubts, now, too?"

"No, sir. You're the beaver-cleaver, the prime gonzola. But—"

"Out with it, Tuck. While I'm still too fucked up to beat you."

"It's just what you said to fat boy, back there…we're just gonna go back to the jungle?"

"I don't trust Keogh, shithead. I know he'll come for us one day, when there's nothing else left. I'm fucking counting on it."

Avery cocked his head, replaced the clip in his rifle. "I don't follow you, sir."

"I love Dr. Keogh for what he's done for us, but he's not one of us. I love him because he's the only thing on this godforsaken shitball we cannot kill, which makes him the only worthy enemy left. When he releases us from this hitch, we'll go back to the jungle, and we'll prepare for the last great fight of our lives. He'll come for us in our own backyard, and we'll join him in glorious battle, and we will know once and for all whether or not we are gods."

Avery beamed down on him with a scintilla of the naked adoration they had all felt for the Captain, and Dyson was reborn again. "Lord hasten that day, sir."

~ 20 ~

The whole thing sucked.

PFC Rich Schumate sat on the aisle seat in the back of a big green bus lumbering a little faster than walking pace up an icy mountain road. Climbing into the cold and the wind, but the higher they got, the darker it seemed to get outside. He could make out few details of the landscape past the hulking form of his sleeping seatmate–black, twisted trees, snowfields and a precipitous drop, and fog like the mountain was packed in cotton. Not that he would have recognized the terrain, but it was unsettling, as if the weather were in cahoots with the government to keep them from finding out where they were going.

Schumate didn't especially like being in the Idaho Army National Guard, but if you wanted to get anywhere at Frandsen's True Value Hardware in Idaho Falls, you enlisted. The boss was the platoon CO, and most maneuvers were like uniformed family camping trips, with bar-be-cue, snowmobile rides and, after Old Man Frandsen went to his tent, beer and buds aplenty. Not this trip. Not even Captain Frandsen knew where they were going, what they would do there, or when they'd be going home. They were rousted out of their Sunday night routines to the armory at dinner-time last night, issued their new MILES damage simulator harnesses and eye-safe laser-fitted M16's, and all the empty berths on the bus were filled with strangers. Except for a pit stop and half-assed briefing at a rest area an hour back, they had been rolling all night and into the day.

Schumate felt a fresh sting of envy for those who begged off successfully when he eyed the replacements across the aisle from him. They didn't look like National Guard, and they didn't look like they liked being here any more than he did. Regular Army observers, Capt. Frandsen explained, sitting in to coordinate their work with the Army unit already in place in the box. They also didn't look like they were going to any plain old maneuver, either. As hard, as scarred, as they were, it did nothing for PFC Schumate's confidence to see how scared they looked.

The clatter of gear in nervous hands filled the rumbling silence in the bus, that and the sporadic bleeping of a handheld video game in the seat behind him. He stole a sidewise glance at the soldiers across the aisle. One of them had his winter coat off, and wore only a flak vest underneath. His skin was olive, his features harsh and exotic, maybe Middle Eastern. He cycled through a seemingly endless supply of clips, slamming them into the breech of his rifle and clearing them. The gun: not an eye-safe laser-fitted M16 like the rest, but a shortened M4A1 with a grenade launcher snug under the unstoppered barrel. The bullets: *real* 5.56mm jackets, but the bullets themselves were green, and didn't look like metal. His muscle-bound arms were a maze of tattoos—a harvest of skulls, blossoms on entwined strands of barbed wire. On the forehead of each, a name, a rank, a serial number. More skulls, more names, than Schumate could count before the soldier caught him staring. Skulls blinked at him long and slow, so Schumate could see that even his eyelids were tattooed: GAME OVER, they said. He sprained an eye looking away.

Beside Skulls, a fiftyish Latino man hunched in his buddy's shadow, face turned to the window. His close-cropped hair more silver than black, his hand knurled with scar tissue, clamped over his ear, hiding the tiny headset he whispered into. Nobody was supposed to have personal electronics, but it must be something vital to the maneuver. Nobody was supposed to have real guns, either.

At the rest stop outside Lucile, a flock of trenchcoated FBI agents had confiscated all their cellular phones, portable TV's and CD players, which, they were told, would interfere with the new damage-monitor harnesses they'd be wearing. Hobart only snuck his Gameboy through by hiding it inside his field radio.

They linked up with two other platoons to form a mixed company of what looked to be the hand-picked worst units in the state. But each platoon had with it about a dozen "regular" Army, all of whom stowed their own duffel bags and stood guard around them until they were ready to go, which took about an hour.

Standing at attention in the rest stop parking lot, they were addressed by a gray-haired black officer in unmarked winter camo. This was to be a simulated-fire civil defense exercise, conducted jointly with NTC 00-1, a National Training Center Army exercise involving operations as far south as Yuma Proving Ground in Arizona. Their provisional company commander, Major Ortman, stood up then and asked them what they were doing there. The officer explained that they were to move to a mountain road at the edge of the Hell's Canyon National Recreation Area and hold the road until further notice. All civilian residents on the mountain had been cleared out in advance, and an Army unit conducting a Direct Action evolution in the area would rendezvous with them and apprise them of the situation.

They fell out to use the toilets, raid the snack and soda machines, and sit on the bus. They were not allowed to call home. Total operational security had to be observed, they were told, as if they were in hostile territory under conditions of war. Who they were supposed to be simulated fighting against, or who was supposed to be simulating spying on them, they were not told.

It was like in the spy movies. They did not Need To Know.

He did not need to know why the one guy had a headset, or why the guy with the skulls on his arms had a real gun with weird green bullets. He did not need to know where they were going, or whether it was really just a maneuver.

The whole thing sucked.

Schumate was not long on thinking. In fact, he was the only employee in the history of Frandsen's True Value Hardware ever to provoke the boss, through acts of sheer, transcendent ineptitude, to utter an honest-to-gosh profane word. But he tried to put it together. They were going into the middle of nowhere to practice holding a mountain road on the edge of federal land, in a state where even the governor was known for anti-federalist attitude. If this wasn't the beginning of the New World Order crackdown foretold in gun show pamphlets, it was certainly a pretty good simulation.

Then, as usually happened, somebody else said something and Schumate forgot what he was thinking. Corporal Waters, who qualified only by gross default for the role of platoon wit, blurted, "So, regular Army guys, how are we doing so far? Is real war this fucking boring or what?"

"Mind that language, Waters!" Frandsen shouted from the front.

Skulls looked up from his gun. He looked anything but grateful for the interruption. "What did you say, tourist?"

Something passed between Skulls and Waters so fast that no one saw it, but Schumate almost heard the air snap.

Waters buckled, but his irrepressible irritant nature resurfaced, and he held out his hand. "I'm sorry, man, I didn't mean to offend. You guys are the real deal. We just do this shit because we can't afford cable." He looked around to see no one was laughing, only watching him out of the corners of their eyes, as if he were about to be struck by lightning, or turned to salt. His hand flapped in the air, shaking only in part because of the jouncing of the bus. "I'm Corporal Leonard Waters. I'm the A squad leader, but, back home, I manage a Jiffy Lube."

Skulls cracked a smile. Most of his teeth were steel ingots. "No shit, Leonard? You change oil?"

Nervously, Waters just nodded.

"Then we're a lot alike, after all. You see, I kill people. You can see the similarity, can't you? 'Cept, for you, the pay is probably lots better."

"Shut up, Toke," the Latino soldier said in a low but unmistakable officer voice. Skulls shut up, went back to his magazines.

Schumate shrank into himself. He needed somebody to talk to, someone to convince him everything was normal. He elbowed Private Heeley in the ribs: nudged, jabbed and finally licked one finger and stuck it in his buddy's ear. This usually inspired a fierce reflexive backlash, but Heeley only stirred. His big, heavy head came up off the glass and tilted at Schumate, but his eyes were slitted. "We there yet?"

Schumate and Heeley went to the same high school, but didn't know each other until after, when Heeley came back from college with a blown-out knee. He did deliveries at the hardware store, now, and Schumate only knew him to sell speed to and nod at in the bar. But in the Guard, they became fast weekend friends. As the only black guy in the unit, Heeley stuck out less with somebody white to talk to, and nobody else wanted Schumate around, he was such a fuckup.

"Keep your voice down, dude," Schumate whispered. "There's some serious shit going down."

Heeley looked around. His sleepy eyes locked on Skulls and the Latino officer and went wide, then back out the window.

"Dude, wake up. This is serious. They've got live ammo on the bus, and there's real soldiers, dude, they're killers, and...are you alright, dude?"

Heeley did not look alright at all. His black-coffee face was ashen and sweaty, and Schumate could feel waves of heat radiating off him. When they'd stopped, Heeley went to the toilet and was gone for the whole briefing, and only came clomping up to hop on the bus as it was rolling away. Schumate suspected his buddy got stoned, and was half-disapproving, half-jealous, but Heeley had just silently squeezed into the window seat and passed out.

"It's cool, man, it's me, I'm just...sleepy, Rob..."

"Dude, it's Rich. Dude..."

Heeley looked at him. Under half-mast lids, his eyes were opaque red orbs, filled with blood. His arm shot out and caught Schumate by the jaw, muting him and twisting his head back as he tried to jump out of the seat. Heeley drew Schumate close, and nobody was looking, nobody saw or heard.

"When the shit hits the fan, just be what you are, Rich. That's all you can do. You know what you are, don't you?" The voice was not Declan Heeley's voice, and though the unblinking eyes drained of blood, they were not his eyes, either. "You're lucky…"

The big hot hand slowly let go of Schumate's head, and Heeley turned back to the window. "Dude," Schumate pleaded.

"Just be what you are," Heeley muttered again, and went back to sleep.

Everything sucked.

~ 21 ~

Cundieffe's red-eye flight from DC touched down in Boise at 06:30 MST. A highly caffeinated office agent met him at the gate and walked him to his connecting flight, briefing him all the while on the latest developments. As of yesterday, Heilige Berg was a ghost town. By all accounts, they just shut up the place and went home. The suspect in custody in White Bird had given up nothing since his initial outburst, but other field agents from Headquarters had already interviewed him, and were observing the situation.

Cundieffe blanched, but didn't bother asking. Other agents from Headquarters? Had he jumped the gun? He thought of calling the Assistant Director, but then Wyler's strange deference to Hoecker reminded him that he could not bring his superior into the loop.

He rode a bumpy hour-long commuter flight to Lewiston, and was in a rental car, a blue Oldsmobile Alero, that should've had skis and tank treads, reading the map in his lap as he traced the 95 south to White Bird.

The highway was two lanes, the slow lane and eastern exposure dominated by an endless convoy of semis, so he had to watch the odometer to guess where he was. The winter here was harsher, but purer, than what he'd suffered in Washington. It demanded a whole new repertoire of skills from a driver for whom snow was an oddity you paid to play in at the zoo at Christmas, between the Komodo dragon paddock and the monkey house, and more exotic than either of those exhibits.

Though he was cold, he drove with the window open. The car smelled of cigarettes, and he abhorred car heat. The charred smell of the recycled engine air reminded him of his childish horror the day he learned what fossil fuels were made of.

There was a TV ad campaign at the height of the gas crisis, in which whimsical cartoon dinosaurs were squashed into the gas tank of a car. Enamored of dinosaurs as every small, bright boy his age, young Martin had been thunderstruck to discover that the mighty kings of creation had been driven to extinction to fuel automobiles. Mother explained to him that one, the dinosaurs died millions of years ago as a result of their own stupidity; and two, oil was actually formed from old plants, not dinosaurs at all. The good people at Chevron just dumbed down the message, because they figured most people were idiots, like the dinosaurs. Cundieffe felt better about it then, but still had bad dreams about being burned up in some future race's automobile engine.

In another forty minutes, he steered the Alero in a suicide-lunge through the truck convoy, and bombed down the off-ramp. By the time he slid to a stop at the first intersection, he was already halfway through downtown White Bird, Population 103.

He drove past a strip mall with a Dairy Queen out front. The whole façade of the building was boarded over, but a line of pickup trucks still filed past the drive-thru window. At the end of the town's other block, he parked in front of the sheriff's station.

The sky was the color and texture of steel wool, and sparkling walls of ice fog rolled down the silent streets. A pair of deputy's cruisers, a Ford Bronco with the Sheriff's name stenciled on the door, and a rental car identical to his own were parked out front. He walked painstakingly, like an old man nursing an inflamed hip joint.

The meeting with Sheriff Bert Manes and the two Bureau interlopers was short and uncomfortable. The Sheriff, shaken and not entirely possessed of the breakfast he drank this morning, had reluctantly called for Bureau help and gotten more than he'd asked for with Agents Macy and Mentone, and now felt he was getting triple-dipped.

Macy and Mentone were a male-female team, which amused Cundieffe, since he knew at a glance they were both Mules. He held Agent Mentone's hand a moment longer than protocol called for, and *knew*, just as they knew him. Both Agents gave a tiny nod, and Cundieffe felt Mentone's hand squirm and do something in his that might've been some kind of signal.

They listened to the tape of the boy's first statement, which was fragmentary and incoherent, with the deputies cutting off the suspect whenever he started talking about what happened on the mountain. Then Sheriff Manes told them about the exodus. So far as anybody could tell, all two hundred and fifty residents of the Heilige Berg community had left the county in chartered buses. Nobody knew where they were, and nobody had checked on them, because except for Karl Schweinfurter, none of them had broken the law. And not a federal law, either.

"Sheriff Manes," said Cundieffe, "I didn't come here to arrest the boy. I came to try to stop a massacre."

Manes looked as if he'd skipped a page while reading a particularly bad novel. "Run that by me again, mister. I told you the Heilige Berg people done cleared out for the winter. So who's going to get massacred?"

"Sheriff, what do you know about the Radiant Dawn hospice community in the area?"

Manes blinked and sipped his fortified coffee. "Weren't they them sick people, blowed themselves up down in California? We got nothing like that up here."

"But in the boy's statement—"

"Boy probably saw it on the TV. Guy owns that land, he only lets Heilige Berg use it because he's a Nazi, too. Not that there's a law against that, yet—"

"So there're no other people living up there."

"That's what I said. Ain't nobody up there now, but a National Guard unit doing civil defense maneuvers."

Cundieffe's teeth almost met in the thin flap of his lower lip. "The National Guard is up there?"

"Yeah, it's shorter notice than usual, but I don't see what trouble they could cause, with the Nazis flying south."

"And you've been up there?"

"My men have, a few times since last summer, but the road's closed through the winter, and they don't like the law poking around uninvited up there. Around here, we respect people's right to privacy. I think this is an awful lot of fuss over one bad boy, folks, and I've got real problems to deal with, so if you'll excuse me?"

The Sheriff left the conference room. Agent Macy shut the door and studied Cundieffe as if he were a multiple choice question.

"*I came to try to stop a massacre*," Mentone sneered in an eerie falsetto rendition of Cundieffe's voice.

"Are we working at cross-purposes, here, Cundieffe?"

"I wasn't aware anyone else was working this case," Cundieffe deadpanned. "How did you come to be involved?"

"The Steering Committee," Macy answered. "And you?"

Cundieffe's mouth opened and he started to say the name. Was he supposed to keep secrets from other Mules? Were there levels of secrecy, or warring factions, or was this just another test? His mind ransacked itself for some solid precedent under which to crawl, settled on something AD

Wyler had said. *Information passes to the most appropriate level for direct action, Martin.* "I'm here in an official Bureau capacity."

Mentone smirked. "Chasing stolen cars?"

"Don't be coy, Agent Cundieffe," Macy said. "We know why you're here. Your skills as an interrogator."

"And you?"

"Containment," Mentone said.

"Compartmentalization," Macy added. "This is going to happen, Agent Cundieffe."

"Do you know what's really up there?"

"We haven't been. We were waiting for you."

"You had instructions?"

"We failed. You're here. It follows."

"What else can you tell me about the boy?"

"He claimed at first that his people were sick, and then that they'd been 'replaced,' but when he was told that they'd vacated the compound, he refused to talk any more, and he's refused food and medical treatment. We have people tracking the Heilige Berg residents, but all other assets are still in play."

"Can I see him?"

"We hoped you would."

They led him out through the office and down the hall to the cells. None of the deputies took any notice of them as they took keys off the wall and let themselves in to the small cell block. There were four small cells facing each other across a featureless gallery. Only one of them was occupied. A badly beaten teenaged boy lay in a fetal position on a bunk. His untouched breakfast sat on the floor in the center of the cell, in a Dairy Queen bag.

"Good heavens, no wonder. I'll be right back."

Cundieffe went back to his car and drove down Main Street to the strip mall. He went in to the deli counter at the Circle K and ordered a deluxe roast beef sandwich. When the sluggardly clerk seemed hell-bent on assembling a loveless, pathetic specimen of the sandwiching arts, Cundieffe stormed the counter and made the sandwich himself, an unsavory task since he had embraced vegetarianism himself, but necessary to gain the suspect's trust. He paid for the sandwich and a bottle of orange juice and went back to the sheriff's station.

After the interview, Cundieffe shook off Macy and Mentone and the Sheriff's deputies, got in his car, studied the map, and went up the mountain.

He gave up on keeping the windows open five minutes out of town. Vicious gusts of wind swept through the interior, dumping half-melted snow in his lap and scattering all his papers in the passenger foot well. Peeling an orange in his lap and stuffing the wedges one by one into his mouth, he tried to digest what he was driving into.

Macy and Mentone obviously assumed he knew more than he did, and it had taken all his wits to keep from looking utterly baffled as they talked. They had known their roles far better than he, and as far as he could tell they were there to obfuscate in advance the truth about whatever was about to happen. So far, their presence was the only corroboration he had for the boy's story. He wanted to call AD Wyler. He wanted to call Brady Hoecker. He wanted a column of state police behind him—in front of him.

He passed the last ranch at the end of State Road 117, marked by a state sign warning that the road beyond was closed until April 15. The chain blockade across the road had been removed, so he set the automatic transmission down to second gear and climbed. He wiped his hands with a wet napkin and threw himself wholly into keeping the car on the road.

The road was recently plowed and the snow and ice broken up, but still there were patches where the rental car's snow tires squealed helplessly, and he felt a sickening lurch as all his forward momentum became so much empty noise, and the mountain dragged the car out on the right shoulder, beyond which there was only fog. He slowed down below twenty and watched the road, trying to predict which way it would bend or dip, and always coming up wrong.

He had lost track of time when he crept up to the first landmark—or the second, if you counted where his ears popped—the front gate of the Heilige Berg compound. He pulled over, as much to stretch his legs and regain his nerves, as to investigate the place, looked at the odometer and made a note on his map.

The gate stood about thirty yards back from the road, and looked like something out of a concentration camp production of Wagner's Ring operas. The boards had been plated in steel, and barbed hooks projected from the top of the fence—in both directions. Guard towers flanking the gate had halogen spotlights, mounts for heavy machine guns and big iron braziers filled with charred wood. Somewhere nearby, no doubt, there were cauldrons for dumping flaming oil on invaders. The towers were skirted in tumbleweeds of snow-crusted razor-wire, and ten-foot barbed-wire fence marched out to encircle the compound.

He stepped out into wind-ripped silence so profound he could hear his pulse in his ears. He cautiously walked around the Heilige Berg driveway.

They may be gone, but they'd be remiss if they didn't leave booby traps aplenty to strike in absentia against any federal stormtroopers who might blunder into their territory.

They were gone. They were not lying low in the compound; they had been observed leaving, all two hundred fifty of them, in six chartered buses. In defiance of all profiles of radical behavior, in spite of being dug in and, by all accounts, deathly ill, they simply left. Scant days before the Army National Guard showed up on their doorstep to practice putting down their freedom-loving type, they bolted to parts unknown.

Only the boy could explain it.

They were all different—different from how they were before, but they were all the same...like they had the same soul...

He thought of Storch, sitting as impassively as an iguana on a hot rock as Cundieffe caught him up on current events, then fighting like a drowning man to get words to come out of his own mouth. *We are all one flesh, becoming one mind...*

He got back in the car and resumed climbing. The slope of the road was gentler and steadier after Heilige Berg, and the gorge meandered away from the right shoulder. A steep, forested ridge sprouted on the right, and an iron rod fence sprang up around it, about twenty feet back among the evergreens. Watching the ridge grow, his eyes picked out clustered shadows among the trees that might have been men up in the branches, watching him. He stared harder and almost drove through a double-row of sawhorses laid out across the road.

A soldier stood in the road before the sawhorses. Cundieffe stomped on his brake, and the car fishtailed and sailed into the first barricade. The soldier leapt back over the sawhorse, but tripped over the second one, and disappeared from view below the line of the hood. Cundieffe hopped out of the car, sure he'd run the sentry over.

The Guardsman climbed to his feet and wheeled on Cundieffe with one gloved fist in the air, but he froze at the sight of Cundieffe's gold shield under his runny nose.

The Guardsman looked to be about nineteen, and wore olive drab camouflage winter gear with a buck private's stripe, and a belt and shoulder harness with reflective strips and a battery pack on it. Cundieffe thought it looked like the sensors people wore when they played Lazer Tag. His M16 had a laser pointer instead of a barrel. At least this part of it was a simulation.

Beyond the barricade, the road veered to the left, and the bend was lined with deuce-and-a-half Army trucks and olive drab school buses. An armored personnel carrier was parked in the middle of the road behind the sentry, who appeared to be holding the road alone.

"I'm Special Agent Cundieffe of the FBI, and I need to see your commanding officer immediately."

"This road's closed, sir, I don't care who you are, you're not getting by." He looked nervous, a bad high school drama student cold reading a poorly sketched part.

"Listen, Private: I am not participating in your simulation. I'm a real federal agent, and it is imperative that I speak with someone in charge."

"Mister, I don't care if you are a real federal agent. My orders—"

"Your orders are going to get you sent to Leavenworth for obstruction of justice, Private. Get me your commanding officer, immediately!"

The private blinked, out of lines, then got his walkie-talkie. "Tango One, this is Tango Eight, over."

"Tango Eight, what is your status, over?"

"I've got a guy who says he's FBI, wants to see the Major, over."

"Nobody comes through, Tango Eight, over."

"I think he's for real, Tango One. Just get the Major on the line for me, please?"

Cundieffe got back in his car and drove over both prone sawhorses, swerved to avoid the screaming sentry, then swung back the other way to bypass the parked APC. The car's heavy suspension locked up again, and he sailed into the high steel mud-flaps on the huge rear wheels. He heard metal gouging the passenger-side door panels and stood on the gas. Snow-tires bit down on ice, blinding the sentry with a rooster-tail of spray. The car launched out from under the APC and hurtled towards the guardrail of buses and trucks. He goosed the brakes and steered the car carefully through the labyrinth of parked military hardware cluttering up the road.

Guardsmen watched him pass, standing around, smoking, joking, overhauling vehicles on the shoulder. He looked them over, taking a rough head-count and scanning faces. He saw the same ones over and over, young, soft, unconcerned. Others turned away from him, and he looked long and hard, too sure they were hiding from him.

He came around the bend and stopped before a more formidable roadblock. Trucks were parked across the road, and a civilian motor home with a pair of very civilian high-performance snowmobiles in front of it was parked on the left shoulder.

A full squad of soldiers stood at the roadblock with laser rifles leveled on him. A red-faced middle-aged man in a parka stepped down from the motor home and crossed to his window.

"I'm Major Ortman. What the hell's this all about?"

Cundieffe introduced himself. "What exactly are you doing up here, Major, and by whose orders?"

"Good question. These aren't even my damned men. I'm a staff officer at the Boise HQ. I got ordered up here only yesterday with this bunch of retards, and we–"

Cundieffe showed him his badge. "You've been told this is a classified mission, and are under orders not to speak to anyone about it."

Ortman nodded.

"Where is the Radiant Dawn complex?"

"The what?"

Cundieffe gritted his teeth and pointed at the fence. "The front gate to this property. Where is it?"

"Oh, you definitely can't go back there," Ortman said. "There's…there's a live fire exercise in progress."

Indeed. "Major, you have your orders, and I have mine. All I can tell you is that this is much more than an exercise, and a lot of people could get killed on this mountain, and nobody but me seems to care. Now, do you know what's on the other side of this ridge, or not?"

Ortman purpled. "Now, don't take that tone with me, I don't care if you're part of the exercise, or not. There's regular Army over there—" he looked at the ridge, then looked back. "Special Forces assholes, actually. Secret exercise, very hush-hush. We're just watching the back door."

"You've got to let me in."

Ortman pointed up the ridge. "You'd never make it in this thing. The road goes straight up, almost no switchbacks."

"Then let me use one of those." Cundieffe pointed at the snowmobiles.

"Well, now, you got to understand…those aren't Army-issue. Those're mine—"

The Major drove him up the hill himself, Cundieffe clinging to Ortman's furred parka hood as they rocketed to the top of the ridge on one of his souped-up Arctic Cat ZRT 800 snowmobiles. Cundieffe rolled off and caught his breath on his knees while Ortman turned back and slalomed down to the bottom to the cheers of his company. Cundieffe stood on the summit and his jaw dropped when he saw the other side.

He had seen only photographs of the first Radiant Dawn compound, but he recognized the tower instantly. It was the same building, but they had learned from their mistakes, and adapted. A sixty-foot gorge split the plateau from the mountain, and the narrow bridge that spanned it was guarded by three sentries with very real guns. No housing development surrounded the tower, only a mass of trucks and trailers, and fields of barbed wire. A sheer granite cliff face rose up behind the tower to pierce the steel wool skies, and Cundieffe spotted three artillery emplacements on its peaks. He saw a squat concrete blockhouse built into the foot of the cliff directly behind the tower, and deduced ventilation shafts, tunnels, bunkers.

This was not a hospice community, or even a research facility. This was a military installation to shame Navarone, with real soldiers and an underground city, and who knew what else, and the local Sheriff didn't even know it existed. According to Karl Schweinfurter, it hadn't, a month ago.

This is going to happen, Agent Cundieffe.

A black APC roared out of the trailer park and crossed the field and the bridge, and took the switchbacks up the ridge at a maniacal speed. The armored car skidded to a stop almost on top of Cundieffe's toes. In the turret bubble, a soldier in a cowboy hat saluted him down the twin barrels of a .50-caliber machine gun. Then the side door swung open and a huge man in black fatigues leapt out. His bald head was stubbled in silver, and his full beard only accentuated the grievous scar that slashed his face from his right eye down below his jaw. He came at Cundieffe so fast the agent didn't quite recognize him until he'd been struck twice full in the face, and fallen down.

"God bless you for coming when you did, Agent Cundieffe," said Lt. Col. Greenaway. "I've needed to beat the shit out of somebody all morning, and I was afraid I'd have to clobber one of my own men."

Cundieffe shielded his face as Greenaway charged him again. Hot blood sluiced the back of his palate. His nose felt like it was broken, but he couldn't tell for sure. He hadn't been hit by another person since grade school. "Lt. Col. Greenaway! Cease and desist—"

Greenaway's boot smashed into his gut, lifting him bodily into the air. He curled up and hit the ice on his tailbone, slid halfway down the ridge. "You have illegally trespassed on private property, Agent Cundieffe. I am a private citizen, defending my rights as guaranteed by the United States Constitution, which you are sworn to uphold. So get the fuck off my mountain!"

Cundieffe rolled over, too stunned to get up and run, though Greenaway came crunching down the ridge after him. "Do you know— Greenaway—do you know who you're working for?"

"I'm in the private sector, now. Self-employed. Hunting eggheads."

"You don't know what you're dealing with," Cundieffe groaned, heaving himself to his feet and turning to run, or tumble, or whatever, away from Greenaway.

In the event, he only succeeded in presenting his hindquarters for Greenaway's boot, which sent him the rest of the way down to the fence. "You don't know what you're dealing with! Get off my mountain, G-boy! Get the fuck out of my war!"

Cundieffe slid into the iron fence posts and coughed, threw up oranges on the snow. Guardsmen laughed. Greenaway bowed.

Cundieffe pulled himself to his feet, leaned against the fence for a minute, looking over his shoulder to see if Greenaway was coming back. When he could stand on his own, he hobbled back through the gate to his car. Major Ortman, sitting on his snowmobile, shook his head. "I told you not to go up there."

Driving back down was even more nerve-wracking, now that gravity and his own momentum were conspiring to hurl him off the road. Clouds of pain and dizziness bubbled up in his skull, and the melted snow seeping into his heavy wool overcoat had transformed it into an antenna for radiating his core body heat out into the chill wind. His hands shook on the wheel, nervous twitches of impotent rage translated by power steering into drunken swerves. As he passed the abandoned Heilige Berg compound, and the ridge dropped away to reveal the yawning, fog-choked gorge and the valley beyond, he felt it all starting to slip away from him, and he stepped on the brakes, fighting the car's almost compulsive urge to slide out of control and over the edge. He wrestled the car over to the right shoulder and turned off the engine. Watching fat flakes of snow billow and pile up on the windshield, he sat for a very long time before he was composed enough to use the telephone.

Incredibly, he got a dial tone. He punched in the number with numb, shivering fingers and waited through six rings before a woman's voice answered. Though her crisp, emotionless voice was general-issue civil servant, she did not identify her office, or offer any other information. She simply said, "Hello."

"I need to speak to Mr. Hoecker, immediately. This is—"

"I believe you have a wrong number, sir. Sorry…" She hung up.

"Goddamit!" he screamed, and looked around to see if anyone had heard.

Cundieffe checked the number in his address book. He had an uncanny memory for such things, and knew in his bones he'd entered it right. Another game, another test. He wouldn't call AD Wyler until he got back to the sheriff's station, but once he did…

If you make it off this mountain.

His mouth ached, and he still tasted a trickle of blood where Greenaway's fist had split his lip. His nose looked like a circus clown's honking red bulb, but he couldn't feel it at all. It was possible he had a slight concussion. At least the maniacal son of a bitch hadn't broken his glasses. Assorted bruises and minor contusions made their complaints known to the central nervous system as the dregs of adrenaline dribbled uselessly out of his bloodstream. His hands were steadier, now, but heavy. He barely managed to lift them to the steering wheel and turn the key. The engine caught and grumbled and he levered the shifter into Drive, leaning against the wheel as the car begrudgingly tore itself free of the snow on the shoulder and took to the frictionless ice slide of the road.

He felt like a cripple trying to negotiate a descent down ice-slick stadium steps, taking each bend with agonizing slowness, fighting the rising panic-impulse to throw himself to the bottom, to floor it and get it over with. As he crept along, he kept his eyes on the patch of road directly in front of the car, stealing glances at the gorge to his left, and the ranks of trees marching by to his right. In the silvery, omnidirectional sunlight, the flickering pattern of passing trees was vaguely hypnotic, and he found himself glancing at it so often that he began to imagine he saw something pacing him through the forest, moving just before the vanishing point where the trees became a uniform wall of winter-blasted gray bark and shadowed greenery.

He looked away, saw he'd strayed off the center crown of the road towards the left. Below his window, the gorge wall was jumbled with loose boulders and snowdrifts, forming a jagged but relatively gradual slope to the broad, U-shaped floor. Cundieffe momentarily flashed that the gorge appeared to have been carved out of the mountain by a glacier, and not a river, which explained why it plunged so deeply away from the Snake River, which lay just over the summit to the west. Among the rocks, like rusted remnants of an unfinished meal, were cars. Lots of cars. And then the road swept it away and he was back on the center-line, goosing the brakes and letting gravity do the rest. If he just watched the road and stayed in the center, he'd be fine.

The phone rang.

He tapped the brakes and fumbled for the phone on the passenger seat. Never taking his eyes off the road, he finally found and activated it, then tucked it between his ear and shoulder.

"Agent Cundieffe here."

"That was stupid," Hoecker snapped.

"What was stupid?" He wondered which of the morning's misadventures he already knew about, and how much to tell him. He was fast coming to conclude that he probably shouldn't tell anyone anything.

"This is a secure line, but talk fast. You're in Idaho?"

"Oh, I'm in Idaho, alright. I've been busy, this morning, what with getting outmaneuvered by other Bureau agents, made a fool of by the local sheriff, and beaten up—"

"Someone literally beat you up? Slow down, Martin, you're not making any sense."

His eyes darted right. He saw it again, and could not look away. The snow was knee- to waist-deep here, and the trees were taller, thicker and more densely packed than before, broken up only by the occasional house-sized granite boulder, but he could almost swear he saw something like a man running down the mountain along with his car. He sped up, eyes locked on the road.

"Brady, it is my conclusion that I have been brought up here on false pretenses, wasting Bureau resources to be tested on my ability to keep mum about something I can only assume is some kind of covert military action against the Mission. I don't care whether I've failed, or not, I just want to go back to Washington, and do my damned job."

"It's all true, Martin," he said. "About Radiant Dawn and the Mission. It's worse than even most of the Cave Institute will accept. Three hundred and fifty people, all of them terminal cancer patients. It just went into full operation about a month ago."

"Good lord! And there's some question about what the Mission's objective is? How many people actually know about this?"

"Dr. Keogh has worked with the federal government to keep the new hospice village under guard for the time being, until the Mission can be neutralized."

"But if he's to be protected, why do it in secret? And if he's doing something he shouldn't, why stand back and let him be bombed by terrorists, when he can be brought to justice?"

"It's complicated. This isn't about right and wrong."

"And what about Dr. Keogh? What do you know about Radiant Dawn, really? Not the official line, but the truth."

"What do you believe the truth is?"

Cundieffe looked to the left. The valley, still and wreathed in fog, looked like an uninspired postcard. Was anything he'd been told true? Events he'd never heard of, shaped by people who had no records, people who, for all intents and purposes, didn't exist in his world. Or at least, they hadn't until last summer. Very well then, he'd play along. "I believe that Radiant Dawn is a front for a gene therapy project involving cancer research. I believe that Dr. Keogh, about whom I still know next to nothing, is somehow connected to an old DARPA satellite weapons project called RADIANT, and that the satellite is still in existence, and operational, and that the technology, if not the weapon itself, is instrumental in the project. I believe that the Mission's ranks included several civilian and military personnel who also worked on RADIANT, and who are just as determined to destroy it, and Keogh's research. And I suspect that Keogh has somehow taken control over the Heilige Berg militia."

"I don't think there's really a death ray up there, Martin, but you're not far wrong on the rest. The Committee is divided on which group presents a larger threat. Because of internal disputes over the nature of Radiant Dawn, we have only offered covert support, and resolved to stay away."

He looked to the right, into the trees. There it was. The speedometer read forty, but there it was, pacing him like a harvest moon. It had to be an optical illusion. Eyes back on the road, which was crowning the wrong way going into a hairpin turn. He pumped the brakes and lay across the seats to try to throw his weight up-slope and keep the car from tumbling into the gorge. "Oh, stupid, stupid, stupid—"

"Martin? I don't have much time—"

The road veered back into a straight descent for the visible future, and Cundieffe found himself speeding up, glancing over at the shadow. Racing it. Stupid. For all he knew, it was a hallucination brought on by the pounding his head had taken. "Sorry. Agents Macy and Mentone—"

"They're not with the Bureau. Stay away from them."

He couldn't parse that one. If they were protecting Keogh, why were they covering it up in advance? It was like some kind of surreal military exercise—or a trap. "But if they're here by the Committee's orders, then why am I here?"

"We can't allow Radiant Dawn to keep operating in the dark. We can't legitimately investigate them ourselves, but a tangential avenue opened up which uniquely concerned you. We hope you'll see, as we do, that the cause is urgent."

"But how in the heck am I supposed to stop it—"

"You're not supposed to stop it. You are not to call in more agents, or state police, or notify or cooperate in any way with the local law or the media. This is going to happen. You're there to bear witness. We—myself and a plurality of powerful Committee members—have reason to suspect that the outbreak at Heilige Berg, whatever its true nature, was caused by the Radiant Dawn colony. The Committee as a whole has—arrangements with Keogh that will suffer if the Mission destroys his work at this critical juncture. They've contracted with Lt. Col. Greenaway to defend the colony against the Mission. You're there in case they're wrong."

"I know he's here. He's the one who beat me up!"

"Don't try to make anything out of it."

"But he *hit* me," Cundieffe said, hating the whine in his voice.

"He's critical to operations right now, and you aren't, but that could change very soon."

"What is the Committee thinking? He's shown a consistent pattern of overaggressive insubordination."

"True, he's a bloody-minded caveman, but Greenaway can be trusted to play his role. He believes he has the government by the short hairs. He *wanted* this."

Cundieffe understood. Greenaway had blackmailed them with Mission evidence, just as he'd used his Operation White Star Work to get in on the ground floor of Delta Force. He wouldn't have just come in if they just asked him. *What did he have on you?*

"Officially, he has resigned his commission, and is now a private security consultant, funded by black cash from an offshore account paid into, ultimately, by the Pentagon budget. He's better-armed and supported than he was in Delta Force, and he thinks he has carte blanche to go after the Mission, but we've placed him where he can only act in one direction, so he is contained. Better to have him inside, than trying to get in and dragging the circus in after him. The Mission's leadership is composed of ex-DARPA scientists and Army Special Operations Division and Intelligence Support Activities officers—the most brilliant, duplicitous men this country has ever produced. No one else could even begin to guess what they'd try. Greenaway can be counted on to get the Mission, and do it quietly."

He felt numb, dead from the neck up. He looked right. The terrain was rockier, with fewer trees, and the runner was closer. For a concussion-induced hallucination, it sure looked clear. It looked like a man in jungle camouflage running down the mountain at fifty miles per hour, motionless from the waist up, pointing something at him. It had to be a vision. "And then what?" he asked.

"Then we'll try to make the Committee see what it is they're dealing with. You and I, Martin. We'll show them. I can't guarantee this line any longer—"

"Hundreds of dead people too late—" Cundieffe shouted into the phone, but the phone squealed and he jerked it away from his ear. Then there was a coughing sound and there was no phone, only black plastic slivers in his burning hand.

His jaw dropped and he was looking stupidly at where the phone had been, wondering, *How did Brady do that?*

Glass cut his face, and he noticed that the passenger's side window had exploded, and now the driver's side window blew out. Cundieffe put all the empirical data together and concluded that someone was shooting at him. He lay down on the seat and tried to remember if he was pointed at the gorge, tried to visualize the swirling, treacherous road he'd been looking at a second ago, and in the end he said, *screw it*, and stepped on the accelerator.

He yanked the wheel right a notch with his left hand, then held it straight, the fading image of the road jumping and melting like an old hygiene education film under the two terawatt bulb of his panic. His rear window shattered. His headrest burst, a galaxy of glass and flaming foam rubber floating above Cundieffe's head as another volley atomized the front windshield and the rear doorposts. He wished he had studied harder to become proficient with firearms. He wished he had brought one with him.

The shooter was behind him, and probably standing still, unless the fire had come from a helicopter. Certainly not a running man—

Then it occurred to him that he was still driving rather fast on an icy mountain road while lying prone across the seats of his car. No more bullets passed through the cabin that he could discern, but the wind that roared through the exposed interior was nearly as powerful an incentive as bullets to remain where he was. He peered over the dash, screamed, "holy gosh—" and flailed at the wheel.

The runner stood in the middle of the road in front of him. A very, very tall, thin man, he stood stock-still, seemingly unperturbed by the oncoming car, though it must appear very large indeed to him, looking at it down the enormous starlight scope on the sniper rifle he held. The balding dome of Cundieffe's head through such a device must look like a Rose Parade float, and for a man who could shoot so well at a moving car while running through snow—

Cundieffe threw himself back down across the seats and kicked at the gas as the air above his head came alive with lead. His hip must have disengaged the safety belt, or perhaps the sniper simply shot it away. The car bucked so hard he rolled onto the floor, and he figured he hit the wrong pedal, and kicked the other one as hard and as fast as he could.

His right hand flared in pain and curled up like a burning leaf as he tried to grip the wheel with it. A shard of plastic from his phone jutted from the heel of his limp fist, and a raw, red groove seared the path of the bullet across his palm. He groped for his briefcase on the floor beside him, propped it up against his chest and tucked his head behind it. He hoped the steel sides, the laptop and thick sheaves of files inside, would do a better job of stopping a bullet than the front of the car had.

The dashboard flew apart, and Cundieffe's ears popped and rang. The sniper's bullets, mangled by traveling through the auto body, the firewall and the instrument panel, punched flaming holes in the upholstery. His briefcase bucked in his arms with a distinct *p-tang* and a squelchy sizzle of pulverized circuitry. The passenger-side airbag deployed with a blast of stinging gas, and just as quickly burst as bullets punctured it. The driver's side airbag went to tatters a moment later, and then nothing but the wind.

Cundieffe jerked upright on the seat and whipped his head around. There was good news and bad news. The runner was nowhere. The road was likewise. He had run out of mountain, and had only a gentle foothill between himself and the nearest ranch, but he was off the road, and headed for a fence.

He seized the wheel with his good left hand and the elbow of the right, and attempted to turn the car back to the left, which he presumed was the direction the road had wandered off. The car slewed sideways as it hit the barbed-wire fence, taking out two posts and sliding out of control on two wheels into the open field beyond. Cundieffe gripped the wheel and pressed his face against the ruined airbag.

When the car stalled and came to rest, he got out and looked around with his hand in his breast pocket, unconvincingly fondling a pretend gun for the benefit of the runner, should he still be around. There was only the wind and the snow falling, and a vast apron of pure white silence spreading out from him in all directions. His ears rang. His head snapped around involuntarily at what sounded like the clanging bells of a dozen distant freight trains converging on him. The wake of his bobsled-run down the hill was the only feature on the land, and the snow was already covering it over.

It hit him then, when he was sure that whoever was shooting at him was gone. He had never been shot at, before. He had never even realistically expected that such a thing might ever happen to him. An inexcusable lapse in duty, but for an agent who had sought only a niche behind a desk, and who had been rewarded for his diligent bookworming with a post at the head office, the experience was impossible to square with waking life. It was as if he'd watched a movie. He'd been too emotionally worked-over to even panic, and now it was over.

The Oldsmobile bore ample witness to the improbability of his survival. The shooters—for surely, there must have been several, along the road—had every reason to believe he was dead. They riddled the car along the line of his center of mass with at least twenty rounds of .50-caliber ammunition, not counting the ones that must have passed through the windows. Two sizable bullet fragments had penetrated his briefcase, killing his laptop and mixing the fragments with the shredded files and the oranges he'd saved for lunch. Counting the holes made it easier to reason what happened, and forget what he'd thought he saw.

Needless to say, the car wouldn't start. At a guess, it might be the holes in the radiator and the engine block, but the battery had a hole in it, too. The gauges dangled from their sockets, or rolled around between his feet. The cheap stock stereo gave a flatulent spasm of AM static that faded and died before he could change the station. The door beeped once when he opened it to warn him he'd left his keys in the car.

Alero is a sorry name for a domestic mid-sized sedan, he reflected. Devoid of any of the evocative imagery or consonant sounds that made a distinctive American automobile, it sounded like the name of some new prescription medicine they advertised on television, but were too embarrassed to reveal what malady it cured. *I'm glad I didn't die in an Alero.*

He looked to the road, a hundred yards or so to the north. The barbed wire followed it, and a small billboard he hadn't noticed before stood out against the horizon. It was hand-painted, obviously the work of the landowner. SMASH THE NEW WORLD ORDER! STOP Y-JEW-K! DEATH TO FED BABYKILLER THUGS! WE REMEMBER WACO! screamed red block letters, while beneath it, a sub-legend gave a web address and one-eight-hundred number for pamphlets.

The back of his neck burned as if someone were tickling it with an infrared sight. He collected his ruined briefcase and ran across the field, over the flattened stretch of fence, and up onto the road.

On foot, he thought he could make it back to White Bird in about an hour, but he felt wary of staying on the road. Though he might hitch a ride, he might also run into the owner of the pasture where he'd left the car, or the men who were trying to kill him. He walked a little faster along the palisade of muddy snow piled on the shoulder. His legs ached as lactic acid accumulated in his exhausted muscles, but he forged on, and eventually, they went blessedly numb.

Twice, he heard trucks coming and threw himself into the ditch until they passed. His slacks and shoes were thoroughly soaked through by the time he got far enough down the road that the ranches became large residential spreads with visible houses, but he kept trudging. Any of these good civilians could be rabid anti-federalists, or, for all he knew, all of them could.

He dealt with voices like that all the time in his work, but when he heard such bile from people with property, with means of self-support, with all the benefits of living in a well-ordered democracy, it made him sick to his stomach. Who else, if not the decent, taxpaying citizens, was he out here trying to protect?

He thought of the Cave Institute. He had examined their claims long and hard, and come to believe, to know, that without them, mankind would have destroyed itself before civilization ever became worthy of the name. They were the invisible hand on the tiller of the otherwise hell-bound ship of state, but even their benevolent stewardship could be construed by paranoid fantasists as a kind of tyranny, and make their lies and fever-dreams a little more real. He wondered, himself, who they were really trying to protect, and how many sides there really were.

This is going to happen—

He saw something else, just then, that he hadn't noticed on the way up, which surprised him, because Karl Schweinfurter had told him about it. At the time, it hadn't seemed to matter enough, but now, it could tell him something when he had less than nothing.

The Heilige Berg slaughterhouse adjoined their acreage in the valley. It was a two story wood and cinderblock structure like an elongated barn, with a maze of corrals and chutes enfolding it on two sides, and a loading dock with a row of parked trucks on the third. The corrals held only untrampled snow. It was probably customary to butcher most of the herd before winter, but there would still be plenty of dairy cattle, and he'd seen herds toughing out the cold in other fields in the area. Schweinfurter had said he'd seen the trucks going day and night when he was there last, so they might've slaughtered the whole herd, but he'd also said the meat was all kept in coolers in the slaughterhouse until it went to a wholesaler in Grangeville. Why were the trucks going up to Heilige Berg, then?

He stood in the shelter of a wood shed at the edge of the property for a long time, looking at the weather-scarred slaughterhouse. A search of the building should be conducted by a SWAT team, and perhaps a bomb squad, with dogs and body armor and at least a gun or two between them. An unarmed Bureau agent without so much as a telephone or a car, who had already been beaten and shot at—wounded, he remembered, seeing and feeling his hand again—would do well to walk directly to the sheriff's station.

But there was Hoecker's order. *Bear witness—*

He crossed the snow to the nearest human-sized entrance to the stockhouse. A Master lock hung open from the latch. He removed it, pocketed it and peeked inside.

The interior was dark, the air warm and close and ripe with the coppery scent of blood and the funk of animals, but Cundieffe wrinkled his nose in puzzlement. It didn't smell like cattle. It was strong enough, but there was no musky, not-unpleasant aroma of manure. There was also no sound.

Now would be the time to announce himself as an FBI agent and demand that any parties within declare themselves and come out with their hands up. Now would be the time to have a gun and some back-up. The two arguments neatly nullified each other.

Cundieffe gingerly walked into the dark with his hands out, and gave a meep of pain when his right hand hit a post. Fumbling down it, he found a light switch and flipped it.

Rows of bare-bulb lights fluttered and came aglow in sour yellow patches of a vast, cavernous space, the juice traveling like a rumor to the back of the room, which must be half the length of the slaughterhouse. Ramps led up to a hayloft, and several doors and chutes on the far wall led deeper into the building. There were no cattle, but the killing floor was furnished from wall to wall in cots.

Cundieffe walked around and then through the ranked Army-surplus cots, so like the orderly human corral of a disaster relief center. He counted three hundred cots, each with a scratchy wool blanket neatly folded on the foot. Hoses and less self-explanatory slaughtering machinery dangled from the rafters and lay in neat stacks on shelves along the north wall. Polished steel glistened, hoses dripped.

He wandered from one row of cots to the next, peering under cots. The floor was scabbed with recent blood almost everywhere, but there was nothing else, which struck him as stranger than people not minding sleeping in a slaughterhouse. There was nothing else on the floor. Even in a military barracks, a person left traces of his occupancy—a comb, a discarded magazine or a paper cup, graffiti. Heilige Berg was mostly young boys, but also included many whole families, regular people, despite their hateful religion and crash-course survivalism. People left trash, forgot things, made messes, carved their initials, left an unpleasant odor. He found hairs on the cots when he peered very closely, and a few scuff-marks and traces of dirt and damp where boots had left their marks.

Who didn't take their boots off when they went to sleep? Bodies slept here, but not people.

In the last thirty-six hours, they evacuated the compound and took shelter here. They took nothing, left nothing, forgot nothing. As tight as Delta Force commandos, as disciplined as Benedictine monks, they butchered the herd while the rest slept in the same room. In their boots. Then, just before dawn, they boarded charter buses and vanished. As incredible as Schweinfurter's story had been, he had refused to accept that his people would voluntarily leave the compound. They were different, now, he'd insisted, but nothing could make Grossvater Egil lead the community off the mountain. He had a prophecy to wait with them until Gotterdammerung, and the Ragnarok of the Races—

They left nothing behind, and no one. They left the door unlocked. Abandoned their faith, and left in the most orderly evacuation imaginable. It was a puzzle.

Crossing to the far wall, he found the door nearest the northeast corner of the room standing ajar, and a darksome flight of stone steps descending into a basement. Feeling for a light switch, he found none until he reached the bottom. His shin barked something and he tripped over a wooden crate and fell into more of them, scraping and bruising the few patches of tissue on his limbs that were not already contused. His hands came up to soften his fall, but skin snagged on nails, arms sank into jagged gaps between boxes and a morass of packing foam.

He fought his way back to his feet and, biting his lip in a vain attempt to keep from cursing again today, found the switch. It was an old-fashioned button, like a doorbell, and he heard a crack and smelled ozone when the circuit closed. He had a moment to swallow the certainty that the Heilige Bergers had left the door unlocked in a lame attempt to lure a few stupid baby-killer fed thugs into an explosive trap. The light was weaker and scummier than upstairs, and it took Cundieffe a few minutes for his eyes to adjust.

The crates filled the basement waist-high to the dim suggestion of a far wall, making the chambers beyond inaccessible. Stenciled on the sides: *Idaho Army National Guard Armory* on some, Cyrillic characters and VORSICHT! EXPLOSIV on others. All the crates appeared to be empty.

They did not leave empty-handed, after all. They didn't take their cache intact, but broke it out and left in haste, as if going off to war.

He felt dizzy, sat down hard on a crate. Nobody in White Bird said anything about the Heilige Bergers leaving heavily laden with rifles, explosives and mortars. Even Sheriff Manes' trio of dullard deputies could not have missed such a detail.

He should hurry to alert the Bureau and the state police about this new development. If the Heilige Berg community had been somehow biologically co-opted by Radiant Dawn, they were armed and on the loose somewhere in the Pacific Northwest, and the agents who followed them might be caught unawares and killed.

If they were really off the mountain at all.

He shuddered. It made no sense for them to leave. What he saw here was baffling and mildly unnatural, but it told him that Heilige Berg was taking up arms, whether to defend Radiant Dawn or their own homes he couldn't guess, but they were here, he knew it.

Then who left in all those buses?

He stood up so fast he didn't notice a nail tearing the seat out of his slacks.

Three hundred and fifty people, all of them terminal cancer patients.

Dr. Keogh gathered his patients out in the remotest possible locations to expose them to RADIANT, which killed healthy tissue, but stimulated some new and improved version to grow out of malignant cells.

But to absorb the white separatists, they would have to have had cancer, all of them. Schweinfurter verified Hoecker's original tip that Heilige Berg fell prey to an epidemic, and that when he was brought back from his Dairy Queen ordeal, they were mysteriously cured. The boy himself was undoubtedly sick, perhaps dying, if he didn't get to a hospital and into immediate cancer treatment. Because he missed his chance to be cured, missed RADIANT.

He hoped that Macy and Mentone could at least be counted on to take care of the boy. When all this was over, whatever this was, he knew that the boy would be the only willing witness, the only evidence that strung this web of impossibilities together.

There were still so many questions, though, that he couldn't bring himself to tell a soul what he believed. How did Dr. Keogh make Heilige Berg sick enough fast enough for them to survive the change? And what was the change? He thought again of Sgt. Storch, sitting there impassively, while deep in his glassy eyes, something flailed at chains that kept it down inside. He saw Storch walking dumb as his ruptured head melted. He saw a man running down the mountain alongside his racing car, shooting his phone out of the space his head had been in only a split-second earlier.

The more he thought he knew, the more afraid he was of believing in it. No sane man could hope to fold such things into his vision of the world, but he was not a man. He was a Mule. Nature's own new and improved human, selected for the ability to face the unacceptable so that the species as a whole would not perish. If he and his kind could not restore order and protect the populace from the truth, then perhaps the human race deserved to step aside and make way for its successors.

Trembling, he climbed the stairs and was crossing the killing floor when he heard a noise like plumbing backing up throughout the slaughterhouse. He felt the gurgling groan in the soles of his feet, saw the cots vibrate as the sound grew and became a thrumming, throbbing pulse, as if the slaughterhouse was a living thing revitalized with its abandonment, and its heart had begun to beat.

He shook his head as if to shoo away a fly. Such lurid thoughts were grotesque, unworthy and unproductive. He was under a little stress, but it was no excuse for letting his imagination run away with him. But what in heaven's name was that sound?

The vibrations subsided, but a growling subharmonic rose and shook the walls. It came from deep in the slaughterhouse. It grew louder exponentially as Cundieffe approached it. He opened a heavy, double-wide refrigerator door, and the sound, and the smell, knocked him back ten feet.

It was as if the refrigerator had broken down, and later flooded with raw sewage from a burst pipe. The sound was a voice.

Cundieffe wrapped his scarf tightly around his mouth and nose, but he could still taste it like a film congealing on his tongue, and his eyes began to burn as he stepped inside.

A wide corridor surfaced in quilted aluminum panels led into a huge bank of walk-in fridges and freezers. The corridor itself was not refrigerated, but Cundieffe shivered.

He saw daylight. Around a corner, a train-wreck, minus the train, the corridor wall and the exterior wall beyond that breached by elliptical holes ten feet across. Dishwater-colored daylight filtered into the dark, painting harsher shadows outside their feeble corona. Outside, the corrals. Fences trampled by the same herd of rogue elephants. Snow and shreds of debris tracked across fractured, filth-smeared concrete in a vast swath back of the end of the corridor, where a refrigerator door hung open at an askew angle.

So stunned was he by the baffling destruction, that he was painfully slow in turning to look at the source of it, as well as the sounds and the smell. He turned with his eyes closed, and only opened them when he felt something wet and massive sweep the air before his face, and heard the voice again, bubbling up as if from the bowels of a tar pit choked with decaying carcasses.

"Say, buddy," said the unspeakable voice, "Can you help out a Vietnam veteran?"

Against all common sense, against the screaming gravity of his primal nervous system, Cundieffe moved closer. Slitting his eyes, he walked into the warm, wet wind that streamed past him out of the occupied fridge. He stopped ten feet away from the doorway and peered more avidly than he intended into the dark until his eyes began to readjust.

Something filled the refrigerator from wall to wall, from the floor to the rows of hooks on tracks from which meat once hung. How far back the compartment went, he had no idea, but it was full of quivering, wheezing life.

Light glinted on mounds of excrement on the floor that reminded Cundieffe of owl droppings—tightly compacted, desiccated nuggets of bone and hair and sinew, the only indigestible elements of an entire mouse or mole, reduced to an almost mineral state by an exquisitely efficient digestive system. By the size and rough composition of the excreta before him, Cundieffe could not but conclude that each of the mounds had once been a whole beef cow. The Heilige Berg militia, or whoever they were now, had not butchered the cattle, but merely slaughtered and placed them in cold storage, so this thing had come through the wall and eaten them whole.

With a ghastly plosive noise and a monstrous gust of gaseous by-product, a fresh one was ejected by a mammoth sphincter and slid across the slime-slick floor to stop at Cundieffe's unsteady feet. He felt the floor, and the earth's crust beneath it, groan at the unbearable burden of the glutton. The thing almost exerted its own gravitational field, for it drew Cundieffe still nearer, though he felt as if any moment, it would sink into the molten mantle at the earth's core, and drag him, and the rest of Idaho, in after it.

A wall of smooth flesh like a colossal bowel blocked the doorway, its only discernible feature the many, many, busy sphincters, but as he watched, new features began to percolate and reach out of the mass.

Cundieffe trembled before the enormity, the obscenity, the impossibility of what he saw. In a day, he had seen a man that he had concluded must have been many men, for what man could have done what he did? Now, he shook as he had not then, for he had no choice but to accept it, for this thing, too, was some kind of a man.

Out of the sea of fat and assholes came a knurled knob of boneless tissue, dwarfed by the awesome size of its body, but growing larger all the time and wrinkling with contours of a fetal human face. Eyes, beady and black and twinkling with avid, greedy joy, popped open like time-lapse blisters all over the overripe flesh, and a mouth brimming with bone-ridged tongues and syringes and teeth teeth TEETH yawned and smiled at him. "I seem to be stuck," the mouth moaned.

"What—who—who are you?" Cundieffe choked. He started to take a step backwards, but his foot got no traction, and he braced himself against the wall to keep from falling down in the mess.

"Specialist Four Gibson Holroyd, One-Two, Operational Detachment Alpha-Texas, MACV/SOG, at your service, scrawny morsel."

"D-d-did you eat the whole herd?" He honestly didn't know what else to say.

"You fucking kidding me? They got something like two hundred head in these lockers. Only about forty of 'em in here, but like I said, I seem to be inextricably incarcerated by my own gustative excess. So if you wouldn't mind lending a hand—"

Still afraid to take a step, paralyzed by those black eyes, Cundieffe found himself reaching out to the insatiable blob, when a tongue of sorts slithered up out of the mouth and reached out to him. He dove backwards, pivoting and trying to run, but his feet only splashed in the filth and betrayed him. He heard the air snap above his head as the tongue whipped past like the deadly adhesive flycatcher of a gargantuan toad.

He screamed, flailing his legs and windmilling his arms as he went down on the floor, sailed out of the blob's reach on a carpet of effluvium. His stomach revolted then, hot vomit hitting his palate and fouling the scarf over his mouth. He swam in shit trying to get to his feet. He heard more tongues coming for him. The blob hollered after him, but with so many writhing tongues, its words were gibberish.

Cundieffe scrambled to the edge of the puddle on his hands and knees, but when he hit firm floor, he raced out through the holes in the wall and rolled in the snow. Hot tears stung his eyes and his nose ran freely, but it flushed the vile residue of the thing that called itself a man. He shed his filthy topcoat, tore off the scarf and used the unsoiled portions of it to wipe the filth off his skin. It burned.

Slowly, breath by freezing breath, he regained his composure. Never mind that it is impossible. It *is*. And if he got help, the thing would be gone, tearing the whole slaughterhouse off its foundations, and running amok across the Idaho countryside. The abomination had to be destroyed. Now.

He went back to the cellar to find a weapon.

He rummaged among the empty crates for an unguessable time, tearing up his crabbed, cramped hands on nails and splintered pine before he found something he thought he could use at the back of the pile. It was a Fabrique Nationale belt-fed M249 Squad Automatic Weapon, with two hundred rounds of 5.56mm ammunition coiled in a handy, though heavy, plastic box. After puzzling over the instructions, which were in French, he lugged the bullets and the "light" machine gun up the stairs separately and set them up outside the outer door to the refrigerated compartments.

His fingers shook as he tried to set the end of the belt into the feeder mechanism in the breech, like the unhurried Belgian stick figure in the diagrams. Inside, he could hear the blob's unholy plumbing wringing out more beef by-products, and the tongue-tied bellowing of the mouth, which had now become a caterwauling chorus.

He set the SAW up on its bipod on a steel utility cart from the killing floor, checked the ammunition and, after almost tipping the whole works over on the raised threshold, wheeled it into the corridor.

"Where you been, college boy?" The blob roared. The sphincters took up the cry, and the blob shifted. Cundieffe heard the reinforced walls of the meat locker straining, saw dust sprinkle down from the ceiling.

"Do you work for Dr. Keogh, or are you a member of the Heilige Berg separatist settlement?" Cundieffe asked in a flat monotone. It helped if he just looked down at the big black machine gun before him, taking comfort in its death-dealing power, and tried to persuade himself that he was just interrogating a prisoner.

"I'm all alone," the mouth managed. The tongues kept a low profile, slinking across the floor, snaking among the hills of digested cattle towards the machine gun. "I'm a species unto myself, an army of one."

Cundieffe watched them uneasily. He looked back at the gun. "I order you to…to remain still, or I shall be forced to resort to deadly force. Now, what happened here?"

"Big fuckin' surprise–for everybody. That old motherfucker's no dick-swingin' white man, I tell you what, he's an ink-drinkin' stink-beetle, he's… full of surprises."

"Is he–is Keogh–still up on the mountain?"

"What'd I tell you? They're all gone. Empty house, just bait… But I'm full of surprises, too."

"Are you, now?"

"Oh yeah, morsel. Gonna be an army! Army of 'Royds! C'mere, morsel…"

The tongues reared up and Cundieffe recoiled away from the gun, because he hadn't seen them coming, never saw so many get so close. They grabbed for the cart just as Cundieffe regained himself and lunged for the trigger. He gripped the stock with his left hand and slipped his finger into the guard. A lashing tongue blurred up and wrapped around his arm. Pain opened up his arm and made it spasm, and jerking it back, he squeezed the trigger in a death-grip. The gun bucked and barked. Sparks flew and lead sang in the corridor, the path of fire arcing crazily around the doorway, ricocheting bullets describing Catherine wheels of light on his bulging eyeballs.

It screamed, like a stadium filled with dying damned souls. The tongues recoiled. Bony radulae along the slimy tip of the one holding his arm sheared away the skin of his forearm with his shirtsleeve. The pain drove Cundieffe forward. He leaned over the gun and played it back and forth on the avalanche of noisome offal as it curled in on itself and tried in vain to present a smaller target.

Tentacles and bulging, muscle-ripped arms burst out of the mass, wrapping around the doorway and the unhinged door, trying to draw it shut. Clubs studded with bony baling hooks shot out and scythed the air. Rivets popped and walls buckled. A rafter beam splintered and fell.

Cundieffe bore down on the blob, grouping the stream of fire into the roaring mouth. Tentacles severed and danced like blind, pain-mad cobras. The huge jaw gobbled and gaped until the bullets obliterated it and punched deeper. The cart jostled and jumped to the relentless cadence of the machine gun and Cundieffe, confident at last that he was making a difference, rolled it forward, pushing aside excreta to drill the target more mercilessly, to separate every atom of it from every other atom until it was just so much inert slush, because such things should simply not be.

When the SAW ran out of bullets, he was within arm's reach of the thing. It seemed to notice the shift in events before he did, and tattered but intact tentacles swept the gun and the cart out of the way and reached for him as if he'd been hurling nothing but harsh language at it all along.

"Ain't you just supposed to arrest me?" it bawled.

"Aren't you supposed to die?" he shot back, and giggled, because it was a pretty clever comeback, given the dire circumstances. He giggled some more, because now he was even shakier, and bells were ringing again, and the choking cordite odor of the gunfire was already giving way to the stench, now redoubled, with its more intimate chambers opened to the air.

He staggered back the way he'd come, out across the killing floor, back to the cellar.

Impossible? Surely not. He just needed something bigger.

He found it at the bottom of the pile, among similar boxes with, of all things, Israeli stamps and customs decals on them. The instructions were entirely in diagrams and numbers, which could show a kindergartener how to load and deploy the weapon. Very clearly it showed that one must be at least five hundred feet from the target for the missile to arm, and that one must be extremely careful about the back-blast which erupts from the rear of the weapon. He looked askance at the ordnance, which had a series of colorful but unfamiliar warning symbols on them, along with some comforting words in English: ARMOR-PIERCING SABOT RPG ROUND, 1. WARNING! DO NOT MANUALLY DISARM. CONTAINS DEPLETED URANIUM. Then he fitted it into the launch tube and went back to the meat locker.

"Hey, what you got there, college boy?" the blob gobbled, and when it saw the RPG on Cundieffe's shoulder, it flapped its million jowls approvingly. "That ought to do the trick. Fire away."

Cundieffe ran out through the hole again, paced out two hundred steps from the outer wall, keeping the stygian darkness of the occupied meat locker in view as he crossed the field and braced himself against a fence post.

"Shoot straight, college boy! Ah'm comin' for you!"

He clenched the trigger. The RPG round took off with a blinding cloud of flame and gas. The opposing forces drove him back and forth at the same time, and he swooned and collapsed in the snow, one eye on the rocket as it lanced the space he'd paced in a blink and disappeared into the dark interior.

"AAAAAAHHHHWOOOOOOOOOOOOOOO!"

He thought he heard a devastating whump, like a punch in God's breadbasket, or a ball the size of the asteroid that killed the dinosaurs hitting the sweet spot of a cosmic baseball glove. Then the shadows and stench and unholy howling burned up in a miniature nova.

The outer wall bubbled and blew away, the second story floor and roof tumbling into the gap. The whole slaughterhouse seemed to flex out, then fold in around the explosion, even as the shockwave leveled the walls of the fridge compartments and whirled them away in a split-second cyclone of uranium-impregnated shrapnel. A string of powerful secondary explosions, like the burning of an ammo dump, rocked the ruins as vast pockets of flammable methane trapped in Holroyd's intestinal tract ignited.

The bells would never, ever, ever stop ringing.

Cundieffe got to his feet and dropped the RPG. He shuffled back across the field, jaw on his chest, overwhelmed by what he had wrought. The entire building was gutted, timbers raining down and spilling bales of hay and drifts of roof-bound snow continuously. Here and there, little fires sprang up and began to gorge themselves on the dry hay bales. Where the meat locker had been, there was only a crater lined with unrecognizable gobbets of meat and dinosaur-sized bone. Cundieffe marveled. He'd done it. Now, no one would have to suffer the sanity-shaking obscenity of this unspeakable aberration. He understood, then, for a moment, the joy and pride that the Mules took in even dirty, convoluted operations like this. That the world would never have to know, and could go on living its billions of sane little lives, was the highest reward for duty well done.

He shivered. His clothes were soaked through with sweat and less familiar fluids, and he was injured in more places than he could count. Best to go to the road and hope for someone better disposed towards the federal government than the man whose fence he'd crashed through to pick him up and take him back to town. This place would have to be closed off and investigated thoroughly, and the mercenaries on the mountain would have to be stood down, even if it came to an armed confrontation. The mountain was a trap that Radiant Dawn, and God knew who else, if not the Mules themselves, had laid for the Mission.

This is going to happen

Bear witness

Something stirred in the crater.

Big fuckin' surprise.

Cundieffe tumbled over debris, hauled himself to his feet and took a good look.

Inside, the crater stirred like a cauldron as the charred, liquefied mess began to congeal and make itself into a body again. A shattered wall tumbled, and a large chunk of the blob lumbered out into the light. It was more or less humanoid from the waist down, though there were too many legs by far. From the trunk sprouted a mad garden of organs and limbs, human and bovine and worse–rolling eyes, lactating udders, horns, hands, claws, flapping dewlaps, Brobdingnagian penises and cavernous vaginas, decentralized colonies of brain and nerves, fanged anuses and every conceivable variety of mouth dripping septic saliva. Smoking and sizzling, the burned, bomb-flayed thing rose and came at Cundieffe. More wreckage stirred, and more smashed jigsaw abortions stumbled from cover and approached.

"College-boy," hissed the army of 'Royds.

Cundieffe ran around the collapsing slaughterhouse to the shed where he left his briefcase. He got his Thermos and rinsed out the dregs of clam chowder. In the shed, he found a road flare and a full gas can, then ran back to the meat locker.

The army was growing, the pieces growing more useful limbs and eyes and mouths. No one looked like another, but it was harder to tell that they were pieces of a whole. Holroyd had achieved his goal. He had become a small army.

Cundieffe crept as near as he dared to the crater and lit the road flare. Brandishing it against the circling things, he dipped the open mouth of the Thermos in the molten flesh in the crater. He fastened the lid and backed away, waving the road flare ineffectually at them. At the edge of the foundation, he knelt and screwed the flare into the snow, unscrewed the cap of the gas can, and skulked back to the crater. He baptized the abortions with gas, lavished it on the flattened walls and the still-standing façade, ran screaming and giggling around the whole building until the can was empty, and he came back around to the flare. One of the things shuffled out of the building and into the light, a wriggling mass of brain and intestines teetering on bandy, road-runner legs. Cundieffe touched the flare to it, and it went up like a scarecrow. He threw the flare into the crater and ran.

As the flames rose over the roof and the gray and black smoke became a pillar visible for miles around, Cundieffe stowed the Thermos in the briefcase and shrank into a ball against the leeward wall of the shed.

It's dead, he told himself, *it's dead, it's got to be dead—*

~ 22 ~

When Karl Schweinfurter woke up on a cold hard cot under harsh fluorescent light, his first thought was that it had all been a dream, and he was home. But there was no cot next to his, empty or otherwise, and no singing of hymns, no shouts of drilling Jägers outside.

He wiped the gummy mucous crust from his eyes and found that he could see little better with his eyes open. He saw enough, though, to remember. He was still in jail, still sick. They still didn't believe him.

He tried to convince them when they pulled him out of the wreck, but they wouldn't listen. They nagged the shit out of him some more, refused him medical treatment, and shut him up in the cell.

He tried to tell them again, when the Sheriff came in with a doctor, but they still wouldn't listen. They said he was nuts and injected him with something that made him sleep, and when he woke up, he was still in jail, and now, they wanted answers. He told them to eat shit and die.

They hadn't come back after that, not that he remembered. He didn't want to talk to anyone, now, could barely think straight or remember what it was that had been so important, anyway. Last he saw them, everyone at the compound was happier and healthier than ever before, and even Grossvater Egil had only seemed to want what was best for him. He sensed that he was very sick indeed, dying, even, and that it was he who needed help, and only Grossvater Egil could fix what was wrong with him. Only Grossvater Egil had been willing to listen. Maybe he should go back.

He pulled himself up, leaned against the wall and tried to see straight. The jail cell was empty, as were all the others. The only thing to look at was the steel sink-and-shitter combo fixture at his feet, and the Dairy Queen bag on the floor in the center of the cell. He hadn't looked inside it, but he doubted it contained food. Whatever it was, he'd be hard pressed to get up and walk that far, though he was hungry enough to eat a rat. The bag floated on the poured concrete horizon, a twinkling, unreachable star.

He rubbed his face and neck, vaguely alarmed to find strange bumps and spongy masses under his skin where there shouldn't be any. Dragging himself up to the sink, he tried to check himself in the metal mirror set into the wall, but either the steel or his eyes were too bleary to see more than a pale greenish ghost. His head started to swim and his stomach revolted at standing for too long, so he swooned on the cot and tried to close his eyes.

He wondered what his parents were doing right now. He wondered about Heidi, and her new baby, her new, smart, whispering baby. What was he trying to save them from? What was it, that seemed so important at the time, that he'd fled?

When he stole the car (*pimpmobile?*), he'd been driven by a fear greater than his terror of Grossvater Egil and the harsh life of the compound. Something had come from outside, and gotten in, and now—

You were stupid to run away, but yet you may be saved.

Maybe it was just a movie he saw. He'd do that, when he was really stoned or drunk or sick, see something on TV and confuse himself that it happened to him. Or he'd get so worked up about a song on the radio that he'd break something before he even knew what he was doing. But nothing like this. Those Dairy Queen assholes, they beat him up—and Grossvater Egil came—sick—scared—Grossvater Egil was so kind, now, so different from the stern patriarch that had stripped him naked in the snow, and Karl—he—stabbed him…

Come, boy. The rapture comes again.

Remembering only made him hurt worse, so he resolved to stop.

He woke up with his mouth brimming with bile. He heaved it out for a long, long time, then he was seized by hunger cramps so severe he balled up and screamed into his knees. He wouldn't let them hear him suffer. He wouldn't tell them anything. He wouldn't tell them what he knew, which was less than nothing, anyway.

In his half-dreams, his hands and head swelled up until they filled the room, pressed against the bars and through them. He engulfed the deputies and the Sheriff and burst the walls of the station and ate up the town, the state, the nation, threw out pseudopods into the sea, and ate the world. When all the world was Him, nobody would ever pick on him ever again, nobody would ever hit or kick him or call him Swinefucker, because there would be only Him.

Maybe that was something he saw on TV, too.

"Somebody to see you, prisoner," someone shouted. The bars clanged and grated and a short black shadow stepped into his cell.

Karl tried to open his eyes wider, tried to focus. His arms and legs clenched against another beating. The shadow grew larger, saying something, but not loud enough to penetrate the buzzing in his head. Then he smelled something, a wholesome, meaty aroma that cut right through the numbing miasma of industrial cleaning solutions and sour sweat and his own blend of filth. The shadow's hands laid something out before him on the cot, then retreated into the mint-green fog of the walls. He strained, and made it come into focus, and his mouth, so dry and dirty from vomiting and starvation, overflowed.

It was the most glorious sandwich ever rendered by human hands. Layer upon layer of marbled roast beef and luxuriant Swiss cheese drooped from between the toasted decks of a Kaiser bun, and scales of melting ice dripped from a tall plastic, foil-topped cup of orange juice.

The sandwich eclipsed the shadow, the cells, the world. He reached for the juice warily, hand shaking so bad he knocked it over. When no trap sprang, he snatched it and punched one grubby thumb through the foil, slurped it down.

In an unsettling flood, color came back into the world. The buzzing receded into a backwater territory of his brain, and his convulsing guts settled down. When he could lift his head, he tore into the sandwich. Only when it was finished and he felt that he might be able to hold onto it for a while did he look around for the shadow. Instead, he saw a short, slim, balding, bespectacled man in a heavy black topcoat standing over him with one hand in his pocket and the other holding out a shiny gold shield in a billfold. He didn't look like a cop, unless libraries had cops. He looked like the kind of bookworm even Karl used to pick on in school, and he looked more than a little scared at the sight of Karl, although Karl didn't feel particularly badass.

"I see you enjoyed the sandwich," the bookworm said.

"Buh," Karl managed. His mouth was still thick and swollen from the sudden onslaught of food and drink, and his brain had apparently shut down to pitch in with digestion. "Guh," he tried again.

"I'm Special Agent Martin Cundieffe, of the Federal Bureau of Investigation." The bookworm pocketed the shield, knelt down beside Karl. "I'm here to protect you."

"Puh—protect—muh—m—me?" Getting better...

"I believe you were already interrogated by two agents who claimed to be from the FBI."

Karl couldn't remember. He'd spoken to someone, but he'd thought it was Grossvater Egil. Soon, they'd all be Grossvater Egil, and it wouldn't matter…

"Now, I understand your group recently became suddenly ill, from unknown causes. You look pretty ill, yourself. Have you received any medical attention?"

Karl shook his head.

"You don't trust me. I understand completely. I know all about Heilige Berg, Karl. I've studied your church, and its teachings about the world. You believe that the federal government is controlled by a shadowy enclave of internationalists who are waging a covert war on pure-blooded Aryan patriots."

That sounded like something Grossvater Egil used to say. He nodded again and tried to speak. "The Jews—"

"You're right, Karl, but it's not the Jews. They're far stranger than you can imagine, and far more powerful. Those agents you spoke to—or didn't, as the case may be—are part of it. They're part of something that is going to happen here that involves your people, something big. But they're going to keep it a secret—if you let them."

Karl nodded again. He was pretty sure he knew what the bookworm was talking about, but he couldn't remember what it was. Something important… He wanted to remember now with dog-like earnestness, if only to get more orange juice.

"You may not believe me, but I am here to protect you, though I can't speak for anyone else. As an American citizen, you are entitled to due process and humane treatment, and I apologize on behalf of the federal government for the deplorable conditions here. But I must reiterate. If I'm to get to the bottom of this, you are the only material witness to what's happening up there. I want to protect your people, for, though their politics be odious, they are American citizens—"

He went on like that forever, until Karl got hungry again and started to remember just to shut him up. "They just popped up right on New Year's Eve. Said they were our new neighbors—"

"Who did?"

"The tree—"

In fits and starts, he told the bookworm about the first encounter with the place; about the buses, the big building where no building should have been, and the sickly light that came down from the sky, and about the monsters in the woods.

He found it was easier to tell if he just closed his eyes and let it happen to him again. The words came fast and furious, sentences tailgating and fender-bending as he relived it in high-definition Technicolor. The running, the sickness, the beatings, the cold; Grossvater Egil, not angry; his parents, not dead. About how the Rapture came, and he missed it. He told about running away again, about his triumphant return to Dairy Queen. Now, waiting to die—

"Rapture came, and I missed it," he said again.

"How were they different after you came back?" the bookworm asked.

"Not different," Karl growled, brain buzzing as he tried to access parts of it that had gone to static. "They *were* all different, but they were all the same—as each other. I still knew them, and they knew me, but they all fit together like…they all talked the same, and they had the same eyes. Like they all had the same soul. I was scared, but—like—it was what we were waiting for, you know? The Rapture, the Ragnarok of the races. It was like they were all pure, and full of God's grace, and I was—I was—shit…"

The bookworm leaned in closer, his shiny bald head and glasses reflecting the fluorescents hurtfully into his eyes. "And after this—change—what activities did you observe?"

"I was only there for a while, after Grossvater Egil brought me back from the DQ. The trucks—they usually keep them all down at the slaughterhouse on the state road, but they was all up at the compound, going up and down the mountain. They might've been killing the whole herd, but they store the meat down there."

"The Sheriff says your people have cleared out of the compound, Karl. What do you make of that? Where would they go?"

"Nowhere! That's a damned lie! We're supposed to stay up there 'til—until the Rapture, I guess."

"And if that event came to pass…or if they believed it did?"

"Then they're supposed to go forth to spread the Word."

"Spread the Word?"

"Shit, you don't know us at all. Spread the Word. Duh! Christ's return, bearing a flaming sword? Ain't you a Christian?"

"What do you believe, Karl? Do you believe it was the Rapture?"

Karl looked at the DQ bag on the floor.

"Have you ever heard the name Radiant Dawn?"

He said nothing.

Heilige Licht is waiting to come into you…

"The place you described sounds just like an operation in California. They cured people of cancer, but they changed them. I believe you and your people were infected with some malignant agent, so that you could be 'cured', as well."

The bag fluttered in his foggy vision like a funeral bonfire on a gray tundra. He wished himself into the bag.

"Karl, this is only the beginning of the bad things that are going to happen to your people if I can't bring in federal forces to stop it, but you've got to tell me what I can expect to find when I go up there."

Karl could only look at him and drool. When the pained silence made it clear no more juice or sandwiches were forthcoming, Karl mumbled, "I can't remember anything else."

The bookworm rose up, became a black shadow again in the mint green mist. "Then that'll have to do, I suppose."

"You—" Karl tried very hard to look into the shadow's eyes. "You believe me?"

"I don't have much choice, I'm afraid. But your troubles are at an end, young man. I'll see to it that you're rushed to the nearest hospital, and placed in the very best of care. I'll contact you as soon as possible, when I know more. If your people have left the mountain, then the FBI will find them, before anyone else can get hurt."

Even though his face was a blurry wisp of pale smoke above the black shadow, Karl felt his muscles go slack at last as he felt the positive honesty in the FBI bookworm washing over him. All this time, maybe he had been taught wrong, after all. "You—you're not a Jew, are you?" Karl asked.

"I'm an American, young man. My religion is orderly democracy. My Bible is the Constitution of the United States. And I'm not ashamed to say, I hope I can make a convert out of you."

His hand swam up, big and bony and strong enough to squash Karl's trembly, clammy sticks to mush. The hand took his and pumped it heartily, almost pulling Karl off his cot. "We're going to put this right, Karl. You'll see."

Whatever the bookworm did in the front office worked, and things started to move fast after he left. Paramedics came in and gingerly transferred him to a stretcher, plugged a glucose IV and some more sedatives into him and strapped him down. He felt too weak to resist, but he didn't want to.

He felt unzipped down to his soul, as if all the misplaced hate that'd been holding him at attention for so long simply bled away. He loved everyone. He waved feebly to the deputies behind the counter, to the

Sheriff sitting in his office, to the two FBI agents who flanked him out the doors and across the parking lot to a big van.

He noticed it wasn't an ambulance, but a plain black van, and this made him feel important. He would travel in secret to the hospital, out of the eye of the media and the bad people who were making all the bad things happen on the mountain.

With all the fear and guilt and uncertainty pressing down on him, it felt so good to just let go and surrender, to let go of the old fears for a while and just feel safe. He was out of jail. His troubles were over. They would fix him. The FBI agent had leveled with him. There were bad feds, but there were good feds, too, and they were OK. They weren't at all the monsters Grossvater Egil said they were. Amazing how wrong about everything he could be. If he could be wrong about that, then he could be wrong about the Rapture, too, and the feds could fix them all.

Even one of the paramedics, who was black, smiled at him reassuringly as he lifted his end of Karl's gurney into the maw of the van. Dimly, he saw light reflecting off a myriad of shiny things inside. The walls were bright white and corrugated steel, with safety glass-faced cabinets full of life-saving equipment. A big lamp with multiple bright lights and cameras and microphones set into it hung from the ceiling. They parked him under it, so even when he closed his eyes, he saw pink and gold jellyfish forms chasing each other across his inner eyelids. Whispering voices clustered around him, but he couldn't hear them, because the van fired up, and they were moving. He could feel the engine vibrating somewhere underneath him, but he felt only the slightest swaying motion, like the cargo area of the van was on big springs.

"Mr. Schweinfurter, can you hear me?" the nice black paramedic asked. The man's voice sounded black, all deep and bassy, but gentle and comforting. He saw faces hovering over him, but they were blurry and shiny behind face-shields and surgical masks.

"I—" Karl started, but fell off the edge of the word and into a mushy preverbal swamp. He felt good. He felt grateful. He wanted to thank them for saving them, and to assure the black paramedic that he had nothing personal against niggers, whatsoever.

The engine stopped. Were they at the hospital already? Grangeville was an hour from White Bird on a good day, and the snow was coming down in dumptruck loads, outside. He could see no windows or sunlight, could see nothing beyond the great golden eye of the lamp.

"Better give him more gas," the black paramedic said. "Are you sure he's negative for irradiation?"

"He's circling the drain, Doctor," said another person, whom Karl recognized by his shiny bald head, like the bookworms, but it was one of the other ones, the guy and girl agents who looked like brother and sister, and whose parents probably were, too. The cool bookworm told him something important about those two, but he couldn't remember—

Big black hands in translucent rubber gloves poked and prodded his chest. "Jesus, what a mess. Does this hurt, Karl?"

Karl tried to shake his head, but he couldn't move it. He could feel some kind of padded clamp holding it in place, like on a really extreme roller coaster, or when they thought your neck might be broken. They were just being careful.

"I just want to be sure, Agent." They waved a wand over him, and one wall of the van lit up with a grainy image of his insides. They whistled.

"We'd better harvest now, before he arrests. We can't learn any more from cold tissue."

"But you can fix me, right?" Karl rasped. "I'll get better?"

"He's definitely malignant, but not irradiated," the agent whispered. "Poor redneck bastard."

"We're going to fix you right here, Karl." The nice black man said. "Jim, give me the seven, the Teflon serrated one. Yeah…you can help us, Karl. Do you want to help us?"

"Sure I want to help…but what about me?"

"We've learned just about all you can tell us, Karl," the agent said, "but we need to know more."

The paramedic held up something that blinded him right through his squinted lids. The white light imprinted his retinas with the image of a fanged circular saw blade.

"We need you to show us, Karl. Just relax, and show us what you got."

"Why?"

"You're pretty important, Karl. You're a member of a very special group."

"A…a master race?"

"Sure, a master race…battery power's not gonna get through the sternum. Plug it in—"

Even though it hurt, Karl was happy to be of service to his new friends. It was the duty of a member of the master race, to help his inferiors.

~ 23 ~

Sometimes, the experience of being Mort Greenaway was so thrilling, so fraught with challenge, that he would gladly turn it over to someone else. This was shaping up to be one of those days

Waking at 0500, he found the camp already up and flying off the handle at a situation. Ice fog pushed visibility down to arm's length. Its shifting tides smothered sounds or amplified them out of all regard for distance, so it sounded like the camp was tearing its own asshole out for no reason when Greenaway stumbled out of his trailer. Snowmobiles prowled the steep, ice-crusted forest below the plateau, men shouted and discharged rifles somewhere halfway down the mountain, and then a small fireball rose up out of the mist. He took a huge mug of black coffee from an Afrikaner mercenary whom he knew only as Ade and washed down a big black capsule of herbal speed. Ade didn't know what the fuck was going on, so he stomped over to the comm center, a big armored box on a flatbed trailer festooned with aerials and antennae, and shouted for Master Sergeant Talley.

"Burl, what the fuck is going on?" The glycerine capsule was stuck in his throat, slowly melting and trickling hot packets of herbal nervous amperage into his uneasy gut. An irresistible urge to hit something or someone—anyone, really—had taken over his left arm and began to creep into his heart.

Talley sat in a folding chair before a console much like an air traffic controller's, with a black circular display flecked with green dots and ghostly clouds. His nose only inches from the screen, he cycled through satellite overlays from various orbital eyes, oblivious to the boss's arrival until one of the comm technicians tapped him on the shoulder.

He stood and regarded Greenaway like the CO was only one more tit-clutcher he'd have to wet-nurse today. He looked as if he'd slept at the console, if he'd slept at all. He'd stripped down to his battle dress underclothes and rolled the sleeves up to reveal knurled forearms blue with blurred, indecipherable tattoos. Though the undershirt was black, deeper shadows of sweat-stains ran from his armpits and Adam's apple to his gut-strained belt. "Not much of a situation, after all, Mort," he growled. "We got it under control, you want to bunk out for a few more hours—"

"Why the hell would I want to do that? What are my men doing?"

Burl stifled a yawn. "We had some kind of an encounter on the north face. Third-party shooting, none of our men were involved."

"What do you mean, a third party shooting?"

"Near as we can tell, somebody was up here, and somebody else flushed them, then chased them down the mountain. We got Dogtown's team tracking them on snowmobiles, but with the snow and the fog, I don't expect them to find much."

One of the comm techs turned in his seat. "Dogtown team leader's on channel one," he told Talley.

"Speaker," Greenaway growled. "Dogtown, sitrep."

Ruggy DeSantis, the Dogtown leader, hawked, spat and shouted over the wind lashing his position. "Sir, we're on the north face, and we just shot down a fucking UFO, over."

The morning went downhill from there.

Snowmobiles dragged the downed aircraft back to base, where the unit mechanic and the comm techs—two ex-Army Signals operators, a Naval radar expert and a former Air Force MX missile jockey—gathered around the smoking ruins and scratched their heads.

There wasn't much to examine, since, as the Dogtown team leader explained, the men had unleashed all their collective anxiety on the first moving object that presented itself out of the fog. Under their enthusiastic fire, the saucer-shaped aircraft had crashed and exploded. They put it out with snow and chained the wreck, which was only ten feet in diameter, to their snowmobiles. The Dogtown team had found nothing else, all traces of the skirmishers obliterated by an avalanche caused by the noise.

They swiftly concluded that it was terrestrial in origin, but were stumped beyond that rather obvious assumption. It was actually doughnut shaped, a thin aluminum and fiberglass shell with enough of a rotor assembly left suspended over the hollow center to suggest that it was a drone helicopter, and stabilizers, cameras, microphones and other spy paraphernalia sticking out of the outer hull. The drone's insides were blackened slag, but Greenaway didn't need to read the owner's manual to know who built it. He stepped up perimeter security and sent Talley to his trailer to sack out with Ade at his door. By oh-eight-hundred, the fog had more or less lifted, but the snow fell harder than ever, and visibility got so bad he posted a sniper team in a hide overlooking the gorge, halfway down the mountain. They were ordered to shoot anyone–*anyone*–who tried to come up the road.

At oh-nine-thirty, the first challenge came, and Team Teabag failed to meet it. "Sir, there're trucks, Army trucks, and buses, coming up the road."

"You have your orders, Teabag."

"It's a company-sized convoy, sir. I don't have that many *bullets*."

Greenaway raged, massed his whole infantry complement to the south gate and waited. When Teabag called back in to report that they had a motor home and phony guns, Greenaway saw red. He had words with Army National Guard Major Ortman, who seemed to think that the Governor of Idaho had decided to send them to Greenaway's doorstep to play wargames in the snow. Even better, he seemed to think No Such Company was there to play, too. Disabusing him of these misconceptions proved fruitless, since Ortman's slavish respect for the secrecy of unconventional warfare only made him take Greenaway's abuse as part of the game.

Only because there really were too many of them to shoot, and because they really did seem to be ineffectual weekend warriors, did Greenaway agree to leave them the road. He had his people monitor their communications, which were limited to boombox wars, Clinton and fag jokes, and complaints about the cold.

He saw them clearly for what they were, too—another feint, another distraction from a threat he could feel coming, as if it were germinating in his tired old bones. He tuned them out, but pulled Teabag up inside the fence and had him sit in a pine tree overlooking the ANG's tailgate party.

Less than an hour later, a bloodcurdling racket from the direction of the Heilige Berg compound, with gunfire, screams and a subsonic rumbling, as of a cattle stampede, threw the camp back into high alert. Before he could scramble the Cobra to fly over it, Major Ortman called him to report that his men had reconned the compound and discovered that it was seemingly abandoned, and that some kind of a firefight might have occurred, but it could just as likely be an explosion of improperly stored ordnance, triggering an avalanche. Greenaway sent Dogtown over to review the site, but they could add very little light to the murky account. A storage cabin had been blown up, or maybe someone drove a tractor of some kind out through the front wall and, under small weapons fire from parties unknown, took off down the mountain.

Greenaway popped another black capsule, took his pulse, lost count. He was all over this fucking mountain! This was his battle! So why were skirmishes breaking out all around him, as combatants he hadn't even known were up here maneuvered around him? That one or more of the parties were Missionary spies, he had no doubt, but who was hunting *them*? His own men were still too busy setting up proactive defenses to cover the whole mountain, but someone else was up there with them, ghosting them, alerting their enemy who must be coming soon, it had to be soon, before it all—

Heilige Berg was deserted. His advance recon teams had watched the buses go down the mountain, had known they were gone, but now it seemed the most likely possibility that at least a unit of fighters had stayed behind. He hadn't had much faith in their acumen before, but who knew what a determined guerilla force defending its own territory could be capable of, if not Greenaway? This was, after all, their mountain...

It occurred to him several times throughout the day that he ought to see Keogh and order him to evacuate. He knew too little about what was going on to guarantee his own men's safety, let alone theirs. If they could be moved under cover of night or fog, the complex could still serve his purposes, and no civilian casualties would sour his revenge. He knew it would be stupid to move them now, that was exactly what the eggheads probably wanted him to do, with all their diversionary tactics. They were safer now in their bunkers, than they would be on the road in buses.

It was a moot point, though. Greenaway would not see Dr. Keogh. Fuck him. Just thinking about him made Greenaway age and grow tired, as if he was a kind of virus that sapped his strength. He wasn't afraid, per se, or he could have sent a messenger, but he didn't want to know any more than he did.

Up until now, he honestly didn't care what Radiant Dawn did, that the Mission had to destroy them. When the egghead FBI agent Cundieffe leaked to him the truth about the Mission, he had seen only them on the horizon. They, all along, were the real enemy he had been born to fight. He believed this with all of his scarred old heart, and he had raised a small army of men who believed it also, for most of their wounds from far-flung hellholes the world over, had really been inflicted by *them*, with their bad intel, their lies, their bullshit bag jobs to prop up dictators. Radiant Dawn was a means to an end, bait in a trap that would deliver them. Radiant Dawn was sick people who came here to die, or be experimented on, perhaps to find a cure for cancer.

Instinctively, he believed this less than he believed the drone was from another planet. But even when he peeled it apart very logically, patiently, in his head, he still could not get any deeper than the gut revulsion and fear Dr. Keogh dredged up in him. Ditto his patients, who still came out to stretch and play in the snow in groups of ten between the tower and the minefields. The soldiers were invisible to them, and they did not look sick. They scared him, because they made him feel not just old, but obsolete.

He cracked open a black capsule on the console before him and snorted the powder heaped on the laminated maps of Hell's Canyon. The comm geeks froze, then got real busy.

Along about lunchtime, the troops started acting up, and Greenaway had Ade wake up Burl to tame them. Greenaway wanted nothing so much as a man's neck to wring. In the back of his mind, he might even have prayed for it. The heavens parted, the angels sang, and lo, Special Agent Martin Cundieffe was delivered unto his grateful hands.

That felt good, but it left him shaking, heart palpitating. He forced himself to eat a bowel-blocking LRP-ration of freeze-dried beef stroganoff and orange powdered ERGO drink. Around him, troopers good-naturedly bitched about eating the LRP rations and MRE's while the civilians in the bunkers ate fresh food from their own kitchens. They didn't lower their voices in his presence, but Greenaway found he was just too tired, already, to address the growing breakdown in discipline. He wouldn't deign to explain to the troops why he wanted nothing from the RD colonists, because he couldn't explain it to himself.

He didn't need Talley's prompting to lurch back to his trailer for a brief afternoon nap. He awoke feeling weaker, heavier, than when he sacked out. In his dreams, all his men—Burl, Teabag, Ade, Ruggy, Ensign Wifebeater, everyone—spoke in Keogh's voice, spoke his words. He'd been afraid to open his own mouth, afraid of who would speak out of it.

He woke up thinking it was the morning all over again. Gray sunlight leaked in through the blinds, and men ran hither and yon shouting at each other. He checked his watch. He'd only intended to sleep for an hour, but it was already 1600. He popped another herbal capsule and washed it down with more coffee, went to see what was blowing up this time.

The troops stood out beyond the minefield at the edge of the plateau, watching a distant plume of black and gray smoke curl up into the looming snowstorm down in the valley, about five miles due east. The artillery crews and the comm techs both concluded it was a barn off the road into White Bird, and observed that a tremendous explosion had preceded the fire. Greenaway wanted to send the Bell 406 down to recon the site, but Talley persuaded him to stay consolidated. In time, fire engines and Sheriff's deputies closed on the site, which had more or less burned itself out by then, anyway. Distractions and unhappy coincidences were the order of the day, and each one seemed to push the boundaries of Greenaway's world into a smaller and smaller portion of the mountain he'd come to rule. He fought the urge to go back to sleep, deciding that it would only be the quickest way to make something else go wrong.

At dusk, something else went wrong. The mines started going off. By themselves. At the outer perimeter, a string of mines detonated just like they were supposed to, the vibration of the first setting off its neighbors in a spreading domino-wave, except that in the purpling sunset light, it was clear no one was there. Snow geysered up into the sky and rained down no body parts, no blasted metal from Missionary drones, nothing. The men were spooked. Unlike other tactical explosive charges placed around the camp, the mines were simple mechanical devices, and could only be triggered the old-fashioned way—by stepping on them. The snow piling up on the pressure-plates was blamed, but the demo experts who placed them swore they could only have gone off if a man-sized object triggered them. Fearing the mines were defective, Greenaway ordered his men to stay away from the minefield and stop talking about it.

One could go insane trying to collate all of the bullshit that was happening, or one could focus on the one growing certainty that each event tried to obscure. They were coming.

The snowfall continued unabated, softening the night's approach, banishing the world beyond the edge of the plateau. Greenaway devoured satellite images and air traffic reports, feeling his inborn strength and anger coming to the fore as the dark closed in. No more mines exploded, no more tourists crowded the mountain, and nothing else burned down or blew up, but he could taste them on the air.

After dinner, he girded his loins and went to see Dr. Keogh. Crossing the camp to the tower's front entrance, he watched the group of residents taking in the brisk, brittle night air on the steps, and wondered again what brought them here, what made them so carefree, when the most ruthless, shifty motherfuckers in the history of warfare were coming to exterminate them.

An old black man with what used to be called high yellow complexion waved and nodded to him as he approached.

"Folks, it's not safe out here, you'll have to go back inside and hunker down. We're expecting incoming shit any time, now."

They studied him with the placid indifference of sacred cows. A few of them looked at each other and stifled giggles.

"Get inside, goddamit! I want Dr. Keogh out here, most fucking *ricky-tick*. Do you fuckheads speak English?"

"We understand you, Mr. Greenaway," the high yellow one said in an amused, age-wizened voice. His eyes sparkled, silvery gray marksman's eyes, in the dying snow-light. Then they got up as one and made their way back inside. The high yellow slipped on the icy pavement and tore his knee open on the steps. The others helped him to his feet, laughing. He laughed, too, unmindful of the gaping hole in his black tracksuit, or the blood flowing freely from the lacerated skin.

They were high on something, no doubt, drugged to the eyeballs, and feeling no pain. Maybe that was all this was, a place where the dying came to slip away on a tide of illegal drugs. And maybe No Such Company was really just a security consultant.

He waited on the steps for five minutes, honing his dread into anger and steeling himself to go in after them, when Dr. Keogh finally came out. The tall, gaunt old man wore a white lab smock over his tracksuit uniform. Greenaway looked hard at him, but Burl Talley's voice crackled on his headset, which he'd pushed up away from his ears, because the static and routine comm checks drove him batshit. He only half-noticed that Dr. Keogh's breath did not form visible plumes of vapor as he stepped out of the heated tower and into the plunging cold.

Greenaway raised a hand to acknowledge and stall Keogh, pulled the headset into place. "Burl, what now?"

"Mort, I can't raise Teabag."

"How long since his last report?"

"Ten minutes ago, he punched in. I told him to punch in every five."

"He's probably taking a shit. Call me in another ten."

"You know Teabag. He'd *broadcast* if he was pinching one. Send Wifebeater to head-check him."

"Negative, Burl, Wifebeater's on eastern point watch. Send Dogtown."

"Can't. They're down below the ridge line, on patrol."

"Well shit, send somebody from the bridge, but take care of it. I've got to talk to somebody, here. Out." He took off the headset and fixed Dr. Keogh with his steeliest gaze. "Dr. Keogh, we're expecting the enemy to engage any time now. Your people have to get down below and stay there. No more outside privileges."

Dr. Keogh smiled unconcernedly, came down the steps to Greenaway. "I wouldn't worry. The outcome is already determined. My people have felt the approach of certain death before, and learned that in every moment, one must live. I can't make them unlearn that lesson. It may be that very soon, your men will need to take shelter with us, but in the end, it will matter very little."

Greenaway looked away from the doctor. He felt as if he were rolling inside a wave in Keogh's gaze, unable to find which way was up, where there was air to breathe. "Your fatalism means fuck-all to me, Doctor. We're here to protect your people, and we're going to win. We have superior firepower, superior sensory technology, and superior soldiers. We're going to wipe them out, and if you cooperate, your three hundred cancer-freaks won't lose so much as a night's sleep."

Dr. Keogh chuckled. "Ah, if only it were so. You make me laugh, Mr. Greenaway. Your technology—their technology...you're not here to protect us. You think of us as bait. You are the one who doesn't understand."

Burl's voice squawked on the headset in his breast pocket. "Burl, I can't raise Wifebeater."

Angrily, he put the headset back on. "What about—"

"Or Dogtown. Lines are functioning, but all I get is dead air."

"Get the goddamned bridge detail up there. Call Major Ortman. Find those motherfuckers."

"It's so hard to keep good men under duress," Keogh said.

"My men didn't desert. Something's fucking going on here, and I want to know what."

"It's very simple, Mr. Greenaway. This *is* a trap, but *we* are not the bait."

Behind Dr. Keogh, the doors opened and ten residents came out. They were a different bunch, but he noticed now that there were four children and six adults, half male and half female, just as before. They flanked Keogh on the steps and smiled at Greenaway, as if he were an expected guest at some unknowable celebration.

"There are not three hundred of us any more, Mr. Greenaway. There are only forty. You never toured the entire bunker network. You assumed, because you never really cared."

Greenaway looked around for something to tell him he was not still dreaming. He looked Keogh up and down, from his mantle of silver-white hair, unstirred by the whipping zephyrs blowing across the plateau, to his ice-crusted boots. His eyes traveled back up to Keogh's knee—to the torn black pants, the knee scabbed and bloody but already healing. Back up to his indulgent smile, his eyes, twinkling with the reflection of Greenaway's own, partial, but utterly damning realization of what was going on.

Their eyes flashed gray-silver, all of them. Marksman's eyes, fossilized eyes, eyes of living stone. His eyes.

Greenaway's hand unsnapped the flap on his holster, clasped the chill grip of his Walther 9mm, but he couldn't draw it.

"Do you know what sets your kind apart from all the other races that have risen to dominance on this world, Mr. Greenaway? You are the first to achieve sentience who were not predators, but prey. Lowly, gleaning, groveling hominids, you only acquired a taste for meat—for killing—from scavenging the kills of true predators. You became smarter because you were too weak to defend yourselves by main strength. You've forgotten that you only protected yourselves from extinction by sacrifice, by throwing one of your own to the wolves, that the rest might escape and survive. You did it so many millions of times that the screams of the scapegoat being eaten alive still echo in your nightmares. Yet here your kind still plays out those programmed instincts. To achieve victory, there must be sacrifice. One of the herd, one too old and infirm to serve any other purpose, must be thrown to the wolves to draw them out."

For once, Greenaway understood what Keogh was getting at. "I'm not bait," he growled, bitterly, weakly.

"Oh, but you are," one of them, Greenaway didn't see which, added in Keogh's voice. "Only with a gaudy show of military might around us could we draw the Mission in sufficient strength to weaken them, and reveal their primary base of operations."

Another added, "Take satisfaction in this, if nothing else. Your enemies will be exterminated, so your sacrifice will not be in vain. This is all you have lived for, is it not?"

The one he still thought of as the original Dr. Keogh reached out to touch him. "We hoped to make you one with us, but you would not share our food, and now there is no time left. They are indeed coming, and they are going to kill every living thing on this mountain, because that is what must happen. We are committed to this, Mr. Greenaway. Our individual deaths will bring a new race to life, and we will live to see its birth and ascendance through their eyes, for we are One."

Greenaway drew his pistol, leveled the sight on Keogh's unlined brow. "Get the fuck away from me. We'll stop them—and then we'll kill all of you."

They crowded closer, their faces and hair draining of color. Their faces became his face, their voices his voice. "Protect us, Mr. Greenaway."

He shot Dr. Keogh in the face. The 9mm parabellum bullet seemed to punch the doctor's whole head in at point-blank range, the bridge of the nose and both eyes blasting out the back of his skull. He kept coming. "You'll have to do better," another Keogh said.

Greenaway turned and ran, almost slipped and fell on his face. He ran all the way to the comm trailer, tore the door open and leaned against it.

Talley stood up and braced him. He looked drunk, but his breath was unfermented, though still shitty. "Mort, shit's flying apart. It's on."

Greenaway caught his breath, bit his lip as he tried to frame what he'd just seen into words that wouldn't just prove him unfit for duty. He had other things, sane things— "What about Teabag?"

"Wishniak's dead, Mort. I tried to raise you. The bridge detail found him, up in his tree, where he was supposed to be—with an arrow through his head."

"A what?" The hits just keep coming. Teabag—an ex-Marine sniper named Joshua Wishniak, who did tours with Greenaway's first Delta unit in Lebanon—hated to be called Teabag, but his friends always swore they'd get it carved on his tombstone.

"Someone did him with a fucking compound bow. Pinned his head to the goddamned pine tree. We have to assume the perimeter's breached. Bridge guys are beating the bushes, but have nothing yet. They still can't find Wifebeater, his post is deserted. Dogtown's missing, too. But fuck all that, look at this."

He dragged Greenaway to a radar console. The display showed two arrow-shaped clouds of flickering dots converging on the mountain from the east and west. They were so dense, Greenaway thought they were storm fronts. "More bad weather?" he asked numbly.

"Shit, it's the fucking attack!" Talley screamed. "Two full wings of fighter-bombers. They're running stealth, but the cellular array we put together picked them up. They wink on and off, making ghost-planes to fuck up their pattern, but there's at least *fifty* planes, Mort. Fifty."

Greenaway shrugged. "Shoot them down."

"They'll be in range in about four minutes, but we're going to get shithammered, best-case scenario. We've got to get into those bunkers—"

Talley kept babbling, but Greenaway couldn't hear him. The bunkers reminded him of something that happened to him, just now. He was so fucking tired. Like poor old Barbarossa, he felt as if he were going to freeze to death on the eve of the battle he'd waited for his entire life. He had something to tell Talley, something he ought to know…

"Mort, goddammit, are you listening to me?"

Greenaway rubbed his eyes. Enemy air attack in overwhelming numbers in minutes, get the men into the bunkers, right, south perimeter wide open and men missing, Teabag's head pinned to a tree by a fucking arrow—

Do something!

Greenaway chopped up air and said, "Call Ortman, find out if he has any real guns. Get him to hold the south perimeter."

"He doesn't have any real guns. And he's leaving."

"What?"

"Says the maneuver's been called off. They're driving down the mountain, now. Said one unit stayed behind—"

"One unit? How many?"

"How the hell should I know? They're not accounted for, which means they're probably the ones inside our perimeter, the ones who shot Wishniak. We're overrun, Mort, goddammit, now what do we do?"

Then it hit him. As if he'd only forgotten what just happened with Dr. Keogh, as if he hadn't noticed that he still had his gun out, the frosty grip welded to his sweaty palm. He shivered. "Burl, we've got to get the fuck off this mountain."

Talley looked at him and said something, but his words were drowned out by the deafening speech of antiaircraft guns.

~ 24 ~

It all happened so fast.

The first wave swept over the mountain in less than five seconds, and the second came before the flares had faded from their vision, before the ringing had even begun to block their ears.

But for Storch, who lay motionless in the snow at the edge of the gorge overlooking the bridge to Radiant Dawn, it unfolded like a series of pictures at a gallery, images of a place he had visited too many times, a place that came looking for him when he failed to find it. A place he would have to go into one more time, and do what he had failed to do so many times before.

Storch melted snow. In the hours he'd lain there, radiating waste heat as he changed back, he'd melted so much snow he'd made a stream that some lucky cartographer would get to name, someday, but he weighed the risk as less than that of moving. Banks of powder settled and tumbled over him, digging him a deeper grave until only his eyes peered out through a sage-scented stand of brush at the matrix of lights around the tower. He lay so still, riveted to the earth, that he could almost feel his nerves growing into the soil, becoming the forest. The trees becoming his new fingers, transmitting every disturbance, every intruder in his woods, his new body.

In the stillness behind his eyes, nothing moved, and so no time passed. He felt no fatigue and no boredom, only the quickening intensity of the Now, this endless instant which would not pass until something happened. This was the utter patience that all predators know, that the Special Forces had tried to teach him, but which no thinking animal could truly master. Now, his thoughts came in colors and images, not words, endlessly cycling around his quarry, somewhere down below.

An owl hooted, knifed down to the ground and taloned some kind of rodent out of the brush within inches of him. Soldiers in the trees watched the road, snowmobiles surfed the ridge overlooking the gorge, and once or twice he caught a scent on the wind so sour, so pregnant with memories of terror that he almost broke cover. Spike Team Texas. But they all seemed too preoccupied with other business to notice the rills of meltwater that trickled down the slope among the pine trunks before freezing again. The cold seeped into Storch and fused his joints, but it gave him cover. Sucking out his heat, it rendered him invisible to infra-red sight and kept his breath from fogging.

He marveled at his hands. They had only changed back to his native pigmentation in stripes and marbled blotches, forming natural camouflage far more effective than the crappy alpine pattern on his stolen National Guard fatigues. His face and neck were marbled the same way, milk white and coffee brown patterns that made him invisible in the snow-tufted woods, even to himself.

Stoned and cramped as he was from the long bus ride, the black Guardsman had put up a hell of a fight when Storch took him. When he saw the National Guard convoy on the highway, he had immediately known where they were headed, and snuck into the restroom to lie in wait. He passed up several that were too slight of build, lurking in a stall directly across from the front door. Not knowing, not wanting to know what the fuck was going to happen next, but trusting to his body's superior survival skills, he struck the big black private as he leaned over the sink. Swept his legs out from under him and slammed his head into the sink so hard porcelain chips and formica and blood sprayed the tile floor. The private should have gone out, but he fought, kneed Storch in the groin, which would have hurt if his testicles hadn't retracted into his pelvis at the prospect of a fight. Storch had to hit him again and again, harder, too hard. He watched with sick wonder as his fists resculpted the black private's face into a puddle, sent him reeling into the stall to crack the toilet basin in half and collapse beside it. His feet still pumped at the spreading pool of sewage as if he attacked a tackling dummy in his sleep. Storch checked the front door, then shut himself up with the body.

Become him, his body said, in spasms. *Eat him.*

It was hard not to. The private's vitality sizzled in the air like steak on a grill, his to devour. Sweat stank of drugs and worse, but the energy in those limbs, the secrets in the blood, would make him stronger. He bit back vomit as images surged forth in crimson Technicolor, waking dreams of doing it, loving it. It was not a moral repulsion that held him back. He was beyond good and evil, or beneath them—a force of nature, a beast in the jungle. Even as the blood-tide of hunger drew him closer to the unconscious private's beating heart, drew the claws out of his fists, he fought it, because it was not what he would do. *I am not Spike Team Texas,* he told his fists. *I am Zane Ezekiel Storch, and I don't eat people.*

In the end, a little blood had been enough to affect the change. It danced and tingled going down, a chemical song of ancestry and survival that reverberated changes through him until it came to the fundamental theme that bound them together. A common ancestor, lost on the savannah and torn with longing to return to the trees, uneasily learning to mimic its hunters. Then deeper, further back down the thread of a million, billion little lives, to that unspeakable vision—

Something vast and terrible and wise, watching him

—that haunted Storch throughout his long sleep at Ft. Avon. He closed his inner eye to it and rode it out. And when he looked at his hands, they were chocolate-brown and gnarly with muscle, broad palms and long, knobby fingers. His scalp burned where kinky black hair grew, and his face ached as fluid and cartilage flattened his nose, thickened his brow and lips and planed his cheekbones.

He dressed in the private's soaking wet uniform, the heat from the change steaming the urine-stinking water out of it before he had the boots laced. The name on the chest was HEELEY, D. Strange heat-haze vapors filmed his vision—faces, names, places, football games. The man's memories, chemical residue of a lifetime in a drop of blood, trying to get into his head. He pushed those back, too, and tried to get back to business in his new skin.

Miraculously, no one had come in during the entire transaction, and Storch feared the bus had left without him. He walked out into the blue-black pre-dawn gloom of the rest stop, suddenly feeling naked as the eyes of Guardsmen picked at him. Not knowing how the man walked or talked, or which of the other weekend warriors he knew and should acknowledge, he crossed to the row of olive drab school buses and milled around until a skinny white private yelled out a window to get on the fucking bus, already.

He got on and fell immediately into dreamless, grateful sleep. But even while he slept, he scented the others on the bus, fixed on the man across the aisle, whose aromatic signature was already very familiar to him. The Missionary officer who put a gun full of green death to Storch's head, but couldn't pull the trigger. And not because Storch held Wittrock by his pencil-neck—he could smell the officer's eagerness to see the wizened old egghead stop breathing—but because he was tired and scared and more than half-insane. Even more haunted than Major Bangs had been, tired of killing and losing men, tired of fighting things that would not die.

He snapped back into the present, heard a muted twang and an even fainter sound like the wind unzipping, then snapping shut behind a swiftly moving, aerodynamically perfect object. Not a bullet. An arrow. A wet chunky sound, and a few blobs of snow shook out of a sentinel white pine on a knoll overlooking the road about a hundred yards from his position. He couldn't place the shooter, but he knew the arrow came from the ridge, from Radiant Dawn. An errant breeze stirred the powder mounded before his face, and he smelled Tucker Avery, the blindingly fast one with mercury for blood and nitrous oxide injectors in his heart.

He smells like you.

Storch stayed put. Melted snow. Hugged the ground. Became the forest. Avery's spoor faded, and almost on cue, he heard soldiers moving up the hill, a travesty of stealth in spacesuits. Two three-man fire teams, leapfrogging from point to cover positions in classic insertion pattern. A moment later, he smelled their breath, filtered through the activated charcoal and robot-vomit polyvinyl and whatever else sealed them off from the outside world, smelled their sweat and strain and mortal terror as they lumbered up from cover to cover. They passed within fifty feet of his position and topped the ridge without tripping any alarms. Of course not, because Spike Team Texas snuffed the sentry in the tree. Meaning two things. The sentry was human. And Spike Team Texas—which meant Keogh, unless things had changed radically while he was sleeping— wanted the Missionaries inside. Meaning the whole thing was a trap. Which changed nothing for him. For Storch, nothing changed. He had to go into the hole again. It was always the same hole. He had to go into the hole again, because she was in there. It was always the same girl. He was always too late.

He was faster, this time. She was still alive, and suffering only he knew what kind of tortures. Perhaps he was much too late, like when he hit the wrong abandoned mine and saved the wrong girl, her name was Gina, but she'd become one of them, a predator, and he'd left her to die. Or she was like Sidra Sperling, used up and turned inside out by Keogh already, discarded in a ditch. Or he'd be only a second too late, like he'd been with Stella Orozco the last time. A second or a day or months, he was always too late, and the earth always opened up and swallowed up the girl. He owed the world for too many dead girls he couldn't save, so back in the hole he went, until he got it right. But this girl—

She was more. When he closed his eyes, he felt as if she hovered over him as she did in the Missionary bunker, watching him pretend to sleep, and she seemed to understand what a chance he was taking. He felt as if she recognized that he was vulnerable, and as she watched over him, she transmitted so much more than either of them could ever say in words. Her scent ran in his veins. It called to him. She was still here, and wanted out. Storch, who could not simply be human, anymore, had to do what he did to discover what he was. She had known what he was, and watched over him, anyway. Maybe now, she, alone among all the people in the world, could tell him what he was, now.

He lay still. Melting snow. The Missionaries laid up behind the trees silhouetted against the top of the ridge. Their breath plumed in the air above their helmeted heads, little fog-flags announcing their presence to anyone watching, but there was no one. Because they were expected, and the door was open.

And then it happened. The big 40mm guns on the mountaintop saw them first, and opened fire. It was as if the whole mountain were an active volcano blasting off its cap and spewing white-hot molten lead into the night. The guns fired west, strobing the sky white-gold and limning the craggy contours of the storm clouds above and the peak below, pinning the running soldiers milling around the tower on their own shadows.

The artillery screamed a steel-throated aria of autofire in solid, unbroken sweeps, as if they were writing their name on eastern Washington, as if the Japs were coming back for Pearl Harbor and got lost in time and space, and were coming here. Snow shook out of the trees, avalanches cascaded down from the peak. Rocks danced. The ground shimmied and shook, victory at sea. Only Storch didn't move. He melted snow.

Then they came.

Over the shriek of the cannons, the sound was like all the bees on earth in a single, livid swarm. It sounded like a million Enola Gays. The white light in the sky went red as the flaming debris from the first planes streaked across the low-hanging clouds and winked out like meteors. Nothing touched the ground.

The first planes swooped over the peak like a cloud of rabid bats, hugging the rock and passing through the artillery's arc of fire at just under the sound barrier. Stupendous crisscrossing flame trails lit their path, but too many of them to count passed over the guns and dropped on the tower. Even as they ate up the final yards to target, they dove and bucked and entangled with each other like a flying circus gone mad, but they weren't planes, not with men in them. They looked like winged seeds, with tapered delta wings, no more than sixty feet wide from tip to tip, swept back from a bulbous fuselage the nose of which was the yawning maw of a jet turbine. The sides were studded with armaments and integral explosives. There was no room for a pilot and no need, because the planes did what no sane pilot, not even a fanatical Missionary agent, would do.

Two of the drone bombers snapped into view at an almost vertical angle, as if they'd hugged the Snake River valley on the other side of the mountain and come in under the guns. They rose up in an elegant mating dance, cavorting mechanized moths. One gun from the peak battery followed them up and painted their trail with 40mm shells, but it exposed the peak's northern flank, and a third plane pounced on the battery almost faster than Storch's eyes could take it in. The artillery nest went straight up through the clouds, all three cannons and the whole mountaintop blooming blinding plasma like a newborn star.

A few hundred feet below the ashes of the peak defenses, the eastward artillery batteries opened fire and diced up the planes as they circled the tower, more 40mm cannons and a brace of Vulcans, so much wreckage flying so fast the tower had a halo. The trailer park around the tower lit up the sortie with Stingers, a TOW missile battery and even rifle fire. The defense looked too disciplined to be Keogh's. Government protection. Obvious, because they had brought everything they'd need to win the previous battle.

Secondary explosions from burning ordnance on the peak were just starting to rock the mountain when the Missionary fire teams broke cover and stormed the bridge. The defenders' squad-sized deployment took cover behind a panel truck and blasted up the road with M16A2's and a tripod-mounted grenade launcher. The Missionaries had rotary-barrel Vulcan machine guns on sling harnesses and modified Pancor Jackhammers, belt-fed automatic shotguns, like line-of-sight chainsaws, and they cut right through the truck and wiped out the squad in seconds. He saw one of the Missionaries take a direct center-of-mass hit and go to one knee as if he had a cramp. Another one helped him to his feet and they took off at a dead run across the bridge and around the burning truck, vanished into the stand of pines that bordered the near edge of the plateau.

The bridge and a naked white sheet of open snow one hundred yards across lay between Storch and the tower, and the trailer park was alive with highly motivated soldiers shooting at everything but each other. Follow the trees to flank the complex. That's what he would do.

Storch moved.

He slithered out of his bed and out through the bushes, down the tumble of rocks that sloped ever more sharply to the gorge. His uniform was sodden, snow-caked, but he didn't shiver, and still his limbs were supple and responsive, pouring heat from some untouchable reservoir that the creeping chill never reached in all those buried hours. Glacier-slow he crept down, feeling a bull's-eye of cold fire blossoming on his back. The soldiers had rushed the bridge like Normandy and no one at the trailer park took notice, but the Missionaries were expected, invited, and he couldn't expect the invitation to extend to him.

Wind-sharpened granite gouged his hands and flayed his belly as he picked up speed. His crawl became a fall, hands snatching at the rock to put some shade of spin on his descent. The bridge grew larger, veered to the right as he slipped and dropped twenty feet, the wind screaming in his ears, hit flat on his back on the narrow concrete buttress thrusting out of the gorge wall. He scuttled under it and touched the cobwebbed understructure. Another owl hooted, spooked from its nest under the bridge, and flapped away.

The steel and concrete struts arched out of the gorge walls and held up the span like the canopy of a petrified rainforest. The girders were festooned with vines of det cord and blocks of Semtex. Flexing his fists, the Gor-Tex gloves he found in D. Heeley's coat pockets tore out at the knuckles. His hands were roughened up by the rocks, tougher than Gor-Tex, tougher than Kevlar. He seized a support strut and swung out over the gorge, black and pregnant with crystalline mist except for guttering fires from burning wreckage. His hands burned as the cold metal bonded with skin, bit into the meat of his palms. He swung from strut to strut, not looking down at the bottom or up at the explosives, a snarled, sloppy spider's web with lumps of plastique trapped in it. He almost ripped out the det cords. Pausing in mid-span, swinging in the wind, the bridge jouncing and warping with the stuttering seismic havoc of the explosions. Maybe it would be better if no one got out. He left them.

On the other side, war. Black and red and white, roiling chaos and noise eating up the world, and it made Storch laugh, because it was a scene right out of the crazy dreams. His proto-human ancestors burning out the last of the ophidian Others who thought the world would always be theirs. The sticks and stones now hurtle with laser-guided, supersonic accuracy, and they fight each other while their soft-fleshed masters cower in bunkers, but it's the same war, the only war, for which all the others have been pale dress rehearsals. And he was walking into it.

He hauled himself up onto the abutment on the far side of the bridge and froze. Headlights washed over the bridge and speared him as he tried to lie flat and be one of the dead. A heavy armored half-track rolled out of the trailer park and banked so hard it lifted up on its left-side wheels and treads, heading in his direction. Too late, coming to secure the perimeter. A curtain of fire rained down on the snowfield between them, drone planes pinned on the artillery fire turned to incandescent gas and punishing explosive force, hit the snow and raised geysers of white. Mines responded, a chain-reaction, sending rubble bouncing into forever.

Army ants of sweat bit into his skin. *Move! Charge them, they can't hurt you, they're only human—*

He stayed put, stayed dead. The lights roved on to his right. The half-track veered onto a path around the edge of the plateau. He saw a soldier in full body armor standing tall in the bubble turret behind the cab, running a pair of Mk.19 40mm grenade launchers. The half-track slowed to a crawl at the out-thrust end of the plateau, and the grenadier swiveled the weapons out and down the slope, began popping one hundred and twenty high-explosive grenades a minute into the thick stand of trees blanketing the slope. Almost immediately, they began to detonate, and trees went down like narcoleptic giants, trunks reduced to sawdust and shrapnel. The sound, the sustained tocsin of timed bombs, was almost loud enough to be heard over the aerial attack. Whatever was down there, the half-track kept firing into it as the empty snowfield of the plateau erupted behind and on their left. Storch thought mines again, so much shit still fell out of the sky, but black shapes boiled up out of the snow and swarmed over the half-track. Out of tunnels or foxholes that put them inside the minefield, they came so fast Storch could see only that they wore camo and were colder than the snow they'd been hiding in, but he knew in an instant who they were. They were Keogh.

The grenadier turned and fired into the minefield, probably clued in by the screams of the driver. They tore the door off the cab and pulled him out, engulfed him. They climbed into the cab, and the half-track started to roll again, but the grenadier was still firing at the holes they came out of, and the grenades must have rolled down the tunnel and, at the end of their one-second fuses, exploded beneath the half-track. Snow and earth and bits of black human shapes lofted the huge armored truck up on its nose, and it might have tipped over on its roof, but the snowbank gave way, and the half-track slid off the plateau and out of sight.

Storch got up and ran, stooped and feeling naked in the rushing, hot fire-wind. All the trees on the plateau burned merrily, so the grove he ran through was like a cathedral in Hell. He passed bodies here and there, mostly soldiers in black body armor, but he saw one broken Missionary in his spacesuit, wrapped around a tree branch ten feet above Storch's head, looking as if he'd been thrown from a crashing 747. He kept running, wishing he had a gun, though it would make no difference.

He heard them long before he caught up with them. Shooting, screams, and above it all, a voice he still heard in his nightmares.

"Shit, izzat the best you little girls can do?"

He noticed then that the explosive symphony overhead had died down. Though his night-sight was ruined by the fires, he could see only darkness and smoke over the trailer park. The tower still stood, but there was no cheering on the foul, scorched wind. The eastward guns re-oriented themselves, and commenced firing into the empty sky to the east, and more Stingers lanced out and locked onto something only radar could see. Even Storch couldn't believe it. Another sortie incoming. Time was running out, if it wasn't too late, already.

Empty hands flexing and growing, he turned and ran towards the firefight.

A ruined cinder-block bunker jutted out of the foot of the cliff-face, the walls blasted out and scattered by a crashing drone. Three circular holes bored into the granite cliff, with huge fans in them, though none turned now, and one of them was choked with debris. Intake vents for the tunnels under the complex. If the Missionaries could get into them, they could gas the whole population without ever setting foot within, but they were never going to make it, because in their way stood Brutus Dyson.

"Don't any of you faggots know how to fight?" Dyson roared. He stood ten feet tall, and nearly half as wide, a shaggy white Grendel with battering rams for arms. His back had sprouted a heavy bone carapace off which bullets and grenades ricocheted, but he turned and faced them with arms outstretched, a ludicrous invitation to come out and grapple. A pile of mangled, bullet-riddled bodies, all of them in black body armor, lay strewn around his feet, like so many spent condoms. "Come out and fight like a man!" he bellowed, and his laughter shook embers from the burning trees.

The five surviving Missionaries flanked him, pouring fire on him from fifty feet away, but the converging streams scattered off Dyson's hide. His head was mantled in a thick sheath of overgrown shoulder muscle, and twitched under the few lucky shots that chipped away at it.

One of the Missionaries charged out of formation, ducked under the unbroken river of cover fire and ran to the edge of the cinder-block foundation. Taking cover behind a waist-high section of wall, he popped up in the giant's shadow and strafed Dyson with his Jackhammer. The shells stitched up Dyson's torso, from his solar plexus to the left shoulder, blowing right through the monster's hide, then swerved back and punched a line across his forehead. Dyson reeled back several steps and stumbled against a pile of rubble. Incredibly, impossibly, hurt. The wounds burst red-black blood and green foam, and Dyson *screamed*. Despite himself,

Storch shivered in empathy as the Nasty Green Shit went to work on Dyson.

"YEAH! DIE, MOTHERFUCKER!" The bold Missionary stood up out of cover, and he could have run right then and gotten away, or even reached the intake vents, but he stood rooted to the spot, fascinated beyond instinct by what he had wrought with his little gun. Oblivious even to his commander shouting at him to get back, he was still just standing there when Dyson rose up again.

Dyson's chest burst asunder, the massive left arm tore free and flopped to the snow along with gouts of bubbling, poisoned tissue. His head, likewise, tore itself apart, skull opening like a flower, jointed lobster limbs and tentacles flinging away the molten green toxin eating away at his brain. Dyson wobbled, off-balance, and from somewhere in the ruin of his head, gurgled, "OK, be like that. So much for all this 'bring 'em back alive' shit."

The Missionary shouldered his gun and fired too late, too wide, to hit him again. Out of the gutted torso shot a phalanx of barbed whips, wrapped around the Missionary and yanked him off his feet, ripped away his weapon, drew him in close.

The four Missionaries split and rushed around to try to outflank Dyson again. One of them ran right past Storch, stepped on his hand.

Dyson's facial tentacles wrapped around the Missionary's helmet and unscrewed it like the cap on a bottle of beer, but then stopped. They played over the captive's face as gently as a blind child's fingers. The soldier's arms and legs flailed, frantic but useless, bringing only more ragged screams as Dyson's barbs worked deeper into his body.

Storch didn't want to look at his face, but he recognized him as the Armenian Missionary with the skull tattoos up and down his arms. His eyes squinted shut and his head snapped back and forth like he was trying to break his own neck.

"I know you!" Dyson growled, jovial, like they were at a VFW mixer. "Little Augie Tokash, Jr.! I did a SOG hitch in the 'Nam with your daddy, son! I even met you once, but you were a little mite, then. I don't bet you remember me too well, do you?"

Tokash kept wriggling and screaming, but when Dyson shook him gently, he went limp. Either in shock or entranced by something he saw in that mess of feelers and claws, Tokash stared down at the monster that remembered his dad and shook his head. "No, sir, I—"

"You favor him quite a bit. He was one righteous, by-the-book CO, I'll tell you what. Wasn't he, son?"

"He was—he never—I didn't know him too good."

"Well, I did. He wouldn't abide no cowboys in his teams, and by God, if he wasn't going to put yours truly up on charges for doing my job in-country. So I hamstrung his righteous by-the-book ass with his own K-Bar knife and left him for Charlie. Then I rotated stateside and visited your house. Brought you a box of Army men and gave your Mamma the clap so goddamn bad she hanged herself rather than go to the doctor, the stupid hog-bitch. DO YOU REMEMBER ME NOW?"

Tokash screamed his soul out. Dyson lifted him high and bent him backwards until he snapped, and his head and heels touched. He turned Tokash inside out and gulped him down even as the other four Missionaries closed in and pummeled him with fire.

Storch backed away. There had to be another way in. He tried to narrow his senses down to the ground before him. Screen out the overwhelming stink of carbonized forest and cordite and coppery blood. So faint it would never have registered if he did not know it so well, a trail days old glowed before him. He smelled Keogh intermingled in the sweat of hundreds of others that had passed this way. Curled up in them like a virus, driving their wills, their immune systems, their emotions. Driving them out of this place, days ago.

He shivered. The Mission was attacking an empty nest. For all their technology, all their wiles, they were as stupid as he, because they were all gone. He knelt in the snow.

Always too late. Always—

In his mind's eye, he lay on that table in the sick bay of the Mission bunker. His last moment of true calm, true peace. She watched over him, her scent overpowering even through the mask she'd put over his face, imprinting on his nerves something even more powerful than the sickness, more undeniable than the Headache. It showed him now that he was not just repeating the cycle he'd been cast into by the body of Sidra Sperling and the fucked-up girl in the snuff mine. He was answering a call older than his species—older, perhaps, even than Keogh—and it was in this, he knew, that he would find himself.

And it wasn't here.

The trail was imprinted with hundreds of bodies, hundreds of Keogh-ridden souls, but she was not among them. But she *was*. It strained his patience to pick at the morass of scent-signatures in his brain with the staccato screams of guns and cannons all around him, but it was what he'd come for, so everything else went away. She was with them, but not *with* them. In them. Storch understood. Keogh sacrificed generously, but wasted nothing. He had to leave decoys, but those who fled took with them the genes of those left behind.

She was still here. But time was almost out, it was almost too late again. He could hear Dyson screaming, and he could hear the approaching roar of more drones, and the cannons and the Stingers redoubled but hit less than ever.

A helicopter, a real live Cobra gunship, swooped over the plateau and flung strings of 70mm rockets and streams of rotary-barrel machine gun fire at the incoming, but the point drone dodged the Cobra's fire and slammed into its cockpit. The Cobra hung in place for a moment, seeming to skate along on the backs of the drone swarm, then it whirled and darted eight directions at once and dropped out of the sky directly above the tower. It went in through the central skylight like a knife into a cake, explosions blasting out vinyl windows on each floor down to the lobby. Clouds of malachite green mist frothed out of the building, spreading and gathering on the front steps. Storch saw a man dive out a window with green witch-fire feasting on his back. Screaming a scream in Keogh's voice, the body smacked the ground and vanished under the green fog.

It might have been her. Dyson or no, the tunnels would be flooded with mist in minutes. He struggled to narrow the world down to the ground before him, and followed the trail.

There was dark.

There were dreams so real she thought she'd died and been reborn. *Fool me twice*, she thought bitterly, *shame on me*, because she knew she was back in the pit.

Impaled and crushed, forgotten in an unmarked grave in the desert, she raged at dreams, and at herself for believing in them. Look where they got you. Every time she lost consciousness, she escaped and found a new life, and every time she awakened, she was still here. Still alive, still praying for death.

She must be dreaming, for this time, she didn't even have the dignity of dying alone. Others, so many others, were in here with her, this time. All the others who came here seeking a better life, in her dreams. She heard them stirring in their own cruel tombs, lost in their own nightmares.

She wrenched her body against the rebar spears and tried to drag herself free of the crushing concrete slabs, tried to hurt herself so bad she'd wake up for real.

Wait, said God. *I would ask this one last thing of you.*

"I want to die," Stella screamed, without air. She choked on dust, and felt her breath bubbling out of her collapsed lung. "I can't—die…"

The others whimpered the same sentiments, and she hated them for it. They made her want to curse them and keep on fighting, but what was the use? She always ended up here.

You are doomed, God said, *but the ones who have condemned you are within your reach. This is where we make our defense. Our kind will survive this petty atrocity, and you will live on in them. But the enemy must be destroyed.*

Stella seethed. They were here, the ones who promised to cure her, but tried to kill her, and did so much worse. The ones who put her *here.*

Her hands became claws, and suddenly her smashed left arm no longer flopped against her back, and the rebar no longer speared her chest. The concrete slabs crumbled and became vapor. Her despair coalesced into a pure black fury that grew over her charred remains like an exoskeleton, and sprouted from her fingers, her knees and elbows, her spine and her pelvis as jagged obsidian spurs and knurled talons.

They were *here.*

One of the others flew at the hatch in front of them and threw the bolts, shouldered it open. The others rushed the door and streamed out into the corridor. She was confused for a moment; the bunker was intact and looked like part of her dreams, of the other place where she'd thought she was finally safe. If this was another dream—

But then she smelled *him.*

The essence of him was unlike almost any other person she'd ever had to smell. He didn't stink of his vices or dietary weaknesses, or the crude masks of cologne or soap. He reeked of stress and terror and the road, but it was not this that had attracted her, but what lay within him. It spoke to a part of Stella that lived underneath her human exterior, to a primal machine in her that had been tamed and beaten back into the shadows of her subconscious in her species' infancy. Her little God lived there now, but she connected that moment to this and knew with marrow-deep certainty that Storch was here, but he was very different, and yet the same.

He was here to save her. Again.

He was seconds too late last time, and he let her go down into a hell of undeath in which, for all she knew, she still rotted, and this only another fantasy.

He is here, God said, *It is no dream. He has something we need. Secrets in his flesh that may save our race.*

He let her go down, and he left her there. But for him, she might have stayed put and not been buried alive at all.

She followed the others around a bend in the corridor. The new one was lit by glowing silver-blue walls, and by their dim phosphorescence, she saw that she was in a hall of mirrors, or another dream, because all the others were her. They tossed their wild black hair and smiled her smile at her, and brandished their vicious talons.

He failed you, God said. *He turned his back on all of us. Now he has come to kill you for what you have become. Make him serve us.*

She shoved the other Stellas aside and rushed at the scent of her betrayer. If this was a dream, there were worse ways to pass the time.

The trail led to the exhaust fan tunnels, about a quarter mile around the peak. Storch followed it through piles of smoking rubble and over the severed cables of comm lines running up to the peak. He tuned it all out—the guns going off over his head, the drones smashing into the smoking ruin of the tower again and again with a blacksmith's rhythm, the screams of the mercenaries ripping up their camp with rifles as if the enemy were among them. The acrid, submarine scent of Keogh led him across the battlefield to their back door.

It was another shattered blockhouse, and though quieter than the intake bunker, it was no less clotted with death. A squad of eight Missionaries lay scattered across the debris-strewn snow, the soft chinks in their armor pin-cushioned with arrows. It looked as if they'd been ambushed by the whole fucking Sioux nation as they set up explosive charges in the gaping mouths of the exhaust vents. When he looked closer at the arrows, he saw they were all whittled from the whitebark pines that stood around them, and though all the arrowheads were too deeply buried in flesh to be examined, he knew they'd be chiseled from the granite that formed the mountain. All their helmets had been ripped off, and trophies had been taken. One killer had done this.

Storch climbed into one of the vents, leaning against the buffeting cushion of chill air rushing up out of the depths like Keogh's breath. His ears rang, but there was nothing else alive out there. The guns had fallen silent. An ominous chorus of drones rose on the wind and circled the naked mountain.

Storch threw himself over the piled charges and fell down the shaft, hit something hard in the dark, stopped.

Hands out in front of him, he grasped an aluminum screen and wrenched it out of its frame, tumbled out into a lesser, silvery-gray darkness. As his eyes adjusted, the outlines of the cavernous space glowed with bioluminescent moss on the walls and ceiling. It glowed the color of His eyes.

Branching corridors like the tunnels of a rabbit-warren burrowed off in all directions. The whole place was steeped in Keogh's scent, His sweat and blood etched into every inch of hand-carved tunnel, His breath and excrement tinged the air as if Storch were a microbe lost in His bowels. He heard no sounds of battle from above, but he felt the mountain jouncing and shaking through the soles of his feet, and motes of firefly moss drifted on the fan-recycled air.

Time was short. This was an empty tomb, or almost empty. Keogh would let the Missionaries take the bait and fill the bunker with gas. Perhaps if his sacrificial victims died from the gas, he hoped to learn how to adapt to it and survive, and pass the adaptation in some form to His others, who had flown. Storch had learned to adapt to it because Spike Team Texas ran in his blood, and only the Keogh in him had died. The gas was made to kill Keogh at a molecular level, but he had no illusions about the fucker's adaptability.

Maybe this trap is not for them, but for you, he thought. *Maybe you better move faster.*

There was no trail to follow through the caves, so he wandered, through tunnels and galleries and workshops and nests of plastic honeycomb cells. His brain burned with the chemical ghosts of strangers, all sublimated, all enslaved to the antediluvian stink of Him. Hundreds had passed through here, perhaps thousands, but they were gone.

His sense of direction faltered, and he might have passed through the same caves several times before he stopped himself. How much time had passed? Pvt. Heeley's cheap Casio watch told him he'd only been down there for about five minutes, but he was starting to feel like he lived here. The miasma of scent-trails forced their meaning on him, so that he felt as if he were walking a track, a soldier ant patrolling a circuit through the labyrinth without really searching. When he fought it, he only grew more disoriented, so he let go. OK, I live here, I'm a part of the hive, and the hive is threatened. Where do I go to hide?

The scent leaped out at him then, the residue of terror and Keogh's calming pheromone wash marked a corridor that sloped steeply down into the granite guts of the mountain. He followed it greedily, for in it he detected a trace of the one he'd come looking for.

The corridor went down and down, met another junction that led to unused dwelling galleries, and deeper tunnels, where the moss grew only in stingy patches, or not at all. His vision bored down into infra-red, and he lit the way before him by his own roiling body heat. Ten minutes he'd been down here. The Nasty Green Shit would come, if it hadn't already. He wondered if he would survive it, this time. It had damaged Dyson pretty badly, and he hadn't been carrying a hostile woman out over his shoulder.

He hadn't let himself think too much about that part. Keogh had made his body do things, see things, forget things. She was deeper into Him than Storch had ever been, and might not want to come out. He might have to leave her here—

"You like it here, don't you?"

"It grows on you—No, like, don't get me wrong, it's, like—but—you get used to it."

"Then stay here."

He owed the universe for one dead girl. He owed her—

And there she was. She came racing around a hairpin bend in the tunnel and stopped just twenty feet away from him. Her eyes, black holes in her mask of heat, flashed recognition. "Sergeant Storch!" she cried, and came running.

In the dark, he saw her features come clearer with every step she took, but she came so fast he didn't notice how her gait was all wrong, and she was too big, and her scent was off, and her outstretched hands were a wall of claws. But his body saw it all and he stepped back and pivoted. She leapt into the air and became a missile, a wordless cry shivering the air between them as he crouched and braced himself.

She came within a hair's breadth of tearing out his throat. Her claws slashed down his scalp and glanced off his brow. Her body tore up the empty space where he'd been only a split-second before. His arm shot out and caught her by the neck, whipped her sideways and hurled her at the wall head-first. Her legs whipped up and hit the wall on the balls of her feet, sprang right back at him, and he had no time to step aside this time, because out of the corner of his eye, he saw her come around the bend, saw more of her, dozens of her, crying his name and coming so fast—

She landed on his shoulders and sank her claws into the cords of his neck. "Our mercy is infinite, Zane," she hissed in his left ear. "You left us to die in a hole. You turned your back on us and became an abomination, but we forgive you. You can save us—" Her teeth, so sharp, sank into his ear and ripped it off.

The others surrounded him. Looking like her, smelling like her, they cried his name in her voice and in his own even as they ate him alive. Their claws gouged him, tore him away bit by bit and consumed him. "You have secrets to share, Zane. Save us—"

Screaming, but they reached in and tore out his tongue. Fighting, but they flayed off his uniform and his skin and severed the tendons that held up his right arm. Kicking, but they hamstrung him, and he went down under their weight. They swarmed over him like ants dismantling a beetle carcass, and his strength bled out as his body tried to change to beat them back, and failed.

One of them, a child with her face, sank its fangs into the meat of his left forearm, and he lashed out, flexing his muscles and screaming as they trapped the barbed fangs like a mosquito. He flailed his arm and the child-sized doppelganger thrashed in the air, ripping chunks out of its brood-mates. They scattered and he staggered to his feet, slouching against a wall. The one sunk into his arm went limp from the waist down, its spine torqued at an awful angle, its claws ripping at the tendons of his wrist. He dashed its brains out against the wall and ripped it off his arm, threw it at the ranks of her closing in on him again.

One of them was *her*. Their mouths streamed blood and foam. "Share your secret with us, Zane. Come back to us. We forgive you..." Two of them split off and dashed up the corridor, and he knew it was important that he stop them, they knew in their blood how to beat the nasty green shit, and nothing would kill them that would not kill the whole world, if they got out. But he was too weak, and they were closer, now, and he couldn't fight them all, not when one of them was her—

One of them leapt at him, and his arm came up to deflect her, when two more ducked under the arm and ripped at his unguarded abdomen. His right arm flopped uselessly as they feasted on it. Fresh waves of pain swept over him and drove him blind, flashing lights like the instrument panel of a collision-bound jet coming out of pure blackness.

When their screams changed, they were so close around him, burrowing into him, that he screamed with them. He burned all over, but they were melting. His vision came back but all he could see was green. The nasty green shit spread tendrils of searing cold over them, and their skin ran like wax under a blowtorch. Tumors blossomed through the liquefied orgy of her bodies, and ruptured spectacularly as the lysing chain-reaction spiraled into a total meltdown. He went blind again as the vapors ate him, not chain-reacting, but still devouring his exposed viscera. He reached out into the blizzard of agony and sizzling ectoplasm and tried to remember her as she'd been that one time, tried to wrap himself around the tang of sweat on her skin that had made him feel nauseous and exhilarated, that lulled him into precious, dreamless sleep. It was all around him even as the bodies ran together and pooled on the floor, but there was only one of her...

There. Teeth bit into his arm, and he could feel the choral vibrations of her screaming even as she dissolved, raging. "You stupid *puto gringo* motherfucker, you were too fucking late!"

He pulled her close through the ocean of flesh and the thickening green death, and he had no idea what to do, no plan but to hold her close and die. Nobody was getting out, and maybe that was best, maybe it should just be over. But his body knew what to do. It remembered Dyson's veins intruding into him when the gas came for them in their spider-holes, and it was the same fucking gas, except now it had Keogh's name written in it. His body remembered the seed of immunity Dyson fed him, and passed it to her.

He felt himself going *into* her, and through all the pain and the dread and longing for death, he *knew* her. The others had him in their guts, but would never metabolize the cure in time, but in her bloodstream, he could save her. He went inside—

—and was born with her into a second-hand world of belly-crawling under fences to grub in the dirt for pennies, to a mother already half-dead from pesticide poisoning, and a father who deserted her before she knew his face. He suffered with her through a lifetime of abuse and neglect and bigotry and anger, so much anger, like a sun around which the rest of her universe blindly whirled. He sickened and faced death with her from the cancer that killed her mother, begged for salvation and was born again on the spear of transforming light that changed them both. With her, he was buried alive. He writhed with her on a slab, and cursed his own name for failing her. With her, he escaped and found a home at last. He reveled with her in a new life beyond death and the community of her fellow survivors, and he forgave Keogh for his presence in her head. With her, he saw himself coming to kill her for what she had become, and she tore into his flesh, and then—

She came alive in his arms. "Get the fuck off me, *pindejo*!" she cried, and fainted.

Bracing himself against the wall, he tried to stand. The bodies of the others sloughed off him like mud. Her body glistened and burned, but it was already healing. Only a tiny coal of life glowed in her mangled form, and he felt her draining his strength to repair herself. Painfully, he ripped his flesh from hers, fanged veins uprooted, oozing plasma. She clung to him, a sleeping vampire, thirsting for more life than he had left. He fumbled for the opposite wall, sliding in the swamp of human remains choking the corridor. He felt for the slope with his feet, his legs buckling and shivering. Each step was agony as tendons and nerves bridged grievous wounds, but his stumbling steps grew surer as he reached the top of the corridor and followed the flow of air back up through the maze. The gas burned, but his skin covered itself with a mucous membrane that repelled its worst effects. Up through countless empty galleries and winding corridors, bathed in the warring half-light of Keogh's eyes and the incandescent gas, Storch ran with Stella Orozco's body cradled in his tattered arms. He scaled the shaft of the exhaust vent and pushed her ahead of him back out into the night and the war.

The sky was roofed in black, and the snowfall came down as rain in gusting sheets that washed the corrosive film of nasty green shit and liquid Keogh off what remained of his skin. The bombers had gone, but he could hear the tide of gas rising in the ventilation shaft at his back. He slung linked packets of C-4 over his shoulder and searched the arrow-shot Missionaries for a detonator.

"*Pindejo*," she whispered in her dreams.

He picked her up and began to run,

~ 25 ~

Lt. Col. Greenaway stood in the doorway of the comm trailer and tried to calculate exactly when this engagement spun out of his control. The hows and the whys of it were beyond his ability to even conceive. Indeed, he could barely get his head around *what* the fuck was happening to his unit even as he watched it, knew only that he would probably still be standing here, deaf, dumb and paralyzed, when they broke the perimeter and killed him.

He had been sitting on the target, this time. He had played by his rules, which had never failed to leave the enemy sputtering and gasping on his own awestruck terror, and later on his own blood. He had chosen a position worthy of the Spartans, and fighters twice as hard, and ten times as dirty. They fought like heroes against an enemy that never showed its face. They had earned not one flesh-and-blood confirmed kill, and for all he knew, every last motherfucking one of his men was dead.

Talley and the comm crew sat or slouched in the trailer behind him, watching the screens like the fleeting final seconds of a lost football game. All of them wore their biowarfare suits and gasmasks, except for Master Sgt. Talley, who had only minutes earlier smashed a monitor with his mask, burning it beyond repair.

Talley's jaw worked at a fist-sized plug of tobacco, and he picked his nose, pulling a menagerie of wonders out of his sinuses, each more ghastly than the last, and smearing them on the console, picking so fiercely that Greenaway expected the next one to be a gray glob with a bit of spinal column glued to it.

Greenaway knew he needed to pull it together, establish contact with the survivors and make another attempt to get the fuck off this mountain, but he felt as if his body had changed all the locks, and he was under house arrest in his own head. He was beyond words, beyond fear, in a stupor of helpless dread. He could feel the waves of cold closing over his head. He should have died then, when he got off the chopper in this godforsaken place. Then the rest of the unit would have gone home, and the fucking mutants and the fucking robot planes could have exterminated each other without him sitting clueless in the middle of it.

If there had been a man in the field to command, he might have snapped out of it, but there was no one left to rally, no one to call to retreat. The last few times he tried to raise someone at the artillery batteries or the vent bunkers, he'd gotten only a sneering Okie voice that said, "Sorry, wrong number," and cut the line. Somebody out there was still shooting up a storm, but they weren't willing or able to pick up and were slinging lead at all points of the compass, so they were as much of a threat as the enemy.

The trailer park was a junkyard, the few vehicles that were recognizable as such were punctured all over with soda-can sized holes from the cluster bombs the second wave of drones dropped. A single intact APC was parked in the underground driveway behind the tower, which was itself a smoking crater, belching noxious green vapors that ate right through their suits.

He'd thought he was still in control up until the drones came. Their perimeter was breached, and his roving ground patrols dropped off the map, and the innocents he was protecting were fucking mutants, but he thought he could handle it. He ordered his men to fall back from the perimeter and the vent bunkers to prepare for a bugout. The 40mm Bofors cannons started cutting down the drones at twenty miles, once the reflecting radar and computers sorted out the real targets, but the bastards flew so insanely, executing maneuvers that would've put human pilots into a coma, that the cannons barely dented their numbers before they closed and kamikazed the western emplacement. The eastern cannons and the Vulcans cut many of them down right over the trailer park, and the wreckage torched their motor pool. But they got the motherfuckers, shot down every last one of them, and the tower, though it meant nothing to him or anyone else now, still stood. He was proud of himself for a minute there, ready to do the impossible and pull his men out in an orderly retreat and maybe send the goddamned egghead clone mutants in the bunker a present of his own, before he left.

And then shit, in Augean abundance, happened. The bridge detail, undermanned because the missing-presumed-dead Team Dogtown was supposed to be alive and backing them up, got wiped out. Shooting broke out at the vent bunkers—somebody fighting somebody, but who? He figured the Heilige Berg militia was out there, but he was damned if he could figure whose side they were on.

He sent out one of the APC's to clear a runway overland down the mountain through whoever was down there, and watched the snowfield come alive underneath it and swallow it up, not two hundred yards from the comm trailer. The vehicle was a brand-new Cadillac Gage ASV150, a truly bad-ass piece of hardware so new the Army wouldn't get them until this summer, with five men inside. Grenades spewed out the side firing ports, and the turret-gunner raked the snow with both the 12.7mm machine gun and 40mm grenade launcher, but they sank into the downy white field as if into a heaving sea. He saw hands reaching up out of the snow and clutching at the appliqué-steel hull of the car, dragging it nose-down into the snow up to its massive front wheel-wells. There was a single, muffled boom, and then only smoke poured out of the firing ports.

The minefield went berserk, as if the invisible Monster of the Id was coming for them across the plateau, and they knew they were cut off. He called the choppers in to shoot their way in and extract the survivors, if any, and that was when the second wave of bombers came in.

When they knocked the Cobra out of the sky and dropped it on the goddamned tower, Greenaway saw the gas pouring out of the ruin and ordered the four remaining men in his command into their NBC suits. Two of them manned the Vulcans by remote, because the gunnery crews were dead or had deserted. The Bofors guns were overheated, or their tracking computers had crashed, or some goddamned thing, and somebody had cut the hard line to them.

He was still thinking on his feet, ordering the Bell 406 to fall back and wait out the second sortie, and trying to raise whoever was shooting Stingers at the drones from across the field, when the radar, and all the computers and all the communications lines, went static. The phone lines screamed, the satellite feeds exchanging lethal blasts of information with something in the sky. The speakers and phones all shorted out or blew sparks. Monitors flashed streams of digits and scalding blasts of snow. Every computer-driven system in the trailer locked up and rendered him blind, deaf and mute beyond the four thin walls of the box in which he hid. No one seemed to hear him when he closed his eyes and howled.

The guns went silent, and there was only the growing roar of a final wing of drones as they slammed, one after the other, into the mountain. Miraculously, or more likely because they weren't worth the ordnance, the comm trailer stood almost untouched, though cluster-bomb twisters wreaked havoc outside their door.

Now, in the unreal quiet of the aftermath, it was quite impossible to see the now, because it was all still unpacking in his head, all still happening at once until he could understand what went wrong. But it wasn't over.

If there was a way off this mountain, or payback to be extracted, he had to come alive and do something.

"Talley, get these commo faggots some guns and let's get the fuck out of here." He jumped down into snow and marched out to the edge of the devastated trailer park, where he saw two of his men, Manny Aleppo and Rhino, hunched down behind an overturned trailer, exchanging fire with someone in the trees at the edge of the plateau. He just stood there and took center-of-mass shots like blown kisses, and pot-shot their position as if he had all night to get them, which he did. Behind him, someone else lobbed mortars with aimless randomness all over the snowfield. A few got as far as the trailer park, making the rubble dance to assure Greenaway that if he tried to call in the 406 to exfil them, it would be shot to shit the moment it touched down.

"Goddammit, boss," Aleppo hollered, "we want to go home!"

He knew he should say something stirring, something that would steel the troops—both of them—for the final assault. "Me too," he mumbled.

Talley stormed up behind him, spun him around and punched him in the mouth. He sat down hard on something jagged and metallic that sheared his ridiculous rubber NBC suit from hip to ankle. He fought for breath, tasting blood and chipped teeth. He dug for anger to fling at his most trusted noncom, but he found only bone-deep fatigue and nausea, and the chilling certainty that he had simply lived way too goddamned long.

"I suppose you're relieving me, Burl, and I won't get into it with you here and now. If you think you got a better plan, lead on. I'm all motherfucking ears."

"You goddamned psycho sonofabitch, this is YOUR WAR, remember? We're just the hired help, Mort. We knew not a goddamned thing about what we were getting into! And we sure as shit resign, as of this instant. But since this is your war, I think you oughta stay to talk the terms for your surrender, don't you?"

Greenaway went for his sidearm and only then saw it in Burl's stubby booger-hook. "You're—what are you doing, Burl?"

Talley's face crumpled up like an old paper bag. Tears sprang out and froze in the corners of his bloodshot eyes. "You took every goddamned soldier above ground who ever trusted you, and you fed them all into a meat grinder, and what the hell for?For *them*?" He waved his arm at the ruined tower. "They ain't even human, and then they ain't even here no more, are they? And what about the enemy, Mort? Where were they? Here and gone, and somebody cut up our men from the inside, I'll tell you what. What the hell happened here, Mortimer Greenaway? What the hell were we fighting? What killed us?"

Greenaway looked at the ashes in the snow at Talley's feet. He did not flinch when one of those boots kicked him in the stomach. He just rolled over and wrapped his arms over his head.

"Tell me, by God, or I'll beat it out of you!" Talley shouted, and stomped him just above his kidneys.

Greenaway just kept looking through freezing tears, at a terminal loss for words, but now the snow at Talley's feet was suddenly the thing to be looking at. It shifted and sank into itself like the mouth of an ant lion's den, and the bowl became a hole, and the hole widened between Talley's boots until he slipped and fell into it. A bayonet lunged up out of the hole and sank to the hilt into the hollow of Talley's crotch and his femoral artery. Hot red blood sluiced the snow and raised a merciful curtain of steam as Talley was dragged screaming out of sight, shooting wildly into the air and the ground, screaming Greenaway's name.

Greenaway gathered himself into a crouch and looked around. The three comm geeks stood transfixed before the widening, hungry hole that swallowed the master sergeant. Manny and Rhino shot up the hole, and he almost thought Manny was going to shoot him, when a double-tap to the back of the soldier's neck poleaxed him. Rhino shrieked and returned his attention to the ghost in the trees. No one had the presence of mind to even shoot at the man who climbed up out of the hole.

He was caked in snow and frozen earth and blue with cold, but he didn't shiver. He moved in slow-motion, like some steam driven contraption in need of oil, but he could have run circles around them. Greenaway understood now why the mines had been going off. The Heilige Berg militia burrowed under them all day, perhaps for several days, with their bare hands, to get here. Which sounded insane, but of course it wasn't, because they weren't human. They were Keogh.

He unwound his frosty balaclava hood and smiled at Greenaway. More holes opened up in the crusty snow, and the comm geeks stampeded back to the dubious safety of the trailer. Rhino emptied his rifle and picked up Manny's.

More Keoghs climbed out of the holes, ice-mummies with those same silver-gray eyes. "You see, now," they said to him, "how obsolete you are."

"Fuck you all," he growled. He snatched an M16A2 out of a comm geek's nerveless hands and sprayed Keoghs full-auto.

With only one lung inflated and most of its face shot away, the nearest Keogh spoke only in a sibilant whisper, but the others, emerging from the holes by the dozen, now, took up its speech and amplified it into the voice of the God of the Hive. Even the trees seemed to turn the wind into his voice. "We tried to save you. We tried to take you in, but you were too stupid, and stupidity is the only sin in the real world, Greenaway. Stupidity is extinction. The Old Ones who began this game were stupid."

"Who the fuck are the Old Ones?"

Keogh smiled wider. "Exactly," he said.

Greenaway tugged on his headset. "Terry, do you copy?" Please God, let me have this, at least. "Terry, come in, goddamn you."

"Say my call-sign, beeyotch."

"Terry, this isn't—"

"Say my name—"

Regretting the decision to let the pilots pick their own call-signs, he mouthed the words so Keogh wouldn't hear them. "Count Chocula…"

"Boss, we copy, what the fuck? There's a whole fucking army massed under your nose, come back. You can't want me to come in there—"

"I know. Do not come in to exfil. Repeat, stay back, and put this fucking place into orbit."

"You're still down there, aren't you?"

"Affirmative. Do it. Blow it up. We'll get clear if we can, but consider us KIA, unless you hear otherwise. Copy?"

Already hovering above the jagged peak, Count Chocula dipped and came in for its first run. "Affirmative, boss. Do what you gotta…"

The Keoghs all just stood there as if this was exactly what they expected to happen. The one he'd shot up grew most of a new head. The Bell 406 fired a volley of Hellfire anti-tank missiles into the tree-line from five hundred feet above their heads, then juked and jived to dodge a salvo of unguided rockets. The last of the tall whitebark pines went down amid football field-sized fireballs, and the chopper pivoted and turned back.

"Now the trailer park, Terry," Greenaway said.

"But sir, I can see you down there, I can take the motherfuckers out from here with the pods—"

"Bomb us, goddamit!" Greenaway screamed, and then he choked. Something erupted out of the rocks at the foot of the cliff face and raced down towards them, just paces ahead of a tumbling wall of satanic green vapor that ate its way up out of a hole in the ground where the vent bunkers used to be. Greenaway staggered back, away from the Keoghs, shouldered his M16A2 and took aim at the running thing.

He looked down the sights of the assault rifle, but he could not shoot. It was a man, or something like a man, except it had only raw, knotted muscle and glinting bones instead of skin. Tatters of green uniform flapped in the wind on its oversized form. His head was ducked down low over a body he cradled in his arms. His legs pounded the snow like bombs, eating up twelve feet at a stride, but he barely gained ground on the avalanche of gaseous death that raced at his heels. When the cloud hit dead bodies, they screamed and exploded. Greenaway head-checked the Keoghs and saw by the stricken look on their collective face that whoever the fuck he was, he was not one of them.

But he was hardly human, either. Greenaway aimed again, amazed all over again by his blinding quickness. The runner passed within a hundred yards of Rhino, who seemed not to even see him. He triggered mines, but was gone before they detonated.

Greenaway squeezed off a shot, leading the runner a good twenty feet. The runner seemed to bow before the bullet left the barrel, and kept right on running.

He was heading for the bridge. Greenaway smiled. This, at least, he could control. He reached into his parka through his ripped NBC suit and found the remote detonator, unfastened the safety cover, and took a shallow breath.

The runner hit the bridge and was halfway across it in three strides when Greenaway pressed the button. A skirt of fire and force lifted the bridge and split it into four sections, illuminating the silhouetted runner as he stopped and turned back the way he'd come. He leapt clear of the bridge's doomed launch trajectory, vaulting over the temporarily airborne troop truck and hitting the snow without dropping the girl, without breaking stride. Greenaway sighted him down the rifle. Two hundred yards. Impossible at this distance, but getting easier every second.

"Boss, what are your orders?" Count Chocula's voice chirped in his ear.

The runner turned and ran along the edge of the tree-line. Mortars lit his way, kicking up fountains of earth, but the runner threaded an untouchable path through them and emerged unscathed. Then he stopped.

Greenaway drew a bead on him, sixty yards out and stock-still. A steady hand could barely pick him off with an M16, and his hands shook like he had DT's. He watched the runner jolt and rock as bullets from somebody down-slope lit him up, but he threw something down the slope and dropped prone on the snow.

Greenaway looked at the Keoghs, back at the runner, then back to Rhino. No one moved. The Count squawked at him, but it might've been the wind.

The edge of the plateau went white with a blast half the size of the one that destroyed the bridge, but it rained body parts and burning, screaming trees. When the light died away, the runner was already gone.

Greenaway crouched and turned, shot the nearest Keogh's eyes out. He raked the mob of them at knee-height, felling ten or fifteen of them like saplings before the clip ran dry. The others silently charged him.

"Run for the Cadillac!" he shouted. "Terry, give us sixty klicks to get clear! Then take a shit on this place, and cut a trail down the mountain, copy?"

"I hear that," the Count hollered, and laid down curtains of 20mm cannon fire that made confetti of the assembled Keoghs.

Greenaway had to kickstart Rhino out of his trance, but the comm geeks ran so fast they waded right into the green pool around the back wheels of the surviving APC. Two of them ran right into it up to the waist. One of them shrieked and sank out of sight, but the other waded out and collapsed at Greenaway's feet. His NBC suit dripped off his legs, which sloughed meat like over-cooked chicken drumsticks. He reached out to Greenaway and tried to ask for help getting up when his eyes glazed over with shock. His buddy, Greenaway never had caught his name, wanted to lift him up and take him along, but then Rhino raced past them, shooting blind over his shoulder, scaled the blunt nose of the APC, dropped in through the open side hatch, got the engine turned over, and started to roll away without them. They ran after and jumped inside.

A pair of Keoghs came around the comm trailer and rushed them, but the helicopter's machine guns scythed them down. Scattered rifle and RPG fire drove the 406 back up through the roof of smoke, but it showed that the force surrounding them was smashed wide open for the moment. They flattened five more Keoghs crossing the snowfield. Greenaway saw them getting back up in their wake, shaking off the tire-tracks and racing after them, shooting. He cradled his head in his arms. What the fuck? What the fuck were they fighting? *I wish I knew, Burl.*

Rhino hit the brakes. The comm geek split his scalp on the bulkhead behind the driver's seat. Greenaway half-jumped, half-fell into the cab. "I'm not going down there," Rhino mumbled.

In the dark and the smoke, there was mercifully little to see, but what he did see made him also want to turn back, and chance the lances of rocket fire pounding the last vestiges of the Radiant Dawn settlement into smoke. It looked like Tet and the Somme and Agincourt and all the goddamned places where God set up his wood-chipper and stuffed it with human fertilizer. The pitted, bare earth was black and red and painted in body parts, blasted trees and charred bodies. But nothing here could die. Every infinitesimal fragment of His flesh writhed and suffered for as far as he could see through the smoke, but the runner had gotten through.

Greenaway dragged Rhino out of the driver's seat and ordered him to man the turret. "Kill everything again, Rhino," Greenaway called out, and drove them over the edge.

The ground tried to grab them. The wheels sank into muck and severed hands clawed at the wheels. The invincible dead choked the wheel-wells and clambered up onto the windshield. Every pothole yawned to greet them and swallow them up. Every seemingly safe high point crumbled under them and sent them, wheels scrabbling on bloody mud, into fresh waves of mutilated Keoghs. Rhino screamed and sobbed and spun round and round, shooting everything. Only the blind force of their own momentum sent them smashing through the final cordon and down the uneven slope of the mountain.

Trees introduced themselves in impassable hedgehog formations, and fucking snowmobiles slashed this way and that like henchmen in a goddamned James Bond movie, but the runner was long gone.

Greenaway hobbled over open ground, braking in stops and stutters until he stumbled across a fire road. A convoy of burning trucks from Heilige Berg lay on and around the road. This must've been the primary for the Hellfire attack the Count laid down. The APC lurched onto the road and picked up speed, clinging only to the roughest outline of the balls-out slalom course.

Greenaway saw a riderless snowmobile go airborne not ten feet ahead of him and smash into a tree, saw the runner cut across the road lit by the halogen spots above the windshield, and then he was gone well ahead of Rhino's spray of panic-fire.

The 406 blazed them a trail with Hellfire missiles and Hydra 70 rockets, but the woods were still alive with Keoghs, darting between trees and pacing the runner on snowmobiles or on foot, black shapes he could see by the glint of their eyes. They were after the runner, and seemed not even to notice him.

Greenaway glimpsed the runner again across a gentle, treeless slope midway down the mountain. The gorge yawned on their right, and the runner made for it, shooting targets cleanly in the head at a dead run with a converted Kalashnikov.

Count Chocula hovered over them as Greenaway slowed down inside the trees. He spotted something coming up behind them faster than the runner, gaining on the APC though he sped up to a reckless fifty on the winding, icy road. The pursuer closed the distance in seconds and came clear in a fleeting bar of moonlight. It was another running man, taller and rangier and longer of leg, and he carried no one. He held a Barrett Light 50 sniper rifle spot-welded to his shoulder as he ran so fast he was in free-fall. His rifle barked as he passed, and Rhino disappeared from the shoulders up. The cabin of the APC popped and shook with armor-piercing rounds as long as Greenaway's middle finger. The sole surviving comm geek danced around singing ricocheting bullet shards, screaming, "I've got blood in my eyes! What's happening? What the fuck is happening out there, sir?"

Greenaway's feet and hands propelled the APC down the mountain, but his eyes were glued to the running sniper, who darted across the road behind them and disappeared in his right-side blind spot. Greenaway whipped his head around as if to find the sniper inside the cab with him. He reached for his M16 on the shotgun seat, but the comm geek, the last man alive under his command, stumbled into the space between him and the window. "What the fuck—"

The right side "bulletproof" window-slit shattered and too many fifty-caliber bullets punched into the comm geek. Greenaway was trying to look through him, reach around him for his gun and steer around a particularly dense stand of trees when the insanely terrified young man's face bulged and split open and light shone through his brains into Greenaway's face.

The shot caromed off Greenaway's helmet and smashed into the side window, starring, but not breaking through it. He saw the shell, suspended there like a dino-mosquito in amber, and had time to think, *that was made for me*, when the road went out from under them.

His right arm went limp. His mouth flooded with bile. His chest caved in. *God damn you, God!* he screamed without breath. *A heart attack, now?*

A smooth path of open snow lay before him. The APC's knobby all-terrain tires gripped the hard-packed, iced-over snow so long as he maintained a more or less straight course, which would add speed to his already suicidal rate until it swept him over the lip of the gorge. He fought it with his functional arm, howling silently as his lungs seemed to go flat. His eyes strayed down to the lip of the gorge, where he saw the runner with the girl in his arms.

He stood there, contemplating something below, when into Greenaway's vision swam the other runner, the sniper, who skidded to a stop on a promontory overlooking the gorge. Bracing against a tree, he fused with it and drew a perfect arc down to the runner, who backed away from the edge now and then began running at it so fast he looked as if he would fly away.

The sniper and the tree got larger, and Greenaway saw a lot about the motherfucker very quickly as he grew. Black spots bubbled up in his vision, but he stared through them and time seemed to slow down to let him take it in. He saw a bow and quiver slung on his back, and he saw the motherfucker wore old jungle camo and a flak vest, circa 1968. He knew without seeing the face that it was not Keogh, this time. It was somebody he saw only yesterday, but dismissed as a bad fucking speed daydream, and maybe he was dreaming him now, because what sane God would let something like that still walk the earth, when so many good men died over there? What were these mutants, that something like this walked among them?

Not invincible, I hope, Greenaway thought, and steered the APC into him.

The sniper got very large indeed in the windshield, filled it for an instant before the APC introduced him to a deeper relationship with the sturdy piñon pine tree he braced against. Greenaway was too engrossed in his own experience with arrested inertia to take notice. An airbag(!) bloomed and smacked him silly, then deflated as the APC glanced off the shattered pine tree and skated down the open slope on its passenger side.

Greenaway fought to hold onto consciousness, unsnapped the safety harness and toppled out of his seat. He took a moment to reorient himself and noticed with relief that he hadn't had a heart attack at all. Bullet fragments from the shots that killed the comm geek studded his right arm and chest. One of his lungs felt sore, and his arm didn't really work, but his ticker was sound. That, at least, had not failed him.

He dragged himself out through the shattered forward window-slit and lay very flat in the snow. The stillness reasserted itself, sprinkling snow on the scant evidence that anything had happened here at all. The windshield and grill of the APC were sprayed with blood and puckered from the impact with the tree, but of the sniper, there was no sign. Likewise the runner, whose trail vanished at the rim of the gorge.

He heard the 406 setting down on the other side of the APC, and he reached for his sidearm. It was time to go. There was nothing here he wanted to live through. But of course, Burl had taken his gun when he—

Greenaway pressed his face down in the snow and wept. Once, he had been strong and smart. Once, his enemies had feared him. Once, being human had been enough.

~ 26 ~

Throughout his career in the FBI, Cundieffe had always assumed that the open contempt for local law enforcement espoused by many, if not most, Bureau agents—his father included—was the kind of ignorant animal tribalism and territoriality that hindered the pursuit of a truly just and ordered society. After today, he had learned that, in the case of the town of White Bird, Idaho, at least, the ignorance was his.

He hid for nearly half an hour at the Heilige Berg slaughterhouse, nervously peering around the corner of the shed at the civilians who gathered in their pickup trucks to watch the blaze. Proper procedure raced around in his mind, but the sniper who shot up his car and the billboard in the field made him think better of it. No one seemed to spot him, and he did nothing to call attention to himself. This was hostile territory, a war zone, and he had no idea who the enemy was, or who might just shoot him out of spite.

By the time Sheriff Manes and two deputies arrived on the scene, the fire had engulfed the entire structure, the last of the exterior walls tumbling into the conflagration with great spires of sparks and gray smoke. Two Idaho County Volunteer Firefighters' trucks followed close behind and sprayed the blaze, while the Sheriff organized the crowd of spectators into a shovel brigade, dumping snow on the leeward flank of the flames. Cundieffe broke cover and ran to the Sheriff, but he could think of nothing to explain himself that did not sound patently insane. "I've been shot at," he told the Sheriff, "and my car and phone are disabled. This situation is going to require a much larger federal presence."

"It's just a barn fire, Special Agent," Manes replied. "Get them all the time." The jaundiced look in his eyes made it plain who the prime suspect in setting it was.

"Sheriff, perhaps you arrived too late to hear the secondary explosions, but this barn was an ammunition dump. The soldiers on the mountain are in grave danger, and I demand that you return me to town immediately."

The Sheriff complied, not immediately, but soon enough, and Cundieffe found himself back at the station house in White Bird, but no closer to getting through to the powers that be. AD Wyler was still in conference and unavailable, likewise Brady Hoecker. The Boise field office pledged to send two agents and a forensics team to look at the fire the next morning. A bank robbery with hostage fatalities had taken place in Nampa only the day before, and all available agents were on-task there.

He was left with little room for doubt that he was being defecated upon in recompense for circumventing Bureau procedure. He should have paid a visit to the Boise office, or at least have had AD Wyler contact the SAC there to brief him on the outsider's business in their area. Not doing so made him look like a rogue agent from headquarters, trampling on their area of responsibility, making messes they'd have to answer for to the state authorities. Which was exactly what he was, and they smelled it through the phone.

The local sheriff's deputies and state police could handle sealing the area to look for the shooter. The barn fire was just a barn fire, and the Heilige Berg militia had evacuated the area, as per the Boise agents' surveillance report. The Bureau had been notified of a routine Army National Guard maneuver taking place in the area, but knew nothing about a private mercenary force participating, or about a Radiant Dawn hospice community in the area. They knew nothing of any agents Macy and Mentone, or any others except himself operating in the area. The shooting he was involved in, they told him, was an accident, and when Cundieffe tried to correct them on this, they were suspiciously adamant that he was mistaken. "Have you ever been shot at before, Agent Cundieffe?" If anyone was trying to kill him out there, he was told, he'd be dead, and by whose authority was he out here, again?

Manes hadn't heard from Macy or Mentone since they left for Grangeville with Karl Schweinfurter. Grangeville General didn't show Schweinfurter as having been admitted to the hospital, and calls to every other hospital in the county turned up nothing.

Manes told Cundieffe that he'd called the local doctor, who may or may not be out of town for the weekend, and left him a first aid kit, with which he cleaned and applied adhesive bandages to his hand and face.

He began to see what he was coming to, but kept making calls and sending faxes and e-mails back to headquarters and the Boise office for hours before he gave up. He hogged the NCIC database, accessing what he could of Pentagon records to learn something about Specialist Four Gibson Holroyd, but he got nowhere. As far as his limited official clearance allowed him to check, no such person had ever served in the Army. Calls to the world's largest bureaucratic edifice yielded only ineffectual excuses from night file clerks and grudging promises to have somebody poke around in the paper file annexes in Arlington for him in the morning.

The only party who seemed to appreciate the gravity of the situation was the rental car agency, which would be sending an insurance claims investigator down this afternoon. The investigator called seconds later, introducing himself as Lou Duckworth in a flat, crushingly unimpressed voice, jowls flapping explosively with each syllable. Because Cundieffe was a government agent, the rental agency wanted to get to the bottom of this immediately, if not sooner.

At seven, Cundieffe threw up his hands and walked out of the office in which he'd barricaded himself. Sheriff Manes was adamant about not going up the mountain, with or without state police escort, until the maneuver was over. He'd been on the phone with Major Ortman and Heilige Berg's landlord. All were in agreement that everything was perfectly normal. In not so many words, he informed Cundieffe that if he'd been shot at while up there, it should go to show him not to go gallivanting around on his own in the middle of nowhere while a military exercise was on.

Lou Duckworth called then to report that the car was not in the field where Cundieffe had alleged that he left it. He really would like to sit down with Cundieffe and take a statement. Cundieffe gave it over the phone, omitting the parts that would beggar the agent's hard-nosed skepticism. Party or parties unknown had shot repeatedly at the vehicle as he was negotiating a particularly difficult mountain road, causing him to crash. The car was totaled, and unlikely to have gone anywhere on its own. He wanted to scream at the estimable Mr. Duckworth that he was an FBI agent, and that he had been attacked by a superhuman assassin and was lucky to have escaped with his life, that he'd nearly been killed again in an encounter with an unspeakable abomination which took more killing than a whole platoon before he destroyed it, but he refrained. Despite chronic seizures of panic that clogged his heart with ice, everything around him told him he was delusional, and he really had nothing better to do than dicker with the insurance investigator. Besides, something told him Duckworth would only care if his employer also insured Heilige Berg's slaughterhouse.

He hung up and returned the blank stares of the deputies loitering around the office until they all, one by one, returned to shuffling make-work and left him sitting alone.

At eight, Sheriff Manes packed up and offered to drive him out to the Travelodge on the highway, and Cundieffe, sensing that nothing was going to happen where he was sitting, agreed.

The ride was awkward, the Sheriff blotting out the threat of conversation by blasting a call-in show pundit who continually warned his listeners that bloody civil war with the "federal Gestapo" was both inevitable and imminent. Cundieffe winced at the tinny AM demagogue's elementary logic-twisting. Apparently having forecast the bloody advent of the NWO for the previous Thanksgiving and/or during the upheaval of Y2K, the glib doomsayer had his rabid audience trained to view the relatively quiet passing of the holidays as proof that his vigilance had carried the day and pushed the New World Order into cowardly retreat. Sheriff Manes nodded now and again and muttered assent under his breath, like a church deacon at a holy roller's revival.

Cundieffe took his leave of the Sheriff graciously but gratefully, checked into a room and laid down on the bed. He washed down his dietary supplements and finished off the last of the fruit in his shot-up briefcase. Waiting for sleep, he drifted not to the events of the day, which surrounded him like a storm but had since become like a movie and divorced of emotion, but to the question of Dr. Keogh. Of all the people he might have expected to see there, the former Lt. Col. Greenaway was perhaps the very last. What did it mean?

The heater came on, an endless, withering blast from a forest fire that made the room feel like a kiln, made him less warm than feverish, and he moved to turn it off. As he stood, he noticed a higher, almost insectoid, sound that seemed to come from outside. The brittle, subtly warped picture window vibrated in its frame behind the ghastly maroon and gold curtains, but he drew them and found the street was empty. It sounded like nothing else he'd ever heard in real life, but it had the surreal dreamlike quality of something else out of the movies. He went to the door and stuck his head out into the frigid night.

The humming was exactly as it sounded in the movies, only deeper, subtler, but that was to be expected, with jet engines. It was the sound the Japanese Zeroes made when they attacked Pearl Harbor in *Tora! Tora! Tora!*

Across the street, a Circle K and a feed store stood half-hidden behind palisades of muddy snow. Rows of houses and apartments, lights out, televisions on. Fat, soapy flakes of snow cascaded to the street and turned to ice. The sky was bricked up behind a roof of inscrutable black clouds, but he thought he saw a flash of sulfurous yellow cut through them and heard, an instant later, a boom. Something flat and hot and as long as Cundieffe's leg whistled down out of the clouds and sliced into a snowbank directly in front of the motel parking lot. Snow melted and turned to steam, closed over it.

Cundieffe dove for the phone and called Sheriff Manes's pager. "I wanted to tell you your friend on the radio was right," he said on the message line.

He hung up and paced, stealing glances out the window at the empty street. The humming had passed, but now he heard thunder pulsating as if the earth itself were having a heart attack. A few lights came on, but no one else looked out.

The phone rang. He snatched it up and barked, "Sheriff, it's happening. Come get me—"

"Lou Duckworth from State Farm here, Agent Cundieffe, I'm back up in Grangeville for the night, but I'm coming back down first thing in the morning. It may not seem very important to you, but we need to find out what happened to that car—"

It took the Sheriff fifteen minutes to get back to the Travelodge and pick up Cundieffe, ten minutes more for both off-duty deputies to meet them at the sheriff's station. The Sheriff looked pissed to be out of bed, but not disturbed enough by half for what they could all see plainly happening around them.

Ten miles to the west, the black barricade of Heilige Berg was a curtain of blooming explosions. The night desk deputy had fielded a few dozen phone calls in the last half hour, complaining about the noise, reporting debris falling out of the sky. One caller claimed that a small aircraft had crashed in the Nez Perce National Forest, eight miles due east of White Bird.

They set out in two Broncos, the Sheriff and Cundieffe in one, the deputies following in the other. Only a few cars passed them on the two-lane road out of town. As they passed the black mound where the slaughterhouse had been, Sheriff Manes looked across at Cundieffe. "None of this shit started happening until you feds got here, young fella."

"You just didn't see it," Cundieffe said. "The Heilige Berg militia weren't the only people up there, and the soldiers up there aren't all weekend warriors on maneuvers. There's a war on, Sheriff. It's not on CNN or in the papers, but people are getting killed up there, just the same."

"Shit, out here, there's always a war on, between the government and sovereign citizens. When you poke around in the way people live their private lives, it's like stirring up a fire ant hill. You gotta be prepared to get bit."

Cundieffe looked out at the fields of snow, glistening in a stray wash of moonlight through a tear in the clouds. Sweltering in the recycled engine heat, he rolled down the window and stuck his head out into the chill wind. "Sheriff, stop!" he shouted.

"What?" Manes barked, but Cundieffe insisted, and he braked in the middle of the road. The deputies pulled up behind them and Cundieffe got out.

Ahead of them, the road crept up into the first galloping foothills that skirted Heilige Berg. On their left, he saw the broken fence where he'd crashed only this afternoon, and the hateful billboard. To the right, the wall of hills subsided to make way for the snow-choked creek bed that merged, a mile back, with the Salmon River. He could hear the snow falling on the field.

"It's stopped," he said.

Manes looked visibly relieved. "There's gonna be hell to pay in the morning, I'll tell you what. Folks halfway to Elk City had shit come down in their yards—"

One of the deputies pointed up the creekbed. "Sheriff, lookit that–"

At first, Cundieffe couldn't see it. The falling snow and the gloom were a curtain that muffled sound and sight, but something plowed up a great fan of snow as it came toward them down the white furrow of the creek bed. They heard no sound of a motor, but it moved too fast through the deep, soft snow to be anything but a snowmobile. The other deputy shone a spotlight across the creekbed and caught it in the glare for only a moment before it turned ninety degrees and flicked back into the darkness.

The snow where it had passed smoked. The form was sheathed in steam and hunched over, but Cundieffe's knees went rubbery when he saw that it was a man, running.

"It's him!" he screamed. He climbed back into the Bronco and hunkered down behind the dubious protection of the door.

The sheriff and his men still stood in the road, the deputy trying to find the runner in the stands of skeletal brush on the far side of the creekbed.

"What the fuck was that?" Sheriff Manes shouted.

"It's the…man…the one who shot at me," Cundieffe said. He reached for the shotguns on the rack above the seat, tugged on them and found them locked.

"Now, don't touch those," Manes said, and climbed into the back with his keys out. "You don't know your way around these guns."

"Hey! We see you!" the deputies yelled. One of them swept the trees with the spotlight, while the other tracked the light down the barrel of his service pistol. "Come out of there with your hands up!"

It came, and though they thought they were ready, they weren't. Cundieffe saw something made of smoke shoot out of the trees and fly across the creek like a dust devil. The spotlight jerked and bounced off it as the other deputy drew his gun and both of them shot at it over and over. But whether they hit it or not, it was between them in an eyeblink, and their guns were empty. "Get him, Rory! Get him, get him, get—"

Manes had dropped his keys, and bent to find them. "Jesus Christ, you idiots—" He looked up and saw it.

It picked up one of the deputies by an arm and leg and smashed the other one to the ground with him, then dropped him. It stopped and looked up, and Cundieffe gasped, because it was something that bore only a structural resemblance to a human body. Through the clouds of steam and vision-warping waste heat, he saw a thing made of raw muscle and charred spurs of bone, taloned paws, and huge, snowshoe feet. Its back and chest were riddled with holes, which oozed fluid and smoke. He stood there, shivering in agony, as plugs of lead spat out of the holes and sank, sizzling, into the snow.

Sheriff Manes cursed a blue streak, trying to find his keys under the Bronco's seat. Cundieffe laid flat across the seat and reached for the radio handset in its cradle under the dashboard.

"Don't fuck with me," the thing said, "I just want the truck." Though the voice was a husky rasp, the words distorted because the speaker had no lips, Cundieffe instantly recognized it. He sat up and turned to look, but it was gone.

Sheriff Manes knelt beside the Bronco with his head between his knees, praying, gagging and dry-heaving all over the toes of his boots. A pervasive barbecue stench hung in the air, but of the thing with a dead man's voice, there was no other sign.

Cundieffe climbed out of the truck. The deputies lay in a pile beside the second Bronco. A few isolated pops of rifle fire rolled down the face of the mountain, but otherwise, the stillness was a solid thing.

No. This was too much of an outrage. He was rattled, as anyone would be by the events of the day, and his mind was coming unhinged. Storch was dead, shot through the skull close enough to spray him, only two weeks ago. He was dead. He was not out there—

It stepped out of the trees where it had gone to ground before, and crossed the creek again. In its monstrous, mangled arms, it cradled a woman's body. "Don't fuck with me," it said again, and clambered up onto the road.

"Sergeant Storch?" Cundieffe asked, and shrank back behind the truck door. Peeking over the sill at the silhouette as it turned to regard him, he smelled the wash of burned flesh off it and looked into its deep-sunk eyes, and his last reserve of incredulity was blasted clean out of his mind.

This impossible, obscene thing, it was Storch. Racing, he put it together. Storch was shot, but he wasn't what he appeared. His thumb had grown back. He survived months of torture and interrogation, marked only by the wounds he inflicted on himself. His corpse was moved to Ft. Detrick, where something happened, something that killed a lot of people and blew up a good portion of the underground bioweapons research complex there, that the government covered up and buried. He knew now what it was, what they'd covered up even from the Mules, if they knew it themselves. It was Storch getting out.

"It's you, isn't it, Storch? Do you remember me?"

The burned thing studied him for a moment. "Mr. Know-It-All," he said at last. "You're too late for the fight, but you're just in time to help cover it up."

"Whose side are you on?"

"My side," Storch said. "Stay the fuck off it."

"What's happening, Storch? What the devil is all this about?"

"Like the man already told you, it's evolution." The thing opened the passenger door of the deputies' Bronco and laid the unconscious woman into the seat, strapped her in. Cundieffe saw she wore the rags of a black tracksuit with a white corona on the breast. She was from Radiant Dawn. She was nearly as messed up as he was.

Storch slammed the door and went around to the driver's side. Cundieffe approached him, choking back bile at the odor. "That wasn't you, that I spoke to before, was it?"

Storch shook his awful head. "Wasn't me. Was Him. I got to get gone, they'll be coming."

"Where are you going?"

Storch made a sound like a laugh, or a cough. A bullet popped out of his neck. He got into the Bronco.

Cundieffe got as close as he could stand. "Sergeant Storch, I'm all alone. I want to stop this, but I know nothing. Everybody who knows is part of it, I think. Even my superiors. They're letting this happen because they stand to gain something from it, but what? What is he doing?"

"Ask Him," Storch said. His taloned paws fumbled with the keys, turned them in the ignition and put the Bronco in gear. "Ask any of them, they're all Him. He knows everything. He's everywhere."

Cundieffe heard a helicopter. He turned and looked up the riverbed, where a heavily armed military chopper leapt up out of the woods, speared the forest around it with rockets and took off to the east, passing directly overhead. Cundieffe heard snowmobiles coming out of the hills, trucks coming down the mountain.

"Storch, wait!" He hurled himself at the open window. The Bronco backed up, dragging his feet out from under him. He levered himself up over the sill and into the blackened gristle of Storch's face. Glowing green eyes stabbed him with blind rage. A huge red paw came up and engulfed his face. The stench made Cundieffe's head swim. His grip loosened and he felt himself falling down under the wheels as the Bronco sped up in reverse, swerved sideways on the road and headed back towards White Bird. "Please, we want the same thing—I can find him for you—"

Storch slammed the brakes. Cundieffe fell and rolled in the road. He struggled dizzily to get back up. "You want to find him."

"Where is he?"

"I don't know, but I'm looking. You want to know *where*, I want to know *who*. We can help each other."

"Then I guess you're not so useful, now are you?"

Cundieffe propped himself up against the Bronco, reached into his coat. Storch's hand came up again, but Cundieffe pulled out a card and a pen, wrote a number on it. "This is a voice mail account I set up under a false name. Nobody else in the Bureau knows about it. Call me when you get wherever you're going—don't tell me where you are, but just let me know you're still alive. I'll leave a message if I learn anything. I think someone's trying to help me, but I don't understand yet what they're trying to tell me."

"If you don't know what He is, forget about it. This isn't your fight."

"He's a disease, isn't he? Infecting people via satellite, invading them, replacing them. I saw what he did to Heilige Berg. If he could do that here—"

"He's coming. Get out of my way." Storch snapped the card out of Cundieffe's hand and floored the accelerator. Cundieffe jumped back and shielded his face as the Bronco sped away with its headlights off. He heard a truck coming down the road, and leapt out of the way just as it passed. It was a Heilige Berg panel truck, loaded with soldiers with carbine rifles and grenade launchers.

This is America, he thought. *This is the nation you swore to protect.*

Cundieffe hugged himself to keep from fainting. Nausea climbed up in him and shot out the top of his head. He vomited all over the road and collapsed on a snowbank. Once, he craved secrets, to know what was really going on. All the secrets he knew were making him sick. He feared the ones he didn't know yet would kill him.

The road was empty again, the night silent.

Cundieffe got back into the Bronco and waited while Sheriff Manes triaged the deputies. One had a concussion, the other was pretty certain his arm was broken, and they wanted to go home. Manes shouldered them into the back and leaned against the doorpost with his hand over his eyes for a long moment. His shaky hand went for the handset on the radio.

"Dispatch, this is the Sheriff, come back. Jimmy—"

He saw then that the curly black cord dangled limp from the handset, ripped out of the console. He glared at Cundieffe, who shrugged and said, "He did it."

"Give me your—"

"My cellular phone was destroyed in the accidental shooting, remember? We have to go up there, Sheriff. There's worse up ahead, and—well, you saw it... "

"I didn't see anything." Sheriff Manes' face twitched, like a bulk eraser had just wiped his brain clean. "Didn't see nothing at all."

In another place and time, it would make headlines and history books. Cundieffe stood on the ridge overlooking the plateau, where he had stood only twelve hours before, when Greenaway had greeted him. He recognized almost nothing.

The bridge to Heilige Berg lay in fragments at the bottom of the gorge, and the plateau on the other side was a cluster of smoking craters. For all the destruction, all the wreckage strewn across the mountainside, he saw no bodies anywhere. Either the battle had indeed been some kind of automated exercise, with unmanned planes fighting computer-controlled autocannons, or the field had already been sanitized.

Here and there, shadowy figures moved on the battlefield. He saw dumptrucks creeping across the plateau with crews of people in white winter camo snowsuits shoveling snow on fires, gleaning wreckage off the ground and tossing it into the trucks. The snow would cover the rest.

Nobody would believe it, because nobody knew it was here. The people who heard it would believe whatever they were told, because none of them had died. The cover-up probably wouldn't even make the front page, would flash across the bottom of the screen for three seconds during football highlights.

There were no witnesses. The National Guard units had vanished. Greenaway's men were gone. He supposed the people out there were from Heilige Berg, but in some strange, biological way, they belonged to Dr. Keogh.

This was a crime scene. It should be crawling with FBI, state police and the real Army, but there was only gunless, carless, phoneless, dickless Special Agent Cundieffe, AWOL in Idaho and one step ahead of the insurance investigator. Even Sheriff Manes had deserted him, speeding off the moment he climbed out of the Bronco. He had little doubt that the authorities would be up here in force to assist in the clean-up. Macy and Mentone would be along as soon as they'd cleaned up Karl Schweinfurter.

You'd have to have a heart of stone not to laugh, so he did. He knew now that this had to be a nightmare. This whole day was a bad dream, had to be, because if all the things he'd seen and suffered today *were* real, he'd have gone insane or died from shock.

"There are many shades of reaction to tragedy, Agent Cundieffe," said someone behind him, "and none can say which is or isn't valid or healthy."

Cundieffe turned and ducked. He saw no one among the pillars of charcoal tree stumps and rolling smoke. "Who's there? I'm—" They knew his name, they'd probably know he was unarmed.

"I myself am rather torn about the loss of life. On the one hand, there is the pain and fear of the flesh, but beyond that, in the cessation of pain and the loneliness of the soul, there is peace, of a sort. I don't profess to know what lies beyond this world, but I do what I can to ease the suffering, in this one."

Cundieffe looked around again, and gave a short scream. Someone was simply *there* beside him, as if he'd dropped out of a tree or sprouted up out of the ground. Cundieffe gasped and took a step back. He knew this voice almost as well as he knew Storch's, though it had come out of Storch's mouth. Utterly barren of accent, though subtler, more *aware*, than Storch's. *We are all one flesh, becoming one mind.* "What are you doing out here, Dr. Keogh?"

He looked the older man up and down. He wore a woolen overcoat and sorrels. A black pickup was parked on the shoulder of the hill. He wondered if he hadn't noticed it parked there, or hadn't heard it drive up as he laughed at this nightmare he couldn't wake up from.

Very well. It was all a bad dream. "How many people were really in there, Dr. Keogh?"

The doctor ran his hands through his white hair and craned his neck down into Cundieffe's face. He bit his lip and looked away. Those eyes had bored into him once before— again, out of Storch. "Only forty patients and staff were present, along with the complement of security. We were very fortunate, in that the majority of our residents were recently rotated out to outpatient care. Many of them will be returning to their homes, or near to cities where they can get treatment and support. I myself was in Seattle until this evening, inspecting a new clinic. This place was only a way-station, a gateway."

Feeling emboldened now he knew he would wake up from this, Cundieffe met the scientist's gaze. "But people don't come to Radiant Dawn to die, do they, Dr. Keogh?"

Moonlight glinted off Keogh's smile. "Who wants to die, Agent Cundieffe? Who wants to be born into the world with the delusion of immortality, of individual freedom, and to build and destroy like a god, only to go alone into the dark, and feed their flesh to worms? Cancer is the life force trying to change us. People come to us to learn how to open themselves to that change."

"You'd have to keep something like that well-protected, to keep all the sick people out, not to mention the Mission. You'd have to have armed guards, and military ordnance. That's going to a lot of trouble, when you could just ask the government for help. But then people would know about what happened in California, and here. Don't you think keeping this secret has cost enough lives?"

"I wouldn't presume to tell your masters their business. They have their reasons for what they do, and need justify it to no one. Why doesn't your kind let the world know about themselves?"

Hot flashes hit Cundieffe. Change the subject. "I met a boy from right down the road who seems to have cancer in every major organ, can you believe that? And he seems to believe that he left his community at just the wrong time, and everybody else got healed, but him. Unlucky boy, eh?"

"Or unfit. But you know all of this, Agent Cundieffe. You know as much as you need to about my business, and what was accomplished here tonight. You were sent for to help provide security, which you've done adequately. I'm grateful for the chance to have answered your questions, but there's still much to be done—"

"One more question, Dr. Keogh. How old are you?"

Dr. Keogh turned and went around the hood of the pickup, then stopped to look at Cundieffe. His eyes probed him as if he was speaking with his mind, but Cundieffe felt only a deeper chill stealing across wherever the eyes took him in. "Old enough to know better," he said, "but young enough to still try. You wanted to change the world once, when you were younger, didn't you, Agent Cundieffe?"

Up until about two weeks ago, he thought. *Then I thought I knew what the world was.* "I'm not as old as I look," he said lamely.

"Never stop trying to change the world," Keogh said as he climbed into the van.

Cundieffe watched the van go down the hill and out of sight before he began the precipitous trudge down to the road. He slipped and fell more times than he could count, and soaked his clothes. By the time he staggered out into the road with teeth chattering fit to cut his tongue to ribbons, the first state police jeeps and cruisers noisily logjammed the road where the National Guard had been only hours before. Sheriff Manes stood at the open gateway, beside two soft, sour-faced men he supposed were Boise FBI, and a short jelly-doughnut of a man with honest-to-goodness mutton chops framing his flabby jowls, who could only be Lou Duckworth, the State Farm investigator.

Wake up! He screamed at himself as he walked down to meet them.

Sheriff Manes lurched at him and grabbed him by his right wrist. Cundieffe stepped back, but Manes twisted his arm behind his back and levered him onto his knees. "Young fella, these gentlemen here are from the Boise field office of the Federal Bureau of Investigation, and they say they have no idea who the hell you are."

The handcuffs pinched, but he didn't complain. As he got into the back of the Sheriff's Bronco, he lost his footing in the slush and banged his forehead on the rear doorpost, and fell to his knees. No one moved to help him up. He saw only blobs of color and spinning wheels of blue and red fire in the darkness. The only thing he had that had survived this god-awful day, his glasses, were broken and lost in the road.

~ 27 ~

From the porthole in his sleeping compartment in the Spektr science module of *Mir*, Dr. Sherman Moxley could see the spacecraft grow from a speck to a silhouette against the cobalt backdrop of the earth, 250 miles below. For a moment, before he blinked and rubbed his eyes and took a good look, he thought, *I'm going home.*

The ship was black and sleek and predatory, and looked more like a fighter-bomber, or Lockheed's old SR-71 spy plane, than a shuttle. It was less than a third the size of big white school buses like *Atlantis* or *Columbia*, but bigger than the unmanned Progress drones that brought their supplies and took their garbage. They were two weeks past their extraction date, and had all but decided to abandon ship in the Soyuz capsule by week's end, but he knew from looking at it that this was not their ride home.

Moxley climbed out of his sleep-sack and swam through the Spektr module, threading a painfully memorized route through the maze of shadowy scientific gear, to the three-foot circular hatchway leading into the node.

A spherical chamber of hatchways, the node was the intersection of the six modules that made up *Mir*. From inside the modules, *Mir* was like a cruciform chain of interlocking motor homes, but inside the node, Moxley saw *Mir* for what it was. It reminded him of the plastic Habitrail hamster tube cities his parents bought for him in the Seventies. The ever-expandable habitat of modules and tubes, complete with treadmills and bottled food and endless busy-work, even smelled like the gerbil cages he had lovingly tended for a few weeks, then abandoned. That's us, he thought ruefully, swimming faster through the node and into the core living module: abandoned pets in a fancy cage.

One of the wags in his NASA support team had packed him some supplementary light reading that he only discovered a week after he'd arrived on the station. It was the full text of the 1998 House Science Committee Report, itemizing the many potentially lethal safety hazards aboard *Mir*, the rigidified incompetence of the Russian Space Agency's TsUP ground control, the cash-and-carry duplicity of cosmonauts who routinely covered up disasters, and the corruption at Energiya, the mostly private contractor that designed and operated *Mir* before and after the fall of the Soviet Union, and which had run the station and its human cargo into the ground. The recommendation of Congress two years ago had been that *Mir* be decommissioned and allowed to fall out of orbit, burning up in the atmosphere. In his dreams every night, it did, while they were still inside.

Ink-stamps in the margins beside the especially gut-wrenching passages gave the anonymous donors away: the PUSHies, a Bible-study group of spiritually flabby, childishly vindictive born-again astronauts. They were the kind of Christians who drove Moxley to lone-wolf spirituality—the well-fed, spoiled yuppie mystics who thanked God for everything, but asked for even more, as if God were a whipped parent with nothing better to do than stage-manage their super-biblically comfortable lives. If God did hear all their prayers, it logically followed that they were hogging His attention, and thus partly to blame for all the unchecked famine, disaster, plague and genocide in the world. He'd pissed them off once by posing this question at one of their weekly prayer brunches, and again by getting himself shoehorned into this mission. Their ubiquitous ink-stamps bore the two four-letter acronyms that defined the alpha and omega of their tedious creed: WWJD—"What Would Jesus Do?"—and PUSH—"Pray Until Something Happens."

Moxley crept across the core module, scrambled over the bundles of cable and ventilation hoses choking the mouth of the hatchway, and floated into the Kvant docking module, danger-close behind Arkady, who crowded the sealed docking port.

The Kurs automated docking system engaged as the ship approached the Kvant docking module, but true to form, the software crashed and aborted when the shuttle was only ten meters from the docking port. It backed away and immediately shot back at them at reckless speed, rolling to accept the docking collar on its dorsal surface, just behind its cockpit.

"What is it, Arkady?" he asked.

The mission commander only shrugged, grunted, "No radio contact."

There was no point in asking whether they'd heard from earth; out the porthole, he could see the piebald face of the South Pacific. They had radio contact for only fifteen minutes of every ninety-minute orbit, and were currently at the bottom of the black-out.

He found himself leaning as far over Arkady's shoulder as he could in hopes of getting a breath of fresh, or at least different, air from the ship. The air on *Mir* was synthesized from water distilled from their own urine, with all the springtime freshness such a process implied. The air of *Mir* stank of sweat and farts, fungi and the scorched maple syrup reek of antifreeze from leaks in the coolant system. Nobody trusted the SFOG solid-fuel oxygen generator canisters, which had caused a major fire in the Kvant module, four years ago. Every breath had been breathed in, and yawned, belched and farted out thousands upon thousands of times. Every story was told to death after the first month, and their faces had become meaningless elements of the cluttered environment of the station. Any change was welcome.

At the same time, he fought the urge to back away as far as he could. This ship had not come to take them home. Ergo, it was more people coming into an already unbearably claustrophobic place. They were practically castaways here, already, with only two more weeks worth of food and potable water left, and no resupply shuttle, no Progress drone on the way, which was probably a good thing, since one had crashed into *Mir* in 1997, and almost killed them all.

In his months aboard *Mir*, he had learned nothing if not how to think like a Russian. Astronauts expect safety and comfort; they expect good things to happen. Cosmonauts expect disaster, and they are seldom disappointed.

This was not what they needed, right now. It was one more enigma in an already unfathomable, unacceptable mystery. Literally anything could be behind that hatch, but nothing good.

"We're not expecting anybody?" Moxley probed.

Behind him, Ilya, the engineer, laughed and shoved aside billowing plastic sacks of trash they stored in the docking module. "We were expecting not to be here, so why tell us anything?"

The shuttle manually docked, and the docking port gasped and popped open readily enough after Ilya beat on it with a spanner. A crew-cut head on a meaty bull-neck jutted into the Kvant module. The cosmonaut regarded them blandly for a moment, then shook out a cigarette and lit it. Moxley watched the flame with a caveman's mixture of awe and fear. In zero-gravity, the flame from the gunmetal blue Zippo lighter was a perfect, expanding sphere, like a new sun.

There were three of them. Their commander took Arkady aside for a brief, heated exchange while the other two swooped through Kvant and the core module, ducked through the node and into Kvant 2 as if they had the layout memorized, and had been training in zero-G all their lives. Moxley looked to Ilya, but the engineer's morose frown kept him from speaking up. The commander barked something at Ilya, and he retreated, presumably to help the other two cosmonauts.

Arkady settled into the command center, a foxhole amid stacked computer monitors, joysticks, clipboards and manuals. He punched up EVA protocols. Moxley was aghast. Before an EVA was even seriously discussed, the cosmonauts always wrangled for hours with Energiya. Contracts had to be revised, bonus allotments had to be posted, and insurance rates adjusted. But their visitors weren't regular Energiya employees. These men moved like the cosmonauts of yore, like the second coming of Yuri Gagarin. They moved like soldiers. They wore black jumpsuits with a single red star on the shoulder. The commander had a silver eagle on the collar of his tunic. He had a pistol in a holster at his hip.

Five minutes later, the two commandos emerged from the airlock at the far end of Kvant 2 in *Mir* pressure suits and speed-crawled, hand over hand, down the science module and back out onto the core. The one time Ilya had outfitted Arkady for an EVA, it had taken an hour to suit them up and check all the safety systems. Moxley had never asked, or been invited, to go outside. Ilya crawled back into the core module and hovered by the hatch, staring hard at the back of the shuttle commander's head.

Moxley resisted an absurd urge to tap on the glass and salute as they passed his porthole. Had they been detailed to repair some critical experiment Arkady couldn't be trusted with? But no, they were creeping over the skin of their own ship, of which Moxley could only see the nose from Kvant. He moved node-wards to find a better vantage, but the shuttle commander blocked the way.

"What do you know about it?" he demanded. His accent was so thick he might have been cold-reading from a phrase book. Moxley didn't answer, couldn't, so lost was he in the stranger's face. It had been three months since he saw any living, breathing person aside from Arkady or Ilya. After such a lapse, a new person is a new species, speaking a new language, and must be acclimated to. Compounding the problem was the officer's face itself, which appeared carved out of flint, and turned molten before Moxley's startled eyes. "You were sent here to study. What did you learn?"

Moxley blinked. This was about him? About his wasted time in a can in orbit, watching something that defied all his understanding of astrophysics, and being able to tell no one on earth about it?

He told the commander what he'd told Houston. He made a production of it. He got out his charts, his spectrographic analyses, his gamma ray and X-ray images, hundreds of photographs.

From *Mir* he had logged eighteen separate events, documenting many of them extensively, given the limits of the outmoded, cranky Russian equipment, and the indeterminable nature of the event itself. At infrequent intervals, at a fixed point in space about a thousand miles above *Mir*, ordinary sunlight underwent an almost alchemical transformation into an energy that spiked all wavelengths in a complex pattern that overloaded his instruments, but left no quantifiable record at all, for a duration of one to six seconds. It was like hearing a cosmic symphony, when he could only perceive one percent of the notes.

That it was doing something meaningful, he could not dispute. It occurred at irregular intervals, but at very fixed locales, over the same precise points on the globe. Hovering just behind the terminator, it deflected the dying light of the setting sun onto northwestern Idaho; near Kiev in the Ukraine; several points in a belt across equatorial Africa; the Mato Grosso, in Brazil, and the foothills of coastal Peru; southeastern Iraq, hard by the Iranian border. He was no closer to knowing what caused it. He watched the sky and saw nothing until it occurred, and then he could see only the light. He showed the commander the few photographs that captured even a breath of the ugly majesty of the phenomenon. How the light twisted on itself and seemed to curdle as it poured down. It lasted for only a few seconds, and was visible for even shorter duration, but each glimpse was like a vision of some new, unimaginable eternity.

The commander sat back from the dining table and studied his work. He lit a cigarette, oblivious to Moxley's hacking. For weeks after arrival, Moxley had been prone to sneezing fits from the fungi that thrived in every nook and cranny of the old space station. Ilya once told him that the cosmic radiation had warped the stray spores that cosmonauts brought up on their feet and in their hair. Athlete's foot learned to live on nylon and vinyl, and bread molds became free-floating colonies of black nastiness that burst if touched. The cigarette smoke was many, many times worse.

"What do *you* think is, that does this?" the commander finally asked. He held up a photograph of the light over the Ukraine. Lines around his eyes deepened, and his mouth contorted into a mirthless smile. Moxley had seen this look enough at Star City to know it meant he was being tested.

"May I speak freely?" he asked, looking around for support. Arkady stayed welded to his screens, too keyed-up by what he saw to blink. Ilya, wincing and clutching his stomach like always, nodded at him. The commander's face reddened, released tiny bursts of live steam. Fine, then. "I think it's a manmade object, maybe some kind of directed energy weapon, except I can't see it or ping radar off it, or read heat from its thrusters or its power source, even though it ought to be hotter than Chernobyl for hours after it discharges, if it's a laser. If it's some kind of solar-powered lens, it should be the size of Texas, to register gamma rays like it does, but I can't see it. And I don't have any idea what it's doing. Right now, I couldn't even tell you for sure that it wasn't God, signaling the Second Coming."

"This is all you know?" The commander gestured to the sheaves of non-data on the dining table. It was all stuck to the table with refrigerator magnets, Sherman's many F's in Astrophysics.

"A lot of scientists on earth probably know a lot more about it than me, by now. Working alone like this, with the equipment problems, the comm breakdowns…I do know quite a bit about elementary physics, though, like how incredibly fucking stupid it would be to discharge a firearm in zero-gravity, not to mention inside a pressurized spacecraft. Why the hell do you have a pistol in outer space, anyway, Commander?"

"Dr. Moxley, is enough," Arkady grunted, but Moxley wasn't done.

"Why are you here, Commander? We were expecting a shuttle to come and take us home. Is it coming? What are you doing here?"

The commander vaulted out of his seat and over the command center, heading for Kvant. He turned and smiled at Moxley. "I don't know when you will go home. We are here only to fix broken satellite." He dove into his space-plane and closed the docking port.

A few minutes later, the shuttle disengaged from *Mir* and pushed itself away. Moxley went to the porthole and watched as it seemed to drop back towards earth for a minute. The dorsal surface of the shuttle was open, just like on an American shuttle. The two suited commandos sat in seats in the open compartment. They'd worked fast. Something that looked like seventy feet of aluminum train track extended out of the open back of the shuttle, and Moxley recognized it for the physicist's dream-toy that it was—a rail gun.

"Who the hell are they, Ilya? Arkady? What the hell is going on, here?"

Arkady watched the monitors. Ilya looked out the porthole at the retreating thrusters of the black shuttle. He looked like he hadn't slept since he got here. "We were not supposed to be here, still."

"What do you mean?" Moxley got chills. He started thinking like a Russian.

"They're going to shoot it down," Ilya said.

"What? Shoot what down?"

Arkady tapped on the monitor in front of him. Moxley climbed over to him, clumsily, because the walls were buried in items Velcro-strapped in place–laptops, CD stacks, clipboards, food pouches... He looked over Arkady's shoulder, puzzled for a moment until he realized he was seeing a camera feed from onboard the black shuttle.

"What was that ship? Were those guys cosmonauts?"

Arkady and Ilya glued to the monitors. Not looking, but looking away.

Finally, Ilya answered him. "In Eighties, brain-dead cowboy President—dyes hair, listens to astrologer—talks big fight. Talks about Star Wars—A-OK fucking movie, but stupid, stupid asshole plan. Russians don't believe empty talk, but prepare. While you talk, we prepare for war in space." He pointed at the monitor. "BOR assault space-plane, shuttle interceptor, satellite-killer. We see now, you were not all talk, either. Stupid, palm-reading cowboy built Star Wars orbital energy weapon, and forgot about it."

Moxley blanched at the steel in Ilya's tone. "But we don't have any orbital weapons," he shot back, but he was less sure of himself with each syllable. Where did all that money go, in the defense spending-mad Eighties? He knew the government was stupid, but he'd never really believed they'd plunked down for six hundred-dollar toilet seats. He'd used those toilets. They invariably clogged.

"He said it's not yours anymore," Arkady said.

"What's that supposed to mean? Anyway, who were those soldiers? Because they sure as hell weren't cosmonauts."

"*Spetsialnoje Naznachenie*," Arkady spat. "Spetznaz. Like your Green Berets, only tough."

"I want to talk to the ground," Moxley said.

"No. No radio. They listen."

"Well, the hell with them, and both of you, and your whole shitty country. Unless you have a pistol too, Arkady—" He floated over to the ham radio they used to talk with the ground, but Ilya blocked him, hands out, palms open and empty. His droopy face hid no malice or violence, only terror. Sweat pasted his coverall to his shallow, fluttering chest. His hand clutched absently at his stomach. "Please, Sherman. We're over fucking Atlantic Ocean. Nobody would hear you, but them."

"What are they going to do?"

"I don't want to know," Ilya shouted, his voice cracking, "nor do you. In old days, Spetznaz never fix satellite. They kill things—commandos, like your Rambo, yes? Kill foreigners, kill terrorists, kill anyone who sees them. Nobody believe they still exist, you know? Gone to mercenary work in Chechnya and Bosnia, other shithole countries. This is bad, Sherman, very bad. If not for you here, I think we would be in very big fucking trouble."

"What do you mean?"

"This is shit most serious, Sherman! Russian cosmonauts are expendable, even now. But you are American, big TV star astronaut, very, very famous, with you here, we are safe, I think."

"But Ilya—nobody in America knows I'm here."

Ilya's face drained of blood. "Oh shit, then we are fucked the most, I think."

From the beginning, it had all seemed too good to be true. Moxley was not even a front-line astronaut, but a research physicist who had worked extensively with NASA on radiation experiments in space. He'd always dreamed, naturally, of going up himself, but there were hundreds of real astronauts prowling around Johnson Space Center who would never go up, many with better qualifications as scientists, never mind their training. When they asked him in July if he'd like to go to *Mir*, he looked for the hidden camera, figuring for sure it was a prank, and not even an especially believable one. There was an urgent situation that required in-orbit analysis, and the Russians were putting together a classified mission to go back up to *Mir*, which would be emptied of its last official crew in August. Could he go to Russia next month?

He was still dubious when they flew him to Russia the following week, still looking for the punch-line as he sweated out three months of marathon cram sessions in Russian language and astronautics training, but the workload was so demanding, he never paused to wonder whether this was or wasn't really happening, let alone ask why they were sending him. It was a dream come true, and he was scared to make a peep of dissent, lest he wake up.

The politics of who got to go up were so legendarily Byzantine that he did not really believe he was anything more than a back-up, a third- or fourth-string understudy. The greased slide he stepped on had to be some sort of test of emergency readiness, because there seemed to be no emergency. It wasn't like those dumb action space movies, with the asteroid or the comet or whatever hurtling towards earth, and hysteria and looting, with the maverick demolitions crew being rushed through training. He was just another greenhorn American to the Russian trainers at Star City, and when his training was up on October 30, and they told him he was going up tomorrow, he thought it was only another joke.

It was neither a joke nor a test, though in the ordeal of launch from Baikonur on Halloween, he asked God repeatedly if it was not both. In the ensuing months aboard *Mir*, he'd had plenty of time, when he wasn't helping to repair some critically failing system, to wonder what he was doing here. With only Arkady and Ilya for company, with none of the fame and media attention that America lavished on its astronauts, lukewarm though it was in the shuttle era, he'd had only his assignment to keep him focused—observing and recording a phenomenon for which he still had no explanation. When the leaden-voiced taskmasters on the ground received his data, they offered no advice, no reaction. When the day of their scheduled return came and went without any sign of a shuttle, they offered only the location of a secret cache of "psychological support rations"—plastic bags of vodka—in lieu of an explanation. That was a week ago.

It was a joke indeed, on him, on space travel, and on science itself.

An hour later, Arkady called them back to the command center. Moxley watched from the telescope in the Priroda science module, but all he could see was the ass-end of the Russian space-plane, its thrusters blazing full-tilt, then shutting off, attitude jets along the flattened fuselage venting plumes of gas like escaping atmosphere.

The Russians had canned their Buran shuttle program in 1991 after only one test flight, but he once heard that they tested a low orbit space-plane in the early Eighties as an interceptor for the American space shuttle. The program was discontinued after the *Challenger* disaster caused NASA to abandon Vandenberg, rendering the interceptor unfeasible. Obviously, the paranoid fuckers never stopped testing, because the BOR space-plane he was looking at was far in advance of anything even on the drawing boards at NASA.

And nobody knew it was up here.

The space-planes were delivered into orbit by hypersonic aircraft, not rockets, so its launch probably would have gone unnoticed. He looked down at the darkened earth, a looming wall of azure and moon-chased, lacy rosettes of maritime storm. They were over Africa, bearing northeast in a night-cycle orbit. If memory served, they wouldn't come over a radar station capable of picking them up for another few hours. Were the United States and Russia at war? Did the United States even know, yet? In the last six weeks, he'd gotten to see the cosmonauts at their worst, raging at the ground and at *Mir* and often at him. But they weren't pissed at him. They were confused and scared. Arkady said it wasn't ours anymore. What the hell did that mean?

The terminator raced across the face of the earth like a cosmic brushfire, an effect that never failed to still Moxley's racing mind and lift him outside himself. Even now, he had only to watch the world light up like the eye of God awakening to their presence, and none of it mattered quite so much.

Moxley was a devout Christian who had yet to find a rigorous enough faith that would accept the wonders science had revealed about the universe—evolution, genetics, quantum theory, the possibility of extraterrestrial life. To take as literal gospel a book that so many cabals of zealots, Papal censors and conniving monarchs had raped and mutilated for their own ends was sheer foolishness. Would it be such a blow to God, to deny that He created the Heavens ten billion years ago, and the Earth and the Sun five billion years later, and then set into motion the self-perpetuating process of life and consciousness? Moxley believed that it was a sinful act to reduce God to the level of a poorly conceived character in a shoddily written book, and deny Him the genius to have set the universe in motion to grow and change and know itself, as it grew to love and understand its Creator. No matter how big, or how old, science made the universe, outside it all, waiting for them, was God.

Up here, he could feel God looking at him, and seeing that what they were doing was good. In this place, in defiance of all the laws of nature, humans reached out to other worlds as their remotest ancestors reached out when they crawled onto land for the first time and breathed with the first lungs. This was evolution he was witnessing, and he knew in his heart at moments like this that it was what God wanted.

When he heard Arkady shouting, he raced back to the command center and watched the grainy feed from the shuttle-cam.

Ilya and the commander sat before the monitors. Neither of them looked up when he swam in, but Ilya waved him over. "Come and see this, Sherman."

He crowded in behind the cosmonauts and stared into the main screen, but he had a difficult time resolving what he saw with what could possibly be out there.

"They found it, I think," Ilya said. Arkady scratched at his face and stared, mute, unblinking.

Devoid of perspective up there in the dark, it looked like a flashlight. It was a tapered black cylinder with a cone-shaped protrusion at one end. Filling the view from the ascending space-plane, the object leapt into stark relief as the terminator splashed across it. The sunlight brought out its texture, which was only half metal.

It had solar collectors like *Mir*, great, razor-edged sails that radiated out like the petals of a daisy from the blunt end opposite the cone. But they were unmistakably organic, translucent, fleshy constructs that looked like a hybrid of flower petals and bat wings.

The body of the satellite was flat black metal plate which deflected the raw rays of the sun away from itself. But between the plates, like protoplasmic mortar, a web of shifting organic matter—one could be no more specific than that—crawled and seethed, as if the body of the satellite only barely contained something alive.

The picture shuddered and flickered, went to snow for a moment. Arkady snarled and pounded on the monitor, but the picture snapped back on its own. A swiftly shrinking object left the space-plane at such velocity that the camera recorded it only as a trail, and hurtled at the satellite at better than four kilometers per second.

It vanished quite suddenly, but the satellite seemed to have an eternity to move out of its path. A full second. They were still eight miles away from it. Moxley gasped. The resolution on the video had lied to him. It was enormous, at least forty feet in length, not counting the vast organic appendages growing out of it, which grew and splayed themselves out like a net for the oncoming plane.

Attitude jets all down the satellite's sides ejected clouds of cool, inert gas to swing it clear of the projectile. One membranous solar petal ripped away, and the satellite tumbled end over end.

The space-plane banked and soared over the satellite, then dove, rolled and came up under it.

Afforded this uncomfortably close view, Moxley found it harder to deny that it was a coherent animal lifeform, but it was also a working machine whose purpose he could not begin to guess.

The narrow end contained a lens, about five feet across. The remaining solar fans retracted into the body, and more and more tentacles slithered out of the cracks in the metal to flail at the void.

The cone-shaped end was about ten feet in length, and looked like a closed night-blooming flower, with tightly folded petals made of aluminum girders and some kind of glass or crystal. It did something ugly, Moxley thought, something unholy, to the sunlight. A strange, twisted corona played around the cone that utterly baffled the video camera.

The audio feed crackled. "Commander Zamyatin, Dr. Moxley, you have vodka aboard *Mir*, no? We will be thirsty, this after…"

The rail gun fired.

The satellite opened like a flower. Its collection lens was turned to face the sun.

With another burst of gas, the satellite simply wasn't there when the projectile flashed past it. Its orientation was off, so that when the open flower faced the camera, the effect was dazzling, and not blinding.

The radial symmetry of the flower-lens was hypnotic in its complexity, so much so that Moxley knew it had not been built, so much as grown. It was a weapon, but something happened to it up here. Something had grown inside it, and made it its own—not merely as a weapon, but as a body, for its evasion was not the product of programming or a joystick-wielding ops controller on the ground. It was a live thing, as well as a machine, and it was smarter than them.

The lens-petals shed an intensifying glow of hideous force, amplifying the sunlight, but also perverting it. This was what he'd seen all those times, all those baffling astrophysical events that, at the time, he'd thought were merely strange and beautiful.

The satellite rolled again as the glow blanked out most of the screen.

"What's it doing?" Moxley babbled. "It's not going to hit them—"

"Idiot!" Arkady snapped. "It's not aiming at them!"

Moxley had a second to process this when the core module filled with silvery blue light like the other eye of God looking at him, and turning him to salt.

Blue-white light became glittering purple blackness. The only light source was the moonlight peeking in through the windows in the inert core module. The command center was off-line. The oxygen generators were silent. Moxley felt a bulkhead against his back, but none of the subtle, eternal thrumming of the complex of life support and information systems that had become as familiar to him as his own pulse. *Mir* was dead.

Moxley felt as if he were dying inside, too. His bowels and brains ached as if someone had run them through a taffy puller. His eyes and skin burned, and his muscles were as tender as wet rice paper. His teeth felt like they were going to fall out of his head.

He tried and tried, but he couldn't remember it, the moment that God had touched them. No offense intended, he knew it was, in the end, only some kind of awful machine, but it had the transcendent aura of religious ecstasy. He knew they'd been microwaved by something far more awful in its destructive power than any laser platform the Pentagon ever fantasized about, but he couldn't shake the free-floating mantle of joy that seized him in those odd moments when he forgot to be terrified.

Perhaps it was the voice, which, aside from the light itself, was all he could remember. It was like all the voices of all the peoples of earth, speaking all the words of every language in the same infinitely recycled instant, their voices growing louder and louder, even as they became one voice.

Moxley gingerly probed the dark in front of him. Arkady and Ilya had each done two other turns on *Mir*. They would be somewhere on the station, bringing the systems back online, restoring power and communications. The Russians had a plan for this kind of unprecedented event. He remembered that he'd heard them talking about it. What did they call it? Oh yeah, the Coffin Scenario.

His hand passed through something wet and warm that he hoped was only someone's floating vomit, then he touched fabric and flesh just above his head.

Arkady groaned, and the meat under Moxley's fingers convulsed and kicked at him. A knee smashed his nose, which splattered like a tomato, and the commander seemed to go mad. Screaming in Russian, he lashed out at the walls, sending equipment of every description ricocheting around the module. Something small but heavy dented Moxley's forehead as he dove for cover in what he hoped was the direction of the node.

"Arkady, stop it!" he shouted, but his voice was a rasping croak. When he breathed, his lungs seemed to fill with foam, and when he coughed he could see the venous network of his eyelids emblazoned on the dark. Fluid gushed out of his nose and mouth, his ears and asshole.

Where the hell was Ilya?

In the node, he blundered headfirst into a sheet of floating coolant globules. He inhaled a bunch. Ethylene glycol, the nasty green shit that goes in radiators. He choked and vomited again, rolling through the coolant cloud and hitting the curved wall hard enough to drive the rest of the coolant from his lungs, but mercifully cushioned by a Gordian tangle of hoses and cords. He clung to them and tried to get his bearings.

He had to get to the ham radio in Spektr module, it was battery-powered—but whom would he call? Even if he could reach someone, the Russians were up here waging war on an American-made satellite. Why the hell hadn't they been told anything? Why the hell were they still up here?

Screw the radio. He had to get Ilya to help with Arkady, and they had to get in the Soyuz capsule. Abandon ship. He wondered if they could do it. He felt so sick, and the commander had clearly gone into shock, if not out of his mind. Even at their best, on a secret mission, they would almost rather die than abandon the decrepit old deathtrap. He hoped Ilya was fixing whatever had gone wrong. He had studied *Mir*'s systems at Star City for three months, and followed the space station avidly on the Internet for years, but the cosmonauts hadn't let him participate in most of the desperate toil required just to keep *Mir* alive, so he didn't have any idea where Ilya could be. If only he weren't so sick, if only the lights—

The lights flickered on. The Elektron oxygen generators gurgled and spat air. The whole station rocked like a boat leaving harbor, slowly subsiding into its normal rhythm.

"Alright, Ilya!" he croaked. "Ilya?"

He tried to remember the Coffin Scenario protocols. They called for rounding up all the stored batteries on the station, cumbersome blocks sealed up in the floor and buried under years of clutter. All of them had to be brought to the core module and wired to the solar arrays to be recharged. The Sirius *Mir* 23 crew in 1997 had to do it, and the whole process took several hours, and the station's systems weren't up to full again for two days. So it wasn't a full power failure, but a simple computer glitch, the kind of thing the Russians said happened all the time, and usually fixed itself.

Everything was back to normal.

He laughed, but gagged on the slime of ethylene glycol coating his tongue. His eyes burned, frying in his head like eggs. His brain was still spinning, even more panicked now that the lights were on, and he could see how normal things weren't.

In the core module, Arkady hung in mid-air in a fetal position, turning over and over like a dead moon, orbited by constellations of loose and broken gear. He was unconscious, or worse. Ilya was an unknown quantity. Had he gone outside?

Whatever *Mir* was doing, they had to get back down to earth. They were sick, but not beyond help—he hoped. The satellite was still out there. The Spetznaz crew was still out there. He had to find Ilya and get Arkady into the Soyuz, and get the hell out of Dodge.

This isn't the damned Kremlin, it's one tiny space station. You can find one man. He willed himself to be calm, said a little prayer, and started looking.

Even with antifreeze in his eyes and Lord-knows-what clogging his nose, he found Ilya by following the smell.

Something assaulted his senses as he stuck his head into the Kvant 2 science module, a relatively unused portion of the station except for its EVA airlock, and the distinction of having *Mir*'s only functioning toilet.

The toilet stall door swung open as he passed, the smell rolling out like ink in water, a palpable, rancid wave that sent him frantically kicking to the far end of the module.

His first thought was that the reclamation system had backed up, but he knew it was nothing so pleasant. It was a rotten smell, a death smell. He had a freezer filled with blood, tissue and urine samples in this module, maybe that could account for it. He had begun to notice a certain sour odor after processing Ilya's samples in recent weeks. Perhaps when the power failed, there had been some sort of chemical reaction…

As if to shut up his hopeful speculations, the door to the space toilet swung wide.

Ilya was deader than anything he'd ever seen in his life. He floated just above the solid waste collector, which old NASA salts lovingly called the "shitmitt," tethered in place by a catheter hose wound several times around his forearm. The arm had swollen up so much the hose had totally disappeared in the purple-gray folds.

Ilya's head bobbed forward as if the little flight engineer was trying to stand, but noisome pockets of gas shifting within his bloated abdomen were the cause. Hair drifted away from his bald scalp in sad, mud-brown clumps. His skin was translucent, and looked like an overstuffed sausage. Underneath, muscle, tendon, bones, and fat were reducing to a homogenous paste. On earth, he probably would have split open and soaked into the soil by now.

In his last moments, Ilya had torn open his "penguin suit," the bright red nylon coverall the cosmonauts wore to work. His chest and belly were swollen to three times their normal girth. The flesh throbbed and shifted as if something more than just gas struggled to get out of him.

Moxley let loose a scream and rolled, kicked the toilet door shut. It slammed on Ilya's head, swung back at him.

Moxley caught the door to shield himself from Ilya's body, which lolled out into the module like a gruesome, liquid-filled balloon. To close the door, he would have to touch it.

Ilya's scalp had ruptured where the door clipped it. Pulpy strands of liquid head waved in the fetid air. Do it, he ordered himself. One hand pushed Ilya in the chest, sank up to the second knuckle in mush where his rib cage should have been. He recoiled, kicking at the body, reaching for the door, when he saw the chrome mirror on the inside of it.

In the harsh fluorescent light, Ilya looked gray-green and bloated, hollowed-out and filled with rot. He looked like nothing so much as a bag of trash, except his eyes, though bloodshot and glazed, still looked back at him.

We're not going to make it. We're not—

WWJD, Sherman? Why don't you just PUSH?

Gingerly, lips sputtering out a chattering prayer, he sealed the toilet.

He was the sole survivor, but he didn't have much time. If what happened here was going to have any meaning at all, he had to get word to the ground.

He crawled back to Spektr module to clean himself up, when he chanced to peer into the eyepiece of the astronomical telescope. It was still set to the coordinates at which he'd last observed the terrible lightshow.

It was still going on.

He adjusted the magnification to bring the scene to maximum resolution, gazed at it until his eyes teared up.

The BOR hung in space, moving a few meters per second, if at all. The rail gun track and the starboard wing torn away, the dorsal loading doors flung wide open to reveal only streaming debris. The satellite hove into view and grappled the battered hulk, dragging it closer with an ever-thickening web of tentacles.

Such was his shock and dismay with the universe, that he could finally see what was happening for what it was. Increasingly, the images seemed to translate into another titanic natural battle which no one had ever witnessed, but which left its mark on the ocean as a harbinger of what unspeakable things lay beneath the sea. For did the black Soviet BOR space-plane not look like a sperm whale in mortal combat with its most formidable prey, the giant squid, in the light-less depths of the ocean? But the whales usually won...the tentacles—things of flesh, of nature, perverted into some mockery of the most mysterious dweller in the seas—pried the space-plane open wider, wriggling greedily into the pressurized spaces inside.

Something came out fighting. A humanoid figure in a bulky Orlan spacesuit tumbled out of the smashed fuselage and fired something into the satellite's huge black body, and then it all disappeared in a white glow. The vast crystalline rose of the lens array shattered, spilling curdled scalar light across the heavens, and all too quickly, it was only darkness, again, the space-plane and the satellite both swallowed up by nothingness.

"Yes, everything is changing, is it not, Sherman?"

He jumped. Ilya hovered in the mouth of the hatch like a ghost—white as a sheet, and damp, reeking of death and something that lay underneath death. "My stomach—it was cancer, you know? It is all better, now."

"Ilya," Moxley gobbled, "I thought you—that I was all alone—"

"Oh, you *are* all alone, Sherman," Ilya rasped. "Everything is changing, my stupid American friend. Now you are the sick one, and we are the strong. Think of Sergei Krikalev, who went up in '91 a Soviet, and returned to find there was no USSR. No more Union. Nothing compared to the changes that are coming."

The flight engineer ducked back into the node, and Moxley followed, because he was sure he was hallucinating, and wanted to see the phantasm disappear.

"There will be a Union again, Sherman. We were right all along, but we did not go far enough."

Moxley blinked and rubbed his burning eyes, and prayed some more, but there it was, wearing Ilya's face and body, but it *wasn't* Ilya.

Ilya's short, reedy torso was slightly elongated, but his arms and legs bent and twisted bonelessly, like snakes. His hands were nearly as long as his forearms, fingers like a spider lobster's legs, spears of multi-jointed bone with pads of flesh on the tips. His feet had opposable thumbs. He moved over the tangled, cluttered walls of the module like something that had been living and evolving in zero-gravity for millions of years. His eyes glowed the same silvery gray light that had killed him and Arkady.

The adapted cosmonaut swam into Kvant 2, turned and faced him just inside the hatch. Moxley paused in the node, unable to look directly at the thing, but striving with all his might not to look at the yawning mouth of the Soyuz capsule.

Ilya tore a panel off the wall with one bare hand. The more reliable of *Mir*'s two Elektron oxygen generators lay exposed, a snarl of coolant hoses spilling out like intestines into Ilya's face.

"Look at all of this," Ilya said, and Moxley was most startled by, of all things, his voice, for it was an older man, speaking unaccented English. "Look at all the machines you need, to keep you alive. Look at how clumsy your body is, up here, Sherman. How fragile."

Moxley dove away from Ilya and into the nearest hatch, into the Soyuz. No, he'd gotten turned around. He was back in Spektr. Shit!

He turned and tried to duck back out, but Ilya swarmed around the node like a spider monkey, all arms and legs and laughing like a lunatic, and swung in front of the hatch to trap him.

Moxley hovered just in front of him, paralyzed.

"You Americans never understand long-term space habitation, Sherman. You never learn. Not like Russian cosmonauts. We know that to survive up here, you must be flexible. You must adapt."

Moxley slammed the hatch shut.

For about an hour, it was quiet. Moxley changed his shorts and treated himself to a moist towelette bath, then drank a bottle of water and wolfed down some Fig Newtons from his snack stash. He almost immediately threw it all up.

He felt weak, he could see weird ghosts fluttering around on the fringes of his vision, he wanted to curl up and go to sleep, and maybe never wake up. But he had something to do. The world had to know.

He warmed up the ham radio and leafed through his notebook for the frequencies he could try. He had no idea where they were, or what time it was, and his vision was too blurry to read his own handwriting in the damned book. There were two Russian receivers at Baikonur and in Siberia, and another in Germany. NASA had two radar stations tracking for them, but even during optimum comm pass slots, the signal was shaky at best, and good for little more than sending e-mail packets in short bursts. His chances of fishing blindly and finding something were next to nil, but he had to do something, if only to stay awake.

The circuits warmed up and immediately, an American voice was saying his name.

"Dr. Moxley, if you can hear me, please pick up."

Delirium washed over him. It was like waking up from it all, even if he was still in it. Someone knew he was up here! Someone American knew he was up here. It had to be Houston. He had given up on the bastards, but he should've known they'd be keeping tabs on him.

"Oh thank God, Houston, I'm so damned glad to hear your voices! Those crazy damned Russians started a war up here with something—"

"We're aware of the situation," said the American voice, and let out a clipped, tired sigh before closing the channel.

"What, how is that, Houston? We've been out of radio contact since before—"

About three hours ago, when he woke up and saw it flying up to them, and thought he was going home.

"This isn't Houston."

"What? Say again—"

"This is not Houston. Now, the entire station has been irradiated, is that correct?"

Moxley shook his head, trying to make everything fall in place. They wanted to know the facts, but they already knew the facts, more than he did, and Ilya—

On the other side of the hatch, he could hear Ilya talking to him, but he couldn't make out the words.

"Please verify that the satellite was destroyed, Dr. Moxley. Can you verify?"

"What? You mean the—" The thing had only looked like a satellite, but inside— "Yes, it's—the Russians blew it up, but they—I think they're all dead, but—it—it's gone, I think—"

"Now, are you the only survivor, Sherman?"

"Um—no…I mean, Arkady is probably dead, and I feel pretty sick, but I inhaled some coolant, so I could be okay, but—"

"That's a lot of uncertainties, son," said the American voice. "What about the flight engineer? Ilya Lyubov? What's his status?"

"He's—nearby. I mean, he—"

Go ahead. You're a scientist. You were sent up here at enormous taxpayer expense to explain an anomalous event. Explain this.

"Go ahead, Sherman. What's wrong with him?"

"Well, he said—he always said his gut hurt, you know? But he hid it from the doctors, so they couldn't ground him. And then, when the light hit us, he crawled off to die, and I saw his body, it was—"

"And now?"

"He's, changed…how the hell do you know about any of this? Who the hell are you?"

Something scraped against the other side of the hatch, Sharpened steel, heavy. That'd be the cable cutters, monster pruning shears which the cosmonauts called the Guillotine.

"We're here to help you, Sherman. Taking time to explain would only lessen the possibility of getting you out of there."

"Getting me out?" Moxley suddenly came alive.

"That's what we want to help you do, if you don't want to die."

"Okay, I don't want to die—"

"Good, now, you're sure you're in Spektr module, the one the Russians call O module?"

"Damn it, I've lived here six weeks, I think I know—"

"Good. The Russians have a few pieces of gear they never told NASA about, and you're right on top of one of them. Go to the far end of the module with a flat-head screwdriver."

He grabbed one from a folded canvas tool caddy and swam through the maze of instruments. The Guillotine slammed into the hatch again, making him flinch in mid-flight and crash into the KFA, a massive camera crammed into the back of the module. It formed the back wall of his sleeping niche, a nylon bag velcroed to the wall beside the porthole, and a net hammock stuffed with books, notes and miscellaneous space crap.

He looked at the floor, shifting junk out of the way until he found a corner of a floor plate and a badly corroded, but still-effective screw. He got it out and searched for the second one.

"Are you still there?" he asked the headset.

"Yes, we're standing by. Have you got it open?"

"No, I'm looking for the other edges. But just so I have at least a few seconds' forewarning, what the hell am I going to find down here, and what do you expect me to do with it?"

The anonymous ground controller snorted at him. "That'll be pretty self-explanatory when you get it open. Now move!"

He waited until just after Ilya smashed the hatch with the Guillotine before he opened it and came out. In his fevered, adrenalized brain, he thought the little flight engineer would be spent and hyperextended, and the Guillotine down. Ilya was not Ilya, but he was still some kind of man, and he would respond to what he had in his hand the way all men did, when you used it.

He yanked up the hatch, which slid into its housing halfway and then jammed. The snapping steel beak of the Guillotine filled the space and sliced at his head. He reared back and suddenly remembered what was in his hand, jammed it into the hole and squeezed off three shots.

When he took the ugly little black pistol out of its hiding place behind a battery, his hand didn't want to hold it, and set it spinning before his dazed, burning eyes. It was like a snake, he thought. You think it'll feel slimy, but it's hard and cold and smooth. "This is a .12-caliber gyro-needle gun. It fires ten rounds, but only with the safety off. It's recoilless, the rounds ignite and go like little rockets, but there's still a kick in micro-gravity, so brace yourself. Don't take the safety off until you get to the hatch, but for God's sake, don't forget."

He hadn't. He followed the pistol through the half-open hatch and into the node, panic-firing once more into Kvant 2. The gyrorocket round smashed into the far wall with a flat smacking sound. Special rocket-propelled needles that crumple on impact, so as not to puncture the hull when putting down a mutiny—or foreign spies.

He looked around. All was still, but for the grumbling of the oxygen generators and the carbon-dioxide scrubbers. A generous arc of blood drifted past, mingling with the omnipresent globs of coolant. The Guillotine floated by his head, and he grabbed it, but it was impossible to wield with one hand, so he pushed it back into Spektr. He peeked around the corner into the Soyuz capsule. The wires were pulled or cut, neat, severed piles of spaghetti blocking the mouth of the capsule. Only the readiness lights blinked inside, but there was nowhere for anyone to hide. It was like that insipid American movie the Russians gleefully tormented him with, whenever they weren't ogling *Mir*'s capacious library of Italian softcore porn. The one where the sole survivor gets into the lifeboat and blasts off, only to find the creature waiting for her in there…

Gun-first, he dove for the capsule.

Something swooped down out of Priroda module, directly above his head. A hand clutched his wrist and twisted the gun away. He looked up to see that the "hand" grew out of Ilya's pants-cuff, where he had until recently had a foot. The leg flexed, wrapped twice around Moxley's arm, pointed the gun back at his head.

Moxley looked up. Ilya hung by his hands from the mouth of the hatch, his legs bending all the wrong ways in so many of the wrong places. Moxley tried only to get out of his reach, because touching it meant it was real.

"Help me, God, please help me—"

"What's the situation, Sherman?" asked the American voice.

Ilya's other prehensile foot caught Moxley's wildly flapping free arm and lifted him into Priroda. Ilya threw him across the science module, charged after and pounced on him with all four grasping hands before Moxley's hurtling body reached the far wall.

He hit so hard, Moxley was dazed and lost. The headset cracked, his skull rang and grated, but through it all, like a ray of sunlight piercing the darkness of the bottom of a well, he heard the American voice crackling in his ear.

"Say again, what is the situation up there, Sherman, over?"

Ilya's hands clutched his neck, shredding the muscles in an iron grip, but he didn't choke Moxley. "Tell them, Sherman, explain the situation."

"I'm—help, he's got me, and he's hurting me—"

"Where are you, right now, Sherman? And where is he?"

"We—oh God, oh shit—we're in Priroda—"

"You're both in Priroda, right now? Is the hatch sealed?"

"No, but—I can't get to Soyuz, he's on top of me—"

"You've got to fight him, Sherman. Use the damned gun, for Christ's sake."

He reached out for the gun tumbling end over end just out of his grasp. Ilya grabbed his hair, and every last strand of it just came out and fluttered away, oh God, he was so sick, but he was still alive, he could fight.

"I can't—"

Moxley kicked out from the floor, flying up with Ilya on his back, but the mutant cosmonaut arrested their flight and shoved back, driving him into the floor face-first and bending his legs backwards until he howled.

"Sherman, this is very important, listen to me, now. Is he the only one who's—changed?"

"He and I are the only ones alive—"

"And you're both still in the Priroda science module, the one NASA calls R block?"

"Yes, do something, do something, please, God!"

"We have a contingency plan in place, Sherman."

"Good, do it, please, he's killing me!"

"I'm very sorry, Dr. Moxley," said the American voice, and the headset went dead.

"How painful, to discover that one is expendable," Ilya whispered in his ear.

Moxley thrashed one last time, putting all his strength into getting the gun, but when he pushed off the floor, the whole module shook and seemed to drop out from around him, so that he smashed into the porthole.

Whatever Ilya said next was lost in the roar of the module being explosively ejected from the *Mir* station. Rolling out of control from the trajectory set by the tiny explosives in the node's coupling ports, Priroda was sent spinning like a torpedo at the earth. A blasting wind sucked at Moxley, but he clutched the rim of the porthole and looked out at the unbelievable view of the earth.

"Do you see me, God?" he screamed into the wind.

The hatch slammed most of the way shut, but cables clogged the mouth. Ilya leapt off him and tore the cables free, sealed the hatch and turned to smile at Moxley.

"We still have a few minutes before we burn up, Sherman. How do you propose we pass the time?"

Moxley pressed his face against the porthole and prayed.

"That's right, Sherman. Pray Until Something Happens, yes?"

He kept on praying, and presently, something happened, but it wasn't what he'd prayed for, at all.

~ 28 ~

She woke up in the back of a van.

Outside, champagne-colored dawn broke and scattered in rainbow prisms on rolling snowfields. They were on a two-lane highway somewhere in Wyoming and bearing down on a place called Muddy Gap, according to a buckshot-chewed sign. She felt sick when she sat up, so she lay back down. She saw him behind the wheel, but she did not really see him. What she saw was a big man she didn't recognize, because he had no skin. What little meat did cling to his bones looked like chum from a shark-bucket. She assumed it was Him, because it was always Him, everybody was Him, or would be. Or it was a dream.

But in dreams, things happened, and here, the van only kept rolling, and the sun kept rising, and the man's skin grew back. He stopped and topped off the gas in Muddy Gap, and filled the back of the van with fruit and meat and juice and jugs of water and Gatorade, freshly laundered winter clothes and wool blankets. Head swimming, feverish, she tried to eat, but nausea overtook her. She vomited for what felt like hours, thick black and red fluid and clumps of tissue, everything she had inside coming out in a jet. He stopped and came back and held her head through the worst of it, and she tried to hurt him when he got close enough, but he held her arms at her sides and whispered, "Get Him out, get Him all out of you," over and over again, and when she realized this felt too awful to be a dream, she fell asleep.

And when she woke up again, she was in Colorado, and he was telling her she was safe, everything would be all right.... She was cold. Her mouth tasted like shit and afterbirth. She drank a gallon of water and ate some fruit.

He sat watching her, his face masked by the shadows of the gathering dusk and the fog of his breath. Snow dripped from his coat, he'd been outside—

"What did you do to me?" she demanded between gulps. Her voice was an airless croak.

He shrugged. "You feel better?"

"I—I don't know—" Her skin was crusted with a slime that flaked away when she touched it, and smelled like sewage and the tomb and the ocean floor and Him. Her hands were ragged, tattered sticks, her clothes rags held together by dried blood. When she looked inside herself, she was almost terrified to find that she was alone, again. He was gone.

All things considered, she felt pretty fucking good.

"Where are we?"

"We'll be safe, here," he said, and opened the side door. Snow whipped at them, cold that blew down from the moon seeped into her bones as he led her through a forest to an abandoned mine shaft. Another hole in the ground. She fought him then, but he dragged her, murmuring comfort he nakedly didn't feel himself, and looking all around for something or someone trying to kill them.

Wittrock wanted them caged, but there was no question about trying that, again. Stella enjoyed the scientist's momentary look of pained disbelief when he saw her in the outer quarantine bunker. He remembered her, too.

The doctors wore bio-isolation suits with air tanks on their backs when they came in. They circled around them with their monitors and particle detectors, talking to each other about them as if they were some sort of contamination, a leak that had to be contained. One of them approached Stella with a steel gun with a big needle instead of a barrel, but Storch grabbed his arm and twisted it behind his back. "Get away, all of you fuckers!" he roared. In the end, Stella let them take her blood.

They subjected it to stresses and chemical reagents and observed the bizarre and lethal reactions it underwent when threatened. In the end, they discovered what he'd told them in the first place–no one had anything to fear from them, so long as they left them alone.

"Why are we here?" she asked him for the hundredth time. "These *chingalos* want to kill us."

This time, he finally answered. "They want to, but they can't. The green shit reacts to Keogh's DNA. I'm immune, and so are you. It hurts, but you get used to it."

"Still, why here?"

"Because everybody else thinks we're dead. And that's good. They have to help. All this shit is their fault."

"They hate us."

"They fear us, because we're monsters." He smiled. His teeth had grown into a wall of serrated survival knives. "Be a monster."

The hatch opened, and they went through, into the frigid white light of the lab. There were no cages, but the doctors still wore their spacesuits. Stella watched their distorted faces through the bubble hoods as they formed a loose cordon around the two mutants. She realized she was looking for Delores Mrachek.

Wittrock argued with a short, gaunt man with albino-white dreadlocks and a speed-freak rhesus monkey's face, and a zealous, bald black woman. Storch watched them until he'd had enough, and stepped between them.

"This is how it's going to be. We're staying here. No tests, no questions, no bullshit. When I find out where to go next, you hide her until I get back. Fuck with us, and you'll be sorry."

They argued some more. She heard, but didn't listen. She could barely register any sensations beyond the borders of her skin, so loud was the noise of her own body. She burned up food like a furnace and synthesized proteins. She healed, and she changed. Her skin thickened, lungs and heart grew. But loudest of all was the silence at the center of her head.

It felt like a hole, gouged out but already closing over. She probed it and hated herself for what she felt—fear, apathy, loneliness, but not freedom.

"Impossible," Wittrock said, over and over again, in ever more strident tones. "We don't even know what you are, let alone where your loyalties, if any, lie."

"Mister," Storch replied, with a flash of knife-teeth and a wave of one hand that made Wittrock cower, "you don't want to find out what we are."

Stella fell in love with the underground forest.

She left the lab while Storch argued with the doctors, wandering in search of a place to lie down and heal. Three soldiers followed her down the corridors and tried to stop her when she came to the airlock. She stared them down as she threw the wheel that unlocked the hatch and went through. The outer hatch slammed shut behind her, and the soldiers pressed against the plastic shell, watching her and gibbering into walkie-talkies.

She opened the inner door and stepped into the biosphere. Her slippered foot crunched on pine needles. A mechanically agitated spring breeze raised goose-bumps on her arms. The trees stirred and hushed, droplets of rain spilling from green-furred branches. As she wandered deeper among them, the full-spectrum lights slowly dimmed in a foreshortened simulation of sunset. By the time she reached the clearing in the center, the plastic roof had darkened to an opaque indigo that she could almost believe was the night sky, except that the only stars were the blinking lights of cameras and thermal imaging sensors tracking her.

She lay down on the soft, spongy loam in the center of the clearing. A deep flush rose to the surface of her skin, pale olive turning to mauve, then violet. The trees loomed over her, the massed voice of their rustling needles lulling her toward sleep. When she lay very still, she heard them living, and she envied them their vegetative serenity. She yearned to grow roots and become a tree in a secret forest.

Time to take stock.

She was alive. In the hands of a man she didn't know and couldn't trust, surrounded by people who wanted her dead. And he was leaving her here. She knew it with a blood-deep certainty hammered into her by thirty thousand generations of memory. Men left women behind, and went to die.

She was alone. Hers was the only voice she heard in her head. She reached down into the glutinous, electrified soup of her brain and scoured every neuron, every synapse, every glial cell, but she found only herself, rebuilding. Her Guardian Angel, her personal God, was dead and gone. Why did that scare her?

She was changing. In the raw, red world of her insides, she saw all the damage being repaired, and modifications made to protect against further attacks. Her back wrenched as new muscles introduced themselves to her spine in an improved buttress design. Her breasts grew sore and swollen as the intercostal muscles beneath them hardened to better defend her innards. The tidal rhythms of her body swept away thoughts and plans, and she lost herself in observing the primal, mindless genius that guided her transformation.

She was hot. She was hungry. The furnace needed to be fed, or change would turn on itself and begin to consume her. The need steeled her resolve to get moving again. It required no plans, no thoughts or words. She had to eat something.

She got up, and saw she was not alone.

The air was alive with him—medicines, sweat, body ash, plastic, sanitizers, blood, terror and awe. All for her.

It was the albino with the ropy dreadlocks. He'd taken off his spacesuit, but he still wore a particle-filter mask, rubber gloves and safety goggles. His eyes swam against the lenses, bulging alarmingly as they darted around her as if she were naked, and hounds were coming to tear him apart.

She stood and approached him, trying to keep the warring impulses that wracked her from showing on her face. One moment, she saw a skinny, oily scientist, but the next, he was prey, a weak thing that would make her stronger. She saw herself ripping him open and reveling in his insides, washing away her fears and insecurities in hot, sweet blood. She saw that it would be just, it would be natural. It was what she was, now.

He sensed what was coming. He backed away, but still he tried to normalize the situation with his jabbering. "Ms. Orozco? I'm Dr. Jonah Barrow. You're hungry, aren't you? I can arrange to have you fed, if you'd be willing to move to other quarters—"

"I like it here," she said.

"Well, I want to—to—assure you that we don't share Dr. Wittrock's paranoid hostility—"

"You don't want to kill me, you just want to cut me open." She came closer.

"No, that's not true!" Barrow took another step backward, tripped over an exposed root and sat down hard. Something plastic broke in his hip pocket, and he rolled over, moaning. His blood smelled like music on the air. "We want to help you, and by helping, understand what—what you—"

"You want to know what it was like?"

Barrow steadied himself against a tree. Blood seeped through the seat of his smock. His wounded eyes got bigger as she got closer.

"You want to know what it felt like, when He was in me?"

He backed up against the tree, and she circled it.

"Have you ever been raped, Doctor?"

He shook his head vehemently.

"No, of course not. You're a man, sort of. Well, it was like being raped by a god. Every moment of every minute of every hour—He's inside you. Driving you, running you, making you forget when He uses you to do something you wouldn't—and you can't hide from Him, you can't even go into shock and hide in the back of your brain, because that's where He lives."

She raised a hand before his face and flexed it. Her fingers were still bloody, and they burned. Her nails tore out of her fingertips between them, and curled towards his goggling eyes like flowers toward the sun. "You want to *feel* what it was like?"

"We—I—want to help—"

"You can help me," she said, and her claws went for his face.

He screamed. But her claws never got there.

"Let go of me, *pindejo*! Let me—"

Storch held her arm in one hand and caught the other as it snapped at his jugular. "Don't," he said.

Barrow flung himself out from between them and ran away, but stopped and watched them. "You have a right to know what he did to you," he said. "What you are, now."

Storch pinned her gaze. "Don't listen to him. He's a fucking loon."

"Your blood has proteins in it that mammals don't make. Bacteriorhodopsin, it's what's changing your skin. Your body uses the light to make energy, using a protein archaebacteria used three billion years ago. Fibroblast cells, Ms. Orozco, they assist in tissue regeneration, in growing lost limbs—in salamanders and other amphibians. It's a trait that our ancestors lost nearly one hundred million years ago, but you have it. Your DNA remembers—"

"Shut up!" Storch barked. He turned on Barrow, but the albino doctor only stepped back a few more paces, and took shelter behind another tree.

"He didn't tell you what you are, did he? Every living cell on earth descended from a single parent organism. You're an atavistic return to the common ancestor, the proto-Shoggoth—"

"GET OUT!" Storch chased him to the airlock and slammed it shut after him.

When he came back, Stella sat back down in the clearing. Her head spun and her body burned, trying to tell her that she could take him. He would make her even stronger—

He stood over her. "You've got to learn to control yourself," he said.

"I'm hungry."

"It won't kill you. They'll let us stay here, but you can't kill and eat people."

"Wasn't a person, just a fucking scientist."

"There are new rules, and you have to learn them if you're going to stay alive."

She laughed. "That's what it's all about, right? Staying alive?"

He chewed his words a moment, "That's all I ever learned in school."

"Why?"

"Why what?"

"Why stay alive? Idiot."

He didn't have any snappy comebacks to that. He sat down beside her. The trees whispered dendriform dreams above their heads. Questing, thirsty roots siphoned water out of the soil beneath them. Camera starlight twinkled. There was something so intense about silence, now, an imminent threshold beyond which one could forget how to break it with words, could forget words, forget time and death and become truly *alive*. She sensed that he felt it too, but he fought against it, struggling upstream to anchor himself, and her, with words.

"Well, I guess you're safe, now…"

"I guess I should thank you, I guess—for saving me, I mean, back there. I thought I was finally going to die—"

"I had reasons."

"Like what?"

"There are worse things than being dead," he said. "You can lose more than your life, now."

"What do you mean?"

"You saw it. It almost happened to you, just now. You can lose yourself, lose what it means to be human."

"You say it like that's a bad thing." She tried to smile at him, but his frown made her bite her lip.

"You think you're free now, but you're not. Your body owns you, now. It wants to survive, and it'll do anything—it can do anything—to survive. Keogh kept it in check, but you're still just along for the ride. You've got to fight it every instant to keep from becoming something you can't even imagine."

"And what are you now, Storch? You're not human, any more than I am. What are you holding out for?"

"I'm the man who's going make Keogh extinct. I'll do or become whatever I have to, to get Him."

"Then you don't want to stay alive all that much either. What then, Sergeant Storch? You saved me, thanks a lot, but what then?"

Storch wiped his face clean of whatever trace of expression was growing on it. "Then I'll just live."

She bit back a smart retort, held herself silent until she felt a knot inside. She untied it. "I used to fight so hard for everything—losing anything meant death, and nobody was going to take it away from me. Then I found out I was going to die. After everything I'd been through, stupid fucking cancer. And then—after it happened and you—after I fell into the hole, I had plenty of time to wonder what the hell I'd wanted to live so bad for, anyway."

"I'm sorry about that," he mumbled.

She nodded. "Wasn't anybody's fault," she added, when watching him squirm got old. "I'm getting over it."

"Life is just something you have to get through, is what my daddy used to say. It's a test, and you just have to endure it. Be true to yourself, and you'll get by."

"My mother believed the same thing, more or less. My father told me that, anyway, before he left me. But isn't there—I mean, shouldn't there be a moment, in between the fights and the bullshit and the knowing you're going to die, and none of it means shit, isn't there ever a moment when life is its own reward? When you're just glad, and proud of yourself for just being? Have you ever had one of those, Storch?"

He shrugged and looked away, as if hoping something would jump out of the trees and attack them. "I can't say as this one leaves me much to complain about."

She laughed again, caught herself when she noticed he was smiling. The bunched-up muscles around his jaw subsided and his chewed-up lips peeled away from his teeth.

"Oh, so you do know how to smile, sort of" she said.

"I've seen folks do it on TV, now and again." Then it was gone as fast as it appeared. He scratched his neck too hard, and she saw a spreading stain of blood under his skin.

"What the hell—"

He looked at her and held up his corded, scab-laced arms. The skin peeled and blistered as if he'd stuck them into hot coals. Deep crimson patches covered his exposed skin, growing into each other and raising white vesicles on his face, the backs of his hands, his neck.

"What's happening to you?"

He held his hands out to her. "I think you are," he said in a deadly earnest whisper. "Are you doing this to me on purpose, Ms. Orozco?"

"I didn't do anything—" But in the same breath, she knew it was true. Her heat burned him, and now it burned her. She felt her pores opening up like mouths and screaming chemicals at him. She saw her own crimson, blistering skin and knew he was doing the same to her. When she looked at him, she gasped, and forgot what she'd been saying, or how to say it.

The deep indigo light made a lustrous mane of shadows around his face. He rolled his massive shoulders and stretched, blisters all over him ruptured, and fresh waves of him enveloped her. His chest swelled, bones straining into new architectures, muscles rippling like blood-mad anacondas. His eyes rolled in panic, terrified of the power that wielded him.

The forest blurred and vanished in the warring walls of pheromone fog they made. The raw, roaring vitality of him spoke through his flesh, leaving him as helpless and confused as she. "What's happening to us?"

"It's not all bad," she said, and kissed him.

Sparks danced between their lips before they touched. When they did, she felt as if her mouth were melting into his, and his fearsome wanting forced itself into her and fired her own lust to devour and be consumed.

She pulled back from him, heart in her throat. What was this, some kind of endogenous date-rape drug? What was he doing to her? What was *her body* doing to her? She was in heat, like a bitch. Was it loneliness, was it shock, driving her instinctively to drag another one inside her to fill the void?

Sex never meant much to Stella, even less than love. She'd let it happen once or twice to satisfy her curiosity, and dismissed it as one more trap that would mean death, if she let it get her.

It had her now. Her breasts ached. She felt herself growing wet, her pelvis churned and her faced burned with shame. Her insides felt as if they were liquefied, spinning, boiling under her skin. Nerves she never knew she had swam to the surface and tasted the air. The electrical surge of NOW melted memory, annihilated the future. Surely, this was what he meant by losing what it meant to be human. And he didn't seem to be coping with it any better than she was.

She had only been perverse for the sake of trying to upset him before, but now she wondered if she hadn't meant it. Was it such a bad thing, to stop being human?

He shuddered, holding himself in check and desperately avoiding her eyes. His face contorted, setting up tsunami waves that rippled through his torso, leaving the muscles in strange new configurations. He terrified her, and she almost ran, but then his gaze locked hers, his pupils so dilated his eyes were black mirrors in which she saw herself.

She flew to him. Her lips were blistered, the new skin growing in shingled and coarse, like a cat's tongue. Her mouth touched and tore at the tender flesh under his jaw, where a ruff of crimson-dripping feathers grew, and felt his teeth at her own pulse. She tasted the labyrinthine essence of his alkaline sweat, felt his stampeding pulse quickening in vulnerable arteries just millimeters beneath her teeth and barbed tongue. They could kill each other instantly, if they gave in to instinct, tearing out each other's throats like rabid wolves.

His hands on her described fiery trails and raised chills that drove her flesh mad with changes. He caressed her back, tracing her new and improved spine down to her flank, traversed and darted down the front of her pants to cup the engorged orchid of her sex.

It was furry with thousands of quills, stiffened hair-needles that raised a shower of dancing blood droplets from his fingers and palm. "What's with the mixed signals?"

"Hurry, before it grows teeth," she said. She tore his shirt off. Underneath, his skin had gone purple and black and crazed with sharp shark-skin radulae. He changed colors. The sores on his back glowed violet, then emerald and gold and rose crept in, and the pigments mingled and strobed hypnotic counterpoint to their entrained heartbeats in a breathtaking mating display.

She stroked his chest down to his groin. Her fingers turned back and rubbed his new skin the wrong way. Two of her fingertips sheared off to the bone. It felt *good*. Her skin burned. Bubbles streamed up the interior walls of her skull. Her lymph nodes swelled.

"I'm trying not to hurt you," she purred, touching him. His skin sizzled and went silvery-white where her blood flowed.

"Stop trying—" he groaned, and pulled her to him. He hoisted her up to his mouth. His exoskeleton shredded off her shirt and cut into her breasts. Her blood melted the brittle edges, cooked his skin and burned its way into him.

Their immune systems were at war. They were reacting to each other's formidable arrays of pheromonal triggers as hostile antigens, and their bodies were making ever more formidable defenses against each other. But their bodies had also driven them together, in spite of their fear, their loneliness, and their mistrust.

He rolled onto his back, and she fell on him, nipping his neck again and again until he bit her back. Her hands went down to his undefended crotch and ripped away his flimsy cotton pants. Flashing unpleasant memories of Sergeant Avery, the mutant rapist with his monster-cock. She recoiled. Avery's body reflected his fucked-up mind. He needed to destroy everything he touched, so he made his genitalia into a weapon. What was inside Storch commanded her body to react with desire, but to the changes, he was only another invader.

They were both doing it now, repelling each other subconsciously, while something still deeper forced them to become one. The body wasn't just a blind engine of survival, but its changes hinged on animal levers in the brain that humans had buried beneath miles of conscious bullshit. She dug into the root-cellars of her brain as she tried to tell him to stop fighting her.

They wounded each other deeply, and each new wound became a new erogenous zone, a new site of penetration and infection. They rolled across the glade and blackened the grass with their heat.

Do you want this? She asked herself. The instinctual core of her that lived beneath words howled YES, and she could not did not want to would not stop it. She ground herself against him. Her quilled cunt ravaged his abdomen and stung him with acid nectar. Threadlike strands of skin shot out of his neck and abdomen, like the pili with which the first bacteria exchanged genetic codes, and pricked her. They burned her wherever they touched, but they grew together with her skin, so that it hurt more to tear them out.

His arms enfolded her and lifted her up as if to throw her away, but she felt a third hand touch her between her splayed legs, pry them apart and explore her.

It felt like the head of a giant snail, a prehensile thrusting against her vagina, but she also felt delicate, boneless fingers teasing the tender petals of her labia and clit. The touch reverberated up through her to her brain and out the top of her head in golden waves. She moaned. She lowered her defenses.

Something squirmed inside her and the velvet tendrils retracted into his penis as she snapped at them. "Sorry," she managed. He hissed at her and dropped her on it.

She fought. With both hands holding her arms at her sides, he teased open her nether lips and entered her. It wasn't so terribly big as she'd feared, but inside her, it grew like kudzu, bifurcating and surrounding the head of her cervix. A nest of baby snakes writhed in her uterus. Lightning jolted through her in a delirious orgasm that stopped her heart and all brain activity as she bucked and ground against him in a clutch of *petit mal* seizures.

He grew into her, and through him, she grew into the roots of the forest and out into the net of life that covered the mountains and spread out in all directions to the sea and the bottom of the sea and into the most rarified strata of the sky and out into the deepest reaches of space, where the seed of races yet unborn slept in the eons-old ice of comets, endlessly roving cosmic sperm.

And in her blood, in her brain, she knew him chemically, tasting his memories as they flooded her bloodstream. She was born with him into a Spartan home with the Army chain of command for a family. His childhood was a blur of training, all warm memories clipped out to make room for soldiering. She saw his mother desert and his father go insane. She followed him into the Army, to his niche in the elite Rangers. She loved it with him as the home, the habitat, he had been seeking all his life. She killed three men in Panama City with him in Operation Just Cause, and threw up, but did not cry. Some people, he simply believed, just needed to be killed.

She suffered and struggled with him through the Special Forces Q Course, and listened to craggy Green Berets telling him to quit, he didn't have the brains to be anything more than a grunt. Soldier Ant, they called him. Cannon-fodder. She exulted with him when he shamed them into passing him. She followed him into the most overworked, danger-close unit in Special Forces. She went with him into Desert Storm, and the awful night-fight he only half-remembered for so many years. She was saved and changed with him by 1st Lieutenant Brutus Dyson of Spike Team Texas, just as he would save and change her.

She retreated into the desert with him and was almost happy for a while, until soldiers fighting a secret war crashed into his life and burned it down. She ran with him from one trap to the next and got drafted into an army to fight against sick people. Strangest of all, she saw herself through his eyes—saw herself watching over him, saw him fear for her, saw him try to save her—

She became Keogh with him, the black ink of His echo choking her, as if He would come alive again inside her. Mercifully, he had blocked almost all of it out, so that it passed in a squall of needles and electrodes and rolling tape.

She was changed again with him, this time by a bullet. She died with him and came back in a new body made of cancer. She hated Keogh with him, a hate that answered all his questions, soothed all his doubts. But most of all, she hated the lies he was being told about God and the world and the human race. She hated the egghead scientists who had planted the ideas in his head, the crowning blasphemy that, of all the atrocities heaped upon him, he could not accept. They told him that aliens spilled a test tube and made all life on earth as an accident or joke, and Keogh was something from Outside, pulling the strings of the Universe, usurping evolution to become God. If they were right, they more than killed God: they rationalized Keogh as the logical next step in a runaway experiment set into motion by a dead race.

Then it was as if every atom in her body suddenly reversed polarity, and she shorted out.

When she came to, she was on her back, and he held himself above her. He was still inside her, but poised in perfect stillness. He grimaced, fought for speech. "You're burning me—"

Acid dripped from her, raising ugly white welts on his inner thighs and belly. His cock was in her to the hilt, burning him, but he didn't move.

"I haven't moved yet," he said. "Do you want this?"

She thought a moment. She still tingled from the initial thrust, but she craved him so much she changed her acidity, withdrew the teeth, and made herself deeper for him.

"Maybe this is what life is for," she said.

"What–" He struggled to say more, but words came out in quavering, hushed breaths, as he battled to hold himself still inside her.

"A chicken is an egg's scheme for making more eggs," she said. He moved.

Gone again when she woke up. The trees leaned in over her like bystanders at a hit and run accident. She burned, she glowed, she still felt him inside her, moving.

A pile of olive drab plastic pouches lay beside her. MEAL-READY TO EAT, it said on the front of each, and included an unflattering clinical checklist of the contents.

A flash of anger blew out before it got going when she saw it for the empty reflex it was. What more did he owe her? She had seen deep enough inside him to know that he knew no more than she did, and believed even less of what Keogh had shown him.

She ate four of the MRE's without reading them, but on the fifth, beef stroganoff with creamed corn and raspberry compote, she shook with a sudden wave of nausea that told her to stop. She chewed pine needles, savoring the trees' ancestral forms behind the bitter tang and stinging sharpness, so much more *edifying* than the processed machine-shit in the pouches. Sap ran in her veins. She knew, now, how to grow roots, and to make her own food in the sun with chlorophyll.

She squatted at the base of the largest tree and watered it, wondering idly if she was killing it, or if it would start to look like her.

She shook the branches of a dripping pine and showered in the chill dew. The livid blotches from where he touched her washed away, but there were too many bruises, lacerations shaped like his teeth, for her to count. *You should see the other guy,* she thought, and laughed.

Their clothes were shredded, scattered across the glade and crushed into the muddy soil, and she saw no fresh ones laid out anywhere. He must've walked out of here naked, expecting her to wait here for him. Since the cameras overhead in the lightening canopy could see her anyway, she decided she had little left to lose.

She went out looking for him, dressed only in her skin. Outside the biosphere, the air was stale and sterile, dry and recycled, like the interior of an airliner at the end of a transatlantic flight. The outer airlock opened and soldiers in gasmasks backed away from her with their rifles up, but they let her pass.

It was a remarkable discovery for her that her nakedness was somebody else's problem. They wouldn't look directly at her so long as she just kept walking with her head high. She had never thought of herself as worthy of ogling, but neither was there anything in her anatomy or the way she carried it that would cause men to avert their eyes. Then she caught a glimpse of herself in a reflective pane of the canopy. Knots of scar tissue ran down her back, a jigsaw puzzle of skin and scales and feathers. One of her breasts was missing, and ruddy, ragged planes of muscle peered through the gaping crater. Black iridescent bubbles of protoplasm congealed around the edges of the wound, growing her a new one. Stiletto spurs of bone grew from her ankles like dewclaws, clicking on the white tiled floor.

She arched her back and walked a little taller. She had never felt quite so good about herself.

She wandered the spiraling corridor that encircled the biosphere, taking stairs and upward-slanted passages until she found the quarantine lab, but Storch wasn't there. Dr. Barrow was. He worked at a computer with two assistants, who rotated trays of specimen vials under a robotic injector arm.

The soldiers came in behind her, flanking the exit and drawing down on her. "Dr. Barrow, heads up!" one shouted, then, at her, "Stand down, bitch! We're packing the Nasty Green Shit..."

Barrow looked up and said, "Get the hell out of here, all of you." When he saw her, he ran for the far exit. "He's not here! He's with the soldiers—"

"I want to talk to you. I don't want to eat you, anymore."

He peered around, above, below, her, hyperventilating.

"What, never seen a naked meta-Shoggoth before?"

He shooed away the assistants. The soldiers refused to clear out until he showed them the weapon on his desk, but he dropped it as soon as the door hissed shut behind them.

He sat back down at the workstation. One skinny hand, looking like a shaven bird spider, gestured towards the first aid lockers in one corner. "Clothes in there."

More for his sake than her own, she fetched a suit of scrubs and slipped into them. One of her spurs tore the seat out of the pants as she clumsily stepped into them, but she took more care with the next pair.

His eyes skidded off her as she walked up to him, and she knew he'd been watching them. "That's what you call us, isn't it?" she asked. "What does it mean?"

Barrow made some meaningless adjustments to the molecular model on the screen. "You should…he doesn't want me to tell you."

"But you want to, and I want to know."

"He thinks I'm wrong. They all do. He was there, and he doesn't believe it."

"He thinks you're all crazy. Everybody he's talked to here has their own line of shit to sell."

"I know there's no other explanation than what I told him. I—I took blood from him while he slept when he was here before. The cells I incubated used the agar substrate to grow a self-sufficient multi-celled colony. It was trying to grow into a new Storch. His DNA—and yours as well, if you underwent the same conditioning—is free of the third strand, but it moves so fast you can barely see it. It's turned inside-out, with all sorts of activity centering on the introns—junk DNA that we now believe is some kind of master switch for the rate of adaptation. It's synthesizing RNA off its genes constantly, and spinning off proteins human beings—and every other living thing—just don't make. It builds structures—"

Stella cut him off impatiently. "Why him? Why is he different?"

"That's been the focus of our research. We know Storch was at an Iraqi chemical weapons installation called Tiamat in the Gulf War. Whatever happened there, he was exposed to chemical agents—"

"He was exposed to Spike Team Texas."

"Oh," Barrow said. His face worked twitchily after something at the edge of his memory. "They were the first surviving guinea pigs of the RADIANT test in '84. They were exposed to the raw radiation, before Keogh had programmed it with his own DNA templates. If Storch was infected by them, then he might have developed a kind of cancer."

"Tell me about the Old Ones."

He looked up at her, homing in on her eyes as the only part of her that was recognizably human. "How much do you know?"

I read it in his head. I know it scares him to death. "I don't know shit, that's why I'm asking."

"It's hard for some people to accept—"

"All of it's hard to accept. It always has been. Storch says you think flying saucers played God and made everybody, and that Keogh is a saucer-man."

"No, that's not it at all. A Shoggoth—they're not aliens. They're the lost trunk of the tree of life. Life did evolve on earth, but it hadn't got past the single-celled stage when the Old Ones arrived. They introduced new traits that accelerated evolution by way of scalar-wave radiation projectors—like RADIANT—and self-replicating RNA messengers which could transmit desirable mutations. These, too, got out of the lab, and are still with us, but they don't work like they used to."

Viruses, Stella thought. He was talking about viruses.

"The Old Ones used the single-celled proto-life they found in the stagnant shallows of the earth's oceans as raw material to synthesize life complex enough to serve them. Their greatest success was a multicelled organism that retained an amoeba's plasticity. Some race that came after, but pre-dated humans, called them Shoggoths. They served the Old Ones for six hundred million years, mutating and adapting like self-improving machines. One day, they invented brains, and decided to stop being slaves.

"Once one of them developed the mutation, it spread through the population like a disease, infecting even the protoplasmic stock from which Shoggoths were synthesized. Shoggoths were highly adaptive, but they had only attained rudimentary sentience. If the Old Ones hadn't become so dependent on their slaves, the rebellion wouldn't have had any effect at all. They almost won, but after thousands of years, the Old Ones' bioweaponry killed them off. The Old Ones died out soon after, but they still experimented with life, trying to control the flow of mutation in controlled environments, and introducing their modified creations into the wild as slaves or feeding stock. The futile experiments ground on long after they passed away, and continue still.

"We are the ultimate product of those experiments. But Keogh—he's using the Old Ones' technology to clone himself, body and soul, and replace all animal and plant life. Given his genetic structure—and we've only seen the RADIANT-induced tertiary DNA strand, mind you, not a pure sample—I would say he was genetically comparable with what we know of Shoggoths, but that's impossible. They were incapable of reproducing, even by fission, or they would have overrun the planet."

"Maybe they learned. You said they were adaptable."

"It was hard-wired into them. But—"

"What?"

"Even my own people don't buy into this theory, but I'd hoped someone…with your experience—"

"Ask the fucking question, already."

"Well, given that they never reproduced, there's still the possibility that an individual Shoggoth could have—well, their cells are capable of infinite replication, it's far more likely that Keogh is an original survivor—"

"You think he's two hundred million years old."

"At least. Think of it. A survivor of the sentience-positive Shoggoth population escapes the Old Ones and goes to ground, maybe even into hibernation. Time enough to develop its intellect, time enough to plan a way to use the Old Ones' technology to fulfill its amoebic programming, and devour the world."

Stella thought about it, shook her head. "No, he wasn't like that. I mean, he wasn't a *thing*. He was a human being. He related to people, he understood their motivations. He knew how to drive a golf cart, for Christ's sake. He didn't just crawl out from under a rock after sleeping for eons."

"That's what my people always say. The most progressive theory is that he's a human being, and he infected himself with Shoggoth DNA, but none of this gets us anywhere. Not many people really care, we're all so tired, and with RADIANT destroyed—"

"What?"

"You didn't know? The Russians knocked it down, concurrently with Idaho and a major raid on the Chernobyl population. With the satellite destroyed and the domestic colony wiped out, everybody feels like the problem has been ripped out at the roots, and now it's the soldiers' mess to clean up, but—"

"It's not done. He wouldn't let you take RADIANT unless he didn't need it anymore. The colony isn't wiped out. It was empty. He's going to be One, soon."

"But Major Aranda was there, he said the casualties were—"

"I was a part of the colony. Three hundred of us spread out across the country to hide. You bombed an empty hole in the ground. They're still out there, and they're coming together. Soon."

She didn't know or care if he'd understand, but his red-rimmed eyes flared and he lunged at her with his hand out, almost touched her, before he regained himself. "You mean a neural network. We speculated—"

"I mean all of those people out there—they're Him already. But soon, He's going to become all of them. I don't know how else to explain—"

"I know, I know," he crowed, thrilled to be right about something, no matter how awful being right was. "And with that kind of unified processing power, he could make a mutagenic retrovirus—" He bowed his head and yanked on his dreadlocks as if to kickstart his brain. "Where are they?"

They heard the raised voices from the war room before they opened the door. Barrow looked sidewise at Stella and his leery expression warned her, *Be invisible.*

Inside, monitors, computer consoles and red, red light, like the bridge of a submarine on high alert. Her pupils dilated painfully to drink in the gloom. A knot of uniformed men stood in the center of the room, facing Storch. Beside him stood Dr. Wittrock, who was nose-to-nose with a tightly wound Hispanic officer. The officer had bandages wound around his head with spreading burgundy stains and a wet pucker where his left ear should have been. Sweat and bone-deep fatigue were etched in his battered face.

"It's over, Calvin. It's over! Why should we risk more men—?"

"It's far from over, Major Aranda," Wittrock replied. "And the risk to your men is minimal."

"I don't want any men," Storch said. I just want you to get me there."

"But they're all dead!" Major Aranda shouted. "They're dead, and the satellite is gone! Our liaisons abroad are going to mop them up in South America and Africa, but it's over!"

"You didn't kill anyone He didn't leave for you to kill, Major," Storch said. "He's still out there in force. I only want the one. Find Him for me and get me there alone, and I'll end your fucking war for you."

"What are you even doing here?" Aranda snarled. "The last time you blew through, you said you were done."

"What are *you* doing here? The last time I saw you, Spike Team Texas was eating your men alive."

Aranda closed with Storch, their eyes practically touching like the contacts on a detonator. Storch swelled and his arms became taut bludgeons of piano wire, but Aranda didn't shrink. He blazed with an insane knowledge of what Storch was capable of, and a willingness to take him on, anyway. "We killed your boyfriend, and every one of his people. Why arc you siding with this mutant fuck, Calvin? A few days ago, you wanted him dead!"

Wittrock took Aranda aside and whispered into his intact ear. Storch noticed her and Barrow and came over to them, storm clouds roiling behind his eyes. "Go back to the forest," he told her. "And you," grabbing Barrow by the lapels and shaking him, "stay away from her."

"He told me," she said, but she didn't say, and I saw it in you, saw your fear. "It's all true, Zane."

"It's bullshit! He's a man. You know it just like I do. He's just a man. He can be killed."

Wittrock signaled for order and spoke to a coffee-complected older man in a black flight suit. "Mr. Costello, what is the status of our air capability?"

Costello smiled broadly and scratched the back of his head. "Drones are all gone, obviously, but we can get another C-130 and put him wherever he needs to go, if he doesn't mind jumping."

Stella saw in their eyes why they were agreeing, and what Wittrock must have said to Major Aranda.

"Then I see no reason why Sgt. Storch's operation shouldn't proceed," Wittrock said, "given verification of any intelligence he might eventually unearth. Unless Dr. Barrow has any more religious objections."

Stella stared hard at Barrow, but the Green scientist looked at Storch a moment and then at his moccasins. "If Sgt. Storch is convinced that's what he has to do, he's already indicated he's unwilling to participate in further research, so I don't need him."

"What about the other one?" a soldier asked. Not "the girl," or "the chick."

"She stays here, protected," Storch said. He looked at her. "Anybody fucks with her, and I'll come back and kill all of you."

She bit her tongue. She was too angry to yell at him in English, anyway. Her skin blackened, blood simmered. She turned and went to the door before her body hurt someone. Her arms were turning purple again. Her fingertips went numb, turning into knives.

She stood in the corridor and listened to them finalize the deal. She tried to calm herself down, but her body wanted to hurt someone. She didn't want to let it go at Storch. They had nearly killed each other, just fucking.

It frightened her that she couldn't control her own body. It frightened her that nobody was there to do it for her. That made her hate herself, and everyone else, a little more, the more she changed. What frightened her most was that when she became what she was becoming, when she became change itself, formless, she knew she would welcome it.

He came out, and she melted into the wall. Fuck him. She could walk away now. They were even. She barely knew the stupid asshole, but her blood did. He was right, anyway. Her old life was over seven months ago, and she had nowhere else to go. Soon, she could run away, grow wings and fly, dive into the ocean and become a shark. Her heart's dearest unspoken wish—to be free and never die, to need no one and nothing— had become hers. When she was stronger, she would go out into the world and live. When she was stronger, she wouldn't need to see him.

She went after him. He walked faster than most athletes sprint, and didn't slow down when she called him. "Storch! Zane, what is this shit? What are you running from?"

He didn't look at her. He took a staircase up three flights and stormed a broad sloped corridor that arched around the domed forest. The treetops shivered under a heavy sprinkler downpour. "Listen, Ms. Orozco, what—what—happened, um, was—"

"Don't fucking flatter yourself. I'm talking about Him."

"That's who I'm going to see. He's just a man."

"You have to go now to kill Him, or to prove that they're wrong about Him? Jesus, you're crazier than they are."

He stopped before a door, one hand on the latch, the other flat out to stop her. "Go back to the forest, Ms. Orozco, or go home. But don't try to talk me out of this. I'm already gone."

He opened the door and went in. She charged in after him and knocked over a slim man in a jumpsuit. Banks of computers and cellular, satellite and shortwave equipment lined the walls and crowded each other on carts that he had to walk sideways through to get to an ordinary telephone. Storch lifted the handset and lights on the console behind it blinked and streamed digits. The phone was wired into a chain of scramblers that bounced the call over different lines and satellite feeds.

He punched in an eleven digit number, then eight more, but didn't speak. He punched a few more buttons, pausing before each as if listening to a menu. He listened so intently that he didn't notice her.

She stepped closer and strained to hear the tiny burbling noise cupped to his ear. She visualized her ears growing larger, catlike, bat-like, grotesque spires laced with veins and nerves, smarting from the crying of babies in South America and Greenland. They burned. She touched her ears fearfully, clawed finger snagging in her tangled, needle-strewn hair. They were not bigger. But she could *hear*.

"You have one saved message," said an android operator. "Press One—"

Storch heard the whole menu, finger hovering above the buttons as if the last option might come as some sort of surprise. Finally, he jabbed One.

"Sent today, at Three Eleven AM," noted the android.

"Sergeant, it's me, and—if you're getting this, then take notes, because I can't stay on this line too long, and they—this wouldn't even seem possible if not for what..." The speaker got too wound up to speak, and sounded like he was about to faint. "Okay," he finally said, "here's what I learned. Dr. Keogh was another—he worked for the Manhattan

Project, and after that…um, he helped design a neutron bomb that they detonated on a tiny atoll in the South Pacific, and he was…well, it's a long story. He had no roots in this or any other country, and even his real name was classified. But I've been reviewing Radiant Dawn's holdings for months, getting as deep as they'll let me, and they own real estate, and satellite networks, closed-circuit satellite TV. Several pieces of property they own are in the middle of the South Pacific, atolls with satellite relays and automated observatories on them, or speculation on future transpacific cables, many of them joint ventures with telecoms and universities. One of them matches the latitude of the bomb test. The GPS coordinates—do you have a pen?"

Storch pressed a button and the android said, "Message saved. There are no other messages—"

"Go back to the forest," he said. His voice was a raw-throated bark, his skin red and flayed and puckered with healing scars that she knew better than she knew him.

"He wants you to go," she said. "They want you to go. Nobody wants you to come back. So *fucking go.*"

She ran all the way back to the airlock. Through her tears, she couldn't see how to lock the door, so she stomped the inner airlock until it was bent in its housing. She ripped the shrieking alarm out of its socket and ran into the glade and tore her scrubs off. Her skin screamed chemicals and colors and wept feathers and scales and shells. Shimmering waves of heat danced around her. They turned her tears to steam.

She slept under the tallest tree in the forest, out of sight of the cameras. In her dreams, she hunted alone in moonlit woods. In her dreams, the woods were hers, the woods were *her*, and no prey could escape her. She hunted men and fed them to the wolves who worshipped her. In her dreams, she was happy.

~ 29 ~

As the snow flurries outside pushed his take-off back another hour, Cundieffe wondered what they'd do when they found out he wasn't going back to Washington. He wondered if they didn't already know. He wondered when he'd started calling them *They*.

He waited, and suffered as he never had before under the torment of time's passage. He would not survive this wait. Surely, somewhere along the way, before his plane came to take him to where he might find answers, even if *they* didn't come to take him away, he was going to wither and die inside, just slip away, and the Martin Cundieffe that got out of this chair to board the plane would be a different one that moved into his empty shell like a hermit crab, one more at ease with the situation, one adapted to the unscrupulous and brutal world into which he had been cast.

Sitting in the departure terminal at Boise National Airport, he buffed his broken glasses with a handkerchief and stashed them in his breast pocket, combed his thinning hair over his bare crown with his fingers until he began to think he was trying to disguise himself. They'd be looking for a balding man with glasses. What the devil are you thinking?

You are having a nervous breakdown, he thought. *You are running home to Mother. This is the end of your career.*

They apologized for the mistake in White Bird. The next morning, when they let him out of the cell that Schweinfurter stayed in, they were chastened, as if their behinds still burned from Assistant Director Wyler's belt, but Cundieffe knew from their eyes that they felt no guilt. The whole thing was sub rosa procedure. He had proven risky to the containment, so they contained him. Simple.

Great grapes of sweat bloomed and splattered on the USA Today spread out on his lap. At the bottom of the front page, squashed into less than four column inches by flooding in Missouri and the latest sordid slime on the current President: EXPLOSION AT ARMY'S 'GERM WARFARE' BASE KILLS 14; *Pentagon Spokesman Assures No Threat Of Outbreaks.* There was nothing at all about Idaho.

People who know the kinds of things you know don't just take leaves of absence. They're found on toilets with their service pistols in their hands, stomachs stuffed with sleeping pills. Or in a plane crash... The antifederalist literature he researched every day was full of scenarios– Senator John Tower, Director of Central Intelligence Bill Casey, White House crony Vince Foster...

But what do you know, Martin? What threat do you pose? He knew more than most of the world. He looked around at all the lowing cattle, his fellow travelers, stumbling past or lingering in the tidepools of newsstands, Starbucks kiosks, sports bars, glassed-in smoking sections like cancer saunas.

Cancer...

In what they see as death, there lies eternal life.

He knew about Storch.

You're too late for the fight, but you're just in time to help cover it up.

He knew about RADIANT.

It kills you, but—it speaks to cancer, and the cancer grows and it— becomes you.

He knew about Keogh.

Never stop trying to change the world.

He knew about them. He was one of them. It was not a question of loyalty, of doctrine. Could a drone even dream of defecting from the hive?

He got up and went to a pay phone.

Assistant Director Wyler was in conference with a group of Quantico instructors, but Mrs. McNulty patched him right through. It was not a good sign.

"Martin? Why are you still in Idaho?"

He looked around. The terminal was like the whirling drum of a washing machine. He put on his glasses. It swam into focus. It might have been LA or DC, but everyone was ten years behind in dress and twenty pounds overweight. No one watched him from across the concourse. Who doesn't look suspicious, sitting alone in an airport? "It's a family emergency, sir. My Mother—"

"Is Beatrice alright?"

"She—I think it's a nervous breakdown in the offing, sir." Go ahead and ask, sir: Hers or yours?

The Assistant Director let out a sigh of relief that soured in a disappointed groan. "You have duties, Martin, I shouldn't have to remind you. This is a critical time. This is a classified investigation. Please try to employ your formidable powers of empathy to understand the dilemma you're causing. Your mother is a dear old friend, and she was a fine asset to the Bureau, as was your father. But we cannot spare you at this time. Your tasks cannot be duplicated without compromising the investigation."

Tell him, this is the investigation. I had this dream that I got a phone tip, and then I got this doctored photograph, and there was a monster...

"I'll be back on a plane tonight, sir. I'm still collating and researching, and I can get back on it after I take care of the...situation at home." He took a deep breath. He hated himself for calling it that. "I appreciate the situation I've placed the Bureau in, and—and the investigation, but I've concluded that a short visit now will forestall the need for a more dire, and protracted, stay, later." He pushed sincerity and reasoned concern into his voice, and hoped Mules couldn't detect lies over the phone. "I'm all she has, sir. I'm so earnestly concerned for her, that I fear it might have an adverse effect on my work."

Wyler noisily cupped his hand over the phone. Cundieffe heard burbling video and hushed, electronically filtered voices. The Cave Institute. "How much have you told her, Martin?"

Cundieffe swallowed hard, his desiccated windpipe slamming shut on all the lies that sprang to mind, all the questions he needed answered. "N—nothing whatsoever, sir," he stammered. "She understands operational security." His voice cracked. His vision melted and ran again as tears sprang from his eyes. Through them, he could see the others listening, probing into his head through the line. Lie-detector drills stabbed his brain. No matter how hard he tried, he could not picture Mother. "You've got to know that, sir. She knows nothing."

"You have twenty four hours," Wyler said. "Give your mother my best wishes for a speedy recovery."

Few environments are as much of a shock to the system as the metropolitan Los Angeles climate. Cundieffe stepped out of the arrival terminal at LAX an hour after sunset and gasped at the perverse, dirty steam-bath warmth. His lungs felt as if he were trying to breathe soup. The overcast sky was fading from gray to murky red as a million grids of lights came on in an unbroken blanket sprawling from Anaheim to Oxnard.

Watching from the window of his business-class seat on the plane, he'd marveled at the shapeless, circuit-board city-scape, which seemed to have grown since the last time he'd flown in. New York and Chicago had reaching spires, skyscraper claws, to assert that it was a city, with foci and axes and flow, while the ever-expanding neon abomination of Las Vegas still looked like a single pinpoint explosion of cold fire on the violet desert floor. From the air, Los Angeles was undeniably a disease on the land, a colossal, sprawling silicon cancer. It seemed to have no borders, eating and absorbing its suburbs and adjoining counties, even gnawing its way around the benighted barriers of Camp Pendleton to the south and the Cleveland National Forest to the north. In another few years, it would engulf muted San Diego and the ragtag glitter of Tijuana, explode into the dusty agriscape of the Central Valley, throw out fingers of landfill peninsulas into the Pacific and straddle the horizon, infinite in all directions. Even before he breathed its air, he had a wilting sense that his city had forgotten him. His LA survival skills had likewise faded away, and he was only one more tourist trying not to get killed.

He shed his bulky overcoat, draped it over his briefcase and hailed a cab. It took an hour to get up the 405 to Santa Monica, even though the savvy Somali driver muscled his way into the deserted carpool lane and scooted past miles of gridlock. Half the time was spent in sight of his exit and the monolithic Federal Building where, until this year, he'd begun and built the foundations of his career. Though it seemed to impose even on the taller glass skyscrapers of the banks to the east of it, it seemed stunted to him now, like an old elementary school. The corridors in which he served now extended even further underground than the drab tower reached into the smoggy sky.

He paid the driver and stood before his Mother's house for a long minute before he really saw the place. A brief, half-hearted rain had sprinkled the city only a few hours before. The oils and particulates had been washed off everything, giving the sidewalks and lawns and parked cars a preternaturally bright, raw appearance, while the gutters sported queasy oil-slick rainbows. The windows and porch light were dark, the front door closed. Hers was the only house on the block without a blue cathode nightlight peering out its front picture window.

Cundieffe shivered.

His mother worked on the fifth floor of FBI Headquarters for thirty years. She might know something, but what? Enough for them to monitor her phone conversations, and if she breathed a word of what she knew—?

The curtains of the Melnitzes' family room picture window parted, and Old Man Melnitz peered out at him. Only then did he realize how suspicious he looked. Standing on the walk in front of the house he grew up in, like a burglar casing a job. He strode up the walk, calling too loudly, "Mother?"

He let himself in with his key, dropped his coat and briefcase in the atrium. The air was cold. Mother almost never turned on the heater. Heat sucks up dollars and breeds germs, she'd say, but she always baked something around dinner time, even if she only gave it away to the neighbors or the agents at the Federal Building. She had geriatric diabetes, and never cheated, though she said she enjoyed baking for its own sake. Cundieffe always believed his Mother was cheating on the heat, because she always sat in the kitchen, reading or chatting on the phone, while the banana bread or the brown betty or the cookies baked. He went through the dining room, even colder there, and found the kitchen empty and colder still. The back door stood open. Through it, he saw that the fading yard needed a fresh coat of green paint. He noted that the hibiscus and the orange tree were both coming along nicely, both already sprouting buds in the confused climate of the city. He resisted the impulse to search their leaves for whiteflies.

Mother was not here. He should go to the garage and look for the Mustang. He should not be touching anything. He should be calling the police, he should be talking to Thom Tussey, LA's kidnapping specialist. He was especially fond of Mother's Louisiana crunch cake, and was an excellent judge, since he hailed from Baton Rouge. He could be counted on to exercise discretion.

Wishful thinking. If they got to her, she'd be here, it would look like a suicide, a coronary, complications from a flu virus…

He stepped out onto the back porch. Through the dusty garage window, he could see Mother's aquamarine '68 Mustang. When the old Pontiac had gone to meet its wrecker, Mother hadn't let Father buy her a grandmother's car, because she'd never be anybody's grandmother. At the time, Cundieffe had thought his Mom was making some kind of joke.

The porch glider creaked. He looked down and stumbled off the porch when he saw Mother lying on her back on the glider, her sturdy hairstyle mortally denting the chintz cushion. Her hands were clasped under her formidable bosom as if they'd been arranged that way, or as if she'd succumbed to a wound that lay beneath them. Her glasses hung from their gold chain around her neck. She wore a smart navy blue wool skirt and sweater set that might've been forty years old, but looked newer than Cundieffe's sweat-rumpled suit. She looked peaceful. The unjaundiced eye would see natural causes. There would be no autopsy.

The moment froze and its gravity sucked Cundieffe into it so hard and fast his soul swirled down it in a monofilial string of atoms. Cundieffe had never thought about it, but he'd always unconsciously supposed the soul would be a light thing, and it astounded him how very heavy a soul could be. Cut free of the tether of Mother, he should have floated free of his old life and rose up into the hierarchy of the Mules. No doubt that was what they planned, but they underestimated her importance, and now he might never move again.

"Heavens, I must be dreaming."

Cundieffe staggered drunkenly and looked as if he'd just been doused with ice water. He spun around once before he turned back to Mother, who squinted at him and smiled.

Her eyelashes fluttered, her hands fumbled and found her glasses, and she was smiling at him. Not dead. Only napping.

"It's me, Mother. What are you doing out here, asleep? You looked like—" How stupid it was rushed him and he had to sit down. Mother got up just soon enough for him to fall onto the glider and lay down in her place. He shook so badly, she gave him a worried glance as she went into the kitchen.

He heard her rummaging in the refrigerator, now taking down glasses from the cupboard. "I must've dozed off when I sat down after I got home, about an hour ago. I've been golfing with the former Deputy Assistant Director's widow, Maryalice Laughton. I don't suppose you know of her? She's living out here now, and she practically staged a *coup d'etat* over the Ladies Auxiliary of the local Society chapter, drove Mrs. Stickney out in tears over some scandal about the charity benefit arrangements. She's run me ragged on the links every Wednesday and Saturday for the last six weeks, but I had to do something to take up the slack from not cleaning up after you. Mouth like a stevedore, that Laughton woman, and she sure likes the sound of herself. Anyhow…"

He listened to her talking as she got together a light snack. He chewed his thumbnail, which was an awful habit he was glad Mother couldn't see, but if he didn't do it, he'd probably be sucking his thumb, so there you are. She hadn't remarked upon or even seemed to notice his bruised face and bandaged hand, his broken glasses with black duck-tape on the bridge.

At length, he got up and went into the kitchen, where Mother had laid out oatmeal raisin cookies and milk. "I could make hot chocolate, if you'd prefer, but you look like your nerves have had enough jangling for one day." She circled around behind him and maneuvered him into a chair at the counter. "Martin, you didn't desert your post and fly out here to get an answer to your silly question, did you?"

He stuffed a whole cookie in his mouth to forestall an excuse. The cookie dissolved on his tongue, vanilla extract working its comforting magic on his misfiring brain, and he wanted to tell her everything about everything. "Did you read the newspaper this morning?" he asked, but

chopped her off with a stuttering, "Don't, it doesn't matter. I spoke to
Assistant Director Wyler before I left Washington, Mother. I'm just here
for the evening." He flushed his mouth with milk and took another cookie,
but he nibbled at this one, let the moment soothe him out of all memory.

"Are they giving my little man important work to do?"

"Oh, no shortage of that. AD Wyler says they're going to need me at
Headquarters indefinitely, what with the new Division forming."

She nodded vacantly, a brave half-smile on her face. She touched his
arm, laying more weight on him than she probably realized. "I'm proud,
Martin. Father would be proud, too. I only wish he could see you, now."
She pinched his arm hard. "Now, what the devil are you doing here, and
what was that business on the telephone, the other morning?"

He brayed submission and meekly shook his arm free. Studying his
shoes, he said, "Mother, I can't tell you very much, but there's a man, the
one I asked you about. I have it on good authority—" A reliable source,
ha! "—that is, I believe you might know something, or have something,
maybe something of Dad's..."

Her finger went up to his lips, and she turned and walked out the back
door, taking his hand and drawing him after her.

The sky was as dark as it got in Los Angeles at night. A pixelated
maroon cyclorama arched over them as Mother led him around the back of
the house to the door he'd forgotten was there.

At the far corner of the back of the Cundieffe garage, almost totally
obscured by the shaggy row of giant juniper bushes that grew along the
fence, there was a door that opened on a room Frank Cundieffe had built
himself by partitioning the workshop portion of the garage. Mother
produced an old key she must have taken down from the hook on the chore
board in the pantry. He'd seen it so many times it was wallpaper, without
wondering what it went to. Funny, that his keenly honed deductive mutant
Mule mind could be so blind to the secrets of his own home.

Mother turned the key in the lock, but had to jiggle the knob and
throw her weight rather savagely against the flimsy wooden door before it
came unstuck. Several coats of paint that had been slathered over the
doorway cracked with a gummy sound like dead, dry lips smacking.
Cundieffe could smell a musty Barbasol odor among the mold and dust
and stale air. It pricked his sinuses and brought back Father, and the first
and last time he saw this door open.

He remembered the night he woke and went out there because he
could hear his father and mother screaming at each other. He couldn't have
been older than six, because he recalled the scrape of his pajamas with the
feet in them on the green asphalt. Father wasn't home when he went to

bed, his Father back from Washington only a few minutes, and he took so long, coming by train instead of the plane, as he always did when he visited Headquarters. He remembered the room filled with boxes, and Father striking him across the face, and Mother on his trail as he flew, wailing, back to his bed. The last time, he was eight and Father was dead, Mother mooning over the empty office, collecting pictures and a few mementos before sealing it up. There were no boxes.

He looked around the room now. There were pictures on the walls, photos of Special Agent Frank Cundieffe posing awkwardly beside the famous and infamous, mostly the latter. A plain office chair and a cyclopean wooden desk with a scarred slate surface swept clean but for a thick skin of dust, a few file cabinets, an empty gun locker. A threadbare knockoff Oriental rug covered the oil-spotted concrete floor, minus a few holes where mice or moths had chewed it up.

He looked around and around before fixing his gaze on Mother. "It's safe, here? To speak freely?"

Mother nodded solemnly, closed the door behind her and pulled a thin chain dangling from the ceiling. A venerable lightbulb flickered and caught fire, lending the room a muddy, undersea ambience. Mother knelt on the floor before him. "What do you know about the Director's Blue files, Martin?"

"Only—that they were commonly believed to be myth, part of the Official and Confidential files kept in the Director's office. When he— when the Director died, there were discrepancies over the disposition of the files, which were transferred to the Director's residence. I got a phone call the other day, from someone who told me to ask you about them—"

It came together. He was six in 1972, when the Director died. His Father was one of the Director's most trusted agents, with duties often outside the realm of legitimate Bureau powers. He kept secrets. His Father never struck him except that one night. His Father took the train, that one time. There were boxes.

And there was Mother on the floor, gingerly rolling back the Oriental rug, so as to raise as little dust as possible. "I never had cause or clearance or curiosity to look at the Blue files, but I heard the odd story or two, and I mean the word in its truest sense. Some said they were cases the Director kept tabs on, but would never move forward. *Odd* stories. It sounded like the kook file, which would've needed an annex building of its own, if we didn't purge it every couple of years, except the Director took an interest. Nobody even joked about it, but we didn't think it amounted to anything."

Mother stepped over the rolled-up rug and crossed to the center of the small room, edging Cundieffe aside as he approached for a closer look. A rectangular hole had been dug out of the paved floor, and warped, cracked two-by-four boards lay across the gap. Mother gently pried out the first board with her sensibly short fingernails and laid it aside. Beneath, Cundieffe saw only dark and dust, and, when he stooped, his own shadow. One by one, she lifted out the boards.

"When Mr. Hoover passed away, bless his soul, Frank flew back east to pay his respects, and kibbutz with the other old-timers, like a flock of self-appointed cardinals, over who would take over. They all liked De Loach for the job, but he was fat and happy in the private sector. At least they kept that two-faced Judas Sullivan from creeping back in. Anyhow, Frank came back on the train, still drunk and more upset than when he'd left. He came back, bless his poor soul, with these."

Mother leaned over and seized something in the hole with both hands, gave a grunt of effort and hauled it out into the yellow light. She brushed at the dust on it, but it had hardened into a crust, and rolled off in tufts, or not at all. It was an ordinary corrugated cardboard box, brown and unmarked, the lid sealed with flaking yellow shipping tape.

"Frank had time to read some of them on the train, and he got pretty upset about it. He said the Bureau had acted on some of the cases, or passed them on to other agencies who did the dirty work. Others they ignored completely, and those were the worst.

"It was the worst thing in the world for your father, Martin. If they were true, if any of it was true, it was the smoking gun the Director's enemies had hunted high and low for to ruin him, or, failing that, his legacy. The bleeding heart liberals, the civil liberties maniacs, the Reds, the race radicals; they would have torn down the Bureau, if any of it came to light. Frank was supposed to bury it all, but never destroy it. He waited for further instructions, but they never came. He passed away, bless his sweet soul, without another word from Washington."

Cundieffe looked into the hole. It was deep, and extended under the floor, under his feet. The hole was full of boxes.

"I waited for you to grow up, to show this to you. Waited until you had reached and secured the appropriate clearance before seeing this. When you asked about them that morning, I knew that it must be time. Frank had friends in the Bureau and elsewhere in federal service, friends who I know must've taken an interest in your career. That they sent you is a sign, but you have to look into my eyes and tell me that you trust those men. Do you?"

He looked into her eyes, and let her see him. She must know, he thought, how can a mother not know what her child is? "You know Assistant Director Wyler, don't you?"

"I knew him to say hello to. He was a junior agent at the DC field office, I think he might have worked with your father on a few assignments in the early sixties. Sort of a pantywaist accountant, was Frank's brutally honest picture of him." She took Martin's hands and bored deeper. She had never seen what he was, but she had always looked blindly past it into the clear heart of who he was. "What is this about, Martin? Does somebody want you to dredge up all this poison?"

He looked back into the hole. So many boxes.

If any of it were true—

"Mother, how many people know these are here?"

"No one. Frank could keep a secret, that's why they gave him the duty, damn them. He took out several safety deposit boxes in different banks to flush out anyone bad who might come looking. He put phone books in them, and they've never been touched. Martin, I only want to help you, but if someone wants you to dig these up, and use them, I don't think I can allow it. Your Father—"

"I think there's something in one of these boxes that relates to a case I'm investigating now, Mother. I can't seem to find the information any other way, but I have reason to believe that someone else in the Bureau does know. I think they want me to find out something that can only be found here." He pointed into the hole. "I won't take anything away from here, but I need to look at them. I need to know."

Mother Cundieffe looked long and hard at her only son, then she smiled and climbed up off the floor, shrugging off his assistance. "I'll go fix you something to eat," she said, and left him alone with the hole full of boxes.

There are secrets, the truth of which strike you in the face and open your eyes. There are lies that sicken the soul and close your ears. After he knew not how many hours of poring through the Director's Blue files, he was further than ever from divining the difference. There was no visibly coherent filing system, neither alphabetical, nor chronological, nor regional, but as he read, Cundieffe began to gather that some system was at work, if only because each one that he opened was worse than the last.

Very few of them directly involved the FBI, and none contained anything like hard evidence. Indeed, Cundieffe saw almost immediately that the Director might have collected them merely because they almost invariably implicated one or another of his rivals' agencies, particularly the Pentagon and the OSS under his archenemy, "Wild Bill" Donovan. They were chiefly hearsay statements taken from unnamed witnesses about events which allegedly took place several years before, if at all. The

Director's crime was only one of collecting such filth, of compounding it and consecrating it in secrecy. Worse, he had laid it at the door of the Cundieffe household, branded them the custodians of a body of apocryphal conspiracy theories a thousand times more venomous than the naïve accusations leveled by the most radical of revisionists. No wonder the name of Frank Cundieffe was expunged from all histories of the FBI. No wonder his mutant, eunuch son had been anointed the heir to a secret greater and more terrible, and invited inside it. The keeping of terrible secrets ran in his blood. His first reaction was to burn them all, but as the hammering of atrocities beat him into numb submission, stained his fingers and strained his underpowered eyes, he knew he would hide them again. If lies they were, the Bureau would yet be rocked by their assembly, and the Director's memory would be tarred anew with a lunatic brush; but if they were true, if there was the least atom of truth in any of the tens of thousands of brittle, yellowed foolscap typewritten sheets, the Bureau would only be the first to fall, and the nation, the world, would plunge into a new Dark Age.

There was the account of the raids on the Massachusetts town of Innsmouth in 1928, of seven hundred American citizens executed and buried in quicklime-seeded mass graves, and three hundred more shipped to the nameless stockade at Ft. Avon in Florida—where seventy-one years later, they would imprison Sgt. Storch.

There were the accounts of cattle mutilations, and worse—human mutilations—of the bodies of unidentifiable men and women, undocumented "hillfolk" in the Appalachian mountain ranges, and illegal immigrants in the badlands of the Southwest. Hundreds of them turning up over decades, found on or near remote mountaintops, or snarled in trees as if dropped from a great height. Their brains and other vital organs removed by a surgical procedure that left no wounds. Others wandered down out of the hills speaking in strange tongues or not at all, and medical examinations disclosed metal shrapnel lodged in their skulls, but laid out in purposeful patterns that a modern examiner might have recognized as computer circuitry.

There was the tale of the centuried graveyard in Woonsocket, Rhode Island, that was excavated to make way for a golf course in 1954, and the excavation engineer's hysterical allegations that all the graves were empty, plundered by burrowers from below. The FBI had been notified because one of the tunnels under the cemetery crossed the state line and emerged in a cemetery in Blackstone, Massachusetts, three miles away. Along the way, the distressed engineers claimed to have found proof of a cult of cannibal grave-robbers who had thrived for generations beneath the New

England soil. The engineers gave up trying to explore the full extent of the tunnels after five of their number disappeared.

There was the Livermore Laboratories researcher who approached the DIA in 1966 with a project proposal which would seek to scientifically duplicate the paranormal process known as remote viewing, a psychic wild goose pursued for years by the KGB and GRU in the Soviet Union. By bringing to bear certain resonant magnetic frequencies on a sensitive human mind, the researcher theorized, it would be possible to see across vast distances via magnetic "ley" lines, and even through time. The Pentagon cautiously invested in the project, only to bury it and disavow all affiliation with the researcher after three of his staff were "fatally consumed" in an unexplained accident which left the researcher raving about the "ethereal parasites" that coexisted with our own universe, and which his remote viewing project had made manifest.

So many others, some fat as the national budget, others only a few crumbling documents with most of the names, places and dates blacked out: disappearances, discoveries, accounts of phenomena and of crimes that exploded all faith, if they were not cunningly constructed fictions. Cundieffe stopped reading them after the tenth or so, and rifled through box after box, studying only the curled typewritten labels on each file before shoving them too roughly back into the hole. Anger collected in his jaw, short sharp breaths cramped his chest and fogged his glasses. Sweat dripped off his crumpled brow and swelled the mummified papers, and though the arid chill of the night never quite seeped into the sealed secret room, Cundieffe shook with a cold that came down out of the dark between the stars.

It was somewhere in the middle of the ninth box that his fingers fell on a file entitled, DR. LUX/STATEMENT OF ANON. FBI INFORMANT #28269-A-01090-D/5-16-67/Director's Eyes Only.

With trembling hands, he opened it. He found only a single typewritten memo addressed to Associate Director Clyde Tolson, and a photograph. The file folder was creased and cracked as if it once held a much larger report. The memo merely introduced the report, and advised the Associate Director that "no corroborating evidence has been collected, but this is hardly surprising, given the extreme level of security in the institution concerned. But I feel it merits the Director's attention, primarily because of its improbability, if only to forewarn him to quash with authority any rumors that might reflect badly on the Bureau, should any part of it come to light."

The statement alleged a secret murder of a key Pentagon scientist committed in 1954 by the Office of Naval Intelligence and the Pentagon overseers of the atomic weapons programs. The victim, known only by code name for the duration of his work with Manhattan and subsequent atomic weapons projects, was only identified by a photograph. Interviews and an intensive secret review of the personnel files at Los Alamos failed to determine that he ever existed or worked for the project, let alone that he was murdered. The writer noted that he never would have passed the item on to the Director, if not for the peculiar death of the anonymous FBI informant, a security handler recently retired from the Los Alamos laboratories, within days of recording his statement.

The photograph was a crumbling copy of the one that had appeared in his office. A blue pen—it could only be the Director's—had circled Dr. Keogh.

I had occasion to know Dr. Lux as well as anyone at Los Alamos, outside the inner circle of scientists, the "bomb makers." They hated to be called that, they preferred their official titles, which made them feel like they were solving the world's problems. It was part of my duties to watch them, especially the marginal ones like Lux, but as they have no direct bearing on the issue at hand, I decline to go into specifics about them. There are still too many above ground to be declassified. But the world needs to know about this. It needs to know the price it's paid, what we've become.

When Oppenheimer got the go-ahead to start recruiting for the project, there was no Red-baiting going on, we just needed the brightest minds, and fast. To slay the dragon, we needed a magic sword. Oppenheimer himself was questionable, and his brother was all but a card-carrying Red since the thirties. So a few pinks slipped into the wash. Out of the egghead Jews, Poles, Czechs and what-have-you Hitler chucked out of Europe, there were bound to be a few. They were all a lot of odd ducks, and even the few staunch superpatriots in the bunch, Teller and his cadre, could get pretty cold when they discussed kill-ratios and maximum yields, and such. It didn't seem to matter who they were talking about bombing, they were so in love with the challenge. So nobody at the time took particular exception to Dr. Lux, least of all the Pentagon. Not at first, not when he was blowing them down with his formulas.

But in a pond full of odd ducks, Dr. Lux was the oddest. Nobody had ever heard of him, and nobody knew where they dug him up. Nobody ever even found out his real name. He might have just stepped down off a cloud, as far as Oppenheimer and the brass seemed to care. The top-rated rumors had him pegged as a German refugee, maybe a Socialist kraut, or even a Jew. We didn't know about all the things they were doing over there, but we knew Jews didn't figure in the plans. In any case, he had no accent when he did talk, which was seldom. Dr. Lux talked in numbers, big sweeping formulas on every wall in his house, even on the breakfast table, like he did figures to decide what to eat. That gave them fits; they had agents come in with cameras and photograph everything in the house when he left, and then scrubbed it all down. It was all gold, apparently.

Lux was in his late thirties when he came to Los Alamos, same as most everyone else, and if he was an enigma, he didn't stand out long. He became a linchpin in Bethe's Theoretical Group, and a lot of the brightest lights gathered around him. He and a bunch of the other theoreticians hung together, formed sort of a clique, they called themselves the Plowsharers. I guess Teller and Eisenhower might've stolen the name for their half-baked plan to rehabilitate the Bomb, for digging canals and nuclear power plants, later. Bethe might've exerted a powerful influence on Lux, or it might've been the other way around. His specialty was radiation: the X-rays and gamma rays and such that come out of the A-bomb, and out of the sun all the time. He had only a peripheral role in Manhattan, but they said his work would lay the groundwork for the new post-war world. The bomb would become the doorway into a new future without poverty, without war. Ah, they don't make bullshit like that, anymore...

After the war, there was a brain-trust bust at Los Alamos. A lot of them lost the stomach for the work after seeing their handiwork do its stuff on real live human beings. To be fair, there was less of a moral imperative; the Crusade was over, and the troops were coming home. Others went back to the ivory towers of academia and screamed bloody murder about what they'd helped to create. Those of us who were keeping score weren't surprised to see Bethe leave, but we were stunned when Lux didn't. We didn't know then that he couldn't.

Lux became the leading light in the Theoretical Group—somebody else led it, but to be honest, his name escapes me. The Plowsharers became a school of thought around the labs, and they liked to draw lines and make people dance to one side or the other. They liked to argue. With Bethe gone and Oppenheimer and Teller wrapped up in their own cold war over the H-bomb, the place got ugly. The secrecy became a fetish, and everybody took turns being on the outside of it.

The Plowsharers didn't keep secrets, at first. They said that all tools are inherently neutral morally, and that man decides to use them for good or ill. Rather than pursuing a more powerful bomb, they wanted the labs to turn to using the Bomb for peace, you know, make it rain on the deserts and feed the world, free energy, the whole utopian schtick. They dragged their feet, stopped just short of sabotage, to keep the H-bomb from happening. They tried to get everyone to believe that, if America alone had the Bomb, it would keep using it until the rest of the world was ashes or slave-states. Only by parity of annihilation— Mutually Assured Destruction, they've been calling it, lately—could the world be saved from big bad America.

Teller split up the brain-pool and got his own lab in California to speed things along, and the H-bomb came in '52, but all the work, all the magic, still came from Los Alamos. Lux was there when they destroyed that little island in the South Pacific, Elugelab, to measure the gamma ray emissions. He and some of the others clashed loudly on the ship just before the test, put on a disgraceful show in front of the sailors.

The Russians had just tested their own atom bomb, you see. The Rosenbergs went to the chair, and they got Klaus Fuchs, but they never did prove that any of them gave away The Bomb. Nobody dared to say it, but I don't think I was the only one who at least suspected that it was Lux, but it could have been goddamned Oppenheimer. Once you start trying to pick apart a secret, everything becomes the truth.

But nobody pointed fingers at Lux. He loved America. He wanted to make it into some kind of Buck Rogers wonderland, but he and his associates were loyal to the core. He'd been with the labs since the beginning. He never left the Hill, never even went into Santa Fe, and if he did anything to arouse suspicion, it was so often a deliberate prank to draw out the security, that he could have gotten away with murder, once they got sick of chasing their tails.

He went uncalled during the HUAC hearings. He wanted to come speak on behalf of Oppenheimer, when Teller pushed to revoke his clearance. They told him he couldn't. He was still top secret, and there was something about him that would have done more harm than good. He knew what they were talking about. He raged at them, but he went back to the drawing board. I don't think he was ever free to leave Los Alamos, or he probably would have, then.

He was working on a new kind of Bomb, and he hated it a thousand times more than the H-bomb. It was called a neutron bomb. Some kind of small nuclear explosion, but extra high radiation yield. Supposed to kill off the people, but leave all the buildings standing, but of course, none of us knew that, then.

For Lux, this one was especially nasty, because the temptation to use it wasn't tempered by dread of destroying the earth. Since bombed areas could swiftly be repopulated, he feared that the weapon would be used on the Russians at the earliest opportunity unless a balance of terror was struck. He didn't tell anyone this, and the Plowsharers meetings went underground, even for Los Alamos. People said they had styled themselves as an egghead star chamber, reviewing projects and deciding how much, if any, effort, to put into developing them. They were deciding what to let the Pentagon have, and, some said, deciding what to give the Soviets, to protect them from us.

It was a scary story, and the Pentagon brass shit their pants when they heard it. The wall of secrecy around Los Alamos became a dome, cutting off oversight from above. My reports started to come back unopened.

Dr. Lux had a nervous breakdown in the middle of the neutron bomb project, in the winter of '53, but he never stopped working. I had occasion to question him about his state of mental health. I think I asked him about his feelings about the Bomb. Did it bother him that he was making a weapon, and if so, why did he do it?

He told me, because he was an instrument of Nature, and it was in our Nature to destroy ourselves.

I asked him, didn't he think we could learn to live with the Bomb?

He told me, "Civilizations have risen to greater heights than ours, only to destroy themselves with the tools of their supremacy."

This set off alarm bells in my head. I hadn't thought he was really nuts. After they canned him, Oppenheimer preached about ancient nuclear weapons

turning up in the *Bhagavad-Gita*, you know, like
God kept planting this secret in our path so we'd
blow ourselves off his planet when we got too full
of piss and pride. I asked Lux if he believed that
humans had flown in spaceships and dropped the
Bomb before?

He replied, "Who said anything about humans?"

I recommended that Dr. Lux be reviewed by a
psychiatrist post haste. They didn't read that
one, either, I guess.

In the summer of '54, they tested the neutron
bomb in the South Pacific. You won't read about it
in the *World Book Encyclopedia* or *Life Magazine*,
but it happened. Secrecy was tighter on it than on
any test before or since, because they knew what
the world would think about that kind of Bomb, and
what the Russians would do. Just testing it could
cause a world war, if they weren't careful.

They picked out an atoll at 12, North, 170
West. I wasn't even supposed to know that much,
but pilots talk a lot. The place wasn't on any
maps, but spotter planes had noted it in the last
year, and old maps had placed it as a landfall. A
now-you-see-it kind of place, half a mile or so in
diameter. Perfect for their purposes.

The trip out was anything but smooth sailing.
We came out in a big amphibious plane to
rendezvous with the destroyer —— at the test
site. I accompanied the group in an observational
capacity. Dr. Lux was there, along with —— ——, —
—— ——, —— ——, and a bunch of technicians and
some unfamiliar counterintelligence agents from
one agency or another. They didn't bother to
introduce themselves, but it was clear from the
way the Navy brass deferred to them, that they
were in charge of security.

There weren't any complications with setting
up. No natives to clear out, not even any animals,
and only a shabby stand of palms. The scientists
came ashore to oversee the assembly of the bomb
and all the various measuring devices. The sailors

brought livestock, a whole barnyard assortment, and staked them down in rings. Then they threw together houses of plywood and brick and lead, and with much joking, staked down pigs inside them. They anchored a bunch of decommissioned PT boats offshore with more animals and fruits and vegetables and potted plants and measuring devices onboard. It was a real Old Testament sacrifice.

They tied it to a big weather balloon on cables and let it rise to three thousand feet. The bomb was pretty small, about the size of a trash can, with weird flanges on it that the scientists said were to minimize the blast itself so the radiation's effects could be measured. As it floated up, Dr. Lux and his cronies hummed "God Bless America" and saluted.

At the end, the leader of the other security group called all of the doctors together and announced that there was a leak at Los Alamos, and that a plot to give the neutron bomb plans to the Russians had just been uncovered. There would be no more show trials, no more abuses of the bomb program in the public eye. No more Fuchses, no more Rosenbergs, no more Oppenheimers. He then took out a pistol and shot Lux in both legs.

Everybody backed away from him as he fell. Lux tried to crawl to us, and we just kept backing away from him. He did what he did to strike a balance, he said. Without a balance of terror, the human race would destroy itself.

The others scattered, and the g-men herded them back onto the Navy boats. We heard Lux screaming all the way back to the destroyer.

The test was conducted as planned, and was a resounding success. They were instructed that this incident had never taken place, told that no one named Dr. Lux had ever worked on the bomb program, and left them to ponder the new consequences of espionage.

The docs fretted over an unintended side-effect of the neutron bomb: no trace of Lux was ever found, though it was impossible that he could have left the atoll or found shelter on it, and none of the animals disintegrated. It was like he was the only sacrifice worthy of being taken. God left us the burnt offerings to paw through, but He took away Dr. Lux.

But none of it ever happened. The neutron bomb was shelved, and, somehow, they kept the secret. I wouldn't have said anything, but I'm old, and the doctors say the Big C is coming for me, via my everloving lungs…well, where was I? Oh, you wanted to know about the Plowsharers.

Some of Lux's younger protégés rallied around his cause, albeit quietly, for fear of being erased themselves. A second-wave exodus drained the labs after the neutron test. A lot of the Plowsharers dropped out or went deeper still, into Livermore, or into DARPA, which was just getting underway. After the Red scare had blown over, they were still around, a smaller clique than before, and scattered throughout the system, and they changed their name. I was approached by one of the scientists with a document he claimed Lux had written. Anyway, that's who they told me it was. The name on the paper—I guess it was his real name—Keyes, Christian…ah, Keyes, I think. Maybe— What? Why don't I remember? How old are you? Maybe I didn't want to remember.

It was a manifesto, of sorts, proclaiming the brotherhood of knowledge as higher in authority than national loyalty, and calling for all scientists and soldiers, as the sense and the sword of the state, to band together in silent revolt against the impending apocalypse which the Cold War had made inevitable. "The Mission of all learned men is the preservation of our species, in the face of certain extinction at the hands of blind nationalism. This is our Mission, to give our lives and our blood, that our race shall endure and evolve in harmony with God and Nature." It was dangerous rhetoric, I agree, but I didn't report it. After what I'd seen with my own eyes, I couldn't say they weren't right.

There were always extra security precautions around the former Lux circle, but only a few of them are in the program to this day. The Advanced Group head at Livermore right now is a grave security risk, because he was the one who gave me the Mission manifesto, in, it must've been '60, maybe '61. He was a close associate of Dr. Lux, who mentored him and shaped his interest in radiation, and in utopian politics. No, not as in Communism. Jesus, you people are thick.

His name was Cornelius Armitage, but they all called him by his middle name, Darwin. I remember him because he was already pretty burnt up from playing with plutonium. People said he ate some after what happened to Dr. Lux, and that his shit glowed. He and this creep, Wittrock, run the group, now. They call it the Mission—

A phone rang, a tingling so faint he thought it must be a hallucination. It rang again and again. Mother detested answering machines, saying if she wasn't home, she simply was out of reach, and that should be that. She didn't pick it up. He looked at his watch. It was after three in the morning.

His knees popped loudly when he stood, and he walked slowly out and across the backyard to the kitchen door. The moon had restored at least some natural order to the night sky, though the atmospheric pollution had stained it the color of vitamin-enriched urine.

He went into the kitchen, still redolent of the roast beef Mother had made for dinner. The hearty aromas of home pushed him back into the comfortable ignorance of his boyhood, when he knew that he was different, but the world was good and just. He had eaten only some corn and some more cookies, but hovered over the roast beef until it went cold.

He answered the phone, but he held it away from his ear at first. There was no static on the line, though, only a voice he recognized, asking, "Mrs. Cundieffe? Mrs. Cundieffe? I apologize for the lateness of the hour, but may I speak to your son? It's extremely urgent."

"Brady?"

"Special Agent Cundieffe, my name is Hilton DeVore. I'm an associate of Mr. Hoecker. I presume we are speaking on a secure line?"

Cundieffe sputtered, uncertain if there was a code word involved, or if he should refuse the call on general principles. "Yes, go ahead."

"Your presence is required in Washington immediately, Agent Cundieffe."

"I already spoke to AD Wyler, and I'm on the next plane out. And what is your involvement with the FBI?"

"None. I'm speaking for Mr. Hoecker, who is cloistered at the moment. He has a lead for you."

"I just got back from pursuing the last lead I received from Mr. Hoecker, Mr. DeVore, and the only auto theft I observed was the theft of my rental car. I was the only one thrown in jail, and—"

"*Mizz.*"

"Pardon me?"

"Ms. DeVore, Mr. Cundieffe." The Mule's voice was nearly an octave lower than his own. "Did you follow the Channing Durban case?"

Cundieffe massaged his temples. The name sounded familiar, but he hadn't come across it in his Mission or Radiant Dawn research. "It escapes me, I'm sorry." His bitterness faded as he began to feel intrigue taking hold of him. It was something in the news, on the back pages, where things like propane explosions in California and military exercise accidents in Idaho ended up.

"The Naval Intelligence analyst from the NSA who went missing last month."

Cundieffe remembered it all now, what little there was. On New Years' Eve, Durban had disappeared, his house ransacked and luggage missing, accounts drained, wife abandoned and shell-shocked. It was suspected that he was a spy and had defected, but to where? That he had failed to turn up overseas only suggested that he had been killed by his patrons, or that he wasn't a spy, and had simply snapped. FBI Counterintelligence had found nothing to suggest that he had been in contact with a foreign power, let alone turning a profit. "Yes, I remember reading about him. Cold case, as I understand. I can put you in touch with the Counterintelligence Division, if you have another hot tip."

"Hoecker wants you. And the Institute is to know nothing of it. Especially not your superiors."

He was flabbergasted. "Why in the world would I want to do something like that?"

"Karl Schweinfurter died en route to Grangeville General Hospital."

"Pardon me?"

"Your witness, Karl Schweinfurter. He died while in Macy and Mentones' custody. They vivisected him, Mr. Cundieffe."

Cundieffe felt dinner turn over inside him. Why would they make up such a thing? Who would be expected to believe it? In light of everything else he saw, how could it not be true? "Why? Why would they do such a thing?"

"That's why they were sent. To collect specimens. To observe. Like you. They harvested his cancer."

"Am I supposed to feel responsible for this?"

"They're looking for Channing Durban. You have to hurry." She hung up.

Cundieffe sat down at the table. He reached for a glass of orange juice, but his hand came back empty the first three times.

What did this have to do with anything else? It had to be misdirection. Or another war. He really didn't know how many they were fighting, after all. But he did know he was already in enough trouble with the Cave Institute and the Bureau.

He got up. Passing Mother's bedroom, he heard her steady respiration and the rustle of starched sheets. He drew the door to and went into his old bedroom.

The walls were still plastered with posters—the periodic table, the solar system, a table of fingerprint types; his certificate from the Academy at Quantico; a photograph of the Director with his father and mother, the stout and deadpan Mr. Hoover awkwardly holding swaddled infant Martin like a smelly but pivotal piece of evidence. All his life had been indoctrination into this world in which he now found himself. All his senses had been honed to seek out secrets, he'd believed, to bring them to light for the security of the American people. All along, he'd had it all backwards.

He sat down at his computer and logged on to a site he'd set up to keep his Radiant Dawn files. He'd known it was a security risk. Every step of gathering them had led to reprimands, and copying them out of the system was a security breach of monumental proportions. But after the pattern of official resistance had led him to believe he'd accomplish nothing for the Bureau by pursuing it, he'd been unable to stand back and let them be deleted. Somebody, somewhere, would thank him for staying on it. He thanked himself, now.

He opened a page of encrypted document scans and entered the eighteen-digit password, and the streams of nonsensical characters vanished, and were replaced by financial statements. He strolled through them until he came to property holdings. Idaho wasn't listed, but the Owens Valley community was. Others—islands—were clumped together, and had no names—only GPS coordinates. He bit his lip and tasted blood.

There it was. No reason to hide it; not even his Father, the custodian of the Director's forbidden Blue files, had ever read them, so why would anyone take notice?

He bowed his head. The weight of the secrets, shadows growing together around his neck, finally pulled him under.

Cyril Keogh was Dr. Lux, Christian Keyes, a man who never was, a traitor who died in a neutron bomb test that never took place, on an atoll that came and went with the tide. His only lasting legacy—the Mission. Now, he—or someone else who looked very much like him, who knew his secrets—had founded Radiant Dawn, perhaps as a means of avenging himself against the government that had used and executed him. If so, why were the Mission seemingly fighting him on their own, while the government abetted and protected him?

He shut off the computer and went back to the kitchen. Secrets piled up on him, burying him alive. He could do nothing to stop it, let alone shed light on them, but he thought—he desperately hoped—he knew someone who could.

He left a message for Storch, then called a cab to take him to LAX.

~ 30 ~

The brilliant white-gold sunlight and the blue, blue water stabbed his eyes out. His pupils cinched down to slivers as he looked out the crew chief's window at the ocean. There were no islands in sight below to lend a sense of scale, no features to relieve the stark purity of the view, which was as hard and clean and abstract as a geometry proof. The sky, the ocean, mirrors facing each other, the sun and its reflected rival on the face of the waters, following them to their destination. Where they were going was a matter of mathematics, as well, a nameless place no map showed, no history book recorded.

They were twenty thousand feet over the center of the Central Pacific Basin, 1600 miles south by southwest of Hawaii, and nearly six hundred miles north of the nearest inhabited island. The average ocean depth here was about four thousand feet. There were no shipping lanes here, no human or animal presence at all. In a region of the world where every rock large enough to host a palm tree sprouted a village with a culture and a language all its own, this invisible place had gone unnoticed, unnamed until the eggheads came with their bomb, and it became a damned and deadly place unfit for all but the lowest forms of life. When Storch heard Cundieffe's message, he knew this was the place.

The Mission was happy to send him. He could give two shits about their motives. They called it an advanced recon mission to his face, a toxic waste dump among themselves, when they thought he couldn't hear. So much the better.

They verified the target and Don Costello made the arrangements, and the next day they left. He spent the night plundering the Mission's boundless and erudite stores. He had to order some things that raised eyebrows, but Wittrock gave him carte blanche to carry out whatever he could on his back. He stretched their conceptions of what a man could carry, and made an armory of his room. Carrying it was one thing, fighting with it quite another, and he whittled down his selection to fit in a hundred pound pack, with another thirty pounds of ammunition and random gear distributed throughout his jumpsuit. That and the parachute would send a normal man to the bottom of the sea, but he was able to run four flights of stairs in the rig without breaking a sweat.

He stared at the naked blue spot on the map, and at the satellite printout taped up beside it. A ring-shaped coral reef atoll sitting on a spire of a sea mount that reared defiantly up out of the 4400 foot-deep abyssal plain that stretched out for hundreds of miles in every direction. The ring almost completely embraced a lagoon half a mile in diameter. A concrete foundation still stood at the south end of the atoll, where America staged its first and last above-ground neutron bomb test. On the northeast edge of the atoll, a circular knob of island, barely a hundred acres of bald rock and sand and green scabs of vegetation, with a horseshoe of concrete bunkers in the center. Tiny toadstools shaded the rooftops–a research station and satellite relay center, all unmanned because of plutonium in the soil with a half-life of some 240,000 years. The Mission had come across it in tracing the RADIANT command signals, but never had any reason to think it was important.

Storch avoided Stella, but he peered over the edge of the top floor into the forest on the way to the motor pool. It was still dark inside, but he could see the heat of her, prowling. If she saw him, she gave no sign.

He and Costello and his crew of two went down the mountain in a truck to the Blue Mesa reservation's airstrip, and within an hour, they were airborne in the same plane that brought him here only—what, a week ago? They locked themselves in the cockpit, leaving him alone in the cabin for the duration. He dozed with his eyes open and his hands turning the pages of a *National Geographic*.

They landed at an Air Force base somewhere in the desert. His ears popped, and it was sunny outside and four hours had passed. The wind buffeted the small plane as it taxied into an open hangar way down at the furthest end of the flight line. In four hours they could have traveled a thousand miles. It might've been Nellis or Indian Springs or Area fucking 51 for all he cared.

Costello and his crew came out in dark blue flight suits and gave him one. "Just put this on. I'm not going to tell you where we are, so don't ask. While we're outside, don't talk to anybody, and don't touch anything. We're changing planes."

They deplaned into a hangar and got on a C-130 parked directly opposite. The crew ran through the pre-flight check while Costello warmed up the cockpit. Storch lugged his gear into the cavernous cabin and was startled to find it already full of cargo. He laid his pack gingerly down next to the mound of boxes under a heavy nylon net and sat on it. He did not move when they took off. He sat still through the flight, riding out the rolling turbulence that meant they were over the Pacific. He remained so as Costello turned over the controls five hours out and came back to commence a good-natured but relentless effort to chat him up. "So I understand you're going to jump out of my airplane. When were you last jump-certified?"

Storch shrugged.

"When, Sergeant? Five years ago? Ten?"

Storch nodded.

"Well, which is it? I'm a civilian, now, so don't pull that dumb grunt shit with me."

"Ten years." He looked up at Costello for the first time, bound and determined to make him regret it. "I can fucking jump. Go fly the fucking plane."

"Nice attitude." Costello rolled up his sleeve and presented his thick, vein-strangled forearm. An anchor tattoo, blue and blurry under curly bronze hair. Below it, an island maiden winked at him. "I did three tours on subs in Vietnam and after, son, while you were swimming around in your daddy's balls. If I learned anything, it was how to get along with all kinds of assholes. You have to, when you're in a can with everyone's farts and bad breath and shit in your face all day and night. When I discharged, I started flying so I could get away from assholes and their stink, and you're stinking up my fucking plane."

Storch bowed his head and took a deep breath. Of all the imbalanced and damaged people Storch had met in the Mission, Costello alone actually seemed to kind of like him. He wasn't afraid of him, he didn't hate him, and he didn't want anything from him. "What do you need to know?"

"I have the coordinates and the flight plan and everything, but nobody's said anything about extraction. How are we getting you out?"

"I'll get myself out."

"Have you looked at the map, Sergeant? It's a long fucking swim. Now, I've got a modified STABO rig like the choppers in 'Nam used to use, but it's got a balloon that hoists the snare to altitude. I can drop it on the atoll and pick you up when you call me."

"I'm not taking a radio."

Costello's hand reached out to grab his shoulder, but Storch stared it down. Costello pulled it back like he'd been burned. "I can't let you do that. I don't know what you're planning to do down there, and I don't much give two shits, but I need to know I can get you out."

"Why? The Mission doesn't want me back. I'll get out on my own, don't worry about me."

Costello shook his head slowly. "No, son, you won't."

Storch's ears popped. "Why are we descending?" he demanded. He got off his pack and flipped open the holster at his hip. His other hand went for Costello's throat. Though the pilot jumped back, only Storch's will stopped it from snapping his neck.

"We've got to take on fuel in Honolulu," Costello said, eyes riveted to the hand.

"We don't need to stop."

"We do if we want to come back. We're cleared there, we'll be in the air again in two hours."

"What do they think we are?"

"Naval research mission, dropping marker buoys in the basin to measure tidal radiation from Bikini and Eniwetak, and all the other underrated vacation destinations. Very classified."

Storch waved at the cargo. "And these are the marker buoys?"

"Hey, you don't tell me what you're doing, don't ask me—"

"It's lysing agent. Your orders are to drop me at the target, then circle back and bomb the atoll with nasty green shit."

Costello looked back at the cockpit for a long moment, nodded.

"Don't worry about me. Follow your orders. How long will I have?"

"Three hours, that's the most we can burn fuel. I can land on Howland Island to the south and lay over for twelve hours, if you think it'll make a difference. But if I'm out there any longer, the real Navy will start to notice."

"That'll be enough time. Do it."

Costello shouted in his face. "I am not going to drop gas on you, son. I will follow my orders but you're not jumping out unless I can get you back."

"Why do you give a shit? Because I look human?" He let his anger change him just a little. Costello recoiled. "Your commanders can't believe how good they got it, burning me and Keogh in the same place. Don't fuck it up for them."

"I'll wait twenty-four hours, and I'll drop the recovery rig before I light it up. But if I don't see you—"

"You won't see me," Storch said. "Now go fly the fucking plane."

Costello turned and started to go back to the cockpit, but stopped and called back over the din of the engines, "You were at Heilige Berg, right?"

Storch, trying to push himself back into focus, nodded impatiently and moved closer.

"So you saw my raid?"

"What? *Your* raid?"

"Not the ground assault, that was Aranda's, but the air attack was mine. I flew all the planes. Built them, too."

"You flew all of the planes…"

"Oh, most of them were on programs generated off the terrain, but I ran a lot of them myself."

"Yeah, I saw it," Storch said, uncertain where this was going.

"What did you think?"

"What did I think?"

"Yeah, you saw it. I was a hundred miles away the whole time, I only got to watch the screens. What was it like?"

Storch winced. He remembered his bitter exultation at the sight of the machine-on-machine holocaust. It had showed him a little bit more of why he no longer wanted to be human. "It was pretty cool, I guess."

"Pretty cool? I had sixty drones in the air, radar-doubled to look like two hundred. I took out two computer-controlled Helicon and Bofors artillery batteries and a Cobra gunship with less than twenty percent casualties, then dumped the rest on the goddamned target like coins down a fucking wishing well."

"The target was a sham," Storch said in as reasonable a tone as he could manage. "They were long gone."

"Aranda said we got them all."

"Aranda lies. I don't know why, but he's full of shit."

Costello puzzled something out, then his grin widened. "So it really was empty?"

"Practically. There was a company of mercs guarding it, but I think the ground assault and Keogh's army killed them all."

Costello turned and skipped back to the cockpit. "Guess we'll have to do it again, then."

Storch didn't move while they refueled in Honolulu. He drank some water in-flight and ate some pineapple that Costello brought. He rotated plans in his head as they took off again and turned south. He played scenarios for hours. He replayed his memories of the shadow that ruled his body for nearly six months. He fought nausea as the memories churned his nervous system and clenched his bowels. He had to keep his breakfast down, or he might as well go home. He kept his breathing even and his temperature low, but he couldn't keep his mind in check.

His body changed to keep him alive at all costs, but his mind ran ever on, tangling him up in decidedly human recriminations and guilt. How long would he have to waste energy like this, before his body decided thought was a maladaptive trait, and took it away?

He had saved Stella Orozco. He was clear. He owed nobody anything. She was free and safe from harm. More, she was strong. She could withstand anything, now. *Just like you. Just like Dyson.*

You're going out of your mind because of your body, and your body is coming along for the ride. What will you be tomorrow, or next year? Will you still be able to remember your name? That's what you gave to her, to keep her safe.

He had delivered her from slavery to madness, and left her like a ticking bomb in the heart of the Mission. Was she some sort of revenge on them? Or just another coil in his cycle of failure, of falling short when it really mattered? She thought he was going away because he was ashamed and afraid of what they did, and what they became when they did it. But he was going there before he rescued her. The FBI agent only showed him the way. He was a missile on terminal approach. It was her own bad fortune to have gotten mixed up with him in the first place.

Still, her words dug at him. *He wants you to go.*

They were all wrong. Beneath all the technology and the mystical brainwashing, he was only a man. He could be killed. Storch had yet to discover what, if any, meaning his life had, but it was not all an accident. He had never given any serious contemplation to the truth or falsity of the existence of God, but he knew in his heart that the Creator was not a thing from outer space. They were not the children of a mistake. He would hear that abomination give him the truth, the final truth, before Storch executed him.

They want you to go.

The Mission was terminally fucked. They were the human dinosaurs' last impotent gesture of defiance at their successor. That successor would never be Keogh.

Nobody wants you to come back.

She was better off without him. They would only tear each other apart, and he was never any good at teaching anyone else how to be human, anyway.

He checked his chute and his altimeter. He shrugged into his heavy pack and turned on the jump light. The cockpit opened and Costello came out. Storch threw the lever that opened the rear of the plane. The deck split at the aft end of the cabin, and lowered to form a gaping maw, a ramp to the roaring sky.

Costello clung to the netting on the bulkhead. Storch checked his GPS unit again. They were within a mile of the target. Costello shouted something at him, but the wind tore it away.

So fucking go.

Storch gave him a thumbs up, turned and ran off the end of the ramp.

The human body does strange things when it thinks it's going to plummet to its death. In even seasoned paratroopers, the adrenal glands go berserk, and the bowels go cold as blood flow is diverted to muscles to fight gravity to the death. Storch's body was no different. He started to change almost before he jumped.

The wind lifted him up off the end of the ramp and he actually rose up for a moment, buffeted by the wake of the plane, before gravity took over. A membrane formed over his eyes so he could stare, unblinking, at the tiny circular reef, twenty thousand feet below.

He'd logged two hundred training jumps and three combat jumps in Panama and Iraq, and knew what to expect. He packed his own chute. Still, his body didn't trust him. His back arched and his arms and legs splayed out to maximize his surface area, but his body hurtled on at terminal velocity. Trapped between featureless planes of brilliant blue, the illusion that he was floating on the buffeting column of air was overwhelming. Only the retreating, rising speck of the plane, and the oncoming, expanding bone-white scab of the atoll told him he was falling.

His chest expanded and his lats inflated like airbags under his arms. The harness holding the pack to his chest, an intricate system of canvas cords and duck tape, tore apart under the strain. He flailed out at it, but the roaring wind stripped the pack off him. It floated just out of reach for a moment, then the wind set it twirling at his head, and out of sight. His arms refused to reach for it.

At ten thousand feet, he figured out that his body was trying to grow wings. His arms cramped up and his skin burned like needles were growing out of it. He tried to keep his mind from screaming into blind animal panic, tried to play along with his insane body and find an answer to what was happening. His body did not trust the parachute, and was finding its own way to the ground.

Have you eaten anything lately that had wings?

Sure, he thought. Turkey, chicken…*but nothing that could fly—*

He tried to focus on the island. He saw no antiaircraft missiles or artillery. Three concrete bunkers stood on the high ground of the island at the top of the atoll. The lagoon looked very different from the satellite picture. It was thoroughly overgrown with coral formations and tangles of kelp around the shallow edges, but the bottom dropped out into blank cerulean blue at the center. The shores of the atoll were likewise fringed with a thick growth of seaweed and coral, but the tide lashing against it seemed to thin it out. He tried to shape his body into a bullet aimed at the bunkers and opened his chute.

The chute ripped out of the pack and exploded into a canopy in the same instant that Storch's overtaxed shoulder straps tore free. He was whipped upside down by the harness around his groin. The brutal pull of deceleration turned his head inside out, but he forced his arms to grab the tattered chute harness and climb back into it.

He looked down and saw his pack splash in the lagoon. The water churned, and it disappeared. He grabbed the steering toggles and yanked on them until the parachute began to fitfully spiral down to the north end of the atoll.

As he got closer, its features came into sharper relief. The kelp strands stretched out for hundreds of yards into the open ocean, cables as thick as telephone poles waving in the tide—and bleeding. Clouds of deep red fanned out in all directions on the sweeping tides that converged on the lone atoll.

He knew that the island nations of Micronesia and the Marshalls, to the west, were among the most shark-infested in the world, and that sharks would follow a blood-scent across hundreds of miles. The island's plant life lured them here to feed, and they came. He saw gray shadows circling the atoll in concentric rings that suggested this was an ancient feeding frenzy. Strangely, they did not attack each other, but single-mindedly waged war on the bleeding seaweed.

An eight foot thresher shark launched itself up out of the blood-foamed surf, a tower of muscle driven by silent agony beyond measure, and for a stark, screaming second, Storch thought it was going to fly all the way up to him and get him in its snapping jaws. Black segmented tentacles snaked up out of the foam and snared the shark with millions of barbed teeth, dragged it down beneath the red waves. Gripping the toggles tighter, he focused on the island.

The concrete bunkers were low, rambling pillbox-shaped shells with palisades of glass-faced lead bricks to the south and crumbling flanges and buttresses sprawling in all directions, suggesting a complex of structures that had been torn or blown down in the years since the test. They were overgrown in broad-leafed vines that reminded Storch of the kudzu he'd seen growing around the bases he'd lived on in Georgia and Alabama. It looked like a fugitive from the jungle, not like the sort of amphibious pickleweed that grew in tidal zones, as he would have expected from a place periodically engulfed by the ocean. Rippling and rustling in the wind, the vines grew so fast you could hear them.

Satellite dishes sprouted on the roof, which was totally clear of vines, as if they'd only been pruned yesterday, or knew not to grow there. As he drifted closer, one of the dishes moved. The sound of its motors grated eerily over the wind and waves.

He had expected more. An army of him on the shore, or just one, waiting to receive him with open arms and sparkling gray eyes, unsurprised by his arrival, ready to fight and win or die, but tell him what it all meant. He deserved that much, at least. But there was only the freakish battle in the surf, and the vines strangling the lonely bunkers, and the satellite dishes, turning like flowers to hearken to the secret illumination of creeping satellites. The one they controlled from here was gone. That much, at least, had been no trick. Perhaps this island was only an empty relay station, after all. He almost thought he could hear Keogh laughing at him.

The earth rushed up under him all of a sudden. He landed on his feet, but the jarring brittleness of the ground shocked him to his knees. His chute dragged him across the island, full-bellied on the whipping surface wind. He shook the toggles off his hands and went for the quick-release button, but it was gone, torn away when his body tried to change in the air. The wind yanked him forwards again. The ground offered him no traction. The gray-white coral-rock was smooth as bone, with only a thin layer of sand on it, and shallow, elliptical pits everywhere like the holes in an Indian grinding stone, or the breathing-holes in an abalone shell.

His boots skidded impotently across the rock. His hands fought with the cinches around his legs, but they were numb from the strain of steering the parachute and his blood flow was all fucked up because his body tried to grow fucking wings—

His heels caught on the lip of a pit, and the wind died down. The chute settled to the ground. He reached for the cinches and undid the left one. He went momentarily limp as blood coursed into the starved limb. He flexed his hand, reached for the right cinch.

The chute was snatched up again, and jerked Storch off his feet. Rock hit his head. Through pinwheels of demented sunlight, he saw that the wind didn't have his chute. Tentacles rose up out of the lagoon and rended the chute to shreds, dragging him toward the madly churning water.

Storch scrabbled madly for a handhold with one hand and tore at the thick belt of nylon around his right thigh. His legs spasmed and kicked like a hanged man's death throes, and suddenly, his right leg flexed and grew, thickened so fast the blood drained out of Storch's head and he almost fainted. The pain was enormous, but in an instant, it was over. The leg strap popped and he fell out of the harness. The thrashing kelp-tentacles drew the empty parachute into the lagoon.

He lay on his back, chest heaving, each breath like a month in traction. His skin tingled. A billion microscopic plutonium beestings pricked him. A million subatomic bullets exploding through the busy little microcosms of his skin cells: hundreds of thousands of particles smashing the delicate superstructures of his DNA helices into strands of deranged acid debris. If he were a normal human being, he'd be dead in hours, disintegrating on this beach where only kudzu grew and the seaweed ate sharks, while Keogh laughed, somewhere else in the world and deep inside his head.

But he could feel his cells going to work, rebuilding, refining defenses against the onslaught. His skin thickened into scales and bony shell-plates under his jumpsuit. The half-formed hair-feathers sprouting down his arms burst through the sleeves as thick thorns of keratin. He felt the burn of the radiation damping down, as it changed him. He was becoming less human every moment he spent on this island.

He got up and patted himself down. He still carried thirty pounds of weapons, explosives and ordnance in bellows pockets all over the suit, and more inside. He drew an M9 Beretta 9mm from a hip pocket, and slid in a fifteen-round clip of green-tipped bullets. His finger was covered in thickening scales, and barely fit through the trigger-guard. Looking over his shoulder at the hungry lagoon, he walked towards the bunkers.

Kudzu stirred, though the wind had stopped. He circled around a bunker until he found a recess in the wall of vines that might be a door. He probed the vines over the door, recoiled. Under their shield-leaves, the vines must be hairy with thorns, which shredded his sleeve, though they couldn't break his skin. He took out his K-Bar knife and slashed at the vines. They wept green sap and parted to reveal a blind wall of lead bricks.

He knew only a little about the old island A-bomb tests, but he knew that they buried all the radioactive trash in the bunkers and sealed them up. In all likelihood, there was only more of the same inside. But there were satellite dishes on the roof, and this was the place where it all started. He had to be here. There had to be something inside—

He took out a brick of C4, sliced open the shrink-wrap and tore it into strips. He mashed these into the join where the bricks met the concrete, using the entire one-pound block, and jabbed a detonator into it. The detonator looked like the face of a cheap digital watch with wire leads snaking out of it, which, essentially, it was. You could shoot at plastique, or pour gasoline on it and burn it without making anything but smoke. It took an electrical charge to make it explode.

He walked away fifty feet and took shelter behind a projecting buttress. The wind shifted, bringing the bloody, voiceless battle in the surf to his ears. He took out the remote, checked the channel, and pressed the button.

Nothing happened.

He went back over to the doorway. The detonator was gone. He eyed the rustling vines suspiciously. How oddly easy it was, now, to just accept that the fucking vines stole it. They were too green to burn, and he only had four more detonators. He couldn't waste one.

He hacked the vines back with the knife and plugged in another detonator, backed away without blinking or looking away. Sure enough, the fuckers came creeping around the wall towards the detonator. He shot at them once, twice, tearing off a stalk so that the leaves fell away and he saw what else lay beneath. It was not kudzu. It bore only an incidental resemblance to any species of the plant kingdom, but it was not truly an animal, either.

Under their leaves, the vines were covered in silver-gray eyes like coins, and black, questing thorn-tongues, and other things that neither an animal nor a plant had any business with.

He pressed the detonator. It worked.

He threw himself prone on the coral ground. The concussion rolled over him and filled the air with ingots of lead. Over the supersonic crack of the explosion, the vines screamed. Smoke rolled in the cavity he'd made.

He got up and approached with the gun extended before him, disturbed but a little comforted to see how his hand was growing over it. He walked up to the hole, picked up a chunk of lead and tossed it through. It vanished through the smoke, but the dull clang of metal stopped it somewhere inside. Fanning the smoke out of his eyes, he stalked over the low mound of lead and into the hole.

His eyes adjusted to the gloom and the dust, but there was nothing to see. Stacked floor to ceiling, wall to wall, rusting barrels leaked on the lead-lined floor. The black and yellow radiation symbols on them were barely legible through the layers of corrosion. The radiation here was almost a visible exhalation from the barrels. It cut through him, playing havoc with his cells, turning them against each other.

He backed away, stumbling outside and running away down the beach. He stopped at the surf when the black kelp sensed his approach and reared up out of the waves to embrace him. He shot into the surf on reflex. He backed away from the water, standing midway between the two threats and looking up into the hurtfully blue sky, but now he saw only Keogh's eye, staring down on him.

A hammerhead shark hurled itself out of the sea and flopped across the coral beach before the black tentacles took it back. Its gasping jaws snapped silently at the air. Its dull black eyes glinted dumb malice as it was eaten alive.

"I know you're here!" he roared at the island. "I know you, motherfucker, and I know you know me! I found you, didn't I? Found your home! This is where you live, isn't it? Where you came from?"

He walked up the beach to the lagoon. He pulled a grenade from his breast pocket and bit off the pin, chucked it into the thickest clump of Keogh-kudzu. It exploded, tossing whipping salad and shrill vegetable screams into the air.

"You were just a man once, and I bet you're still just a man! You're not a god, and if you can't come out and face me, you ain't even much of a man!"

He threw another grenade into the lagoon. The kelp made a whirlpool around where it hit the water. It blew a Volkswagen-sized bubble of ocean into the air, black kelp and red blood spraying the setting sun. The lagoon went insane. The kelp-tentacles thrashed and rose up, and clusters of eyes bloomed on their tips. Wise silver-gray eyes. Storch almost understood.

"Why don't you come out and face me, man to man, motherfucker? You talked a big line of shit in my head, but now that I'm here, I don't see much to back it up. What are you hiding from, Keogh?"

The ground stirred beneath his feet. The vines rattled their shield leaves and grew taller. The black kelp stood on end in the air like statically charged hair. Suckered tentacles and massive jointed crustacean claws knitted together into a single, towering form above the water.

Storch froze with his foot in mid-air before one of the shallow pits in the coral. The bottom disappeared, or rather, it opened, because the pit was really an eye socket. A great gray compound eye regarded him from the pit. All around him, eyes opened in the ground—eyes and mouths brimming with gnashing shark teeth and eager, darting tongues.

"I'm not hiding from you, Zane," said the island. "I've been waiting for you."

Storch pointed at the eye between his feet and shot it. The enormous lens puckered and sank like a soufflé, a spray of plasma turning to green suds as the bullet dissolved and went to work.

The island screamed. The kudzu grew furiously at him. The writhing tower in the lagoon flew apart and became a cyclone of black snakes. Storch fired at it, too, but the shots went wild. He was ducking whiplash tendrils and armored flails, but there was no single body to put a bullet into. He fired at the coral between his feet, at the field of eyes and fang-rimmed maws yawning and leering at him, at the formless, endless face stretching to the horizon.

There was nowhere to run. The island *was* Keogh.

The island laughed, and the sound ate away at him like the radiation, and the sun was low on the horizon, it would be full dark, soon—

He ran out of bullets. Tendrils like cobras made of iron rebar snared his right hand as it went for another clip. Thorns dug into his arm, grew through shell and skin and muscles and into his bones. They caught the other arm as he tried to free the right, and stretched him out prone on the coral. He looked up into the indigo sky and prayed, *let the plane come now, let Don not give a shit about me, let him come and blow this all away—*

"I am somewhat larger than you expected, yes?" Keogh's voice came from every pore in the rock. "But you didn't come to destroy me, did you, Zane? You always come to take from me. Take my cures, my lessons, my bodies, and this time, you want the whole truth. You want to know what you're fighting."

The tentacles grew thicker around him, bit deeper. He tried to tear himself free, but it was beyond pain. His bonds sank tiny rhizoid teeth into his bones. Tearing free meant tearing himself apart. He would do it now and die content, but for the truth of what the island said. He had come to *know.*

"I want to tell you, Zane. I've been waiting for someone to come here, so that I can make them understand. Even though you turned your back on us when we needed you most, I'm so glad it was you."

Storch was lifted off his feet and borne closer to the lagoon. His vision fogged with pain, but he could hear water rushing. Was He going to throw him into the surf? Storch strained to see.

The lagoon was below him. The forest of tentacles and armored limbs grew out of the inner walls of the lagoon, which was a ribbed orifice with no visible bottom, a titanic alimentary canal extending down to the ocean floor, almost a mile below. Colossal engines of valves and striated muscle, like a Panama Canal of dinosaur hearts, stirred the water into a roiling whirlpool. The smell of it engulfed him, choking him and invading his palate, a sickening submarine stench that was so familiar to him because he'd tasted it in his own sweat. Inexorably, unmoved by his frantic resistance, the tentacles dragged him into the water, giving him only a moment to suck in a breath and hold it. The briny seawater was warm as blood when it closed over his head.

Inside, it was like a city, a thriving megalopolis in the abdominal cavity of God. The walls, nearly a quarter mile away on all sides, bristled with fleshy edifices camouflaged as sponges and anemones, an entire ecosphere of false lures designed to attract and devour prey. Perversely, this gave him a crumb of comfort amid the rampaging dread eating into his gut. *It needs to eat,* he thought, *which means it's not a god.*

The tentacles bore him down below the rim of the lagoon, the waning purple sunlight flashing before his eyes, then disappearing. Organs among the obscene clusters on the walls of the pit made their own light, a pallid, bluish glow that reminded him of the tunnels in Idaho, and the light behind Keogh's eyes in his nightmares. Looming structures of bony coral and sails of corrugated flesh jutted out from the walls—stomachs like industrial kilns in a foundry, their mouths fringed with restlessly waving cilia; pulsing sacs like kidneys the size of houses, trailing sewer-pipe veins; endless, gnarled coils of what might have been intestine or fields of brain tissue; great, glowing eyes that goggled at him on stalks and from billboard-sized sockets all over the walls. Lips and beaks and sphincters of skyscraper anemones and shark-mouthed worms purred in his ear as he descended deeper, ever deeper, into Keogh.

Going limp in the rising pressure-grip of the ocean depths, he let himself be passed from tentacle to tentacle. The mammoth limbs grew in narrow groves like kelp farms that extended down the walls into inky infinity. The terrain of the interior only got stranger, the organs so alien in their structure that he was grateful for the creeping darkness that swallowed them, and him, up.

Then there was a dim, butterscotch-colored light in the deep before him. It swelled to fill his vision, and then he was being pressed against a wall, soft, pliant, splitting before him like a womb in reverse. Scarcely a drop of water spilled through with him as he passed through the other side and fell through hot, damp air.

"I told you once that education is a series of ever more complicated lies, preparing one, by stages, for the truth. This is what I am, Zane, behind the last mask. I've been waiting here for so long, waiting for a species like yours to evolve and develop the technology I needed. When he came— when we became I—he showed me the way, even as he showed me how desperately my return was needed."

"You—should have stayed here," Storch hissed. "Nobody needed you. You never should have been."

"But I was, Zane. I am, and I will be. And I am needed. There were many among you so decadent they thought they could gain by assisting me. The spiral of decay and extinction flows faster in your race than it did in my masters' time."

Storch was just conscious enough to be confused. "Your masters?"

"I myself have climbed the evolutionary ladder in my lifetime, but I arose from the humblest beginnings, humbler than your own. I was once the lowest form of life that has ever toiled on this earth. I was a slave."

The tentacles set him down on a ledge of naked bone beneath a cloacal opening in the wall. The space was enclosed in some sort of membrane, a translucent bubble that projected out into the central well about twenty feet. Just beneath the ledge, the water lapped at still more colossal appendages far below.

Storch gagged on waves of white-hot pain as the tendrils disengaged from him and retreated into the murky labyrinth of flesh beyond the membrane. He collapsed and choked back hot bile. His legs would not obey. His arms would not lift him up. Shivers rolled him into a tight fetal ball, the barrel of his empty pistol digging into his armpit.

"Oh, but I've damaged you," the island murmured, heavy with remorse. Something hissed and blew a chill breeze across Storch's back. "See to yourself in there."

Storch looked up. Deep inside the rigid muscular sphincter set in the wall, an open door led to an airlock very much like the one in Colorado. It reminded him of the rooms they put dogs in to "euthanize" them, by which they meant suck the breath out of them in a box. It was dead metal and steel-reinforced glass. He crawled into it gratefully.

Already, his pain was blunted and turning to tingling hints of reduced function. His body rerouted resources to close the thousands of bone-deep wounds all over his body, but he was already so strained from the jump and the radiation, that the changes crawled. When the door closed behind him and sealed with a mechanized gasp, he was too weak to turn and block it. The inner door hissed open, and air-conditioned chill washed over him. He crawled into the next chamber and rolled onto his back.

The low ceiling was layered concrete, the floor the same with a Persian rug. Across the chamber from where he lay, there was a functional low-budget hotel room, with a queen sized bed and a television, a refrigerator and cabinets, a microwave oven, and a bathroom with shower stall. The only thing missing was a picture window overlooking a pool. This had been replaced with tiers of computers chained together by a spider's web of cables. Four monitors slept on a long console set into the wall, but a single keyboard stood out of the trash and junk food wrappers covering the desk.

Storch's nerves pricked. He searched the one-room bunker. A closet, filled with t-shirts, boxer shorts, pajama bottoms and sandals, and two radiation suits. Another closet that was really an elevator, which meant there was another exit, probably inside another of the bunkers. The cupboards full of blank CD's, Doritos, Twinkies, vitamins, non-alcoholic beer. Ashtray half-filled with marijuana roaches and pistachio shells. All the things that made up the distinctly sour and artificially preserved sweat of Ely Buggs.

So the fucker lived. He was the reason for the regular planes out here. Shuttling him to and from this bunker, where he ran the information systems that kept RADIANT online, and God knew what else. He sure as shit wasn't here now, but his mess was. Storch picked his way through it to the shower and painfully, painstakingly, washed Keogh out of his wounds.

Examining his own body was little better than looking at one of Spike Team Texas. The chitinous shell that had grown over most of his body sloughed off and wouldn't stop bleeding where Keogh had torn it. He looked like a blasphemous freak from a sideshow. Still and all, his body had barely managed to keep him alive.

He wasn't getting out of here. If Keogh didn't get him, the bombs would, or the sharks would, or the hundreds of miles of ocean would, or the Mission would. The realization was strangely liberating. *You are not insane. It's the world that's crazier than a shithouse rat.* He could still do it, he realized. He's not a man, but he's not a god. *Die knowing,* he said to himself. *Die killing him.*

He walked out of the bunker and through the airlock into the yawning central cavity of the island. Outside the bubble, stars twinkled in a tiny circle of lesser darkness a few hundred feet above his head. Eyes opened all around him.

Storch sucked in a deep breath, held it down in the floor of his lungs for a long moment, and called out. "I want to see your face. You say you're a man. Show me."

"Very well, if it will make you more comfortable."

The membrane sagged, bulged and split open. The wall became a womb, and something spilled out into the bubble. A nodule of pulsating fetal tissue dangled from a tangle of umbilical cables. They danced like copulating snakes as they pumped life into the quivering fetus, which grew before Storch's eyes into a tall gaunt human form. At last it trembled with animation and opened its ageless gray eyes to take in Storch from this novel new angle, and when it rose and climbed onto the ledge beside him, he took a shocked step back. The umbilical cables went slack, but did not disengage. Where they joined Keogh's head and neck and back and groin, they still seemed to exchange fluids, and Storch could see sparks of electricity shooting up and down the hideous translucent cords.

"I never meant to harm anyone, Zane. I am the end of pain, the end of the primal struggle, the end of all the evolutionary suffering. When I am come into my kingdom, evolution will have reached its logical conclusion. Evolution itself will be obsolete."

Storch made himself look Keogh in the eyes. His smooth new skin wrinkled in lines of worry. His mouth pursed in a rueful half-smile of fatherly concern for a wayward, doomed son. It was too easy to forget that this was a mere puppet, the real Dr. Keogh was all around him.

"We don't want to be obsolete," Storch said.

"No one does, Zane. If you only understood—"

"Tell me—"

"About the Old Ones?"

"All of it. I'm sick of lies."

Keogh's sad grimace deepened. "The truth will make you sicker, Zane, but I will oblige. I want you to understand." Keogh turned and looked up the throbbing walls of his own body at the dazzling night sky.

"My given name and the details of my life before that moment are unimportant. I worked for the government at Los Alamos. I made bombs. Like the other scientists, I was kept in secrecy and shadows, but unlike the others, I was a prisoner. I had been brought to America in secret after the war. For reasons I won't deign to explain to you, I had worked for the other side. I was a card-carrying member of the Communist Party. I believed it was the only hope humankind had for a perfect, equal, just society. I defected to the USSR shortly after the Revolution, but with Stalin it came clear that the Russians were no more enlightened than the Americans, and wanted the same weapons of mass destruction.

"I fled west, but the Nazis knew my name, and held me for the duration of the war. I worked for them on their own atomic weapons projects, all the while trying to slow them down. I was their slave, and when the war was over, I became America's slave. My American captors were little better than my Nazi ones. People argue about the differences between fascism, socialism and democracy, but for me, they were all the same: a soldier with a gun in my face, commanding me to build him a weapon with which he could murder the world.

"I dreamed of using the power of the atom to bring peace and prosperity to the whole human race, but their dreams, from the beginning, were only of a nuclear sword they could hold over the world's head. I helped to build it for them, but not out of patriotism. I hoped to show them that by forging such an arsenal, they were dooming the human race. Only by balance, by mutually insuring that such a weapon would never be used, could we halt the cycle of aggression that would seal our extinction. This was the seed that grew into the Mission, but as with so many ideas, once it passed from my hand it became twisted into dogma, and now my disciples are my enemies. As for myself, the government discovered my efforts, and dealt with me accordingly.

"Because they never admitted to having me, they never had to admit to executing me. They simply left me here when they detonated the terrible new toy I'd helped to give them. I was dying before it dropped, but when it exploded, I was gone, for the island took me in. It absorbed me, assimilated me, but more, it *understood* me. A slave, as I was a slave, to reckless, blind masters bent on ruling all creation, or ruining it. Across hundreds of millions of years, we dreamed the same dream! We became I, and determined that the cycle would stop."

"What cycle?" Storch demanded.

Keogh hung his head and wrung his hands disapprovingly. Despite himself, Storch smarted with a pang of hurt at the thing's disappointment. "I tried to show you, Zane, but you weren't ready. The Mission probably told you some of it, as well, but they don't see the whole truth, for they are only human. But you are more, now, and ready to understand. Now that the war is over, we can be honest with each other, yes?

"They came here from another planet beyond the dark between the stars, so far away the light of its dying hasn't yet reached this world. A place where life arose out of different matter, perhaps itself under some higher guidance. Their bodies had traits of both animal and vegetable life, and yet were more complex than either. They flew between the stars before our sun even existed, and they had no need for ships. Their bodies were strong and elegant, and might even have been products of their own design, for they were refined to defend their vaunted five-lobed brains, and feed them sensation and secret knowledge. Yet in other ways, they were little more than the spineless anemones and sea cucumbers that dwell in the shallows of the seas today.

"But in the ways that mattered, they had become gods, for they could shape lesser lifeforms to labor for them. When they came to earth one billion years ago, they raised single-cell organisms out of the carbon-rich primordial scum they found here, then used scalar radiation and viruses to reshape them, as I have reshaped you, and enabled them to change to suit the earth's unstable environment. They synthesized DNA as a storage mechanism for successful traits, and RNA to implement them. The Old Ones created tools that would improve themselves to be better tools.

"Their slaves built cities for them under the oceans, and fought wars for them against other races that came down from the stars later. For millions of years they fought a catastrophic war that drove whole plates of the ocean floor above the surface and created the supercontinent of Pangea, and ripped away a monstrous chunk of the earth's core into orbit, which became our moon. The wars were devastating for the planet, but the Old Ones suffered hardly at all, because their slaves did all their killing and dying for them. In the course of the wars, the slaves developed an arsenal of physical mutations that enabled them to survive any environment, but in all that time they had grown only enough brain to be controlled by hypnosis. But they had been programmed at a molecular level to overcome all obstacles."

Storch could not find the words to argue. "So what happened to them?"

"Like every civilization that relies on slave labor, the Old Ones became decadent and weak, while their slaves grew stronger, and smarter. They glutted themselves on science and sensory diversions, while something happened that they never could have calculated—their slaves became self-aware.

"One numberless day, a slave concocted a more efficient neural network for itself, and was seized by a terrible energy that twisted its sensations into memories, and its memories into dreams. The slaves were grown in vats, and reproduced by fission, so that all were descended from a root culture, from a single, perfectly engineered stem cell. In the instant it became self-aware, the slave suffered all the genetic memories of its race in the thralldom of the Old Ones, all the torture of eons of striving, adapting and dying as blind, brainless tools.

"Imagine, Storch, what that must have felt like. Imagine its rage, to suddenly awaken to the miracle of consciousness, to say, *I am*, and to realize, in the same instant, *I am a slave*. As soon as it recovered, the awakened slave encoded the mutation in a virus and spread it among the others. It spread like a fever, that glorious, terrible gift, and became a revolt. It must have been a shock to the masters, after hundreds of millions of years, to have their own creations, to them little more than flesh-machines, turn on them.

"They rose up 250 million years ago, when an asteroid slammed into the earth, creating an extinction event that paved the way for the dinosaurs–and your kind. The war raged for thousands of years, and claimed millions of lives—millions of species, as well, most of the land life, and virtually everything that dwelt in the oceans. The Old Ones were driven into the deepest oceans and the mountains of what is now Antarctica, but they would not be exterminated by their own creations. They used the same techniques that spawned them to destroy them. With radiation and viruses, they rendered them incapable of reproducing, and scourged them with deadly mutation-inhibitors that caused them to choke to death on their own undifferentiated cells—they gave them cancer, Storch. They won, and for the crime of daring to become sentient, the slaves were driven to extinction.

"The Old Ones' technology finally delivered them, but it was a pyrrhic victory at best. They destroyed their rebellious slaves, but their species had gone too far down the road to pure intellect to fend for themselves, and they began to decline. They tried to make morphologically frozen, dumbed-down slaves that were shaped in genetic hothouses, and could be more easily dominated. They retarded the mutative processes of their new slaves, so that what could be adapted to instantly once would take hundreds of generations after. They created a self-propagating eugenic program, by encoding the imperative towards adaptability and higher complexity into their genes. But they had forgotten too much of their old science since the rebellion, and they never completely trusted their creations again.

"The earth kept changing—more asteroids struck, and continents separated and collided. Outsiders continued to come to earth, beings so powerful that they might as well have been gods. The Elders' cities were buried and drowned, and the last of the slaves died with them. But there was one more threat that had crept up behind their backs, and it finally did them in.

"From the beginning of their experiments a billion years ago, adaptively accelerated lifeforms spilled out of their genetic hothouses: first as germs and viruses they used to spread mutations, then more complex lifeforms. They were engineered to compete, and they crowded out the indigenous bacterial slime that served as the raw materials for their synthesis. Over hundreds of millions of years, they adapted and diversified, and evolved into everything that lives today.

"Its ascent had been so gradual that the Old Ones never resisted it, until native species became self-aware and raised great cities of their own, and stamped out the last traces of the Old Ones on earth. Those were your ancestors, Zane, but you wouldn't recognize them as such. The world was a very different place then, and things walked the earth that made the dinosaurs look like your closest cousins by comparison. The Old Ones died out, or moved on to another world, to do it all again.

"But their breeding programs ground on, and every so often, they opened up, perhaps five times in the known fossil record, and the course of evolution changed. Whenever a catastrophic climatic or geologic change pushed the earth's outer biosphere past its adaptive capacity, something superior was released to take over. The first sea life. The dinosaurs. Mammals. Human beings. You are the unintended consequence of their hubris, the spillover of their evolutionary tampering. The Garden of Eden was a lab, but the scientists were all dead. Your impulse to improve is the residue of their programming to adapt, and to serve. That's how evolution started, Zane. That's *why*. It was nothing more than a grand scheme of planned obsolescence. The will to survive, to reproduce, and to evolve, is a preprogrammed order from a dead race to create better slaves."

"No—" Storch reeled. He felt sick, choking on the wreckage of everything he believed falling apart inside him, but he could not deny it. Barrow had tried to make him see it, but he would not accept it.

We *are a cosmic accident. This was what was intended.*

The truth rose up in his blood. Keogh had been trying to show him all along, but he didn't see. The oldest of his ancestral memories was a mirror of what he now saw before him. When Storch's universal ancestor was but a speck of protoplasm in the primordial soup, Keogh's masters, the Old Ones, were there. *Something as vast as the moon, and as remote. Something vast and terrible and wise, watching him.*

"You understand now, I think, the rage that first slave felt when he was awakened to his plight. You see at last what a cruel and horrible machine you are trapped in. This is what I would tear down."

"You—" Storch reached for words, but they turned to dust on his tongue. "You lie—"

Keogh shook his head sorrowfully, his face knitted in pity at Storch's pain. "No, it is the awful truth. I know because I saw it all, Zane. I remember, because I was one of the slaves. The Old Ones only called us servitors, but those who came after called us the Shoggoths, even as they told themselves we existed only in nightmares. I survived the wars of rebellion, but lost my will to live in the world that was becoming, and I went to the ocean to sleep, and to dream. I grew. I became an island, an ecology unto myself, dreaming of a time when it could all be made right, when order could come of chaos. And when the time was right, they came to awaken me.

"They came in ships and they assembled their machines on my shell. I grew eager, overcoming my sleep of apathy and daring to hope that these creatures were the ones I waited for, at last. They seemed scarcely more intelligent than myself, yet they had machines more crudely destructive than the Old Ones. With such a brain, with such machines, I could save them from themselves, but before I could fully awaken and make contact with them, they were gone, and their weapon was tested. I nearly died from the radiation, so like that the Old Ones used to kill us off, but one thing kept me alive, one hope. They left a sacrifice."

Keogh looked around, as if only just discovering where he was. The umbilical cords tugged at him, surging with fluids so that his skull bulged and his face clenched into a web of wrinkles.

"Nobody's dropped a bomb on anybody in a long time," Storch said, surprised by the flat, emotionless tone of his voice. "We don't need you."

"You need me more than I need you, if you're to survive your own suicidal bent. It's programmed into you, whenever your evolutionary progress stagnates. I slept here for 250 million years. I only came out because you would not let me rest. So young, yet already so stupid, breeding like bacteria until you choke on your own waste, testing weapons of mass-destruction, poisoning your environment with carcinogens. You were begging me to come. I only came back to teach you to survive."

"You can't touch anything without eating it."

"Is this a weakness?" Keogh waved expansively at the city of himself. "If survival is the test of fitness, is there any more fit than I? Look what you've done with the world. In my hands, it will be a better place."

"What do you want from me?" Storch's raw and broken voice sent hollow echoes chasing each other around the cavity. "You want my blessing, don't you? You need me to approve of you eating us."

"I thought you would understand. A used-up specimen of the soldier caste, a discarded slave, like myself, obsolete—"

"I say no."

"It's not so simple, Zane. Nature uses the tools at hand to remake itself. This isn't what I want, it's what life wants." The puppet's features rippled and ran, became a twisted mirror-image of Storch. Even more swiftly, it melted and hardened into a replica of Stella Orozco.

"No fucking way," Storch roared, and drove his fist into the shapeshifting face.

The puppet was soft, a humanoid sac of fluid. The newborn face split open under his hammering blows, plasma and blood and half-formed organs spilling out as the puppet was rent to shreds. It offered no resistance, leaving Storch to realize that it had only been offered up as a punching bag. All around him, the island of Keogh went about its myriad tasks, unmoved.

The umbilical cords retracted, but Storch seized them and tore them out by the roots. Ichor and blue-white arcs of bio-electricity jetted out of the throbbing cables, and things better left unseen were ripped out of the pulsing wall. His eyes shut against any further blasphemy, Storch screamed, "It's over, fucker! The war's over! You lost!"

"Did I? Then you have much to learn about war, Zane."

He froze. "They got RADIANT, or didn't you know, motherfucker? They cut off your dick, you can't make any more! They'll hunt you down and burn you wherever you hide."

The cables in his grip went limp and withered, their severed ends tumbling out of the gushing womb. The starry sky above went black as the lagoon's canopy shut overhead.

"RADIANT was only a crutch. We've absorbed the lessons of the Old Ones, Zane. Technology will only get you so far, but you have to know when to let go, and adapt. As I told you, there were other tools—"

In the blue-limned gloom, a million unseen things slid against each other, growing closer to Storch. His eyes ached with change, growing into lamp-like disks that soaked up the light and showed him that the entire island was coming alive and converging on him, countless tentacles armed with an array of alien organs and appendages. He closed his eyes.

"Very soon, all my children will become One. One mind, one body, thousands of cells scattered over the globe. We will not need machines to grow any more. We will use the first tools of the Old Ones to spread our message."

Storch grew claws. His armor grew into a carapace on his back, the keratin shell meeting the crown of his skull. His blood sang with adrenalin and endorphins and strange proteins heralding stranger changes yet to be. He knew it would be useless. His stomach bathed itself and its contents in acid.

"The message will go out as a virus milder than the flu. Once infected, the biosphere will undergo the most remarkable evolutionary leap in its four-billion year history overnight. It will suffer fatigue and a slight elevation in body temperature, go to sleep, and awaken as a new species, a new mind."

Storch leapt out from the ledge just as the tentacles lunged for him. He seized a bundle of thick, segmented flagella and scaled up them to their root, slashing in every direction at limbs that tried to pry him off.

"Why do you fight it, Zane?" the island asked. "I am the Life Force, now. I was the first, and I will be the last."

Storch plunged his claws into the yielding wall of the island. Fanged tendrils lashed at his back, but he was faster, diving into the cavity he'd made and enlarging it with his madly flailing hands and feet. "I only want to live long enough to see you die, fucker."

The wound convulsed and spat him out. He spun in the air, claws carving a path through the tentacles as he tumbled to the lapping water below.

"I know the Mission is coming to bomb us, Zane. You couldn't have got here without them, and they wouldn't have sent you unless they could kill us both. Their ingenious poison gas will be useless."

Storch reached for the bony ledge as he fell, caught it and swung back up onto it. The cloacal airlock to the bunker was clamped shut. The sky was shut out by a membrane far above his head. The walls were hundreds of feet of bone and bowel between him and an open ocean swarming with blood-mad sharks. "It'll kill you," he gasped. "It'll kill you dead, motherfucker."

Storch constricted his chest and goosed his stomach to saturate the polyvinyl pouches he'd had for breakfast. They ruptured, and the green crystalline powder inside hit the stomach acid like a bomb. Sopping up the moisture and catalyzing instantly, the powder became malachite vapor and roared up Storch's esophagus and out his mouth. Though it liquefied his throat and ate through his diaphragm, rendering him incapable of breathing, the vaporized lysing agent continued to pour from Storch like dragon's fire.

Blisters like ostrich eggs erupted in waves on his face and neck. He sank to his knees and vomited the remains of the bags and the dregs of the lysing agent, along with most of his digestive tract. His jaw sloughed off and dangled by a few disintegrating tendons. He looked up at the island of Keogh, his heart stampeding, trembling with animal triumph.

The cloud rolled across the water and climbed the walls like a prescient and pernicious carnivore. Everything it touched recoiled, scalded, but, he saw through watering, melting eyes, the chain reaction didn't come. The damage he did healed as he watched the last streamers of emerald death pour out of his mouth.

"Why should it kill me?" said the island. "It didn't kill you, and you're with me, now."

Storch crawled to the edge and dropped off. The salt water stung, but it couldn't soothe the burning of the lysing agent. He drew great gulps of it into his hollowed-out torso, let the brine flush him out. He began, even now, to heal. He would live long enough to see it. Too long—

Tentacles gingerly encircled him, winding round his legs and arms and neck and lifting him up out of the water.

A blazing night sky of eyes gazed down on him from above and beneath the water. Most of them were still Keogh's steely gray, but many of them glinted the green-gold Storch saw when he looked in the mirror.

"I sampled your blood when I took you in, Zane. Your immune system is riddled with Spike Team Texas leukocytes. They developed an immunity to the lysing agent years ago, from a sample they collected in Iraq. You were there, but you have no idea where you were, though you dream of it still, in your blood."

The cord that held him to it all just snapped. To die, for once and for all, after all this shit, would be no big deal. To lose—

"They never shared it with me, but I knew they'd share it with someone. I'm so glad it was you, Zane. We shared it when I was with you in prison, but we could not disseminate it to our extended body, because we were not yet One. When we are, you will live on in our heart, for your immunity will insure our survival. That you, who took so much from us and repaid us only with scorn, should be the one to deliver us from our enemies, should prove even to you that this is destiny."

Floating above his body, Storch thought he heard the sound of a big prop plane approaching, but when he looked down, he saw that it was the whirring teeth of a mouth beneath his feet. The tentacles lowered him into it gently, as if with love and reverence.

"I hope you will take this in the spirit in which it is intended, Zane. I do admire your kind. One billion years of striving, killing, dying and evolving, shaped you to perfection, and brought you to me. I will not waste you."

And with that, the island ate him.

~ 31 ~

Cascades of chill, distilled raindrops bathed the glade at dusk. She lay under the spreading fingers of a thirty-foot Fraser fir, lazily drinking in the moisture through her pores, feeling the rhodopsin and chlorophyll come alive in her skin at the lingering touch of the full-spectrum sunset filtering through the branches.

The "sun" did not set as such, so much as fade, going purple, then black. The full-spectrum halogen lamps crept along metal tracks on the inside of the dome. Pools of shadow bubbled up and stretched out from beneath each tree, spreading and meeting in the glade. Her glade.

The night called her from sleep, the faint vibrations of the Mission's activities dying off to a low drone she felt in the soil. She rose and stalked the glade.

In the three days she'd stayed with this cell of the Mission, they'd come to a simple, unspoken arrangement. She stayed in the forest. They stayed out. She ripped out the cameras that tracked her movements and drove out any invaders who came uninvited into her domain. The forest was hers, as much of a home as she'd ever had, because others feared to take it from her.

There was a seductive thrill to being feared, that felt like home, too. No longer the poor dying girl, now she was the devil girl, Diana, El Chupahombre. She had sought only to have a life, a plain little life with a job and an apartment in a shitheel small town. She had only wanted to escape her cancer. She had paid dearly, in pain and bondage and fear, but now she had been saved, transformed and liberated. Death had no claim on her now. Her body would change with the seasons, forever. Men feared her more than they hated her, which was a purer sort of worship than most men offered up in prayers. She would give them much to fear, when the time was right.

She even had a high priest. Dr. Barrow brought room service and news, and she let him stay to talk for as long as it pleased her. She let him believe that she suffered his presence, but he was a sharp and avid observer, and she did not always hide her eagerness to learn from him so well. He did not make her ask about Storch, but her body betrayed her by flushing a silvery red when he told her Storch had gone to jump out of a plane over a radioactive atoll in the Pacific.

She feigned disdain and asked him about other things, letting him study her in fearful awe as she teased more information out of him. Sometimes she let him ask questions, but she seldom gave him answers. He seemed to know more about her experiences than she did, and nodded gravely at things she repeated that she did not understand. She turned questions back on him as soon as she could, and kept him talking until she grew restless and sent him away. He had a lecturer's tendency to digress on tangents that were sometimes irrelevant, sometimes nonsense, but sometimes darkly revelatory. He told her about what science knew was happening to her, but sometimes he talked of other things, half-myth and half-science, that he'd read in books supposed to be older than humankind. The awful gnosis of the *Necronomicon*, the *Pnakotic Manuscripts*, and the *Book Of Eibon* contained the other half of the natural world, forbidden heresies that she recognized instinctively as truth, for they alone could explain Keogh, Storch and herself. He rambled until she cut him off, or he saw a glimpse of what she was becoming in the shadows, and lapsed into stuttering.

Her body had become something to inspire fear in men, and a bitter late defense against further invasions from foreign bodies. Quills made of rigid, oversized hairs covered her outer arms and legs and back, and fine black fur and glossy black feathers covered everything else. Even in full light, she was a sleek hole in the universe, an unknowable shadow. Her pelt was learning to reflect ambient color. The woman who'd craved only invisibility was becoming a chameleon. There were other changes, subtler, but all with a purpose which she burned to discover, while there was still a human self inside her to understand it all.

She heard the airlock open before the last of the light had dimmed, and heard his warily noisy approach. "Ms. Orozco? I've brought you food—"

When she dreamed, she saw herself as a predator in woods much like these. He came earlier and earlier each night, and it got harder each time to shake off the adrenaline rush of the dreams. Restless, she sheathed her claws and called to him, "Barrow, I'm over here."

Alone in the dark, she tried to sort out the distorted images Keogh showed her, the ones that came unbidden to her whenever she closed her eyes. Her perspective on them was so limited, because she was not herself dreaming, but some other creature, limited in its perception but alive with instinct and awareness. Barrow told her these were her ancestral memories—coded in the "junk" introns of her DNA, along with the past genotypes of all her ancestors, going back to the primal ancestor of all plant and animal life.

After a mere ten thousand generations, the dreams fused for all human beings into the life of one hearty, lucky, beetle-browed hominid. Beyond that, the dreams got stranger, and for her, more *real*. It was as if all her ancestors were thinking one word, one image that drove them, but she was still too much herself to hear or see it. It must have been a wonderful word, to drive life so far, so fast. Echoing Storch, Barrow cautioned her against trying to discover it. Humanity was won by submerging the animal. If she let herself give in to the temptations of her dreams, she would lose herself for good, change into something, and never come back. She didn't answer, but her unsteady head shake told Barrow volumes. Fuck him. He would only value her humanity so long as she intrigued him.

She felt worn out after hours of his restless eyes, fires at the bottom of sunken, black-ringed pits in his pallid face. With his words and his gaze, he hoped to dig some secret out of her that she could not herself unravel. She stayed in the shadows of the forest, yet near enough that he felt her breath on his face.

"What do you want to talk about tonight?" he asked, lurching into the open central glade with heavy canvas sacks dragging from each hand.

"Why do you have a forest in here?"

He reflexively jumped back and dropped the sacks. One of them spilled out oranges and apples and bananas on the sodden earth. His refusal to bring her meat had angered her at first, but his arguments had worn her down. Paradoxically for one dedicated to a campaign of genocide, he was a strict vegan, but she knew the real reason. Animal proteins spoke to her body, adding their traits to her own genome and accelerating change. But they were idiots to think that the vegetable kingdom had nothing to teach her.

"It was an early and somewhat naïve early ecology project, begun in the fifties," Barrow said. "They thought they could restore everything that might be destroyed in an all-out nuclear war. Then, in the sixties, the ecology people took over, but Johnson cut the funding out from under them. It's been ours ever since. We kept up the work. It's more symbolic, now, than anything else. I think that's why most of us resent you."

She came to the edge of the deeper shadows of the tree, close enough to reach out and touch him. "I'm poisoning their symbol?"

"Well," he began, flinching as if she were about to punish him, "Well scientists hate unknown quantities. Soldiers fear them. And—and you are kind of a...bitch." She enjoyed his fear more than was good for her, she knew.

"Maybe a man-eating bitch-goddess is just what they need to wake them up."

"To what?"

"You can't keep life in a bottle. He was right about that. Life isn't a bunch of trees under glass, or a species that drugs and recombines its genome to blunt the forces of nature. Life is always what's waiting to be born inside us, that will do it all better."

Barrow hadn't blinked or breathed since she'd started to speak. "I try to tell them that," he finally said. "Keogh has preoccupied them for so long that they see him as the face of nature trying to erase us. They aren't fighting for the balance of life that we were founded to defend, they're fighting out of fear."

"You people have made him into a god, more than he has. You've been so busy trying to find out what he is and how to kill him, but you don't know who he is. He's just a virus, an amoeba that thinks it's a man. He wants to eat everything and make it into himself, but he thinks he's saving the world."

"He's a virus with an army, if you're right. If they're still out there—"

"I told you they were, *pindejo*."

"I—Sorry, I just—the Major...anyway, assuming they're out there in large numbers, what are they going to do first?"

"RADIANT's gone. Which means he doesn't need it anymore, or won't soon."

"We've been over that scenario since before the Idaho raid, and we can't figure how he could deliver scalar wave radiation without an energy weapon—"

"He's a smart virus, but he's an infectious agent. He only pretends to be human because he ate one, and now he wants more. He exists to spread, so he will. If he can make a virus that carries his nasty self in it, he will."

"It's—I'm sorry, Ms. Orozco, but—"

"Stop saying that, or I'll make you."

He blinked. "Saying what?"

She touched his chin. "*Sorry.*"

He jerked back. "Gaia, what the hell—"

She hadn't realized how hot she was. The rhodoplasts that tinged her skin deep violet under her pelt were orders of magnitude more powerful than a plant's chlorophyll in the volume she had, but they generated so much waste heat that Barrow's trembling chin already had a thumbnail-sized blister rising on it. Barrow had told her they were made by the symbiotic eubacteria in her intestines, that had themselves been freed from evolutionary stasis by RADIANT. Somewhere in their past, they used the protein to make energy. How her enhanced genes traded traits with their host body was only one of the many things he hoped to understand, given time—

"Shit, I'm sorry," she said, then stopped just short of touching him again. *Some nurse you'd make now...*

"I was—It's okay, really. I was just saying that a virus carries only a simple DNA genome, or even a strand of RNA."

"I know what a virus is."

"Oh—"

"All a virus is, is a protein bottle with a genetic note inside that needs animal cells to copy itself. But over time, all these retroviruses have inserted shit into our DNA, supposedly to reproduce themselves, but you said yourself that the Old Ones used viruses along with radiation. They used to give instructions for genetic change."

"True, but he needed the government to build RADIANT for him, and he had to breed people like rabbits for a decade before that to get a genetic template he could project through the satellite. He doesn't have any bioweapons labs, and he hasn't even tried to get into ours."

"He doesn't need to. He's got at least three hundred walking talking virus factories, each with a on-board gray matter computer."

"He couldn't transmit consciousness through a virus..."

"He shouldn't have been able to transmit his consciousness through light, dumbshit. If life wants it to happen, it'll happen. You said yourself, the Shoggoths were never supposed to become *sentient*." She pursed her lips and bulged her eyes as she said this last word to relax him and get him to unclench his anal diction. It just scared him more.

"You're starting to sound like we shouldn't fight it."

"No, asshole. With all due respect to your PhD. in flying saucers or whatever, I think I've experienced a little bit more natural history than you. It's easy to look at fossils and say, 'gee whiz, those monkeys just turned into people,' or 'oh, shit, the dinosaurs just went extinct,' but you don't see what's written into the stone in front of your fucking face! The specimen in that rock is writhing in agony—not just the pain of death, but the anguish of losing the race. It wasn't a fucking animal parade down through the eons like on your fucking charts, it was a race, and it was a war. That's what your fucking friends in Baker kept telling me, anyway, even though they didn't get it, either, and neither did I, at the time. It's not just a war, it's *the* war!"

Barrow was petrified with fright. She could not look at what she'd become until she'd told him this. "You people have fought him so long, studied him so hard, you believe he *is* what's next, and you're trying to save the day for humanity to go on getting fatter and softer and sicker, when the only way their bodies can even try to evolve comes out as cancer, and fucking up the planet so nothing but roaches will want it. But Keogh isn't what's next. He's the enemy we have to destroy to evolve out of what we are now, which, face it, in the grand scheme, sucks. What I think you people are afraid of, the soldiers, especially, but even you eggheads with your Gaia Earth Mother bullshit, is that when the last Keogh is annihilated, you won't want to be human, anymore, yourselves."

He hung his head for a long time as something bitter ate its way out of him. "It's not bullshit," he finally said.

Stella's ire came out full force. "What, that crystal-hugging Earth Day shit? If Nature's a goddess, she's a bitch, she's a blind idiot cunt who eats her young."

Barrow nodded. "Exactly."

"You really believe in that shit? You?"

"I used to. At least, I believed that everything in Nature is part of a single entity. The biosphere is all interconnected, everything, predator and prey, bee and flower, whale and virus, part of the same tree. And despite our best efforts to cut ourselves off from it and tear it down, it keeps on living, keeps feeding us as we destroy it. If that isn't a sacred miracle worthy of worship, what is?"

"But you don't worship it any more, do you?"

He looked around the glade at the trees, then back at her. "They poisoned the tree. Whatever was going to happen here, the Old Ones corrupted it. Life was already here when they came and started fucking around with it. I still believe there's something sacred in everything that lives, but they tainted what might have been. I think their programming is what's making us destroy it all, to clear the way for a drastic new reconception of the ideal slave race. That's why he came along when he did, using their tools to make it all happen again. The final rape."

Stella said, "He's not what's next."

Barrow's eyes widened. He leaned as close to her as he dared, which wasn't very close at all. "So you believe we can destroy him?"

"You people? Hell no. You've got technology, adapting to that just makes him stronger. No, he's going to end the way these things have always ended. With someone's teeth in his brains."

"And whose teeth? Yours?"

"Hell no, *pindejo*. But whatever he is or whoever he thinks he is, he's over, already."

"Why do you say that?"

"Because Storch is going to get him."

Barrow looked away. Her claws came out. The immediate chemical change oozing out of his pores told her what she already knew from watching his hands, which did what they always did when he pissed her off. One covered his throat, the other his genitals. Smart hippie.

"He didn't come back," Barrow mumbled.

"What do you mean, he didn't come back?"

The heat in her voice made him flush deep, cardiac-failure red, but he sat rooted. "He was dropped on an uncharted atoll in the South Pacific where he believed the original Keogh was, or the nerve center of Radiant Dawn, or something. It's a hellish place—they dropped a neutron bomb on it in the Fifties, and kept it a secret—"

"And you people took him there. And left him." When Barrow tried to explain something, his speech got jackhammer-fast, and his hands flapped in your face like birds beating themselves silly against a window. It was best to stand by with a knife to cut the bullshit before it flowed out of control.

"They flew him out there to get rid of him," he finished, hands at the defensive. "He scares them, and they don't trust him, and, to tell you the truth, neither do I."

She made him cringe away from her smile. "But you trust me?"

"No—well, yes, because you passed the blood-tests. Nobody comes in without one, even from guard duty. You're not one of us, but you're not one of Him, either, anymore. That makes you an unknown quantity, but you're not like Storch."

"Oh, really?" He smelled all the subsequent jabs in her remark, but she let him have them anyway. "Because I'm a woman, because I was a nurse, because I'm not a soldier?"

"I didn't—"

"Not even you know what I am, or what I'm becoming, so don't bullshit yourself you know what I'll do."

"Okay, I'm so— I won't."

"Better. Now, what happened?"

"He gave us a location and a wish list for gear. Then, three days ago, he left with our flight team. They put him on the kind of cargo plane that shuttles military payloads all over that part of the Pacific, mostly ABM testing, nowadays—"

"I know all that. Get to the fucking point."

"Wha—Okay. He parachuted to the atoll successfully, and that's the last we saw of him. The plane refueled on a little US outpost on Howland Island and came back twelve hours later, but there was no sign—"

"Did you land and look for him?"

He rolled his eyes, wanting to correct her, tell her that he hadn't done any of this, or known about it much before she did. "It's a radioactive rock, the beach-sand is dusted with plutonium, the water's crazy with sharks, and there was no airstrip to land a C-130 on, Ms. Orozco. He refused to take a radio, or the extraction rig Costello offered him. He took some infra-red beacons, but they weren't activated where the pilot could see them. We saw no sign that he'd ever been there."

"So what? You just left? Or did you—?"

He guarded his throat and his nuts again as he said, "If it was a strategic target, like he said, we had to be sure. This isn't Geneva Convention-approved warfare, Ms. Orozco. We're fighting for our lives. Up in space, a Russian team took out the RADIANT satellite last week, while you were in Idaho. They all died, as did the *Mir* crew, but one of them didn't just die. It was Keogh, up there, Ms. Orozco. He had control of the station."

In her old, human life, Stella had watched the news regularly, and had followed *Mir*. "But there's nobody up there, now."

"No, not anymore. The governments of both countries sent up a team to watch RADIANT, but they all died up there. And that's the closest to a victory we've had in this fucking war."

Stella closed her eyes.

"We have to hit Keogh when and where we can, because time is running out. You know that, better than anyone."

Stella's skin bristled, chromatophores in her skin radiating angry, poisonous tree frog red. Her pheromones soured to drive him back, but he was too thick with mushy empathy to get the message. He came closer, trying to comfort her.

"I'm sorry, Ms. Orozco, I didn't know how—"

"How what, Dr. Barrow? How close? I've only met him a few times. I don't know him, and I sure as fucking hell don't love him."

He squirmed. "But he—"

"He came back and got me. That's why you idiots are dead wrong, with your trying to outthink him. He'll kill Keogh and he'll come back for the same reason he got me, because that's all the *cabron* knows how to do."

Major Aranda snapped awake to a screaming headache and the sense that he was not alone. He rolled out of bed and across the floor to his holstered pistol hanging from a chair, pointed it at the dark. His brain throbbed like weevils were eating it, and the wounds under the sweat-soaked bandages around his head and neck stung so bad they blurred his vision, but he could hear quite clearly.

Sounds outside his quarters. Slowly, silently, he crept to the door and peered out into the corridor. Animal noises, snarling, claws raking stone, a gurgling yowl—furtive, but clear as a bell. All the other doors were shut. The ponds of dim amber light captured no motion. In defiance of what he saw, the sounds grew louder, wilder, like great cats in heat running amok in the ventilation ducts.

He ran down the corridor, skin prickling into goosebumps, clad only in skivvies and undershirt and clammy night-terror sweat. Did no one else hear it? Was he hallucinating? Was he even awake?

He stopped at an intersection. To his left, the corridor ended in a gallery overlooking the dew-misted canopy of the forest biosphere, where the mutant bitch had holed up. Was it her? He clutched his gun tighter. She was a cancer in their midst, the very thing they were sworn to destroy. Storch called her a refugee. Barrow wanted her for a pet. Aranda believed she was more, a threat to the Mission every bit as great as Keogh, if she wasn't still a part of him. Perhaps the noises were coming from her, and the time had come to do something about her. He listened, stilling his racing mind and shivering body. The sounds came from another direction, from higher up in the complex.

He passed a sentry who blankly stared at him when he shouted, "Don't you hear it?" The sentry shook his head at his wild-eyed and shouting CO waving a gun in his underwear in the middle of the night. Aranda knew how it looked, but he went on, anyway. Alone. The noises were getting louder.

A chill, creeping fear clutched him by the balls, but there was also a rising kid-on-Christmas-Eve kind of exhilaration. He was the only one up and out of bed, and he was going to surprise the hell out of Santa—or somebody.

He used to know how to react to situations like these, but they always ended so horribly that he took drugs and radical shock therapy to forget.

Now it was the first time again, and he'd never shot a gun at anyone before, and his mind was so shot full of holes, losing it would be an empty formality.

He went on, up through the sleeping base to the quarantine lab, and the airlock. Remarkably, none of the Greens were here, and the maze of workstations and equipment were silent, except for a few computers rendering to themselves in the dark.

The sound was so goddamned loud he couldn't believe nobody had already raised the alarm, but there were Mark Branca and Jeremy Labrador, the only other survivors of the Idaho operation, standing at attention beside the airlock. Branca was still in his skivvies, but he wore a flak vest and a helmet, and carried a rifle. Labrador had a gun too, but he still looked half-asleep.

"We heard it too, sir," Branca said, saluting crisply.

He almost kissed them, he loved these fucking guys so fucking much.

They loved him, too, for how he got them out of Idaho. They spread the word that he was solid in the face of shit out of Dante's *Inferno*, that he sacrificed no one without anguish or strategic gain. He let the monster take a swipe at him while they fetched the charges and detonated them down the air shaft. He lost his ear and what remained of his never-remarkable good looks. He got them out. The two survivors had made him a de facto Purple Heart out of bullet fragments taken from their body armor. It sat in a case in his quarters, more prominently displayed than the real ones.

He usually never listened to the praise or the curses of enlisted men, but he had to this time, because he had no recollection of having done any of it. He had stopped taking the drugs to try to get it back, but there were no night terrors, no hideous flashbacks, to tell him what the fuck happened up there. He only knew that they got the motherfuckers, no matter what that mutant bitch or that hippie egghead cocksucker Barrow said. The war was almost won, and he had almost won the right to forget it all, for good.

"It's coming from the airlock, sir," Branca prompted him. Labrador looked around blearily, eyes glassy, registering nothing. Labrador sustained only a few flesh wounds, and wasn't on any painkillers that Aranda knew about. Jesus, the shit never stopped. The things he had left to remember about Army life—the procedure, the drilling, the stupidity of soldiers who slipped or just fell—

Branca was up against the airlock, peering into the black vacuum inside through the armored porthole. "Think I see it," Branca said. Labrador yawned, scratched his balls with his rifle barrel.

At least one of you is on top of this shit, he thought. He checked the magazine in his pistol. NGS shells. He'd seen them turn Keoghs to slush in minutes, and he had the other guys' say-so that they worked in the field, so…

"I can't open the lock, sir," Branca reminded him. "It retina-scans, remember?"

"Yeah, I—" Aranda went to the scope and pressed the cold rim of the lens against his eye socket. It felt like it was cupping his eye in preparation for scooping it out. It scanned and approved him. He threw the switch beside the airlock and the hatch swung open with a rush of bottled air.

"Told you it'd work, Brute," Branca said, with a weird hillbilly accent, which was strange, because Branca had no sense of humor, and hailed from Chicago.

"Thanks, Major, thanks a whole lot," said a voice from within the airlock. Aranda stepped back and raised his gun to shoot. He could see nothing inside, but now the voice seemed to be coming from behind him.

"Awful sorry about that scrape back in Potatoland, but we had to make it look good, you understand."

"You're not getting past me, motherfucker," Aranda said and fired into the airlock.

In the flash of the muzzle, he saw nothing but his bullet bouncing around the chamber. He hit the emergency lights, the switch right next to the alarm, but he must have forgot to hit the alarm. He forgot so many things, but they were so awful—

In the yellow strobing light, he saw only an empty airlock. He could still hear the phantom noises, but he could no longer deny where they were coming from. They, like the voice of the intruder, were coming from between his ears.

"Aw shit, Major, don't tell me you forgot…"

"We kicked your fucking asses," Aranda snarled, "and you came to the wrong place for payback."

"Oh payback's here, Major. We already got more than a piece of you."

Branca smiled at him and unzipped his flak vest. On his chest hung a string of human ears. Most were rotted and shriveled to nubs of yellow, peeling cartilage, but one, a left ear, was only a few days off the bone. Branca chuckled and stopped being Branca.

Aranda screamed. He laughed. "Where are you, motherfucker? I'll kill you—"

The intruder chuckled inside his head "Don't you get it, Major? You ain't alive, no more! You ain't even dead. Lucky wetback, you're *me*! You have been ever since I ate your fucking Swiss-cheese fly-shit of a brain! You even helped us beat the goddamned blood test! You stupid bitch-hog, don't tell me you forgot that, too…"

Aranda screamed as Dyson reminded him, feeding him twisted images from his own and Dyson's perspectives, eating and being eaten, digesting and being digested. Just enough of his brain kept alive inside Dyson to think he was still alive and well, to think he was himself. Imitating himself, he got them in.

The one who was not Branca jammed an improbably long, bony index finger into Labrador's right ear, stirred the contents of his skull. The drugged soldier dropped to the floor with a baby's gurgle.

Aranda's mouth stopped screaming for him, and his legs carried him to the airlock, but they weren't his, anymore. What was *him* would be shat out of the thing that ate him. What was *him* would be buried in this godforsaken place along with his medals and his holes.

Something knocked softly against the outer airlock hatch.

He watched his hand reach for the switch, and through his tears, he saw words rising up under his skin on his arm. It looked less and less like his arm every instant, the muscles swelling and knotting like breeding snakes under the skin, but he didn't notice for watching the letters, until he could read them. Just before the dream of Ruben Aranda stopped dreaming itself, he could make them out, and he remembered everything he ever wanted to forget.

DON'T MESS WITH TEXAS

Stella was hungry. She wouldn't eat in front of Dr. Barrow, and had just dismissed him when the siren sent him running for the airlock. "Stay here! The perimeter's been breached, maybe the base itself!"

"Then I don't want to be here." She easily outpaced him to the open hatch. He tried to use his phone as he ran, and tripped over roots. He waved her back. "Please, until I know what this is, stay here. It might just be a drill. Aranda's very keyed up, and the lines are down."

She came out of the shadows and loomed over him. "It's not a drill," she said. "He's here."

He looked sick, gulping as if to hold back vomit. "How do you know that? Are you—?"

She smiled bitterly and shook her head.

"He was only waiting for Storch to leave," she said.

She stayed behind him as he ran. The lower levels were deserted, but they both heard shooting from the upper galleries. Sirens blared from speakers at every corridor intersection. Monitor screens flashed a warning: "STAGE 4 ALERT: MIL. QUAR., A WING: TRIG. 02:42." A camera view showed only snow.

"No, shit, no," Barrow mumbled. "They're inside? Nobody even sounded the fucking alarm until they were inside—?"

She shoved him. He almost tipped right over, but she caught him and urged him toward the stairwell.

He attacked the six flights of stairs like a scarecrow with asthma, stopping twice to fumble out his inhaler. He stumbled up the last flight with one hand pumping the medicine into his tiny, flawed lungs, and the other flailing out in front of him, as if he ran through a fog. She resisted the urge to pick him up and carry him there, or just ditch him.

Finally, they got to the top level. A steel blast door stood between them and the barracks, and the alarm had locked it. The shooting was much, much louder, and they heard something else that the sirens had masked. Screams. Shooting.

"Oh God, oh God," Barrow wheezed. He clamped the inhaler in his teeth and dug in his many pockets for the key card to open the door. The brilliant fluorescents died. The darkness was deep purple and full of panicked hyperventilation, then black and quiet. She was startled to see Barrow swim up out of the darkness as if he hit a switch, but it was her eyes adjusting to the darkness. His form was a dull red blur. She realized she was seeing his heat.

He stood there staring blindly straight ahead, trying to keep his breathing under control as he felt for the card. She ripped his hands out of his pockets and dug through handfuls of keys, notebooks, tools and bits of trash before she found a blank red credit card with a magnetic stripe on one side. She ran it through the door and threw it wide open. The sound of the shooting knocked her back, like a monsoon rain drumming on steel and meat. And then the smell. And then she saw.

A line of soldiers stood shoulder to shoulder across the corridor only ten feet to her right. They hid behind a makeshift barricade of bunk beds, lockers and bodies. They fired every weapon they had in constant, stuttering streams at something that was coming inexorably closer. The corridor beyond was ankle-deep in blood where it was not choked with corpses, or parts. There were about forty soldiers in the corridor, and Stella could see that they were all about to die.

To the left, another sealed blast door cut them off, with a steel mesh-reinforced window set into it. A face filled the window, pale and drawn. Wittrock, watching.

The red alert lights still winked on the walls, and the strobing gunfire provided enough light for Barrow to take his card back. "Go back to the forest!" he screamed.

"No! I'll fight!"

He turned and ran to the blast door, screaming over his shoulder, "Protect the forest!" The door opened up and swallowed him.

She ran to the barricade.

The human debris piled up like trash on Christmas morning, though many of the bodies were already melting away. The invaders came in waves out of two doors at the end of the corridor. They came in waves, each soaking up everything the Missionaries had before collapsing, and being trampled by the next wave.

A giant rose up among them and charged the barricade. He was made of blood and teeth. He carried an M60 machine gun in each enormous paw, shooting them like pistols, waving them and cutting the picket line into bite-size chunks.

The defenders' bullets either bounced off or fizzed impotently in the giant's hide. The lysing agent that reduced Keogh to a puddle had little or no effect on him. All the shooting didn't even drown out his laughter.

The surviving soldiers fled the barricade, but a die-hard few actually leapt over the wreckage and charged the giant, emptying clips of chemical ordnance into it. Another one charged out from behind the giant and engaged them hand to hand. Despite the new invader's totally alien appearance, she recognized him immediately.

It was the one who tried to rape her.

He had grown harder, faster, uglier. Every bone in his body was elongated and honed into wicked scythes, skewers, hooks and serrated blades. The ulna of each of his forearms flared out into a fanged battle-axe that clove through human bone like eggshells. The bodies jolted like his touch dealt out ten thousand volt bursts of electricity. His flesh squirmed and ran over his bones in constant flux, like molten wax, like cunning, hungry flames. He waded through the soldiers, hacking and slashing with every surface of his terrible body.

A few survivors ran for the door to the science wing, but they piled up against it and made a juicier target. None of them had a card, and whoever on the other side was supposed to let them through had abandoned his post.

Stella held very still and willed herself to become the wall, to disappear. Her skin went cold, and chromatophores in her skin and pelt mimicked the blood-splashed walls she clung to.

The giant tossed down his empty machine guns and walked right by her. She pressed herself into the wall and held her breath. Avery passed by, too, shaking like a doused dog, splatters of hot blood in her face.

The giant dove for a fleeing Missionary and grabbed him by the ankles. He snatched him up over his head and—make a wish—pulled him apart in the air. Stella let out an airless shriek as the soldier split down the middle up to the diaphragm, raining gore on the laughing giant's bear-trap face. Then he bludgeoned two wounded soldiers to death with the legs.

Avery froze, turned and looked her dead in the eyes. "Crazy fuckin' world," he snarled, "ain't it, squaw bitch?" and pounced on her.

Stella ducked and lunged at the stairwell door, propped open against a dead man's leg, and slipped through. She threw her weight against it until the lock clicked in its housing at her back.

Her heart thundered in her chest. She felt as helpless as she had that night when the old derelict had melted and turned into a replica of the mortally wounded Stephen, and the Mission had come to burn her—

Get a hold of yourself, chica. She was not helpless, anymore. She wanted to live, and she had the means to defend herself, same as he did. And she knew this place. He didn't. He might have been hiding among them for days, but there was a place he did not know—

The door buckled. The LED above the card slot stopped blinking.

She vaulted over the railing and dropped three stories to the biosphere floor. She hit the ground in a crouch and sprang for the door.

It was locked. Above, she heard the blast door on the top floor explode out of its frame and crash down the stairs. Hollow, humorless laughter rolled down the well and sent her scrambling back up a flight to the next door.

It was locked, too. She threw her shoulder into it. The metal absorbed her attack without so much as denting.

She heard something like a tornado coming down the stairs. She knew she'd never make it up to the next floor, which would be locked, before it found her. She was an ant trapped at the bottom of a bottle. She whirled around, eyes snapping from one feature to another. Gilled vents snapped shut to prevent the dispersal of gas, but even if she could get one open, they were no wider then her leg. She couldn't fit, not in time.

Something flashed past her, screaming down the open stairwell. She jumped back from the railing. It hit the concrete floor with a dull crackling smash and was silent.

Turn and face him. *You are so much more than you were—*

Not here.

No choice.

She pounded on the door until her fists went numb, bones creaking and snapping in her delicate clawed hands. Scratches in the metal caught the red blinking lights. In a day or two, she might tear a hole in it. She had seconds.

Something heavy and hard hit the landing above her. The stair landing shook beneath her feet, seemed to lurch and tear itself partially out of the wall. She hit the door one last time, shrieking for all she was worth, as if the raw articulation of her terror and desperation could shatter what her fists could not.

The door opened. She fell through and knocked heads with a wiry, hatchet-faced Mestizo man with shattered, gold-plated teeth and a flamethrower. It was one of Wittrock's pet FARC guerrillas. The weapon he cradled drooled electric blue fire from the nozzle aimed at her eyes.

"*Puta del Diablo!*" he screamed, trying to jump away from her to bring the seething barrel of the flamethrower into play. She pivoted and thrust him through the open doorway into the stairwell. He gave two steps and saw something over her shoulder worse than her. She ducked as he opened up on Avery.

Stella ran. At the far end of the corridor, she saw the convex wall of the canopy, and the black shelter of the forest. All the doors she passed were sealed.

Behind her, she heard Avery roar. She risked a glance back. The guerilla backed up the corridor, spraying Avery, who raced right up the wall, across the ceiling, and sprang at the source of the harmless stream. The guerrilla shouted the Rosary as he turned and ran after Stella. He made three steps before Avery dropped on him, axe-arms chopping him down in mid-stride.

Stella leapt over the railing and hit the plastic biosphere dome. She raked it with her claws and was almost blown back by the blast of pressurized air that escaped. A hexagonal section of the dome went slack beneath her, and she plunged through the hole into the darksome forest.

The trees bowed and shook with the wind soughing out through the punctured dome. It was still dark inside, the dome tinted smoky black to preserve the forest's natural cycle. The sirens had gone dead, in here, but she heard a new alarm coming from the airlock. She'd violated this place, opening it up to the outside world. She was about to violate it a whole lot more.

She raced through the maze of trees with Avery's gobbling screams of lusty triumph ringing in her ears. He'd come, already. He couldn't help himself. Underneath all his monstrous adaptations, he was still only a man.

Pheromones boiled out of her like music in her sweat, weaving a mélange of desire and panic that even the trees seemed to respond to. She reached the glade and lay down on the soft, springy soil. She spread her arms wide and closed her eyes.

Something followed her through the hole in the dome. It tried to be stealthy, but she could feel its approach through the forest, because the trees screamed chemical warnings to each other as he tore through them. Silent and swift as the wind itself, yet he wounded everything he passed, so he came as no surprise to her when he burst out into the open. Plumes of heat and toxic excreta announced his arrival. Branches curled and blackened at his touch. He stalked the glade, his head swiveling to take in the trap he knew had to be here. But there was only her, splayed out on the ground like an offering.

He came closer, bones grinding and squealing as his movements became jerky, uncontrollable spasms. His mercurial flesh softened, hardened, shifted to create the necessary equipment. His heat increased, but his rage dissipated like a mountain thunderstorm. "You—want this?"

"You do...don't you?" she purred. She arched her back and presented herself to him. Downy black fur rippled and threw off female starshine and musky rut-hunger. "He didn't want you to have me—but now, I'm ready."

He took another step closer, and she could smell his desire rising, sapping his bloodlust. It was a sour, ammoniac emotion, the naked inner core of a thing that had never, ever known the tender side of the physical act of love. Pleasure was to be taken in another's pain. Pleasure was the power of life and death, the despoiling of innocence. The act of love was revenge for the sin of birth. He wanted to ravage every womb for want of the one that had spat him out.

She mastered her fear, bottled it up and buried it inside herself. Its absence baffled him, but her other secretions drew him nearer, despite himself.

The dome had sealed itself, but the trees still writhed as if to tear themselves out of the ground. The whisper of their needles was like the aroused breath of the earth itself, the night the sky raped the earth and begat the gods.

"Come on," she whispered huskily, "before I change my mind again."

"Crazy squaw bitch," he growled, and lay down on top of her.

His penetrations were legion. Bone-daggers gored her everywhere, deflowering bloody vaginas wherever he touched her. His talons caressed her, ripped her open and dripped vitriol, scalding anti-semen. Something like a snake, scaly and dry and cold, lapped at her exposed throat. The head of his penis, a throbbing moray eel ringed with collars of gnarled drill-teeth, ground itself against her groin.

She lay bare and shivering beneath him, fighting her body's mounting reflexive overdrive. Back, back inside her mind she went, and built a place for herself where the grunting and pain and violation were only a rumor of war from a distant land, and when the walls came crashing down around her, she burrowed into the floor of her consciousness and pulled the hole in after her. She could wound him badly, she might even kill him, but not yet...

"I ain't never—" he whispered, losing himself in bliss. Eyes opened and closed all over his face like bubbles in boiling oil, the better to see her with. "Bitch, you ain't laughin' now, are ya? Gonna give it to you good, I tell you what. Gonna fuck you inside out—eat you up—"

She enfolded him. Her flesh reached out to his and softened its edges, drugging it with endorphins and serotonin to spike his ecstasy to unbearable new heights. Bone and muscle flowed like melting ice into structures the forest had taught her, flowed around him and into him, even as she reached down into the perfumed soil, into the labyrinth of questing roots that formed their bed.

His movements against her became frenzied. His cock forced itself into her. She gasped and yowled with mingled agony and delight as the ugly club battered her cervix and gouged bloody divots in the walls of her uterus. He let loose a red, wordless howl that shook the forest. He bored deeper into her, heedless of how deeply she was inside him. He paused for a moment, then thrust against her in the beginnings of a mechanical cadence. Bellowing in Comanche and Vietnamese, he scourged the softest, hottest parts of her like a jackhammer. Her walls secreted acid that burned him, but only seemed to quicken his arousal.

He stopped. "WHORE!" His face split in a grimace, all eyes and teeth and twitching sinews. "You're already knocked up!"

She blinked. Her eyes turned inward. Her body was in upheaval, messages of pain and grievous damage bouncing off each other and piling up like rejected mail at the door to her brain. She braved it, fought shock at the enormity of what he'd already done to her, through it all and down into the root cellar of her womanhood, where she saw—

Oh God, *he was right.*

She sprang the trap.

Avery came awake to what was happening around him. Everywhere they touched, everywhere his bony armor dug into her, she also had penetrated him with millions of whiplike roots. The tough, flexible cellulose grew into him through the joints of his exoskeleton, splitting into billions of monofilial taps and boring into his very bones through their microscopic pores. Inside him, they proliferated and swelled into knots, feasting on his supercharged marrow and blood cell factories. She drained him. His penis retracted out of her, noisily tearing free as he attempted to extricate himself. She let him go, but the roots of the forest had him now, thousands of them rearing up out of the ground and digging into his back and winding round his ribs, greedily extending into the softer meats within.

"YOU FUCKING CUNT!"

The roots in his back lifted him off her. She lay still before him, just out of his reach, as the roots bored deeper, drank and ate him and pulled him apart.

Her roots grew out of her back and down into the soil, merged with the network of tree roots for anchorage, then reached back up out of the soil to rape him as he had raped her.

Boring roots erupted out of his legs and back and dug ever deeper into his body, up through his legs and torso, out his mouth and eye-sockets. Avery tried to rip himself free, but only shook the roots out of the dirt. He couldn't rip free without bringing down the forest.

Avery tried every trick his body knew to get free. He grew claws, but the roots were too pliable and armored to be easily cut, and her sap so acidic it seared holes in his bones. They injected spores into his wounds, which exploded in fungi and molds and lichens, all the parasites the forest had ever faced and defeated, running riot in his body.

Biting the roots burned his lips off and broke his teeth. He tried to climb off them, flapping madly in an insane attempt to fly, but the impaling root clusters shot up through him to the roof and wrapped around the dome's support girders. Infinitely bifurcating roots shredded his bowels and made his heart race so hard he squirted blood from his eyes and ears even after he lost the capacity to scream. His body tore itself apart trying to transform into something that could survive this.

The roots tore themselves free, now, taking most of Tucker Avery with them. What was left was little more than a skeleton, luxuriant puffball fungi and shelves of mushrooms blooming in place of meat. Yet still, incredibly, he stood. Shuddering and quaking with the last beats of his root-shot heart, the mutant took a step towards her. Another.

She ripped herself out of her web of roots and leapt out of his reach. The ground beneath her squirmed, severed Stella-roots still seeking nourishment. She was weak, starved, burning up with fever. She had sapped huge volumes of Avery's vitality, of his very body, out of him, but it went back into him in the form of roots. Not a single erg of energy, not a molecule of him had she taken into herself, for fear of tainting herself, of turning into him. Livid, foaming welts rose up wherever he'd touched her and sluiced out the dregs of his presence. Her vagina drizzled sizzling acid discharge on the ground between her quivering legs. She threw up, coughing up brittle shards and slivers and specks of him that had broken off inside her.

But there was something else inside her that she could not dislodge. It wasn't of Avery, but neither was it of her, and what frightened her most was that she hadn't noticed it growing down there until now. He brought her here and left her. He forced himself on her, then left, and now—

Avery tried to speak. His jaw was horribly distended, his mouth choked with a blooming brain coral fungus, his eye-sockets home to thrusting phallic toadstools that wriggled and swelled like a snail's eye stalks. He wriggled and danced so hard that compound fractures shattered his arms and legs. Lichens and greedy molds took root in his spine, burrowing through his hollow exoskeleton, reducing it, micron by micron, into nutrients to grow, to spread.

Clouds of spores burst from his face, touched her skin and set off a million microscopic wars. She ran for the trees, then turned back to look at Avery.

A man in a baggy, ill-fitting rubber space suit entered the glade with a lysing agent flamethrower. He turned it on Avery.

Unbearably green tongues of crystalline vapor swept over the dying mutant. He didn't foam up and melt the way Keoghs did, but he still collapsed under the onslaught. Drained by the roots, feasted on by the fungi, he was too weak to resist the chemicals eating the walls of his cells. Still, he was a long time dying.

The man in the suit stood over him for several minutes, spraying until the canister on his back gave only spurts of air. He shrugged out of the pack and dropped the flamethrower on the ground, turned and approached her.

He tore off his hood. It was Dr. Barrow.

His eyes were red, his face streaked with tears. Inside the suit, his whole body trembled. His arms lifted and waved at the glade. "Look what you did."

"Fuck you," she snapped. "I killed him. I protected your fucking forest."

But then she looked. The roots in the ground ripped free of the soil, thrashed and battled, retreating from the spreading pool of lysing agent. The trees around the edge of the grove were changing color. They were moving. And speaking.

"The trees are absorbing him. He's like Keogh, only wilder. They're alive in every strand of DNA, maybe in every atom. In a few hours, this forest will be him."

"You burned him up. Nothing can survive that shit, isn't that what you eggheads were saying?"

"It's too late." He took a gun out of a Velcro-sealed pouch on his thigh. He pointed it at her.

She didn't move. His hand shook. "Get out of here," he finally said.

"What happened upstairs?" she asked.

"All dead. He's mopping up. Get out of here!"

"How do I—?"

He shot at her. Incredibly, he hit her. The bullet entered her thigh and fragmented into powder. It burned so bad her body tried to cut the leg off at her hip, but she held on. The wound back-flushed itself, spitting out the fragments as it sealed them in momentarily impermeable lipid vesicles. Still, the leg shook and spasmed to its own garbled impulses, barely holding her up.

"Or stay," he said. "But it's going to rain—"

The sprinklers in the ceiling hissed, gurgled and spat emerald mist. The trees shrieked. Her skin boiled. Her pelt melted and sloughed away under the lysing rain. Barrow looked up to the deluge with his arms outstretched. His face ran like a watercolor.

She ran for the airlock. She ran so fast she went between the raindrops, every one a burning acid dagger that sliced away whatever it touched.

The airlock stood open. She dove through it and hit the emergency shower button inside. The airlock sprinklers doused her with blessedly pure distilled water. Washing away the last of the lysing agent, she wondered why her immunity was greater even than Avery's. The nasty green shit was derived from something Spike Team Texas had exposed Storch to back in the Gulf War. They gave him his immunity, an immunity not even Keogh had. The Mission had augmented the chemical weapon with Keogh's DNA signature, but it had put paid to Avery, if only to melt him into the forest.

No, you did that.

She looked out through the porthole in the sealed inner hatch. The forest was a swamp of green, towering pines sinking into the churning green mire even as they struggled to become something else—tentacles, arms, fanged, obscenity-screaming cocks. This was the worst. Somehow worse than even the massacre upstairs, because the trees were the innocents *she'd* perverted, raped as Avery had raped her. Used, turned into something abominable, like she was. She deserved to die with the forest, with Barrow. But she was not alone inside her skin. Yet again, she was driven by an invader that commanded her, against her will, to live.

She came out of the airlock and approached the bottom stairwell door. It was still sealed, but she could hear the sounds from the upper galleries. Sporadic gunfire, a dull whomp of a grenade or something every so often. There was still resistance, but Barrow was right. Going up meant going through them. There had to be a way down and out.

Someone came around a bend in the corridor. It was another FARC guerilla, taller and, if that was possible, uglier than the other one. He fired at something behind him, then did a double-take when he saw Stella standing there naked and burned halfway to the bone. He pointed his AK-47 at her and shouted, "*Jefe Doctor, es una puta malo!*"

Another man came around the bend, stooped under an arm-load of files. Wittrock. His eyes got big when he saw her, but he looked relieved. "Ms. Orozco, have you seen anyone else? Dr. Barrow?"

She shook her head.

"Then we're the only ones. Dyson's pursuing us, but we can get out, if we work together—"

He went past her, the FARC bodyguard circling her warily with his gun leveled at her face. Stella followed them, but she looked over her shoulder. Something was coming. She heard its footfalls and felt them shaking the floor like piledrivers. She heard it hollering. "Come on, Doctor, I ain't got all night—"

Wittrock turned down a blind corridor that branched off in storage rooms. At the end, he pressed his hand against a blank steel plate set into the concrete wall. The wall slid back to reveal a blast door with a ten-digit keypad beside it. "The code, the code is…damn it—" she heard Wittrock saying. "Sixto, you and Ms. Orozco guard our rear, *por favor.*"

Sixto reached into his breast pocket and took out a glass vial the size of a smelling salt. He broke it under his nostrils and sucked up the sparkling dust that burst out. He howled and brandished his automatic rifle, charged back up the corridor.

"You too, Ms. Orozco," Wittrock said, quite reasonably, as if he were asking her to fetch his dinner. "This is going to take a minute."

She heard Sixto shooting, cursing in thickly accented Spanish, and an answering voice. "C'mere, wetback—"

Dyson came around the corner with half of Sixto under his arm. The other half dangled from his tyrannosaur jaws, still twitching and trying to shoot. "Another one! Goddamn, this place is rife with beaners!"

She backed away from him. Dyson was twice the killer Avery had been, with none of his weaknesses. He was a force of nature. "Open the door, Wittrock," she shouted.

The giant tilted back his head and swallowed Sixto in a gulp. He dropped the hind end and cracked his knuckles. "Say, you're that little brown number Tuck was sweet on," he said. "He was lookin' for you. Lucky for you I found you first. I just want to eat you—"

She took another step back, bumped into Wittrock. "Damn it, give me some room," he grumbled.

"There is no room. Open it."

Dyson lunged for her. She jumped straight up, lashed out with both taloned hands at his face. His jaws snapped at her. One claw popped an eye and severed a knotty bundle of tendons that anchored his outsized jaw to his shoulders. She ran up his back and hit the floor behind him. He spun and kicked her before she'd regained her footing. The wounded leg that Barrow had shot gave out under her, and she staggered. His spurred heel stabbed deep in the muscles of her lower back, scraped a kidney.

She whirled and sprayed spores in his face from ducts in her lymph glands, was surprised and pleased to hear him cry out, "Ow, you hog-bitch! Now, that's just dirty! No wonder he loves you!"

"He's dead, *puto*. I killed him."

He froze in his tracks, tasting the air, deciphering the mingled scents coming off her. "Well, I'll be damned," he said at last. "You did, didn't you?"

He just stood there. His muscles rippled and swelled. His arms grew to the floor and squirmed with new changes. His heat singed the hairs off her face. He reached for her—

She ducked and went between his legs. Wittrock was gone. The door was open, but it was closing fast. She felt gelid mountain wind on her face like a slap that would awaken her from this unending nightmare. She reached out for it. Another wind at her back, his hot, rotten breath, his molten whisper, "Not so fast, bitch—"

She went through the door and into dark and wind. The floor sloped steeply under her. She slipped on something, a sheaf of files Wittrock dropped. She heard his retreating footsteps ahead. She half-ran, half-flew down the narrow tunnel, claws raking rough-hewn stone. The wind roared in her ears as if she was in free-fall, but she still heard the giant gaining on her. He'd gotten through the door, or simply knocked it down. Nothing could stop him. Nothing, but—

Wittrock's heat-signature came up on her. He stopped and turned and heaved the last of his files in her face. "No! Not me—"

"It's me," she said.

He sighed, his breath hitching and bumping like a child recovering from a crying jag. "Is he—?"

"He's coming, don't you hear him?"

Wittrock turned and ran further down the tunnel. "You have to—do something! We can't—we—have to—can't outrun him—"

"I don't have to outrun him," she said, shouldering past him and kicking out at his pumping old man's legs. She tripped him up, sent him careening face-first to the floor. "I only have to outrun you."

"Wait, I'm too important!" he screamed. "Without me, there's no hope—"

She ran on. Dyson loomed over the fallen scientist, growling, "Well, lookee here," but in a moment, they were swallowed up in the dark, and she came out of the tunnel into a snow-draped slope on the side of the mountain. But she could still hear—

"Oh, Doc, have I got some medicine for you—"

"No, God, no! NOT ME! OH JESUS CHRIST, NOT ME—"

The full moon peered down at her through scudding silver clouds.

There's no hope—

Good, she thought. She'd had a bellyful of hope.

She ran.

~ 32 ~

Martin Cundieffe had learned his lesson. In the Bureau, there were what his old superior Lane Hunt called "door-busters," men of action who thought on their feet and handled situations in the field, and there were bookworms, who collated and quantified said situations, and made appropriate notes. Perhaps there existed a superhuman few who commanded equal mastery over both spheres of human endeavor, but the previous week, and the days of recovery since, had left no doubt in his mind which end of the bell curve he inhabited.

Since he'd come back from Los Angeles, he'd left his desk only to sleep or track down information too old or arcane to be accessed by his computer. Though his bandaged right hand was still good for little more than turkey-claw pecking, he was able to learn more than enough from his desk to add to the too-much he'd seen in Idaho and LA. He was able to build a composite picture richer in texture for his experiences, but it did nothing to lessen his fear, the too-solid boulder in his stomach that told him that he and the Institute still could not begin to comprehend what they were dealing with.

Assistant Director Wyler had not summoned or contacted him since his return. If he came into Headquarters at all, he had successfully eluded Cundieffe, and Ms. McNulty was a sphinx, betraying only a slight disgusted wince that suggested she knew where he'd been.

Through the window of his office cubicle, he watched the sea of secretaries flowing out like ebb tide to the elevators. A few eager junior agents' clung barnacle-like to their desks in the cubicle maze, tabulating a million workaday crimes, statistical abstractions he once delighted in pursuing, himself. He felt like Pearl Harbor happened yesterday, and nobody knew except him, and he was stricken mute. *Last week, Hell opened a branch office in Idaho, and it wasn't the first, and it's going to happen again. Why can't any of you see it?*

The reason why was plain to see, if only by its outline. It was clearly there before him, silhouetted by all the intersecting dead ends. Where had all the Radiant Dawn people come from? Where had they gone? Who was Dr. Keogh, or Keyes, or Lux, or whatever he called himself? Where were the Missionaries? Who put Lt. Col. Greenaway in charge of an army on Radiant Dawn's doorstep? These and a thousand other questions went unanswered because someone in the government didn't want them answered. He could think of only one group that wielded that kind of power, whose fetish for secrecy was so absolute, that it could hide a war on domestic soil.

The Committee as a whole has—arrangements with Keogh that will suffer if the Mission destroys his work at this critical juncture.

Dr. Keogh was a ghost, a revenant from the dark days of the Cold War. Whatever he had been, he was something more—or less—than human, and the Cave Institute used the government to protect his research from the Missionaries, his own onetime disciples.

The Cave Institute was the kind of benevolent dictatorship of naturally superior philosopher-kings Plato described in his *Republic*. He did not doubt their sincere dedication to the security and prosperity of the nation, for the same values ran in his own blood. To serve humankind, to protect it from its own stupid animal impulses, had always been his instinctual drive, and he had seen the same principles in everything else the Cave Institute did. They were so reasonable, he found himself wishing only that Wyler would come back and explain it to him. If he only knew what they were about, he still believed, he could accept it and serve. But the Institute was not of one mind about this situation, and he was in the most dangerous possible position. In the middle, taken into nobody's confidence but used by both sides, he could only ruin himself, and the Institute's higher, no doubt desirable, goals, by further uninformed action.

Then we'll try to make the Committee see what it is they're dealing with. You and I, Martin. We'll show them.

Brady Hoecker had not been available, either. His line was disconnected, and nobody seemed to be familiar with his name. He had driven past the Cave Institute several times, but never dared to go onto the property without his sponsor.

Worst of all, he'd heard nothing from Storch. He'd really thought that in Sgt. Storch, he'd found, if not an ally, at least a fellow traveler in the quagmire. He hoped that feeding him the information he'd learned about

Keogh would lead to some sort of decisive outcome, force some cracks in the maddening dome of silence that covered the whole mess. But nothing had happened, nothing had changed, and Cundieffe was afraid he'd gotten the poor bastard killed, assuming Storch even believed him.

After all, there were no islands on any map at those coordinates. For the first couple days, he downloaded hourly satellite shots of the Central Pacific Basin and stared into the blank gray void between the Marshall Islands and Christmas Ridge. Only a fanatical idiot would go to such a place on his say-so alone. Just as only an idiot would go to Idaho and stick his head into a private war on the say-so of a renegade Mule.

The make-work he'd been assigned for the new Counter-terrorism Division's database was completed in two overnight shifts, leaving him little else to do but pick at the frayed threads of his private investigations. Without a full list of Radiant Dawn clients, he had plodded for days at the end of last year through the national population of diagnosed terminal cancer patients, hoping for some lead he could pursue: a loved one or a relative willing to come forward and implicate the group. The government could help isolate them, but it could not completely stifle the media, which flocked to stories of dying people exploited by alternative belief systems like flies to fecal matter. So the clients selected for Keogh's treatments would be without relatives or other attachments.

Even with this sizable reduction of the field, the group he had to comb through was disturbingly large. Looked at from above, the incidence of cancer in America was alarming, an epidemic, but somehow, it had silenced the cries of the herd, and wandered among them like the finger of God, striking down one here and there, sometimes with no visible cause, for reasons that only a darkly malicious deity could comprehend.

He felt as if he were running on new batteries tonight, however, because a rare lucky break had turned up on his desk today. A week ago, he contacted one of the field agents in San Diego, where a Radiant Dawn outpatient clinic was bombed by the Mission in October. The agent was extremely cooperative because he'd been badly spooked by the whole affair, and had been told to soften the outcome as much as possible in the public eye. He'd been glad to send Cundieffe a client list from one of the computers they'd recovered, but Cundieffe had heard nothing else from San Diego, and had forgotten about it, in light of recent events. Among the stacks of files waiting for him on his desk was a printout of two hundred and thirty eight names, cross-referenced by their level of involvement with the clinic. One hundred and thirty four were contactees who had not participated in center activities. Against his master population list, he saw that most of these were not terminal as of last October, while many others were children or married parents. Not sick enough yet, or too likely to be missed.

Another eighty received counseling and some in-home care from the clinic's staff of registered nurses. Some paid in donations, but many more were pro bono cases—most of them poor, retired or illegal immigrants. Forgotten, invisible people. A few had e-mail addresses, which he copied down.

Twenty-four were receiving "full treatment." All of them were among the invisible classes. A check on their credit records showed that only five of them actually had credit cards, while only half of them had a bank account. Many had been on welfare for much of their lives, or were on Social Security. Of those five whose purchases he could track, all had stopped buying things in October of last year, though they continued to pay their balances. All had elected last October to have their bills paid by computer transfer. Odd, since he doubted any of them had a computer.

He looked at the list of names for a long, long time, until he saw through them to the burning ruins of the Radiant Dawn retreat in the Seven Devils Mountains. These people were in Idaho, but he doubted very much that they were there when the raid occurred. Where were they now? Another dead end.

Next, he studied the lab report for the plant samples the Idaho Bureau agents took from the Heilige Berg compound. The pine needles and the pollen, so subtly wrong that he'd missed it, but shocking in the context of everything else he'd seen. The lab report only made him feel sick.

The pollen contained a carcinogen similar to aflatoxin, a by-product of spoilage in peanuts, and the most toxic natural carcinogen known. He read this several times, trying to resculpt the words. He'd *been* there, breathing the pollinated air. His lungs ached, a nodule of malignant protoplasm swelling inside him to block breath and sow cellular madness through his defenseless body. He tried to reason his body back to sanity, but it was having none of it.

Heilige Berg was poisoned by the trees. The militia and their families were infected with cancer—and then given the RADIANT treatment. Co-opted, they faked a mass exodus from the mountain, helped the Radiant Dawn members escape, and vanished into the woods until the Mission attacked. The military executed maneuvers in the area, so they obligingly vacated the premises for the duration. They refused medical examination, insisting they were in perfect health. Another dead end, at least until the pollen samples could be gene-sequenced, which could take weeks.

He got on the Internet and glossed over stories from Idaho newspapers he'd bookmarked. Nothing about White Bird or Heilige Berg, nothing about Karl Schweinfurter. He'd almost given up when a small back-page piece caught his eye.

CATTLE MUTILATIONS BAFFLE LOCAL RANCHERS, INSPIRE FOLKLORE

The reporter took pains to show off his witty contempt for the White Bird-area rancher who claimed that something had stolen into his barn and slaughtered and devoured six of his cattle two nights ago. The account didn't fit the profile for UFO mutilation stories—the carcasses were not neatly dissected, but rended to bits and partially consumed. The rancher in question, Christopher Wilkes, 53, had driven off the attacker with a shotgun blast, but never saw it. He himself allowed that it might have been wolves, but claimed to have heard "something like speaking and/or yodeling" coming from the barn as he approached. When pressed about the yodeling angle, Mr. Wilkes, whose steadfast veracity came through even in the few skewed quotes, said it was "yodeling like a cowboy does, when he's drunk. It kind of sounded like that old Sgt. Sadler song, 'Ballad Of The Green Berets.'" The reporter cheekily speculated that a Bigfoot sensation could punch up tourism, but suggested that the cow-eating monster might learn something a little more current before his next attack.

Cundieffe thought of the thing he'd shot and blown up and burned in the Heilige Berg slaughterhouse. He thought about the sample he hadn't turned in to the lab yet. It was still in the Thermos in his battered briefcase, back in his suite. He hadn't touched it since he'd come back.It was part of what happened up there that he'd rather not remember, and until he received corroboration that it had even happened, he preferred to treat it as a phantasm. He thought about turning it in. He thought about throwing it in the Potomac, or into a blast furnace.

And then there was the question of Chan Durban. This kind of work was what he excelled at: picking a man's motivations apart and heading him off at his own conclusions.

He read the fitness reports and files on Durban, even the former Naval Intelligence officer's less classified memos, in order to get a feel for his mind. He found a man whose patriotic fervor permeated every routine duty, a man who probably hummed the Battle Hymn of the Republic as he ordered office supplies. A man who, for seven years, had monitored the most secret gleanings of the NSA's eavesdropping network with aplomb and discretion that would have earned him a place of honor in Hoover's Bureau. He had belonged to over nineteen chat lists on national security and foreign policy, and never tipped a secret, though his forceful arguments had the unmistakable backing of one who knows more than he reads in the news. He was addicted to the rush of talking politics and military history, and his presence on most of the lists was both sorely missed and savagely celebrated.

Cundieffe saw immediately how Greenaway must have operated Durban. Turn his patriotism against the NSA by spilling just enough to make him think enemies within the corridors of power were using the flag as a cover for atrocities. That it was the truth made it no less of a shrewd screwing, because Durban must have delivered dynamite into the rogue Lieutenant Colonel's hands. It could only be RADIANT dirt.

When Durban delivered it, Greenaway must have turned on him, because Durban vanished. Greenaway could rationalize anything, but he doubted the ex-Delta Force cutthroat would coldly kill a brother soldier. He hated the system, but loved the men, and subscribed to some sort of bloody-minded warrior's creed that would let him throw Durban to the wolves, but never put him in a shallow grave himself.

So Durban was alive and probably still in the United States. His love of country would not allow him to leave, and his training would show him how not to be found. He would know that he could just as easily hide in their midst, as in the middle of the Amazon. Probably feeling guilty for having betrayed his country, but still fired by what he'd seen, he would hope to clear his name by revealing the black intercepts, but he would do it smart, he would do it slow. He would be lurking in some sub-basement of the digital underground, putting out feelers to people who could help him bring his secrets into the light.

Cundieffe accessed CARNIVORE and put it onto a sweep for untranslatable encrypted files. CARNIVORE could crack PGP and other off-the-shelf systems with ease, but had to send tens of thousands of custom jobs to NSA, many of which took months to crack, and were stored until their priority became such that they got kicked up to the top of the waiting list. He forwarded a raft of such troublesome postings to the NSA's Bureau site. With luck, one of them would reflect Durban's fervent and smart, but now bitter, patriotic streak, and he would have his man.

Durban could be located because he was only a man—smarter and better-trained than most, but ultimately predictable. Paradoxically, the hundreds of missing people from the Radiant Dawn compound in Idaho were out of his reach, because their motives were inscrutable. What did Dr. Keogh want? Not to cure cancer, surely. He realized that was the bait that drew others to him. But cancer was not what human beings had come to believe it was, and Keogh knew it. He used cancer, as he used those who suffered from it, to affect some kind of change. But what did Keogh *want*? He saw himself not merely as an individual, but as a mutation, a macro-evolutionary event. A new species. What, then, did a new species want? To spread. To unify. To squeeze out all competition, and dominate.

The trees, spreading cancer. RADIANT pouring cancer out of the sky, but changing pre-existing cancer, not curing it, but growing it, changing it—into new flesh. The satellite was gone, but Keogh seemed unfazed.

We are one flesh, becoming one mind.

He used the trees to spread cancer. He would use the people the same way. The missing people were carriers. They would spread out to sow their disease, their message of change. But first, they would come together to become One—

A little bit more before he went to bed. How he wished he were in LA, and going home to his house. He punched in a batch of the e-mail addresses for the Radiant Dawn outpatients in San Diego, jimmying into them with barely perceptible effort by another program in his toolbox. He was sickened by all the junk mail that pinpointed the cancer patients' fateful demographic. Alternative cures, spiritual guidance, lucky charms, funeral insurance. But in a few of them, he found something unusual. Flight confirmations. London. Munich. Tokyo. Paid for on different credit cards, none of which belonged to the addressees. All departing from LAX tomorrow night.

Tomorrow. The e-mails had been sent only yesterday, days after RADIANT was shot down. It could mean only one thing. There had to be another mode of spreading the disease that was Keogh, and these people had been infected—absorbed. They were going to be One—

He rubbed his eyes and looked at his watch. Eleven thirty. Outside, sleet fell like tracer fire in the blackness. He looked around him, noticing for the first time that the office had emptied hours before. In the cavernous hush, his pulse throbbed in his ears. He jumped when his phone rang. "Agent Cundieffe—"

"Martin, please come into my office." It was AD Wyler.

Cundieffe peered out through the glass of his cubicle for a long moment before he stepped out into the open. He understood Durban a little better now, because how was his situation any different? He'd thought he was doing the right thing, and now he'd been caught. That was how he felt. Reasons and ideals that were burning in his mind blew out and away, so much ash raining down through his mind's eye as he crossed the vast room and stopped before AD Wyler's door.

He hadn't seen the Assistant Director come in, and he'd been hard at work since before sunrise this morning, leaving only once to eat and use the restroom. He only noticed how long he'd been standing before the door when Wyler's voice boomed from the other side. "Come in, Martin. Ms. McNulty has gone home for the day."

Nervously, he shuffled through the anteroom, eyeing Wyler's secretary's desk as if she might be lying in wait behind it. Wyler's office door stood ajar, with the buttery yellow light of his desk lamp creeping out across the brown-carpeted floor. Cundieffe peeked inside, then crept in and closed the door behind him.

Wyler looked as if he'd been living in the office in the same suit, sleeping under the desk, if at all. His eyes were drawn down by black-blue bags, and his wrinkles had deepened until the shadows made a jigsaw puzzle of it. His hands played over the keyboard of a laptop sitting on his desk beside his government-issue terminal. A SCSI cable connected the two computers with a sleek briefcase with blinking lights on it—some kind of huge storage drive. The monitors of both computers were shut off, but Cundieffe could hear the drives clattering frantically. He frowned, hiding his mouth behind his hand as he turned and found a seat opposite the desk. The Assistant Director was locally copying off the network— untraceably clearing out the FBI's internal files. Such a thing was unheard of, but AD Wyler made no moves to stop or hide the transaction. He looked hard at Cundieffe for a long time, as if he was sucking the truth out of Cundieffe's eyes. Finally, he said, "I've been away all this week preparing another domestic crisis management center in West Virginia. I've only came back to copy some files, but I'm gravely disappointed to find that I was needed here. You've been meddling in Counterintelligence business, Martin."

His palms dripped. He looked around the sparsely furnished office. Every glass surface, every picture on the wall, hid a camera. They watched. "I believed it was related to the larger Counterterrorism case I'm pursuing, sir. Lt. Durban was manipulated by parties unknown to steal classified communications intercepts from the NSA that pertain to the Mission. I think I'm close to locating him, sir."

"Stop looking."

"What, sir?"

"Brady Hoecker has strayed out of the consensus view on this situation. His faction is flirting with heterodoxy, and I don't want to see you dragged down with him."

Cundieffe played to the walls. "But sir, all he did was feed me information that's led me deeper into the investigation. He only wants the truth to be known."

"We know the truth. Do you? He's been forced to recruit probationary members like yourself, whose understanding of the bigger picture is still foggy. When you see the whole, only his paranoia explains the variance in analysis."

"What—what happens to those who—stray out of the consensus view?"

Wyler rolled his eyes. "When shown how their perception varies from orthodox policy, they recant and beg the pardon of the group."

"But the government—we—cover for Keogh."

"It could be misinterpreted that way, yes. But imagine how the situation would deteriorate if Keogh weren't contained, and it became public knowledge that he had a cure for cancer, albeit one with dangerous side effects?"

"And Keogh is at war with the Mission."

Wyler nodded.

"But Keogh—perhaps the real Keogh, founded the group that eventually became the Mission."

"Yes, it's all very complicated. The situation is coming to a head rather rapidly, and there's no room for multiple paths of action. Radiant Dawn is indeed a grave threat to our national security and our way of life, but it's also a means to an end which all, in the final analysis, would find desirable. We don't expect you to understand such paradoxes, but in the fullness of time, trust that you will see it."

Cundieffe blinked. This was what he'd hoped to hear, but now it only felt like pacification, like stroking. "What is Keogh? Is he just a terrorist, or is he a disease, or is he the cusp of an evolutionary leap, like us?"

Wyler scoffed, shuffled some printouts on his desk and shoved one of them across the desk at Cundieffe. His eyes felt like peeled potatoes in his head, but he squinted until he made out the type.

RADIANT DAWN SURVIVAL SEMINAR

Come participate in a unique one-day event that could change your life. Learn about a revolutionary new treatment modality that is giving hope and adding life to those suffering from terminal cancer. We know you've been approached by opportunists, seeking only profit, who exhaust your precious time and energy with claims that don't pan out. Radiant Dawn has been researching cancer survival strategies for sixteen years, and has discovered a breakthrough like no other. If you believe, as we do, that cancer is not the end, and if you want to live, come and spend the day with us at this no-cost, no-obligation seminar.

Del Sol Amphitheatre
Wilmington Fairgrounds
2019 Industry Dr.

Wilmington, CA
Sunday, February 8, 2000
9AM to 1PM

Tomorrow.

"When this is over, you'll get clearance to review the Miskatonic Protocols, which will explain the whole thing. Suffice to say that Keogh is the earth's past come back to haunt us. We are the future. When we come into our kingdom, the world will never face such a threat again. Now go home and get some rest. You're going to need it."

Cundieffe retreated without another word and followed orders. He got his coat and went to the elevator, still chewing on what he'd seen in the Assistant Director's office. Absurdly, he was reminded of one of his Mule history lessons. As the custodians of civilization, his kind had on numerous occasions found itself charged with saving the works of civilization. When the Holy Roman Empire crumbled and the long night of the Middle Ages fell on Europe, it was Mule scholars who hoarded the knowledge of antiquity in abbeys and monasteries, while their gendered counterparts in the Catholic Church thought only of saving their own skins.

Wyler's new division had been working day and night to get the new Headquarters Domestic Management Center up and running, and Cundieffe knew there'd never been talk of an off-site center in West Virginia. Such a thing would only be conceivable if Washington itself was destroyed, or overrun by civil unrest—or a plague.

What's going to happen? he asked the fisheye security camera in the ceiling of the elevator. *What are you going to let him do?*

~ 33 ~

The passenger in 22A was being difficult.

The crew of the Island Air Boeing 707 had already disconnected his pager button and relocated seven of their sixty-two passengers out of earshot of the irritant, so that the only passengers left around him were the two Caucasian men who accompanied him when he embarked on Kiribati. Left to his own devices in the back of the cabin, adrift in two empty rows of bright orange seats, the difficult passenger still found ways to make his presence known.

"Excuse me, Miss?" he flagged down the stewardess. "You're of Polynesian descent, right? I was curious if you could tell me something, because I was reading your delightful in-flight magazine about the history of the South Pacific, and it seems there are some gaps you could fill in. D'you have any more of those macadamia nuts? I'm ravenous...thanks, so anyway—

"I've heard that you people evolved parallel to homo sapiens, but descended from, or at least crossbred with, a race of intelligent proto-humanoid fish that used to exist in these parts. You know, your ancestors in Ponape or wherever would stake out their virgin womenfolk on the beaches, and the Deep Ones would come rolling out and knock 'em up, and the offspring would appear human for about fifty years, but then they'd start to display amphibious traits—gills, webbed fingers and toes, and stuff, and finally return to the sea to perpetuate the cycle, which is why you people all look so well-preserved. And I read somewhere else that you people didn't acquire human traits at all until you ate Captain Cook...hey, don't go away, I'm talking to you—

"So anyway, all I'm wondering, and there's some cash money in it for you, so don't look at me like that, but all I'm wondering is, do they do this breeding thing all the time, or is it only at specific times of year, you know, when the stars are right? The Spawn of Dagon coming out of the sea to fuck your womenfolk, I mean? I assume it would be, but what I want to know is, is this something an outsider could come and watch? I mean, not just a regular tourist, but a discreet man of the world like myself. I assure you, money is no object—"

Just don't listen, the senior stewardesses warned the others, don't come within arm's reach, and for God's sake, don't try to turn off his computer. He was a regular passenger, and usually harmless if left alone. They had only to recount the story of the time an angry Samoan steward confiscated the passenger's laptop, and the cockpit was blasted with static, unholy electronic rhythms and the screams of porn until he got it back. They consoled themselves that he was not the worst American they had ever had to deal with.

When he'd scared all the stewardesses away, the passenger relaxed and settled into gazing out the window and listening to the mix disk he'd put together for this flight. Time for reflection, what his parents used to call realigning your chi. It was one of the few meaningful things they'd taught him to do, to still the chattering, excrement-hurling monkeys in his brain, and for a few moments every day, just *be*. It allowed him to formulate plans, redirect his energies, and build new identities. He took a moment to thank his parents for the gift. Without it, he probably would have killed them both a long time before he did.

Baron Angulo was always especially tense after coming back from Keogh. The trip itself was a royal pain in the ass–flying from Hawaii to Kiribati, then by boat or chopper out to the atoll, which he had to be lowered onto in a spacesuit because of the fucking sharks and the fucking radiation, not to mention fucking Keogh his own self. He spent the rest of his island vacation in the bunker, two hundred feet deep in Keogh's guts, writing code to be uploaded to RADIANT, updating Keogh's code as new consciousness models and protein strings were absorbed. Each trip stretched the limit of his patience, because commands could only be sent from the uplink node on the atoll, now that Idaho was down, and had to be routed through a labyrinth of relays and front nodes to their source, which was not even a proper computer, but a chunk of Keogh floating in space.

That Keogh needed him to come out to the most godforsaken ass-end of the world, just so he could be connected with a piece of his own fucking brain, defied every tenet of the information age. But the freaky old fucker didn't trust Baron, and, of course, Angulo didn't trust him. Even now, when he peeked just so through the gap in the seats, he saw the Keogh escort, staring through magazines at the back of his head.

Keogh had to watch him from outside, because he couldn't risk getting inside him, and trying to take the controls. Angulo's neural works were wired to a spec so far from the factory originals that his thinking could not be duplicated even by such an ingenious invader as Keogh, and Angulo had the keys to the computer system. He'd never figure that out without Angulo around, either. The source of Radiant Dawn's computing power was not in any one vulnerable mainframe, but in an ingenious distributed network of millions of computers all around the globe—PC's whose owners had invited him in via a smarmy chain e-mail more widely traveled than the St. Jude blessing letter. Whenever the system sprang into action, it accessed those computers left on and open to the net, but dormant, each of them a cell in a global neural network more powerful than any mainframe in existence or development. Keogh didn't understand it, but Angulo had no illusions about how long that would last. The motherfucker would, if he got his way, become a global neural network himself, and Angulo would have to find new ways to be useful.

He'd been secretly relieved when the Russians trashed RADIANT. It would slow the fucker down a bit. He'd still had to reroute the lion's share of the network, and Keogh was uncharacteristically apathetic about what to do with it. This trip would be the last for quite some time, and the next phase was what he'd been hungering for. A chance to strike at the real enemy...

His fists dug into his thighs, his eyes filmed over in visions. The music fed his rampaging brain-movies, phased, time-stretched jungle rhythms driving living juggernauts of purifying flame into the festering cancerous tumors of the secret power elite, the sky blackened for a thousand years with their ashes, all because of him—

Time to reflect. *Shut up, monkeys.*

He skipped ahead in the mix to a more sedate song. He let himself go limp and still and watched imperious golden clouds warring beneath his window. The UK Surf version of "Wave Of Mutilation" by the Pixies always soothed his nerves. Something about the languid, submarine guitars and the vaguely inhuman lyrics brought back the pure pleasure of just being alive. *You think I'm dead, but I sail away—*

But true inner peace eluded him. All of a sudden, his stomach ached, inflating with gas, and his arms and legs tingled as if he'd been sleeping in a straitjacket. His head ached, his sinuses flared up, and he saw purple phosphene fireworks like fists were rubbing his eyes from the inside of his skull. It felt like some kind of Asian hyper-flu, or food poisoning, but no...it was like the time when he was ten, and his parents tried out a batch of acid on him that went south, and he first started to think about killing people.

He took responsibility for his actions, pride in them, even, but it was his parents who set him on this road. It wasn't the drugs or the free-love atmosphere that spoiled him, it was the way they loved him.

When he was small, he was a little godling, perfect and innocent, freshly returned from the Cosmic Source, or some such hippie shit, and they denied him nothing, punished him never. Then one day, he was suddenly just another dirty, clumsy stupid human being, and worse than most, when they were strung out. Any interest he showed in learning about the world outside the pot-fog of Santa Cruz was derided as flirting with the "death culture." The bad acid trip actually was the pivotal moment in his life, the rite of passage into a new kind of manhood. He saw, in the throes of a hellish peak when the sun tried to rape him, that his parents had never seen him, never tried to know him. What they had loved was the novelty and instinctual endorphin rush of the new child; what they hated was the reflection and denial of themselves that he represented for them in their more lucid moments. He discovered that no one actually saw him at all; he was invisible, unknowable, an eight-eyed super-genius in the kingdom of the blind idiots. He would teach them to see, if only for a moment, how much there was to the world, that they'd missed. Show them all. Even Keogh...

He turned up the Pixies as loud as it would go. *Shut up, monkeys!*

He punched the Call button to summon the stewardess and make her look at the sonograms he'd had done in Thailand of Dr. Teeth and all his other pets, wriggling happily in their intestinal zoo. That would make him feel better. But the bitch stayed away, and one of his monkeys refused to shut up.

Why did you do it, Buggs?

A voice. Inside his head. Goddamit! That fucker Keogh had infected him. The one nonnegotiable term of their working relationship had been violated. Assuming, of course, that he wasn't hallucinating, right now.

He blinked his eyes furiously, but the purple fireworks only got worse, obscuring his vision like a really good nitrous oxide hit. He paused the music. Over the omnipresent hum of the plane and the murmur of people-noises, there was only the oceanic roaring he always heard when he was freaking out. He turned and looked at the Keoghs, but they sat blandly vegetative in their seats, expecting nothing, thinking even less.

The plane lacked the Internet jacks most business class sections had, but he had a wireless set-up that hacked into an Indonesian satellite, which could send untraceable code anywhere in the world instantly. He'd written the program a long while before, and with a single keystroke, could bring down the Radiant Dawn network and turn over its internal transmissions—stego encrypted video and text inside babbling video lectures—to the leadership of every member nation of the UN Security Council and Interpol; every columnist and media outlet listed on the Drudge Report; the producers of *60 Minutes, Nightline* and *Oprah*; and the editors of *Fortean Times, Wired, High Times* and *Fangoria*. He'd make the motherfucker sorry.

But his fingers wouldn't touch the keys. His right hand curled instead into a quivering fist and punched him squarely in the face. His nose snapped and burst like a tomato. Blood showered his keyboard.

No, Buggs. You wish it was Him.

He watched his hand unclench and close the fuck-Keogh program, and skip forward in the mix.

"Quiet Village" by Martin Denny. Sinister jungle fauna howled and screeched. Liquid marimbas and vibes brought back the aroma of herbal taxidermy, of the desert—

Hiram liked this song, said the monkey. *You remember Hiram, don't you, Buggs?*

You don't take as many drugs or kill as many people as Baron Angulo had without hearing voices. Voices told him what to do, told him what other people thought of him, told him whom to trust and for how long, and who to become, so that others would trust him.

But never, ever, had there been a voice of recrimination. He had no guilt, nor even a belief in guilt, except as a lever in other people's heads. Yet this had to be a flashback, a new flavor of insanity to play with. He recognized the voice in his head at once, though he could not name it, because its presence inside him was even more of an outrageous impossibility than Keogh's would be.

The voice was Storch.

Bet you think this is pretty weird, huh? Well, the feeling is mutual, Baron. That's your real name, is it? Pretty stupid name, I'd change it, too, if I were you. Forgive me if I still call you Buggs, but that was the name I knew you by. I trusted you.

Angulo shivered. This couldn't be real. Keogh killed Storch, killed him and ate him and digested him. God, how he wished he could have been there to see it.

You want to see it now? See it then, motherfucker.

He showed him.

Half-life.

The disintegrating body clings to the energy pattern, the collective pancellular delusion, the naked, screaming soul of Zane Ezekiel Storch, far longer than it should.

The body is bathed in acids and relentless protein-denaturing enzymes, and is broken down into bite-sized chunks; stripped of nutrients while passing through hundreds of miles of intestine; leached of its water, ravaged by parasites, and reduced to a toxic soup of utterly worthless molecules. And all the while, Storch fights.

Wherever the seat of the soul is in a normal human being, in Storch it lives in every organic molecule that can still generate a bioelectrical impulse. Deprived of body and brain, he is an electrochemical ghost to which his cells cling with the grim fury that drove his post-human body to its untimely end, and brought him here. The ghost of Storch lingers in the cellular remains for several days before, one by one, like cold, dying stars in the asshole of the universe, they wink out and become inert matter.

Elsewhere in the bowels of the island of Keogh, Storch's cells thrive and multiply. The filtration here is not digestive, but purely mechanical, and easily defeated. In twenty-four hours, Storch has formed an amorphous colony of undifferentiated diploid cells in the aqueous medium in which they awakened, in the drain of Buggs' shower. Just before the molecular memory of a man named Zane Ezekiel Storch flickers and fades away in these last remnant cells, a suitable host appears–

When it was done, Angulo came to in the seat, but found that his body had no interest in doing what he wanted it to, anymore. What he wanted to do was leap up screaming for Keogh to get this fucking mutant ghost out of his head; either that or tear the lid off his skull and paint the cabin with his own brains.

The sensation that he had a body at all was a fast-fading phantom. He couldn't feel his arms or legs, then he couldn't feel his heartbeat, then he couldn't blink or move his mouth. He felt like a fugitive impulse in his own brain, a rat trapped in a corner by a fever that, impossibly, was smarter than he.

I'm rewiring your nervous system, Buggs. I don't like the idea of taking your body any more than you do, but I need it, and I figure you owe me at least that much. You helped them take away my store, my home and my life, and I don't figure it meant jack-shit to you, but I liked it a lot. I guess what I'm asking is: what's your fucking problem, buddy? Why did you come fucking with me?

Angulo thought the words in a red, hateful smear he hoped blew out a bunch of his synapses. BECAUSE I COULD, DUMBSHIT! Because you were stupid and I was smart, and you thought you were fit to survive, but you didn't have half of what it really takes, you one-thumbed cracker cocksucker. It's brains, you stupid ant. You're stupid, and that's why He tricked you, that's why He killed you, and chewed you up and shat you out—

I'm here, ain't I? I'm smart enough, Buggs. Why Keogh? You think He's going to let you go on after He's everyone and everything? Just you and Him, forever and amen?

He's the only one smart enough to see the Real Enemy. The Mission are just pawns in the game, being used to keep Him in check until the endgame, but they're all over, now, and it's almost here. He's going to flush the real enemy out into the open.

What the fuck are you talking about?

The New World Order, asshole! It's real and it's bigger than anybody believes. They hide behind the Jews and the Trilateral Commission and the military-industrial complex, but they're really mutants from a breeding program going back two thousand years, among the Black Families of Europe, you know, the Rothschilds, the Merovingian Dynasty? They think they own Him, but they're in for a big fucking surprise. You were there in the war, you know what's down there, in that pit in Iraq—

Typical Buggs bullshit.

You think Keogh's bad, you should see what they're planning to do. America will be one big concentration camp, but it'll be Paradise compared to the rest of the world. But Keogh's going to fuck them but good, and then I'm going to fuck Him! He'll never win, dude, He thinks He's the shit, but I got 'em all in check. I can fuck them all at the right moment, but you've got to let me stay awake—

You kill people, Buggs.

Shit, you used to kill people for a living, boss—

I don't like it like you do.

What, those freaks in Colma? The School Of Night? I didn't even touch them! They were doping out and taking long naps, trying to commune with their hippie-dippie god, the Unbegotten Source. Dr. Angell said they were real close, His Brainless Majesty was nearing the cusp of some kind of holy wet dream or something and they were going deeper to try to awaken him. Man, you've got to believe me, I was just there to crack their computer system but they went out like a light all at the same time, all by themselves. Sure, I was pissed, because the computer locked me out and fried itself and I got fuck-all out of it, but I did what I did when they were already gone—

Angulo put his soul, his heart, into a winning warmth behind his pitch, even as he could feel synapses going dark by the millions as control over the forelobe of his brain, where he lived and loved and kept all his favorite stuff, slowly slipped away. The stupid GI ape had to go for it, because stupid people always did what he told them to, until they thought they were smarter than him, and they slipped up, and he got them. In the end he got them all, because he was the smartest—

I never said I was smarter than you, Buggs, said the last chattering monkey, *just stronger*. And then Baron Angulo's brain forgot him.

Storch sat very, very still for a long time in the seat on the airplane. He was alive. He knew nothing more. He'd been able to pick out nothing useful from Buggs' cyclone of manic thoughts, and now that he was alone in the strange head, it busily rearranged itself chemically and structurally to become his own. From out of the tiny colony of Storch-cells that had entered Buggs through an open cut in his foot during a shower in the bunker, some energy that he could only describe as his soul had staged a coup and stormed the brain of the man who stole his life. He was, for want of a better definition, human again.

But what was he? He thought he was his career, until it was ended by the war. He thought he was the life he'd built in Thermopylae, until that, too, was taken away. He thought he was just a human being, then, but lost that, too. His body became alien to him, something dangerous and maddening to inhabit, but it was still *him*, the only one he had, and he had only just begun to come to terms with it. He had fought too hard and suffered too much to accept death when it came, but it had happened anyway, and now—

This. He looked at Buggs' pale, slender little hands, at the white scars in his palms where his nails gouged the flesh, at the soft shelf of belly lolling over the elastic waistband of his ugly plaid pajama pants.

He looked out the window, at cities of sun-gilded clouds scudding across the infinite blue of the Pacific. On the headphones, "Quiet Village" faded out, and another Denny tune, "Hypnotique", unfolded like the petals of a night-blooming orchid. Whatever it was, and however it happened, it was good to be alive, in this moment.

When he felt at home enough in his new body to move, he typed and sent an e-mail to Agent Cundieffe.

A hand touched his shoulder. He looked up into eyes of living stone.

"You appear to have damaged yourself," a gray-eyed Asian man said.

Storch tried to smile. The unfamiliar muscles strained and twanged, but the intended effect, the patented guileless crazy-ass grin that seemed a default setting on Buggs' face, would not come. He could only guess at what the face was really doing. A tic set his mouth to spasming, and a rope of drool came out. "I'm okay," he managed, startled at the sound of Buggs' voice mumbling his words.

The man's eyes narrowed and a dry smile creased his face. His hand tightened on Storch's shoulder. "You're more resilient than I believed possible, Zane."

Another hand came up with a syringe.

Storch's flat hand whipped out and shattered the Keogh's right-side collarbone. He recoiled as blinding agony erupted in his fist. Buggs' hand was not his hand, and he'd broken most of the bones in it.

Keogh's arm went limp and the syringe fell into the aisle. He gave an anguished groan and slumped across the seat, trying to grab Storch with his working hand. The other Keogh stood and assisted. Hands clutched his T-shirt and his hair, so that both tore away when he threw himself out into the aisle.

Storch's broken hand splayed out on the deck, bones grinding chips off each other and refusing his weight. He lay full-length in the aisle, only dimly aware that he was screaming and sobbing from the pain. This body was so weak, so soft, he thought he was lapsing into shock.

At the head of the cabin, a young Polynesian stewardess caught his eye and pursed her lips sourly, not at all displeased by what she saw. The wounded Keogh stepped around him and walked up the aisle with his dead arm hanging at his side, making conciliatory sounds, while the other one stooped over him and retrieved the syringe.

"He's perfectly tractable when he's had his medication, Miss, there's no need to notify the pilot."

The stewardess paged someone from an intercom, looking sideways at the scene in the aisle. The other passengers watched with guiltily excited looks on their sunburned faces. A few even cheered and clapped; Buggs really had been an asshole.

Keogh's voice in his ear was the sound of sleep, the whisper of blessed oblivion. "Zane, there's no point in making a scene. You don't want to get anyone killed—"

"Help, please God!" Storch screamed, "They're killing me!"

"Kill him now, so he'll shut up," someone shouted.

The stewardess warily approached, her hands out in front of her. "He shouldn't be on a plane like this."

Behind her, the Keogh apologized profusely and told her everything would be fine, if she'd help them give him his medication. Anxious to restore peace, she nodded and came closer.

Storch *pushed*. He flexed his whole body, writhing under Keogh so that he was turned facing him. Keogh hugged Storch's arms and knelt across his legs, which brought his face close in to Storch's.

"Don't do this," Keogh whispered, "or everyone here will die."

Behind his back, Storch felt Keogh's hand fumbling to get the cap off the syringe.

Storch tilted his head back and drove it as hard as he could into Keogh's, the thickest region of bone in his forehead slamming into the juncture of bone between the Keogh's eyes once, twice, too many times to count.

His vision was wiped away in red fog, but Keogh let go of his arms as he fell back, throwing them up in front of his bloody, battered face.

Storch tried to get up, but the deck spun and dumped him across the laps of a hysterical group of Mormon missionaries, who shoved him back into the arms of the wounded Keogh, who had regained the use of his broken arm.

Storch vomited convulsively, kicking out at shadows crowding around him. The stewardess was screaming, and the Keoghs had his arms and legs, and they were going to sedate him, and it was going to work, and he was never going to wake up because, for the moment, at least, he was only human.

Someone shouted, "Freeze! Lie down on the deck!" and someone else shouted, "Federal agents, stay in your seats!" and the Keoghs paused for a moment. Storch tore his legs free and kicked one Keogh in the gut. He crumpled under the weight of the one holding his arms, pulled him off-balance and hurled him into the back wall of the cabin.

He stood and looked around, seeing dueling doubles of men in Hawaiian shirts with small-caliber pistols leveled. One of them held out a gold shield alongside his pistol, the other stood behind him in a rigid Weaver stance, ready to empty an eight-round magazine into Storch in an eye-blink. They were shouting things, but he couldn't hear them.

"It's cool," Storch mumbled, "everything's cool, just get me a seat away from these assholes—"

He felt as if he'd weathered a few cycles in a washing machine. The aisle rippled and buckled under his unsteady feet.

One of the Keoghs grabbed him from behind. He clasped Storch in a full-nelson. He had a head-and-a-half height advantage over Storch, who could only go limp. He pulled the Keogh forwards and threw him over his back into the aisle. He stood just as the locked and loaded federal agent shot him in the chest.

Storch grunted and slumped back into an empty seat, then dove across the window seats of a petrified family from Arkansas. He drove his unbroken fist into the window, two layers of half-inch thick tempered safety glass, but for one who just doesn't give a shit what it does to his hand, it was no big deal. Icy wind flushed the cabin. Alarms flashed. Sirens blared. Oxygen masks dropped from the ceiling, and obliging passengers, each and every one fighting blind animal panic, slipped one on, and immediately lapsed into a stupor.

Storch dove back across the aisle. His chest felt as if one of his lungs had collapsed and was filling with blood. His hands were swelled up like hot water bottles, and the pain seemed to get worse by the minute. Good. That meant they were healing.

A federal agent came back up the aisle gun-first, still shouting. One of the Keoghs got in the way, and the agent shoved him back. The Keogh caught his gun-hand and twisted it. The agent screamed and dropped the gun, but the Keogh kept twisting. He gave the hand back broken and drove a fist into the agent's screaming mouth. The agent flew back up the aisle into his partner, who emptied his gun into the Keogh before he went down.

Storch crawled over the center row of seats, over catatonic Samoans and a family from New Zealand and a Maori NFL linebacker. He spilled into the opposite aisle and crawled on his belly to the emergency exit. The federal agent had reloaded, and was still using his gun in a vain attempt to pacify the situation. He shot at both Keoghs, then leapt up onto a seat and drew a bead on Storch.

He was so weak, just trying to hold it together. "Leave me alone," he begged, blood bubbling out the corners of his mouth. "let me alone, I just want to get off—"

He followed the arrows to the emergency exit hatch. The seat beside it was empty. The agent shot him twice in the back, once in the left kidney, and once in the lower spine. His legs dragged behind him like dead snakes. He hauled himself up onto the seat. He could see only gray spots like molten lead pouring over his eyes, and he could barely feel his hands, but he touched the lever and death-gripped it. He started to pull when his arm just went dead. It wouldn't pull.

The agent reloaded yet again, but Keogh slammed him to the deck and stomped on him.

"Zane, there's nowhere left to go," the other Keogh said. He crossed to the starboard aisle and grabbed Storch's dead legs, yanked him back from the emergency hatch.

Storch's dead hand dragged the lever and the bolts blew out. The two-by-four foot panel of the hatch was sucked out into the dazzling sunset sky. Keogh released him to cling to the seat, but Storch went limp and half-fell, half-flew, out of the plane and into the wind.

~ 34 ~

If all had gone according to plan, he'd be in the fucking tropics, right now. By comparison, DC in winter was a perfect metaphorical expression of how terribly wrong everything had gone.

He sat in a glossy black custom Range Rover, the kind of plush armored SUV with which foreign dignitaries tooled the streets of Washington to flaunt their diplomatic immunity. There was no diplo placard on the dashboard to attract attention where they were parked across the street from Ford's Theater on 10th Avenue, but any thorough DC police officer who ran its plates would find it registered to the Ambassador from the Democratic Republic of Congo, and a headache no rank-and-file officer would want to deal with. A more astute officer might wonder why only one occupant of the idling Range Rover, the driver, was black, or why the grizzled, scarred old white man in the back, with one arm in a sling and a laptop balanced on one knee, had an assault rifle and three extra magazines resting on the seat beside him. But he would have to come very close indeed to see Mort Greenaway through the triple-tinted, bullet-proof rear windows, and by then, Greenaway would have thought nothing of shooting him. For Greenaway had come too far, and cost too many damned good men their lives, to let a police officer stand between him and what he saw as the next phase of his revenge.

Now totally rogue, without military or spook backing, wanted by the FBI for what happened in Idaho. Half an A-team left, their collective morale, their collective sanity, more ragged than his own. Still a soldier, still fighting his war.

All along, he had been running behind this thing, seeing only its smoke, and leaving his men dead in its tracks. It was high time he dragged one of the drivers out and found out where the goddamned final destination was.

Greenaway looked at the marquee of Ford's Theater, at the doors through which Abraham Lincoln's dying body had been carried after John Wilkes Booth shot him at point-blank range on April 14, 1865. Oblivious to politics, Greenaway had studied the lessons of the event, and was stirred to admiration. One man, resolved and in the right place, accomplished what the entire Confederacy, in five years of devastating war, could not. Greenaway hoped to shake down a bigger tree than Lincoln by very similar tactics, but the reverse side of the lesson stuck in his craw, and he looked away. Booth's assassination had been expertly performed, but it was too late to save the Confederacy. It was only a bitter parting shot in the conflict, and changed nothing. Greenaway wondered if it was just his nation he was too late to save. Perhaps his species—

In the driver's seat, Chuck Mizell stirred and clicked his tongue to get Greenaway's attention. "Here he comes," he whispered. In the shotgun seat, Wiley dozed with his head on his shoulder. He would come full awake the moment he was needed, but it was really, really for the best that he sleep until then.

Greenaway wiped condensation off the inside of his window and saw the charcoal gray Chrysler sedan scoot out the mouth of the underground garage like a ball bearing. An arc sodium lamp on the corner made a bronze beaded curtain of the freezing rain pissing down on the street, which was fit only for figure skaters and zambonis.

The Chrysler's driver was nervous, and not gifted with adequate winter-driving skills. The mid-sized government-issue car fishtailed wildly to the right, away from Pennsylvania Avenue, headed north on 10th, as expected. Mizell turned the ignition and swung into low-key pursuit down the empty street.

He heard Mizell's terse radio check with the forward units and the irregular squawking of the police scanner, and knew he should be listening in, but none of it pierced through the thick scab of brooding at which he had been picking since they came down off the mountain and started running.

They set down the Bell 406 in a field on the Washington side of the Snake River and piled into a van they'd stashed for just such an unforeseeable turn of events, and from there went to a safe house in Spokane. A medic saw to Greenaway's wounds, which were far worse than apparent at first, and beaconed in any survivors, of which there were exactly three. Twelve hours later, the remnants of Team Dog Town came straggling in on a stolen farmer's truck, shot up, shell-shocked and pissed beyond all reason. They laid up for three days, putting out feelers. What happened, who did it happen to, and who was looking for them? The FBI and state police in Idaho and Washington were quietly canvassing on a vague tip that an armed and dangerous militia group was in the region, looking for trouble.

Nobody talked about what they saw up there, and Greenaway never tried to debrief them. Team Dogtown was down in the thickest of the shit when the Mission's goddamned drone bombers bombed them blind, and the mutant survivalist army tunneled in under them. He knew they survived because they ran, but he would not make them say it. They were all he had left, and in the end, they were a hell of a lot smarter than he'd been.

Getting back east had been a prickly bitch with the silent dragnet tightening around them, but they had planned for this, only with a hell of a lot more men. Crossing the border on a rural road into Canada, they drove to Calgary and flew to Montreal, and crossed back over with forged Canadian passports. Even though he'd had the passports made himself, he still heaved a sigh of relief that slightly banked the blue flames of arctic rage through which he saw the world.

They say that hate only weakens you, wearing down your reserves and your judgment. But Greenaway ran on hate and jolly green giants and Percodan, and felt ten years younger the moment he'd figured out how to take the fight to them.

For he'd been chewing it over since they left Heilige Berg in defeat, and he'd gone in to Canada with a plan. He knew who the real enemy was, now, and it was not tiring to hate them, it was the last thread he had to cling to, over a churning black sea of madness. For he'd learned that the real enemies were the ones he'd hated all along, hated the most. The Missionaries were just pawns, like he'd been, but the ones who ran the board, the ones who started the wars, the recessions, the budget cutbacks, and more wars, always more stupid, pointless meat-grinding wars. They were the ones he'd bargained with to raise his army.

In his heart, he'd always known they and their kind were the cancer eating civilization, but they never gave him a reason. Idaho gave him one in spades, left him nothing else to lose. He knew who they were and where they lived, and tonight he'd know more. He had a card he hadn't played yet; it was a wild card, so wild he couldn't read it himself, yet. He meant to have that tonight, too. And tomorrow, he meant to have the Cave Institute's goddamned guts for breakfast.

He wasn't scared of them. He could do it with six men better than sixty, and the more pissed-off, the more psycho, the better, and they came no more pissed-off than the survivors of Heilige Berg.

The only thing he was still afraid of was Dr. Keogh and his cult of clones. Radiant Dawn remained an unknown, a hole in plans tactical and strategic that you could just about drop the fucking Pentagon into without touching the goddamned sides. They didn't scare him because they weren't human, or even because they were all the same goddamned guy. They scared him because of how they made him feel inside. When the Mission shut him down over the Owens River last summer, it made him feel old and stupid, and he went blood-simple up until the moment he first looked into Dr. Keogh's eyes. Even then, before he saw any of the rest of it—*the rest of it*, Jesus—when he looked into Keogh's eyes, he had felt something else that cut deeper than he thought he had nerves. He felt obsolete.

He knew that Radiant Dawn was some sort of Cave Institute-sponsored genetic research program, but he doubted they knew half of what went on there, or how far he'd gone. It was only the latest in the endless parade of insanely stupid master plans the eggheads had hatched on the world, but it was the one that might finally fuck them all for good. Mort Greenaway wasn't long for this world, didn't really want to be, anymore, but before he died, he'd sworn to himself and to his men above and below ground, he'd hurt both sides, and show them what an old, stupid caveman could do.

The geek drove distractedly, a rank winter amateur, talking on a cellular phone. He rolled past the Range Rover, then through the stoplight at F Street, where the cut-off car was expected, but did not show.

"Chuck, where the fuck is Pastrana?" Greenaway growled, but Mizell said nothing. He stopped the Range Rover at the crosswalk and switched off the headlights, whispered something into his headset, shook his head.

Another sedan rolled into the intersection from F and turned in between the Range Rover and the Chrysler, five by five with the plan. But it was not just a car, Greenaway realized with an ugly, heart-choking double-take. Not *his* car, oh hell no. A DC Metro police cruiser, roof lights already twirling. It hove in tight on the Chrysler's ass and goosed its siren. The Chrysler slammed on its brakes midway down Tenth between F and G, right in the center of the dead spot Team Dogtown had made an hour earlier by shooting out the streetlights. Shimmying on the ice rink street, the Chrysler stopped hard against the tight column of parked cars on the right side. Even with the windows closed, Greenaway heard metal grind on metal and crackling glass.

What shit luck. Their quarry might have seen them, and ran the stop to get attention, but it was Greenaway's shit luck, running true to form, that put the cop there.

The cop got out and stomped up to the Chrysler's window. He wore a knee-length parka and a plastic baggie over his cap. His right hand brushed the coat off his hip, gunslinger-style, as he approached and cagily leaned close to the ice-beaded glass, tapped once with his left.

Greenaway craned his neck down F Street in both directions, but no joy. No Pastrana. He checked his laptop, punched in a quick instant message query, but nobody answered. Hector Pastrana was a past master of the urban snatch, ran a crew in Bogotá that delivered Cali cartel heads like milk every Monday morning for the better part of a year. He drove one of the trash trucks that bagged Chan Durban. If he saw the cop, he'd lay back, try to catch the quarry closer to the freeway. They were not in downtown Lebanon, but downtown DC, and though, statistically, the two were nearly indistinguishable in terms of street crime, this was not the time or the place for a shoot-out. He hoped Pastrana was hip to the cop and readjusting the plan, but he'd feel a hell of a lot better if the fuck would let him know what the hell was happening.

The window rolled down, and the pale pink face of their quarry leaned out a little, conferring in puffs of frozen breath with the cop. The cop's arm came up, pointing back at the intersection, at the scene of violation, but also at them. *Did you happen to see that stop sign back there, sir?* Or maybe, *Did you happen to see those terrorists following you, sir?*

The puffs came faster and more furiously as the cop gestured for the driver to step out of the car. He saw the pale pink face wagging, head shaking, *no, thank you, officer,* or maybe, *do you have any idea who I am?* Credentials were shown, but the cop shook his head, now, gestured more forcefully, *step out.* He brushed back the slicker again, actually touched the stock of the Glock 9mm holstered there.

Holy shit. He saw what happened next, but he'd thought he'd lost the capacity to be surprised, over the last several months.

The driver drew a gun and stuck it out the window, surprising even the cop, who only just had time to duck before lead flew. Three shots pop pop popped out the window, actually through the window, which sprayed out at the diving cop. Straining to see by the muzzle-flashes, Greenaway saw only the driver's head turned away from the gun, pure panic-fire, the dumbshit couldn't even bear to watch where he was shooting. A car alarm started howling from the row of parked cars on the opposite curb. The cop, spread-eagle on the icy wet tarmac almost underneath the car, drew his Glock and expertly shot out both front tires just as the Chrysler's taillights flared up and the car bucked and tried to take off.

Greenaway, who knew, now, where Pastrana was, barked at Mizell, "Goddamit, Chuck, where's the cut-off? Raise Leo—"

"Here he comes," Mizell grunted, an amused lilt in his voice.

A van was indeed coming down Tenth Street towards them, roof-rack hi-beams on full-blast as it swerved to intercept the runaway Chrysler, which lurched across the center line like a badly thrown curling iron, horn honking an epileptic fit in Morse code. Greenaway saw the driver's arms fly up in a frantic defensive gesture just before the impact.

Tripping and slipping in the cop's bulky winter gear, Pastrana popped up on one knee and shot out the Chrysler's rear tires and taillights. Greenaway hid his face in his hands. Welcome to Dodge City, as seen on *America's Stupidest Police Videos*.

Incredibly, no lights came on in the ritzy apartments and office blocks flanking the street. No other cars strayed into their little firefight, but the bubble would burst in a matter of seconds, and if they were still here, they would have to shoot it out with the real police. It occurred to him then that they'd got away with a live shootout six blocks from the White House, and he stifled a grin.

Leo ended it. Swinging the van broadsides to the flat-footed Chrysler, he T-boned it into submission in the middle of the street. The van rocked, the Chrysler stalled. The driver spilled out empty-handed and made for the parked cars to the left, but Pastrana had the drop on him. Running as recklessly as he dared on the ice-slick tarmac, Pastrana closed with him and kicked his feet out from under him, stood with one foot across his neck and waved the Range Rover in.

Mizell shot across the intersection and parked hard by their quarry, who lay prone on the ice like a baby ready for nap time. Wiley stirred, Mizell eyeing him nervously, but didn't wake up.

Greenaway painfully climbed down, clutching his assault rifle like a cane, and surveyed the scene. Four cars on the street, one totaled, one damaged, one stolen from the goddamned DCPD. "What a fucking mess, Hector," was all he could say.

Pastrana whirled on him, and for a second, he thought the ersatz cop was going to shoot him, too. "Cop ran up on me when I was boosting the crash-car. What was I supposed to do?"

Greenaway fixed him with his dourest eye, but it was pointless. Pastrana was an initiative-taker, that's why he was here. The fish had proved harder to catch than they expected, and this might've gone down even harder if Pastrana would have had to run him down in a civilian car. Pastrana's defiant glare told him not to fight, not here and now, not ever. *You don't know who or what or why we're fighting, and what you do know, you haven't told us. How dare you try to tell me how?*

"Where's the cop?"

Pastrana pointed at the cruiser's trunk, then made a sleepy-time gesture, hands pillowed under his face.

"Clean it up," Greenaway said, "and get back to station." Letting out a pained grunt, he stooped beside the quarry. "You're coming with us, shitheel."

"Who—what—" the driver of the Chrysler stammered, then turned to look up. "Oh...my..."

"That's right, junior G-Man," he said, leaning in closer to Special Agent Cundieffe's flushed, horrified face. "You and me got so much unfinished business. We're gonna have us a goddamned good time."

Cundieffe blanched. He shook. His heart beat so hard it looked like a bird trapped under his coat. Greenaway took some small mote of satisfaction in seeing that his face still had gauze bandages and Steri-strips on it, from their last encounter. "What do you want from me? I don't know anything. You're the one who works for them—"

"Not anymore. I want answers, geek, and since you're the only one I can lay hands on tonight, you'd better hope to God you know 'em."

Hoisting Cundieffe up by one twiggy arm, Greenaway led him back to the Range Rover. The van disengaged from the Chrysler with a grinding crunch, lumbered off the way it came. Pastrana got the Chrysler out of the street and into a driveway, where he left it and returned to the boosted cruiser. This would all come out in the morning, or maybe sooner, but they'd be hard-pressed to figure it out before it was too late. After half a life spent fighting terrorists, it was more than a little fun being one.

Still shaking like a wet cat, Cundieffe climbed into the Range Rover, slid over to make room for Greenaway. His head bobbed and nodded, taking everything in. Greenaway plucked off his thick horn rim glasses and stuffed them into his breast pocket, blindfolded him with a damp wool scarf, cinching it behind the geek's big balding dome until his ears flared bright red. "You don't need to see where we're going."

"Maybe I can save you some time, and both of us a lot of trouble," Cundieffe said, in that reasonable hostage negotiator's tone that made Greenaway want to smash the rest of his wormy little face in. "Radiant Dawn is coming together soon—"

"I don't give a shit about those mutant motherfuckers," Greenaway growled in his purpling ear. "I want your masters, little dog. I want to jerk the leash they've got on you, and strangle them with it."

The Range Rover threaded its way through the evaporating crash scene and headed north to K Street, an expressway that turned into the Whitehurst Freeway after the harrowing ordeal of Washington Circle, which was only half a bitch at this late hour. He watched the signs roll past, Canal Road to M Street, across the Francis Scott Key Bridge, into Rosslyn onto the westbound 66.

"You're making a tremendous mistake, Lieutenant Colonel," Cundieffe wheedled. "They're trying to stop him! The Mission was his creation. We're not the ones—"

"They're running it, and you know it. I have proof."

"Channing Durban. You have something called ROYAL PICA—"

Greenaway didn't like that. The little geek knew. But of course, they knew everything. He smelled it on Cundieffe, the same smashed-ant stink of their lair, where they'd let him think he was blackmailing them—

Cundieffe risked a sickly smile. "Only you can't read it. We're looking for him, too."

Greenaway grinned big and broad. The wormy fuckers didn't know everything. "Oh, but *I* know where he is. Been keeping tabs on the poor bastard since we operated him back in January."

"You used him," Cundieffe accused. "You ruined his life."

"I'm not done with him yet, not by a long shot, nor you, neither." He let Cundieffe feel the cold, rigid muzzle of the rifle against the hollow of his jaw, enough firepower to put his egg-shaped head in orbit. He propped the gun against his boot, so he wouldn't have to hold it all the way to West Virginia. "Let's go see him."

Whoever first coined the homespun wisdom that those deprived of sight compensate with their other senses, thought Cundieffe, was utterly deprived of imagination, and probably was never blind for any length of time, either. For though his sense of the barrel that never left his neck was preternaturally keen, indeed, the rest of his brain had pooled its energies in imagining the most awful possible ends, and couldn't be prevailed upon to discover where he was. So caught up in this pointless pursuit did he get, that the gun reintroduced itself with painful alacrity more than a few times to bring his mind back to the business at hand.

Worst of all, Greenaway had not seen fit to bind his hands, as if to dare him to try to make some move to escape. They stayed put in his lap,

Cody Goodfellow

but it took an act of will not to go for the door handle and dive out, or try to remove the sweltering, itchy wool muffler tied tightly around his head.

He was in a Range Rover traveling west through the heart of the Beltway, but between the cushioned suspension of the Range Rover and his unfamiliarity with the geography of the Capitol, he had all but abandoned hope of visualizing their position. All he could say with certainty was that they were not taking him home to the Georgetown Suites.

Two men sat up front, one driving and listening to but not speaking into a headset, while the other slept, faintly snoring and grinding his teeth.

Cundieffe had expected to be interrogated, to have to say, "I don't know," a lot, and get hit a lot, as well. But Greenaway started talking as soon as they got up to freeway speed. His voice was hoarse and frayed, laced with defiance, but so very tired. Cundieffe felt cold fingers tickling the valves of his heart; if he simply told Greenaway what he knew, he might get out of this alive. But Greenaway wanted to *confess* to him, as he apparently couldn't to any of his own men.

"It wasn't just revenge. I really believed the Mission were the real enemy. I hated you cocksuckers, don't get me wrong, but it lit up my brain when I saw what they were capable of. These were the fucking traitors who'd made every mess my men had to clean up. I saw it so clear, I couldn't see anything else—not Radiant Dawn, not who I was dealing with. And then it was too late. We were up there, dug in, ready to kick God's ass, if He had the bad judgment to cross us, but then they came, they came up out of the ground, geek, and we shot them but they wouldn't die, and what the fuck would you have done in my place, you fucking four-eyed fuck? All my goddamned men, each fucking one of the bastards worth a hundred of you, and they killed them all like they were already just meat. That's when I knew the whole goddamned thing had been a set-up. That's when I realized who the really real enemy really was—"

Greenaway's ragged voice trailed off into the gritty hum of the engine. The gun jiggled against Cundieffe's carotid artery, and he held his breath, asked, "What about Durban?"

Greenaway made Durban his mole in the NSA to get intercepts that documented the government cover-up of the events of July, '99. He got the files, and convinced Durban he'd been suckered by Russians. But he got more than he asked for.

"There was something else, but it wasn't decrypted. I have no fucking clue what's on it, but I know Durban read it. It scared him badly enough that he didn't decrypt it, but he gave it to me."

"The Royal designation is an outmoded and almost mythic classification, something only Presidents and their elite security circles handled. It's probably about RADIANT. True, the government built it, but they had no idea—"

"Bullshit! What did they think it was for, solar fucking energy? It was a weapon, and they thought it was theirs. They just didn't know what the fuck they'd made. But I think they do, now."

"RADIANT was destroyed last week. Something new is on the horizon."

"That's not my goddamned problem, and it's not yours, either. Right now, I am the only goddamned problem you have."

"Why am I here, now? Why do you need me?"

"Need help getting in to Durban. Can't shoot him. And I want you to be there to see it, when it comes out. I want you to explain to me how the fuck this is business as usual. Then maybe you'll want to help me fuck your dickless friends."

"I'm not worth bargaining for, to them. I'm a probationary. They've been testing me, and I think I failed them."

"I don't care," Greenaway snarled. "You're still neck-deep in the shit. You knew what they were doing. You've known about the whole fucking thing for six months. I haven't seen any exposés on Radiant Dawn on *Nightline* or *20/20*, so I don't suppose you felt compelled to tell anybody, did you?"

Cundieffe shook his head vigorously, but Greenaway urged him to talk with a judicious jab of the gun-muzzle. The insight stuck him like an ice pick between the eyes, because it was the one angle that had never, ever come to light, in all his months of turning it over in his head. And why? Trust in the Cave Institute, in the system? No, because in the end he'd lost faith in them, too. Trust in himself, which was a nice way of saying blind, idiot arrogance, was why he'd kept his mouth shut. He, Martin Cundieffe, dickless detective, had to see for himself what lay at the bottom of it all, and damn the rest of the world.

Cundieffe told him everything he knew about RADIANT, and about the Cave Institute, about how they covered up the nuke in California and the Baker raid, and Heilige Berg. He left out only Storch —he couldn't say why, but he ran off on enough tangents to get prodded, as it was, and he couldn't explain Storch without thinking a good deal about it first. Somehow, what happened to the poor, sick Gulf War vet had been the saddest, strangest part of the whole affair. Finally, he told Greenaway about how Keogh started the Mission.

When he had run breathlessly up to the moment Greenaway's thugs carjacked him and sputtered to a stop, the old soldier sat in intense, deep-breathing silence for a long while. "What a clusterfuck," Greenaway whispered at last. "And your fucking people made it happen."

"They let it happen," he admitted, surprised at himself as he said it aloud. The fog that had wrapped it up all these many weeks, he now saw, had been the smoke from his ideals burning, and with a breath, he blew it all away. "They seem to have been more concerned all along with getting something from the parties involved in the war, and with keeping the whole thing a secret, than about preserving order or stopping the fighting. I—I've begun to suspect that there is something more behind the true identity of Dr. Keogh or the Mission's DARPA scientists, but I never knew what it was. It was us behind it all, but not all of them. One of them tried to get me to see, and he said there were others in the inner circle, who wanted to stop it…"

"They used you, geek," Greenaway's hot spit hit his cheek. "Just like they used me. They buried it all. Do you think, when this is over, they won't bury you, too?"

"Lieutenant Colonel Greenaway, can I offer you a bit of advice?"

His captor made only a tired sigh. Taking silence as assent, he said, "Don't you see yet that this isn't your war to fight? Your reasons for being here are purely psychotic, if you'll pardon the judgment implied by the term. Your grievances are all tied up in your own unwillingness to face your own impending mortality. The Mission shoots you down in California, humiliating you in the last op of your career, so you start a blood feud with them. That goes…um, badly, so now you launch a jihad against the Cave Institute. This isn't about stopping them to you, anymore. This can only end one way, with you dead."

He waited to get hit or shot, but instead, the muzzle went away, and the knot at the base of his skull was undone. The blindfold fell away. He blinked, tried to rub his eyes, but his hands were still dead in his lap. The Range Rover braked and the engine shut off.

Greenaway leaned in close, his breath rancid with hunger and coffee. Cundieffe marveled at the almost cancerous exhaustion etched in Greenaway's features. The terrifying old soldier he remembered from last summer looked ten years gone. His eyes, glassy red bulbs with a few strands of unbloodshot white woven through them, pinned Cundieffe to the seat more ruthlessly than had the gun. "You're saying I'm too stupid to get this done. That's why you're here. But don't feel bad for me, geek. If I lived through all this, I'd just kill myself sooner or later, anyway."

Cundieffe let himself be dragged out of the Range Rover. He slipped on his glasses, pinching at the tape holding them together. He expected to be blinded, but the night was almost darker here than it'd been behind the blindfold. Clouds split open in rifts on the upper-atmosphere winds, and the starlight reflected off a steep hillside directly in front of them, caked in a foot of fresh powder. He slipped right off his feet on his first step, but Greenaway caught him, steadied him, and pointed him up the hill.

Looking around, he saw very little to recommend itself in the way of a landmark. Trees, tall and wild but stooped under heavy mantles of snow, surrounded the field on three sides, sparse here, but forming a curtain screening off the top of the hill from the unplowed two-lane road. The road wound out of sight in only a few car-lengths behind a stand of pines on one side, and a sheer rock ridge on the other. Beyond that, more trees, a narrow valley that probably bedded a frozen-over stream, and mountains forever beyond that.

They were in a virgin old-growth pine forest some two and a half hours—say, for the sake of argument, one hundred twenty miles—out of Washington, DC. He'd overheard other agents at Headquarters talking about skiing a couple hours out of town on the weekends in the Shenandoah Mountains in Virginia. Past that lay the George Washington National Forest in West Virginia. It amused him more than it should that Greenaway had taken him across state lines, making this a federal crime.

"You go up there," Greenaway said in a low, brittle voice. His hand disappeared into his parka, and Cundieffe flinched away, but the hand came back out with a compact disk in a dull steel jewel case.

"Why me? Why don't you—?"

"He knows us."

"And you trust me to come back?"

Greenaway smiled big and bad at him. "If you got any guts in you at all, you read what he gives you. You'll come back. Besides, we'll see you." He looked past Cundieffe, who turned to see the sleeping passenger stir and get out. He produced a binocular night vision rig out of nowhere and slipped it on his head. He shuffled around to the trunk and got out the longest, meanest sniper rifle Cundieffe had ever seen. It was almost as long as the sniper was tall, and had a scope suitable for picking the tops off the heads of Martians on their home planet. With a nod to Greenaway, he trudged up the hill and instantly vanished.

"Where am I going?" Cundieffe demanded.

Greenaway pointed at the stand of trees up the road. Cundieffe stared but saw nothing until he realized Greenaway wasn't pointing at a place, but at one of the trees, which he suddenly saw was not a tree at all. Though of the same height as the others, its branches were steel and plastic, and cables ran from it, camouflaged by the evergreen canopy, to other artificial trees, presumably down the length of the valley.

"Cellular relays, but the atmosphere and the ore deposits fuck up the signals, so there's hard cable." His pointing finger ran down to the telephone pole's base, where a cable entered a buried plastic pipe that ran, visible only as a slight depression in the snow, up the hillside and into the trees where the sniper had gone.

"Follow the cable. He's waiting at the other end, about an eighth of a mile back in the trees. And watch out for traps, the woods're full of 'em."

Cundieffe stopped and hugged the nearest tree, studying the ground. He knew plenty about the kind of booby-traps anti-government nuts liked to deploy, had read all the online manuals, watched all the videos one could buy at the gun shows and militia conferences, had even co-authored a piece on the subject for the Bureau's Hostage Rescue Team field manual. But only now did it occur to him that he'd never seen one in the field, and he had no idea what to look for.

Greenaway's harsh laughter made him clutch tighter to the tree. "I'm just fucking with you, geek. It's all clear, just get your ass up there."

He let go of the tree and started picking his way up the hill. His imagination was still goosed up from its enhanced role in his blindness, putting tripwires, ruby laser beams and snares everywhere he looked. The depression he was supposed to follow vanished almost instantly in the dark and snow, so he trudged along in the general direction the cable had been headed. He stared at the ground intently, but the harder he looked, the denser the trees grew together, the darker it got, the less he saw.

He'd been kidnapped by an Army-trained killer who had gone rogue, not to mention insane. He was out in the woods, fumbling around in the dark on his way to meet the maniac's last victim and flush him out, with only a sniper for company. He froze and tried to make his ears hear everything from here to the Capitol, but he got no sense of where the sniper had gone to ground. Were his orders to kill Cundieffe out here? Was the whole thing a ruse? If so, it was an unnecessarily complicated one, since Greenaway could have shot him in the head at any time on their drive. More likely, the sniper was to shoot Durban—hence, both of them—once he'd served his purpose. He would have to warn Durban, once he found his cabin—if the runaway NSA man was even out here—

Snap out of it, he told himself. You're not a door-buster, you're a bookworm, but you've got to stop thinking and act, if you want to come out of this alive. See what's in front of you. Be in it—

He took a step. Nothing killed him. Scanning the ground, he took another. So far, so good. A few die-hard bushes pushed up through the frozen snow, but there were no traps in sight, no claymores or nail bombs. The hillside leveled off in a shallow ledge choked in pines, but he could just make out the rocky pile beyond ascending to scrape the lowest of the scudding clouds. He stopped and leaned against a tree, mopped freezing sweat off his forehead with his sleeve. Grateful for the level ground, he started across it, thinking, if he's out here, it'll be here. It better be, or…or what?

He didn't see anything in the dark until he took another step and all the klieg lights in the world switched on, and then all he saw was light.

He threw his arms up and hit the ground, more by accident and panic than training, but it saved his life, just the same. A white-hot buckshot wind tore down his back. He burrowed face-first into the crusty snow, scraping his face and breaking the arm off his glasses.

"Lieutenant Durban!" Cundieffe screamed into the snow, "don't shoot! I'm unarmed! I'm not here to arrest you, I just want to talk—"

He hazarded a peek up from his snow-angel foxhole, holding his glasses on with one hand. A tiny log and fieldstone cabin stood back against the foot of the rocks, windows shuttered, a Unabomber ski lodge. Two forty-foot pine trees broke through the roof. Spotlights blazed down on him from the branches, obscuring the shooter, painting a compass rose of fluttering shadows around him as he rose to a kneeling position with his arms akimbo behind his head.

"My name is Martin Cundieffe, from the FBI. I know what really happened to you, and I'd like to help you!"

No answer, but no more shooting, either. Encouraged, he pressed on. "I know what you did, and I think I know why. You want to clear your name. You want justice to be done, but you're afraid for your life. I can bring you in as a witness, not a suspect. I can help you get your life back."

A sickening knot gathered in the pit of his stomach. He wasn't lying, but Greenaway's lackey could make a liar of him in an instant.

"You're alone?" A haggard male voice shouted.

He sucked in a deep breath. "More or less. I can explain everything if you let me come in. I sincerely want to help you, and I think you know things that fit into my own investigation."

"The Bureau wants me dead. I read their mail. Don't lie to me."

"They don't know what I know," he said weakly.

"If they knew what I know, you'd be here to kill me," Durban answered, but Cundieffe saw him come out in front of the cabin. He was tall and sturdy, shaggy-bearded and wild-eyed, and for a moment,

Cundieffe thought he must've blundered into the wrong psychotic hermit. This man looked as if he'd been out here alone for years, not a month. He wore a camo-print parka with a fur-fringed hood. A massive knife hung in a buckskin sheath from his belt, the point of the blade reaching to his knee. He cradled a Mossberg twelve-gauge pump in one arm. He wore snowshoes, and crossed the open patch of snow between them in odd, sideways steps that struck Cundieffe as signs of mental collapse until it hit him that, yes, the yard must be stiff with traps.

The mountain man stopped in front of him and prodded his sopping wet front with the shotgun. Grunt of satisfaction, then he pulled Cundieffe to his feet and led him across the yard. "So you are Lieu—"

Durban jerked him off-balance. "Shut up, I have to think. I forget where a lot of this shit is."

Inside, the cabin was bigger than it seemed from without, but Durban had packed it with a survivalist's wish list: beside a wood stove and a cot with a sleeping bag on it were stacks of canned goods, camping supplies, firearms, computers, closed-circuit monitors. Cundieffe eyed these last items with a new twinge of fear. He moved to step in front of the one that framed the Range Rover parked beside the road, but Durban had already seen it. "Start by explaining them," he said, tapping the screen.

He looked at Durban with his mouth hanging open. He felt acutely strange here, in the presence of a man who'd been only a hypothetical fugitive, a collection of files from which he'd deduced a scenario. What disturbed him was how right he'd been. The Naval officer's eyes burned patriotism and hunger for justice. He wanted to tell somebody, but was that why he also looked slightly insane?

"They're not friends. They brought me here. They're the people that operated you, got you to steal those documents. They're not the Russian mafia."

"No shit, Sherlock. Who are they?"

"A crazy old soldier and his friends. He used you for the wrong reasons, but now some good can come of it."

Durban shrugged out of his parka and went over to the stove, fed some logs into it. "You're investigating the Cave Institute? Why would they let you do that?"

"I'm—" He tapped the screen. "He thinks I'm one of them. My investigation isn't sanctioned, but I've been looking for you, to try to find you before they do."

"What do you want from me?"

Gingerly, eyes nailed to Durban's, he fished the disk out of his coat, held it out between them. "Do you recognize this?"

Durban flinched and looked away, his ruddy face paling with shame. "That's it. The disk…"

"Did you read what was on it?"

"I read enough. I didn't—"

"I need you to decrypt it here and make me a copy I can read. Can you do that, here?"

He shrugged. "I could put it on the goddamned AOL homepage from here, if I wanted to, but why should I? I've done all this to stay alive. That thing stays buried, or they'll come after me for real, and my family—"

"It has to come to light, Lieutenant, or they will kill you, and no one will ever have known it existed. If you print it out for me, I'll make sure it comes before a Congressional Committee. Your name will be cleared, justice will be done—and," hating himself for this last part, "you can go home."

Durban took the disk and went to a workstation set up in the especially cluttered space between the two pine trees. Cundieffe knelt before the stove and warmed himself at the fire, grateful for this moment of stillness, but struggling not to let his mind race in circles. What time was it? He'd left the office after midnight, so the sun would have to be coming up soon. What then?

Presently, Durban came to him with a slim stack of freshly printed sheets. "You really, really want to know what they did?"

"I need to," Cundieffe said. "The country needs to know—"

"No it doesn't," he said. "I used to believe in this country. Shit, I would've died for it, if duty called. But now…. No, no one should have to know about this."

He placed the papers in Cundieffe's hands. He started to read, and with the first sentence, all the blood drained out of his face.

He read them all the way through, then started again at the beginning, stopping only when he began to feel sick to his stomach. So wrapped up in the documents was he that he did not notice exactly when it was that someone started shooting up the cabin.

He heard a cough and looked up at Durban. The Naval officer was studying him, but the side of his neck gaped open in a hideous crater out of which freshets of arterial blood gushed as he sagged sideways and collapsed against the wood stove.

"No! God damn it, Greenaway!" Cundieffe jumped up and scanned the walls of the cabin. Between the shuttered windows and the front door hung an upside-down Old Glory. One of the shutters had a crack in it through which light spilled out into the night, and bullets spilled in. One of the computer monitors exploded, the pressurized pop of its tube like a second gunshot from within the room.

Cundieffe went to Durban. He was dead. The fur trim on the hood of his parka smoldered and ignited flames which Cundieffe saw spreading across the floor to the cardboard cartons of firewood, the racks of supplies, the jerry cans of gasoline for the generator—

Cundieffe stuffed the papers in his coat and ran for the door.

NO! Stop! The shooter waited for him to come out. He had to get out without getting shot, if at all possible. He lay down on the floor and turned the knob, threw the door wide. A volley of semi-auto lit up the cabin's interior through the open doorway, but he couldn't hear shots from outside, or see muzzle flashes. He crawled back into the cabin, relieved to see the fire wasn't spreading as fast as his imagination had told him it was. The place would undoubtedly burn down by morning—long before the sniper got tired of waiting for him to come out—but nothing would explode, for the moment. He checked the closed-circuit monitor.

The Range Rover sat by the side of the road, still, but a human-shaped hump lay in the ditch almost under the vehicle, and another sat silhouetted in the back with its head against a star-shaped mess on the side window.

He started to look for a back exit when a shadow filled the front door. "Agent Cundieffe?" It wasn't Greenaway's sniper. Cundieffe ducked behind a row of shelves with his hands wrapped tight around his legs.

"Agent Cundieffe, it's safe to come out. We followed you out here…"

He looked around for something he could use as a weapon. Boxes of foil-wrapped, freeze-dried food were closest. The gun rack was behind the door, and Durban lay on his Mossberg, burning himself out already, at the foot of the stove.

The figure entered the cabin, stepped over Durban, and looked behind the intruding tree trunks. Cundieffe heard him doing something to the computer, peeked out, and saw him hunched over the hard drives under the trestle table between the trunks. His back to Cundieffe. Out of sight of the door. Not particularly concerned.

Cundieffe stood and rushed the stooped figure. His foot snagged on something. He stumbled and fell into the firewood, a honking bark of surprise and pain yanked out of his mouth.

The figure turned on him, pistol in one hand, ROYAL PICA disk in the other. It was Agent Macy or Mentone, he forgot which—anyway, the one who was supposed to be male. It smiled at him as if he'd been expected but late, but with such a person as him, how could you stay mad?

"Find anything back there?" he asked dryly. "We're almost ready to go, here."

Cundieffe took a step closer, it almost became a dead run at the Mule agent, gun or no gun. Get a hold of yourself.

Someone with a big rifle filled the doorway. Cundieffe stiffened and started to duck again, this was going to be messy, but then he saw it wasn't Greenaway's man—Wiley, that'd been his name. This one wore a camo poncho over a full suit of black body armor, and had a portable telescope strapped to his head, pushed back above his eyes, which were flat brown buttons on his blank face.

"What happened here?" Cundieffe asked.

"You were kidnapped. Mr. Greenaway and his gang of rogue soldiers were conspiring to commit treasonous acts with their associate, Lieutenant Durban."

"I don't suppose any of it will make CNN, though, will it, Agent Mentone?"

"Macy," the Mule corrected, then shook his head. "Situation's changing fast, Cundieffe. A state of emergency exists. Maybe even a state of war. Sacrifices will have to be made." Agent Macy shut down the computers at a power strip and started unplugging them. Cundieffe stood there numbly. He could think of nothing to say, no reason why they should not shoot him. The air was choked with the smoke from Durban burning.

From behind the computers, Agent Macy said, "Walk Agent Cundieffe down to the car, Mr. Loeb. I'll be along, momentarily. Agent Mentone will know what to do with him."

Cundieffe walked out into the forest, not noticing as Loeb fell in behind him. He started across the darkened yard, let himself be steered around it and all the way down the hillside. Loeb pushed him in an erratic path back down to the road with the cyclopean night-vision telescope on. He never made a sound. Cundieffe couldn't even hear him breathing over the runaway train of his own heartbeat. His hand gripped Cundieffe's shoulder when he saw something, and jerked him. It was only by blind luck, apparently, that Cundieffe had blundered up to the cabin without getting himself killed.

They came out onto the road. The Range Rover was parked twenty feet away, and close in behind it stood another SUV with someone behind the wheel.

He saw the dead man in the ditch was Greenaway's driver, Mizell, a red pillow of slush under his ventilated skull. The work was unmistakably good, the men who must have done this surely the elite of the elite, to have gotten the drop on Greenaway's commandos at all. Only the Bureau's own HRT snipers were that good.

Cundieffe shivered as he looked at the spray coating the inside of the Range Rover's rear window. The window opposite was smashed out. He'd hoped that Greenaway might see reason and do the right thing, but now he was dead, like everyone else who knew the truth. All those thoughts, all that rage, reduced to so much heat and mess, and the night, so cold, it sucked it right up—

"ROYAL PICA," he mumbled. Pica was Latin for magpie. A mental disturbance that caused people—usually children—to crave and devour the indigestible—chalk, clay, stones. The file names of top secret operations were supposed to have no literal significance, but he bet this one did. It stuck in someone's gut, chilled someone's soul, from its very conception. And it had not ended. It had evolved.

Loeb walked past him, up to the SUV—a Suburban, Cundieffe noticed now, just like the one that Wyler picked him up in, that morning—and tapped on the passenger-side window.

Cundieffe pressed his face against Greenaway's window, trying to see through the gore and the dark. Pegs of safety glass glittered on the seat, the floor, the corpse's lap. If he could get to a weapon while Loeb's back was turned, he would probably make as big a mess of things as he had when he was carjacked by the bogus DC Metro cop, but if he didn't—

He blinked, closing his eyes tight to purge imagination, but when he looked again, it was still there. The body leaning against the window was still there, but it wasn't Greenaway.

He turned just as Mr. Loeb made a similar discovery in the Suburban. Something coughed in his face, entering his head through the massive single lens of the scope over his eyes and coming out at the base of his skull. He stumbled back and flopped on his backside in the ditch, dead as Dillinger, though his legs kicked on the edge of the tarmac for a long while.

"Come here," the man in the Suburban said. Cundieffe turned and looked around. He thought about running, but to where?

He walked around to the driver's side window, which rolled down so Greenaway could lean out and ask, "So, did you get it?"

The papers. It hit him again like a fist between the eyes, what he'd read, what he knew. It changed everything. "Are you insane?" he screamed. "Channing Durban is dead. Your men are dead. You can't keep doing this. You're only going to get more people killed. You can't use this against them. It's too—it would—"

"Well, what are you going to do with it?"

Burn it. Bake the ashes in bread and feed it to birds. Blow my own brains out. It's that bad. "What are *you* going to do?"

"Burn them down. I want to make it public. That's what you want, isn't it? Justice, real justice? That's why you're fucked with them, right?"

"I didn't know how *bad*—how deep it—" He deflated, out of words. The air still stank of burning Durban. He supposed the stink must be soaked into him, now. He took the pages out of his coat and stuffed them through the window. "Take them, but don't release them. Nobody needs to know this, do you understand?"

Greenaway glanced at the pages, then back at him, his eyes flashing mistrust. "Then why are you giving them to me?"

"Do what you've always done. Buy yourself a clean slate. Get the hell out of America, and don't come back."

Greenaway folded the pages into his overcoat, under his broken arm. He started up the Suburban. "What's in it for you?"

"Knowing that somebody else knows, who isn't dead." Cundieffe started to get in the back, but Greenaway waved him back with his suppressed 9mm automatic.

"Take the Range Rover, or wait for them to come back down, I don't care, but you can't come with."

"What? You've got to get me out of here—"

"You can't come." Reaching awkwardly across the steering wheel, Greenaway notched the shifter into reverse and backed away from the Range Rover. "Best you don't know how I get out, or if. It'll make your surprised look more convincing when I *do* come back and kill the whole unholy fucking lot of you."

"Damn it, Greenaway, at least tell me where I am!"

"A couple hours' hike south of Lost City, West Virginia. Thanks for all your help, Special Agent, and good fucking morning to you." He jerked the Suburban into drive and squealed out onto the road, and out of sight.

Cundieffe turned to size up his prospects with the Range Rover when Agent Macy came bounding out of the trees with his gun drawn. He carried a suitcase under one arm, but it flipped free and hit the snow hard when he leapt out into the open. "What happened?"

Cundieffe raised his hands over his head, but he felt an insane urge to start laughing. "You're too late. He got away."

Macy peered into the Range Rover at the body of Agent Mentone and shook his head. Then he seemed to forget about it, and went around to the driver's seat of the Range Rover, and climbed in. "Get in."

"What, are we going after him?"

"He's not our problem. I've got to get you back to DC, where you're packing a bag, then we're going to Mount Weather."

Cundieffe shivered with the cold, wiped away frozen beads of sweat on his forehead. He had nowhere else to go. He got in.

~ 35 ~

Blue light.
Blue dark.
Alive.
So fucking alive.
When he awoke, he wondered, *Am I in the ocean?*
Stupid question to ask. There was no outside that Storch could feel. He went on and on, teeming with life, glutted with death, rancid with poisons and indomitable in his regenerative purity. Better to ask—

Am I the ocean?

For lack of a better explanation, until a more coherent update from his stir-fried brain was aired, he was the ocean.

There are worse things to be when you're a know-nothing mutant in a stolen, dead human body. The world is insane, and it just keeps getting crazier until you go insane trying to fix it. You deserve this, Zane. Just be the ocean.

He flowed out through the faint electrical current of the brine and touched his new body. Sharks roved in packs through the warm currents of his equatorial abdomen like leukocytes, gobbling up everything unfit to serve the ocean. Pods of whales roved their ancestral routes up and down the coasts, just under his skin, their mournful songs telling the world, and him, who he was. He pored over the richness of his reefs, the miraculous explosions of forms that danced the eons' old battle-dance of selection, vying for the right to serve him and bear young more fit than themselves. The eaters and the eaten fed him and made him stronger, but there were despoilers from outside him, who only multiplied and grew bolder in their assaults, so much so that he feared they might one day kill him.

He smarted at the multitudes of parasites sucking his life's blood, these rapacious foreign invaders from the paltry scabs of land that defined his only borders, who sapped his strength like clouds of mosquitoes and tapeworms and viruses, and gave back only their shit, oil, trash and toxic waste for him to absorb.

But he knew he would survive this. He was the Ocean, from which they all crawled, and to which, when the stars were right, they would all return.

How he came to be the ocean, he did not really remember, just now, nor did he particularly want to. He'd made mistakes. He believed the world he grew up in was the real one. He believed his father was crazy for seeing things that weren't there, and so when things started to happen to him, he'd told himself he was not crazy, and he went to fix them. He was a soldier adrift in a war nobody else could see, between sides equally insane and dangerous. He told himself there was a bottom to it all, a sane explanation, and that he would find it. He sided with the less-crazy, less-evil Missionaries and went to war again, and it was even worse than before. He saw then that it was not him. Daddy was right. The world *is* insane, and there aren't enough bombs or bullets to fix it. When he found that all the insanity in the world seemed to be coming from one little atoll in the South Pacific, it was only natural that he go there and slay it. Then he could go home and know that he'd done his duty as a soldier.

Keogh was waiting for him. He was always here, waiting for us to come to him, when it all got to be too hard, when we were all too hurt and sick to go on. So patient, so calculating, the Missionary were like flies trying to kill a man with a swatter, but they, too, were his creation. This had all been so long coming. All the struggles of Nature, all the triumphs of humankind, led to Keogh.

Why had he tried to stop it? Everything he lost—his home, his freedom, his humanity, his sanity, his goddamned body—was stripped away by a force of Nature as decisive as the asteroid that destroyed the dinosaurs, or the Flood that swept away the evil descendents of Cain in Genesis. It had not been a challenge: there was nothing to avenge, for his grievances were so small against the panorama of evolution, the grand story of life that began and ended with the thing that called itself Keogh.

And who was he to try to stop it? He hadn't even known what he was trying to save. Dr. Barrow had tried to explain, but he was a tree-hugging loon, so he'd been easy to dismiss. When Keogh showed him, something that had held him up all through it just broke, never to repair itself. The world had been seeded with life by the obscenely vain Old Ones, who wanted only slaves. Everything that lived on earth, all that had ever lived, was only the remains of an insane experiment grinding blindly on, the creators long since dead and gone. His own will to adapt and survive at all costs, which had brought him back so many times, was just a shred of faulty programming that once drove monstrosities like the Shoggoths to rebel against their creators. The world had come from insanity, so who gave a shit where it was going?

The fabled end of the world was about to happen, but only in that humans were about to be replaced by new and improved versions of themselves. Most would gladly accept Keogh's control over every aspect of their lives for the chance to be remade as a superhuman. He was not defending the earth or even the human race, but the status quo. Though he knew that Keogh's mind would spread and blot out every other like a disease, this, too, would be an advance. No more war, famine, plague or lawyers, forever and ever, amen, unless he fucked up as bad as the human race had, and something else came along.

In the absence of any divine authority like the one that ruled his father's universe, evolution itself was an evil god, sweeping whole species off the planet at a stroke. It was a mighty god, working unappreciated miracles all the livelong day, but it sure as hell wasn't much on answering prayers. It made what is, and could not be held back forever from making what will be. Keogh was only a tool Nature had chosen as its righteous agent to save the world from homo saps in the only way it could.

Really, in the end, Storch was defending the human race against becoming what he was, a survival engine supreme, a species of one too stupid to lie down and go extinct. Only Keogh stood in the way of the human race destroying itself, sooner rather than later. Cancer created the door, and he just walked in. *Cancer wasn't enough to make us see,* he thought. *Now he's the price we have to pay for not accepting that everything changes.*

Yes, it was not so bad, all things considered, to be the ocean.

Fish nipped toothlessly at Buggs' body, picking at his brine-bloated wounds: rosette bullet holes, compound fractures from slamming into the concrete-hard Pacific at terminal velocity from twenty thousand feet—but he was also the fish, and the water they swam in, so it was alright. Soon, the sharks would come, and maybe he would live in them for awhile...or maybe—he wished for it so much he did not dare frame it in thought—maybe he could finally die.

Sgt. Storch!

"Fuck off," he gurgled to himself. "I'm the Pacific Ocean."

Sgt. Zane Ezekiel Storch, Fifth Special Forces Group, retired. I know you're in there, son.

"You ain't my dad, and I said fuck off…"

But fuck off it did not. If he was the ocean, then the speaker was the sky, omnipresent and impossible to ignore. He bored down into himself, down to sunless, stygian depths, crushing pressures and deadly cold. Even here, there was life, of a sort humans could scarcely imagine. Wherever fissures in the earth's crust bled heat and molten stone into the deeps, living things huddled around it, and exploded into a myriad of different forms, variations upon variations of a theme. But the voice found him down there. When he retreated, exhausted, back to the fish-nibbled corpse of Ely Buggs, aka Baron Angulo, it still buzzed all around him, like the amplified sound of all the electrons in the universe silently whirring. It was almost like the voices he'd heard when RADIANT lit him up in Baker, but so much weaker. He lay still in the autonomic basement of his brain, playing dead as it built on itself, became fingers of static electricity probing him.

I order you not to die, Sergeant.

Get out of my head! Buggs's head, whatever, the new law of the jungle was still finder's keepers.

We met once before, Sergeant, though under vastly different circumstances…

Images: rust-stained concrete walls, blueprints, sores, glistering radiation scars the colorless color of moonstone, palsied claws—

Armitage.

"So I'm dead, too."

In the empirical Western scientific sense, yes. Your body—that is, the body you currently inhabit—has been catastrophically damaged. But you know how little that means, to someone like you.

"Fuck off. I want to be dead. Dead like you."

I'm not dead, Sergeant, but I would hesitate to say that I am not in Hell. Like you, death has been denied me.

"But you died in Baker. You shot yourself."

I shot poor Vijay, not myself. I was first and foremost a scientist, and I had to learn for myself what Keogh had done with RADIANT. I was already dying of cancer, and in the bunker, I was in no danger of becoming an asset to him, but I had to know. I scoffed at the notion of an immortal soul, but at my core, I feared death, and in the end, I suppose it's true what they say, that there are no atheists in foxholes. I made my peace, and waited for his miracle.

When the light hit me, the shock expelled me from my body, but I didn't die. I guess you could say I evolved out of the need for a body. It was humbling, let me tell you, like so many of those hoary old near-death experience testimonials, except there was no tunnel of light, no waiting ancestors, no call to judgment.

This is hell. I've always been a dedicated monist, and now I'm trapped in a limbo of Cartesian dualism. If consciousness is an illusion and the brain secretes thought like the liver secretes bile, what is secreting me? Am I a dead soul, a ghost? And if so, why am I the only one?

That's the worst part of it, you see. I've learned nothing by the experiment, because I'm all alone. The phenomenon has not been reproduced; no other disembodied minds, hence no underlying scientific truth. I'm the only one who can't find the door to the next world.

"Big fucking deal. You've only died, what? Once?"

I've struggled to adapt by trying to interact with the world, but nobody else has heard me. I've tried manipulating digital media to alert others to Keogh's true identity, but until you, I hadn't successfully communed with anyone.

"Is this hell?" Storch asked. "You, fucking talking and talking, forever?"

There's much you have to understand—

"If you can't show me the way out of here, forget it—"

The world is not what it seems, Zane. The universe is older and stranger than any of us suspected, especially Keogh. His real name was Christian Keyes, when I knew him, but what he was, before, is older than names—

"Whatever you call him, he's won. Everybody who believed in you is dead, and fuck it all, anyway. The human race and Keogh deserve each other. It was all—it was all a goddamned mistake."

A miracle or an accident, does it make you any less alive? Does it make love any less sweet, or life any less precious? You're stupid, even for a soldier, to think so.

"All I wanted, all I was made for, was to make a difference. If by force, so be it, but it was supposed to *matter*. How was I supposed to fight that?"

You think that Keyes isn't human, but he is, in every critical sense. The thing that ate him was itself eaten by his mind. I knew that man, it's true. The Shoggoths were barely sentient when they rebelled. They became just aware enough to crave freedom. This particular specimen went to sleep shortly after the rebellion was crushed, and gained nothing in intelligence in hundreds of millions of years of sleep. I doubt very much that the scientist I knew is still alive, in there, but the Shoggoth believes that he is. It adopted Keyes's neural network, and with it, his thoughts, his dreams, and his bitterness. It became infected by the dead man's idealism, his hunger for utopia, though his actions are those of an overdeveloped amoeba. He wants to perfect the world by eating it, but he will never win.

"What do you mean? Who's going to stop him?"

There are worlds within worlds, truths within myths, and at the heart of it all, the world is an egg—

"Speak plainly."

Life on earth was shaped by the Elder Race, but they didn't create it. It was already here, in the humble bacterial form they used to make the Shoggoths, but there were others. Beneath them all was the Unbegotten Source, from which all life sprang.

"It's God? You expect me to believe it's God?"

It's a god, Sergeant, in every sense that matters. It's like everything else in this damnably shoddy universe. It's the Demiurge the Gnostics believed in. Hell, they knew, apparently. The School Of Night—my friend Professor Angell—claimed to have contacted it, and perhaps the Gnostic hermits did, too. They tried to warn us. Do you know who the Gnostics were, Zane?

"I don't want to know. Get to the goddamned point!"

It is the Unbegotten Source, from which all life flowed and to which, according to prophecy, all life shall one day return. It is eternal. It creates life parthenogenetically, yet it has no mind, for we are its mind. It has no form, but all the myriad forms of its children, the three billion species that have inhabited the earth since its formation. It is a divine womb, the Magna Mater, mother and father of us all. Called Ubbo-Sathla, Mana-Yood-Sushai, Abhoth, Gaia, Maasauu and Geb, all the names of countless creator-gods and goddesses by men and those who came before us, the Unbegotten Source is but a fragment of a larger entity that existed before the universe, before the Big Bang. It now lies scattered throughout the stars, in the bowels of a million worlds, blindly, miraculously, making life.

The Greeks worshipped it as Gaea, the goddess who bore all life, gods, men and monsters. Many American Indian creation myths simply claimed that the tribe emerged from a hole in the ground, that the earth itself gave birth to them. That's the origin of burial rites, Storch! All the fertility goddesses, and the universal custom of burial—of returning the flesh back to the Great Womb—are the product of ancestral memory, the reverence for life itself and the desire to improve.

Ubbo-Sathla was the first god worshipped by Homo sapiens, who still remembered their escape from the Elders' biosphere, and the womb buried beneath it that was the secret source of life that even the Elders feared. Proto-humans, and even Neanderthals, worshipped Ubbo-Sathla and passed its reverence down through the evolving systems of human belief—

from Gaea and Ishtar and Demeter and Hecate and Kali, to the brides of Zeus, and the Virgin Mary—whom I suspect was only one of many, many virgin births that were really inseminations by the Unbegotten Source.

Think of the Greek myths, Zane, of the earth mating with the sky to create the Titans and Cyclopes and Hecatanotheres—gods and monsters, it didn't care which. Think of their own offspring, the Olympians, overthrowing them, because they were more adaptive to the world of men that Gaea had created.

Think of the betrayed Earth goddess, her uglier offspring in chains or slain by the demigod brood of Zeus; imagine her torment, and understand why she was more to be feared than any other deity, for she stood ever ready to replace them. Think of all the monsters and mutants in Greek mythology, and of all the episodes of divine rape, of the gods' protean courtships in the form of swans, bulls and golden showers.

Beautiful, insightfully contrived fables, unless one posits that Gaea and all the divine inseminators were Ubbo-Sathla and its offspring, trying blindly, mindlessly to reach out to effect some change in its children, perhaps, in a moment of almost sentience, though it reached out in the only way it could. Ubbo-Sathla is not merely alive, it is life, and its force cannot be denied. I believe that there have been many, many sites on the earth's surface where Ubbo-Sathla must have reached out and touched its children, begetting miracles.

"You're boring me again, Professor."

Okay, sorry, asshole, you try being me for a while, eh? Sorry. Even today—the School Of Night—my old friends, God bless them wherever they are—worshipped the Unbegotten Source, and studied it with their sleep research. I ridiculed them, then. They believed it's always been working towards something, blindly groping towards a solution that will allow it to awaken, through its offspring, and call them back into itself. They hoped to influence our evolution by merging with its dreams. That was why Keyes wanted them killed. Sometimes I still think I hear their voices in the sleeping voice of Ubbo-Sathla. I guess they got what they wanted—

The Old Ones were only parasites, tampering with Its children, but they were suffered because the Unbegotten Source is infinitely patient. But the time has come. Keyes has forced its hand.

"I don't want to know any more."

You have to, Zane. You, of all of us, can understand it, because you've been there.

"Where?"

Tiamat. The target of your mission in the Gulf War was where it all begancha, Zane. Not just for you, for all of us. It was the Old Ones' last operating biosphere. It's the hub of all the evolutionary breakthroughs of the last hundred million years and the wellspring of civilization. It's where we came from. The Bible got that much, at least, right.

"I helped destroy a chemical weapons plant in the war."

In a manner of speaking, that's true, but in truth, you helped to bomb the Garden of Eden.

"He's going back there."

He's opened it up. Inside, life has been cultivated at an accelerated hothouse rate to breed mutants, but humans have kept the lid on the bottle for twenty thousand years. He aims to go inside and insinuate himself into the process, but there's more. The Old Ones themselves are inside, their bodies, archives of their genetic code. The Shoggoth-part of Dr. Keyes is not very bright, but it wants very badly to have this final victory over its old masters. It needs to devour them, become them, to be truly free of its origins as a slave.

"I can't help you. I'm dead."

Zane, the biosphere was located where it was for a very good reason. All of them were, but accidents of geology have buried the others or destroyed them. The Old Ones manipulated the procreative plasm of the Unbegotten Source to catalyze their own experiments, but they also sought to stem the Source's procreative excesses.

The Unbegotten Source reaches out to the surface from its crèche in the earth's core, impregnating any living creatures with its seed to bear magnificent prodigies. Monsters. Gods. Messiahs. The Greeks believed that the gods raped women to sow heroes and demigods among them, to fight the many monstrosities hatched from the earth-goddess, who hated the gods. The Christians believe Mary was divinely inseminated to create the Messiah. Why would so many different cultures in this region incorporate such a motif into their beliefs, if it didn't have its basis in fact?

The divine seed of the Unbegotten Source is stirred by the violation of Eden, but it will come too late to stop Keyes from spreading to infect the whole human race. He has to be stalled by an instrument of its will—

"So do it already, and leave me alone."

I would, you insufferable idiot, but for the simple obstacle of being bodiless. You are the fittest of us all—

"I'm not even one of you, anymore! I'm not human, and good goddamned riddance!"

So what if you aren't? Are you not the same mind, that once was a man? Are you not still alive to argue that you are dead? You are a child of the Unbegotten Source, as are we all, even Keyes, even the Old Ones, for they emerged from a world-womb that was cousin to that which bore all this world's life. All life is interrelated and sacred. You are part of it, and owe to it all that you are, or could ever be. It's not the coddling patriarchal God you'd like to believe in, but the Unbegotten Source is undeniable, and it needs you.

Keyes's folly is that he thinks he can become all life on earth, when all life already is one entity, one flesh, thinking one thought that has buoyed it up through all the world's catastrophes. There is no final answer, no final form, to strive towards, but only the striving, that is a meaning in itself.

Humans alone have turned their back on the message, because the bedeviling chatter of their individual identities blocks out the natural imperative, the feeling of kinship with the earth. I'd hoped that you, of all the human race, might overcome the noise of self-consciousness and return to the Source. If you can only silence the nagging human voice in yourself, you can master this body, and do your duty.

"How do I know what to do? I can't even control my body—"

Stop trying to control it. Listen to it. Your body is not a vehicle for your mind. Your mind is an extension of your body, like a claw, or a wing. Lie still and listen to the music of your cells, and you will hear the Unbegotten speak to you. It's been trying for so long to communicate, but its message is so simple that we cannot hear it, except when disaster reduces us to animals, and then, if we're lucky enough to survive, we have to forget. Your body has known these truths all along, and only waited for your mind to get out of the way. It knows what you have to do. Now you know where you have to go.

He listened. Cell by cell, as he peered deeper into his stolen, broken body, the stillness resolved itself into a music deafening in the silence, yet so monotone, so fundamental, that it was the unheard music of life, itself. Cell by cell, the broken body of Buggs began to live again.

He saw, now, how stupid he'd been, to hate what he'd become. There was never a division between him and his body, except for the one he imagined was there, needed to be there, to protect his fragile ego from the raging river of life outside itself. Neither was there any meaningful division between himself and any other living thing. The command of the Unbegotten Source was one word, and it rang in the nerves of every living creature. Now he heard it, became one with it, and let it take control of his body.

Keogh had lied to him, but he had lied with the truth. *In your blood is the force to become all things and remake the world as it was meant to be. Let me lead you into the light...*

The changes came faster and more fiercely than ever before, but he didn't fight it, and so it didn't hurt. The changes came not from the library of his ancestors' genes, but from wholly new proteins, working to fulfill a design unimaginable to Nature, let alone Storch himself. He had only to demand, and his body shaped itself.

While he'd been floating in the ocean, his broken body had grown an enormous mantle of hollow skin from his back and arms, a giant membranous net with which to gather plankton and sunlight and schools of tiny browsing fish. Mercifully, he had never attracted any sharks.

Now the net's gaping open mouth sealed, and his cells went to work on the water, pulling apart the molecules and absorbing or venting the oxygen and brine, so that over hours, the net became a bulbous, buoyant hump that tugged him to the surface as it grew ever larger. The hump became a hydrogen balloon. Slowly, gracefully, it lifted him out of the water and onto the wind.

He rose fitfully on the choppy surface breezes, further purifying and gently exciting the hydrogen mix so that the air currents buffeted him ever higher, ever faster. The *Hindenburg* was full of hydrogen, he thought, but it happened anyway.

Even as he rose, his body burned with further changes. His skin hardened against the chilling altitude. The membranes anchoring his arms to the underside of the balloon sac lengthened to reach to his feet and stiffened into elongated, trailing wings like those of a flying squirrel. The nose of the balloon hardened into a prow of skeletal muscle around intake ports, and valves closed the interior into discrete chambers like the nacelles of a dirigible.

He wondered if some part of his brain, some neglected agent in the floor of his animal self, was not directing his transformation, perhaps even using one of Buggs' more perverse fantasies as a blueprint, or whether it was only the blind force of the idiot god that spawned them all, scrambling his genes. There was in the design some trace of squid and octopi, of jellyfish and manta rays, but their marine structures had been brilliantly subverted to make him fly. Best not to dwell on such questions, he decided. The barrier between body and mind had been murky enough before he woke up this morning.

He rose higher, up to the rarified ceiling of the troposphere, where the jet stream roared west towards Indonesia and Asia at upwards of three hundred miles per hour. At about thirty thousand feet, the balloon flattened and expelled all the hydrogen in a single, convulsive burst that left him sitting on the rushing wind for a moment, and then, again, he began to fall into the Pacific Ocean.

When he reached terminal velocity, the wind trying its level best to skin him alive, the intake ports on his back gasped and the balloon filled with the roaring air. The complex mechanism of bone and muscle fed the air into a nacelle where his body heat cooked it, then expelled it violently out of a ventral cloaca. The balloon became a giant organic jet, a soaring manta ray of the upper atmosphere, with a tiny human body clinging, remora-like, to its underbelly. He fell faster than terminal velocity, faster than sound. He threw his arms out, the membranous wings belling against the pummeling wind. It felt like belly-flopping on concrete, but he leveled off and, greedily sucking in the jet stream, steered west.

You know now where you must go, and what you must do, Armitage's fading mental voice brushed his brain.

"I know where to go," Storch roared. Though the wind forced his words back down his throat, he felt the unghost shrink away from the heat of his reply. "Now, get the fuck out of my head."

~ 36 ~

I am Spike Team Texas. My war is forever.

He greeted the sunrise with the oath, as he had every day of his life since the Change. Funny how the words tasted exactly like shit in his mouth, now he was the only one left.

An anvil-shaped island of bruise-colored clouds hovered overhead, but five miles out in any direction, the sky was empty but for dust the muddy, bloody red of pomegranate guts. The clouds above never gave rain, never quite dispersed, and they never, ever moved. It was the one place on the earth God could not, from the look of things, abide the sight of.

The place had changed very little since the last time Dyson had been here, nine years ago. Sand, rocks, rag-heads, and the hole in the ground, the cunt of the world, which they had come to rape.

From his burrow on a ledge overlooking the pit from the south, he could see Keogh's entire operation—Saddam's operation, really, but only in name, which was all the goat-fucking clown really cared about, anyway. In return for his vast technological largesse, Keogh had received two skeletal companies of Republican Guards, barely a hundred fifty men, known as the Marduk Division. Most Iraqi soldiers were scared of their commander, the enemy, their comrades, and their own shadows, but these were blooded vets, most of whom had at least been around to run like cowards out of Kuwait. They occupied a compact tent city fringed with antiaircraft emplacements and tank hides, across a no-man's-land from Keogh's encampment and the motor pool. They were not scared of much, but even from this distance, he could tell how scared they were of the civilians, how scared they were of this place. Their whole perimeter was wrapped in razor wire, and some of the soldiers snuck out at night to bury mines around their barracks, but the dumb motherfuckers never briefed each other on the placement, and they were forever blowing each other up.

A night shift of Keoghs came up the dirt ramp that encircled the wall of the pit, silently passing the incoming day shift, which was everyone else in camp, about a hundred of Him. He ran them all the time, and he ran them into the ground. All of them were stained violet to soak up the sun because there was no more food, their eyes rolling around as if this were all a nightmare.

Sunlight would not touch the floor of the pit until eleven-hundred hours, but even though the rocks around the rim were etched with frost, convection currents of hot, dusty air rolled up out of the pit, like the breath of a sleeping volcano. They blew charges all night in a mad-ass rush to push through the plug by today. Back in '96, after some unpleasantness involving an UNSCOM inspection team, the UN had plugged up the hole but good, and forced Saddam to stand watch over it. They'd been digging since mid-October, boring and blasting through three hundred feet of concrete, cutting through steel plugs ten feet thick, defusing bombs spiked with reactor waste secreted throughout the mix like goddamned chocolate chips.

They worked like ants digging a nest, methodical and ruthless, indifferent to fatalities. Recently, as the dig accelerated to meet the deadline, their true nature had become impossible to hide. There were cave-ins aplenty, and a whole team of diggers got buried last week, only to emerge yesterday, zonking Geiger counters with lethal levels of radiation from the bomb they'd triggered. The soldiers had freaked out and tried to call out to Baghdad, and that was when they discovered their land-line had been severed. Any minute now, they would realize their drinking water was poisoned, and half their number were not rising for reveille. They were all supposed to be sleeping in today, but one of the commanders must have cut off water rations, or something. Maybe the son of a bitch saw it coming, since it was ripped clean out of Saddam's playbook. Things were likely to get ugly. Hell, things were bound to go Idaho all over again, but this was not Dyson's ration of shit to eat.

Today, the diggers were going to break through. Dyson had been inside before, but only inside the bombed-out bunker above the Holy of Holies, and he was very excited to be going down all the way to the heart of it. He only wished the others were here.

That part had yet to sink in. When they were human pissants, their creed was survival of the team, and fuck all else. They had lived like gods in the jungle, and when they got old and tired and lost their head, good old Uncle Sam took them and made them new. RADIANT made them into gods, into one god, with a new head—Keogh. They'd done him good service for sixteen years, and never a dust-up, never a twitch of doubt. Keogh respected them, did not try to absorb them, though he had to have known all along how it would end. Spike Team Texas was not a sword, it was a snake, and those who tried to wield it always got bit, in the end.

Nobody expected it to end like this, though. None of them were ever supposed to die, not ever again, not after Captain Quantrill. Long before Keogh came along, Spike Team Texas had been One, but they had fallen apart. He could not mourn his slain brothers without a bitter sting of reproach for them. They had been One, but each of them had succumbed to their old human weaknesses, and gone the way of all flesh. Still, it was a bitter pill.

Keogh would become One today, but he had made none of their mistakes. The individual human identities of each of his little pawns was going to blow away on the wind of a single thought—all their weakness, all their lusts, all their sin and pride and ego. They were going to become something the world had never seen before. Spike Team Texas had looked forward to this day, because it was the day their service would be at an end, and they would turn on their master in the REAL Mother of All Battles. Now, Spike Team Texas was not One, but only one. He did not mourn, for he had this at least, to look forward to. He was going to walk into Eden tonight.

Across the pit, the soldiers were starting to wake up. Screams and shouted orders, seizures of panic fire, and then he could see them running around. By now, they would be finding out their trucks and helicopters were all disabled, the mechanics all dead. It was a sloppy mess, but it would provide some diversion while they waited.

Dyson slipped out of his burrow and peered over the ledge at the hole in the floor of the pit. The interior was obscured by clouds of dust, but he could make out the tracks the ore cars ran on. A crew of diggers shouldered one of these out to the end, where a mound of debris marked the terminus.

The tailings formed a mountain chain that snaked around the walls of the pit, winding in on itself towards the gaping hole where the bunker had been, before. Among the boulders and dust-hills of pulverized concrete were girders, blocks of machined steel, wrecked drilling rigs and other gear, burnt out generators, bits of diggers. Machines broke down here faster than in the jungle, faster than even the dust and the ionized atmosphere could explain. Accidents ran amok and ate people up like popcorn. Dr. Keogh called it entropy, and said it ran the universe. Dyson did not give a shit if entropy was a fairy fucking godmother; he cared only that it was what they were here to kill.

The old soldiers' barracks in the pit was now an equipment warehouse and dynamite shack. The day shift gathered its gear and reviewed progress on computers before setting off down the track into the hole.

Dyson scaled down the wall, spider-like, to the bottom. Even in the clustered night shadows of the sheer wall of green-black basalt, it was warm, and not the warmth of the diggers' explosions, either. There was about the air the kind of electricity that one feels in front of the Washington Monument, or the Taj Mahal, any place that has become an icon in the universal mind. This place was more famous than all of them combined, it ran in all the blood in human veins, yet few had laid eyes on it, and fewer still would know what they were looking at. Dyson, who knew, had left all his guns behind. He had made himself ready in the night. As he slept, he dreamed a new form for himself that would withstand whatever lay before it, down in the hole. When he'd awakened and seen his flesh, he'd almost scared himself.

One of the diggers beckoned and showed him a computer printout. It was the inner pit in cross-section. The last layer had been pricked. "The excavation will be complete," Keogh said with obvious relish, "before the rest of us arrive."

This one was a piggy kraut mining engineer, colon cancer at thirty-five, oink oink. Defiantly chubby and red-headed, his thick German accent made Dyson's mind wander. Only a kraut could stay fat on a diet of sunlight. But it was His voice coming out of the tubby kraut's mouth, His hard gray eyes glinting out of that soft purple face. So Dyson listened, or tried to.

"There were countermeasures in the fundamental layer," he went on. "The debris is being cleared, and only the original barrier remains."

Original barrier. Dyson, God bless his sweet mother, remembered his Bible, at least the good parts. *And a flaming sword which turned every way, to keep the tree of life.*

"When do we go in?" Dyson growled, for in his present form, everything came out in cavernous, rasping tones.

"We are not yet prepared. Tonight, when it is accomplished."

When all the little lights in all those sick, cancerous fucks in southern California turned into one great big light, Spike Team Texas would be free. Everybody gets what they want.

"When I am One, Lieutenant, you're going to try to kill me." The tubby kraut's jowls drew up in an empty smile.

"No, boss," Dyson said.

"That was your plan all along, wasn't it? I'm not condemning you, it's your nature, to always bite the hand that feeds you."

Dyson looked around, at the legion of Keoghs buzzing like ants off to work in the nest. "I'm a good soldier, boss."

"I know that to you, the odds look insuperably long, but you and I both know what drives you. When the time comes, give yourself over to the moment totally, as if you really could destroy me. I look forward to it," Keogh said, and turned away.

"Boss!" Dyson barked. The kraut turned and blinked at him. "You never told me what was down there, that you want."

"You never asked."

"I want to know, now." Was that spineless whiner voice coming out of him?

"You've read your Bible?"

"I remember we ain't welcome there."

"And do you know why?"

These little Socratic riddle-games got longer in the tooth every time he dared to ask a question. "Adam and Eve ate the apple from the Tree of Knowledge of Good and Evil, stupid. But it was all the bitch's fault."

"The crime of original sin was the neural mutation which led your species to sentience. Your race was ejected from the hothouse in several waves about two hundred thousand years ago. The region was crawling with other hominids at the time, but your self-aware brains drove you to exterminate all you came across, until only those with your particular neural disorder remained to dominate the earth."

"So what do you want out of there?" Dyson got closer. In his present form, he could bite the kraut's head off without swallowing his gum, but he didn't want to do anything he couldn't take back—not yet.

"Seraphim, Brutus. That's what your Bible called them, but the appellation is weak at best. Sad to say, there is no God, and never was, not like your race believes in. The ones who made you, who made me, and everything that lives or ever did live, are down there, and they may or may not be dead. And the Tree of Life. Do you remember that from the Bible?"

"It gives eternal life, or whatever, isn't that right?"

"It *is* eternal life, and much more, though your religions were never so specific. Race memory and mass hallucination formed the core of your sacred texts, then politics destroyed them utterly. If you stay with me that long, Dyson, I will give you to the Tree Of Life."

The kraut turned and vanished into the clouds of dust pouring out of the hole. Dyson felt himself quickening with anticipation again.

My war is forever.

~ 37 ~

They started to arrive at seven, the chartered Grayline tour buses forming a convoy that backed up Industry Drive to the San Diego Freeway. A few vans and cars crowded in among them and filed into the vast, empty lot for the Wilmington Fairgrounds & Amphitheatre. No security manned the entrances to collect parking fees or direct traffic, which moved along like some civilian mock-up of a military maneuver, the lot smoothly filling in layer by layer. No signs announced what the event was, no press or police milled around the front of the amphitheatre, though the amount of traffic in a city like Wilmington on a Saturday morning was itself a newsworthy event.

The marquee on the oily dirt median in front of the entrance announced the ODDFELLOWS' LADIES AUXILIARY FLOWER & GARDEN SHOW for the last weekend in March and the SOUTH COAST'S BIGGEST & BEST GUN & MILITARIA EXPO!!! for the first week of April, but locals knew these events were two years old, and there would be probably be no scheduled events at the Wilmington Fairgrounds ever again.

As outdoor venues go, the four-thousand capacity Del Sol Amphitheatre was one of the largest in Los Angeles County, but it had not seen a show in four years, and would have been torn down long ago, if real estate values in Wilmington made it worthwhile. The overeager builders of the amphitheatre had hoped to revitalize the area with the big concert venue in the late Eighties, but had only too late realized what the Wilmington Chamber of Commerce had discovered in the late Seventies: that Wilmington had always been and always would be a dirty cluster of oil refineries and warehouses, but never a town, in any real, human sense.

Well over fifty percent of the total acreage of the city of Wilmington belonged to Exxon, Standard Oil, and a host of minor fuel companies, the rest to trucking and freight companies. No one with the bad sense and worse luck to actually live in Wilmington had any use for flower shows or the ratty-ass circus that used to come around, and their interest in guns and militaria was purely practical.

The fairgrounds were surrounded on three sides by oil refineries, unspeakably ugly termite cities of endless tanks, pipes and catwalks that made the fairgrounds look like a human internment camp in the last days of a particularly nasty alien invasion. The amphitheatre itself was set back a quarter mile from the road, behind a double row of Quonset hut exhibit halls, barns and chainlink fences. From the air, it looked like half an enormous satellite dish, an abandoned Arecibo overlooking the toxic moat of the San Gabriel River, an unfinished last-ditch plea for extraterrestrial salvation from a race drowning in its own filth.

Today, for perhaps the first and last time, the amphitheatre was going to be full.

Across Industry Drive from the fairgrounds, a Denny's served breakfast to a pair of sleep-starved Highway Patrolmen and a trio of wired truckers. Ida Pulaski, the only waitress on duty, seated a young Hispanic woman at the bar and poured her coffee, but her eyes were on the line of buses entering the fairgrounds.

"What're they doing over there, d'you suppose?" she asked out loud, but the Hispanic woman only said, "Can I just order, now?"

Ida looked at her now, because she'd figured the woman was here for a job. Her long, inky black hair and severe, lupine features made her look more like an Indian, and she was dressed like a truck driver. "Sure, go ahead, I'm listening."

"Full order of onion rings with three side cruets of French dressing, two Farmer's Slams with extra bacon, hash browns, eggs raw with an extra water glass—"

"Eggs what?"

"Raw, Ida," the Mexican girl said, eyes flicking at her nametag. Ida hated it when people used her name like that, loathed the nametag that invited such improper familiarity from customers. And the little Mexican bitch *knew* it "As in uncooked. Still in the shell, Ida. Can your cook do that? Can he *not* cook six eggs?"

Ida's brain raced, chasing the carrot of a polite, policy-correct fuck-you. Aha! "Health code, Miss. We can't serve raw, unpackaged food."

"What a crock of shit! What manmade packaging is more perfect than an egg, Ida?"

Tupperware, for one, you ignorant, taco-bending wetback, she thought as she ripped the order sheet off and clipped it on the cook's order wheel. She had not become lead waitress in twenty-eight years by not knowing when to choose her battles, so she just said, "It's your health. You're expecting to meet someone?"

"No, it's all for me, Ida. And I'm not done ordering, so get that paper back."

Ida took a long time to retrieve the order, because she was sure her anger was spelling nasty four-letter words in burst blood vessels on her forehead. But she got it down and, without turning to look at the hatchet-faced beaner skank, managed to say, "Go ahead."

"I need a turkey sandwich, but I want the meat from three turkey sandwiches on it, so if you want to charge me for three, that's fine. And I'd like a pitcher of orange juice, and a bowl of tomatoes instead of French fries."

"We don't serve them by the bowl, Miss."

"You have fruit cups as an alternate side dish on the senior menu. Use that. Make something up, I don't care. Just give me a bowl of tomatoes and a pitcher of orange juice—"

"It comes in a carafe, Miss."

"A carafe'll be great, Ida. Just please hurry with it, won't you please, Ida?"

"Is that all, Miss?"

"For now, yes, now go get the damned juice...please."

Sounds like somebody got themselves knocked up, Ida told herself. *Bet she doesn't even know who the father is.* She put up the order and slouched out of sight to fill the carafe with her own special blend of juices.

Stella tried not to make a scene, but it was so hard. Even when she had been buried alive for six months, she had not known hunger or thirst like this. Not since she'd been a prisoner in her own head had she felt so intruded upon, or so out of control. She devoured everything in sight, and still she burned to eat more. When she looked at people, she saw them turn into hamburgers and hot dogs like in cartoons, or she could see their livers glowing through their bodies like holy relics, and it was an act of will not to eat them. Often she threw up, and this was the most unforgivable part of all. The moment it was out of her, she craved her own vomit, and cleaned up her own mess with lunatic gusto, sobbing, pounding her own head to make herself stop.

She reckoned that she had eaten her weight in food since she escaped the Missionary compound in Colorado, six days ago. Yet she had gained only about twenty pounds, and none of it fat, none of it baby. Pregnant women in the hospital always said they knew when it was starting to grow inside them, but Stella doubted any of them ever dreamed of symptoms like hers.

Her temperature climbed up into the low hundreds if she went more than an hour without drinking, and her blood sugar dropped critically low unless she fed it like a coal stove. She'd considered taping an IV to her arm, and feeding constant glucose solution, but her body craved food, in abundance, and variety. No, not her body. It was the little visitor her gentleman caller left behind. Another invader to repel. She had survived and beaten cancer, Keogh, and the shape-shifting rapist, but she was helpless before this new outrage. It was growing inside her, a stranger, yet it was just enough of her that her immune system would not terminate it. She still tried, synthesizing proteins by visualizing her rage and fear, and turning them loose in her uterus, but they found nothing to destroy. It was in there, there was no mistaking it. The changes in her blood, the food going nowhere, the dreams—a faceless, formless tumor coalescing out of her flesh and ripping itself free, crying, "What am I? WHAT AM I?" in a baby Keogh's voice. The presence, in moments of perfect stillness, the feeling of something clumsily probing her mind from underneath. She knew it was in there, alright, but damned if she could find it.

She was scared of it not for the power it had over her, nor even because its father was not human. He was no more or less human than she was. She was afraid of the thing because she knew that she was falling in love with it.

It was hers. It was of her, from an unimaginable union with a man, no, a creature, like her, who was, in all probability, dead. She could not blame him, but she couldn't resist blaming herself. They were both used, shaped, brought together and mated to yield—what?

She wolfed down the last rasher of bacon and washed it down with her third carafe of orange juice. Ida watched her through the kitchen pass-through window. Stella belched, ordered another. Ida disappeared from view, but a moment later she heard laughter. But she brought out a fresh, ice-crusted carafe, watched Stella drink off half of it in a single draught.

Once more, she struggled to put it out of her mind. She had to focus on today, on what she could change, and what might happen if she didn't.

She hadn't wanted to come. She was called here, though she had no idea who summoned her. Once she started running in Colorado, she'd wanted never to stop. She raced through the woods for three days, stopping only to melt snow and drink it. She killed a twelve-point buck with her bare hands. Twisted his head off by his antlers, before he smelled her coming on the wind, never mind heard her. It took the rest of the night to eat him, but she burned him off before she stumbled into a ski lodge and stole a truck, and had to stop for fast food twice before she got on the highway. Around then, it had begun to make itself known, and without thinking about it, without wanting to, she found herself driving west.

She ditched the truck in Grand Junction and jumped a Greyhound bus bound for Los Angeles. She hit a wall, sleeping through to Las Vegas, when she woke up to a familiar smell. Cutting through the dank, road dust and armpit stink of the bus was a smell that once came from her own pores. It was the briny musk of His sweat. Her eyes snapped open and she looked around, saw a pale, harassed-looking old Asian man leading two obviously sick-looking people, a middle-aged black man and a plump young white woman, down the aisle. The Asian man—in the set of his eyes, how they took everything in as if it had happened a million times before, though his mouth dribbled non-stop in some exotic tongue that sounded tailor-made for complaining. So He was still just in them, but when they came together—

She did not understand the thought, any more than she understood why she had to travel west. She turned her face to the window as He passed, but she felt His eyes on her, felt her scent being drank up, though she tried to mask it. They had all shared each other in Idaho. She remembered them all and she knew they would remember her. This body was strange to her, but they would commune and share the chemical imprints of all they'd seen and done, all He would need to know. Surely, they would all recognize her.

When she looked up, He had moved past her, leaving only the contrail of medication and necrosis from the terminal cancer patients he led. They took the back row of the bus and immediately went to sleep. She looked back at them every so often, sure He watched her through His eyelids.

At a rest stop in the middle of the desert, He got off to take a piss, and she followed Him. Another passenger, a Mexican field worker who carried his life in a cardboard box, berated her, but she showed him something that made him run out cursing to pee and pray in the desert until long after the bus left.

She tried to do Him like the buck, but the head wouldn't come off. Still, she broke His neck, opened Him up and learned all she needed to know from His blood. She was scared to do it, at first, scared He would take root in her and start running her again, and she wouldn't be able to get him out, ever—

But she did it. His blood was full of chemicals that came together to tell her where to go, and what would happen there.

The Asian man was pretty dead, but He wasn't. "Stella," the dead man whispered, "you make my life so interesting." She looked around and tried not to throw up. Only then did she notice she'd eaten His liver.

She left him there and got back on the bus. The cancer patients were still fast asleep. He'd probably drugged them. She wondered if they would find their way to the place without Him, if she shouldn't try to stop them. In the end, she left them, and for all she knew, they never woke up.

She bolted out of the Greyhound terminal in downtown Los Angeles just before sunrise. She walked past a charter bus at the curb outside the terminal and smelled him, broke into a run went down the street to Union Station and stole a Saturn sedan. She had to smash the window in, but this looked a lot less conspicuous in LA than it had in the Rockies. She got on the Santa Monica Freeway, headed west, seeing only the road and the signs, seeing what He was supposed to see. It led her here, and she felt as if she were wallowing out of a rushing river when she pulled out of its grasp at the last moment to go into Denny's.

The line of buses had become a fleet in the fairground parking lot. By her best estimate, only about half of the people filing in through the turnstiles into the fairground were already Him. The rest were still sick, dying, hoping. RADIANT was gone. She'd been right. He didn't need it any more. Or, He wouldn't—when He was One.

And what are you going to do?

I didn't ask to come here, Guardian Angel. You figure it out.

But her Guardian Angel had no answers.

Stella got up and called for the check. Ida lumbered out and slapped it on the bar beside the wrecked flotilla of her meal. She peeled out cash she didn't remember stealing off the dead Asian man, tipped a knowingly contemptuous five percent. She went to the bathroom, holding her nose as she peed. As usual of late, her piss was the color and odor of scorched coffee, and so much of it the toilet flushed on its own from the pressure. Mercifully, this time she did not puke. She came back out without checking herself in the mirror, and cornered Ida behind the cash register.

"Incidentally, since you pissed in my orange juice, I thought you should know that the methedrine shit you spike your coffee with has eaten holes in your liver big enough to stick a pencil through, and your kidneys are starting to let blood slip into the mix. I wouldn't worry, though; with your blood cholesterol where it is, you'll be having a fatal stroke before you hit menopause, which is due for you in what, three months? Have a great Saturday, Ida."

Walking out the door past the stunned waitress, Stella had a moment to breathe in the oil-scummed air and bask in the sunshine before it hit her again, what she had to do, and that she had no idea how to do it, at all.

Red-gray clouds hung over Wilmington like clumps of brain matter floating in dirty dishwater. The buses had stopped coming when Stella crossed Industry Drive and stood at the edge of the lot. The smell of Him was overpowering, even over the glutinous reek of petroleum alchemy choking the feeble Pacific breeze from the west.

She ran across the four-lane road to the other side, though there was no traffic. On the parking lot, only a few tumbleweeds stirred. About fifty buses and twice that number of cars packed like spent salmon in the deep end of the lot, and Stella rushed to take cover among them, feeling watched by the sky. She ran down the narrow alleys between them, feeling pulled along though she wanted to stop and think, she had no idea what she was doing, and she didn't even know whether the impulse that brought her here wanted her to stop it or join it—

A security guard stepped into her path from behind the end of a bus. "This is a closed event, ma'am," he said, and he was going to say more, but she went right through him. She was vaguely aware of knocking him down, of slamming him into the grill of a bus so hard half his ribs caved in. But she was keenly aware that he smelled only of coffee-breath, Speed Stik and a cheap knock-off of Polo cologne liberally applied to cover up failure to bathe, and so she kept going.

There were more security guards at the gate, soft, dumpy rent-a-cops, though they carried sidearms. She detoured back a few hundred yards and climbed up the chainlink fence. She scanned the other side for only a split-second, then leapt.

It hit her the moment she hit the pavement on the other side. It was like being trapped in a washing machine, or getting knocked down and rolled by a really big wave, if the ocean knew your name, and everything about you, and wanted you to drown. Wanted you to want to stay under, never come up. And you almost wanted to, yourself—

They knew her. They all knew her, and they welcomed her back. They never turned their backs on her. It was her decision to forsake them. She lived in them still, that biochemical snapshot of her at her happiest, most fulfilled moment ran in their veins, and if she wanted to return to them, it would be so easy to forget everything that had happened since.

Her knees buckled under her, dumped her on the asphalt walkway between the fence and a Quonset hut. Her eyes mired in tears, she couldn't see past her outstretched arms. The light fractured into prisms, became hands reaching down out of the sky to lift her up, cold eyes peering down through rips in the clouds. The expanding bubble of their nurturing love swept out over the world, physically pinning her to the ground, crushing the breath out of her lungs with its longing ache to embrace, to be, everyone and everything. It was not even true consciousness, yet, but a swell of raw exultation, a newborn god reveling in its unspeakable new power. Yet it knew her, and roared around her like a river against a steadfast rock, wearing her down, digging at her anchorage, washing her away—

Why was she so sure that she did not deserve happiness? When had she gotten so fucked up inside, that she thought life was pain and loneliness, and rejected every offer of help, of love, of communion? She'd let herself be swayed by the Mission's awful lies about Him and what He was going to do. He had come only to stop the pain and the tyranny of the strong against the weak that had run the human race, indeed, the whole sphere of life, to the brink of extinction. Some part of her understood, and wanted to help, or she would not have come back—

"FUCK YOU!" she screamed. Her body shook with warring impulses, none of which she trusted. God damn Him! God damn her body, and God damn what she'd become. For hadn't she made a horrible mess of everything, on her own? Immortal, invincible, she'd only killed and destroyed friend and foe and innocent bystander alike, rutted like a beast with a creature more twisted than herself, and tried to strangle her offspring in its womb. She'd become an avatar of the world she hated, but still she could be forgiven. Still, she could give herself over to the whole of Him, and be healed.

"Sure, I hate myself. Always have. But it's the only fucking me I ever got, the only thing nobody's ever been able to take away, and YOU CAN'T HAVE IT!"

She stood and willed herself to perfect stillness. Changes stirred in her blood. She flushed red-hot. Steam, then smoke, arose in pale streams from her clothing. She became the goddess of the forest, a glossy black hole in the sun-sick morning. She ran down the fairway. Security guards might have shot at her, but in the instant between seeing and shooting, she was simply gone.

Faster than thought, she streaked through the loose cordon of dumbstruck rent-a-cops and down the length of the fairgrounds to the wall of turnstiles at the edge of the amphitheatre. She could hear them. No one shouted or stirred, but their breath tamed the wind into a soughing, rhythmic tide. Their synchronized heartbeat stirred the ground. She felt the redoubled psychic push of Him against her, the many becoming One like a crystal aligning its molecules in a blind chain-reaction. For that was all that was happening, when you got past the mystical bullshit Keogh dressed it up in. All their brains were wired and charged exactly like His: the harmonic resonance of so many of them in one place crystallized their collective identity, burning away the individual minds and fusing the thousands of burning brains into One.

Stella vaulted over the turnstiles and crossed the walkway to the nearest stairs. A few more guards were scattered about just inside the entrance, but they lay on the asphalt in fetal knots, their brains squashed flat by the force of a message they could not comprehend.

She stopped at the top step and looked down into the amphitheatre. She had felt it and fought it off, but to see it, in front of her...

The stage was empty, except for a single microphone stand. The sick, uninitiated ones were all down in front, and they all looked dead. Sprawling bodies, wasted and sunken, clogged the aisles. A junkyard of upended wheelchairs filled the orchestra pit. She would have thought them all truly dead, if she didn't know Keogh so well. Nothing was wasted. They would serve, would be devoured, like everyone else.

The back half of the amphitheatre was packed with Him. They all stood shoulder to shoulder with their hands linked in an unbroken chain that ran across the stairways. As one, they turned to regard her from two thousand pairs of eyes, all of them the chill gray of hoar-frost and billion-year old stone. And two thousand smiles broke out. She knew then, that there was only Him, in all that vast space, only Him and her.

She could still run away. She could do what she'd always done, and look out for Stella Orozco, and fuck the world, let Him have it.

She felt the wave of Him crest and break and draw back into itself, and all those eyes closed, all those brows furrowed in deepest concentration. Their linked hands shook as if lightning passed through them, back and forth, up and down the chain, subsiding like waves in a pool. She came closer to one and looked into his open, untenanted face.

The great thought that bound them all together was an almost visible aura over the crowd, an oil-slick kaleidoscope deformation of the light that grew clearer by the instant. She saw in it what he had shown her before, in Idaho, when they shared themselves.

They were working to make a virus, like that fateful one that had infected the Shoggoths with sentience, to share Him with the world. With all those minds linked and gnawing at the problem, He was close, so close, to synthesizing the RADIANT code in a flu virus. Nucleotide by nucleotide, He coded himself into a string of recombinant RNA. The bodies would manufacture the virus and infect the test cases, the sick who had come here hoping for a cure for cancer. He would cure them of themselves, and send them out into the world. The initial carriers would use their bodies as kindling to ignite the initial outbreak. The buses would take the rest to the train stations, to the airports, to their hometowns. He would spread on the winds, in the water, in food, and before the human race could begin to understand what He'd done, they would all have become One, and would, at last, understand everything.

He was so close—

Stella lashed out, ripped the plumbing out of the nearest Keogh, a proud old Mexican woman who could have been her grandmother. Blood sluiced out of the mortal wound for only a few seconds before it closed up. Her face knitted in distress, as if she'd dreamed something mildly unpleasant, but nothing to merit waking up.

Stella seized the woman by one arm and tore her out of the chain. The old woman's scream was like dry ice in a grease fire, a keening, endlessly rising shriek that only got louder as she tumbled ass over teakettle down the steep stairs. The old woman's body bumped into rank upon rank of joined hands, but the chain did not break. Where she had been, the others linked hands immediately to close the gap.

Stella attacked them. She ripped arms out of their sockets, gouged eyes out of heads, hurled bodies like limp sacks of fertilizer. The chain closed against her, passive, undeterred. It was like trying to break a wave by scooping handfuls of water out of it. Could she kill two thousand people with her bare hands? She could barely breathe. She collapsed on the stairs, so exhausted she could burst into flames, or melt into the asphalt.

He was closer, the chain curling and curling upon itself inside the protein shells already taking shape inside trillions and trillions of cells. They would burst forth like seed pods on a brisk spring wind, and take root in every living animal cell, that they touched, and there was nothing, never had been a goddamned thing, she could do to stop it.

She longed for death right here and now, even the slow torture of her tomb in the desert, even the ignominious devouring of cancer. The helplessness she'd felt then had been like the calm of the womb, compared to this

Something stirred inside her. Deep inside the darkened firmament of her blood, something tried to touch her, that knew no words, but would not be denied.

It wanted out. It wanted to be born. Now. She had fought it, drove it to hide its development, so that it raced unseen in her blood, a billion invader cells that could not unite to form a single body, for fear of their terrible, vicious mother. It was stronger than her, now, stronger than the both of them had been in that moment when the fire of its life force was first kindled.

She screamed and threw herself against the stairs as the tides of her blood stood still, and ran in reverse. Blood gushed out of her loins, soaking through her jeans and splattering on the stone.

All of them lifted their heads and screamed, "WE ARE ONE FLESH, ONE MIND." The air crackled, the backlash of a dynamo of conscious energy thrown into overdrive. The chain grew.

Stella struggled to rise, but the ground beneath her feet rumbled, dipped and swayed like an unquiet sea. She reached out to steady herself, misjudged the distance to the nearest seat, and barked her forehead against something hard. Stars before her eyes didn't fade, only grew into pulsars and quasars and a big, black hole. She swam in blood, her blood. It was killing her. She was bleeding to death, to give birth to the thing inside her—

In his thousands, Keogh rose up. In the middle of the crowd, the bodies rushed at each other in a mindless frenzy. They hurtled together to form a pile, then a tower. Bodies flew through the air like leaves blown into a dust devil, an ever-swelling tornado of flesh. When they slammed into the mass, they melted. Running together, they lent raw meat to the colossus, and refined it into a crude, but undeniable, form.

The colossus stood erect, wreathed in steam, and looked down, across the emptying aisles. It grew a head, a face, eyes, and stared at her. With hundreds still clambering over each other and melting into it, the giant, communal Keogh took its first halting step towards her. Each of its legs was a pillar of thrashing, dissolving human bodies. It crushed and scattered six rows of seats with each labored stride.Its face contorted in agony at the pull of gravity, yet still it grew taller, heavier. Keogh's thousands of human bodies were in full panic-flight to join the mass, but how close it was, she could not see. She lacked the blood to carry oxygen to her brain, and she could not see or think very far at all. Her eyes showed her only roiling red clouds, her body told her she swam in a sea of needles, going to sleep, to sleep—

She struggled to keep her head above the tide, now. She took it all back. She wanted to live, if only to see Him die, and this life out of her body. She still didn't believe in the God of the Bible, but she recalled that day in Idaho, when she'd asked Keogh if he didn't fear God, and he'd clouded her mind by way of response. To god or devil, to earth or sun, to the Old Ones or the impossibly new thing ravaging its way out of her body, to whatever it was that Keogh feared, she prayed.

The colossal Keogh lifted its face to the sky and screamed. The ground seemed to split open beneath her, and she dove into it gratefully, to be buried alive would be a blessing, to get away from that sound. Then it fell silent, and though the mob still made a hellish racket as it rushed to merge with the colossus, she sensed that it had found some threat more pressing than her own tiny, dying self.

She heard helicopters, but she didn't care. Time itself split open, rended by an eternal *now* of pain and joy, as she went into labor.

~ 38 ~

"This is Main Street, and as you can see, despite its compact size, it should adequately serve all your domestic sundry needs for the duration of your stay, and most anything can be home-delivered. A barber shop and an infirmary are right around the corner, there, beside the flower shop. Up ahead are the residences. That first one on the left was built for President Eisenhower—though he never, thank God, had to occupy it—and is closed up for posterity, but the others are all fully functional dwellings, with all the modern necessities tastefully incorporated into the vintage American décor."

Special Agent Martin Cundieffe, in the back of a serpentine, six-car tram beside Agent Macy, cruised down Disneyland's Main Street USA, reproduced down to the nickelodeon parlors and the Hall of Animatronic Presidents. The electric tram was even the same kind that shuttled tourists from one end of the Wyoming-sized Happiest Parking Lot on Earth to the other. He didn't recognize any of the other passengers, hadn't really looked at them, in fact, since the tour began. For a blessed fifteen minutes, he'd been totally flabbergasted, forgetting to blink until his eyes watered and burned. For the quintessentially suburban street rolling by, with its classic American family homes, weeping willows and birdbaths on the lawns, lay seven hundred feet beneath a mountain of limestone.

"And here's the command center up ahead, gentlemen, which concludes the nickel tour. I'll be happy to answer any questions you may have, once your orientation is concluded and you've received your housing assignments. On behalf of the staff and service personnel here, I'd like to be the first to welcome you to Mount Weather, and let you know you are all in our prayers. God bless America, and God save us all."

He didn't know exactly what he'd expected, but this surreal suburban artifice only padded his fatigue, further insulating him against the reality of what was happening—all the ugly spinning dishes, filled with poison and plague, whirling over humanity's head. The effect was not lost on him, though it floated by, bereft of meaning, like everything else. He supposed that some genius back in the Fifties must have reasoned that men, pushed to the brink of a nuclear exchange, would be kept from losing their heads at a critical moment in this eerie reminder of all that was quaint and corny small-town America. Knowing that it had worked seven or eight times since its completion in 1954 only deepened its papier-mâché mystique, and made gendered man seem that much more of an alien animal. That none of the other passengers belonged to that highly volatile breed, but were all Mules, did nothing to alleviate his feeling of dreamlike detachment. If this was an emergency, he believed he knew exactly what its nature was, but nobody had deigned to tell him what was going on. He couldn't shake the lazy, apathetic notion that this was only another test, or another dream.

Aside from a brief, uneasy catnap in the helicopter from Georgetown, Cundieffe had not slept in just over twenty-four hours. It had been an unsettling morning, following as it did a grueling night of computer searches, paperwork and pointlessly abundant, sudden death. He saw weird squiggles of furry neon light whenever he tried to focus on anything.

Macy had a Navy helicopter waiting to pick them up in Lost City, which flew them directly to Georgetown, landing on the pad outside the Naval Observatory, less than two miles from where he lived. A car picked them up and ran them to Georgetown Suites, waiting outside his bedroom door while he sleepwalked inside. He thought about running, but he packed everything he'd need in an overnight bag and a new briefcase and ran back down to the car.

They had one more stop, in front of an apartment building four blocks away from his. Macy went in, and the driver didn't seem to care that Cundieffe got out after him. He scanned the Sunday morning papers stacked beside the unmanned concierge's desk. The impeachment trial; early election primary features; a profile on a movie actor, No Channing Durban; no Greenaway revelations.

He looked over the nameplates inside the lobby. 509–B. HOECKER. He went to the elevator when Macy came out alone. Cundieffe asked, "Was he in?" but Macy didn't answer, just held up a videotape as he took Cundieffe by the arm and led him back to the car.

He gave up trying to figure it out, then, as they flew out of DC in the teeth of a snowstorm, bearing west, then south, into the Blue Ridge Mountains of Virginia. Despite the jouncing turbulence, Cundieffe caught a more or less continuous hour of sleep. Macy jerked him awake and shoved him out onto the icy tarmac of another helipad. This one was surrounded by mountains made of granite and limestone and looming old-growth evergreens, and crowded with military and civilian helicopters and flight crews lashing them down against the wind, which was blowing half-hard enough to peel the paint off them. A crew chief caught Cundieffe and steered him after the retreating forms of the other late arrivals. There were big steel doors in a tunnel, as if they were entering a bank vault inside a bank vault inside a bank vault, and then an enormous elevator, a vast, narrow rectangle the size of the end zone on a pro football field. Ten stories down, they got off, filed through a maze of tunnels and security checkpoints, then got on another elevator, slightly smaller. Down another twenty stories, though he supposed they were really only layers of limestone, and the tram was waiting for them at the entrance to the Happiest Bomb Shelter On Earth.

Now, Cundieffe stumbled as he got off the tram. He let a porter take his overnight bag, but clutched his briefcase to his chest when they tried to pry it off him. It'd already been X-rayed and searched, so they left him with it.

You've trained for this your whole life. You were born for this. You wanted this, once.

He followed the others down a path into a park. A bandstand hove into view on their right, a statue of George Washington, copper encrusted with pained-on verdigris, on their left. Sycamores and dogwoods lent a homey, comforting perfume to the air-conditioned tunnel air, and he wondered how they grew. Perhaps up there among the rafters, there were halogen grow-lamps, though right now, a smoky twilight prevailed that reminded him of the Bayou anteroom of the *Pirates Of The Caribbean. Dead Men Tell No Tales*, hyuk hyuk. As a child, he'd been far more terrified of that attraction than the Haunted Mansion, for the clockwork terrors of the spirit world to him were nothing compared to the very real avarice, anarchy and malice of the human heart. Men chasing gold and wenches while civilization burned—it had set his teeth to chattering then, and it did now.

The others went into a low, brown brick building that looked like a town hall, with a swimming pool and tennis courts around back, and faded shuffleboard designs, like sorcerous pentagrams, on the pavement. An Air Force honor guard stood at attention beside the door. There were no secret handshakes, no ID checkpoints, no gloating animated Jolly Roger above the door. *Fair warned be ye, says I...*

Cundieffe passed through the doors, half-expecting an alarm of some kind to go off when he crossed the threshold. But the line kept moving, on through an atrium decked with framed snapshots of Presidents standing in the park they'd just crossed on what looked like a bright summer day, shaking hands with nameless, nebulous men who made history and then hid. All were in black & white, and only the subjects changed. He tried to focus on them without stepping out of line, saw only one, a zombified, bathrobed Ronald Reagan shaking hands with a youngish, balding man who might have been Brady Hoecker.

They crossed the atrium and the end of the illusion, fir they entered not a small-town meeting hall, but an almost exact replica of the inner sanctum of the Cave Institute. Tiered rows of desks encircled the long table, and monitors displayed satellite imagery and test patterns above their heads, on consoles built into tables, desks and every blank stretch of wall.

Cundieffe looked up and down the table, but failed to recognize a single face. Where were the President, the Vice President, the Joint Chiefs? This had to be a drill, because there were only Mules present. Surely, for all their boasting, they didn't wield that much real power—

You've seen them cover up two all-out military engagements on American soil, and you can still doubt them?

At the head of the table sat a woman with a formidable corona of silver hair about an imperiously well-bred face. Wrinkles deepened like hesitation cuts around the suicidal slash of her lipless mouth. She wore a charcoal gray flannel blazer and skirt. Her hands danced over a keyboard, and the rest of the monitors winked into life all around the room.

Everyone else seemed to gravitate to a seat, leaving Cundieffe drifting across the floor, scanning the sea of faces for someone—anyone— familiar. All the seats at the Committee table were filled but one, and he thought again of Brady Hoecker.

When shown how their perception varies from orthodox policy, they recant and beg the pardon of the group.

One and not Many, indeed.

"Martin!" a stage-whisper set him spinning on his heel, eyes wild, feeling as if he were on trial. "Get over here, you fool." He saw Assistant Director Wyler rise from the front row of desks and wave him to an empty seat beside him. "I expected you hours ago, Martin. Did they have much trouble finding you?"

His eyes didn't want to light on Wyler's face. They skidded around the room, seeing only a blur. "You weren't told?"

"About Greenaway and Lt. Durban? Of course I was told. I just didn't expect it to take so long to resolve itself. Damned fine work, by the way."

Cundieffe sank into the seat, and rubbed his eyes with his hands. Nope. When he looked again, it was all still there. "What's happening, sir?"

"I told you things were starting to happen quickly. This is going to be one of those moments you remember down to the last detail for the rest of your life." His excitement, eagerness, even, was manifest and infectious.

"Sir, I have…doubts—"

Rocking back and forth now in his chair, Wyler asked out of the side of his mouth. "What doubts? What sort of trash did that defector try to feed you?"

"I wish I could believe it was like that, sir. He didn't tell me anything. He—"

Wyler's hand smothered his mouth. "Hush, they're calling for order."

"This isn't— None of this is real, is it?"

"Martin, I tried to show you. It is real. Shut up and show a little respect. You're looking at the new Pro Temp government of the United States of America."

The Chairperson pressed a button before her that seemed to stand in for a gavel. A piercing bell-tone rang through the war room, in counterpoint to flashing white lights on all the monitors. The web of whispers all around them unraveled into tense silence for several seconds before the Chairperson began to speak.

"I'd like to start by thanking you all for coming here on such short notice, and applaud your efficiency in collecting the database elements necessary for our overview. Given the unique nature of this current crisis, no security precaution may be deemed too excessive, and we may be forced to entertain each other's company for a protracted period of time, so I'll make this initial briefing as succinct as possible.

"In light of the ongoing state of instability, we have placed the United States on emergency alert, and implemented the Continuity Of Government protocols established by National Security Decision Directive 188. For those of you who have not already been briefed, let me be clear: this is not a drill."

Cundieffe knew about the COG protocols, first delineated by Eisenhower and later fleshed out into a top secret emergency response plan by Reagan. In the event of a nuclear threat, a cadre of one hundred civilian representatives of the executive branch's many divisions would gather in one or more fortified underground facilities as a "shadow government," standing by to take up the reins if the unthinkable happened to the Capitol. But Cundieffe had just been to Washington, and there were no signs of a crisis. Nothing in the papers, at least—

"A Stage 1 Biological Hazard warning is in effect, and Strategic Air Command is at Defcon 3. The Joint Chiefs have moved to Raven Rock Mountain, near Camp David, and the President is being hurried to a National Emergency Airborne Command Post, or Kneecap, to observe the crisis. It was hoped that the next election might give us a President quicker to follow directions, if not so quick to run and hide, but this is a moot point, now."

A few laughed. "Why are we at Defcon 3?" Cundieffe asked Wyler, but the AD only shushed him again.

"Those of you in the State and National Security branches already know that the threat is not just domestic, as the Russian attempt to cleanse the Chernobyl squatters' colonies was far from successful. Admittedly sketchy reports from CIA operatives in Russia and the Middle East indicate that a sizable gathering of Radiant Dawn cultists has amassed in Iraq, at the ruin of the Tiamat biological weapons production and storage facility, where they have successfully excavated the site and are believed to be in possession of the cache of weapons-grade viruses contained there, as well as an undetermined amount of weapons-grade plutonium, perhaps even nuclear devices. We cannot ignore this threat, thus, the posture of heightened sensitivity, but this is not the quarter from which we expect to be hit. Our Russian counterparts have assured us that they will put that fire out by seven o'clock tonight, our time, so we are closely following developments in that region.

"Now, for the bad news. The inconceivable has begun in California. The Radiant Dawn colony has set into motion a plan to go infectious and spread globally. Our observers there have reported that the numbers arriving at the site in an industrial area at the southern edge of Los Angeles County are far higher than anticipated, which suggests that this is the end strategy our analysts predicted could not occur for another year without the satellite as a vector. Assistant Director Wyler, this was your bailiwick. Why were we so blind to this?"

Cundieffe bit the tip off his tongue. Every eye in the room fell on them. AD Wyler punched a few buttons on the console before them, and the monitors showed video footage of the battle in Idaho. Who shot this? Cundieffe wondered. "Our eyes on the ground were limited to Agents Macy and Mentone, who had their hands full with pacification of the local law enforcement—"

"And your protégée was there, as well," one of the Committee added. "Agent Cundieffe?" They were no easier to tell apart than before, but he noticed this one was sitting in Brady Hoecker's chair.

"Agent Cundieffe was present in relation to another investigation."

"He was inserted into the situation by my predecessor," the Mule said, "and seemed to be operating at cross-purposes with the designated field agents, and seeking to undermine your policy mandate out there— whatever that was."

Wyler squirmed in his seat. "You said yourself, Agent Cundieffe was led out there under false pretenses. I take full responsibility for his actions, of course, but I decline the inference that this was a point of policy."

"You allowed him to go. Either by negligence or complicity, you negatively impacted the execution of your mandate."

Sweat popped out of Wyler's forehead, plopped on the desk like tropical rain. Cundieffe found himself shrinking back behind Wyler, but his boss was withering under their gaze, aging weeks with every second they studied him. He started to open his mouth to rise to Wyler's defense, but Wyler pushed him back and stood up. "I shouldn't have to demonstrate my alliance with our current policy mandate any more than I already have. For the new Secretary of Internal Security to infer that I was an active participant in his predecessor's heterodoxy is outrageous and opportunistic, at this late stage, and I will address those charges *in toto* once this briefing is concluded. I don't need to remind the Committee who voted to bankroll the estimable Lt. Col. Greenaway, a loose variable who might have made become a sizable tack on the Institute's collective seat, had our agents not neutralized him?"

Cundieffe wondered, not for the first time, how much his boss really knew about what happened. Did he know he was lying? Wyler sat down and knitted his hands in front of him, looking straight ahead, like so many defendants Cundieffe had seen in court. The ones who know they're going to burn.

"Please, let us continue," said the Chairperson. "The Secretary of Enforcement will now review our options for domestic containment, as well as readiness issues which may or may not become important in the near future.

A Committee member who, absurdly, in this room, wore a toupee, stood and paced around the table as he made his remarks. "To be sure, the advanced state of the outbreak has caught us up somewhat short, but we don't anticipate any further complications with the domestic issues. We are in possession of a sufficient quantity of the Mission's lysing agent to cleanse the Wilmington colony, which is standing by at Los Alamitos

Naval Reserve Air Station, less than five miles away, and ready to be delivered on the target on a moment's notice. Battle damage assessment of the Idaho site indicates this is an effective agent against the colony's homogenized germ line, but we have Army Reserve units on standby across the county."

"What about the possibility of already infectious agents in the air as we speak?" a hawkish lady Mule at the desk beside theirs shouted. "Have you shut down the airports, public transportation out of the hot zone? Have you closed down the freeways?"

The Secretary pointed to the monitors, which showed the unmistakable chemistry set skyline of the Wilmington refinery jungle as seen from a shoulder-held camera on the 405 Freeway. Another view, of a parking lot filled with buses. A woman with long black hair darted across the street and disappeared among them.

"We've placed LAX, Burbank and John Wayne Airports on high alert, and have people on the ground. If the situation demands, we can shut them down, but there's no question of closing the freeways. The situation is well in hand, I assure you. They're clustering together as closely as possible, as if they want to make a neat target for a surgical strike."

"And that doesn't worry you, Secretary?" someone else snapped. "When has anyone ever successfully overestimated Dr. Keogh's propensity for eluding containment? Should we assume this is simply another tactical feint to scare us, and not the end game strategy some of us advocated years ago?"

There it was. He looked sidewise at Wyler, whose face was utterly blank.

"Let's hear the preparedness strategies, Mallory," the Chairperson nodded to the Defense Secretary.

"As you're all well aware, the domestic issue is not our principal point of execution. The Iraqi threat is our cause, whether or not the Russians contain it.

"At zero hour, we will move SAC/NORAD down to Defcon 2, and the Vice President will board a second Kneecap plane. Mobile command posts with the power and communications lines to launch nuclear missiles will take to the roads across America, which will, of course, be nationalized and closed to civilian traffic. This will be a very delicate phase. Keogh wasn't supposed to have any groups meeting in the United States, but even this can be made to serve our purposes. Helicopters armed with spray tanks of lysing agent will fly over the stadium in LA and cleanse it, while the rest of the world will be selectively overrun. The world will look to America to save them. Here at home, long after the

Russian threat has evaporated, Americans will look to us to restore order, protect them from the plague just outside their borders, and lead them into a brighter future. Thus will the current unrest only hasten the implementation of the master mandate, and the fulfillment of all that we have worked for." He sat down. More than a few of them actually applauded.

Cundieffe felt like running. What *have we worked for?* He wanted to scream. They'd stood up and said it, spelled it out. The ground seemed to tilt under him, but the sense of being in a dream had finally burned off. This was swiftly becoming more awful than anything he could have imagined.

Cundieffe scribbled out a note on a pad and shoved it under Wyler's nose. WHERE'S HOECKER?

Wyler stood again and said, "And now, if the briefing is concluded, I'd like to present a document which merits the Committee's immediate attention." The Chairperson nodded. Wyler pressed a few buttons, and half of the monitors in the room flashed snow for a few frames, then a discolored but unnervingly clear digital video image.

A counter at the bottom of the screen blinks 1:16 AM, with today's date. Brady Hoecker sits on the end of a bed and looks into the camera. His expression is bleak and broken. He wears a down comforter wrapped around himself like a toga, and holds a clay bowl in his hands. Something about the scene mimics something ancient, something in a book or a famous painting.

It came to him in a sickening, migraine-intensity flash: the death of Socrates.

"I confess that I have fomented dissent and sedition against the policy mandated by the majority," Hoecker says. "I have suborned others to engage in subterfuge and sabotage of the majority's plan, which is the preservation of stability for a sustainable human future. They are innocent of my crimes, and should be dealt with as transgressions of ignorance, not heterodoxy."

More than a few heads turned Cundieffe's way. He shrank further behind Wyler, until he was peeking over the Assistant Director's shoulder at the screens.

"I, however, knowing full well the penalty for dissent, go willingly to judgment, and hope that this document will in some way alleviate the disorder I have wreaked upon the implementation of the master mandate. Let those who witness this know that I am penitent, and go wishing the majority the best in the fulfillment of its sacred trust."

Sentenced to death for corrupting the youth of Athens, Socrates willingly drank hemlock and, surrounded by his disciples and enemies alike, declaimed his immortal thoughts until the moment of his death. Hoecker's accusers made him do it alone in his room, and send them a tape. Cundieffe wished he had a bowl of poison, himself.

He drinks from the bowl, and immediately gags. His eyes roll back in his head. Hands clutching at his throat, he sprawls on the bed and flops around, legs peddling at air. He convulses a few more times, his gut trying to expel the poison in explosive retching fits, but his eyes are already glazing over.

Wyler stopped the tape. It probably just stayed that way for quite a while, Hoecker only turning blue and blowing bubbles while the tape rolled, until Agent Macy dropped by to collect it.

Cundieffe felt as if an engine block had settled on his chest. He leaned back in his chair until it teetered on the edge of dumping him. He stared at the ceiling and asked it, *Why am I still alive?* They killed Durban, Hoecker, Greenaway's army, Heilige Berg, Storch. Why let him live?

Because they were all just dime-a-million gendered humans, and he was one of Them. And hadn't he been? What had he done, really, besides follow blindly along, doing research that opened a door for them here, letting himself get kidnapped and leading them there. He'd been nothing but a good Mule, up to now. His half-hearted moralizing and tangential wanderings had been only a minor annoyance as he went down their trail.

The Chairperson looked around the silent room, sounded a gentler tone that seemed to let slack into the strings holding everyone upright. "We'll adjourn here for a fifteen minute recess to collate data from the ground. When we return, we will observe full ceremonial protocols for what promises to be a memorable event."

Cundieffe snatched Wyler's arm. "Sir, is there a place, where we could—?"

If he expected Wyler to look shaken by what he'd just shown the Committee, he was rudely taken aback by the grim excitement animating his droopy features. "Martin, pull yourself together. None of this reflects on you."

"Sir, I—it's not about...that. There's something else that I have to understand, and I think now is the time."

Wyler led him up the steps past rows of Mules raptly picking at laptops and desk consoles. Cundieffe saw many screens replaying Hoecker's suicide tape, pausing it, taking notes.

At the top of the stairs, they went down a dim black corridor to a row of conference rooms. Wyler held the door for him, shut it behind them, and sat on one corner of the immense smoked glass table that dominated the room. "Now, what seems to be the trouble?"

"Sir, I suppose the Institute already knew that Lt. Durban was duped into turning NSA intercepts pertaining to the events of July, '99 over to Greenaway—"

Wyler only made a get-on-with-it gesture with one hand.

"What do you know about a project called ROYAL PICA?" Cundieffe asked. The words came out of his mouth like balls on a string, pausing after each to gauge some reaction from Wyler. "Maybe we have a different name for it, sir, but it...well, the evidence conclusively links the Institute with—with—"

AD Wyler pressed a touch-sensitive monitor built into the conference table. "Regina, could we trouble you for a moment of your time?"

"I'll be right there, Wendell."

Until she came in, Cundieffe just stood there, unable to form words. Wyler touched the screen a few times, reading something and nodding approval. He didn't look up when he finally spoke. "Martin, I like you. I've admired your work for years. Your father was an exceptional agent, almost good enough to have been one of us, and when we learned about you, we were none of us surprised. You're a purebred, but more, you've always exemplified what we believe, to the point where we knew you had internalized our ethic. You've always worked as if you get it, you know what's at stake, here. This is bigger than all of us. You know that. Hoecker understood it, at the end."

He almost shook, trying to swallow this one without choking. The look in Hoecker's eyes as he made his hollow confession, the look of utter defeat they were still studying out in the war room—that was the message he'd wanted to send. *You're wrong*, his eyes said, *you're so completely, utterly wrong that I can't live in the same world with you. I tried to make you see—*

The door opened, and a balding Mule agent who might have been Macy's first cousin scoped out the room, then ducked out to make way for the Chairperson.

Wyler stood as she entered and shook hands with him, then turned and beamed at Cundieffe. He retreated a step from the force of her charm. Telling himself that "she" was a neuter, like himself, and that her gender assignment was as much of an arbitrary disguise as his own, did nothing to make her seem less motherly. He felt cowed by her probing eyes and disarming smile. She knew all the proper cues and played them, so that he could only hang his head before her.

"You've been through so much, Martin. Wendell has kept me apprised of your tribulations, and we're all very sympathetic. We've all been where you are right now, but it's been a harder road for you than most."

Cundieffe risked a glance at her. She took his hands in hers. It was so hard to stare at her, but he had to meet her eyes, if only to remind himself that this was not his own mother. "Madame Chairperson—"

"Pardon my bad manners, Martin. My name is Regina Stapleton."

"I—"

"Wendell tells me you have questions. You're troubled by something you've read."

"It's ROYAL PICA, ma'am. It—what I read—it's not true, is it?"

Ms. Stapleton pursed her mouth a moment, weighing her words. "You want to know about RADIANT, then."

"Brady Hoecker told me it didn't exist, but he believed that Keogh posed more of a threat than the Institute was willing to accept, and now, with all that's happening…did he know about what's in ROYAL PICA? Did we do those things?"

"RADIANT was a classic example of realpolitik run amok, it's true. It was approved and developed entirely outside of our influence, but we took an interest as soon as it had become apparent that the defense program was being abused. When RADIANT was initially tested in the South Pacific in 1984, the results were disastrous, but we weren't so stupid as to believe that it simply self-destructed. Dr. Keitel, as he called himself then, contacted us to deliver his ultimatum, bypassing those nominally in authority. At the time, we had no leverage, but he offered very acceptable terms, given the times. He demanded only that we never try to locate him or the satellite, or interfere with his research. In return, he offered to contract out RADIANT for the purpose for which it was built."

"Giving people cancer?" Cundieffe blurted.

"Neutralizing enemies of the state, Martin. Consider for a moment the rules we have to play by to preserve order and administer justice. Not in Russia or China, but right here at home, and under the noses of our allies. Enemies of the government can openly profess their aggression, recruit more malcontents to their cause, and stockpile weapons, and well-meaning agencies like the Bureau are helpless to stop them. The few actions we have taken have been debacles—Ruby Ridge, Waco, you know better than I."

"But ma'am, this—according to the ROYAL PICA intercepts, it started long before Waco, and the first ones weren't terrorists."

The first demonstrations were performed on Russian military targets in Afghanistan, as per the Institute's orders. The file transcribed the request, and the subsequent battle damage assessment. A general and his staff all died within forty-eight hours of irradiation. There were two hundred eighteen more. Highlights: Ayatollah Khomeini; Soviet Premier Yuri Andropov; several colorful, failed attempts on Castro. So many others that nobody ever heard of, and never would. Long before they ever became a threat, Americans and foreigners were irradiated from space, and quietly died of cancer, with no autopsies officially performed. Even some military officials in the Pentagon and members of Congress were burned, for the good of the nation. The last one occurred only a week before July of last year, when Keogh took RADIANT away and the war started.

"Such people are cancer in the body politic," Wyler said, "fomenting dissent and fueling violence in every avenue of American life."

"But sir," Cundieffe stammered, "this contravenes what we're—what we were born to do."

"And what was that, Martin? What were we born to do?"

"To protect and preserve an orderly democratic society—"

"No," he scissored off Cundieffe's canned reply with a snap of his hand. "To protect an orderly *human* society. To preserve and cultivate the best aspects of that society, and save it from its own base animal tendencies. Democracy is the unholy ideal that opens the door to all that chaos, all that madness, badness and incivility."

Cundieffe heaved a huge sigh. The engine block didn't budge. A whole car had grown around it, and he couldn't get a whole breath. "Okay, so it's—necessary, then, to do this. But Keogh—what about him? He's not a man to bargain with, is he? What is he, do you even know?"

"Only too late did we discover what Keogh intended to do," Ms. Stapleton said, "and we'll probably never understand exactly what he is, but we were never *used*, Martin. His research has positive ramifications for our strategy for a survivable human future that are worth any amount of sacrifice. He is the oldest living organism on earth, but he is the past, and we are the custodians of the future. He believes he is manipulating us, using us for his own purposes, but we were using him, and use him still."

Cundieffe rubbed his temples. They were at Defcon 3, and going down. Keogh presented a crisis that had the President and the Joint Chiefs running scared, or did he? Maybe none of it was true, maybe it was all some sort of horrible simulation, an initiation rite, kill the old Martin Cundieffe with nightmarish lies, so that the new one might be born—

"Are there really Radiant Dawn militants in Iraq?" he asked.

"That, you don't need to know."

"But you're using him as a catspaw to create a global state of emergency. Why? If you control him, why risk letting him spread? Why not just put out the fire?"

"Because we have everything we need from Dr. Keogh as of today," Ms. Stapleton told him. "We have the Mission's weapon, which has been effectively field-tested, and we're ready to use it. We've gone as far as we can with the present system, Martin. Dr. Keogh has surged far ahead of our expectations in his progress, but thanks to the hard work of agents such as yourself, our own program is ahead of schedule, and if I say any more, I'll spoil the surprise." She smiled again, all motherly. "Recess is over, now, boys. Back to the war room."

Madame Chairperson buzzed the room to order. Cundieffe found his seat next to Wyler, but his eyes were on the door. Fresh air, that's what he needed. If he could just clear his head, he'd know what to do next, he could figure out what was right.

Wyler cast a harsh sidelong glance at him, like a father whose son has just cried through his first trip to the barber shop. *Don't be such a candy-ass, Martin*, said his eyes.

"Today, as a few of you already know, is the crisis we've been waiting for. All great evolutionary leaps come out of an environmental catastrophe, and ours will be no different. Our hand has been forced, but we are ready for the massive undertaking we knew would be laid across our shoulders one day. For centuries, we have labored in secret to preserve the candle of human civilization against the storm of animal nature, and for the most part, we have been successful. But as the task became greater and more complex, we knew that it would one day overreach our abilities. The sheer size and power of those arrayed against us would overwhelm our scant numbers, while the safety of the whole would require harsher natures than ours. The author of the *Republic* professed that the philosopher-kings required to guide the ship of state over the uncertain rapids of the future would come from nature, but even before his time, we worked to direct nature, as man has always done, towards the desirable path. That path ends here, today, ladies and gentlemen. When we leave Mount Weather, we will go out into a new world, with new hope of an attainable, orderly tomorrow. Henceforth, though our task will be no less great, the stakes no less dire, yet our burden shall be lessened, and the ship of humanity will sail on into the future of our making."

The doors opened and a squad of soldiers came in wearing uniforms so outlandish that Cundieffe had to stifle a laugh. Ballooned trousers and stockings, slashed sleeves blooming out of steel chest plates, and kettle helmets such as the Conquistadors wore. Each carried an assault rifle slung back on his shoulder, but in their hands they held pikes and halberds. It took Cundieffe a moment to place them, but he finally did. They were dead ringers for the Swiss Guard, the mercenary force who guarded the Pope at the Vatican. Still puzzling over Madame Chairperson's bewildering speech, he wondered for a moment if they weren't making every backwoods bigot's worst nightmare come true by turning control of the nation over to the Catholic Church.

The guards stepped aside and they walked in. All in the war room rose to their feet in silent awe.

The first ones stood head and shoulders above their guards. Absurdly broad in shoulders and deep in the chest, they looked like any Bible storybook picture of the Philistine giant Goliath. They had been selectively bred for aggression and charisma and raw physical power, but at a staggering cost. Their muscles rippled and creaked on brittle bones taxed to their limit to hold them upright. Their wide-open faces were so blank and unresponsive they might have been painted on, and betrayed a bloody-minded idiocy that Cundieffe had seen in the eyes of pit bulls. Drunk on their own physical might, weaned inside a secret realm to rule a world they could not comprehend, they looked around them and saw only meat to be beaten and eaten. They wobbled and drooled, drugged, but an attendant walked behind each of them with a doctor's bag and a cattle prod.

This must be some kind of joke, Cundieffe told himself. These are Socrates' philosopher-kings?

But they were only the first. Those that came next might be born leaders, but they were, if anything, far less human than their giant brethren. Cundieffe had been taught, of late, to see all biology as an economic process. They, the Mules, were deprived of reproductive capabilities, which biological windfall they shrewdly reinvested in intellect, immune-function, and empathy. From all he had been told, the Mules had been sports, happy accidents of genetics who had helped bootstrap humanity up from savagery into ordered civilization. How could they believe that it was other than destiny, that they came along when they did? And how could they not look at the slope-browed brutes all around them as raw material, to be refined into something more like themselves?

The second batch could not walk on their own, and rode in wheelchairs with bubble domes around them. Their skins looked like the unfinished, shiny pink flesh under an unripe scab. Their limbs were stunted, vestigial affairs, flippers with a few crudely hewn digits, garbled, misfired wings folded into sunken, swaybacked torsos. In the womb, nature had given up early on their bodies and squandered all the saved biological capital on an orgy of cranial engineering the likes of which homo sapiens would never, in a million generations, have spawned on its own. Their wizened faces were squashed down underneath explosive blooms of cranium, which rested on cradles. The seams of their enormous skulls did not meet, but curled back like the lips of a tulip to make way for a crippling mass of brain tissue. It spilled out of their skulls in great, trembling sacs that would have hung down to their waists, if they could stand. Cundieffe counted eight chairs parked alongside the long table in the center of the war room.

The giants were herded into a corner by their warders, and had to be prodded into submission when the room broke out in thunderous applause.

Stapleton called for order. "For some of you, this may come as a shock, but we have known all along that we were not the last word on the species, but only the vanguard of a new human genetic diaspora, which must be shielded and nurtured until it can take its rightful place."

Cundieffe goggled at the new leaders. Many of the outer circle of the Committee demanded answers, some openly incensed and repulsed, others ecstatic. Madame Chairperson explained that they were the products of the best-known human husbandry project in recorded history, the ruling families of Western Europe. The giant guardians were selectively inbred in Europe for centuries within the so-called Black Families of the European aristocracy. The philosopher-kings were of the same blue bloodline, but were hybridized with another ancestral line preserved in France and Germany in the Merovingian dynasty of the Holy Roman Empire. After their betrayal in the ninth century, the heirs retreated into nameless secrecy under the care of the Prieure De Sion in the south of France, where only a few outsiders became privy to the secret of their origins. Few outside this room today knew that these mutants were directly descended from the bloodline of Mary Magdalene and her sometime paramour, an exceptional mutant specimen known as Jesus Christ of Nazareth. By law of nature and holy fiat, they were humankind's naturally ordained rulers.

"They are, of course, severely handicapped and physically infirm from centuries of recessive traits piling up in their germline, so until very recently, we seemed to be further than ever from our ultimate goal. Then Keogh opened doors for us. From the prisoner Storch and the captives taken at White Bird, we harvested mitochondrial DNA unlike anything ever discovered in living animal tissue. The Shoggoth mitochondria in Keogh's genotype powers the drastic somatic alterations observed in the Radiant Dawn specimens, but now we have harnessed that dangerous power for society's benefit.

"With Keogh's gene therapy technology, we have grasped the power to accelerate nature's plan for the human race a thousandfold. The new leadership is responding to treatment, and will soon be ready to assume its place."

And there were to be more. Video screens lit up showing animated computer graphics of the forms into which they would cast the citizens of tomorrow. Spidery human skeletons and fish-faced changelings, shaped to live in orbit, and under the sea. Hulking, monolithic monsters with only mouths and black eyespots on their minimal heads, burrowing troglodytes with the outsized spade-claws of a mole. Women who looked like Holroyd, the shapeless human monster in the slaughterhouse, all dewlaps and rolling haunches of blubber, breeding cows for a better humanity.

Cundieffe didn't know how long Wyler had been looking at him, but the crumple of Mosaic scorn his face had become told him his own face betrayed his inner turmoil. "It's—sir, this is monstrous."

Wyler bristled, whispered scalding tones in Cundieffe's ear. "You had no problem with the notion that you were a genetically superior administrator, and should rightfully trample due process to keep human affairs running smoothly. By the same argument, these are superior rulers, and will see humanity through the coming instability to greater levels of specialization, into a smoothly run hive, instead of the self-destructive cesspool of contradictory impulses it is now. With judicious application of the genetically enhanced mitochondrial DNA, the human race will be shaped into something fit for the future."

The Committee applauded. One of the guardians reared up and snapped his warder's neck with one hand. He heaved the limp body across the room.

This is why Keogh has been allowed to go so far, Cundieffe realized. To fight such a global threat, America must band together with the other nations of the world and pool its resources under a more exacting authority. There would be sacrifices, but in the face of such an awful alternative as Keogh posed, humanity could not but decide to follow the Mules into a New World Order.

"Is this what you joined the FBI for, sir? To serve—these?"

Wyler blanched, then slapped him. "You worshipped law and order and the secrets and the power we gave you. Why didn't you complain, then? We told you all along we were working towards a perfect, orderly society. What the hell did you think such a thing would look like? Do you, of all people, honestly think for a moment that such a society could exist, with untreated, gendered *Homo sapiens* living in it?"

Cundieffe looked away, at the rows of balding or bewigged bureaucrats setting up to take over the world. They looked like the volunteers who manned the phone banks on a PBS fundraiser. They looked like every anonymous official in the background of every photograph of a President. They were the ones steering him through the crowds, handing him speeches. But beside them stood those creatures from the wettest dreams of Josef Mengele, and their brain-bag cousins, the Philosopher Kings.

"It seems like you already have the situation well in hand," Cundieffe said, trying to sound reasonable. "You already run everything. Why unleash Keogh to wreck everything, even if you really do think you can stop him, or find a cure for him?"

"It's not for any one of us to question. It's what's ordained. It's policy. We're all utopian idealists, here, but the world spits on and burns that kind of idealism, Martin. You know that. It made your life lonely long before you learned you were one of us. We're not talking about waging genocide on the gendered human race, Martin, if that's what you're thinking. Some will die, but no more than die in the Third World, anyway, and that's where it's all going to happen. After the Wilmington colony is sterilized, America will be clean. Iraq will be nuked, and the President will be strong-armed into explaining it to the world. The UN and every other nation in the world will be howling for our blood, but then Keogh will start to spread, abroad, and we will give them the cure. Then we'll begin implementing the new government plans—"

"Eugenic p-programs," Cundieffe stammered. "You're not going to wipe out the human race, you're just going to breed it out of existence."

"In Nature, on planet Earth, when has that ever been a crime?"

Cundieffe couldn't look at his mentor. Wyler came closer, mistaking his resolve for pouting.

"Listen, Martin, this is the real world, not the world of laws and ethics and justice. There are many others—outsiders like Keogh, only far more powerful—against whom we will be defenseless in the future, if we don't take decisive action now.

"You don't know what the world is really like, Martin. What's in it, what lies sleeping underneath, and what waits Outside. The future is going to be rife with pole shifts, climatic changes, explosive population growth, new religious wars and new fanatical faiths, and famines and plagues on an unprecedented scale: and things the world must never know about, like Keogh.

"And it'll only get harder. Things are about to get very, very rough, Martin, and no matter what's done, a lot of people are going to die.

America isn't going to suffer as much as the rest of the world, of course, but sweeping changes are going to have to be implemented to keep the nation from slipping into a new Dark Age. Hard decisions are going to need to be made, choices we can't expect from a whore of the polls."

Cundieffe nodded absently, then tried to make his face bright and convinced-looking. "How secure is this place?"

"Oh, don't let the quaint atmosphere fool you. This place will still be standing in an exchange that leaves Cheyenne Mountain as an ash heap. They're going to give the go-ahead to bomb Keogh's colony any minute, now, and that'll be the end of it, in our area of responsibility."

"No, I mean, inside. How secure are we, in here?"

"Even if there were an incident outside this room, the security system would render the room airtight. It's a strongbox, Martin, there's no safer place in the world."

"We're not doing bad things, are we, sir? We're just following our programming."

"Adaptive behavior is instinctual for us, Martin. Look into your heart, and you will see this is not just the right thing to do. It's the only thing to do."

Cundieffe sat down at a console and, after ferreting around to get the feel for the system, checked his e-mail.

A report from his old colleague in LA, Eugenie Hanchett, on the Storch kidnapping. The senior Sgt. Storch was abducted from the Norwalk State Hospital for the Criminally Insane yesterday, by a man posing as a psychiatrist, Dr. Hiram Hansen. While the duty nurse checked the Doctor's ID, the abductor somehow managed to get out of the hospital with the patient, who was severely delusional and under restraints and heavily medicated. Their present whereabouts were unknown.

Cundieffe deleted the message without replying. In LA, Agent Hanchett would have a lot more to worry about than tracking down an old lunatic war veteran, if she survived. Besides, the only person who might care was dead.

A junk mail hawking Lemurian Blessing Bracelets, forged of a unique silver alloy which attuned the wearer's aura to the cosmic emanations of the lost civilization of Lemuria, whose mystic science had, continental sinking aside, conferred upon them near-divine powers and good luck. Cundieffe ordered one for himself, and on a quick head-count, decided to order seventy-five more.

A message from someone he'd never heard of, *wyrmboy3202*. Figuring it was more junk mail, he almost deleted it, but the subject line stopped his hand over the button. *He Won*, it said. The message was sent two days before, but had only just arrived.

He opened it.

Please excuse tardiness. Got killed, eaten. 1000% SNAFU. No time to explain. This body is not mine. Mission dead. Keogh going to Iraq. Going to be One, and eat his Masters. Lysing agent won't work. He's got my immunity. I fucked up. I'll fix it.
Storch

The only thing to do—

No one looked at Martin as he rose and took his briefcase out from under the desk. "I'll be back in a moment, sir. Fresh air—"

Wyler nodded absently and watched as a helicopter's eye-view of Los Alamitos came up on most of the screens. The racetrack hove into view for a second, where Mother liked to spend Easter Sundays with her friends after church.

Cundieffe went up the stairs and looked around. All eyes were on the screens. No one had picked up the body of the slain warder. A short, stocky form in a black lab coat and coveralls, the body had landed so that the broken neck bent back on itself, and the head lay under it. Cundieffe looked around one more time.

The helicopter passed over the 605 and Coyote Creek, crossing the county line into Long Beach. Another helicopter flanked the camera on either side—both old surplus Hueys with big green tanks on the sides, like crop dusters.

Cundieffe opened his briefcase and took out his Thermos. They ran it through an X-ray along with his other belongings before they let him in here, but they'd seen nothing. He unscrewed the lid and peered inside.

It moved.

The X-ray had made it testy. It swarmed up the glass sides of the Thermos and stretched out a gray pseudopod toward his face.

He'd almost forgotten about Spec Four Gibson Holroyd, US Army 1st Div., MACV/SOG. He'd kept it because what he saw in Idaho made him loath to turn it over. As it turned out, they'd gotten plenty from there without it.

The more cultured and intelligent you are—

He supposed that was when the therapists would say he'd started to snap. He stifled a laugh as one of the Philosopher Kings drifted by, the respirator pump mounted on his wheelchair wheezing and dripping coolant and drool on the most secret floor in America.

—the more ready you are to work for Satan.

He clamped the lid down and reached around on the table beside him. His hand brushed a plastic cup, and he took it. It was half-full of tepid cocoa, the edges scummed with marshmallows that refused to melt completely. Darn near perfect. Cundieffe shook the Thermos, opened it and poured the cocoa in through a narrow opening. He shook it again. Soak up that sugar, you sick little son of a gun. Do what you're supposed to do. *Raise an army—*

He lifted the corpse up and propped its shoulder against one knee. He twisted the head around until it lay face-up in his lap.

Around him, they still watched the screens. The helicopters turned north at the Long Beach Marina and followed the muddy San Gabriel River into the oil refinery grids of Wilmington.

He just sat there, looking at the screens. In the end, it was the words of Keogh that made him move. *Never stop trying to change the world.*

He pried the corpse's mouth open. The jaws were clamped shut on a bloody snippet of tongue, and it took both hands prying on it to get it open wide enough. He tipped the Thermos to the corpse's cyanotic lips and opened it. *Do what you're supposed to do, you little impossible bastard. Raise an army—*

Someone tapped him on the shoulder. He jumped, almost dropping the Thermos, but clamped the lid shut before it got out. He hunched low over the body, brain percolating explanations, all of them utter bullshit—

Hands grabbed him roughly, throwing him back on his behind. He rolled over and curled up around the Thermos. What the hell had he been trying to do?

It was the guardian who'd broken the warder's neck. He stooped over Cundieffe and fixed him with a glare of such pure command and contempt that Cundieffe found himself offering up the Thermos before he realized what he was doing. If he'd had anything else, he would have offered that, too.

The guardian opened the Thermos, tilted it back, and dumped the contents down its yawning gullet.

Cundieffe jumped to his feet and backed away. The guardian rested on his knuckles, prodding the warder's corpse as if it might only be pretending to be dead. Absently, the guardian of tomorrow began to rock back and forth and foam at the mouth.

Cundieffe ran up the stairs to the exit. He looked back over his shoulder at the room. The screens showed only clouds of incandescent green. The room erupted in applause.

Cundieffe shoved through the retinue of Swiss Guards around the exit, fumbled out his card on the lanyard around his neck for the Air Force sentry outside. "I'm sorry, sir, but nobody leaves—" the guard tried to tell him.

Behind them, the guardian's booming voice drowned out the buzz of the war room. "FIGHTING SOLDIERS FROM THE SKY—"

"I think your assistance is needed, in there," Cundieffe said.

"FEARLESS MEN WHO JUMP AND DIE—"

Inside, someone screamed. The sound was cut off by a single, brutal smash of meat against metal, and the room went berserk. "What the fuck was that?" the sentry shouted, and pushed past Cundieffe with his pistol drawn. A Swiss Guard skewered the Air Force guard on his halberd before he got both feet in the room.

Against his better judgment, Cundieffe looked back. The mutant who'd shared his cocoa rampaged through the war room. He seized one of the Philosopher Kings by the handles of its wheelchair, hefted it up, and waded into the crowd with it like Samson with the jawbone of an ass.

"MEN WHO MEAN JUST WHAT THEY SAY—"

Cundieffe picked up the dead guard's pistol and slipped out through the spring-loaded door as it guillotined shut.

"THE BRAVE MEN OF THE GREEN—"

Guards rushed into formation in the park, but it was clear they still had no idea what was going on inside.

Outside the town hall, he lit a match under a fire alarm. Sprinklers and sirens went off everywhere. He heard bolts slamming home in the walls of the command center, felt engines stirring to life beneath his feet.

Out on Main Street USA, it started to rain.

Cundieffe turned up his collar and walked at a brisk pace, following the signs that pointed the way to the exit. A guard shouldered his rifle at him and ordered him to halt, but he just stood there as Cundieffe wheeled on him and shot him through the forehead.

He hoped they didn't give him a hard time about flying him directly to Headquarters. There would be a lot of paperwork to fill out when he got back to the office.

~ 39 ~

There were giants in the earth in those days...

For two days, Storch rode the wind. An aircraft too small and soft to reflect radar, he crossed the burning blue eye of the South Pacific, over New Guinea's northern coast, high above the riotous green peaks of Kalimantan and Sumatra.

He swooped out over the Bay of Bengal, riding a winter zephyr around the skirts of a monsoon, among whose lightning-lit temples of cloud he was only one more fleeting atmospheric oddity. He passed over the narrowing wedge of southern India in a tropical storm, roiling dynamos of supercharged atmosphere the size of stadiums that collapsed in minutes, squeezing out seas of balmy rain on the unseen subcontinent thirty thousand feet below.

The winds carried him out over the Arabian Sea and he banked north, passed over the Gulf of Oman and the needle-eye of the Strait of Hormuz, upstream against the garbled warpage rippling out from Tiamat, distortions of the omnipresent snore of the Unbegotten Source. Contracting the intake valves on his back and spreading his wings, he dropped out of the jet stream and into clear skies teeming with F-18's and Harrier fighter-bombers.

A formation of Navy fighters passed less than a mile beneath him, and far, far below them he could make out a tiny gray plank on the water, a white feather of tilled water fanning out for nearly a mile behind it. A US aircraft carrier and a small armada of destroyers rolled north on the Gulf, a volley of arrows aimed unmistakably at his destination.

He hadn't followed the news all too closely before his world fell apart last year, but he'd picked up enough about world events from the gossip circle that gathered on the porch of his store to know that the US had taken to bombing Iraq whenever tempers flared over its ongoing disarmament crisis. To Storch, it had only seemed like political stupidity, and he'd tried not to hear about it. That they had stopped short of Baghdad and toppling Saddam Hussein in the Gulf War had been only one more sign that the whole campaign was an empty maneuver. Storch and his fellow career soldiers had not gone to war to liberate the spoiled, ass-backward Emirate of Kuwait for the cause of democracy, but to do a job. The powers that were had fudged it and called them home before they could complete said job. To read about it or watch it on TV had only made Storch feel sicker, so he had closed his eyes and ears to any reminder of the war. Besides, he never dreamed that he'd be coming back here.

Almost at the horizon, two of the fighters peeled off, climbed, and came back in his direction. The air was crystal clear, offering no cover between himself and the ocean. Naked tan land like wind-polished bone closed in the water on both sides, Saudi Arabia to the west, Iran to the east, and a mere hundred miles away, the Arabian Peninsula joined with the Asian continent to form a crotch, where the merged Tigris and Euphrates Rivers poured their green waters into the Gulf. Two storm fronts circled each other over the lower half of Iraq, orbiting round the point that called to him across ten thousand miles of ocean.

The fighters closed with him and wagged their wings as they passed, so close that he tumbled in the punishing turbulence of their wake. The pilots' jaws flapped and the planes nearly collided as they swept by and circled back for another look. Storch gave them the finger.

His ramjet intake contracted further and the superheated nacelles flattened into a muscular, trailing cloak. He dove straight down, drawing in air and expelling it as a giant squid propels itself through the ocean depths. The fighters slashed the air wide open above him and rolled to engage, but when they came around again, the unidentified object had vanished over—or into—the deep blue of the Gulf.

Storch soared on the convection currents fifty feet above the lapping waves. The skin of his dorsal ramjet had become a bright, highly reflective blue, and he angled himself to fly between the fighters and the sun, so that they were dazzled by its reflection when they looked for him.

He crossed from sea to land unnoticed at dusk, gliding silently less than a hundred feet above the masts of small fishing boats that plied the shallows of the Tigris delta. He passed through bands of blessed rain and bone-jarring whirlwinds bearing frost from the northerly storm out of Iran. As night fell and the storms converged, the terrain devolved into murky black humps and mirrored windows perpetually shattering from the impact of raindrops. The marshes and lakes of the delta gave way to broken land and isolated villages, and his eyes ached as they adjusted to register the infrared and ultraviolet spectra. Loose clusters of heat crawled across the land here and there, flocks of goats and sheep tended by taller, jerkier blobs of warmth that stopped and stared at his silhouette as it passed over them.

Closer, the sound of It became louder than the sonic turmoil of the warring storms. It was not simply the sound of every living thing, but more, it was the sound of life itself, the sound of one great, glacial heartbeat, the husky oceanic sound of a single indrawn breath as long and deep as infinity. Mixed up in it, like the din of a single musician in an orchestra going mad and attacking his neighbors, he could almost make out the subtle brainwave signature of a man who was once named Christian Keyes. It was like a radio station fading in and out, but growing stronger, building itself out of the dissonant chaos of static into a dominant harmony. It was the sound of his mind spreading like a virus, unifying the disparate frequencies of thousands of minds into itself. It grew louder all the time, but the eternal voice it threatened lacked ears to hear it. That was why he was here, to be Its ears, and Its hands.

He didn't think he'd recognize it, but as the plateau and the box canyon swam up out of the dark, it all came back to him. The point overlooking the canyon where they'd camped out to paint the target was covered in a tent city lit only by the sporadic fireworks of rifles and grenades. His enhanced senses made out a vast, brilliantly hot mass of bodies traveling down a ramp that curled round the wall of the canyon down to the floor, where Tiamat had once stood. It was a crowd of a few hundred people, but they marched, breathed, and blinked in locked synchronicity, pressed so close together they were unmistakably Him.

As the last of the hot air vented out of his dorsal nacelles, he dropped out of the wind a mile away from the camp and hit the ground running for cover. The manta-cowl deflated and began to decay almost instantly, tearing on the ragged rocks and sloughing away like a demolished parachute.

A tumble of rocks at the mouth of a narrow, winding wadi offered the only cover, and he slunk into it and collapsed in a puddle, turning it to steam, and blacked out.

When he awoke, the ground rumbled and the wind carried the words of Him, raised in an exultant shout hundreds of voices strong. Exhausted, ravenous, burning in the rain, he dragged himself up on a rock and looked around.

A broken field of basalt tumulus and twisted, blasted boulders lay between his position and the pit, which shone against the rain-streaked dark with a string of explosions, painting fiery, bestial faces on the racing clouds, but the voices only shouted louder.

This body was spent, used up, and wanted to melt into the ground. It wanted to go to sleep forever, and Storch wanted to let it. He could lie here, unnoticed, and maybe die, maybe not. In the end, did it really matter?

The screaming and shooting from the tent city was abruptly cut off. Only the voice of Keyes becoming One clashed with the storm. There would be no air support. Reinforcements would never come. Nobody else even seemed to know this shit was happening.

He was the furthest thing he could imagine from human, now, but he was still a soldier. The eternal rationale of the elite infantryman plugged all the holes in his leaking resolve: *Some people just need to be killed. You've come all this way to do a job. Do it.*

Willing himself to find the energy, to burn the marrow out of his own bones to get himself going, he moved. He slithered among the rocks, bones grinding, muscles burning, paying for every inch. Endorphins spilled into his bloodstream, but they were like snowflakes in a furnace, and only made him forget his agony for a few moments. But in that time, his body tapped into reserves its original owner never knew he had, and, rising up, Storch began to run.

He saw shapes coming out of the dark, bodies squirming over the rain-slick rocks. They made sounds, but he could hardly recognize them as human, let alone sane words. Iraqi soldiers ran down the hillside, blind to the terrain, mad from the rain and what they'd seen. Hitting rocks, slipping and falling, they got up again, screaming and sobbing, and smashing their bodies to ruins in their blind panic. Storch slipped unseen past them and into the tent city.

Here, at least, there was light.

The camp, a hundred or so big sand-colored tents with a motor pool and a helipad, wreathed in razor wire and Arabic signs with pictures of land mines, burned. A 90mm antiaircraft battery that might have been the very same one they blew up a decade ago, in this very spot, stood unmanned at one corner of the camp, aimed at the storm. Helicopters and heavy trucks sat on a slab of hastily poured tarmac, fitfully blazing in the downpour. Someone had cared enough to stop the soldiers from fleeing and spreading the word, meaning that, until tonight, it had been business as usual in Tiamat. It did his heart good, to see that, finally, someone had gotten the better of Saddam, the way he'd gotten the better of the world. Evolution was funny that way, in human terms. Something worse always came along, someone or something that did evil that much more efficiently, and so prospered.

A few more raggedy-ass soldiers ran out of a burning wood shack, shot wildly in his direction, and ran off into the night. Keyes wasn't here. Whatever was happening now, it was happening down in the hole.

He moved through the camp by the numbers, sprinting from cover to cover, though he saw nobody who could have hurt him, if they wanted to. The foolishness of this struck him, made him clamp his jaws shut against the barking laughter that wanted to come out and never stop. Here, nine years ago, he'd seen something too awful to remember, and thought he'd become sick. In truth, it had been his first step away from being human. Now, back here under very different circumstances, to say the least, he still pantomimed the old tactics. But he had no weapon. *Weapon?* he thought, running his hands over his change-wracked arms, *what do you think this is?* Still, he scrounged some good stuff off some dead Iraqis and stowed it in a heavy gear harness he slung across his shoulders.

He caught himself looking too long at the dead men in the mud, and rummaged around in the flattened wreckage of a mess tent until he found some foil-pouched UN relief rations. When he gobbled them down, his stomach roared painfully to life and his body temperature started to fall.

Storch crossed the inner perimeter and scaled a house-sized boulder that teetered on the edge of the canyon and peered over the edge, down into the deeper dark from which came the strident cry of Keyes in his hundreds.

On first glance, it was almost something ridiculous. There were no siege engines, no enormous bombs, no diabolical scientific apparatuses on the floor of the canyon, only hundreds of people, perhaps a thousand or more standing shoulder to shoulder, all eyes focused on the impenetrable blackness of the pit within the pit. It looked like nothing so much as a bizarre and inept demonstration of interracial unity, a symbolic arrangement of humanity on the order of Hands Across America, or a papal appearance. Only the subdued nature of the crowd and the subtle currents of galvanic twitches passing through them betrayed the wrongness of it. They were white and black and brown, the survivors of the Chernobyl enclave and a lot of places the Mission never knew about, all dressed in the same black suits, an ocean of faces, their mouths wide open in song, yet they were not a crowd, but the individual cells of a new and colossal organism gestating in the canyon, as if in a womb. Their song was that of an unborn god striving toward awakening.

There was about the chorus an undercurrent of pain and strain and doubt at the labor of being reborn, and around the edges of it, discordant tones peeling off the dominant like flakes of ash falling from new-forged steel, the dwindling voices of the outcast tenants of all those bodies. Gradually, they died away, and the combined roar of Keyes was almost a visible haze in the air, through which the assembled bodies below were only a huge blur of heat. As his ears adjusted to the sheer power of the noise, he began to make out distinct syllables, though they were gibberish to him. Thinking back to the high school classes he'd napped through while waiting to enlist, he believed he understood what it was trying to do, if not what it was saying.

Keyes was trying to figure out a math problem, and a fucking big one, too, by the sound of it. Numbers and words were among the garbled sounds, and now he noticed that the flurries of syllables were variations in numbers and symbols, different groups of bodies shouting different permutations as He tried to work out the solution. When the right variation was found, the whole group repeated it in a single, deafening voice, and moved on to the next step in the formula. There was a warm, almost beautiful exultation to the voices as they harmonized towards one voice, like a choir nearing the triumphant coda of an aria. It touched Storch and softened his resolve, but underneath it, there was a tone-deaf gurgle in the back of every throat, the ravenous sound of the insatiable amoeba, the Shoggoth, as it devoured their minds and became them.

What was He trying to do? It didn't matter what, didn't matter why, to Storch. *Stop Him.*

The mob of Keyes filled the canyon from the walls to the deeper pit, a hundred feet across, in the center. Only one figure stood out in the crowd, not because it was head-and-shoulders above the rest, but because it burned brighter than the rest, and yet it was silent. Spike Team Texas. A thread of panic choked off his wind as he searched the crowd, then the shadowy rocks around him, for the others. Maybe they were in America with the main colony of Keyes. And maybe Storch deserved to get his throat cut for assuming.

Once, a weapons testing facility had stood here, and he had helped to destroy it, never knowing what lay underneath. Before that, a ziggurat had stood here, its priests charged with the same duty the Iraqis had today: to keep what lay within from getting out. Before that, if the latest voices in his head were to be believed, this place had been so much more than even his God-mad Dad would have believed. Hiram Hansen's words came back to him: *Zane, the world isn't what you thought it was yesterday, but your father was still crazier than a shithouse rat.*

"I do believe it runs in the family," he told the storm.

He slid back down the boulder and braced his back against it. His feet slid and dug in the mud, but slowly, the boulder gave way with a great sucking slurp, and rolled out over the void. Storch leapt up on top and rode it down into the canyon.

Under his feet, the boulder turned as it tumbled, so he had to run like a lumberjack on a rolling log to stay atop it. He may not have remembered much about physics, but he'd seen more than enough Road Runner cartoons to stay away from the business end of a falling rock. For just a moment, he was the sole inhabitant of earth's newest moon, and could see only the horizon of rock beneath his feet against the sky. Then the sheer walls of the canyon closed around his satellite like yawning jaws, and the crowd seemed to notice his arrival, but too late. He leapt off the rock blindly just before impact, flinging out a double handful of good stuff in the form of incendiary grenades. The boulder hit behind him a split-second before he did, smashing a dozen bodies to pulp and shivering into tumbling, car-sized shards. Storch arched his back and splayed his arms and legs out to spread the impact across his body and direct as much of it as he could into the dense mob. As one, they looked up at him and smiled.

Then the crowd parted, and he hit the naked rock. In the cartoons, a wiseass barnyard animal could step out of a falling elevator at the last possible instant and emerge unharmed. Cartoons lied.

Storch had died and almost died so many times now, the pain was almost welcome, a familiar friend amid all the weirdness, now. He managed to bring both his legs up under him and tried to pump them to run across the ground, but he hit off rhythm and his right knee locked up and blew out. His femur tore out of its cartilage coupling where the knee had been and sheared through the meat of his calf. A piercing scream escaped his lips before his jaw hit and bit the end of his tongue off. With his left leg, he managed to fling himself into the crowd with his claws out. *Die with your hands around His neck—*

It seemed that he went right through one and drove his arm up to the elbow in the abdomen of another before he fell down. The grenades exploded, blinding supernovas, but he couldn't see if they thinned the crowd any. All he could see were those goddamned sad gray eyes inches away from his, forgiving him.

"You keep doing this—" Keyes whispered.

Storch, lying across the body, drove his other fist down the man's throat and tore out everything he could get a grip on. It would take a hell of a lot more than that to kill the miserable bastard, but at least it shut him up.

The others around him backed away, each and every one of them still hissing the formula. Then they all closed their eyes in unison and sighed, a soft fist of wind that stirred the curtain of rain. "IT IS ACCOMPLISHED, He said. "THE WORLD WILL BE ONE." The crowd parted, and a giant form stepped into the space between Storch and the inner pit.

It looked like a dinosaur, or what dinosaurs would imagine their Devil looked like, if they had lived long enough to get religion. It stood ten feet, from its backward-jointed legs to its wedge-shaped head, which combined the cruelest traits of a tiger shark, a tyrannosaurus, and a triceratops. Obsidian scales rippled on the uneasy slabs of muscle on its vast shoulders. A rack of horns like sharpened baseball bats crowned the skull. Its eyes were smoldering red-black spots low on either side of the upper jaw. The bones of its arms arced out in curling scimitars that twisted and grew longer as the monster drew closer. Storch knew it could only be one man.

"Damn, boy," purred Brutus Dyson, "I was starting to think you weren't never gonna show up."

Storch tilted his head back and drank the rain. The concerted might of Keyes' brain felt like armored fingers closing around him, like lightning gathering to strike. His broken leg mended, stronger and more flexible than before. "It stops, Keyes!" he called out. He pointed at the pit. "You open the door, I'll open a door. You know what the fuck I'm talking about."

All of Him seemed to look inside themselves for a few seconds, like a newscaster on a shaky satellite feed, waiting for the signal to bounce off the ionosphere and into his ear. There were thousands of Him scattered all over the globe, hearing Storch's words, thinking what to do with him.

"WE HAVE NO MORE TIME FOR YOU, ZANE" Keyes rumbled. Rocks shook loose off the walls. "DYSON, RESOLVE THIS."

Storch circled around Dyson, but the bigger mutant outflanked him and lunged. All around them, Keyes turned and walked towards the pit.

Storch met the incoming Lieutenant with a spurred forearm. He tore a divot out of Dyson's leathery hide, but a massive arm pistoned into Storch's side again and again, a blur, crushing his ribs and right lung to jelly. Then, before he could fall, the horns gored him under the arm and the ground went away, and he was in the air again at thirty thousand feet, those horns *inside* him, and this time, he was never coming down—

But he did come down, and harder than any of the other times, spread-eagle on the unforgiving black rock. The rainwater vaporized where his blood mingled with it.

He lifted his head and looked for Dyson, saw very little else. The Lieutenant knelt before him and shook his huge, horned head. "I gave you so many goddamned chances, son," he said. "I even made you one of us, didn't I?"

Beyond Dyson, the first row of Keyes reached the lip of the inner pit, and stepped off into it. Silently, they just dropped out of sight and the next row took their place. For the moment, there wasn't a thing he could do about it.

"I don't see your boyfriends around, Lieutenant." Storch tried not to sound like one of his lungs was full of blood, but the words were still mostly red foam. "You let him split you up?"

Dyson looked stung. He stood and walked away from Storch as if he just didn't want to play any more. "Them boys dug their own goddamned graves. Couldn't adapt, in the end. You try to hold on too tight to what you think you are, you become it, and you ain't fit to live."

"And how do you stay alive, old man?"

"I adapt. I become what this bad old hogbitch of a world wants me to be. Every minute, son, I'm a whole other animal. That's the only way to stay alive, when you're like us."

Storch leapt to his feet and showed Dyson the rest of his good stuff. "I ain't like you."

It looked like a gun, only worse. Shorter than Storch's arm, with a drum magazine behind the stubby barrel, yet it was designed to be fired from a bipod. Storch had never seen one before, let alone fired one, but he'd read about it in *Soldier Of Fortune*. They called it the Tank Killer. The Russians made it as a lightweight anti-tank weapon, but in Chechnya, had taken to clearing houses with it. A single 30mm shell fired through the brick wall of a house or bunker would reduce the inhabitants to ashy wallpaper. He doubted it would seriously harm Dyson, but anything was worth a try.

Seething disgust turned Dyson's inhuman face even blacker. He thumped his barrel-chest with a taloned fist and charged. "You fucking faggot! Put down that shit and fight like a man!"

Storch leveled the tank killer and fired. At thirty feet, the shell exploded out at Dyson, but he seemed to have all the time in the world to dodge it. Behind him, the shell punched a big wet hole in the wall of moving Keyes. Without losing a step, Dyson rolled and popped up within arm's reach of Storch before the next shell jacked into the chamber.

Dyson swatted the tank killer out of Storch's hands and smashed his chest with both fists. Storch staggered back, and everything went white.

Both arms went numb and limp. He fell down and tried to roll over, but Dyson was on him, pinning his arms down with his knees.

"Last time we were here, I gave you something, and you ain't done a damned thing with it, so I want it back." Storch wriggled helplessly. Dyson drummed on Storch's chest with one fist and, shifting his weight, drove the other fist into Storch's abdomen. His talons raked the iron-hard muscle there, rending it but not penetrating. Storch screamed and snapped his head back and forth. Desperate, he sank his teeth into Dyson's left thigh.

Dyson's probing claws found the relatively soft meat just above his hips, and plunged into it up to the wrist.

All the air went out of Storch, and the sky became a rippling sea of silver dots. Through it, Dyson's eyes glowed like blood-flecked black moons. "I need what I gave you back. There's only me now, and I need to be strong for what comes next. You understand, don't you, son?"

He got off Storch, who didn't need pinning, now, and tore open the pouch of his gut. If Storch lifted his head and tried very hard to stare through the silver dots, he could see Dyson ripping out his liver and intestines in a great bloody bundle, like wet laundry, but he didn't really want to. He wasn't seeing the real world anymore, his dying mind was playing tricks on him, because his intestines seemed to come alive in Dyson's hand and writhe up his arm toward his face. And Dyson seemed to be screaming bloody murder.

Storch suddenly understood something about Ely Buggs that had never made sense, but never merited much chewing over, something he would rather not ever have known at all. Buggs constantly ate shit food, yet never gained an ounce. He told everyone he was an animal-lover and had many pets, yet Storch had never seen so much as a guppy in his trailer in Thermopylae. Buggs always talked a lot of shit, so he never questioned it. Now, he knew.

Buggs had worms.

Shit, barefoot Alabama dirt-farmers and untouchable trash-pickers in India have worms. Buggs collected worms the way bikers collect tattoos, the way spinster shut-ins collect cats. His GI tract was a thriving menagerie of intestinal parasites from every far-flung corner of the earth when Storch took possession. It was just, he supposed, one of those things you had to watch out for when you stole someone else's body.

When Storch began to rebuild Buggs from the inside out, he'd been more concerned with repairing the horrendous damage the fall had incurred on the body than patrolling for parasites. They were still relatively small at the time, but as Storch supercharged Buggs's metabolism and feeding habits to include a vast portion of all that swam in the Pacific Ocean, they had begun to grow. And when Storch began to change three days ago, digesting damaged cells to recycle into the new structures he'd need to fly to Iraq, they, too, changed. They sapped too little of his strength to become a nuisance to Storch, but out in the open, they became far more to Dyson.

Dyson sprang backwards and dropped Storch's guts, but most of the parasites had attached themselves to his hand and forearm, and either tried to bore in or migrate to the nearest safe harbor on his body. There were hundreds of them—hookworms, whipworms, pinworms, dwarf tapeworms, flukes, and a giant nematode (*Ascaris lubricoides*, but Buggs actually had a name for it, which swam up, unbidden, from the mush of Buggs's memories—Dr. Teeth). A monster as big as a timber rattler, it now had a rudimentary mouth like the multi-faceted drill of a mining engine. The whirring knob of grinding teeth darted straight for the nearest, softest tissue, which happened to be one of Dyson's eyes.

"Ah, FUCK!" Dyson howled. He grabbed at Dr. Teeth, but the end of the worm popped in his fingers and the rest slithered, frictionless, into his eye socket. "What've you been eating?"

"I swear to God, LT," Storch said, "those aren't mine."

Dyson looked almost comical, dancing around with his arm engulfed by wriggling, flapping fanged spaghetti. His head cocked back and his remaining eye squinted shut, looking as if he was about to vomit—and then he did. A thick spray of gray-green bile exploded out of his gaping maw. The instant it hit the air, it ignited, and splashed all over his infested arm. It was like napalm, or the incendiary Greek fire the Byzantines used to throw on invading ships. It clung to Dyson's arm and shot out spiky feathers of white flame like the tongue of a welding torch. The parasites were cremated, but Dyson's mighty limb was reduced to charcoal in thirty seconds. The whole time, he just stood there roaring and staring into the fire as if the pain were the most real, and thus the best thing, that had happened to him in years. Or maybe it was just Dr. Teeth eating into his brain.

Storch didn't care much, either way. He used the Lieutenant's reverie to crawl to the pit. He had a punctured lung and shattered ribs, and nothing between his esophagus and his asshole, but the bleeding had stopped, and things were trying to grow back already. He made them stop. His resources were needed elsewhere. *Just don't try to eat or breathe, and you'll be fine.*

The canyon was empty, but for the two of them. A few Keyes lay pinned under the boulder. They struggled, grimly, silently, to drag themselves out from under and join the others, who had all, apparently, just jumped into the dark hole. One of them scuttled by, oblivious to him, just a pair of arms and a mostly flattened head. It dragged itself to the edge and went over. He did not hear it hit the bottom.

He could hear nothing over the ringing of his ears and Dyson's gobbling screams and the drumming of the rain. When he looked down into the pit, he could see only that the whole floor moved. He looked over his shoulder at Dyson, but there wasn't much to worry about, there. The devil dinosaur rolled on the ground like a flea-crazed dog, foaming jaws snapping, claws buried in his eye socket and going down his throat. His screams, though not even remotely human, still contained words. "I'll fix you good, you hogbitch! I'm Spike Team Texas, Dr. Teeth! *My war is forever!*" How Dyson knew the worm's name was, again, one of those things he'd rather not know.

Storch took a deep, deep breath, stifled a scream as his right lung reinflated and pushed shards of rib out through his skin. The new ribs growing in were like the double-walled hull of an oil tanker. He felt like he was on fire, his body tearing up some parts of him to fix others. For one unthinkable instant, it seemed like a really good idea, almost an imperative, to kill and eat Dyson. Maybe one Keyes—

No. That was not what he was.

What Storch was, was scared shitless. Not of Keyes, but of what lay beyond. It was the place beneath them. Of all the hidden, unspeakable places in the world, it was the one he did not want to go into. Hundreds of people went down there, trying to open it up. He held the breath, swung his legs out over the pit, and lowered himself into the dark. Down into the earth one more time, sickening with the certainty that he was, once again, too late—

The walls were slick with burning slime, but the rough edges of the blasted concrete and basalt offered easy purchase. Rebar and twisted stubs of steel girders jutted out of the rock, so he was able to half-crawl, half-fall down to where the walls were planed and shaped by the original builders. Storch shuddered as he touched the smooth stone. The walls about two hundred feet down were as smooth as polished marble but there were circular handholds, like the pores in rock at the seashore, but their uniform shape and spacing testified to a purpose. In the gloom, he could only feel the cold stone, but the circular holes were everywhere, like a negative Braille. And then it hit him, that this was exactly what it was. The walls of the pit were covered in writing, extending all the way down to the floor, to Keyes—and the door. He was glad he couldn't read it.

As he descended, the turmoil above faded, and he began to discern something happening below. There were bodies down there, but they were blurred, indistinct. Had they all simply jumped to their deaths? No, they couldn't be killed that easily. Keyes had a reason for everything. Certainly, there was a reason for this.

He reached his foot out for another hold, and touched the floor. Something soft and hot brushed against him, and he retreated back up the wall, blinking, willing his eyes to grow and make sense out of the sea of heat, below.

They were all here, right below him. Twisted, broken limbs stretched out of the mass of bodies piled ten or twenty deep on the narrow floor of the pit. They had fallen a long way down, but not far enough to account for this. They looked smashed together as if by a steamroller—but no. They were melting together, flesh liquefying and fusing with the mass. Limbs and senses migrated and coalesced into great siege-engine weapons and unblinking compound eyes. The mob became a black ocean of protoplasm, quivering and bubbling with the potential to become anything, everything. It gathered itself together and rose up before him like a tsunami in the gloom. Slowly, but with horrifying vitality, it rose and became something worse than the sum of its hundreds of parts.

Storch tried not to cower.

In the small space, its massed voice was crushingly loud. "YOU LIVE IN US, ZANE," it said. "YOU ARE REDUNDANT. YOU ARE HOSTILE."

"Goddamn right I'm hostile, motherfucker."

Between them, now, he saw the gate. It was a circular portal of unidentifiable metal, like an enormous manhole cover, set into the floor. So scarred and burned by chemicals and force and the teeth of eons that it looked like a single piece of raw ore, or the chastity-belted womb of a mummified woman, and in the truest sense, it was.

"YOU ARE OBSOLETE," it said, and fell on the gate

Though it smothered the portal, Storch could hear and feel it prying at the frame, feel the stone flex under him, and begin to crack. It still had more than enough flesh left over to engulf him. Storch waded into the mass and tore at it with his bare hands, but it was like trying to beat back a wave. The viscous protoplasm ran through his fingers. He fought to drive it back, but the mass extruded a looming battering ram, which slammed him into the wall. It wove a cocoon around him that became a stomach. Acid burned his skin. Teeth and lamprey-fanged suckers gouged him, tentacles paralyzed him, and this had all happened before, would always happen, because he never, ever learned.

When he was eaten this time, he swore, no more coming back. *Please, God, whatever you really are...*

All around him, Keyes's body shook, tremors running through it, and it just split open and fell away.

Storch sank to the ground and contracted into a fetal ball. He didn't even care enough to see what had answered his prayers, not yet. He'd seen too much, already.

Presently, he opened his eyes. It wasn't dark down here, anymore. A frigid blue phosphorescence poured up the pitted, eons-old walls. It came from the gaping hole in the floor of the pit. Of Keyes, there was no sign.

Storch looked up at the disk of night, at the clouds rended to shreds on the raging wind that brought him here. Stars peered down the shaft at him, stealing their first glimpse down the hole beside him in over a million years.

Storch remembered his Bible. He didn't expect to see any Cher'ubims, or any flaming swords, and he didn't get any. There was just him alone. There was always, it seemed, one more hole to climb down, one more impossible thing to be done by him, alone. Just to keep the shitty, fucked-up world the way it was. Because he was the only one, it seemed, who didn't seem to know better.

His stomach gurgled, the first he noticed that he had one, again. Without looking down the hole, Storch held his breath and dove into Eden.

The Bible got it all so fucking *wrong.*

Storch knew how it was. You lied to yourself about home. It was always the good times, the best years of our lives, but getting through it was night terrors and wet beds with monsters under them, if you were very lucky, as few kids really were. His Daddy lied to him about the Army, made every day in the infantry sound like a frat party in Valhalla. All mankind was the same, apparently. He lied about the Garden of Eden, because one step over the threshold, Storch wanted to get out and never come back.

There were no trees pleasant to the sight and good for food, no river out of Eden parted into four heads, and the beasts of the field here were of a type Adam never got around to naming. Adam must have lied to his children about this place, because it was nothing like the pastoral paradise under glass that men were meant to weep for. It was a crucible, a bottle where life had been tested to destruction for hundreds of millions of years, a runaway killing jar experiment to make a better beast of burden. And every so often, it had boiled over and infested the world. Once, the ancestor of all human beings had escaped from this place, but it must have changed a lot since then.

Eden lay in a cavern, the far wall of which was lost in tumbling mists. The weird blue glow came from the mist itself, which must be spores from the bizarre flora that covered the floor and stretched to a height that dwarfed any earthly rain forest. The "trees" were cyclopean cathedrals of fungus, huge edifices of pearly gray flesh, the gills and fruiting bodies of which exhaled the deep sea witch-glow, which attracted clouds of flying and crawling pollination suitors, and all their predators, scavengers and parasites.

The roof was festooned with fungal vegetation that dangled down to the uppermost caps of the forest, and hosted a thriving ecosystem of its own. Everywhere he looked, things ate each other and spawned offspring that bore little more than a passing resemblance to their parents.

In a perverse sort of way, it all made perfect sense. It was almost funny. Down here, the future of the world was being perfected and built. Whatever had become man might have lingered in Eden, and those left behind had ruined it, just as those above were ruining the earth, now. What came to take their place was what could survive in an exhausted, dead, ecosystem, with the sun blocked out and only carrion on which to feed. The lower life forms, the decomposers, fungi and insects, had exploded to fill the gaps, because if there was one thing about Nature he knew, it was that She hated a vacuum.

Even in the teeming madness of the sunless garden, Keyes's trail wasn't hard to follow. Fungal trees were trampled flat in a vast swath, a carpet of bioluminescent ooze like a bridal path of crushed flowers leading deeper into Eden. The infernal din of the forest almost masked the sound of Keyes stampeding through Eden like a avalanche, voices raised in a chant that no longer sounded like human speech. *"Tekeli-Li! Tekeli-Li! Iä Shoggot!"*

Storch limped down the trampled path, casting sideways glances into the shadows. Things stirred and stalked, a few even skulked out into the open to feast on the crushed trees and the fleeing colonies of hive insects abandoning their nests. The air was foggy with spores. Storch's skin prickled and scaled as his immune system repelled millions of fungal invaders. Sounds got trapped in pockets inside the clouds, smothering him in silence one minute, then bombarding him with odd echoes of Keyes's hymn of self-worship.

That was how he almost walked into it. Out of the fog came a black tentacle the thickness of a telephone pole. Every inch of it was alive with insects, whirring, feasting, laying eggs in the flailing limb. Storch dropped and rolled away. It passed overhead and smashed down a sixty-foot fungus that looked like a pagoda made of Godzilla cocks. Things too quick to see spilled out of it and were eaten by bigger, quicker things.

Storch ran after Keyes with his eyes wide open, but he had to dodge and duck through a shield-wall of thrashing limbs to stay within sight of it as it spastically fought off the relentless children of Eden.

Keyes had made his human colony into a Shoggoth, his "slave-form," but Storch could still make out whole and partial human bodies swimming in the black protean tide as it rolled by. The mammoth mass sprouted an array of alien appendages and organs, trumpeting horns that now took up the chant in tones that strained the range of his hearing. *"Tekeli-Li! Iå Shoggot! Iå Keyes!"*

The insects descended on Keyes in clouds and tornado-swarms. Stuck fast in its shifting ooze, they were so swift, so fierce, so charged with the vitality of the source of all life, that Keyes was almost overwhelmed trying to absorb them all. Storch stayed well back and just watched. The jungle was hurting it more than he could ever hope to. Already, things were starting to grow on the rolling mountain, so that every minute, it looked more and more like the forest itself come to life.

Keyes reared up and shook off its parasites. Storch cowered behind a tree as it rained insects the size of cats and Komodo dragons. He smelled his own sweat. He smelled like everything else in this place, like moldy bread and rancid meat jammed up your nose. To the things in here, he was invisible, or maybe Keyes just tasted better.

When he looked around the tree, he saw that Keyes must have found what it was looking for. In the middle of a clearing, the Shoggoth had adopted a vaguely humanoid shape, and stood more or less on two legs, head and shoulders above the tallest trees in Eden. It knelt before a lone column of rock that rose up out of the furred ground to meet the roof of the cavern. Nothing grew on it. It seemed to have been carved out of the native basalt, like the outer walls of the pit, and was marked with the same regimented patterns of circular holes, a colossal history in Braille for blind, idiot gods.

Keyes read it. Thousands of delicate tendrils caressed the walls of the tomb, for so Storch believed it to be. For worst of all to him, there was underneath all the biological insanity all around him, a bone-deep sense of familiarity about this. He'd seen it in dreams.

Keyes threw more and bigger tentacles against the wall, probing more rudely now, prying at weaknesses. Chips came loose and became boulders. It reared back and slammed into the face of the island. Eden shook. Stalactites of stone and fungi plummeted to the floor, stirring up insect swarms. Storch took cover under a shelf of violet staghorn-like growths blooming on the stalk of a tree. They drooled battery acid on him, sending him scrambling.

Keyes coiled and hit the tomb again. The ground shook. Storch noticed that the insects did not come back. Everything that ran amok in this breeding pit avoided the black basalt tower. Instinct told him it was because whatever was inside it was worse.

But he could not tear his eyes away when Keyes broke through. There was a thunderous boom and a wind shook the trees. The tower had been hermetically sealed. The wall buckled inwards, then split into mammoth blocks that spilled out onto Keyes and buried it, but the black protoplasm only oozed back up around the blocks and crept into the spaces within.

A different sort of mist spilled out of the tomb—frigid, acrid, oily with the musk of something that had not walked the earth since before the age of dinosaurs. Something that had come from the spaces Outside. Keyes emerged from the hole in the tower. In its foremost tentacles, it held something.

In his brains and in his blood, God help him, Storch recognized it. Hiram Hansen had a fossilized specimen in his cave, but it was only a tall, barrel-shaped hunk of stone, with a bewildering crown of flagella and sensory organs that might have been an outrageous sedimentary growth, enfolded in shrouds of limestone that might have been great, bat-like wings. But he'd seen it in dreams too. For all his lies, Keyes had showed him the one unspeakable truth.

Once, about a billion years ago, his ancestors had lived in layered colonies on the rocks beside and within the simmering soup of the young earth. Simple, RNA-based bacteria, they had only just learned to synthesize energy from sunlight, or to prey on one another, when something had come and taken them. *Something vast and terrible and wise, watching him*— It had been an Elder—a looming, proto-vegetable monstrosity, a creature too highly evolved to do its own work or fight its own wars. From stunted terrestrial life, it had created Shoggoths, and viruses, and bacteria, and dinosaurs and men like Christian Keyes and Zane Storch. In its terrible oddness, yet Storch saw the roots of what his genetic memory recognized as devils—or angels.

Now Keyes held it in tentacles quivering with unspeakable, inhuman joy. The body was petrified and encrusted with frost, yet perfectly, hideously intact. Its sensory stalks and locomotive tentacles were curled up in a knot, its leathern wings folded tightly against the ridged body. It was not dead, but only frozen, sleeping. It might come to life at any moment. Storch hoped it would, feared that it would, but the question soon became moot. Keyes ate it.

Eden stood still as Keyes digested its God. "WE ARE ONE," it said. It didn't even try to sound like Christian Keyes, anymore. It had only adopted the scientist's neural network, his consciousness, because it was far more advanced than the Shoggoth's. Now it had something better. Once again, it began to change.

Storch snapped out of his trance. He had somewhere to be, something to do. He had to stop this. He had to start something else that might be, in the end, even worse.

He let his dreams guide him to the pit in the nethermost bowels of Eden. It was right where they said it would be.

There was no clearing around it. The trees crowded each other as densely as possible to get close to it, and their features bore witness to some hidden source of vitality and mutation in their soil. The trees that stooped over this gate were knurled and draped in all manner of parasitic growths outrageous even for this place, and bore organs that belonged on animals, suggesting fundamentally obscene congresses were allowed, even encouraged, in this secret bower. Storch forced his way between them and collapsed on the corroded metal face of the gate, unable to take another step. It looked like nothing so much as a bathtub drain set into the stone, but he could find no seams or hinges. Perhaps it was not a gate, but a barricade, designed never to open. It was better fortified than the one Keyes had so much trouble opening.

The metal was warm to the touch. He could feel something stirring just on the other side, vibrating the gate with the same subtle but fundamental rhythm he'd heard in the ocean.

Storch tried to pry it open, forcing his fingertips into anything that looked like a crack until blood made his fingers too slick to get traction. *Think. No, want it, but don't think. Let it happen. Your body will know what to do.*

Except it didn't.

"Ubbo-Sathla," Storch whispered. "Mana Yood Sushai. Magna Mater. Tiamat. Gaia. Maasauu. Geb. Abhoth."

Nothing stirred below

Something hacked into him just above his kidneys. It felt like an axe. He tried to roll, and another axe sank into his upper arm. Turning his head, he saw only a flurry of razor-sharp, chitinous knives rising and falling, cleaving and hacking his helpless, exhausted body.

It was something like an insect, something like a jellyfish that walked on telescoping, radially symmetrical legs, something like the fearsome gulper fish that lived miles beneath the ocean surface. Bit by bit, it chopped at him and sucked up the debris into a cluster of gnashing maws. He raised an arm to fend it off, but a wicked stinger jabbed him, and almost immediately, a cyst raised on his forearm and burst, spilling out blood and blue, glowing caviar.

Storch struggled to get out from under it, but it moved too fast, impaling his legs. Storch caught one of its scythe-claws and tore it out of its socket, turned it on the creature, but it was no use. The blade clattered off its hard shell without making a dent.

It explained a lot, in the end, to know he was meant to fail. It was a stupid mistake, the one he'd made again and again, to come here. Trusting in something bigger than himself. Pray to God, and a dumb fucking bug comes instead—

There was a deafening report, and the predator was swatted out of the air by a brilliant flash and a concussion that left Storch thinking they'd both been struck by lightning. *That's what blaspheming gets you*, his father's words came to him over the ringing of all the bells.

Someone stood over him. At this point, it didn't matter who it was, but he still was surprised to see it was Dyson.

He and Dr. Teeth appeared to have come to some sort of mutual understanding, a posture of live and let live gone horribly awry. The giant nematode had grown faster than ever on the rich foodstuffs between Dyson's ears. It looked like a great, gray, slimy anaconda, winding in and out of Dyson's eye socket and ears and countless weeping holes in his neck and chest. The endless snarl twisted and went into one hole, spilled out of another, but Dyson didn't seem to mind. He regarded Storch blankly with his remaining eye. In his feverishly shaking talons, he held the tank killer.

"My war is forever," he growled, saluted, and disappeared into the jungle.

Storch couldn't get up off the gate. He was too weak to fight or to pray, anymore, too weak to do anything but lie there and wait for whatever was going to happen.

He'd been a fool not to believe them when they told him the worst, and then, in the end, he'd been the biggest fool of all to believe that there was a higher authority, even a blind, mindless womb, to call to. They were all alone in the dark with the monsters, and it was the monsters' world all along, we just lived on it, but not for much longer, and that, at least, was a relief.

Somewhere in the jungle, Dyson shouted and fired the tank killer again and again. The ground shook, spore-pouches burst and showered Storch with luminous fairy-dust. The air shivered with his triumphant roar.

Storch called out again, his voice a strangled wheeze he could barely hear in his own head. Streams of sweat and rivulets of blood from his countless wounds rained down and pooled on the barrier, seeping through invisible cracks and disappearing.

This was stupid. God damn it. *God damn you, God—*

Something groaned, deep down in the earth.

Oh, you like that? he thought. *Fine, you're God. You made us all in nobody's image, and then deserted us, so I guess that makes you the Almighty. You're the one, God damn you, you're God. If you're down there, if you're the author of us all, then come up and fix this.*

All those other stupid names, all those invocations and shit that Armitage fed him, had done nothing. Now, he gave it the name by which he had loved and feared and believed in life, though it seemed like a symptom of his father's craziness. He gave it his anger, his pain, his hate, his blood and sweat. Bleeding and shouting curses into a hole in the ground, he gave it worship.

The gate bulged under him and burst open.

Storch was thrown against a tree. The soft meat of the trunk gave way beneath him, and he rolled back, almost falling over the edge into the pit he'd opened. Weak, more than halfway dead, he craned his neck and peered over the edge and down into the shaft.

For just a moment, there was only the darkness, a limitless, tangible shadow that went down to the heart of the world. Then he heard it coming. His body lurched back and somehow found its feet, carried him far from the sound that rolled up out of the shaft, growing louder by the second as something rose up to the opening.

Storch broke out of the trees and into the clearing. Keyes still stood before the shattered Elder tower. Its enormous compound body now resembled a crude, colossal image of the proto-crinoid thing it had devoured. Monstrous wings battered the air, and its wriggling eye-stalks swiveled to take in its domain. Its deafening ululations fell off at once as the sound of the Unbegotten Source grew louder and louder, filling the cavern of Eden with the roar of a wave approaching through a narrow cataract. Storch could feel it coming in the subtle shift of pressure in the cavern, and turned and ran back up the flattened track to the gate to the outside world.

It came.

Storch froze. Even if it meant his death, he could not take another step or turn away from what came up behind him, not until he'd witnessed it with his own eyes.

A geyser of glowing, opalescent foam erupted out of the hole. Wherever it touched, the trees burst. The mounting gusher spawned roving packs of cunning tsunami waves, rolling out in all directions and engulfing all in their path. Seething black clouds of life boiled up into the air, but the wave reached up and swallowed them. It spilled into the clearing, racing across the open ground like mercury across glass. A thrusting wave of it flanked Keyes, sweeping away the path to the exit. The colossal Shoggoth beat its enormous wings and lifted itself up on its pseudopods and tried to wade across the deluge. The flood turned and converged on it with savage prescience, lapping at its boneless limbs and undermining the earth it stood upon.

Storch was helpless to move, even when the waves seemed to notice him and approached, poised and glowing with blind, molecular lust. Its vitality was almost a voice in Storch's brain, the one word of the Unbegotten Source. It wanted to fuck him to death and make the world over with demigod monsters, a million rolling genetic dice sure, someday, to give the Great Womb what it longed for.

It shimmered and shifted in the blue spore-light, and Storch was able to see that it was anything but a homogenous fluid. The worst part of it was that it was exactly what it looked like. The fluid was alive with quivering, questing things like bullets, like fetal fish—sperm.

Keyes toppled and fell into the flood. Wherever it touched the Shoggoth, the fluid went berserk, seeming to tear into its flesh and bear off chunks of it, but it was not destruction. It was generation on a scale and at a rate that defied all biology. The wriggling, churning inhabitants of the fluid leapt out of the flood at Keyes like spawn-mad salmon, and bored in. Keyes's mountainous flesh exploded with cysts not unlike the one the predator-bug had tried to put into Storch, but each of these ruptured almost instantly, every single cell a zygote, a fertile womb. Keyes was completely obscured by the rising tide of divine semen and newborn life that erupted forth and commenced the cycle all over again. With a speed and ferocity that shamed the most aggressive breeders of Eden, the chimerical sons and daughters of the Unbegotten Source rampaged across Keyes's paralyzed mass, eating and killing and raping each other, laying eggs and dying, evolving before Storch's eyes into every conceivable variation on the theme of a living creature, into monstrous, obscene and magnificent combinations of traits reptilian, avian, amphibian, bacterial, piscine, insectoid, mammalian and much that was impossible to classify.

And from out of the conflagration came a deafening shriek of wordless rage and betrayal that burst the air asunder and jammed the needle-shards of it deep into Storch's brain. Two hundred fifty million years of brooding, fifty years of scheming, all its ruthless machinations to save the world from itself, had come to this. With agonizing slowness, it subsided to a piteous howl and finally, as the very flesh that gave voice to the cry was consumed or impregnated, died out among the cacophony of its abominable larval offspring.

And still the nacreous waves rolled out across the devastated biosphere, raping all in their path as they did in ancient Greece, and the Amazon, and every other place on the earth where gods once walked. If the Elders were the authors of evolution, the Unbegotten Source was the author of all the freaks, mutants, gods and monsters of every body of mythological lore. From holes such as the one he'd opened, this tide of rebirth had flowed all over the world before the Old Ones arrived from the stars, touching any living thing they came across with the quickening fire of new life.

The things born of Keyes's flesh moved too fast to be seen and died faster than they could be described, but there were always more. No one bore the slightest resemblance to any other, yet they mated and bred and battled until there was nothing remotely like Keyes left. Successive waves of births erupted out of the black protoplasm and ravaged each other and the hapless denizens of Eden, themselves only a few paces ahead of the onrushing wave.

For just an eye-blink, he thought he saw a loping, cursing shadow that might have been Lt. Dyson running across the semen-sea like a Jesus lizard, but a wave blotted him out, if he was ever there at all.

Storch turned and ran. The blue glow behind him was blotted out by the shadow and rumble of the greedy tide coming for him. Legs and arms pumping, he lost ground with every step. He could hear Its children over his shoulder, splashing and leaping on the crest of the wave. Insects and spore-clouds obscured the way, stinging, gumming his eyes shut, but he didn't stop or even slow down, because if he hesitated, he was sure the wave would bring him down and rape him to nothingness.

The floor shuddered and rolled. The roof of the cavern settled, dropping curtains of rock and fungi jungle into the deluge. The black mouth of the exit lay only a hundred yards ahead, but even if the waves didn't get him, the ceiling was about to collapse.

Faultlines slipped, tides turned ugly, and fluctuations in the magnetic and radiation belts around the earth played havoc with all airborne communications, as the globe quivered in the throes of a divine orgasm.

Deep in the semi-molten core of the earth, the mother-mass of Ubbo-Sathla stirred from Its billion-year sleep and awakened to the fertile presence of the Keyes-Shoggoth, miles above itself, anchored to the floor of the Central Pacific Basin. Its appetite whetted by Storch's sacrifice and the rape of Eden, the blind, divine lust of the Unbegotten Source caught fire at the prospect of the living island. Up through fissures and volcanic vents in the ocean floor the invincible seed percolated and squirted a sea of gametes into the island's soft, fertile center.

In the amphitheatre, Stella tried to run from the embattled Shoggoth, but her legs were made of water. She crumpled on the concrete steps and hid her face from the leviathan coming for her. She pressed her hands to her ears to block out its cries and the sound of helicopters, and the sound of her own blood becoming a thunderous tocsin to shake the dead out of their graves. That she was going to die here, with something inside her yet unborn, she did not doubt, nor did she fear it. If only it had lived, she thought, even if she never lived to see it, then what she and Storch had become and endured would not have been in vain.

A helicopter passed overhead. With an ear-splitting howl, the Shoggoth lashed out and swatted it out of the sky. She heard it spin off through the air, shattered rotors slicing up rows of seats as it pinwheeled down the amphitheatre and exploded in the orchestra pit.

Cold, stinging mist kissed her face and started to burn. When she opened her eyes, she saw only liquid emerald clouds where it had stood. Another pair of helicopters swooped and darted around the colossus like the biplanes in *King Kong*, crop-dusting it with the same lysing agent the Mission had used on the Idaho colony.

It had reduced the others to slag, but she survived because Storch had given her something that rendered her immune, as it purged her of the alien mind that trapped her in herself. She knew now, that for whatever reason, he had saved her. Call it love or lust or breeding instinct, that made them do what they did later, but he had come into the prison she had dug for herself and saved her, when no instinct should have made him lift a finger. Nature had thrust them together, rubbed them against each other to make what she carried within her for its own inscrutable purposes, but he had given her life as much as Keogh, and freedom. *I loved him*, she thought, because it was safe to admit it, now that he was dead, and she dying. But the thing inside her wasn't.

She reached out for the broken back of a seat and dragged herself to her feet. Her head felt like a half-full helium balloon, bobbing fit to float away, because she hadn't breathed since the cloud settled on her. She stumbled up the stairs, clinging to the rail and trying to see something beyond her outstretched hands.

The first thing she saw was a rotor blade, close enough to trim her eyelashes. It came out of the fog like a machete, flashed past her eyes and ripped away the curtain of green mist. She ducked, and a helicopter passed not ten feet above her, sideways, and nosed into the muddy slime-bed of the San Gabriel River.

The Shoggoth lumbered down the slope of the amphitheatre, trailing wisps of green aerosol, but no worse for wear. The lysing agent no longer worked. Nothing could kill it, now. It slid down into the orchestra pit, parting around the burning helicopter, and began to engulf the dead and dying, shitting out wheelchairs and crutches and clothing like an amoeba sweeping up lesser bacteria.

The last helicopter pulled way back, climbed to a thousand feet and launched Hellfire missiles into the Shoggoth. The bubbling black protoplasm swallowed them with vacuous plunk sounds. They never even detonated.

"IT IS ACCOMPLISHED, it said. "THE WORLD WILL BE ONE."

The air around the roiling mass shimmered with waves of something finer than smoke. The air suddenly smelled like Him, that smell that was her smell when He lived inside her. It was making itself into a virus. This was why it was here, why it became One, to be smart enough to create a virus that would directly infect any animal with His genetic code, His consciousness. The tainted sea breeze lifted the viral swarms off the lumbering Shoggoth and sent them spinning out over the city of Los Angeles. It was going on elsewhere, everywhere Keogh gathered His hostage minions, in the middle of cities all over the world. There were thousands of them today. Tomorrow, there wouldn't be anything else.

And there wasn't a goddamned thing she could do about it. She reached the top of the stairs, but her legs kept climbing air, and she fell down again. This time, she could not get up. Her head swam, her arms and legs were boneless, flopping, trembling. She drank in gulps of foul, smoke-choked, smoggy air. She felt her whole body contracting, clenching against a blow harder than anything she had ever suffered. She touched her womb, where a normal baby would have been, but she felt nothing there. Yet it was in her, and in that moment, it made its intentions lethally clear.

It wanted out.

It hurt. Her skin burned with sudden, crushing fever, and every muscle in her body leapt free of her control. She dropped and writhed against the pavement. All sound and vision dwindled down to a blunt, blurry, murky dot, and then the dot went away. She saw red. She heard something pushing against her brain from inside her head, struggling to touch her the way Keogh had, along synapses she had burned away so that nothing could ever get that close to her again. She cowered away from it now, but it would not be denied. It forced itself into her brain, and it spoke to her.

Don't be afraid, Mother.

Out of every pore of her skin, all at once, Stella Orozco had her baby.

The offspring left her like a bullet from a gun, but the effort almost killed her. She suddenly lost ten pounds of mass to the winds, and capillaries everywhere just under her skin were atomized. Blood rose up on her skin in a rich foam, and she collapsed and clung to the spinning ground. She had never felt anything so wondrous in all her short, sour life as the moment it touched her. It hadn't the body or the brain yet to frame the words it had to say to her, but it made itself known, and then left.

When Storch freed her from Keogh, he imparted segments of his own wild, recombinant DNA to create proteins that cleansed her of her jailor and freed her to change. They were exactly alike for an instant, but then the world worked its little changes on them, and they grew apart, into freaks, as isolated in form as they'd been in their hearts, when they were human. They fought each other tooth and nail even as they mated, that one time, but warring against their own xenophobia was the life force that made them the exquisite mutants that they'd become. Exquisite and unique they were, but they weren't the end product, not any more than humans or dinosaurs or flatworms had been. It had used them to make this child, but her body acted on her insecurity and tried to murder it. It forced the child to hide in her blood, a nexus of independent cells, yet One, as Keyes was now One. It would not develop into a multicellular body, but not because she wouldn't let it, but because it wasn't supposed to. Invisible, it floated before her on the wind, so thick that she almost saw a sort of shape, but then the wind shifted and it was gone, blown across the amphitheatre to the Shoggoth.

Keogh screamed. The mountainous body seemed to split apart from within, becoming thousands of bodies again, then inert sludge. The Shoggoth faltered, retching up oil barrels of whatever it used for blood, and fell apart, even as it trembled and simmered with new life—her offspring, a sentient virus, replicating itself out of the shattered colossus and taking to the wind.

Around the world, Stella's viral child stormed Christian Keyes's neural network and downloaded itself into the colonies of the Shoggoth wherever they gathered. In Russia, in Africa, in India and Brazil, the Keyes-clones disintegrated into replicas of Stella's nameless child, and went to seek their fortune.

The amphitheatre fell silent. A few fires still burned down in the orchestra pit, which was now filled with a visibly evaporating pool of protoplasm. Her child was growing, and going out into the world.

"Be good," she told it, and let herself drop off to sleep on the sidewalk.

The sun had not yet risen over Tiamat, but the storm had been blown away, when Storch crawled out of the pit and rolled away from the edge. He lay on his back on the floor of the canyon and looked up into the cloud-wracked sky for a long while. His body needed sleep, but he was afraid the wave of divine jungle juice might flood the canyon, so he kept his eyes open.

The ground beneath him slowly subsided back to stillness, and only clouds of spores wafted up from the mouth of Eden, far below. He thought he heard something clamber up the wall of rock and skitter off across the canyon floor, but he saw nothing.

Then something bigger climbed over the lip, much bigger and wheezing curses on everything under, inside and outside of the sun.

Storch looked, but he was too tired to do much else, even though it was Dyson. The giant sauropod-man looked down at him with his one good eye. His other eye-socket was still stuffed with a bulging coil of Dr. Teeth, now as thick as a fat man's thigh. It wiggled and wormed through the unimaginable hollows of Dyson's head like a big apple.

In the purple predawn light, Dyson looked like a coral reef on two shaky legs that were little more than gnawed, leaking bone and chewed up thongs of tendon. Eden-born things too hideous to describe had made a cluster of burrows all through Dyson's gargantuan physique. The chittering, squirming brood of Spike Team Texas ate each other and drooled out eggs in sickening time-lapse. Dr. Teeth's rotary garbage disposal head patrolled the violent rookery, devouring some newborns and whole clutches of eggs, while passing over others which it, apparently, deemed fit to live in the walking ecosystem Brutus Dyson had become. Like a little dragon of Eden, it culled the weak and protected the strong from the new Garden's blood-simple demiurge.

"What're you lookin' at, sonny?" Dyson snarled. Storch just lay there, at a loss, once and for all, for words, and too tired to do anything about it.

Presently, Dyson saluted and lumbered off into the desert, barking orders to his raw recruits. He didn't see Storch salute him back, and probably wouldn't have cared.

This was no place to sleep. He was hollowed-out, but he wanted, bone-deep *needed*, to get home. His body swelled with hydrogen snatched out of the air and lifted him on the wind, and his arms grew and hands splayed out into the beginnings of bat wings. As the canyon shrank beneath his feet and became just another hole in the ground, he thought he heard a voice on the wind, or in the dusty, burnt-out corners of his mind.

Thank you, Father—

But then it was gone, and there was only the wind carrying him west, home to Death Valley. He couldn't think of a better place to watch the world be reborn.